MURDER MOST
POST𝘈L
Delectable
FELINE

Other Titles in Random House Value's
Murder Most Series

Murder Most Romantic
Murder Most Medieval
Murder Most Divine
Murder Most Confederate
Murder Most Celtic
Murder Most Merry

MURDER
MOST
POSTAL

EDITED BY MARTIN H. GREENBERG

MURDER
MOST
Delectable

EDITED BY MARTIN H. GREENBERG

MURDER
MOST
FELINE

**EDITED BY ED GORMAN,
MARTIN H. GREENBERG & LARRY SEGRIFF**

GRAMERCY BOOKS
NEW YORK

This 2005 edition published by Gramercy Books,
an imprint of Random House Value Publishing, a division of
Random House, Inc., New York, by arrangement with
Cumberland House Publishing, Nashville, TN.

Pages 305-307, 655-656, and 910 constitute an extension of this copyright page.

Gramercy is a registered trademark and the colophon
is a trademark of Random House, Inc.

Random House
New York • Toronto • London • Sydney • Auckland
www.randomhouse.com

Printed in the United States of America

Catalog records for these titles are available from the Library of Congress.

ISBN 0-307-29021-2

CONTENTS

MURDER MOST POSTAL

Homicidal Tales That Deliver a Message

Contents

Introduction

"All letters, methinks, should be as free and easy as one's discourse, not studied as an oration, nor made up of hard words like a charm."
—Dorothy Osbourne (Lady Temple)

"An odd thought strikes me—we shall receive no letters in the grave."
—Samuel Johnson

Although cultural anthropologists have come up with several reasons to account for the advancement of mankind, including our use of tools and trial-and-error problem solving, the development of our ability to communicate might be the ultimate key to our dominance of this planet.

It is man's ability to relate thoughts, abstract concepts, and ideas clearly and distinctly to another human being that fosters growth and learning in human society. Ever since the first caveman sketched out the bison hunts in the Lascaux caves more than sixteen thousand years ago, mankind has constantly been trying to improve our methods of communication, particularly the speed at which we send messages. From smoke signals to drumbeats to the Pony Express and on to the telegraph, telephones, and e-mail, we have always wanted faster, better, more reliable modes of communication.

This is not to say that some methods of discourse have fallen by the wayside. Consider the mailed letter. Until well into the twentieth century, the letter for centuries had been the most popular form of individual communication across any distance. Kings, popes, lords, heads of state, scholars, and authors all used the simple device of pen and paper to plot against one another, gossipmonger, woo and win each other's hearts, and play the intricate games of court and social intrigue still popular in this day and age. In fact, in London, communication by letter was so popular that the mail was often delivered two or three times a day. Of course, this was at a time when literacy was primarily enjoyed by the nobility, thereby limiting the number of letters sent. It was also before the age of advertising, so every letter also actually had a point to it. Nowadays, the U.S. Postal Service would be hard-pressed to try and deliver the mail more than once a day. (Indeed, sometimes they cannot even manage this.)

In today's fast-paced society of fax machines, cellular phones, and lightning-fast e-mail, the emphasis has shifted from content to the incredible speed at which a message can be sent. Accompanying this shift of priorities from literary merit to haste has been an alarming rise in the instances of bad manners being used in composing and sending e-messages, something that a letter writer would never have done in years gone by.

No matter which new ways of communications are discovered in the future, the mail for now is still a fairly effective way to deliver messages, as anyone who has sorted through a voluminous pile of junk mail can tell you. Even the letter itself can send a clear message before it is opened. A letter from a friend can make a recipient smile with the anticipated pleasure of reading it. A letter from a law firm, of course, usually engenders an entirely different response.

In the following twenty-one stories, all by masters of the mystery genre, the mail itself takes center stage, as we reveal tales of purloined postage, larcenous letters, and contemptuous correspondence. The first master of the short mystery story, Edgar Allan Poe, is here with his classic detective tale of a missive gone astray and the cunning way in which it is retrieved. Mystery Writers of America grandmaster Lawrence Block tells of the correspondence between a death-row inmate and the brother of the woman he killed, and of the deadly consequences for both. A series of letters from "Agent No. 5 and Agent No. 6" (Issues of national security prevent us from revealing their real names here) takes us on a cloak-and-dagger chase in search of an unpublished manuscript that is so terrible, everyone wants to possess it. The inestimable Ellery Queen makes an appearance to investigate a puzzling philately theft. We've even taken a step into the twenty-first century with Matt Costello's story of letters in cyberspace, as one man pours out his heart to a chat-room stranger in the last messages he will ever write.

From stolen stamps to murder-by-mail, the stories in this volume are all prime examples of just how dangerous delivering a message can be. So, after you've sorted the pile in your mailbox, thrown out the junk ads, paid your bills, and caught up on your correspondence (and don't forget the stamp!), sit back for a well-deserved break and enjoy these stories of *Murder Most Postal.*

MURDER MOST POSTAL

Like a Bone in the Throat

Lawrence Block

THROUGHOUT THE TRIAL PAUL DANDRIDGE did the same thing every day. He wore a suit and tie, and he occupied a seat toward the front of the courtroom, and his eyes, time and time again, returned to the man who had killed his sister.

He was never called upon to testify. The facts were virtually undisputed, the evidence overwhelming. The defendant, William Charles Croydon, had abducted Dandridge's sister at knifepoint as she walked from the college library to her off-campus apartment. He had taken her to an isolated and rather primitive cabin in the woods, where he had subjected her to repeated sexual assaults over a period of three days, at the conclusion of which he had caused her death— by manual strangulation.

Croydon took the stand in his own defense. He was a handsome young man who'd spent his thirtieth birthday in a jail cell awaiting trial, and his preppy good looks had already brought him letters and photographs and even a few marriage proposals from women of all ages. (Paul Dandridge was twenty-seven at the time. His sister, Karen, had been twenty when she died. The trial ended just weeks before her twenty-first birthday.)

On the stand, William Croydon claimed that he had no recollection of choking the life out of Karen Dandridge, but allowed as how he had no choice but to believe he'd done it. According to his testimony, the young woman had willingly accompanied him to the remote cabin and had been an enthusiastic sexual partner with a penchant for rough sex. She had also supplied some particularly strong marijuana with hallucinogenic properties and had insisted that he smoke it with her. At one point, after indulging heavily in the unfamiliar drug, he had lost consciousness and awakened later to find his partner beside him, dead.

His first thought, he'd told the court, was that someone had broken into the cabin while he was sleeping, had killed Karen, and might return to kill him. Accordingly, he'd panicked and rushed out of there, abandoning Karen's corpse. Now, faced with all the evidence arrayed against him, he was compelled to believe he had somehow committed this awful crime, although he had no recollection of it whatsoever, and although it was utterly foreign to his nature.

The district attorney, prosecuting this case himself, tore Croydon apart on cross-examination. He cited the bite marks on the victim's breasts, the rope burns indicating prolonged restraint, the steps Croydon had taken in an attempt to conceal his presence in the cabin. "You must be right," Croydon would admit, with a shrug and a sad smile. "All I can say is that I don't remember any of it."

The jury was eleven to one for conviction right from the jump, but it took six hours to make it unanimous. *Mr. Foreman, have you reached a verdict? We have, Your Honor. On the sole count of the indictment, murder in the first degree, how do you find? We find the defendant, William Charles Croydon, guilty.*

One woman cried out. A couple of others sobbed. The DA accepted congratulations. The defense attorney put an arm around his client. Paul Dandridge, his jaw set, looked at Croydon.

Their eyes met, and Paul Dandridge tried to read the expression in the killer's eyes. But he couldn't make it out.

Two weeks later, at the sentencing hearing, Paul Dandridge got to testify.

He talked about his sister, and what a wonderful person she had been. He spoke of the brilliance of her intellect, the gentleness of her spirit, the promise of her young life. He spoke of the effect of her death upon him. They had lost both parents, he told the court, and Karen was all the family he'd had in the world. And now she was gone. In order for his sister to rest in peace, and in order for him to get on with his own life, he urged that her murderer be sentenced to death.

Croydon's attorney argued that the case did not meet the criteria for the death penalty, that while his client possessed a criminal record he had never been charged with a crime remotely of this nature, and that the rough-sex-and-drugs defense carried a strong implication of mitigating circumstances. Even if the jury had rejected the defense, surely the defendant ought to be spared the ultimate penalty, and justice would be best served if he were sentenced to life in prison.

The DA pushed hard for the death penalty, contending that the rough-sex defense was the cynical last-ditch stand of a remorseless killer, and that the jury had rightly seen that it was wholly without merit. Although her killer might well have taken drugs, there was no forensic evidence to indicate that Karen Dandridge herself had been under the influence of anything other than a powerful and ruthless murderer. Karen Dandridge needed to be avenged, he maintained, and society needed to be assured that her killer would never, ever, be able to do it again.

Paul Dandridge was looking at Croydon when the judge pronounced the sentence, hoping to see something in those cold blue eyes. But as the words were spoken—*death by lethal injection*—there was nothing for Paul to see. Croydon closed his eyes.

When he opened them a moment later, there was no expression to be seen in them.

THEY MADE YOU fairly comfortable on Death Row. Which was just as well, because in this state you could sit there for a long time. A guy serving a life sentence could make parole and be out on the street in a lot less time than a guy on Death Row could run out of appeals. In that joint alone, there were four men with more than ten years apiece on Death Row, and one who was closing in on twenty.

One of the things they'd let Billy Croydon have was a typewriter. He'd never learned to type properly, the way they taught you in typing class, but he was writing enough these days so that he was getting pretty good at it, just using two fingers on each hand. He wrote letters to his lawyer, and he wrote letters to the women who wrote to him. It wasn't too hard to keep them writing, but the trick lay in getting them to do what he wanted. They wrote plenty of letters, but he wanted them to write really hot letters, describing in detail what they'd done with other guys in the past, and what they'd do if by some miracle they could be in his cell with him now.

They sent pictures, too, and some of them were good-looking and some of them were not. "That's a great picture," he would write back, "but I wish I had one that showed more of your physical beauty." It turned out to be surprisingly easy to get most of them to send increasingly revealing pictures. Before long he had them buying Polaroid cameras with timers and posing in obedience to his elaborate instructions. They'd do anything, the bitches, and he was sure they got off on it, too.

Today, though, he didn't feel like writing to any of them. He rolled a sheet of paper into the typewriter and looked at it, and the image that came to him was the grim face of that hard-ass brother of Karen Dandridge's. What was his name, anyway? Paul, wasn't it?

"Dear Paul," he typed, and frowned for a moment in concentration. Then he started typing again.

> Sitting here in this cell waiting for the day to come when they
> put a needle in my arm and flush me down God's own toilet,
> I found myself thinking about your testimony in court. I
> remember how you said your sister was a goodhearted girl who

spent her short life bringing pleasure to everyone who knew her. According to your testimony, knowing this helped you rejoice in her life at the same time that it made her death so hard to take.

Well, Paul, in the interest of helping you rejoice some more, I thought I'd tell you just how much pleasure your little sister brought to me. I've got to tell you that in all my life I never got more pleasure from anybody. My first look at Karen brought me pleasure, just watching her walk across campus, just looking at those jiggling tits and that tight little ass and imagining the fun I was going to have with them.

Then when I had her tied up in the backseat of the car with her mouth taped shut, I have to say she went on being a real source of pleasure. Just looking at her in the rearview mirror was enjoyable, and from time to time I would stop the car and lean into the back to run my hands over her body. I don't think she liked it much, but I enjoyed it enough for the both of us.

Tell me something, Paul. Did you ever fool around with Karen yourself? I bet you did. I can picture her when she was maybe eleven, twelve years old, with her little titties just beginning to bud out, and you'd have been seventeen or eighteen yourself, so how could you stay away from her? She's sleeping and you walk into her room and sit on the edge of her bed . . .

He went on, describing the scene he imagined, and it excited him more than the pictures or letters from the women. He stopped and thought about relieving his excitement but decided to wait. He finished the scene as he imagined it and went on:

Paul, old buddy, if you didn't get any of that, you were missing a good thing. I can't tell you the pleasure I got out of your sweet little sister. Maybe I can give you some idea by describing our first time together.

And he did, recalling it all to mind, savoring it in his memory, reliving it as he typed it out on the page.

I suppose you know she was no virgin, but she was pretty new at it all the same. And then when I turned her facedown, well, I can tell you she'd never done *that* before. She didn't like it much either. I had the tape off her mouth and I swear I thought she'd wake the neighbors, even though there weren't any. I guess it hurt her some, Paul, but that was just an example of your darling sister sacrificing everything to give pleasure to others, just like you said. And it worked, because I had a hell of a good time.

God, this was great. It really brought it all back.

Here's the thing; the more we did it, the better it got. You'd think I would have grown tired of her, but I didn't. I wanted to keep on having her over and over again forever, but at the same time I felt this urgent need to finish it, because I knew that would be the best part.

And I wasn't disappointed, Paul, because the most pleasure your sister ever gave anybody was right at the very end. I was on top of her, buried in her to the hilt, and I had my hands wrapped around her neck. And the ultimate pleasure came with me squeezing and looking into her eyes and squeezing harder and harder and going on looking into those eyes all the while and watching the life go right out of them.

He was too excited now. He had to stop and relieve himself. Afterward he read the letter and got excited all over again. A great letter, better than anything he could get any of his bitches to write to him, but he couldn't send it, not in a million years.

Not that it wouldn't be a pleasure to rub the brother's nose in it. Without the bastard's testimony, he might have stood a good chance to beat the death sentence. With it, he was sunk.

Still, you never knew. Appeals would take a long time. Maybe he could do himself a little good here.

He rolled a fresh sheet of paper in the typewriter.

Dear Mr. Dandridge, I'm well aware that the last thing on earth you want to read is a letter from me. I know that in your place

I would feel no different myself. But I cannot seem to stop myself from reaching out to you. Soon I'll be strapped down onto a gurney and given a lethal injection. That frightens me horribly, but I'd gladly die a thousand times over if only it would bring your sister back to life. I may not remember killing her, but I know I must have done it, and I would give anything to undo it. With all my heart, I wish she were alive today.

Well, that last part was true, he thought. He wished to God she were alive, and right there in that cell with him, so that he could do her all over again, start to finish.

He went on and finished the letter, making it nothing but an apology, accepting responsibility, expressing remorse. It wasn't a letter that sought anything, not even forgiveness, and it struck him as a good opening shot. Probably nothing would ever come of it, but you never knew.

After he'd sent it off, he took out the first letter he'd written and read it through, relishing the feelings that coursed through him and strengthened him. He'd keep this, maybe even add to it from time to time. It was really great the way it brought it all back.

PAUL DESTROYED THE first letter.

He opened it, unaware of its source, and was a sentence or two into it before he realized what he was reading. It was, incredibly, a letter from the man who had killed his sister.

He felt a chill. He wanted to stop reading but he couldn't stop reading. He forced himself to stay with it all the way to the end.

The nerve of the man. The unadulterated gall.

Expressing remorse. Saying how sorry he was. Not asking for anything, not trying to justify himself, not attempting to disavow responsibility.

But there had been no remorse in the blue eyes, and Paul didn't believe there was a particle of genuine remorse in the letter either. And what difference did it make if there was?

Karen was dead. Remorse wouldn't bring her back.

HIS LAWYER HAD told him they had nothing to worry about, they were sure to get a stay of execution. The appeal process, always drawn out in capital cases, was in its early days. They'd get the stay in plenty of time, and the clock would start ticking all over again.

And it wasn't as though it got to the point where they were asking him what he wanted for a last meal. That happened sometimes; there was a guy three cells down who'd had his last meal twice already, but it didn't get that close for Billy Croydon. Two and a half weeks to go and the stay came through.

That was a relief, but at the same time he almost wished it had run out a little closer to the wire. Not for his benefit, but just to keep a couple of his correspondents on the edges of their chairs.

Two of them, actually. One was a fat girl who lived at home with her mother in Burns, Oregon, the other a sharp-jawed old maid employed as a corporate librarian in Philadelphia. Both had displayed a remarkable willingness to pose as he specified for their Polaroid cameras, doing interesting things and showing themselves in interesting ways. And, as the countdown had continued toward his date with death, both had proclaimed their willingness to join him in heaven.

No joy in that. In order for them to follow him to the grave, he'd have to be in it himself, wouldn't he? They could cop out and he'd never even know it.

Still, there was great power in knowing they'd even made the promise. And maybe there was something here he could work with.

He went to the typewriter.

My darling, the only thing that makes these last days bearable is the love we have for each other. Your pictures and letters sustain me, and the knowledge that we will be together in the next world draws much of the fear out of the abyss that yawns before me.

Soon they will strap me down and fill my veins with poison, and I will awaken in the void. If only I could make that final journey knowing you would be waiting there for me! My angel, do you have the courage to make the trip ahead of me? Do you love me that much? I can't ask so great a sacrifice of you, and yet I am driven to ask it, because how dare I withhold from you something that is so important to me?

He read it over, crossed out *sacrifice*, and penciled in *proof of love*. It wasn't quite right, and he'd have to work on it some more. Could either of the bitches possibly go for it? Could he possibly get them to do themselves for love?

And, even if they did, how would he know about it? Some hatchet-faced dame in Philly slashes her wrists in the bathtub, some fat girl hangs herself in Oregon, who's going to know to tell him so he can get off on it? *Darling, do it in front of a video cam, and have them send me the tape.* Be a kick, but it'd never happen.

Didn't Manson get his girls to cut X's on their foreheads? Maybe he could get his to cut themselves a little, where it wouldn't show except in the Polaroids. Would they do it? Maybe, if he worded it right.

Meanwhile, he had other fish to fry.

Dear Paul, I've never called you anything but "Mr. Dandridge," but I've written you so many letters, some of them just in the privacy of my mind, that I'll permit myself this liberty. And for all I know you throw my letters away unread. If so, well, I'm still not sorry I've spent the time writing them. It's a great help to me to get my thoughts on paper in this manner.

I suppose you already know that I got another stay of execution. I can imagine your exasperation at the news. Would it surprise you to know that my own reaction was much the same? I don't want to die, Paul, but I don't want to live like this, either, while lawyers scurry around just trying to postpone the inevitable. Better for both of us if they'd just killed me right away.

Though I suppose I should be grateful for this chance to make my peace, with you and with myself. I can't bring myself to ask for your forgiveness, and I certainly can't summon up whatever is required for me to forgive myself, but perhaps that will

come with time. They seem to be giving me plenty of time,
even if they do persist in doling it out to me bit by bit . . .

WHEN HE FOUND the letter, Paul Dandridge followed what had
become standard practice for him. He set it aside while he opened and
tended to the rest of his mail. Then he went into the kitchen and
brewed himself a pot of coffee. He poured a cup and sat down with it
and opened the letter from Croydon.

When the second letter came he'd read it through to the end, then
crumpled it in his fist. He hadn't known whether to throw it in the
garbage or burn it in the fireplace, and in the end he'd done neither.
Instead he'd carefully unfolded it and smoothed out its creases and read
it again before putting it away.

Since then he'd saved all the letters. It had been almost three
years since sentence was pronounced on William Croydon, and longer
than that since Karen had died at his hands. (Literally at his hands,
he thought; the hands that typed the letter and folded it into its envelope had encircled Karen's neck and strangled her. The very hands.)

Now Croydon was thirty-three and Paul was thirty himself, and he
had been receiving letters at the approximate rate of one every two
months. This was the fifteenth, and it seemed to mark a new stage in
their one-sided correspondence. Croydon had addressed him by his
first name.

"Better for both of us if they'd just killed me right away." Ah, but
they hadn't, had they? And they wouldn't either. It would drag on and
on and on. A lawyer he'd consulted had told him it would not be
unrealistic to expect another ten years of delay. For God's sake, he'd
be forty years old by the time the state got around to doing the job.

It occurred to him, not for the first time, that he and Croydon
were fellow prisoners. He was not confined to a cell and not under a
sentence of death, but it struck him that his life held only the illusion
of freedom. He wouldn't really be free until Croydon's ordeal was over.
Until then he was confined in a prison without walls, unable to get on
with his life, unable to have a life, just marking time.

He went over to his desk, took out a sheet of letterhead, uncapped a pen. For a long moment he hesitated. Then he sighed gently and touched pen to paper.

"Dear Croydon," he wrote. "I don't know what to call you. I can't bear to address you by your first name or to call you 'Mr. Croydon.' Not that I ever expected to call you anything at all. I guess I thought you'd be dead by now. God knows I wished it . . ."

Once he got started, it was surprisingly easy to find the words.

AN ANSWER FROM Dandridge.

Unbelievable.

If he had a shot, Paul Dandridge was it. The stays and the appeals would only carry you so far. The chance that any court along the way would grant him a reversal and a new trial was remote at best. His only real hope was a commutation of his death sentence to life imprisonment.

Not that he wanted to spend the rest of his life in prison. In a sense, you lived better on Death Row than if you were doing life in general prison population. But in another sense the difference between a life sentence and a death sentence was, well, the difference between life and death. If he got his sentence commuted to life, that meant the day would come when he made parole and hit the street. They might not come right out and say that, but that was what it would amount to, especially if he worked the system right.

And Paul Dandridge was the key to getting his sentence commuted.

He remembered how the prick had testified at the presentencing hearing. If any single thing had ensured the death sentence, it was Dandridge's testimony. And, if anything could swing a commutation of sentence for him, it was a change of heart on the part of Karen Dandridge's brother.

Worth a shot.

"Dear Paul," he typed. "I can't possibly tell you the sense of peace that came over me when I realized the letter I was holding was from you . . ."

PAUL DANDRIDGE, SEATED at his desk, uncapped his pen and wrote the day's date at the top of a sheet of letterhead. He paused and looked at what he had written. It was, he realized, the fifth anniversary of his sister's death, and he hadn't been aware of that fact until he'd inscribed the date at the top of a letter to the man who'd killed her.

Another irony, he thought. They seemed to be infinite.

"Dear Billy," he wrote. "You'll appreciate this. It wasn't until I'd written the date on this letter that I realized its significance. It's been exactly five years since the day that changed both our lives forever."

He took a breath, considered his words. He wrote, "And I guess it's time to acknowledge formally something I've acknowledged in my heart some time ago. While I may never get over Karen's death, the bitter hatred that has burned in me for so long has finally cooled. And so I'd like to say that you have my forgiveness in full measure. And now I think it's time for you to forgive yourself . . ."

IT WAS HARD to sit still.

That was something he'd had no real trouble doing since the first day the cell door closed with him inside. You had to be able to sit still to do time, and it was never hard for him. Even during the several occasions when he'd been a few weeks away from an execution date, he'd never been one to pace the floor or climb the walls.

But today was the hearing. Today the board was hearing testimony from three individuals. One was a psychiatrist who would supply some professional arguments for commuting his sentence from death to life. Another was his fourth-grade teacher, who would tell the board how rough he'd had it in childhood and what a good little boy he was underneath it all. He wondered where they'd dug her up, and how she could possibly remember him. He didn't remember her at all.

The third witness, and the only really important one, was Paul Dandridge. Not only was he supplying the only testimony likely to carry much weight, but it was he who had spent money to locate Croydon's fourth-grade teacher, he who had enlisted the services of the shrink.

His buddy, Paul. A crusader, moving heaven and earth to save Billy Croydon's life.

Just the way he'd planned it.

He paced, back and forth, back and forth, and then he stopped and retrieved from his locker the letter that had started it all. The first letter to Paul Dandridge, the one he'd had the sense not to send. How many times had he reread it over the years, bringing the whole thing back into focus?

"When I turned her facedown, well, I can tell you she'd never done *that* before." Jesus, no, she hadn't liked it at all. He read and remembered, warmed by the memory.

What did he have these days but his memories? The women who'd been writing him had long since given it up. Even the ones who'd sworn to follow him to death had lost interest during the endless round of stays and appeals. He still had the letters and pictures they'd sent, but the pictures were unappealing, only serving to remind him what a bunch of pigs they all were, and the letters were sheer fantasy with no underpinning of reality. They described, and none too vividly, events that had never happened and events that would never happen. The sense of power to compel them to write those letters and pose for their pictures had faded over time. Now they only bored him and left him faintly disgusted.

Of his own memories, only that of Karen Dandridge held any real flavor. The other two girls, the ones he'd done before Karen, were almost impossible to recall. They were brief encounters, impulsive, unplanned, and over almost before they'd begun. He'd surprised one in a lonely part of the park, just pulled her skirt up and her panties down and went at her, hauling off and smacking her with a rock a couple of times when she wouldn't keep quiet. That shut her up, and when he finished he found out why. She was dead. He'd evidently cracked her skull and killed her, and he'd been thrusting away at dead meat.

Hardly a memory to stir the blood ten years later. The second one wasn't much better either. He'd been about half drunk, and that had the effect of blurring the memory. He'd snapped her neck afterward, the little bitch, and he remembered that part, but he couldn't remember what it had felt like.

One good thing. Nobody ever found out about either of those two. If they had, he wouldn't have a prayer at today's hearing.

After the hearing, Paul managed to slip out before the press could catch up with him. Two days later, however, when the governor acted on the board's recommendation and commuted William Croydon's sentence to life imprisonment, one persistent reporter managed to get Paul in front of a video camera.

"For a long time I wanted vengeance," he admitted. "I honestly believed that I could only come to terms with the loss of my sister by seeing her killer put to death."

What changed that? the reporter wanted to know.

He stopped to consider his answer. "The dawning realization," he said, "that I could really only recover from Karen's death not by seeing Billy Croydon punished but by letting go of the need to punish. In the simplest terms, I had to forgive him."

And could he do that? Could he forgive the man who had brutally murdered his sister?

"Not overnight," he said. "It took time. I can't even swear I've forgiven him completely. But I've come far enough in the process to realize capital punishment is not only inhumane but pointless. Karen's death was wrong, but Billy Croydon's death would be another wrong, and two wrongs don't make a right. Now that his sentence has been lifted, I can get on with the process of complete forgiveness."

The reporter commented that it sounded as though Paul Dandridge had gone through some sort of religious conversion experience.

"I don't know about religion," Paul said, looking right at the camera. "I don't really consider myself a religious person. But something's happened, something transformational in nature, and I suppose you could call it spiritual."

WITH HIS SENTENCE commuted, Billy Croydon drew a transfer to another penitentiary, where he was assigned a cell in general population. After years of waiting to die he was being given a chance to create a life for himself within the prison's walls. He had a job in the prison laundry, he had access to the library and exercise yard. He didn't have his freedom, but he had life.

On the sixteenth day of his new life, three hard-eyed lifers cornered him in the room where they stored the bed linen. He'd noticed one of the men earlier, had caught him staring at him a few times, looking at Croydon the way you'd look at a woman. He hadn't spotted the other two before, but they had the same look in their eyes as the one he recognized.

There wasn't a thing he could do.

They raped him, all three of them, and they weren't gentle about it either. He fought at first but their response to that was savage and prompt, and he gasped at the pain and quit his struggling. He tried to disassociate himself from what was being done to him, tried to take his mind away to some private place. That was a way old cons had of doing time, getting through the hours on end of vacant boredom. This time it didn't really work.

They left him doubled up on the floor, warned him against saying anything to the hacks, and drove the point home with a boot to the ribs.

He managed to get back to his cell, and the following day he put in a request for a transfer to B Block, where you were locked down twenty-three hours a day. He was used to that on Death Row, so he knew he could live with it.

So much for making a life inside the walls. What he had to do was get out.

He still had his typewriter. He sat down, flexed his fingers. One of the rapists had bent his little finger back the day before, and it still hurt, but it wasn't one that he used for typing. He took a breath and started in.

"Dear Paul . . ."

> Dear Billy,
> As always, it was good to hear from you. I write not with news but just in the hope that I can lighten your spirits and build your resolve for the long road ahead. Winning your freedom

won't be an easy task, but it's my conviction that working together we can make it happen. . . .
Yours, Paul.

⌒‿

Dear Paul,
Thanks for the books. I missed a lot all those years when I never opened a book. It's funny—my life seems so much more spacious now, even though I'm spending all but one hour a day in a dreary little cell. But it's like that poem that starts, "Stone walls do not a prison make / Nor iron bars a cage." (I'd have to say, though, that the stone walls and iron bars around this place make a pretty solid prison.)

I don't expect much from the parole board next month, but it's a start. . . .

⌒‿

Dear Billy,
I was deeply saddened by the parole board's decision, although everything I'd heard had led me to expect nothing else. Even though you've been locked up more than enough time to be eligible, the thinking evidently holds that Death Row time somehow counts less than regular prison time, and that the board wants to see how you do as a prisoner serving a life sentence before letting you return to the outside world. I'm not sure I understand the logic there . . .

I'm glad you're taking it so well.
Your friend, Paul.

⌒‿

Dear Paul,
Once again, thanks for the books. They're a healthy cut above what's available here. This joint prides itself in its library, but when you say "Kierkegaard" to the prison librarian he looks at you funny, and you don't dare try him on Martin Buber.

I shouldn't talk, because I'm having troubles of my own with both of those guys. I haven't got anybody else to bounce this off, so do you mind if I press you into service? Here's my take on Kierkegaard . . .

Well, that's the latest from the Jailhouse Philosopher, who is pleased to be
Your friend, Billy.

Dear Billy,
Well, once again it's time for the annual appearance before parole board—or the annual circus, as you call it with plenty of justification. Last year we thought maybe the third time was the charm, and it turned out we were wrong, but maybe it'll be different this year. . . .

Dear Paul,
"Maybe it'll be different this time." Isn't that what Charlie Brown tells himself before he tries to kick the football? And Lucy always snatches it away.

Still, some of the deep thinkers I've been reading stress that hope is important even when it's unwarranted. And, although I'm a little scared to admit it, I have a good feeling this time.

And if they never let me out, well, I've reached a point where I honestly don't mind. I've found an inner life here that's far superior to anything I had in my years as a free man. Between my books, my solitude, and my correspondence with you, I have a life I can live with. Of course I'm hoping for parole, but if they snatch the football away again, it ain't gonna kill me.

Dear Billy,
. . . Just a thought, but maybe that's the line you should take with them. That you'd welcome parole, but you've made a life for yourself within the walls and you can stay there indefinitely if you have to.

I don't know, maybe that's the wrong strategy altogether, but I think it might impress them.

Dear Paul,
Who knows what's likely to impress them? On the other hand, what have I got to lose?

BILLY CROYDON SAT at the end of the long conference table, speaking when spoken to, uttering his replies in a low voice, giving pro forma responses to the same questions they asked him every year. At the end they asked him, as usual, if there was anything he wanted to say.

Well, what the hell, he thought. What did he have to lose?

"I'm sure it won't surprise you," he began, "to hear that I've come before you in the hope of being granted early release. I've had hearings before, and when I was turned down it was devastating. Well, I may not be doing myself any good by saying this, but this time around it won't destroy me if you decide to deny me parole. Almost in spite of myself, I've made a life for myself within prison walls. I've found an inner life, a life of the spirit, that's superior to anything I had as a free man . . ."

Were they buying it? Hard to tell. On the other hand, since it happened to be the truth, it didn't really matter whether they bought it or not.

He pushed on to the end. The chairman scanned the room, then looked at him and nodded shortly.

"Thank you, Mr. Croydon," he said. "I think that will be all for now."

"I THINK I speak for all of us," the chairman said, "when I say how much weight we attach to your appearance before this board. We're used to hearing the pleas of victims and their survivors, but almost invariably they come here to beseech us to deny parole. You're virtually unique, Mr. Dandridge, in appearing as the champion of the very man who . . ."

"Killed my sister," Paul said levelly.

"Yes. You've appeared before us on prior occasions, Mr. Dandridge, and while we were greatly impressed by your ability to forgive William Croydon and by the relationship you've forged with him, it seems to me that there's been a change in your own sentiments. Last year, I recall, while you pleaded on Mr. Croydon's behalf, we sensed that you did not wholeheartedly believe he was ready to be returned to society."

"Perhaps I had some hesitation."

"But this year . . ."

"Billy Croydon's a changed man. The process of change has been completed. I know that he's ready to get on with his life."

"There's no denying the power of your testimony, especially in light of its source." The chairman cleared his throat. "Thank you, Mr. Dandridge. I think that will be all for now."

"WELL?" PAUL SAID. "How do you feel?"

Billy considered the question. "Hard to say," he said. "Everything's a little unreal. Even being in a car. Last time I was in a moving vehicle was when I got my commutation and they transferred me from the other prison. It's not like Rip Van Winkle. I know what everything looks like from television, cars included. Tell the truth, I feel a little shaky."

"I guess that's to be expected."

"I suppose." He tugged his seat belt to tighten it. "You want to know how I feel, I feel vulnerable. All those years I was locked down twenty-three hours out of twenty-four. I knew what to expect, I knew I was safe. Now I'm a free man, and it scares the crap out of me."

"Look in the glove compartment," Paul said.

"Jesus, Johnnie Walker Black."

"I figured you might be feeling a little anxious. That ought to take the edge off."

"Yeah, Dutch courage," Billy said. "Why Dutch, do you happen to know? I've always wondered."

"No idea."

He weighed the bottle in his hand. "Been a long time," he said. "Haven't had a taste of anything since they locked me up."

"There was nothing available in prison?"

"Oh, there was stuff. The jungle juice cons made out of potatoes and raisins, and some good stuff that got smuggled in. But I wasn't in population, so I didn't have access. And anyway it seemed like more trouble than it was worth."

"Well, you're a free man now. Why don't you drink to it? I'm driving or I'd join you."

"Well . . ."

"Go ahead."

"Why not?" he said, and uncapped the bottle and held it to the light. "Pretty color, huh? Well, here's to freedom, huh?" He took a long drink, shuddered at the burn of the whiskey. "Kicks like a mule," he said.

"You're not used to it."

"I'm not." He put the cap on the bottle and had a little trouble screwing it back on. "Hitting me hard," he reported. "Like I was a little kid getting his first taste of it. Whew."

"You'll be all right."

"Spinning," Billy said, and slumped in his seat.

Paul glanced over at him, looked at him again a minute later. Then, after checking the mirror, he pulled the car off the road and braked to a stop.

BILLY WAS CONSCIOUS for a little while before he opened his eyes. He tried to get his bearings first. The last thing he remembered was a wave of dizziness after the slug of Scotch hit bottom. He was still sitting upright, but it didn't feel like a car seat, and he didn't sense any movement. No, he was in some sort of chair, and he seemed to be tied to it.

That didn't make any sense. A dream? He'd had lucid dreams before and knew how real they were, how you could be in them and wonder if you were dreaming and convince yourself you weren't. The way you broke the surface and got out of it was by opening your eyes. You had to force yourself, had to open your real eyes and not just your eyes in the dream, but it could be done. . . . There!

He was in a chair, in a room he'd never seen before, looking out a window at a view he'd never seen before. An open field, woods behind it.

He turned his head to the left and saw a wall paneled in knotty cedar. He turned to the right and saw Paul Dandridge, wearing boots and jeans and a plaid flannel shirt and sitting in an easy chair with a book. He said, "Hey!" and Paul lowered the book and looked at him.

"Ah," Paul said. "You're awake."

"What's going on?"

"What do you think?"

"There was something in the whiskey."

"There was indeed," Paul agreed. "You started to stir just as we made the turn off the state road. I gave you a booster shot with a hypodermic needle."

"I don't remember."

"You never felt it. I was afraid for a minute there that I'd given you too much. That would have been ironic, wouldn't you say? 'Death by lethal injection.' The sentence carried out finally after all these years, and you wouldn't have even known it happened."

He couldn't take it in. "Paul," he said, "for God's sake, what's it all about?"

"What's it about?" Paul considered his response. "It's about time."

"Time?"

"It's the last act of the drama."

"Where are we?"

"A cabin in the woods. Not *the* cabin. That would be ironic, wouldn't it?"

"What do you mean?"

"If I killed you in the same cabin where you killed Karen. Ironic, but not really feasible. So this is a different cabin in different woods, but it will have to do."

"You're going to kill me?"

"Of course."

"For God's sake, why?"

"Because that's how it ends, Billy. That's the point of the whole game. That's how I planned it from the beginning."

"I can't believe this."

"Why is it so hard to believe? We conned each other, Billy. You pretended to repent, and I pretended to believe you. You pretended to reform, and I pretended to be on your side. Now we can both stop pretending."

Billy was silent for a moment. Then he said, "I was trying to con you at the beginning."

"No kidding."

"There was a point where it turned into something else, but it started out as a scam. It was the only way I could think of to stay alive. You saw through it?"

"Of course."

"But you pretended to go along with it. Why?"

"Is it that hard to figure out?"

"It doesn't make any sense. What do you gain by it? My death? If you wanted me dead all you had to do was tear up my letter. The state was all set to kill me."

"They'd have taken forever," Paul said bitterly. "Delay after delay, and always the possibility of a reversal and a retrial, always the possibility of a commutation of sentence."

"There wouldn't have been a reversal, and it took you working for me to get my sentence commuted. There would have been delays, but there'd already been a few of them before I got around to writing to you. It couldn't have lasted too many years longer, and it would have added up to a lot less than it has now, with all the time I spent serving life and waiting for the parole board to open the doors. If you'd just let it go, I'd be dead and buried by now."

"You'll be dead soon," Paul told him. "And buried. It won't be much longer. Your grave's already dug. I took care of that before I drove to the prison to pick you up."

"They'll come after you, Paul. When I don't show up for my initial appointment with my parole officer—"

"They'll get in touch, and I'll tell them we had a drink and shook
hands and you went off on your own. It's not my fault if you decided
to skip town and violate the terms of your parole."

He took a breath. He said, "Paul, don't do this."

"Why not?"

"Because I'm begging you. I don't want to die."

"Ah," Paul said. "*That's* why."

"What do you mean?"

"If I left it to the state," he said, "they'd have been killing a dead
man. By the time the last appeal was denied and the last request for a
stay of execution turned down, you'd have been resigned to the
inevitable. They'd strap you to a gurney and give you a shot, and it
would be just like going to sleep."

"That's what they say."

"But now you want to live. You adjusted to prison, you made a life
for yourself in there, and then you finally made parole, icing on the
cake, and now you genuinely want to live. You've really got a life now,
Billy, and I'm going to take it away from you."

"You're serious about this."

"I've never been more serious about anything."

"You must have been planning this for years."

"From the very beginning."

"Jesus, it's the most thoroughly premeditated crime in the history
of the world, isn't it? Nothing I can do about it either. You've got me
tied tight and the chair won't tip over. Is there anything I can say
that'll make you change your mind?"

"Of course not."

"That's what I thought." He sighed. "Get it over with."

"I don't think so."

"Huh?"

"This won't be what the state hands out," Paul Dandridge said. "A
minute ago you were begging me to let you live. Before it's over you'll
be begging me to kill you."

"You're going to torture me."

"That's the idea."

"In fact you've already started, haven't you? This is the mental part."

"Very perceptive of you, Billy."

"For all the good it does me. This is all because of what I did to your sister, isn't it?"

"Obviously."

"I didn't do it, you know. It was another Billy Croydon that killed her, and I can barely remember what he was like."

"That doesn't matter."

"Not to you, evidently, and you're the one calling the shots. I'm sure Kierkegaard had something useful to say about this sort of situation, but I'm damned if I can call it to mind. You knew I was conning you, huh? Right from the jump?"

"Of course."

"I thought it was a pretty good letter I wrote you."

"It was a masterpiece, Billy. But that didn't mean it wasn't easy to see through."

"So now you dish it out and I take it," Billy Croydon said, "until you get bored and end it, and I wind up in the grave you've already dug for me. And that's the end of it. I wonder if there's a way to turn it around."

"Not a chance."

"Oh, I know I'm not getting out of here alive, Paul, but there's more than one way of turning something around. Let's see now. You know, the letter you got wasn't the first one I wrote to you."

"So?"

"The past is always with you, isn't it? I'm not the same man as the guy who killed your sister, but he's still there inside somewhere. Just a question of calling him up."

"What's that supposed to mean?"

"Just talking to myself, I guess. I was starting to tell you about that first letter. I never sent it, you know, but I kept it. For the longest time I held on to it and read it whenever I wanted to relive the experience. Then it stopped working, or maybe I stopped wanting to call up the past, but whatever it was I quit reading it. I still held on to it, and then one day I realized I didn't want to own it anymore. So I tore it up and got rid of it."

"That's fascinating."

"But I read it so many times I bet I can bring it back word for word." His eyes locked with Paul Dandridge's, and his lips turned up in the slightest suggestion of a smile. He said, "'Dear Paul, Sitting here in this cell waiting for the day to come when they put a needle in my arm and flush me down God's own toilet, I found myself thinking about your testimony in court. I remember how you said your sister was a goodhearted girl who spent her short life bringing pleasure to everyone who knew her. According to your testimony, knowing this helped you rejoice in her life at the same time that it made her death so hard to take.

"'Well, Paul, in the interest of helping you rejoice some more, I thought I'd tell you just how much pleasure your little sister brought to me. I've got to tell you that in all my life I never got more pleasure from anybody. My first look at Karen brought me pleasure, just watching her walk across campus, just looking at those jiggling tits and that tight little ass and imagining the fun I was going to have with them.'"

"Stop it, Croydon!"

"You don't want to miss this, Paulie. 'Then when I had her tied up in the backseat of the car with her mouth taped shut, I have to say she went on being a real source of pleasure. Just looking at her in the rearview mirror was enjoyable, and from time to time I would stop the car and lean into the back to run my hands over her body. I don't think she liked it much, but I enjoyed it enough for the both of us.'"

"You're a son of a bitch."

"And you're an asshole. You should have let the state put me out of everybody's misery. Failing that, you should have let go of the hate and sent the new William Croydon off to rejoin society. There's a lot more to the letter, and I remember it perfectly." He tilted his head, resumed quoting from memory. "'Tell me something, Paul. Did you ever fool around with Karen yourself? I bet you did. I can picture her when she was maybe eleven, twelve years old, with her little titties just beginning to bud out, and you'd have been seventeen or eighteen yourself, so how could you stay away from her? She's sleeping and you walk into her room and sit on the edge of her bed.'" He grinned. "I always liked that part. And there's lots more. You enjoying your revenge, Paulie? Is it as sweet as they say it is?"

The Purloined Letter

Edgar Allan Poe

Nil sapientiae odiosius acumine nimio.

—**Seneca***

AT PARIS, JUST AFTER dark one gusty evening in the autumn of 18——, I was enjoying the twofold luxury of meditation and a meerschaum, in company with my friend, C. Auguste Dupin, in his little back library, or book-closet, *au troisième*, No. 33 *Rue Dunôt, Faubourg St. Germain.* For one hour at least we had maintained a profound silence; while each, to any casual observer, might have seemed intently and exclusively occupied with the curling eddies of smoke that oppressed the atmosphere of the chamber. For myself, however, I was mentally discussing certain topics which had formed matter for conversation between us at an earlier period of the evening; I mean the affair of the Rue Morgue, and the mystery attending the murder of Marie Rogêt. I looked upon it, therefore, as something of a coincidence, when the door of our apartment was thrown open and admitted our old acquaintance, Monsieur G——, the Prefect of the Parisian police.

*"Nothing is more hateful to wisdom than too little keenness of insight." (Latin)

27

We gave him a hearty welcome; for there was nearly half as much of the entertaining as of the contemptible about the man, and we had not seen him for several years. We had been sitting in the dark, and Dupin now arose for the purpose of lighting a lamp, but sat down again, without doing so, upon G.'s saying that he had called to consult us, or rather to ask the opinion of my friend, about some official business which had occasioned a great deal of trouble.

"If it is any point requiring reflection," observed Dupin, as he forbore to enkindle the wick, "we shall examine it to better purpose in the dark."

"That is another of your odd notions," said the Prefect, who had the fashion of calling everything "odd" that was beyond his comprehension, and thus lived amid an absolute legion of "oddities."

"Very true," said Dupin, as he supplied his visitor with a pipe, and rolled toward him a comfortable chair.

"And what is the difficulty now?" I asked. "Nothing more in the assassination way I hope?"

"Oh, no; nothing of that nature. The fact is, the business is *very* simple indeed, and I make no doubt that we can manage it sufficiently well ourselves; but then I thought Dupin would like to hear the details of it, because it is so excessively *odd*."

"Simple and odd," said Dupin.

"Why, yes; and not exactly that either. The fact is, we have all been a good deal puzzled because the affair *is* so simple, and yet baffles us altogether."

"Perhaps it is the very simplicity of the thing which puts you at fault," said my friend.

"What nonsense you *do* talk!" replied the Prefect, laughing heartily.

"Perhaps the mystery is a little *too* plain," said Dupin.

"Oh, good heavens! Who ever heard of such an idea?"

"A little *too* self-evident."

"Ha! ha! ha!—ha! ha! ha!—ho! ho! ho!" roared our visitor, profoundly amused, "oh, Dupin, you will be the death of me yet!"

"And what, after all, *is* the matter on hand?" I asked.

"Why, I will tell you," replied the Prefect, as he gave a long, steady, and contemplative puff, and settled himself in his chair. "I will tell you in a few words; but, before I begin, let me caution you that this is an affair demanding the greatest secrecy, and that I should most probably lose the position I now hold, were it known that I confided it to any one."

"Proceed," said I.

"Or not," said Dupin.

"Well, then; I have received personal information, from a very high quarter, that a certain document of the last importance has been purloined from the royal apartments. The individual who purloined it is known; this beyond a doubt; he was seen to take it. It is known, also, that it still remains in his possession."

"How is this known?" asked Dupin.

"It is clearly inferred," replied the Prefect, "from the nature of the document, and from the non-appearance of certain results which would at once arise from its passing *out* of the robber's possession— that is to say, from his employing it as he must design in the end to employ it."

"Be a little more explicit," I said.

"Well, I may venture so far as to say that the paper gives its holder a certain power in a certain quarter where such power is immensely valuable." The Prefect was fond of the cant of diplomacy.

"Still I do not quite understand," said Dupin.

"No? Well; the disclosure of the document to a third person, who shall be nameless, would bring in question the honor of a personage of most exalted station; and this fact gives the holder of the document an ascendancy over the illustrious personage whose honor and peace are so jeopardized."

"But this ascendancy," I interposed, "would depend upon the robber's knowledge of the loser's knowledge of the robber. Who would dare—"

"The thief," said G., "is the Minister D——, who dares all things, those unbecoming as well as those becoming a man. The method of the theft was not less ingenious than bold. The document in question—a letter, to be frank—had been received by the personage robbed while alone in the royal *boudoir*. During its perusal she was suddenly interrupted by the entrance of the other exalted personage from whom especially it was her wish to conceal it. After a hurried and vain endeavor to thrust it in a drawer, she was forced to place it, open it was, upon a table. The address, however, was uppermost, and, the contents thus unexposed, the letter escaped notice. At this juncture enters the

Minister D———. His lynx eye immediately perceives the paper, recognizes the handwriting of the address, observes the confusion of the personage addressed, and fathoms her secret. After some business transactions, hurried through in his ordinary manner, he produces a letter somewhat similar to the one in question, opens it, pretends to read it, and then places it in close juxtaposition to the other. Again he converses, for some fifteen minutes, upon the public affairs. At length, in taking leave, he takes also from the table the letter to which he had no claim. Its rightful owner saw, but, of course, dared not call attention to the act, in the presence of the third personage who stood at her elbow. The minister decamped; leaving his own letter—one of no importance—upon the table."

"Here, then," said Dupin to me, "you have precisely what you demand to make the ascendancy complete—the robber's knowledge of the loser's knowledge of the robber."

"Yes," replied the Prefect; "and the power thus attained has, for some months past, been wielded, for political purposes, to a very dangerous extent. The personage robbed is more thoroughly convinced, every day, of the necessity of reclaiming her letter. But this, of course, cannot be done openly. In fine, driven to despair, she has committed the matter to me."

"Than whom," said Dupin, amid a perfect whirlwind of smoke, "no more sagacious agent could, I suppose, be desired, or even imagined."

"You flatter me," replied the Prefect; "but it is possible that some such opinion may have been entertained."

"It is clear," said I, "as you observe, that the letter is still in the possession of the minister; since it is this possession, and not any employment of the letter, which bestows the power. With the employment the power departs."

"True," said G.; "and upon this conviction I proceeded. My first care was to make thorough search of the minister's hotel; and here my chief embarrassment lay in the necessity of searching without his knowledge. Beyond all things, I have been warned of the danger which would result from giving him reason to suspect our design."

"But," said I, "you are quite *au fait* in these investigations. The Parisian police have done this thing often before."

"Oh, yes; and for this reason I did not despair. The habits of the minister gave me, too, a great advantage. He is frequently absent from home all night. His servants are by no means numerous. They sleep at a distance from their master's apartment, and, being chiefly Neapolitans, are readily made drunk. I have keys, as you know, with which I can open any chamber or cabinet in Paris. For three months a night has not passed, during the greater part of which I have not been engaged, personally, in ransacking the D—— Hotel. My honor is interested, and, to mention a great secret, the reward is enormous. So I did not abandon the search until I had become fully satisfied that the thief is a more astute man than myself. I fancy that I have investigated every nook and corner of the premises in which it is possible that the paper can be concealed."

"But is it not possible," I suggested, "that although the letter may be in possession of the minister, as it unquestionably is, he may have concealed it elsewhere than upon his own premises?"

"This is barely possible," said Dupin. "The present peculiar condition of affairs at court, and especially of those intrigues in which D—— is known to be involved, would render the instant availability of the document—its susceptibility of being produced at a moment's notice—a point of nearly equal importance with its possession."

"Its susceptibility of being produced?" said I.

"That is to say, of being *destroyed*," said Dupin.

"True," I observed; "the paper is clearly then upon the premises. As for its being upon the person of the minister, we may consider that as out of the question."

"Entirely," said the Prefect. "He has been twice waylaid, as if by footpads, and his person rigidly searched under my own inspection."

"You might have spared yourself this trouble," said Dupin. "D——, I presume, is not altogether a fool, and, if not, must have anticipated these waylayings, as a matter of course."

"Not *altogether* a fool," said G., "but then he is a poet, which I take to be only one remove from a fool."

"True," said Dupin, after a long and thoughtful whiff from his meerschaum, "although I have been guilty of certain doggerel myself."

"Suppose you detail," said I, "the particulars of your search."

"Why, the fact is, we took our time, and we searched *everywhere*. I have had long experience in these affairs. I took the entire building, room by room; devoting the nights of a whole week to each. We examined, first, the furniture of each apartment. We opened every possible drawer; and I presume you know that, to a properly trained police-agent, such a thing as a '*secret*' drawer is impossible. Any man is a dolt who permits a '*secret*' drawer to escape him in a search of this kind. The thing is so plain. There is a certain amount of bulk—of space—to be accounted for in every cabinet. Then we have accurate rules. The fiftieth part of a line could not escape us. After the cabinets we took the chairs. The cushions we probed with the fine long needles you have seen me employ. From the tables we removed the tops."

"Why so?"

"Sometimes the top of a·table, or other similarly arranged piece of furniture, is removed by the person wishing to conceal an article, then the leg is excavated, the article deposited within the cavity, and the top replaced. The bottoms and tops of bedposts are employed in the same way."

"But could not the cavity be detected by sounding?" I asked.

"By no means, if, when the article is deposited, a sufficient wadding of cotton be placed around it. Besides, in our case, we were obliged to proceed without noise."

"But you could not have removed—you could not have taken to pieces *all* articles of furniture in which it would have been possible to make a deposit in the manner you mention. A letter may be compressed into a thin spiral roll, not differing much in shape or bulk from a large knitting-needle, and in this form it might be inserted into the rung of a chair, for example. You did not take to pieces all the chairs?"

"Certainly not; but we did better—we examined the rungs of every chair in the hotel, and, indeed, the jointings of every description of furniture, by the aid of a most powerful microscope. Had there been any traces of recent disturbance we should not have failed to detect it instantly. A single grain of gimlet-dust, for example, would have been as obvious as an apple. Any disorder in the gluing—any unusual gaping in the joints—would have sufficed to insure detection."

"I presume you looked to the mirrors, between the boards and the plates, and you probed the beds and the bedclothes, as well as the curtains and carpets."

"That of course; and when we had absolutely completed every particle of the furniture in this way, then we examined the house itself. We divided its entire surface into compartments, which we numbered, so that none might be missed; then we scrutinized each individual square inch throughout the premises, including the two houses immediately adjoining, with the microscope, as before."

"The two houses adjoining!" I exclaimed; "you must have had a great deal of trouble."

"We had; but the reward offered is prodigious."

"You include the *grounds* about the houses?"

"All the grounds are paved with brick. They gave us comparatively little trouble. We examined the moss between the bricks, and found it undisturbed."

"You looked among D———'s papers, of course, and into the books of the library?"

"Certainly; we opened every package and parcel; we not only opened every book, but we turned over every leaf in each volume, not contenting ourselves with a mere shake, according to the fashion of some of our police officers. We also measured the thickness of every book-*cover*, with the most accurate admeasurement, and applied to each the most jealous scrutiny of the microscope. Had any of the bindings been recently meddled with, it would have been utterly impossible that the fact should have escaped observation. Some five or six volumes, just from the hands of the binder, we carefully probed, longitudinally, with the needles."

"You explored the floors beneath the carpets?"

"Beyond doubt. We removed every carpet, and examined the boards with the microscope."

"And the paper on the walls?"

"Yes."

"You looked into the cellars?"

"We did."

"Then," I said, "you have been making a miscalculation, and the letter is *not* upon the premises, as you suppose."

"I fear you are right there," said the Prefect. "And now, Dupin, what would you advise me to do?"

"To make a thorough research of the premises."

"That is absolutely needless," replied G———. "I am not more sure that I breathe than I am that the letter is not at the hotel."

"I have no better advice to give you," said Dupin. "You have, of course, an accurate description of the letter?"

"Oh, yes!"—And here the Prefect, producing a memorandum-book, proceeded to read aloud a minute account of the internal, and especially of the external, appearance of the missing document. Soon after finishing the perusal of this description, he took his departure, more entirely depressed in spirits than I had ever known the good gentleman before.

In about a month afterward he paid us another visit, and found us occupied very nearly as before. He took a pipe and a chair and entered into some ordinary conversation. At length I said:

"Well, but G., what of the purloined letter? I presume you have at last made up your mind that there is no such thing as overreaching the minister?"

"Confound him, say I—yes; I made the re-examination, however, as Dupin suggested—but it was all labor lost, as I knew it would be."

"How much was the reward offered, did you say?" asked Dupin.

"Why, a very great deal—a *very* liberal reward—I don't like to say how much, precisely, but one thing I *will* say, that I wouldn't mind giving my individual check for fifty thousand francs to any one who could obtain me that letter. The fact is, it is becoming of more and more importance every day; and the reward has been lately doubled. If it were trebled, however, I could do no more than I have done."

"Why, yes," said Dupin, drawlingly, between the whiffs of his meerschaum, "I really—think, G., you have not exerted yourself—to the utmost in this matter. You might—do a little more, I think, eh?"

"How?—in what way?"

"Why—puff, puff—you might—puff, puff—employ counsel in the matter, eh?—puff, puff. Do you remember the story they tell of Abernethy?"

"No; hang Abernethy!"

"To be sure! Hang him and welcome. But, once upon a time, a certain rich miser conceived the design of sponging upon this Abernethy for a medical opinion. Getting up, for this purpose, an ordinary conversation in a private company, he insinuated his case to the physician, as that of an imaginary individual."

"'We will suppose,' said the miser, 'that his symptoms are such and such; now, doctor, what would *you* have directed him to take?'"

"'Take!' said Abernethy, 'why, take *advice*, to be sure.'"

"But," said the Prefect, a little discomposed, "I am *perfectly* willing to take advice, and to pay for it. I would *really* give fifty thousand francs to any one who would aid me in the matter."

"In that case," replied Dupin, opening a drawer, and producing a checkbook, "you may as well fill me up a check for the amount mentioned. When you have signed it, I will hand you the letter."

I was astounded. The Prefect appeared absolutely thunderstricken. For some minutes he remained speechless and motionless, looking incredulously at my friend with open mouth, and eyes that seemed starting from their sockets; then apparently recovering himself in some measure, he seized a pen, and after several pauses and vacant stares, finally filled up and signed a check for fifty thousand francs, and handed it across the table to Dupin. The latter examined it carefully and deposited it in his pocket-book; then, unlocking an *escritoire*, took thence a letter and gave it to the Prefect. This functionary grasped it in a perfect agony of joy, opened it with a trembling hand, cast a rapid glance at its contents, and then, scrambling and struggling to the door, rushed at length unceremoniously from the room and from the house, without having uttered a syllable since Dupin had requested him to fill up the check.

When he had gone, my friend entered into some explanations.

"The Parisian police," he said, "are exceedingly able in their way. They are persevering, ingenious, cunning, and thoroughly versed in the knowledge which their duties seem chiefly to demand. Thus, when G——— detailed to us his mode of searching the premises at the Hotel D———, I felt entire confidence in his having made a satisfactory investigation—so far as his labors extended."

"So far as his labors extended?" said I.

"Yes," said Dupin. "The measures adopted were not only the best of their kind, but carried out to absolute perfection. Had the letter been deposited within the range of their search, these fellows would, beyond a question, have found it."

I merely laughed—but he seemed quite serious in all that he said.

"The measures, then," he continued, "were good in their kind, and well executed; their defect lay in their being inapplicable to the case and to the man. A certain set of highly ingenious resources are, with the Prefect, a sort of Procrustean bed, to which he forcibly adapts his designs. But he perpetually errs by being too deep or too shallow for the matter in hand; and many a school-boy is a better reasoner than he. I knew one about eight years of age, whose success at guessing in the game of 'even and odd' attracted universal admiration. This game is simple, and is played with marbles. One player holds in his hand a number of these toys, and demands of another whether that number is even or odd. If the guess is right, the guesser wins one; if wrong, he loses one. The boy to whom I allude won all the marbles of the school. Of course he had some principle of guessing; and this lay in mere observation and admeasurement of the astuteness of his opponents. For example, an arrant simpleton is his opponent, and, holding up his closed hand, asks, 'Are they even or odd?' Our school-boy replies, 'Odd,' and loses; but upon the second trial he wins, for he then says to himself: 'The simpleton had them even upon the first trial, and his amount of cunning is just sufficient to make him have them odd upon the second; I will therefore guess odd';—he guesses odd, and wins. Now, with a simpleton a degree above the first, he would have reasoned thus: 'This fellow finds that in the first instance I guessed odd, and, in the second, he will propose to himself, upon the first impulse, a simple variation from even to odd, as did the first simpleton; but then a second thought will suggest that this is too simple a variation, and finally he will decide upon putting it even as before. I will therefore guess even'—he guesses even, and wins. Now this mode of reasoning in the school-boy, whom his fellows termed 'lucky,'—what, in its last analysis, is it?"

"It is merely," I said, "an identification of the reasoner's intellect with that of his opponent."

"It is," said Dupin; "and, upon inquiring of the boy by what means he effected the *thorough* identification in which his success consisted, I received answer as follows: 'When I wish to find out how wise, or how stupid, or how good, or how wicked is any one, or what are his thoughts at the moment, I fashion the expression of my face, as accurately as possible, in accordance with the expression of his, and then wait to see what thoughts or sentiments arise in my mind or heart, as if to match or correspond with the expression.' This response of the school-boy lies at the bottom of all the spurious profundity which has been attributed to a Rochefoucault, to La Bougive, to Machiavelli, and to Campanella."

"And the identification," I said, "of the reasoner's intellect with that of his opponent, depends, if I understand you aright, upon the accuracy with which the opponent's intellect is admeasured."

"For its practical value it depends upon this," replied Dupin; "and the Prefect and his cohort fail so frequently, first, by default of this identification, and, secondly, by ill-admeasurement, or rather through non-admeasurement, of the intellect with which they are engaged. They consider only their *own* ideas of ingenuity; and, in searching for any thing hidden, advert only to the modes in which *they* would have hidden it. They are right in this much—that their own ingenuity is a faithful representative of that of *the mass*; but when the cunning of the individual felon is diverse in character from their own, the felon foils them, of course. This always happens when it is above their own, and very usually when it is below. They have no variation of principle in their investigations; at best, when urged by some unusual emergency—by some extraordinary reward— they extend or exaggerate their old modes of *practice*, without touch- ing their principles. What, for example, in this case of D———, has been done to vary the principle of action? What is all this boring, and probing, and sounding, and scrutinizing with the microscope, and dividing the surface of the building into registered square inch- es—what is it all but an exaggeration *of the application* of the one principle or set of principles of search, which are based upon the one set of notions regarding human ingenuity, to which the Prefect, in the long routine of his duty, has been accustomed? Do you not see he has taken it for granted that *all* men proceed to conceal a letter, not exactly in a gimlet-hole bored in a chair-leg, but, at least, in *some* out-of-the-way hole or corner suggested by the same tenor of thought which would urge a man to secrete a letter in a gimlet-hole bored in a chair-leg? And do you not see also, that such *recherchés* nooks for concealment are adapted only for ordinary occasions, and would be adopted only by ordinary intellects; for, in all cases of con- cealment, a disposal of the article concealed—a disposal of it in this *recherché* manner—is, in the very first instance, presumable and pre- sumed; and thus its discovery depends, not at all upon the acumen, but altogether upon the mere care, patience, and determination of the seekers; and where the case is of importance—or, what amounts to the same thing in the political eyes, when the reward is of mag- nitude—the qualities in question have *never* been known to fail. You will now understand what I meant in suggesting that, had the pur- loined letter been hidden anywhere within the limits of the Prefect's examination—in other words, had the principle of its concealment been comprehended within the principles of the Prefect—its discovery would have been a matter altogether beyond question. This functionary, however, has been thoroughly mystified; and the remote source of his defeat lies in the supposition that the Minister is a fool, because he has acquired renown as a poet. All fools are poets; this the Prefect *feels*; and he is merely guilty of a *non distributio medii* in thence inferring that all poets are fools."

"But is this really the poet?" I asked. "There are two brothers, I know; and both have attained reputation in letters. The Minister I believe has written learnedly on the Differential Calculus. He is a mathematician, and no poet."

"You are mistaken; I know him well; he is both. As poet *and* mathematician, he would reason well; as mere mathematician, he could not have reasoned at all, and thus would have been at the mercy of the Prefect."

"You surprise me," I said, "by these opinions, which have been contradicted by the voice of the world. You do not mean to set at naught the well-digested idea of centuries. The mathematical reason has long been regarded as the reason *par excellence*."

"'*Il y a à parier*,'" replied Dupin, quoting from Chamfort, "'*que toute idée publique, toute convention reçue, est une sottise, car elle a convenue au plus grand nombre.*' The mathematicians, I grant you, have done their best to promulgate the popular error to which you allude, and which is none the less an error for its promulgation as truth. With an art worthy a better cause, for example, they have insinuated the term 'analysis' into application to algebra. The French are the originators of this particular deception; but if a term is of any importance—if words derive any value from applicability—then 'analysis' conveys 'algebra' about as much as, in Latin, '*ambitus*' implies 'ambition,' '*religio*' 'religion,' or '*homines honesti*' a set of 'honorable men.'"

"You have a quarrel on hand, I see," said I, "with some of the algebraists of Paris; but proceed."

"I dispute the availability, and thus the value, of that reason which is cultivated in any especial form other than the abstractly logical. I dispute, in particular, the reason educed by mathematical study. The mathematics are the science of form and quantity; mathematical reasoning is merely logic applied to observation upon form and quantity.

The great error lies in supposing that even the truths of what is called *pure* algebra are abstract or general truths. And this error is so egregious that I am confounded at the universality with which it has been received. Mathematical axioms are not axioms of general truth. What is true of *relation*—of form and quantity—is often grossly false in regard to morals, for example. In this latter science it is very usually *untrue* that the aggregated parts are equal to the whole. In chemistry also the axiom fails. In the consideration of motive it fails; for two motives, each of a given value, have not, necessarily, a value when united, equal to the sum of their values apart. There are numerous other mathematical truths which are only truths within the limits of *relation*. But the mathematician argues from his *finite truths*, through habit, as if they were of an absolutely general applicability—as the world indeed imagines them to be. Bryant, in his very learned 'Mythology,' mentions an analogous source of error, when he says that 'although the pagan fables are not believed, yet we forget ourselves continually, and make inferences from them as existing realities.' With the algebraists, however, who are pagans themselves, the 'pagan fables' *are* believed, and the inferences are made, not so much through lapse of memory as through an unaccountable addling of the brains. In short, I never yet encountered the mere mathematician who would be trusted out of equal roots, or one who did not clandestinely hold it as a point of his faith that $x^2 + px$ was absolutely and unconditionally equal to q. Say to one of these gentlemen, by way of experiment, if you please, that you believe occasions may occur where $x^2 + px$ is not altogether equal to q, and, having made him understand what you mean, get out of his reach as speedily as convenient, for, beyond doubt, he will endeavor to knock you down.

"I mean to say," continued Dupin, while I merely laughed at his last observations, "that if the Minister had been no more than a mathematician, the Prefect would have been under no necessity of giving me this check. I knew him, however, as both mathematician and poet, and my measures were adapted to his capacity, with reference to the circumstances by which he was surrounded. I knew him as a courtier, too, and as a bold *intrigant*. Such a man, I considered, could not fail to be aware of the ordinary policial modes of action. He could not have failed to anticipate—and events have proved that he did not fail to anticipate—the waylayings to which he was subjected. He must have foreseen, I reflected, the secret investigations of his premises. His frequent absences from home at night, which were hailed by the Prefect as certain aids to his success, I regarded only as *ruses*, to afford opportunity for thorough search to the police, and thus the sooner to impress them with the conviction to which G———, in fact, did finally arrive—the conviction that the letter was not upon the premises. I felt, also, that the whole train of thoughts, which I was at some pains in detailing to you just now, concerning the invariable principle of policial action in searches for articles concealed—I felt that this whole train of thought would necessarily pass through the mind of the Minister. It would imperatively lead him to despise all the ordinary *nooks* of concealment. *He* could not, I reflected, be so weak, as not to see that the most intricate and remote recess of his hotel would be as open as his commonest closets to the eyes, to the probes, to the gimlets, and to the microscopes of the Prefect. I saw, in fine, that he would be driven, as a matter of course, to *simplicity*, if not deliberately induced to it as a matter of choice. You will remember, perhaps, how desperately the Prefect laughed when I suggested, upon our first interview, that it was just possible this mystery troubled him so much on account of its being so *very* self-evident."

"Yes," said I, "I remember his merriment well. I really thought he would have fallen into convulsions."

"The material world," continued Dupin, "abounds with very strict analogies to the immaterial; and thus some color of truth has been given to the rhetorical dogma, that metaphor, or simile, may be made to strengthen an argument as well as to embellish a description. The principle of the *vis inertiae*, for example, seems to be identical in physics and metaphysics. It is not more true in the former, that a large body is with more difficulty set in motion than a smaller one, and that its subsequent *momentum* is commensurate with this difficulty, than it is, in the latter, that intellects of the vaster capacity, while more forcible, more constant, and more eventful in their movements than those of inferior grade, are yet the less readily moved, and more embarrassed, and full of hesitation in the first few steps of their progress. Again: have you ever noticed which of the street signs, over the shop doors, are the most attractive of attention?"

"I have never given the matter a thought," I said.

"There is a game of puzzles," he resumed, "which is played upon a map. One party playing requires another to find a given word—the name of town, river, state, or empire—any word, in short, upon the motley and perplexed surface of the chart. A novice in the game generally seeks to embarrass his opponents by giving them the most minutely lettered names; but the adept selects such words as stretch, in large characters, from one end of the chart to the other. These, like the over-largely lettered signs and placards of the street, escape observation by dint of being excessively obvious; and here the physical oversight is precisely analogous with the moral inapprehension by which the intellect suffers to pass unnoticed those considerations which are too obtrusively and too palpably self-evident. But this is a point, it appears, somewhat above or beneath the understanding of the Prefect. He never once thought it probable, or possible, that the Minister had deposited the letter immediately beneath the nose of the whole world, by way of best preventing any portion of that world from perceiving it.

"But the more I reflected upon the daring, dashing, and discriminating ingenuity of D——; upon the fact that the document must always have been *at hand,* if he intended to use it to good purpose; and upon the decisive evidence, obtained by the Prefect, that it was not hidden within the limits of that dignitary's ordinary search—the more satisfied I became that, to conceal this letter, the minister had resorted to the comprehensive and sagacious expedient of not attempting to conceal it at all.

"Full of these ideas, I prepared myself with a pair of green spectacles, and called one fine morning, quite by accident, at the Ministerial hotel. I found D—— at home, yawning, lounging, and dawdling, as usual, and pretending to be in the last extremity of *ennui.* He is, perhaps, the most really energetic human being now alive—but that is only when nobody sees him.

"To be even with him, I complained of my weak eyes, and lamented the necessity of the spectacles, under cover of which I cautiously and thoroughly surveyed the whole apartment, while seemingly intent only upon the conversation of my host.

"I paid especial attention to a large writing-table near which he sat, and upon which lay confusedly, some miscellaneous letters and other papers, with one or two musical instruments and a few books.

Here, however, after a long and very deliberate scrutiny, I saw nothing to excite particular suspicion. At length my eyes, in going the circuit of the room, fell upon a trumpery filigree card-rack of pasteboard, that hung dangling by a dirty blue ribbon, from a little brass knob just beneath the middle of the mantelpiece. In this rack, which had three or four compartments, were five or six visiting cards and a solitary letter. This last was much soiled and crumpled. It was torn nearly in two, across the middle—as if a design, in the first instance, to tear it entirely up as worthless, had been altered, or stayed, in the second. It had a large black seal, bearing the D——— cipher very conspicuously, and was addressed, in a diminutive female hand, to D———, the Minister, himself. It was thrust carelessly, and even, as it seemed, contemptuously, into one of the uppermost divisions of the rack.

"No sooner had I glanced at this letter than I concluded it to be that of which I was in search. To be sure, it was, to all appearance, radically different from the one of which the Prefect had read us so minute a description. Here the seal was large and black, with the D——— cipher; there it was small and red, with the ducal arms of the S——— family. Here, the address, to the Minister, was diminutive and feminine, there the superscription, to a certain royal personage, was markedly bold and decided; the size alone formed a point of correspondence. But, then, the *radicalness* of these differences, which was excessive; the dirt; the soiled and torn condition of the paper, so inconsistent with the *true* methodical habits of D———, and so suggestive of a design to delude the beholder into an idea of the worthlessness of the document;—these things, together with the hyperobtrusive situation of this document, full in the view of every visitor, and thus exactly in accordance with the conclusions to which I had previously arrived; these things, I say, were strongly corroborative of suspicion, in one who came with the intention to suspect.

"I protracted my visit as long as possible, and, while I maintained a most animated discussion with the Minister, upon a topic which I knew well had never failed to interest and excite him, I kept my attention really riveted upon the letter. In this examination, I committed to memory its external appearance and arrangement in the rack; and also fell, at length, upon a discovery which set at rest whatever trivial doubt I might have entertained. In scrutinizing the edges of the paper,

I observed them to be more *chafed* than seemed necessary. They pre-sented the *broken* appearance which is manifested when a stiff paper, having been once folded and pressed with a folder, is refolded in a reversed direction, in the same creases or edges which had formed the original fold. This discovery was sufficient. It was clear to me that the letter had been turned, as a glove, inside out, re-directed and re-sealed. I bade the Minister good-morning, and took my departure at once, leaving a gold snuff-box upon the table.

"The next morning I called for the snuff-box, when we resumed, quite eagerly, the conversation of the preceding day. While thus engaged, however, a loud report, as if of a pistol, was heard immedi-ately beneath the windows of the hotel, and was succeeded by a series of fearful screams, and the shoutings of a terrified mob. D——— rushed to a casement, threw it open, and looked out. In the meantime I stepped to the card-rack, took the letter, put it in my pocket, and replaced it by a *facsimile* (so far as regards externals) which I had care-fully prepared at my lodgings—imitating the D——— cipher, very readily, by means of a seal formed of bread.

"The disturbance in the street had been occasioned by the frantic behavior of a man with a musket. He had fired it among a crowd of women and children. It proved, however, to have been without ball, and the fellow was suffered to go his way as a lunatic or a drunkard. When he had gone, D——— came from the window, whither I had followed him immediately upon securing the object in view. Soon afterward I bade him farewell. The pretended lunatic was a man in my own pay."

"But what purpose had you," I asked, "in replacing the letter by a *facsimile*? Would it not have been better, at the first visit, to have seized it openly, and departed?"

"D———," replied Dupin, "is a desperate man, and a man of nerve. His hotel, too, is not without attendants devoted to his inter-ests. Had I made the wild attempt you suggest, I might never have left the Ministerial presence alive. The good people of Paris might have heard of me no more. But I had an object apart from these consider-ations. You know my political prepossessions. In this matter, I act as a partisan of the lady concerned. For eighteen months the Minister has had her in his power. She has now him in hers—since, being unaware that the letter is not in his possession, he will proceed with his exactions as if it was. Thus will he inevitably commit himself, at once, to his political destruction. His downfall, too, will not be more precipitate than awkward. It is all very well to talk about the *facilis descensus Averni*, but in all kinds of climbing, as Catalani said of singing, it is far more easy to get up than to come down. In the present instance I have no sympathy—at least no pity—for him who descends. He is that *monstrum horrendum*, an unprincipled man of genius. I confess, however, that I should like very well to know the precise character of his thoughts, when, being defied by her whom the Prefect terms 'a certain personage,' he is reduced to opening the letter which I left for him in the card-rack."

"How? Did you put any thing particular in it?"

"Why—it did not seem altogether right to leave the interior blank—that would have been insulting. D———, at Vienna once, did me an evil turn, which I told him, quite good-humoredly, that I should remember. So, as I knew he would feel some curiosity in regard to the identity of the person who had outwitted him, I thought it a pity not to give him a clew. He is well acquainted with my MS., and I just copied into the middle of the blank sheet the words—

"——— ———*Un dessein si funeste,*
S'il n'est digne d'Atrée, est digne de Thyeste."

"They are to be found in Crébillon's 'Atrée.'"

An Act of Violence

William F. Nolan

June 20, 1994

To Janice Coral Olinger,
Having read every word you've written, I feel I know you well enough to address you as "Dearest Janice," but of course this would not be socially appropriate. I'm a fellow writer who stands in your very tall shadow—but (to my honor and delight) we have shared many an anthology contents page together. Thus far, nine of my humble tales have been selected for anthologies in which your fine work has appeared. But I doubt that you read my contributions or even know I exist, since you probably have no time for the work of obscure writers such as myself. (I know how busy you 'are: *Conversations with Janice Coral Olinger* lists ninety-eight books in a thirty-year career span, and at least twenty-five of these are major novels. Amazing output!) But, hey, you don't have to know me because this letter will serve to introduce me to you.

My reason for writing at this time is to extend my sincere and heartfelt condolences on the very recent death of your husband, Theodore N. Olinger. I know that you and "Ted" were both very devoted to one another and that his sad passing (isn't cancer a bitch!) was a severe blow to you emotionally. Ted (if I may so refer to him) was a wonderful poet and an astute critic, and I realize that you both shared an intellectual and creative seedground as well as an abiding physical attraction. Your sex life with Ted is naturally none of my business, but a strong sexual bond was evident from your mutual behavior in public. The way you held hands and *touched* each other at that P.E.N. awards dinner made this very clear to me. (Yeah, I was there.)

Anyhow, please accept my deepest sympathy at this immense and tragic loss in your life. I trust that once you have weathered your period of mourning you will again return to the role you were born for: that of a supreme artist of the written word.

> With profound respect and good wishes,
> Alex Edward

P.S. My address is on the envelope in case you wish to reply— and I *do* hope you will wish to do so.

July 30, 1994

Dear Janice Coral Olinger,

Well, the Great Wheel of Time grinds ever onward and I see that more than a full month has gone by without a reply from you to my missive of 20 June. That's fine, really it is. I had, of course, hoped for a reply, but I am certainly not surprised that I failed to receive one. In view of your personal family loss, this is quite understandable, and I bear you no malice. I'm sure your mail has been piling up from many other devoted readers and that you simply have not been up to answering it. (Bet you get a *ton* of letters!)

However, now that you have been granted suitable time to pull yourself together, I *would* ask that you be kind enough to honor me with a personal reply.

I'm excited about your latest novel, *Whose Blood Is It, Anyhow?* (what a bold and splendid title!) which I have had the pleasure of reading as they say "cover to cover." (In fact, I was up most of last night lost in those final, dynamic chapters!) May I say that I am truly awestruck at the passion and artistry evident on every page of this epic work. Your short stories are marvelous watercolors, but your novels are many-layered oil paintings. (At least, that's how I think of them.) And your dialogue . . . wow! No one in America today handles dialogue with your deft, incisive touch. Just one example (of oh, so many!): when your dying politician, Arthur (invoking shades of Camelot, right?) bids his final farewell to Morgana (a clever reversal of character names in terms of darkness and light), their exchange left me literally breathless. The entire scene was illuminated by your brilliant dialogue. *Viva! Bravissimo!*

I could go on for pages about *Blood*, but I'll let the critics rave for me—as they most certainly will. Let me just say how much your work has inspired my own, how your fire and passion have transformed my life. I am a better man, a better human being, because of Janice Coral Olinger. *Salud!*

By the way, to prove whereof I speak, I have every one of your books in mint first editions, with each dust jacket carefully protected by a clear plastic cover.

As a writer, you are numero uno. No one else has your heart, your spirit, your expansive imagination. I stand in humble awe of your powers.

Enough. Write to me soon and let me know your reaction to this letter. I eagerly await your response.

> With sincere admiration,
> Alex Edward

August 25, 1994

Dear Janice Coral Olinger,

I'm frankly perplexed. All these weeks have gone by and I
haven't heard a peep out of you. I know you received my letters since my return address was plain on each and I never
got them back from the post office. Have you been ill? On a
trip? Away on a lecture tour? What's the problem? All I have
asked is that you take a few minutes to reply to someone who
has shown his deep and sincere respect for your boundless
creative gifts. Truly, I don't see why you can't write me a letter (however brief) acknowledging my existence. Why do
you continue to ignore me in this disturbing fashion when it
is obvious I so greatly admire you? (It seems that common
courtesy alone would dictate a reply.) I repeat, what's the
problem?

Last night I reread your short story, "The River Incident"—
which rightfully earned the O. Henry prize in '82 (go,
Janice!). And once again I was struck with your employment
of raw violence within the context of a higher sense of
morality. Your characters *transcend* death, even though they
may themselves die or cause others to die. In "The River
Incident," when Cara shoots her father on the riverbank, her
act is not an act of violence, but of release. (Obviously, this
is what the O. Henry judges realized.) Knowing there is no
hope for the old man's future, knowing that life has become
a terrible burden on him, Cara sends a .45 slug into his brain,
allowing him ultimate freedom and a release from the crip-
pling cage of his body. (Which is exactly what the great lady
poet Sylvia Plath accomplished with her suicide; I *know* you
agree.) "Go, my father, go," she says, pressing the barrel
against his temple and pulling the trigger. She is sending him
on a wondrous journey. Thus, her act is one of great compassion.

I am curious. What was your motivation for this story? Did it
come out of your own life—or did you hear about an incident
like this when you were growing up in that house by the river
in Maryland? (The story has a ring of stark truth which cannot

be denied.) Or did it all flow from your incredible imagination? Please, write and let me know.

Devotedly yours,
Alex Edward

⌒

September 2, 1994

Dear (silent) Janice Coral Olinger,
Here we are into September and I've had *no* word of any kind from you. I am baffled (and, I must confess, somewhat hurt) by your continued silence and lack of human response. Why are you treating me in this manner? Why are my letters to you being ignored? Why am *I* being ignored? It is obvious from what I've written how much I admire you and your works. I have made this abundantly clear. Why, then, have you chosen to bypass me utterly, as if I don't exist? I simply do not understand why you cannot spare a few random minutes for me (no matter *how* busy you may be).

This is not like you, not in character with your work. Your books, for all their overt violence, are extremely humanistic at their core, and I know you to be a gentle, caring person, a creature of warm compassion. (What was it Ted said of you in that *Newsweek* piece? . . . that you were "a vessel of tenderness.") One look into those round dark luminous eyes of yours clearly reveals your compassionate soul. Well, what about sending some of that compassion in my direction? I could *use* a little. All I'm asking of you is a simple note, after all. A few kind words, letting me know you appreciate my devotion as a dedicated reader. Is this too much to ask? I think not. Right now, with my letter before you, write and let me know you *care*.

Vaya con Dios!
Alex Edward

⌒

October 15, 1994

Janice Coral Olinger,

I find that I can no longer address you as "Dear." Your cold, unresponsive silence has rendered such a salutation impossible. I checked my files today and find that I first wrote you a letter (and a fine, warm one it was!) on 20 June—almost *four full months ago*! I followed up this initial missive with those of 30 July, 25 August, and 2 September, all without a *single word* back from you. There is no excuse for this kind of rudeness. You insult me with your stubborn refusal to respond to my letters. It is no longer possible for me to maintain positive feelings toward you. Your cruelty has also tainted your work, and this is most unfortunate. I now look at your shelved books and mourn the past. You have wounded me deeply. Additionally, you have made me look like a fool. I wrote to praise you and got nothing back. I'm becoming very angry at you, Ms. Olinger—or however the hell you like to be addressed. Just who do you think you are, some goddess living up in the clouds? You live right here on good ole Mother Earth, just like I do. We both breathe, eat, and shit, like everybody else on this lousy planet. You're no goddess, lady. You may know how to write novels and stories, but you sure don't know much about common courtesy.

And what do you say to this?

In frustration,
Alex Edward

December 10, 1994

Olinger bitch . . .

Again, you have chosen to callously ignore my letter of 15 October. You obviously don't give a flying fuck about me, or my opinions, or my words, or anything else having to do with Alex Edward. Normally, I'm a real easygoing guy, patient, reasonable, quick to forgive and forget—but you've gone over the line. Your snotty silence is just too fucking much. I will *not* be treated this way. Not by you or by anybody. Let me state my position loud and clear: either I get a letter of apology from you within the next ten days or I'll be over to your house in Baltimore to give you a Christmas present you *won't* like. Remember what the witch said to Dorothy in that Oz film . . . "and your little dog, too!" Well, I'll also have a present for that witless little pansy poodle you lug around in your arms for all those dust jacket photos. I think you should know that what you are doing is directly promoting an act of violence. You are really one rude bitch and if I don't hear from you this time, I'm sure as hell going to pay you a personal visit.

Think I'm bluffing? Just blowing off steam? Think I won't act? Then think again, sister, because you are dealing with a guy who has your number. The way you mistreat people means you don't *deserve* to go on living.

It's like in that *Harper's* story of yours, "Dark Angel." Take my word, unless your apology is in my mailbox by 20 December ,I'm *your* Dark Angel come Christmas.

This is one letter you better not ignore.

Alex E.

PRESS ANNOUNCEMENT—FOR IMMEDIATE RELEASE

On the morning of December 26, 1994, in the den of a private home at 6000 Roland Avenue, Baltimore, Maryland, the body of noted writer Janice Coral Olinger was discovered by neighbors. She had been shot once in the left temple and had died instantly. Her white poodle, "Snowball," was found lying beside her. The dog had also been shot to death.

Local police were called to the scene. Lieutenant Angus Campbell of Baltimore Homicide has issued this public statement:

Several handwritten letters, dated from June into December of this year, were found on the desk of the deceased. They were all signed "Alex Edward."

Ms. Olinger's father, A. E. Coral, was for many years a prominent Baltimore banker, and was known to have a violent temper. Police records show that he had frequently been cited for physically abusive incidents involving his wife, Barbara, as well as Janice Coral (later Janice Coral Olinger), their daughter. Records indicate that Janice Coral left the family home as a teenager and apparently never saw her father again. His initials, A. E., stand for Alexander Edward, which correlate with the signatures on the letters.

In the opinion of Dr. Thomas F. O'Rourke, a respected Baltimore psychiatrist, the emotionally shattering death of her husband, noted poet Theodore Olinger, caused a fracture in Janice Coral Olinger's personality. She took on a second, wholly separate identity based on the male persona of her violent father and, as "Alex Edward," wrote the series of deranged letters leading to the tragedy.

Her death, by gunshot, was apparently self-inflicted. The police department theorizes that she first shot her pet, then put the weapon to her own head. Dr. O'Rourke explained it as an "acting out of what her father might have done to her had she remained in the family home." (The banker was later jailed for attempting to murder his wife, Barbara Coral, and is now serving a term in the Maryland state prison.)

The death of Janice Coral Olinger is tragic and senseless, the product of what Dr. O'Rourke describes as "a lingering and ultimately fatal childhood trauma." Funeral arrangements are pending.

The Corbett Correspondence

"Agent No. 5 & Agent No. 6"

Merrivale Hall
Dunseaton
Reading, Berks.

November 1st, 1995

Dear Agent No. 6,

How refreshing to have a female operative in the Secret Service! You are an example to us all. That clapped-out Volkswagen is the perfect camouflage for you, though a trifle Third Reich for my own taste. However, it is the ideal complement to the Luger pistol you keep strapped to your right thigh.

Calamity! Delightful as it was to have you as my guest at Merrivale Hall last night, there has been an unforeseen consequence. A few hours after you left, Balzac, my butler, happened to try the door of the bedroom where you slept. It was locked from the inside! Balzac alerted me at once and I produced the master key, which I keep hidden in my wardrobe beneath a pile of discarded false mustaches. We gained entry to the bedroom to be met by a hideous sight.

Lying in the middle of the floor was a dead body. He (for the corpse was patently male) was an Oriental gentleman with a sinister cast of feature. His shoes were of such contrasting sizes—four and ten, respectively—that we can only assume he walked with a pronounced limp. There were no marks of violence upon him, but a steady trickle of blood was coming from his mouth, staining my Turkish carpet, a treasured gift from a grateful government in Ankara.

There was, alas, nothing in the man's pockets to suggest his identity. Grasped tightly in his left hand was the manuscript of an unpublished novel by someone called James Corbett. My butler and I agreed that we were gazing at a murder victim.

To preserve the good name of the Department, I wish to solve this crime rather than hand it over to those baffled buffoons at Scotland Yard. I am in urgent need of your help. Did anything strange happen in your bedroom last night? Is the murder connected in some way with Halloween? Was the room unoccupied when you departed this morning? And who is James Corbett?

Needless to say, I questioned my staff closely. They are four in number. Balzac is above suspicion, having been with me for twenty years, presented by a French administration indebted to me for services rendered. I would likewise exonerate Deeck, my valet, who, though American and thus subject to fits of grandiosity, is utterly trustworthy. About my cook, Dante, I am less sure. He can be temperamental.

Garbo, the maid, is another unknown quantity, having been recently bestowed upon me by a thankful Swedish parliament for my success in exposing the Stockholm Scandal.

I ask two special favors. Can you throw light on this mystery? And do you know a technique for removing bloodstains from a Turkish carpet?

Yours in desperation,
Agent No. 5

                A safe house,
               a secret place,
         somewhere in England

November 2nd, 1995

Dear Five (let's be informal),

You don't surprise me one bit. Without disrespect to your hospitality, I had one hell of a night (or what was left of the night after you abandoned me in such haste after chancing upon my Luger). You call it the bedroom where I slept, but I had no sleep at all. Shortly I'll explain why.

First, I must tell you about James Corbett, the writer of the manuscript you found in the dead man's grasp. Corbett was a prolific author of mystery novels—he claimed seventy-three—written between 1929 and 1951. In those more trusting times many of his books were bought by the unwary, but by the 1950s he was ready for oblivion, his work turgid and unreadable to a public weaned on Fleming's James Bond. I tried reading Corbett myself, and I'm at a loss to understand how such drivel was ever published. How could anyone seriously devise a plot revealing the villain as an unknown twin? Corbett tops that: in _The Monster of Dagenham Hall_, twins are present from the beginning and he produces an unknown triplet. In another work, which I skimmed, a character produces a "single-chambered revolver." Elsewhere, someone is "galvanized into immobility." I could go on; Corbett did, for twenty-two years.

Here is the crunch. For some arcane reason, over the last couple of years dealers in used books have been deluged by requests for Corbett novels. Prices have gone crazy. I heard of one woman in California who said she would kill for a copy of *Death Comes to Fanshawe*. Another, in Bethesda, Maryland, is said to have her Corbett collection insured for a million dollars; it is kept, unread, in a bank vault. Madness on this scale is dangerous. It has thrown the book market into turmoil and is even threatening the stability of the money markets. Instead of hoarding Impressionist paintings or uncut diamonds, people are putting their fortunes into Corbetts. Inevitably, all this activity attracted the attention of the security services. Recently the CIA and MI5 called a secret meeting. I was given a mission to investigate.

I won't go into the tortuous trail that led me last weekend to your ancestral seat, except to state that I was acting on alarming information from an impeccable source. London had been advised that an unpublished manuscript by Corbett had been discovered in a Tibetan monastery. This script is said to be so unspeakably dire that in 1938 it was rejected by every publisher in London. Imagine the excitement! What mutilations of the language, what contortions of plotting, could sink below anything Corbett ever had in print? A novel worse than *Devil-Man from Mars*? The script will be coveted by all who are infected with this Corbett-mania. In auction it will fetch an unimaginable sum, maybe as large, I was told, as the entire British budget. It will destabilize the international money markets and make the Wall Street crash look like a blip.

My mission is to seek and destroy. The Corbett manuscript *must* be shredded or incinerated. My name has been circulated as an expert capable of validating a genuine Corbett. The CIA calculated that this might persuade the possessors of the manuscript to make contact. Obviously they did.

My petal, I urge you, for the sake of us all, for the future prosperity of our children and our grandchildren—if that script is still in your possession—DO NOT READ ANY PART OF IT. DO NOT ALLOW YOUR SERVANTS TO READ IT. Destroy it at once.

For the record, here is what happened in the bedroom. Soon after you limply quit the room, I heard a tapping on the door. Thinking your vigor might have been restored, I blithely unlocked and discovered Balzac, your butler, who handed me a sealed message. I assumed it was from you, perhaps apologizing for what had happened (or failed to) between us. But the message was apparently in secret code. I devoted the rest of the night to trying to crack it, without success.

The rest is a blur. Sweetie, did you know that the bedroom you gave me has a secret passage behind the erotic tapestry? As dawn was breaking, I heard a sound from the general area of the Roman orgy and the whole thing moved. A secret door! Instinctively, I used my training in the martial arts and swung a stiletto heel toward the intruder's marriage gear. He fell at my feet. I didn't stop to examine the size of his shoes or the contents of his left hand. I rushed through the secret passage and came out at the railway station, where I boarded the first train. My Volkswagen must be still on your drive. Only today, with the aid of a Tibetan/English dictionary, have I translated the message. Roughly it runs:

Honored Lady,
We shall shortly give you an opportunity to examine the first female private eye novel ever written, Farewell, My Handsome, *by James Corbett. Your expert valuation is awaited with interest by the owners.*

Honeybunch, I am sorry about the inconvenience. What is one dead man between agents? But PLEASE heed my warning and destroy the Corbett. You can save the world from financial ruin. And the best I can suggest for your carpet is to stain it red.

I eagerly await your reassuring reply.

Devotedly,
Agent No. 6

Merrivale Hall
Dunseaton
Reading, Berks.

November 3rd, 1995

Dear Sexy Six,

Let me first put your mind at rest on one score. It was not lack
of desire that made me leap out of your bed so unceremoniously. I despised myself for having to leave you at the very second when your Luger was about to go off with a bang. This was
such uncharacteristic behavior on my part that I consulted a
doctor next day.

Blood tests revealed the presence of a drug that inhibits performance and causes loss of nerve at the critical moment. It
must have been administered to me in my soup. The drug is
made from a poppylike flower that only grows in the vicinity
of Florence, where it is used by the local maidenry to control
the bambino rate. My temperamental cook, Dante, is a native
of Florence. He made the soup.

On the other hand, it was Garbo, the maid, who served it to
us, under the supervision of Balzac, the butler. All three had
the opportunity to spike the master's soup. I incline toward
Dante as the culprit. He has been surly toward me ever since
I caught him standing outside the maid's window, serenading
her with a mandolin. I happened to be with Garbo at the time,
tucking her into bed with a concern for the bodily comfort of
my female staff that has always made me a model employer.
Dante was understandably vexed when I leaned naked over
the balcony and asked him to play "O Sole Mio!"

Your warning about James Corbett came too late. A curiosity
born of my Secret Service training made me read *Farewell, My
Handsome*. It was excruciating. An Albanian telephone directory has more narrative drive. The novel features a female private eye called Miss Marbles who has the attributes of Sherlock
Holmes, Dick Tracy, and Boadicea rolled into one. A woman
of advanced age, she keeps a derringer in her ear trumpet and

a stiletto beneath her wig. Her walking stick is also a blowpipe and she fires poison darts—having first removed her dentures—with alarming accuracy. Needless to say, she is a mistress of disguise.

There is worse to come. Since the dead courier was of Oriental origin, I decided to read the book backward and made AN AMAZING DISCOVERY. *Farewell, My Handsome* conceals a second novel called *Devil-Woman from Venus*. Instead of using twin characters, Corbett has outdone himself this time by writing twin novels, back to back! I thought at first I'd made the greatest literary discovery since the Rosetta Stone. Then I read *Devil-Woman* through. It beggars belief. Its protagonist is yet another female private eye, Dame Agatha Tea Cozy, who learns the state secrets of enemy powers by seducing their agents while wearing a rare perfume that makes her irresistible. The perfume can only be obtained from a demented, one-eyed French apothecary in Tours. A bizarre coincidence. Balzac, my butler, is a native of Tours.

I need your help more than ever, my Lugerbelle. Self-defense is not murder. You were right to kill the bearer of bad Corbett. Big questions remain. Your nocturnal visitor would have needed a key to open the subterranean door to the secret passage. Who gave it to him? Balzac has a key (and unfulfilled ambitions of being a novelist). Deeck, my valet, has one as well, though it has mysteriously gone astray. Dante's key turned up in my soup last night. And Garbo's key, alas, is in her bedroom door—she wants to be alone.

We found your Volkswagen on the drive, but we also found a bomb attached to its exhaust pipe. It was defused with great skill by Deeck, who, it transpires, was taught Bomb Disposal as part of his routine work as a civil servant in Washington, D.C. Do you see what this means? They wanted you to authenticate the Corbett manuscript and then blow you up for your pains! I couldn't bear to lose you, my angel. Thank God we frustrated their dastardly scheme.

Who is behind all this? If one Corbett novel could cause a financial earthquake, would not two bring an end to civilization as we know it? How can I tell if this double-barreled drivel really is authentic Corbett? When can you come to view it? I ask for two reasons. First, the fate of humanity may hang on your word. Second, I miss you dreadfully. (My doctor was highly complimentary about the love-bites you left upon my anatomy. He had never seen such fearful symmetry outside a tiger cage.)

The bloodstained carpet is no longer a problem. It and the dead body have both vanished, and there have been unconfirmed sightings of them heading across the channel in the direction of Tibet.

By the way, I hid the Corbett manuscript in a lead container and buried it fifty feet under ground. When I dug down this morning, to make sure that it was still there, I met Deeck digging his way up. Am I wrong to trust my valet?

Come soon, my darling!

Excitedly,
Five

⌒

Still a safe house, I think,
a secret place,
somewhere in England

November 4th, 1995

My Poor Demented Five,

Didn't I implore you in the name of everything you hold dear NOT to read the Corbett manuscript? Your latest letter plunges me into despair, because it is obvious that Corbett has driven you out of your mind. You underestimated the power of his prose. I know of others who ended up as gibbering idiots after reading just a paragraph from one of his books, and I had hoped to preserve you, my genial host, my pajamaed playmate, from a similar fate.

Too late.

How can you expect me to believe this nonsense about reading the book backward and discovering a second book? You
say *Devil-Woman from Venus* beggars belief. I say that your
story does. This is clearly the product of a demented mind.
Dame Agatha Tea Cozy, indeed!

Can I believe any of the rest of your letter? Is it really worth
my while agitating my gray cells to probe the mysteries of the
master's soup, the key to the secret passage, the bomb beneath
the Volkswagen, and the valet with the burrowing instinct?
Are you trying to tell me in coded language that you fear
Deeck is a mole? I am desperately concerned for more reasons
than I can reveal at this stage. I will only state that a theory
about your domestic staff is beginning to form in my brain.

Dear Five, for the sake of those few unfulfilled minutes we
spent together, I am willing to give the benefit of the smidgen
of doubt I still entertain as to your sanity. If you will dig up the
Corbett manuscript and send it to me at once, then I shall see
for myself if *Devil-Woman from Venus* is a figment of Corbett's
imagination, or yours.

I remain your impatient, ever-loving,
Six
P.S. I rather care for Lugerbelle as a name.

Merrivale Hall
Dunseaton
Reading, Berks.

November 5th, 1995

My dear Lugerbelle,

How can you question my veracity? Have you forgotten that
moment of truth we had in the blue bedroom at Merrivale
Hall? Why do you doubt my sanity? I have been trained by the

British Secret Service—the envy of lesser nations—and am therefore impervious to brain rot and to corruption by the written word. For the sake of what (almost) happened between us, you must believe me, my divine darling. You are the only woman who has seen me in my Union Jack pajamas without laughing. For that reason alone, I will never lie to you.

There is Malice Domestic in my household, and I need you to plumb its ugly depths. To convince you that I speak in earnest, I am enclosing a number of items.

(1) An article from the *Tibetan Astronomy Journal* about a UFO (Unidentified Flying Oriental) seen crossing the Himalayas on a bloodstained carpet.

(2) A report from an independent geologist proving that a fifty-foot hole was dug in my garden on the third day of this month. Soil samples attached.

(3) An infrared photograph of Deeck, my valet, burrowing into the main lawn last night. When questioned about his nocturnal recreation, he put it down to the fact that he was born prematurely when his mother became overagitated while watching the film of *Journey to the Center of the Earth*. "I can't help it," said Deeck. "I have to dig. It's in my blood."

(4) Fragments of the bomb found beneath your Volkswagen. Since it is November 5th, we detonated it as part of our Guy Fawkes Day bonfire celebrations.

(5) One of the poppylike flowers used to make a drug that can render a man impotent. The flower was found hidden beneath the chef's hat of Dante, my cook, but—and this was a shock to me—Balzac, the butler, was wearing it at the time. A French-Italian conspiracy?

(6) Garbo's membership card from an organization called Corbettaholics Anonymous. When people get the urge to read Corbett, they rush off to a therapy session and talk themselves out of it before committing suicide instead. Corbett in Swedish! Ye gods!

Every member of my staff is a prime suspect, and only you can pick out the real culprit or culprits. The future of the English language hangs in the balance. Save it, my dove. I am sending you the manuscript of *Farewell, My Handsome* along with its Siamese twin, *Devil-Woman from Venus*. I am sure that they are genuine—they even bear Corbett's signature.

To ensure safe passage, the manuscript will come inside a reinforced steel strongbox, inside a picnic hamper, inside a coffin, inside a bulletproof hearse. The vehicle will be driven by Deeck, the Maryland Mole. The four suspects will deliver it to you in person, so that you can authenticate the document and nab the villain in one fell swoop.

If it is bona fide James Corbett, you must destroy it at once in the name of justice, freedom, linguistic integrity, and the spirit of international harmony. Unless, of course, its value is so immense that we can afford to retire from the Secret Service on the proceeds. In that event, my pumpkin, I would like to offer you my hand in marriage and my heart in perpetuity. Pronounce it a best-seller and I am your agent.

Yours with drooling passion,
Five
P.S. Where shall we spend our honeymoon?

A safer house,
more secret,
somewhere in England

November 9th, 1995

My Incorruptible One,

Before you read any of this, pour yourself a large scotch. Now knock it back. All of it. And pour yourself another. Ready?

You are going to be gob-smacked by what you read, but bear with me, dear heart.

The hearse arrived the day before yesterday with its precious contents intact and your four untrusty servants aboard. Believe it or not, they had an uneventful journey. I questioned them all in depth, and your sanity and integrity are not in doubt. Each of those bizarre incidents happened, no question. Now I shall explain.

First, has it ever occurred to you why you were appointed Agent Number Five? Think about it. For me, there is no difficulty. I am Agent Number Six because I was recruited shortly after they gave you your box of false mustaches and sent you back to Cambridge University to learn the spy trade. I was the next in line. Simple.

But have you ever speculated about Agents One, Two, Three, and Four? Have you never wondered why you were not introduced to them? Probably, being the upright fellow you are, you decided that, as this was the Secret Service, you had better not ask. I can now reveal that, until four days ago, they were all employed in your household. To you they are known as Balzac, Dante, Garbo and Deeck. Number One, "Balzac," is the kind of spy known in the jargon of our trade as a sleeper, which is why he has been in your service as butler for twenty years. Number Two, "Dante," the temperamental cook, is in fact the world's foremost authority on passion-reducing drugs. His presence was necessary because Number Three, "Garbo," your maid, is the Mata Hari of the Service, the beautiful woman who extracts secrets by seduction; she has to be subdued at times. Number Four, your American valet "Deeck" with the burrowing tendency, is a CIA mole who recently defected to our side in order to devote himself to the study of the subversive writer James Corbett.

You must be asking why this formidable quartet infiltrated your domestic staff. It was on the instruction of "M," our spymaster. Their quest—and mine—was to probe your integrity and discover beyond all doubt whether you were reliable. The British Secret Service has had too many unfortunate episodes in the past with Cambridge men. Yes, my fearless Five, you were set up, put in the frame, and tested to the limit. I, too, joined in the deception, as did Harry Kirry, the well-known corpse impersonator. The Oriental gentleman in my bedroom was only Harry performing his turn. A pale face, a little stage blood, and the ability to stop breathing can produce wonderfully deathlike effects.

The bomb attached to my car was genuine, as you discovered, but it was put there to add credibility to the operation. I was hoping to get rid of that old beetle once and for all.

The Corbett manuscript was also a "plant." It was genuinely written by James Corbett, as "Deeck" will attest, but the claims I made as to its value were much exaggerated, simply to see if you could be tempted by the lure of money. You were not. You behaved impeccably, passing every test we set you. Even Garbo has sworn to me that nothing happened between you and her, naked as you were when Dante spotted you on the lady's balcony. In fact, Garbo erroneously believes you must be undersexed, for you are the first not to have succumbed to her charms. I didn't disillusion her. She has her professional pride.

All of this has been reported to "M."

What none of us anticipated is your discovery that the Corbett novel, read backward, is *Devil-Woman from Venus*. Using the manuscript in the deception was my idea, and now I must tell you something in the strictest confidence. That manuscript has been lying in an attic in my house for years.

You see, in civilian life I am Constance Corbett, the granddaughter of the author. In Grandpa's lifetime the script was rejected by every publishing house in Britain, but none of them had the wit to read it backward, as you did. What we have, my brilliant confederate, is a property that must be worth an enormous sum, notwithstanding its literary limitations. It is unique. It will be a sensation. That is why I shall not be destroying it. The final part of your penultimate paragraph said it all (though I liked the ultimate paragraph, too):

Its value is so immense that we can afford to retire from the
Service. Grandpa's book is a surefire best-seller. You, brave-
heart, can remain an agent, but not of the secret kind. You are
to be my LITERARY AGENT. You will find that the skills required
are not dissimilar.

I accept your proposal of marriage, on one condition: that you
do not ever call me "Con." So pack your Union Jack pajamas
at once, and jump into the Volkswagen and hit the gas. I can
hardly wait for our joint debriefing.

What a happy ending!

Your devoted Lugerbelle

Between 1929 and 1951, James Corbett published more than forty
novels, including the immortal Devil-Man from Mars, Death Is My
Shadow, Her Private Murder, The Monster of Dagenham Hall,
Agent No. 5, Murder While You Wait, and Vampire of the Skies. The
study of this British mystery "legend" became a Malice Domestic tradition
when William F. Deeck, the world's leading Corbettologist, began writing a
regular "Corbett Corner" feature in Malice's newsletter, The Usual
Suspects, and in other mystery periodicals that illuminated Corbett's bon
mots. It also led to such Malice panels as " 'He Sat Up Like a Full-Blown
Geranium': The Genius of James Corbett." In this story, two renowned
Corbettologists pay a skewed tribute to this mystery author, "a master,"
says Deeck, "of the language. Unfortunately, no one knows which language
it was."

Agent No. 5 and Agent No. 6 are, respectively, Edward Marston and Peter
Lovesey. Now retired from the Secret Service, they have published nearly forty
books between them and are living happily ever after at the Corbett Institute for
Demented Authors.

Agony Column

Barry N. Malzberg

GENTLEMEN:
I ENCLOSE MY short story, "Three for the Universe," and know you will find it right for your magazine, *Astounding Spirits*.

Yours very truly,
Martin Miller

~

Dear Contributor:

Thank you for your recent submission. Unfortunately, although we have read it with great interest, we are unable to use it in *Astounding Spirits*. Due to the great volume of submissions we receive, we cannot grant all contributors a personal letter, but you may be sure that the manuscript has been reviewed carefully and its rejection is no comment upon its literary merit but may be dependent upon one of many factors.

Faithfully,
The Editors

~

Dear Editors:
The Vietnam disgrace must be brought to an end! We have lost on that stained soil not only our national honor but our very future. The troops must be brought home and we must remember that there is more honor in dissent than in unquestioningly silent agreement.

Sincerely,
Martin Miller

~

Dear Sir:
Thank you for your recent letter to the editors. Due to the great volume of worthy submissions we are unable to print every good letter we receive and therefore regretfully inform you that while we will not be publishing it, this is no comment upon the value of your opinion.

Very truly yours,
The Editors

~

Dear Congressman Forthwaite:
I wish to bring your attention to a serious situation which is developing on the West Side. A resident of this neighborhood for five years now, I have recently observed that a large number of streetwalkers, dope addicts, and criminal types are loitering at the intersection of Columbus Avenue and Twenty-fourth Street at almost all hours of the day, offending passersby with their appearance and creating a severe blight on the area. In addition, passersby are often threateningly asked for "handouts" and even "solicited." I know that you share with me a concern for a Better West Side and look

forward to your comments on this situation as well as some kind of concrete action.

Sincerely,
Martin Miller

~

Dear Mr. Millow:
Thank you for your letter. Your concern for our West Side is appreciated and it is only through the efforts and diligence of constituents such as yourself that a better New York can be conceived. I have forwarded your letter to the appropriate precinct office in Manhattan and you may expect to hear from them soon.

Gratefully yours,
Alwyn D. Forthwaite

~

Dear Gentlemen:
In May of this year I wrote Congressman Alwyn D. Forthwaite a letter of complaint, concerning conditions of the Columbus Avenue–West Twenty-fourth Street intersection in Manhattan and was informed by him that this letter was passed on to your precinct office. Since four months have now elapsed, and since I have neither heard from you nor observed any change in the conditions pointed out in my letter, I now write to ask whether or not that letter was forwarded to you and what you have to say about it.

Sincerely,
Martin Miller

~

Dear Mr. Milner:
Our files hold no record of your letter.

N. B. Karsh
Captain, # 33462

~

Dear Sirs:
I have read Sheldon Novack's article in the current issue of
Cry with great interest but feel that I must take issue with his
basic point, which is that sex is the consuming biological drive
from which all other activities stem and which said other
activities become only metaphorical for. This strikes me as a
bit more of a projection of Mr. Novack's own functioning than
that reality which he so shrewdly contends he apperceives.

Sincerely,
Martin Miller

Dear Mr. Milton:
Due to the great number of responses to Sheldon A. Novack's
"Sex and Sexuality: Are We Missing Anything?" in the
August issue of *Cry*, we will be unable to publish your own
contribution in our "Cry from the City" Column, but we do
thank you for your interest.

Yours,
The Editors

Dear Mr. President:
I was shocked by the remarks apparently attributed to you in
today's newspapers on the public assistance situation. Surely,
you must be aware of the fact that social welfare legislation
emerged from the compassionate attempt of 1930 politics to
deal with human torment in a systematized fashion, and
although many of the cruelties you note are inherent to the
very system, they do not cast doubt upon its very legitimacy.
Our whole national history has been one of coming to terms
with collective consciousness as opposed to the law of the jungle, and I cannot understand how you could have such a position as yours.

Sincerely,
Martin Miller

Dear Mr. Meller:

Thank you very much for your letter of October eighteenth to the president. We appreciate your interest and assure you that without the concern of citizens like yourself the country would not be what it has become. Thank you very much and we do look forward to hearing from you in the future on matters of national interest.

Mary L. McGinnity
Presidential Assistant

Gentlemen:

I enclose herewith my article, "Welfare: Are We Missing Anything?" which I hope you may find suitable for publication in *Insight Magazine*.

Very truly yours,
Martin Miller

Dear Contributor:

The enclosed has been carefully reviewed and our reluctant decision is that it does not quite meet our needs at the present time. Thank you for your interest in *Insight*.

The Editors

Dear Senator Partch:

Your vote on the Armament Legislation was shameful.

Sincerely,
Martin Miller

Dear Dr. Mallow:

Thank you for your recent letter to Senator O. Stuart Partch and for your approval of the senator's vote.

L. T. Walters
Congressional Aide

Dear Susan Saltis:
I think your recent decision to pose nude in that "art-pho-
tography" series in *Men's Companion* was disgraceful, filled
once again with those timeless, empty rationalizations of the
licentious which have so little intrinsic capacity for damage
except when they are subsumed, as they are in your case, with
abstract and vague "connections" to platitudes so enormous
as to risk the very demolition of the collective personality.

Yours very truly,
Martin Miller

⌒

Dear Sir:
With pleasure and in answer to your request, we are enclosing
a photograph of Miss Susan Saltis as she appears in her new
movie, *Chariots to the Holy Roman Empire*.

Very truly yours,
Henry T. Wyatt
Publicity Director

⌒

Gentlemen:
I wonder if *Cry* would be interested in the enclosed article
which is not so much an article as a true documentary of the
results which have been obtained from my efforts over recent
months to correspond with various public figures, entertainment stars, etc., etc. It is frightening to contemplate the
obliteration of self which the very devices of the twentieth
century compel, and perhaps your readers might share my
(not so retrospective) horror.

Sincerely,
Martin Miller

⌒

Dear Sir:
As a potential contributor to *Cry*, I am happy to offer you our
"Writer's Subscription Discount," meaning that for only five
dollars and fifty cents you will receive not only a full year's

subscription (28 percent below newsstand rates, 14 percent below customary subscriptions) but in addition our year-end special issue, *Cry in the Void*, at no extra charge.

Subscription Dept.

⌒

Dear Contributor:

Thank you very much for your article, "Agony Column." It has been considered here with great interest and it is the consensus of the Editorial Board that while it has unusual merit it is not quite right for us. We thank you for your interest in *Cry* and look forward to seeing more of your work in the future.

Sincerely,
The Editors

⌒

Dear Congressman Forthwaite:

Nothing has been done about the conditions I mentioned in my letter of about a year ago. Not one single thing!

Bitterly,
Martin Miller

⌒

Dear Mr. Mills:

Please accept our apologies for the delay in answering your good letter. Congressman Forthwaite has been involved, as you know, through the winter in the Food Panel and has of necessity allowed some of his important correspondence to await close attention.

Now that he has the time he thanks you for your kind words of support.

Yours truly,
Ann Ananauris

⌒

Dear Sir:
The Adams multiple murders are indeed interesting not only for their violence but because of the confession of the accused that he "did it so that someone would finally notice me." Any citizen can understand this—the desperate need to be recognized as an individual, to break past bureaucracy into some clear apprehension of one's self-worth, is one of the most basic of human drives, but it is becoming increasingly frustrated today by a technocracy which allows less and less latitude for the individual to articulate his own identity and vision and be heard. Murder is easy: It is easy in the sense that the murderer does not need to embark upon an arduous course of training in order to accomplish his feat; his excess can come from the simple extension of sheer human drives . . . aided by basic weaponry. The murderer does not have to cultivate "contacts" or "fame" but can simply, by being *there*, vault past nihilism and into some clear, cold connection with the self. More and more the capacity for murder lurks within us; we are narrow, and driven, we are almost obliterated from any sense of existence, we need to make that singing leap past accomplishment and into acknowledgment and *recognition*. Perhaps you would print this letter?

Hopefully,
Martin Miller

Dear Sir:
Thank you for your recent letter. We regret being unable to use it due to many letters of similar nature being received, but we look forward to your expression of interest.

Sincerely,
John Smith for the Editors

Dear Mr. President:
I intend to assassinate you. I swear that you will not live out
the year. It will come by rifle or knife, horn or fire, dread or
terror, but it will come, and there is no way that you can AVOID
THAT JUDGMENT TO BE RENDERED UPON YOU.

Fuck You,
Martin Miller

Dear Reverend Mellbow:
As you know, the president is abroad at the time of this writing, but you may rest assured that upon his return your letter,
along with thousands of other and similar expressions of hope,
will be turned over to him and I am sure that he will appreciate your having written.

Very truly yours,
Mary L. McGinnity
Presidential Assistant

Graduation

Richard Christian Matheson

J ANUARY 15

DEAR MOM AND DAD:

It has been an expectedly hectic first week; unpacking, organizing, getting scheduled in classes, and of course fraternizing with the locals to secure promise of later aid should I need it. I don't think I will. My room is nice though it has a view which Robert Frost would scoff at; perhaps a transfer to a better location later this semester is possible. We'll see.

I had a little run-in with the administration when I arrived; a trivial technicality, something about too much luggage. At least more than the other dormitory students brought with them. I cleared it up with a little glib know-how. As always. Some of the guys on my floor look as if they might be enjoyable and if I'm lucky maybe one or two will be interesting to talk to as well. But I can't chase after "impossible rainbows." That should sound familiar, Dad, it's from your private collection and has been gone over a "few" times. A few. But maybe this time, it's true. Anyway, the dormitory looks as if it's going to work out well. Pass the word to you-know-who. I'm sure it will interest him.

The dinner tonight was an absolute abomination. It could easily have been some medieval mélange concocted by the college gardener utilizing lawn improver, machinist's oil, and ground-up old men. And I question even the quality of those ingredients. I may die tonight of poisoning. Maybe if I'm lucky it will strike quickly and leave no marks. Don't want Dad's old school to lose its accreditation after all. However, I'm a little concerned that the townspeople will be kept awake tonight by the sound of 247 "well-fed" freshmen looking at their reflections in the toilet bowl. Today while I was buying books an upper-classman called me green for not getting used ones. If he was in any way referring to the way my face looks right now, he should be hired by some psychic foundation. He can tell the future.

Anyway, Mom, I certainly do miss your cooking. Almost as much as I miss my stomach's equilibrium. Ugh.

The room gets cold early with the snow and all. But I have plenty of blankets (remember the excessive luggage? . . . guessed it) so that poses no difficulty. I'll probably pick up a small heater next week, first free day I get. For now I'll manage with hot tea, the collected works of Charles Dickens, and warm memories of all of you back home. Until I write again, I send my love and an abundance of sneezes.

Here's looking achoo . . .

Yours regurgitatively,

February 2
Dear Mom and Dad:
Greetings from Antarctica. It is unbelievably cold up here. If you can imagine your son as a hybrid between a Popsicle and

a slab of marble, you've got the right idea, just make it a little colder. In a word, freezing. In another word, numbing. In two other words, liquid oxygen. I may be picking up that heater sooner than I thought. I see no future in becoming a glacier.

I met my professors today, all of whom seem interested and dedicated. My calculus class might be a trifle dreary, but, then, numbers put a damper on things any way you look at it. The other courses look promising so far. Tell you-know-who that he-knows-who is genuinely excited about something. I'm sure he'll be cheered by that forecast of future involvements.

Burping is very popular in my wing of the dormitory and some of the guys have been explaining its physical principles to me, complete with sonic demonstrations to validate their theories. One guy, Jim, who looks a little like a bull dog with slightly bigger eyes (and a much bigger stomach), apparently holds the record in two prestigious areas: he drinks the most and belches the loudest. For your own personal information files, he also seems to know the fewest words a person can possess and still communicate with. I estimate that the exact number of words is a high one-digit counting number, but I could still be going too easily on him. His belches, however, are enormously awesome. He is able (he whispered to me when I bumped into his drunken body in the hallway last night) to make time stand still temporarily with one of his burps.

Furthermore (he said), that would be one of his lesser efforts. Were he to launch a truly prize-winning belch (he said), civilization as we know it would be obliterated and the earth's atmosphere rendered noxious for two thousand years. Personally, I feel he exaggerates a bit. Maybe fifteen hundred years.

Jim doesn't stop burping until one or two in the morning, which makes studying a degree harder. It's like having a baby in the dorm, with Jim erupting and gurgling into the A.M. hours. Except that he weighs three hundred pounds. But I'm learning to live with it. Occasionally, he gets to be more than a petty annoyance and I get upset, but it's really nothing to worry about. So tell you-know-who to not put himself into a state. I'm fine.

If we could harness the secret of Jim's aberration and regulate it
at timed intervals, perhaps Yellowstone Park would be interested. Oh well, he'll probably quiet down soon. I miss you all a lot
and send my fondest love. Until I thaw out again, bye for now.

Bundlingly yours . . .

P.S. Avoid telling you-know-who I'm "cold" up here. He has
this thing about that word.

February 22
Dear Mom and Dad:
An enlivening new roommate has entered my monastic quarters. He is slight in frame and says very little; a simple kind of
person with a dearth of affinities, except for cheese, which he
loves. I call him Hannibal owing to his fearlessly exploratory
nature. You see, Hannibal, while not easy to detect, is very
much present. He comes out to mingle only during the evening.
The late evening. More precisely, that part of the evening when
I like to try and catch some sleep. Hannibal is evidently on a
different schedule than I.

In short, I have mouse trouble.

Hannibal, in all fairness, is but one of the offenders. He is
joined each evening by a host of other raucous marauders who
squeal and scratch until dawn, determined to disturb my rest.
They're actually quite cute, but are, regardless of angelic
appearances, a steadily unappreciated annoyance.

I mentioned my visitors to some of the other students in the
dormitory and they said I wasn't the only victim of the
whiskered nocturnal regime. They advised setting traps and,
failing that, to use a poison which can be purchased from the
student store. It is rumored to yield foolproof results. I know
it sounds altogether like a cross borrowing from Walt Disney
and an Edgar Allan Poe story, but, regrettably, I must do
something.

As an alternate plan, I thought of possibly speaking with a brainy flutist I know from orchestra class, who is quite talented. Whether or not he would care to revivify a Gothic tale simply for the benefit of my slumberous tranquility is something we will have to discuss. Also the question of playing and walking at the same time may come up. But I'll try to circumvent that aspect. It's a slightly off-beat gig but it seems an improvement on the other method. I'll speak with him.

My classes are going fairly well, with no serious laggings in any subject despite the effects of Jim and Hannibal's henchmen upon my alertness. Thanks for the letter and a very special thanks for those fantastic cookies, Mom. They were delicious. You really made my day. And the traveling scent of your generosity made me quite sought after for a "little sample" of what food can really taste like. Jim went ape over them and said he wouldn't mind taking the whole next box off my hands. Which is something like a man with no legs admitting that he, occasionally, limps. Good old Jim. He'll probably eat himself to death one day. Although it would take him at least two days to do it right.

In light of the popularity of your largess, I have determined that everybody else must have the same immense regard for the school cook I do. He is acquiring a definite reputation, the likes of which has been shared by a handful of historical figures. Lizzie Borden, Jack the Ripper. The man has no regard for the human taste bud. All in all, I'm convinced that our chef will most assuredly go to hell.

Anyway, Mom, thanks again for the cookies. They were eaten with rapturous abandon. And you may have saved several students from ulcers. What better compliment? All my love to everyone back home. Including you-know-who.

Thwarted by burps, squeaks,
and bad food . . .

P.S. I think Jim (our resident sulphur spring) finally knows what it's like being kept up at night. He too has mouse trouble. (At least someone will visit him.)

March 9

Dear Mom and Dad:

Got in a small amount of trouble today as a result of being late to class and complicating matters by arguing with my professor over a dumb thing he said about me.

You see, in Philosophy I, as it is taught by Marshall B. Francis, you are not allowed an impregnable viewpoint. It must always be open to comment. And he says he likes to analyze. I told him he likes to shred and butcher. Whereupon he requested a "formal presentation of my personal philosophy of life's purpose."

Since, as you know, my philosophy responds unfavorably to direct assault, I refused. Mistake number one.

He told me if I didn't cooperate he'd have me leave the class and withdraw all credit from my participation thus far. I thought this unfair, so we started yelling at one another and in the clouded ferocity of our exchanges I accidentally slashed him on the cheek with my pen. It wasn't deep, but it scared him a lot. It wasn't at all like it may seem; I say that only because I know what you're probably thinking. Believe me, it was just a freak accident with one lost temper responding to another.

We talked in the infirmary later and he said he understood and would allow me a second chance. After that kindness, I volunteered my philosophy without hesitation (rather sheepishly), and he smiled at my completion of the apologies. He said that sometimes you have to be willing to fight for your beliefs and that he respected my actions in class, saving the accident, of course. I think we'll be great friends by the end of the year (if he doesn't get infected and die); however, philosophers consider life to be a danger so I guess it wouldn't surprise him too much.

It is still very cold with no trace of warmth. Jim continues to noisily burn (or is it burp) the midnight oil much to the chagrin of everyone in the dorm. If a sonic boom occurred during the evening, it would be completely overlooked. Buried.

Once again, my love to all of you back home, and I sure would like to hear from you, so please write. Better not tell you-know-who what happened to me today. He'll get the wrong impression. He has enough people to worry about as it is.

With new-found philosophy,

P.S. Hannibal is no longer with me. He and his men are squeaking across those great Alps in the sky. That poison really was foolproof.

⌒

March 18
Dear Mom and Dad:
My social horizons are expanding here in Isolation City. In one day, I met the remainder of my floormates (truly a rogues' gallery) at a party and also a very nice girl who works as my lab partner.

I met my across-the-hall neighbor quite by chance over a game of poker. I beat him over and over and he had to write me a few IOUs. When I asked him what room he was in (so I might stop by and "collect"), it turned out to be the room directly across from mine. It's weird how you can overlook someone who is right under your nose. Anyway, he's a nice guy, but is badly in need of tutoring in the finer points of the gentlemanly wager. He is absolutely the worst gambler I have ever encountered. I suspect that his brain has decomposed from excessive exposure to Jim, who is his favorite card player. They play to one another's caliber it seems. Two drunks leading each other home.

My neighbor's name is Marcum Standile Jr. As a rather unusual point of insight into his personal life, we figured out tonight (in my room after the party) that Marcum owes roughly $40,000 to various other dormitory inhabitants with whom he has played poker. This sum is exceeded only by Jim's, whose debts accrued in two short months amount to a figure which is something akin to the annual budget for Red China. Perhaps my training in calculus is coming in handy for once.

I'll write more about Susie later. Everything is pretty good academically speaking and the sun is even occasionally making a token appearance. Miss you very much and send all my love.

With endless computation,

P.S. Got a letter from you-know-who. Guess he took the accident a little too seriously. Tell him to relax.

~

April 4

Dear Mom and Dad:

I'm rich! Marcum got his monthly allotment from his financially overstuffed folks and came through with over $400 for yours truly. So far, this much money has me in quite an influential position since word of my monetary windfall has spread like an epidemic. I am popular beyond belief. I've considered opening up a loan service (with determined interest) so as to make the entire endeavor worth my expended energy, as well as expended funds. An idea which I took from a movie with George Segal, *King Rat*. The entire prison camp where he was being held captive by the enemy, had less money than George so he became the nucleus of all existing finance. The concept appeals to me. I'll probably just buy a heater and an electric blanket, though. Fancy dies so quickly in a young man's heart. Sniff.

I am referred to alternately as "Rockefeller" or "pal," depending on the plight of who I'm speaking with. I never dreamed any one person could have so many "pals." Last night, someone pinned a sign to my door that says "Fort Knox North." It's only right. Being rich is such toil. Tell you-know-who I will use it wisely.

My lab partner and I have become even better friends in the past few weeks. I think I mentioned in the last letter that her name is Susie, actually Susan Johnson. What I failed to include in that brief description is that she is kind of like my girlfriend, stunningly beautiful, intelligent, and popular, and maybe the first girl, since Beth's death, that I really care about. Without pouring forth excessives about Susie, I'll simply say that I know you'd love her. She is quite a unique person and around here that's a godsend, the prevailing ambiance being composed of uptight females. I only hope that she feels the same about me. But that will come in time. I think it would crush me if she were just experiencing feelings of friendship. But I suspect that her eyes are the best spokesman for her affections and they tell me everything is going perfect. Tell you-know-who not to hold his breath. She isn't at all like Beth, so don't let him even attempt to connect things. Beth was just something that happened. I'm sorry about it, but it was, after all, an accident and I think I would resent you-know-who making more of this than there is. Or maybe making less of it. It feels right to me. Not like with Beth. So please keep you-know-who off the subject completely; it's not fair.

By the way, I think I might make the dean's list, so cross your fingers. Philosophy I is going very well and Marshall B. Francis and I are becoming friends of the close variety. As I predicted.

I miss you all very much and send my love. Please write.

With Krupp-like fortune;

P.S. Thanks for the latest batch of cookies, Mom. I'm not sure I can eat all of them myself. Plenty of willing mouths around here, though.

⌐

April 17
Dear Mom and Dad:
Terrible news. Remember Jim, the guy who belched and kept everybody up? He was found this morning, in his room, dead. The school won't issue any kind of statement, but everyone thinks it might have been suicide. I don't think there was a note or anything, and it could have just been an accident.

If it was suicide, it would have made a lot of sense, speaking strictly in terms of motivation. He wasn't a very happy person, his weight and all making him almost completely socially ostracized. He was only eighteen years old. It's a shame things like this have to happen.

It certainly is going to be quiet around here without his belching and carryings-on; which is kind of a relief even if the circumstances are so tragic. Nobody has mentioned the funeral, but I hear his parents are going to have him buried locally. That's the nicest thing they could do for him. He really liked the college and the town and everything, and although unhappy, was happier here than he would have been anywhere else. It's going to be abnormally quiet around here. Maybe with the improved conditions we'll get some new scholars out of this dorm. I know I'll sleep better. Still, I feel as if every death has a meaning; a reason for happening. I may bring that up in Philosophy I. Anyway, it's a damn shame about Jim. Marcum lost a great card partner.

On a slightly cheerier note, Susie and I are still seeing each other, but I have a difficult time figuring her out. Maybe she isn't the demonstrative type. If that is the case, I can understand her reticence, but if not, I can't help wondering what's wrong. We talk all the time, but she doesn't seem to be able to let me know she cares. It's odd because Beth was similar in that way.

I'm sure time will make its own decision. Sound familiar, Dad? It's another one of your polished "classics." What would life be without my father's inimitable cracker-barreling? A bit more relaxing perhaps . . . Incidentally, the loan business is beginning to take shape. I'll write more about it later. For now, it's looking quite hopeful. Monte Carlo, here I come.

Pass the word to you-know-who, about my business. It's what he likes to hear. Former client makes good and all that stuff.

Miss you all very much and send my deepest love.

Destined to be wealthy
(but in semi-mourning),

P.S. My room is starting to bother me. Maybe a change!

April 25

Dear Mom and Dad:

You-know-who wrote me a letter I received today. He wants me to come home. The onslaught of Jim's death along with the isolating geography up here has him surprisingly alarmed. He feels that the milieu is just too strenuous for me to manage. I disagree with him completely and feel that I'm taking Jim's death very well. I'm not overreacting beyond what is reasonable. After all, Jim and I were almost complete strangers. Maybe the ease of detachment comes because of that.

I wrote you-know-who tonight after dinner, but I think a word from you might help to quell his skepticism. I know you told him about the death out of good conscience, but, as I recommended, it may have been a bad idea. All in all, I couldn't be happier and the thought of leaving depresses me very much. I think my letter will stand on its own merit, but a word from you would assist the cause enormously.

Business is in full swing here at Fort Knox North. I've made over fifteen dollars in interest this week. Once again, I'm baffled as to how to spend the newly mounting sums. Perhaps a place where liquor and painted women are available to book-weary students? However, I'll probably squander my gain away on decent food. The indigenous delicacies are becoming as palatable as boiled sheet metal. Really disgusting. I look forward to a meal by the greatest cook in the known world. I hope you're listening, Mom.

I talked to the dean of housing today about changing rooms and he told me (morbidly enough) that the only available room is Jim's. It seemed grisly at first, but I gave it serious thought and am going to move in tomorrow. It's been cleaned up (all but boiled out) so there is no trace of anything that indicated someone lived in it. Or died in it. For obvious reasons, I think you would agree, telling you-know-who would just fuel the flame. He can't expect everyone to react to death the same way. It doesn't spook me to be in Jim's room.

I wonder, though, if his spirit will inhabit my lungs and create zombie burps. All, no doubt, from your cookies, Mom. He was really hooked. Phantom gases are an interesting concept, but don't exactly arrest me esthetically. Quiet, I think I hear a cookie crumbling.

My studies are going exceptionally well. Something interesting happened in Philosophy I today. Remember I told you I was going to mention the point about Jim's death maybe being the happiest salvation he could have chosen? Well, I made the point and nobody would talk about it. They all seemed disturbed about the personalized nature of the question since it wasn't just a hypothetical inquiry. Some people even made peculiar comments. People are unpredictable when it comes to death.

Things are "OK" with Susie. We're supposed to go to a concert tonight. Will tell you about that in next letter. Miss you all hugely and send my fondest love.

Sleeping better,

P.S. Susie may get my class ring tonight. Lucky girl.

April 26
Dear Mom and Dad:
Something ghastly has happened. It's hard to even write this letter as I am extremely upset.

Susie and I returned from the school auditorium sometime after midnight, following the concert, and sneaked into my dormitory room to listen to some music. I had planned to ask Susie how she felt about me after we settled down. The concert had been very stimulating and we were both being quite verbal, competing for each other's audience as many thoughts were occurring to both of us. We talked for several hours and were almost exhausted from the conversation before quieting down.

As we sat listening to the music, on my bed together, I bent over to her cheek and, kissing her gently, asked her how she felt about our relationship and where it was going. She was silent for what must have been minutes. Then she spoke. In almost a pale whisper she said that we would always be good friends and that her regard for me was quite sincere but that she couldn't feel romantically about me ever. She didn't explain why, even though I asked her over and over.

Maybe the fact that I was tired had something to do with it, but I began to cry and couldn't stop. Her admission had taken me entirely by surprise. I had thought things were just beginning to take shape.

I guess Susie sensed that my hurt was larger than even the tears revealed and she got up from the bed to walk to the other side of the room. Working things out in her mind, I guess. She walked to the window to let in some air. As she raised it I could feel the cold wind rush in, and I looked up to see Susie's hair blowing as she kneeled near the window, looking out over the fields. It was so quiet that the whole thing seemed like a dream; the cold air plunging in on us, the music playing with muted beauty for us alone, the near darkness making shadowy nothings of our separateness.

Susie leaned out the window, and I watched her, transfixed, thinking that what she had said was a story, that she was only playing. She only continued in her silence, staring into the night's blackness.

I guess she wanted more air or something because she raised the window, and as I rose to help her with it, a screaming cut the air.

She kept screaming until she hit the walkway below. Then there was silence again. She was taken to the hospital and operated on for a fractured skull, broken shoulder, and internal injuries.

She was pronounced dead at 6:30 this morning.

The police questioned me today about the accident but seemed satisfied that it was a tragic accident. They could, I'm sure, see my grief was genuine.

I am left with almost nothing now. Susie was everything I worked for other than school, and without her here, that means nothing. I am thinking of coming home. You-know-who needn't say anything to you or me about what he thinks. He's wrong. And, at this point, I don't need advice. My treatment will be mine alone from now on. I don't want interference from him anymore.

I am very seriously depressed. I keep thinking that had Susie told me long ago that she cared we wouldn't have spent so long, last night, in my room. If only she had cared, everything might have been different. I think these thoughts must occur to anyone who loses someone cherished. I didn't think something like this could happen to me. I find it hard to go on without someone caring. If you don't care about someone who cares about you, why should you even exist? Without that there is no reason.

In deepest hopelessness,

P.S. Maybe no letters from me until I feel better.

April 28
Dear Mom and Dad:
Things are no better with me than my last letter reported. Since Susie's death I am unable to concentrate on studies and am falling seriously behind in my classes. I sit alone most of the time in my room, watching the fields as the winds create giant patterns. Before today, I had thought it the most beautiful view in the dorm.

Speaking of the dorm, I now find myself unable to associate with any of the other residents. They all remind me of Susie. I almost hate this building because it remembers everything that happened in it. It will not forget anything and each time I get inside it I feel subsumed by its creaking examinations of me. I am now easily given to imaginings about many things and question all things. I trust only myself now.

My loan business is being attended to assiduously with the scrutiny of a watchmaker fearing he has left out a part from a shipment of hundreds of timepieces. I am losing money now. The clientele is not paying me back punctually or with owed amounts adequately covered. Everybody on my floor and many people scattered throughout the building have taken out loans. Almost none have returned them. I am almost at my wit's end trying to get the money. But you can't torture people to get it. I'm really getting desperate. I have such contempt for those who borrow things and either refuse to return them or consciously allow themselves to let their obligation slide through negligence. Negligence should beget negligence. It's only fair that way.

I have been going to concerts the past two nights. They seem to help me relax. I despise returning to the dormitory more and more. Every time I get inside I feel suffocated. I realize that I must try to adjust and get back into the swing of things, but it is not easy. I am trying. Tell you-know-who.

That's all I can tell you. I can't foresee much of anything now. My dearest love to both of you. Please write.

Confused with sickness,

April 30
Dear Mom and Dad:
Last night, almost as if the dormitory knew my hate for it (like a dog who senses its master's loathings), it took its own life along with the lives of many inside its cradling horror.

As I walked back from a 10:30 concert (Chopin) at the campus center, I came upon the dormitory burning bright orange in the night. Firemen say it was caused by an electrical short circuit or something. Nineteen students were eaten by flames, unable to escape the building. The remains were charred beyond recognition and teeth and dental records are being matched to discern who the students were.

It doesn't seem to matter who someone is once he is dead. Only what he did while he lived. An honorable life will not tolerate an impure death. But the life that deceives and cloaks its meaning with artifice and insensitivity cannot die reasonably. Perhaps Marshall B. Francis would have something to say about that. All death seems to need is an attached philosophy to resolve its meaning. Otherwise it is just an end. I may talk to him.

There is nothing left for me now of course. I am numbed by the death which surrounds me here. My room and belongings were destroyed in the fire, and the purpose of my schooling has become inconsequential to both myself and what I want.

I will try another school, in another place. Things must be different elsewhere. Somewhere there must be a safe place. A place where things such as what I have seen haven't happened. If there is, I will find it.

I'm catching a plane tomorrow at noon and should arrive at about 5:30. My love to you until then.

Forward looking,

P.S. I got an A in philosophy. Hooray!

Someone Who Understands Me

Matthew Costello

Welcome to Chat Room 13!
Attending: 2
>> Nightmover
>> Paladin

WHO WOULDN'T HAVE BEEN curious?

I mean, there was so much talk about virtual sex and virtual relationships in cyberspace, you'd have to be a mole to be uninterested.

And I am not a mole.

I also had the number-one prerequisite of someone seeking adventure on the net: time . . . and lots of it.

It wasn't always that way.

But these days, I had—

>> **What changed, Paladin? How come *you* had so much time?**

Oh . . . sorry. Didn't think you'd be interested.

You see, my company sold paper goods, real paper made from real trees. Imagine giant forests ripped down to make a zillion telephone books, and that was our business.

But paper was an endangered species. Now we had the paperless office . . . and everybody acted as if that were a good goddamn thing. Hey, the World Wide Web is filled with pages and pages that— ta-da!—don't use paper.

The paper business started to collapse. It was only a matter of time until my boss waddled into my cramped little office and said, "Jack, I'm afraid I have *pre-tty* bad news."

Only a matter of time . . . and I had plenty of time.

>> So you went on the Net?

Yes. I surfed, I skipped, I zapped from page to page, with my office door locked and not a hell of a lot of work to do. That's what I did . . . until I found ChatWorld . . . and I met Cynarra.

>> Cynarra? Nice screen name.

Yes. Though I immediately wondered whether it was real. Cynarra . . . it sounded like something out of a novel. We started chatting. And when I came back the next day, she was there, waiting for me. It became something . . . to look forward to.

>> And you're married . . . I presume?

Yes. Married. *Imprisoned* is more like it. I guess I could have divorced my wife—but what would my life have been like? All the money we had was Bev's money, old money from her old family. And I was about to be unemployed. If I left Bev, would I end up on the street? The idea of living in an old refrigerator box wasn't too appealing.

>> No kids?

Our two kids were all grown. Out of the house and glad of it. It was just Beverly and me. Bev and Jack, sitting in their co-op, quietly seething.

>> Sounds like you were ready for some fantasy.

Oh, yes. Fantasy, reality. I was ready for *something*. At first, Cynarra and I simply talked. She seemed cloaked in mystery. She described herself as a "dark-haired, dark-eyed beauty." I thought about that *a lot*. Later she said she had full lips and a sexy smile. We just talked at first, but then—

>> **You developed a cyber relationship? Cool!**

Yeah, cool. A cyber relationship. I was at work, talking to Cynarra. Always waiting for her to come on-line.

>> **Did you use your real name?**

No way. I used my "screen name"—Paladin. Remember that old show, Paladin? *Have Gun, Will Travel?*

>> **Nope. Paladin? Before my time. Sorry.**

No problem. So . . . I was Paladin and she was Cynarra. And I described myself to her, embellishing it a bit. I said I was tall . . . even though I'm only 5' 7". I didn't think that she'd ever see me. I said I was slender and muscular, with deep-set blue eyes. Ha—well at least I do have blue eyes.

>> **And then?**

>> **You still there?**

>> **Paladin . . . ?**

Sorry. I felt this pain . . . in my stomach. Sharp pain. But—where was I?

>> **She was Cynarra and *you* were Paladin.**

Yes. So we started talking about intimate things.

>> **Sex?**

Well, I don't want to make it sound like we just talked about sex, that we only tried to get each other hot and bothered. It was more than that. She opened herself to me, she told me about the slob she was married to, how badly he treated her . . . how she couldn't stand him.

I started feeling bad. for her. No, worse than bad. I felt as though, in all my copious free time, I wanted to protect her.

She told me that her husband came home and smacked her.

Once she told me that she had an ugly bruise on her cheek where he slapped her. And she told me that the only thing—the only thing!—that made her feel better was knowing that I was out there, waiting for her.

>> **And how were things at your home?**

Oh great, terrific. I'd come home . . . and Bev and I wouldn't have two words to say to each other. Then, when she went to sleep, going to bed so early as though she actually had something to do the next morning, I'd creep in the den and use our home computer to check for any messages from Cynarra. I knew that she couldn't log on—but there might be a message.

I soon discovered that the only thing I lived for were words from Cynarra.

>> So . . . you arranged to see her?

No. That's the funny thing.

What happened started out as a joke. We were just kidding. And I wrote: "Wouldn't it be great if we could get rid of our respective spouses. If somehow they were *dead*, and we could be together. Wouldn't that be great?"

>> And you were kidding?

Right. I mean, we—

>> Hello?

>> Still there? Paladin? Are you—

Sorry. Started coughing. Couldn't stop. Anyway, it was a joke. I mean, I had never seen this person, my dark-eyed Cynarra. Most likely she didn't resemble her description at all. But that didn't matter. No, not when she fired me with this incredible fantasy. Then she typed something interesting.

She wrote, **<<There are poisons, you know. Undetectable poisons.>>**

The first thing I wondered was whether ChatWorld was secure. I mean, could anyone eavesdrop and listen to our private tête-à-tête? But that was a big selling point of ChatWorld. . . their motto . . . "Let yourself go . . . it's your own private world . . ."

>> Like now?

Exactly. Like now. No one can "hear" us. So, Cynarra told me about a Web site, a place called Dead.com. She told me to check it out.

>> Dead.com. Sounds cheery.

That Web site was creepy, lots of pages dealing with death and mutilation. And sure enough, there was a page on poison. And on that page I found something called a fungoid colloidal suspension.

>> Sounds yummy.

Toxic mushrooms, fermented and turned into a slightly sweet mixture. It causes intense gastral pain, contractions, hemorrhaging, and— it was rumored—a death that was virtually unrecognizable from—

>> Yes . . . ? Unrecognizable from—Paladin?

Sorry again. The person who died from that poison was most likely to be diagnosed as having a spontaneous hemorrhage.

>> Neat.

Now, Cynarra and I talked about almost nothing else. There were still those tender moments when we imagined touching each other, caressing . . . but now we had a new shared enthusiasm. We imagined being *free*.

>> So you went down to your local mushroom store.

No. No, I had to search the city to find out where you'd get these stupid mushrooms. But it turned out that they are a vital food source for the Munghip Lizard, a small green lizard from the Central Amazon. If you had a Munghip as a pet, you absolutely *had* to have these mushrooms. I told Cynarra.

>> She went there too, eh? Quite a run on toxic mushrooms.

She didn't tell me that she did that. I thought: maybe for her this was all a fantasy, and I was helping her create this fantasy. I didn't know if she was serious.

But I told her what I was going to do. I told her that she had me entranced, that I didn't care what she really looked like . . . if she was bald and toothless. She was my *Cynarra*, and she gave me the dream to be free.

>> *And* financially secure.

Yes. If this worked, I'd have the money I needed to live. That wouldn't be a problem. When the ax fell, when the business collapsed, I'd be okay.

>> So when did you do the deed? Was it a dark and stormy night?

It was morning. A gray November morning, barely light, the cloud cover so thick. I had the mushroom mixture fermenting for the five days—exactly as called for by the recipe. Then I went to the fridge and found Bev's container of Trim Grain. That stupid diet beverage of hers looked like quicksand. It was marsh sludge. It sloshed around in the container and left a gritty film on the sides.

>> Guess it would mask the mushroom brew, huh?

Sure. And I didn't have to put a lot in. A single teaspoon was terminal. But I put a couple of extra tablespoons in—just to be sure. A little overkill wouldn't hurt. I shook the container a couple of times.

Bev always had a couple of glasses of the stuff every day, always trying to fight that middle-aged spread.

I went to work. I waited for Cynarra.

>> **And she didn't show up?**

No. She did. I didn't tell her what I did. I wanted to wait to make sure it worked. I was afraid that she'd be shocked.

>> **But it was *her* idea.**

Or her fantasy . . . her game. I wanted it to be done, a—what do they call it?—*fait accompli.*

We chatted a bit. Then, after lunch, I went back to ChatWorld, but she wasn't there. But there was a message. She had run out . . . she had some errands to do. She said that she'd be back.

I was so nervous, so damn excited I took a walk.

I got back to my office late. The office manager got on my case . . . but it didn't matter. Not anymore. I went to my computer terminal, expecting Cynarra to be there, back from her chores.

>> **But she wasn't.**

Yeah. And I felt alone. I wanted to *share* this with her. She helped make it happen and now I was all alone.

So I left work early. I left, and returned home.

>> **And found? Paladin?**

>> **Paladin, you there? Hey, come back . . . Paladin.**

I'm back. Couldn't type for a minute. Where was I?

>> **You went home . . .**

Yes . . . I went home . . . went back into the apartment. And as soon as I opened the door, I knew something was wrong.

>> **How did you know that?**

I don't know. It was something about the sound of the place, or maybe the smell. Something that said . . . a bad thing has happened here. I felt shaky. I went to the kitchen. To fix myself some tea. Steady myself.

>> **You didn't want to go find the body?**

Not yet. And there was a chance, a slim chance that Bev wasn't there. Maybe she had gulped her Trim Grain and run out for a milkshake. Maybe she collapsed in Baskin Robbins while some pimply-faced college kid watched her writhe on the linoleum.

>> **Nice Image.**

I used my Winnie-the-Pooh honey dipper to put some honey in my tea. I zapped the cup in the microwave. I liked my tea hot. I was scared.

>> **Who wouldn't be?**

The microwave beeped, and I took out my tea. I took a sweet sip, nearly burning my lips. The phone rang. A jarring sound. But I ignored it. The machine picked it up . . . but there was no message. Don't you hate that? When people call and leave no message.

>> **Sure. Detest it. When did you go look . . . ?**

It took a few minutes, but finally I was ready. I took a breath, and walked with my tea into the living room . . . and it was empty. Then I went into the bathroom. An obvious place, I thought. Especially if someone was feeling stomach pain. Head for the porcelain throne, try to puke the poison out.

>> **And the bathroom was—**

Empty. So . . . now it was time to check the bedroom. And I began to worry that maybe today, of all goddamn days, Bev had skipped her precious Trim Grain. It was damned unlikely . . . but anything could happen. I walked back to the bedroom.

>> **Yes.**

>> **Come back! Hey, friend, don't leave me hanging.**

>> **You there?**

Barely. Can hardly see straight. But might as well . . . try.

So, I went to the bedroom, and there she was, curled on the floor, still in her flannel nightgown with faded blue flowers and dotted with a zillion cotton nits that screamed "throw us the hell away."

>> **Nothing too sexy, eh?**

And there was a pool in front of her where she had thrown up. A bloody pool. Her eyes were wide open . . . I had to walk close to see that. I stepped over her body, and looked at her eyes. Whatever pain she had been feeling was right there. Easy to see that she had been feeling real bad before she died.

>> **And you called the police?**

No. That was my plan. Call the police. Tell them I came home to find her like this, and pray that the mushroom mixture was masked by the blood and fluids. But then I saw something . . . in the den . . . glowing.

>> **An angel of the Lord? Just kidding—**

The computer screen was *on*. I walked over to it. Bev had turned on the computer. For some reason she had been typing something. A message . . .

>> **And the message said—?**

But you must know what it said?

As soon as I saw it I knew how stupid I had been, how *completely* stupid. I stood in front of the screen, and felt my stomach go tight. Because the message said:

>> **Don't kill me!**

No. The message read:

"Paladin, my love.

I used *your* courage to become brave, to do what I wanted to do. By tonight, my husband will be dead. I put some of the same poison, my love, in his honey. Meet me soon in our regular chat room!

I love *you*.

Cynarra."

I looked at the screen. My tea was all gone. The tightening in my stomach didn't go away, it got worse. Until—like now—I can barely breathe.

It's funny. I logged on. To tell someone . . . and I stumbled into you. Another faceless person in ChatWorld. Another—

>> **Outstanding! Hey, this is an absolutely *outstanding* story, my man. You've *got* to publish this.**

>> **Hey, you still there Paladin? The log shows that you're still on-line, still in the room.**

>> **You reading this, Paladin? Believe me, this is a great story and you have to upload it to the archive.**

>> **Paladin?**

>> **Paladin??? Hey, hit the keys, guy!**

>> **Paladin . . . ? Well, if you aren't going to chat, I'll go find someone who will.**

>> **Sheesh. I'm outta here! :(**

Nightmover has left the chat room.
Attending Chat Room 13: 1
Welcome Paladin!

Letter to the Editor

Morris Hershman

DEAR MR. HITCHCOCK:
I'M writing to you because I've heard of you and I want your advice about something. My friends say I ought to be a real writer, anyhow. I write letters very good.

What I figure, though, is that maybe you can tell me if I ought to be as scared as I am.

Like I say, this thing really happened. If you want to make a story out of it maybe I could collaborate with you on it. I've got the story; all you'd have to do is write it up.

Anyhow, this happened to me on Brighton Beach. In Coney Island, you know, in Brooklyn.

When I go out there I usually bring a blanket in a paper bag, unroll it on the sand, take off my pants and shirt and, with my bathing suit already on instead of shorts, try to catch me a little sun. I park myself near the peeling wooden sign that says Bay 2. A lot of people near my own age come out there, in the twenties and thirties. I can lie on the sand and look up at the boardwalk. Though it's plastered with signs saying that you need shirt and pants to go walking up there, that doesn't really matter.

It happened just this afternoon, the thing I want to tell you about. You know what it's been like in the city: 93 in the shade, people dropping like flies. Even on the beach today, the sand was like needles under your feet.

When I'd waited for half an hour and none of my friends showed up, I went into the water. Usually I walk in up to my ankles, then dive in to get the rest of me good and wet.

Well, I swam out past the first buoy. Like all the rest of them, it's red on top and with what looks like barnacles on the sides. All of a sudden I saw a guy coming almost head on into me. About twenty feet or so away I heard another man yell, "Sam!" and then there was the sound of bubbles.

The fellow had disappeared (the guy I'd been looking at call him number one so you won't get confused) and then he showed up above water with the crook of his arm on the other guy's neck, pulling him in.

"This man's hurt!" he shouted.

I can scream pretty good, too. "Give 'em room!"

On the shore they tried artificial respiration. I went along to watch the hefty lifeguard in his white shirt, the victim's legs between his, jumping up and down like clockwork. I won't forget it as long as I live.

How long that's going to be, maybe you can guess.

Anyway, this fellow who'd brought him in stood off to one side. He wore a bright-red rubber cap and a bathing suit with white stripes at the sides. He was a beanpole of a guy, the kind who probably never stops eating, though. His large brown eyes stared right past me.

"Poor guy, whoever he was," Beanpole said to anybody who'd listen. Then he stopped and pointed. "Look!"

I did, but all I saw was the usual beach scene: the kids selling ice cream or tin-bottomed paper cartons of orange drink or cans of cold chocolate, or cellophane bags with potato knishes inside. You can always recognize the sellers because they wear white sun helmets like in movies about big-game hunters in Africa.

At my left a guy wandered from girl to girl, trying to strike up a talk—"operating," it's called nowadays. A lot of acquaintances run into each other at Bay 2 because they've mostly been to the same summer places: White Roe, Banner Lodge, Tamiment, Lehman, whatever you like.

At one blanket, people gathered around a uke player who was picking out "Blue-Tail Fly." He stopped to tell a singer something about one of the downtown social clubs for older unmarried people. "I'm going down for a dance tonight at the change-of-life club," he said.

Then I saw what Beanpole had been pointing at. Two men, clearing a path for themselves, inched their way along the lines of blankets. Between them they carried what looked like a white gauze pad folded in two. It turned out to be a stretcher. They covered up the guy with a sheet over his face, so he couldn't even breathe.

"I guess they're taking him to the first-aid station," I said to a small blonde next to me, remembering the wooden shack on Bay 6 or 7 that looks like it was on stilts and with a spiral staircase that takes you up to the dispensary.

The blonde shook her head slowly. "No, it's the ambulance for him and then the morgue. I saw him earlier in the day. He was a very good swimmer."

At my side the Beanpole nodded. "He must'a gotten cramps or something. We were way out, past the fourth marker. Nobody in sight except . . ." And he turned to me like he'd just noticed I was there.

I introduced myself. He mumbled that he was glad to know me, but he didn't mention his name. His eyes were hard and bright.

"How much of it did you see?" he asked quietly.

"I saw you practically on top of him and trying to get a grip on him. You did a hero's job out there. Nothing to be ashamed of, believe me!"

I had made up my mind not to go in swimming today, and when my friends came around a little later, I told them what I'd seen and spent the afternoon lying in the sun.

Once I felt somebody's eyes on me. I looked up and there was Beanpole, not too far away. He was asking a girl the name of the book she was reading, but every so often he glanced in my direction. I lay back and closed my eyes and forgot it.

But when I was going home by way of the Brighton local, I started to ask myself questions. Once I remember I looked up at my reflection in a subway window glass; I might have been a skeleton.

Well, as soon as I got home to Snyder Avenue, where I live, I started writing this letter to you. I was supposed to take a shower and go down to a State of Israel bond rally at Twenty-third and Madison, but I don't think I will. Not tonight. For all I know, maybe I'll never go to a rally again in my life.

It's this way: the blonde girl at the beach told me that the dead guy was a good swimmer. If he'd been in trouble, well, any old hand at swimming knows enough to float around till he can save himself. I'd heard the victim calling "Sam!" before he went under, like Sam was right near; but Beanpole said he never knew the dead guy.

The idea I've got explains why Beanpole behaved like he did, the way he kept looking at me. I've been thinking hard, and now what I saw looks completely different. I had told Beanpole, "I saw you practically on top of him." The way I remember it now, Beanpole was holding the guy *under* water, not saving him. Beanpole kept him under water till it made no difference one way or the other.

But maybe I'm wrong. Maybe Beanpole is a right guy, after all. Maybe.

I figure it like this, though: I'm the only one who saw it happen, and he knows that.

Like I say, maybe I'm all wrong. Beanpole could have gotten so bollixed up trying to save the guy he went around afterward like he'd flipped his lid. He looked calm to me, but maybe some guys carry all their feelings inside them, like a guy does if he's worked up to kill somebody.

Well, that shows what you can think about in the morning. It's almost morning here, and I can look out the window and see dawn touch the rooftops across the street.

I guess I'm all wrong, crazy with the heat or whatever you'd call it.

But it'd be so easy for Beanpole to find me. After all, he knows my name and it's in the phone book. All he has to do is come in right now and shoot the top of my head off.

But even if he did the truth would come out. This letter alone is sure to do it. If I hear anybody coming, I'll stop writing and hide it as quick as I can. It'd be found by the police, afterward. I'm sure Beanpole's name and address were taken this afternoon, and plenty of people got a good look at him.

Anyhow, that's all of it, and like I said at the beginning I want your advice about whether I'm right to be as scared as I am. Should I go to the police and tell them all this?

To show you the way a guy can get nervous; just this minute I could have sworn I felt a draught on the back of my neck, like the door had been quietly opened by somebody, and

The Coveted Correspondence

(A Father Dowling Story)

Ralph McInerny

1

FATHER DOWLING THOUGHT THAT there were two major motives for an interest in genealogy: A person either wanted to contrast his current eminence with humble forebears or to wallow in the lost past grandeur of the family.

"Where does that leave Sally Murphy?" Marie Murkin asked.

"The Irish are different."

Marie humphed. "Don't tell me about the Irish. I married one."

Silence fell. Marie looked as if she regretted alluding to the long-since-departed Mr. Murkin, gone now into that bourne from which no traveler returns—at least word of his demise had never reached her—but simply gone, here one day and gone the next. It had turned Marie into a grass widow, prompted the beginning of her long career as housekeeper in Saint Hilary's rectory, a post that justified, if only in

her own eyes, a freewheeling curiosity about the people of the parish.
Sally Murphy had been reluctant to avail herself of the opportunities
of the parish center where seniors gathered every day under the capable direction of Edna Hospers. Not that it was a regimented day. Edna
simply created an atmosphere in which the elderly men and women
could enjoy themselves. Sally had finally succumbed to Marie's urging,
become a regular at the parish center, and apparently was soon boring
others to death with stories of her uncle Anthony.

"Edna hasn't mentioned it," Father Dowling said carefully. He was
not yet sure what Marie was up to.

"Oh, she wouldn't," Marie said with great conviction, and then
added in an altered voice, "if she is even aware of it."

There was an ancient enmity between the housekeeper and Edna
Hospers, nothing seriously disruptive, but an endless flow of ambigu-
ous criticism from Marie and of impatience from Edna when Marie
tried to make inroads into her fiefdom in what had once been the
parish school.

"Someone has complained to you, Marie?"

"I am a victim myself."

"Tell me about it," the pastor said, closing his book. It was clear
that Marie had some point that she would eventually make and there
was no use in his kicking against the goad.

Sally Murphy was not a woman who, on the face of it, one would
expect to draw attention to her family, either present or previous generations. Her brothers, after tumultuous teenage years, had joined the
navy after a kind of either/or was presented to them by the judge, and
had kept in sporadic touch with Sally over the years, postcards arriving
from brigs and jails around the world. After dishonorable discharge
from the navy, they had joined the merchant marine and continued
their adventures. Meanwhile, Sally's parents, proprietors of a tavern
that passed from being a respectable neighborhood watering hole to a
somewhat unsavory dive, enjoyed their wares as much as they sold
them, and ended up in perilous health that had taken them to fairly
early deaths. Not, all in all, a background one would be inclined to celebrate. But Sally's claim to fame was oblique, her uncle Anthony on
her mother's side.

"She insists that he was a famous writer."

"What was Mrs. Murphy's maiden name?"

"Fogarty, but he wrote under a pseudonym."

"Did she say what it was?"

Marie sighed, "I hesitated to prod her into more lying, but I did ask."

"Well?"

Marie closed her eyes, in search of the name. They snapped open. "Connor Tracy."

The pastor sat back, his eyebrows lifting.

"Have you heard of him, Father?"

"Oh yes."

Marie looked crestfallen but then she brightened up. "Of course she would pick a real writer to brag about. That doesn't make him her uncle."

THE REPUTATION OF F. Connor Tracy had known the usual literary ups and downs. As a young writer, his short stories had captivated readers of *The New Yorker*, the *Atlantic*, and *Partisan Review*. Only a Catholic could have written them, but their interest far transcended his coreligionists. Indeed, Catholics came to them later than the general reader. No Catholic college could claim him because no college could. When he came out of the service in 1945, discharged at Great Lakes, he had spent a few weeks with his parents in Aurora, sitting on the porch and looking at the Fox River move slowly southward. Acclimated once more to peace, he decided to set about doing what he had pondered doing while a marine. He wanted to be a writer. The GI Bill would have supported him at the college of his choice, but his ideal of the writer was a man of the people, who lived and worked as others did, and wrote besides. And so he had. He moved to Wisconsin and took a job with a county highway department and at night, in the room he rented in Baraboo, he wrote. Eventually he sent manuscripts to New York and they were invariably accepted. Later he would admit that since this is what he had aimed for, he had not been as surprised as he should have been. With success, he quit the highway crew and moved to Ireland where he could live cheaply and devote himself entirely to his writing. Alas, there his craft found the formidable rival of the local pub. The two decades left him were spent producing the fiction that would offset the tragedy of his life.

"He received the Last Sacraments," Sally said to Father Dowling when, having determined that her story about being related to the great writer was possibly true, he sought her out to talk about it.

"Thank God. How do you know?"

"The priest wrote to my mother."

"Ah."

"She put that letter with the others she had received from him."

"From Tracy?"

"From Tony, she would say. That was his name."

"Where did the pseudonym come from?"

"F. was for Fogarty. The others are family names as well."

"He has always been a favorite of mine."

Sally beamed in a proprietary way. "I must confess I've not read much of him myself, Father."

"What happened to the letters your mother received from him?"

"Oh, they came to me."

"You should be careful of them."

"Of course."

She mentioned them as well to the journalist who interviewed her, alerted by those who were moved by Father Dowling's acceptance of Sally's story. Katherine Reynolds, a local writer, was with Sally when she was interviewed.

"I know every story by heart," Katherine said.

She also knew a good deal more about the writer than Sally did, and her remarks formed the staple of the story in the *Fox River Tribune*, the title of which, nonetheless, was "Niece of Famous Writer Fox River Native." Sally's mention of the letters nearly derailed the interview. Katherine begged to be allowed to see them, to read them. "Just let me touch one," she said, breathlessly. The adverb was the journalist's but anyone who knew Katherine would have found it accurate.

"Did you see the story in the *Tribune*?" Father Dowling asked Marie Murkin.

"The three-car accident?"

"The interview with Sally Murphy."

"You'd think she'd written the stories."

"She has a right to be proud, Marie."

"And what is Katherine Reynolds's excuse?"

It seemed best to drop the subject. Marie apparently thought that Sally's sudden prominence diminished the housekeeper of Saint Hilary's. But he couldn't resist a little dig.

"They might want to do a story on your letters, Marie."

"What letters?"

"You must have kept those of your many suitors."

"I had one suitor and I married him and lived to regret it."

2

THE STORY PROMPTED Father Dowling to take a volume of Tracy's off his shelf. The novel, remembered as good, proved better than his memory suggested, and for the next week and a half the pastor of Saint Hilary's worked through the slim oeuvre of F. Connor Tracy. He read slowly, wanting to prolong the pleasure, if pleasure was the word. Tracy had a melancholy imagination which in the bogs and pubs of Ireland exuded a keening music that gripped the soul and made the heart heavy with an all but unbearable sorrow at the follies and failures of men. Phil Keegan on a visit picked up a volume, frowned at the jacket, opened it and read a line or two, then shut it and returned it to the table. Father Dowling introduced the inexhaustible topic of the Cubs to forestall any negative remark from Phil. It was not necessary for salvation to enjoy the fiction of Tracy but to denigrate it could not be considered morally neutral.

"Funny you should be reading him," Phil said, not rising to the bait of the Cubs.

"Rereading," Father Dowling said and then, because that sounded smug, added, "He was always a favorite."

"I hope his letters are worth something."

"His letters?"

"His niece had a collection of them he had written to her mother. They're missing."

"Tell me about it."

Sally Murphy had been enjoying the quasi celebrity the story about her uncle's letters had conferred upon her. She had begun to annoy others at the parish center because of the frequency with which she brought up the connection. There was nearly a fight when old Agnes Grady suggested that the writer had lost his faith and wrote only about degenerates.

"He writes about the Irish," Sally had protested.

Agnes nee Schwartzkopf just lifted an eyebrow. Sally demanded to know if Agnes had read anything of Tracy.

"I don't read that sort of thing."

"You don't read any sort of thing," Sally said hotly.

It was Katherine who soothed the troubled waters. "No one could read the letters he wrote Sally's mother without being transported."

She spoke with a calm authority that carried the day.

Katherine had attached herself to Sally, having received permission to read the letters in the Murphy home. Her suggestion that Sally keep them in a safe deposit box at her bank had not been taken up. Katherine had embarked on a campaign to edit the letters; something she offered to do gratis.

"It would be a privilege, Sally."

"But they're private letters."

Katherine explained to Sally that nothing was more common than to publish the letters of the great, particularly those of great writers. Sally did not think many breaches of decorum constituted a new moral code. Her lips became a line and she shook her head firmly at the renewed suggestion and finally Katherine had let it drop.

"It is selfish to want to keep such a treasure to oneself," Katherine told Edna Hospers, needing some outlet for her frustration and finding it in the sympathetic director of the parish center.

"Would there really be such interest?"

"Edna, any publisher would snap it up. As for the originals . . ."

"What do you mean?"

"Someone recently paid ten thousand dollars for an old pipe that had belonged to Tracy."

If a mere object elicited such a covetous reaction from collectors, what would dozens of letters written over an extended period of time and in the very hand of the great writer bring?

"Sally would never let them go."

"I don't think she should! But she has no idea of their value."

When he was told of the exchange, the pastor had been remind-ed of the chiding tone of guidebooks written by British authors, lamenting the way the natives failed to keep up the artifacts and buildings that brought tourists from afar. Why didn't the Italians restore all the churches in Rome? Since there was at least one church in every block, this would have proved a vast enterprise. So Katherine chided Sally for thinking of her uncle's letters to her mother as letters to her mother rather than as messages to the world at large.

When the letters were missing, there was no need to speculate on what had happened. Sally said it outright.

"Katherine has them, of course. I want them back. I don't care if you have to arrest her."

"How long have they been missing?"

On this Sally was vague. The last time she had definitely laid eyes on the correspondence had been a week before.

Katherine was not at home. She did not answer her phone and there seemed little point in leaving more messages on her answering machine. The police made inquiries but Katherine had left no trail. It was Edna's thought that Katherine had simply lost patience with Sally's intransigence and acted on her own.

"Taken them to a publisher?"

Edna nodded. "You had to hear the fervor with which she spoke."

Calling all possible publishers of literary correspondence would have been a formidable task, but Phil Keegan was prepared to under-take it. In order to give it focus, he got a court order to enter Katherine's house, hoping to find some indication of what she might have done with the letters. That is how the body of Katherine Reynolds was found.

3

PERHAPS IF SHE had been found earlier, Katherine would have been thought to be asleep or unconscious. The blow that freed her from this

Vale of Tears had left no visible mark, and only a close examination by the coroner revealed the lesion on her head. She had been struck from behind and fallen forward onto a sofa, this breaking her fall, and then apparently rolled gently to the floor. Her still open but unseeing eyes prompted Edna, who had accompanied Cy Horvath, to speak to Katherine as if she could hear. And then the stillness and strangeness brought a gasp before Edna cried out. Cy had already seen the body and its condition and was on the phone to Dr. Pippen.

Given the reason for the court order, Cy, unable to do anything for Katherine and Edna having been taken away, began the search for the letters. Letters he found, but only of the kind that any household would contain—bills, junk mail—until he came upon half a dozen replies from publishers in response to the inquiry Katherine had indeed presumed to make. All but one of the publishers was interested. Indeed, on Katherine's answering machine were several messages from publishers who had not wanted to trust what was now somewhat disdainfully referred to as snail mail.

"Did you find a copy of the letter she sent, Cy?" Phil Keegan wanted to know.

"No."

"I suppose we can ask one of these publishers for a copy."

"Why?"

"It should tell us whether she had the letters in her possession."

Cy had an impassive Hungarian countenance and it would have been difficult to know what his reaction was. Agnes Lamb who had returned from guiding Edna to solace and sanctuary wrinkled her nose as Keegan spoke.

"Those answers tell the story, don't they? That and the fact that she is dead."

"Maybe."

Maybe not, however. The search for the letters suggested that someone else had been searching the house, perhaps in quest of the letters.

"They must have found them," Agnes said.

"Maybe."

"That would explain their not being here," Agnes explained patiently.

"If they were here in the first place."

Agnes started to laugh and then stopped, not wanting to be amused all by herself. Neither Phil Keegan nor Cy Horvath seemed to think the captain's agnosticism was misplaced.

"We are going to proceed on the assumption that she was killed for some letters she didn't have?"

"We are not going to proceed on the assumption that she had the letters."

"That's the same thing."

The silence suggested that she had been guilty of a solecism.

WHEN PHIL STOPPED by that night, he brought Father Dowling up to speed on the investigation. This did not take long, since all the results were negative. It was not certain that the one who had murdered Katherine had got what he had come for, if he had indeed come for the letters.

"Was anything else missing?"

"Nothing obvious. But we don't have an inventory so it is difficult to say. He was a very neat thief, and murderer."

"He?"

"Inclusive. We don't really know that either."

Several publishers had been contacted and one had faxed a copy of the letter received from Katherine. It was an enigmatic epistle.

> I am writing to ask if you would be interested in publishing a collection of some forty-seven letters written by F. Connor Tracy to his sister over a span of some twenty years, all of them after he had settled in Ireland. My preliminary study of the letters suggests that they have great importance, both biographical and literary. In some of the letters, he begins sober and ends drunk, traceable not only by the handwriting but also by the repetitiveness, but all in all they have an elegiac quality that admirers of his work will recognize as his peculiar voice. On the other hand, some of his reminiscences of childhood strike a whimsical even nostalgic note not normally associated with his outlook.

"What do you think, Roger?"

"That she was a bit presumptuous. I gather that Sally had not authorized such an inquiry."

"Does the letter suggest to you that she had taken the letters?"

In one sense, it emerged, she had. A school notebook was found in her bedroom in which were transcribed more than a dozen of the letters. Apparently Katherine had taken advantage of the time Sally had allowed her with the letters to copy them.

"She asked if she could take notes," Sally said. "I didn't dream she would copy them out word for word."

It was clear that Sally was not yet fully convinced of the intrinsic value of her uncle's letters. She had accepted the publicity and had herself exploited them, but apparently expecting that at any moment someone would question their importance.

"She was right about publishers being interested in the letters."

"What good does that do me now?"

"You're sure the letters are missing?"

"Of course I'm sure."

Father Dowling looked at Edna but she avoided his eyes. This was a delicate matter, but he had promised Phil Keegan he would try.

"It occurs to me, Sally, that if Katherine put the letters away in a different place . . ."

"She did that all right. In her own house." But Sally's expression softened. "God rest her soul. Imagine getting killed over some old letters."

"That's my point, Sally," Father Dowling said.

Sally looked at him blankly.

"Sally, if I can imagine the letters are still here, someone else can, too. Perhaps the same person who killed Katherine."

"But he has the letters now."

"But what if Katherine never took them? What if they are still here, in this house, and the killer comes to the same conclusion . . ."

Sally's hand went to her throat and she moved closer to Edna on the couch.

"Why don't you and Edna conduct a thorough search?"

Sally's reluctance was gone, indeed she was eager to turn the house inside out to see if the letters were there, even while professing that she didn't believe for a minute that they were.

If they were, they were not found by Edna and Sally.

"It was a long shot," Phil said, shrugging. "Chances are the killer got the letters."

"You sound surer now."

"Well, if Edna Hospers couldn't find them I doubt they are in Sally's house."

"I don't suppose a thief would be stupid enough to try to sell them immediately."

"How would he go about selling items like that?"

Roger put Phil Keegan onto Casper Barth the rare book dealer. Meanwhile there was Katherine's funeral to preside over.

McDivitt pulled Father Dowling into his office when the priest arrived at the funeral home for the rosary that night at 7:00.

"Am I early?"

"There are half a dozen people," McDivitt said in hushed tones. "I could understand it if the weather was bad."

"We'll start fifteen minutes late."

This calmed the funeral director. He offered Father Dowling a little something, knowing it would be refused. He himself poured a dollop and tossed it off. When he put the bottle back into a drawer of his desk he chuckled. He drew out a card and held it up for the priest to see. *Let McDivitt replace your last divot.*

"I hope you don't plan to use that."

"Good Lord, no. I was given it at our last convention. Undertakers have a strange sense of humor, Father Dowling."

"I wasn't aware they had any at all."

"You'd be surprised."

"I am."

At 7:15 they went into the viewing room. There were a dozen people there now, all wearing the expression one saves for wakes and funerals. Most of those there were regulars at the parish center. Sally's absence seemed conspicuous, and Father Dowling thought less of her for it. Whatever Katherine may or may not have done, she was dead now, cruelly murdered. Sally might have chosen to be flattered by Katherine's interest in her famous uncle, but she seemed to resent it. Father Dowling nodded to the mourners and then took his position on the prie-dieu set up beside the open casket and began the rosary.

Repetitive prayer is conducive either to meditation or distraction and Father Dowling found his mind straying. What was it Hamlet's uncle had said? "My words fly up, my thoughts remain below, words without thoughts never to heaven go." Of course it was another distraction to remember that. He put his mind to concentrating on the mystery being commemorated by the decade they were reciting. When he finished he felt that he had been engaged in physical labor. It occurred to him that Katherine looked serene and peaceful lying there. He might have mentioned this to McDivitt but it would have seemed lugubrious.

Others had come in while the rosary was being said and Father Dowling was delighted to see that Sally was one of them. She was speaking with a man Father Dowling did not know. Phil Keegan had brought Marie Murkin with him.

"Katherine's beau," Marie said of the unknown man.

"I hope you locked the rectory doors, Marie."

She narrowed her eyes. "The answering service is on."

This was a device that Marie abominated, particularly when she was on the receiving end of someone's recorded message. Those who reached the rectory heard only "Saint Hilary's," a beep and silence. It was Marie's theory that everyone now knew enough to speak after the beep. "If they haven't hung up, that is."

Hanging up was what Marie did when, after enduring many rings, she was answered by a taped message made God knows how long ago.

That remark seemed oddly apropos when Phil Keegan asked Father Dowling to listen to the tape that had been taken from Katherine's answering machine. Her cheerful message, addressed to the world at large, brightly inviting the caller to leave a message long or short after the beep, was a voice from beyond the grave. The microcassette was all but full with messages going back nearly a year.

"Who is Hughes, Roger?"

There were several messages from him, usually saying that he would arrive at such and such a time at O'Hare. Hughes was the name that had been given for the man Marie had called Katherine's beau. It had been the pastor's understanding and, he learned, that of Edna as well, that Katherine was single and seemed to have no inclination to change her marital status at her age. She had been forty-seven when she died. The messages from Hughes began two months before.

Hughes had been at the funeral but Father Dowling did not have an opportunity to speak to him.

"I did," Marie said when he lamented this.

"Ah."

Silence. She wanted him to ask what she had learned. He knew she was incapable of not telling him. All he had to do was wait. Marie's willpower had strengthened in the hard school of the rectory under Father Dowling's teasing regime, and it was more than an hour later that she came into the study and began to talk before she had taken a chair.

"He is from Indianapolis. He was almost the exact age of Katherine. Her little book on Tracy came to his attention and he got in contact with her."

"And visited her?"

"Who knows what might not have happened if Katherine had lived." Marie's sigh seemed freighted with the mystery of things.

"Did he go back to Indianapolis?"

"He has to work."

"At what?"

"The main thing is whatever he felt for Katherine has been cruelly crushed."

"Didn't you ask him what kind of work he does?"

"What difference does it make?"

"Probably none."

"Probably."

4

THE WILD-HAIRED young man in the corduroy jacket chose not to waste his sweetness on the desert air of Fox River. Instead he poured out his story to a reporter from the *Chicago Tribune* who, once she had acquainted herself with recent events in Fox River and received assurance from the book review editor that F. Connor Tracy was indeed a major writer, pulled out all the stops. The natural son of the famous writer had come to the area to visit the ancestral spots of his deceased father. There were anecdotes of his father, vignettes of his childhood, a vow to make good his claim to be the heir of the literary property of his father.

His putative cousin was shocked. "My uncle never married and never had any children. Period."

This was the sole quotation from Sally Murphy in the story, but she had no sooner put down the phone than she called Tuttle the lawyer, demanding that he put a stop to this desecration of the memory of her uncle. Tuttle assured her that he would treat it with the same vigor he would treat an attack on his dear departed father.

"It's those letters that are causing all this," Sally said when she went to Tuttle's office.

"The letters." Tuttle scratched the tip of his nose with the wrong end of a ballpoint pen, creating what looked like blue veins.

"You must have read about them."

"I want it in your own words."

There was the distinct sound of snoring from the lawyer's inner office. He rose, kicked the door, and shouted, "Peanuts."

Sally half expected a vendor to appear and supply Tuttle with a package of peanuts. But the snoring stopped.

"My associate," Tuttle murmured. "Go on."

He paid close attention to her narrative but his spirits sank as he did so. Letters from a drunken brother in Ireland? She called him a writer but he was certainly nobody famous like Elmore Leonard or Louis L'Amour. But Tuttle perked up when she unfolded the story from the *Chicago Tribune*. He hadn't read a paragraph before he tipped back his hat and said, "Libel. We'll sue for libel."

"He's just a boy. He has nothing."

"I mean the paper."

"Oh."

Here was an opportunity Tuttle could warm to. He would be David, the *Tribune* would be Goliath, the outcome had a biblical inevitability.

"I want the letters back, too."

"Your cousin take those, do you suppose?"

"Don't call him that."

"Did he?"

"I don't think he was even in the country when they were taken. I gather he just got off the boat."

"Boat?"

"Just arrived."

Tuttle's loyalties wavered as he imagined a young man newly arrived from a foreign land being pounced upon by a huge metropolitan newspaper and then by relatives he had never before seen. If only Sean had come to him before Sally Murphy had . . . But Sally's connecting of the death of Katherine Reynolds with what she was saying brought home to Tuttle that the job being offered him might have all sorts of possibilities.

"You think she was killed for the letters?"

"I'm lucky I wasn't."

"They must be pretty valuable."

"Or life is held pretty cheap."

"That too."

After she left, Tuttle roused Peanuts Pianone and over shrimp fried rice at the Great Wall pumped his old friend about the status of the police investigation.

"I'm not assigned to that."

"What have you heard about it?"

Peanuts dipped his head, now to the right, now to the left, raising his eyebrows as he did. But that was it. Tuttle doubted that Peanuts had even heard of Katherine's murder. His career as a policeman consisted in putting in time until he was eligible for a pension. His family connections gave him tenure and the department preferred that he remain uninvolved in police work.

"Why do you want to retire?" Tuttle asked. Millions would kill to get Peanuts's situation; it was better than retirement.

"Stress."

Tuttle went around to Saint Hilary's to have a chat with Father Dowling. The pastor was thick as thieves with Phil Keegan. Marie Murkin told him the pastor was busy. "This will only take a minute," Tuttle said, brushing past her and heading for the study. The housekeeper was clinging to his arm when he stopped in the open doorway.

"You make an impressive couple," the pastor said, and Tuttle felt the grip on his arm go. There was a young man seated in an easy chair, holding a bottle of beer, grinning at the new arrivals.

"Sean, this is Tuttle the lawyer."

"I've already met Marie," the young man said, half rising and extending a very large hand.

"The writer's boy," Tuttle said, recognizing the young man from the *Tribune* article. The boy beamed.

"How do you know that?"

"You're famous. I am your cousin Sally's lawyer."

"She denies the connection."

"There wasn't much about your mother in the article."

Father Dowling broke in. "Tuttle, I can see that you have much to talk about with my young visitor. Sean, come back tomorrow for lunch. It's just after the noon mass. Come for that if you like."

A noncommittal nod.

"You sure you don't want to spend the night here?"

"The *Tribune* is footing my bill at the hotel."

Tuttle was on his feet. "We will leave you to your devotions, Father Dowling. Young Sean and I will go somewhere for a beer."

"This stuff is like water," Sean observed, then apologized to his host.

"It is not Guinness, I grant you."

"You want Guinness, we'll have Guinness," Tuttle promised.

The pastor showed them out, the housekeeper seemingly having disappeared. Tuttle got Sean into the passenger seat and then set off for the hotel at all deliberate speed. There they could charge everything to the boy's room and be in effect the guests of the *Tribune*.

The luxury of the modest hotel seemed sybaritic to Sean and Tuttle himself was far from immune to its charms, the chief of which was watching the young Irishman scrawl his name on the bills as they came.

"It's a lot better than where I stayed at first."

"Before you called the reporter?"

But Sean waved the topic away. Some minutes later, Peanuts arrived. Tuttle did not think it seemly to keep Peanuts from this bonanza.

"If only they served Chinese food."

"You'll complain in heaven," Tuttle chided.

"Not if there's fried rice."

The human mind is a wondrous thing. That night Tuttle awakened from a just and well-fed sleep to find that of all the badinage of the evening, what had stuck in his mind was young Sean's mention of a period prior to calling the reporter. The newspaper story had the reporter meeting Sean as he flew in on Aer Lingus. It was the kind of detail that interested the police. Tuttle was not surprised when he learned, later that day, that Keegan and Horvath had taken young Sean downtown for questioning.

5

MARIE MURKIN GREETED Phil Keegan coldly and let him find his own way to the study. Nor did she offer him refreshments.

"What's wrong with her, Roger?"

"Sean."

"Ah."

The newspaper accounts of the arrest were decidedly unfriendly to the police. The suggestion was that in desperation they had decided to frame a young immigrant. The fact that neighbors of Katherine's would testify that they saw the young man in the neighborhood prior to the killing did little to right the balance. Nor had Sally's belated statement that Sean had come to her door and she had turned him away as soon as she saw what he was up to.

"Besmirching my uncle's reputation," she scoffed. "I was having none of that."

The fact that Sean did not have the missing letters was regarded by the prosecutor, if not the third estate, as an exonerating factor. Perhaps he would not have resorted to violence if he had come into possession of the letters themselves. So went the theory, but the theory was soon exploded by Tuttle's discovery.

The little lawyer came to Father Dowling in a moral quandary. He had come upon information injurious to his client but as an officer of the court he could not withhold evidence.

"Evidence of what?"

"Father, he had the letters. The missing letters. He had checked a bag with the porter of his hotel and he asked me to pick it up and keep it for him."

"And the letters were in the bag."

Tuttle nodded. "They'll hang him, Father."

Even if he told Tuttle he could conceal the letters, he knew the lawyer would not believe him.

"Let me talk to Sean first."

The young fellow sauntered into the visiting room and plopped into a chair across from Father Dowling.

"Well, I must be a goner if they're sending me a priest."

"Would you like to talk as penitent to priest?"

"I didn't kill that woman, Father."

"But you had the letters."

He slapped his forehead. "Has he told the police?"

"He won't be able to keep them a secret from the police, Sean."

"You know, Father, I never got the chance to sit down and read them. That's all I wanted, to see what my father had written when I was this age or that. Had he never so much as alluded to my existence in writing to his sister? It's in a parish record out in Sligo. I've seen it myself. Maureen Shanahan, son; father Anthony Fogarty. That's his real name."

"You have some claim to the letters then."

"I don't want them. Not now. I wanted Tuttle to give them back to Sally Murphy."

"So you took the letters from Katherine?"

"I went there, yes, The door was open and I called and went in, the way we do in Ireland, and there she was, lying on the floor. I thought she was asleep. Truth is, I thought she might be drunk. I knelt down next to her. That's how I discovered the letters. She had hidden them under the couch. I took them—borrowed them really. I never meant to keep them."

It was all too easy to imagine what Phil Keegan and Cy Horvath and the others would make of this alibi. The letters would equivalently hang him, as Tuttle had said, but of course there was an embargo on the death penalty in Illinois.

"THAT BOY WOULDN'T hurt a fly," Marie Murkin declared, filling the pastor's coffee cup. Sun illumined the dining room curtains and became polychrome in the prismed edge of the mirror over the sideboard.

"Perhaps he thought he wasn't. It was an unlucky blow."

"I believe his story."

"It's too bad you won't be on the jury."

Sean's story that he had entered the house of a woman just murdered and had taken the letters he happened to discover when he knelt beside the woman to see if she was asleep was not a logical impossibility, but it did not rank high on the scale of plausibility. Of course his story explained why he had been seen in the neighborhood, and why he was in possession of the letters, for that matter, but his instructions to Tuttle suggested someone with much to hide.

"I have a professional obligation to believe him," Tuttle said, not a ringing endorsement.

"What can I say?" Sally Murphy said. "It all comes from his telling that preposterous story."

But it was not a preposterous story. Monsignor Hogan in the chancery had connections in Sligo and had provided Father Dowling with a photocopy of the parish record in which the name of Anthony Fogarty, American, was given as father of the child Sean. The mother had gone to God due to complications in a later out-of-wedlock pregnancy. Sally held the photocopy at arm's length, wrinkling her nose as she studied it.

"What's to prevent any man's name being used on such an occasion?"

"I doubt that the priest would be party to something like that, Sally."

If Sally did not share his doubt she would not of course say so, not to his face, but Father Dowling could see that she was indeed convinced. Whatever her distaste, the young man from Ireland was her uncle's son and thus her cousin. But even her distaste had lessened. A shocking claim, repeated, loses its shock value, and the fact of the matter was that few others seemed to react as Sally had. Of course the godless newspapers took it as gospel that a country like Ireland must be rife with hypocrisy. If the country would only join the modern world, Sean's mother would have gotten an abortion and that would have been the end of it. Not that they said that, of course. Sally did not expect consistency from the devil's disciples.

"I almost wish I could believe his story, Father."

Such sympathy, and it was widespread, would not keep Sean from being tried for the murder of Katherine Reynolds. Even if he had not meant to kill her, he had entered her house as a thief and had struck her down when she confronted him.

"Of course if his story is true, someone else must have killed Katherine."

6

LATER, EYES CLOSED, tipped back in his chair, drawing on an aromatic pipeful of tobacco, it occurred to Father Dowling that in one sense there were many possible suspects. There were the publishers to whom Katherine had written, any one of whom would have seen the value of her literary trove. But they were far away, and it would have taken a dark view of publishers to imagine them flying to Fox River to burgle and kill, even for some very valuable letters. Acquired in that way, they could only be possessed, enjoyed; they would bring nothing further unless the owner revealed that he had stolen property. The unlikelihood of this did not stop Father Dowling from asking to see that correspondence with the publishers that Katherine had inaugurated.

TUTTLE'S INVITATION TO sit at the defendant's table, gently refused at first, became a week later less off-putting. Marie was appalled.

"It puts you on his side."

"A murderer's side?"

"That's the whole point of the trial."

"What kind of a world would it be if priests avoided murderers?"

Marie was certain there was a logical flaw involved here but she did not have time to point it out. Of course she was right. Sitting at the defense table would be a public act, suggesting he was less concerned with mercy for the wrongdoer than that he be found innocent of a crime. But a series of phone calls to Indianapolis had so clouded things that Father Dowling told Tuttle he was prepared to accept the invitation.

"Better late than never."

"Things are going bad?"

Tuttle drew a finger across his neck while emitting a chilling sound.

From his vantage point at the front of the courtroom, Father Dowling had a good view of the little balcony from which a dozen spectators looked down over a large clock at the proceedings. Brendan Hughes was a most attentive observer in the front row, his arms on the railing, his chin on his folded arms. The note Tuttle passed him while a neighbor of Katherine's was on the stand identifying Sean as the man she had seen lurking in the neighborhood the day the murder had occurred had an address on it. An airport hotel. Hughes was waiting for him in the lobby.

"I think you're expecting me," Father Dowling said, as Hughes rose eagerly at the mention of his name.

"He said you'd be wearing a collar. I saw you in court."

"I understand you teach English."

"Celtic literature. F. Connor Tracy is a favorite of mine."

"Could you identify his handwriting?"

"Yes."

Father Dowling withdrew from his pocket one of the letters that had been recovered from Sean. Hughes's eyes brightened at the sight of the envelope.

"This is an authentic letter from the writer." He took another envelope from his pocket. "But I want you to look at this one first."

Hughes took the second envelope impatiently. It was not sealed and he soon had the single sheet of paper in his hands. His eyes glided over it and then he looked at Father Dowling. "This is a fake."

"And this one?"

Hughes's reaction to the other letter was completely different. He nodded, he smiled, he held the pages as if they were sacred. "This is one of the letters. No doubt about it."

"I wish I could say that you have been a great help to the guilty party."

"What will they do with him?"

"I'm not a lawyer."

"You really do look like a priest."

Hughes in turn really looked like a professor. He was a learned man, and a delightful conversationalist. But Father Dowling did not discover this on that first occasion. The fingerprints on the bogus letter matched those found in Katherine's house, a fact determined within an hour after Father Dowling turned it over to Phil Keegan. Much later that night, Phil came by the rectory.

"He admitted it, Roger. Cool as could be. I had to stop him and tell him to get a lawyer."

Katherine had shown Hughes some of the letters on a previous occasion, she had shown him her transcriptions of others. His desire to have them became overpowering. The combination of the letters and Hughes's amorous attentions were more than Katherine could resist. She agreed to take the letters.

"In fairness, Father, she had no idea I meant to steal them. She thought we were merely cutting a corner for the good of literature. Those letters belonged in the public domain. When she realized what I intended, she objected. She snatched at the letter she had shown me and I pushed her away. I had no intention to harm her. Or to let the young man go to prison. I was agonizing over what to do if he were found guilty."

"You are lucky to have Amos Cadbury as your lawyer, Brendan."

"What will happen to the letters?"

Sean and his cousin Sally entered into an agreement with a publisher to bring out an edition of the letters. The obvious editor would have been Brendan Hughes, but that of course was out of the question.

"And the originals?" Father Dowling asked the cousins.

Sean beamed. "They will go to the Notre Dame library, Father."

"That's very generous of you, Sally."

"Oh, they'll pay for them."

And there were other mementos and papers that the two of them could make available to the world of letters with adequate compensation to themselves. Tuttle in turn would actually collect a fee for his successful defense of his client.

"Peanuts wants a leave as a reward for tracking down where Hughes was staying." Phil said this in a neutral voice.

"Will he get it?"

"Roger, he's been on leave ever since he joined the department."

A Nice Cup of Tea

Kate Kingsbury

SAM WILSON WAS AS regular as high tide. I reckon there wasn't a man in Rainbow Bay who couldn't set his watch by him. Every morning, just five minutes after Maisie put the kettle on the stove, we would see Sam come whistling up the path with the mail. That's why, when he didn't appear at the usual time last Wednesday, Maisie just about had kittens.

Maisie is my older sister. We don't look much alike. She is thinner than I am, and taller. Her hair is iron gray while mine is milk white. We both wear glasses, but I still have all my teeth and I smile more than Maisie does.

We don't get out much anymore. Maisie doesn't see too well, and the damp gets into our bones and triggers our arthritis. That's the trouble with living close to the ocean. Not that I mind all that much. I never was one for socializing, even when my Harry was alive.

Maisie's looked out for me ever since our parents died in an avalanche when I was only eleven. Maisie used to be a schoolteacher until she retired several years ago. She taught biology to fifth graders— a waste of time, if you ask me.

The only thing those kids are interested in nowadays is how to attract the opposite sex, and what to do with them when they succeed. They don't need biology lessons to find that out.

Maisie never married. She used to say there wasn't a man on earth good enough to make her give up her freedom. Personally, I think she frightened the men off. Those who were brave enough to get close to her, that is.

Maisie made a great teacher, but she doesn't know much about being a woman. She liked to take charge, and you either do things her way or not at all. Most men don't like that. At least, my Harry didn't. He always said that marriage should be a partnership. Though I always let him think he was the boss.

Maisie made a big fuss when I told her I was getting married. She was afraid that Harry wouldn't take care of me as well as she had. But then she didn't know my Harry the way I knew him.

When he died a year ago last November, Maisie came to live with me. I think she'd been waiting forty-eight years for that moment. That's how long Harry and I were together. I miss him a lot.

Maisie's highlight of the day is when the mail arrives. I don't know what she expects to find in there. More often than not we get nothing more than some fool advertising circular trying to sell us magazines we don't want, insurance we don't need, or storm windows we can't afford.

It doesn't matter to Maisie. She treats every piece as if it's a letter from the President himself. At least, she did so until last Wednesday.

Life in our little town can be pretty dull, especially in the winter. There's only one main street, and no big stores like the ones in Deerport a couple of miles up the road.

Visitors tend to stay away from the beach when the cold, wet wind comes roaring in from the Pacific Ocean. They call it Rainbow Bay because if you stand on Satan's Point between the twisted pines and look west, straight out to sea, you can nearly always see a rainbow. I always wish on a rainbow. At least, I used to. I don't go up there anymore. It's not much fun without Harry.

Maisie isn't impressed by rainbows.

In fact, there isn't much that excites Maisie. She spends most of her time in the backyard when the weather's good. I must admit, the garden has never looked better. Except for the yew.

Maisie has always wanted to live in England. She visited there once. Now she drinks tea out of English bone china cups and keeps a curio crammed full of English figurines. She even has a picture of Queen Elizabeth over her bed.

One day she decided we needed English topiaries in the backyard. She took a pair of shears to the yew and hacked at it for hours. She said she was forming peacocks, but by the time she was done, the hedge looked as if it had been attacked by a giraffe with hiccups.

Sam said he liked it, though. I think that was when Maisie decided she liked him. Sam was one of the few mailmen I've met who truly believed in the carrier's code. You know . . . through wind and rain, and whatever else the Good Lord chose to put in his path.

Mind you, Sam was no youngster. His face was as wrinkled as a boiled handkerchief, he had no hair to speak of, and sometimes I wondered how he had the strength to ride that bike of his in the teeth of a nor'easter.

But his smile could warm your heart on a cold day, and the twinkle in his eye could make a woman feel like Miss America. He was quite a ladies' man, our Sam.

Maisie always had a cup of tea ready for him, every morning except for Sunday. Sam loved Maisie's tea. "A cup of your tea can keep me going for the rest of the day," he told her. "Never tasted tea like it. You should sell it. You'd be a wealthy woman in no time."

But Maisie isn't much of a businesswoman. She prefers to give the stuff away. She packages it in hand-sewn pink silk bags and gives it to people for birthdays and Christmas. I reckon just about everyone in Rainbow Bay has tasted Maisie's tea at one time or another.

It was raining last Wednesday, and blowing up for a winter storm. I could see the cedars at the edge of our yard fanning the rhododendrons. Sam would need a hot cup of tea, I thought as I watched the big, sooty clouds roll across the sky.

But the tea grew cold and bitter while we waited for him.

"He must be ill, Annie," Maisie said. "He's never this late." She kept getting up and going to the window, until she made me feel dizzy. "The tea will be too strong," she said. "I'll have to take it off the stove."

"Well, pour it out," I told her. "We don't have to wait for him."

She looked at me as if I'd suggested she walk down Main Street naked. "We always wait for him," she said, "and we'll wait for him today."

Maisie makes the best tea in the world. She dries and blends her own, from the leaves of herbs and flowers, and every one of them tastes different. I look forward to my tea and muffins in the mornings. I didn't want to miss out on them just because the mailman happened to be late.

"But if he doesn't come, we won't get to drink the tea ourselves," I said. I was getting a little annoyed at her. Not that it did any good. Once Maisie has made up her mind, the Good Lord Himself wouldn't be able to budge her. I resigned myself to waiting for Sam.

He was getting ready to retire from the post office. He was due for a nice pension, and the mortgage on his house was all paid up. He told us about it, the last time we saw him.

"All I need now is to find a woman willing to cook and clean for me," he said, with a sly wink at Maisie, "and I'll be all set. I reckon it's time. It's been lonely since Ellen died last year, and it'll be lonelier still when I don't get to bring the mail to all my charming ladies."

He'd been talking about "finding a new woman" for weeks, but when he said it that last morning, Maisie got more fidgety than I ever saw her before.

I wondered if she was thinking about Louise Daniels. Louise is a member of our gardening club, and quite the chatterbox. She used to be pretty at one time, until the years caught up with her. She wears a lot of makeup and stinks the room out with her perfume. She dyes her hair a horrible red. It's been permed so much you can see patches of scalp in the frizzy mess.

Louise lives by herself in a room over the beauty shop on Main Street, and I think she's pretty lonely. She's always talking to the members of the garden club about Sam, telling us what he said to her and what she said to him. It's mostly the same things Sam said to the rest of us, but we let her go on thinking she's the only one he paid attention to. I guess, deep down, we all feel sorry for her.

Maisie doesn't like Louise. But then Maisie doesn't like a lot of people.

I have to admit, I looked forward to Sam's visits, too. Sam knew everything there was to know about everybody. He was the first one in town to know that Eleanor Madison was expecting a baby in the spring (except Eleanor and the doctor, of course), when we'd all gone to her wedding just before Thanksgiving.

I remember when he told us about that. I thought Maisie was going to swallow her dentures. She was almost as shocked as she was the time Sam told us that the mayor was in trouble with the IRS for evasion of taxes. Or that Beatrice Harrington's son had been expelled from college. I think Sam knew about that before Beatrice did.

Anyway, when Sam didn't come last Wednesday, Maisie kept insisting that he must be ill. She wanted me to make him some chicken soup.

"Call the post office, Annie," she said. "Ask if he came in this morning. Perhaps the mail is late arriving and he's waiting for it." Maisie doesn't like talking on the phone. She says she likes to see people's faces when she talks to them. That's the only way she can tell what they're really thinking.

Well, I called Pauline, the head clerk at the post office. What she told me shocked me speechless. Poor Sam had died.

She'd heard that it was a heart attack, Pauline said. He was alone in the house and died sometime during the night.

I hung up the phone and stood there for a minute, trying to get my heart to believe what my ears had heard. Sam . . . dead. We'd never see him again. Never hear his cheerful whistle or feel warmed by his compliments again. It was a great loss, and I don't think I fully realized just how devastating a loss until that moment.

"What's the matter?" Maisie demanded, in the kind of voice she must have used on her more unruly students.

It was then I realized I was crying. "It's Sam," I said, hunting for a tissue in the pocket of my sweater. "He died of a heart attack last night."

Well, I thought Maisie was going to drop dead herself. Her face went this dreadful gray and she grabbed ahold of the table to steady herself. "Sam? Heart attack?"

She said it so faintly, I barely heard her. Seeing her look so awful like that made me forget my own misery for the moment. I hurried over to her and made her sit down in her chair. Her hands were as cold as an Arctic wind, and her expression reminded me of the time we'd seen Father Jamison's pet poodle run over by a tractor.

I'd never seen such a terrible look on a man's face as I saw that day when the priest carried that pitiful, broken body to his car. The memory of it haunted me for weeks. It was that kind of look I saw on Maisie's face when I told her about Sam.

"We'd better have that tea now," I said, rubbing her hands. "It will make you feel better."

Maisie jumped out of that chair as if she'd been stung by a yellow jacket. "I don't want any tea," she said, and her voice sounded as if she were choking. "I'll never touch another cup of tea as long as I live!"

She rushed out of the living room and I heard her bedroom door slam. It got awful quiet after that. I thought I heard her crying, but when I crept down the hallway to listen, she must have heard the floorboards creak. I couldn't hear any sound at all from that room.

It was two days later that I heard the news. Sam hadn't died of a heart attack, after all. He'd died of food poisoning. Betsy Mae told me, when I went into the bank to deposit the pension checks.

Betsy Mae loves to gossip. She has sharp eyes that never miss a thing. Her hair is blonde, except for the roots, and she wears teenager clothes. She hasn't been a teenager for at least twenty-five years.

"Poor old devil," Betsy Mae said that day. "He must have kept something too long in the fridge. Chicken, I shouldn't wonder. They say it's the worst thing to hang on to. That's the trouble with men living all alone. Don't know how to take care of themselves. Not like us women, that's for sure."

I didn't really want to talk about Sam. My voice didn't hold up too well whenever someone mentioned his name. And it seemed as if everywhere I went, people were talking about him.

"Mind you," Betsy Mae said, looking at the pension checks as if she'd never seen one before, "I don't reckon he would have been alone that long. I heard that he and Louise Daniels were getting very friendly, if you catch my drift. Too bad he waited so long to make up his mind about her. He might have been alive today."

She scribbled something on the deposit slips and held them out to me. "Just goes to show, you have to live for the moment. That's what I always say."

I took the deposit slips from her and tucked them inside my purse. I said good-bye and started to leave, but Betsy Mae was in a talkative mood, as usual.

"How's Maisie doing?" she asked. "I saw her in the post office the other day and she said her arthritis was playing her up."

I looked at Betsy Mae, wondering if I'd heard her right. "You saw Maisie?"

"Yes, and she told me she was mailing a package of tea to Louise Daniels for her birthday." Betsy Mae leaned over the counter as if she didn't want anyone else to hear what she said. I thought that a bit strange, because I was the only customer in there at the time.

"To tell you the truth," she said quietly, "I remember thinking she hadn't done a very good job of wrapping the gift up. It was in a paper bag tied around with string. No tape on it or anything."

That didn't surprise me. Maisie never could wrap up a package. Her Christmas gifts always looked as if Santa's reindeer had used them to play football. Since she'd lived with me I'd done all her packaging for her.

"I did wonder if Louise would ever get the tea," Betsy Mae was saying. "But I asked her yesterday when she was in here and she told me she'd almost finished it. She seemed surprised that Maisie would send her a birthday present. Specially since it wasn't her birthday."

Not nearly as surprised as I was, I thought. In the first place, Maisie hardly ever went out without me. She didn't like to drive because her eyes are not what they used to be. I didn't even know she'd left the house. And what was she doing sending Louise Daniels a birthday present when she'd made it plain to me that she didn't like the woman?

"I bet Louise is going to miss Sam," Betsy Mae said, studying her fingernails. They were long and pointed, painted bright red. One of them was cut right down to the quick. She's always cussing about breaking them. I don't know why she doesn't just cut them all short. That way they'd all be the same length.

"I'm sure we'll all miss him," I said, edging away from the counter. "I have to go now, Betsy Mae."

She went on talking as if I hadn't spoken. "I don't mind telling you, I'll miss him. He was like a breath of fresh air coming into this stuffy place. Brightened my day. Always had some juicy bit of gossip to tell me. I don't know how he found out so much about everyone. My Joe reckons he read everyone's mail, and that's how come he knew so much."

I could feel the tears starting to sting my eyes, so I just nodded and hurried out of there. I didn't want Betsy Mae to see me cry. She'd pester me to find out what was wrong. I could just imagine what she'd say if she knew a foolish old woman like me was breaking her heart over a man who preferred someone like Louise Daniels.

All the way home I kept thinking about what Betsy Mae had said. Maisie must have slipped out while I was taking my afternoon nap that day. Why hadn't she told me she'd been out? Obviously because she didn't want me to know that she'd mailed a package of tea to Louise.

That was not at all like Maisie.

The more I thought about it, the more uneasy I got. We had never kept secrets from each other before, and I didn't like the idea of her doing it now.

As far as I knew, Maisie hadn't been out of her room since she'd heard about Sam dying. I'd taken her meals in to her, but most of the time they came back untouched. She wouldn't even drink her tea. Maisie was taking Sam's death very hard, indeed. Harder than I was, in fact.

I thought about that for a long time, too. And I didn't like what I was thinking. It was time, I decided, for some straight talk between my sister and me.

Maisie wouldn't open the door when I knocked at first. I was just about to give up when I heard the bedsprings creak. The door opened a crack and Maisie peered at me through the opening. "Annie?" she said, as if she were expecting someone else. Her voice was quavery and I could tell she'd been crying a lot.

"Of course it is," I said, trying not to sound annoyed. After all, I was heartbroken about Sam, too, but I managed to go on living. "Who else would it be?"

"I thought—" She shook her head, as if she didn't know what she thought.

"I want to talk to you," I said.

"I don't feel like talking right now."

She started to close the door, but I held it open. "Why did you send Louise a package of tea?" I asked, watching her face very closely.

I could tell, by the way her eyes slid away from mine, that she knew that I knew. "It was her birthday," she said. "I thought it would be a nice gesture."

"It wasn't her birthday, Maisie. You don't know when her birthday is."

She looked at me then, and her face wore that stubborn look I knew so well. "I thought it was last week," she said.

I knew I would have to come right to the point. "Sam was poisoned," I said. "I think he opened the package meant for Louise."

I couldn't believe I was actually saying those words to her. I couldn't believe she would really do what I knew she had done. But after a moment or two, her face kind of crumpled up, and she nodded. My stomach felt as if somebody had kicked it.

"What did you put in the tea, Maisie? What kind of poison?"

"Clippings."

I barely heard her, but I could read her lips. I pushed the door open wider, and this time she didn't try to stop me. "Clippings from what?" I demanded.

"The yew."

Then I remembered. Of course. The English yew, one of the deadliest of poisonous plants. I could feel the shudder go all the way down my back to my feet. "Oh, Maisie," I said. "Why? How could you? Everybody loved Sam. I loved him."

"I loved him, too." Her eyes were bright with tears when she looked at me. "I loved him more than anybody. I didn't know he would open the package."

"Sam opened a lot of people's mail," I said. "Everybody knew that. How do you think he knew so much about what was going on in town?"

"He shouldn't have stolen the tea," Maisie said. She walked over to the bed and sat down, making the springs creak again. "I didn't know he would steal the tea."

"He must have replaced it with some of his store-bought tea," I said, trying to work out in my mind what had happened. "You know how much he loved your tea. Betsy Mae told me that Louise got the tea you sent to her, and she's perfectly all right."

"Betsy Mae knows?" Maisie said, her voice going up a notch or two.

"Not about the tea being poisoned. At least, not yet." I tried to think what was best to do. "I suppose everyone will know sooner or later," I said. "The police will want to know why you did it."

Her face went chalk white when I said that, but her chin went up. "I won't tell them," she said, and I could tell by her tone she meant it. "I won't have everyone laughing at me."

"I don't think they'll be laughing," I said, trying not to let her see how much I was hurting inside. "Why did you want to kill Louise?" I asked her, although I thought I already knew the answer to that.

"Sam was going to ask her to marry him. I thought if something happened to her, he might eventually get around to asking me."

Even though I'd half-expected it, hearing her say the words so matter-of-factly shocked me. "You wanted to marry Sam?"

"You've had a husband," she said, making it sound like an accusation. "You were so wrapped up in Harry you didn't need anyone else. All I ever had was loneliness. I wanted to know what it was like to be married, to be loved by a man, at least for a little while before I died."

"I always thought you were happier living alone," I said. "You never told me . . ."

I didn't know how to finish the sentence, but she finished it for me. "That I envied you? No, I never told you. But there wasn't a night went by when I didn't long for someone to love me, the way Harry loved you."

There was such a look of sorrow in her eyes, I almost cried. "So what are we going to do now?"

"We don't have to do anything," Maisie said, sounding more like herself. "No one has to know Sam was poisoned. No one will suspect me. We can just pretend it never happened."

"I don't think I can do that," I said. "I need to think about it."

"There's nothing to think about." She narrowed her eyes, and for a moment she looked like someone I didn't know at all. "You are not going to tell everyone your sister is a murderer. What would people say?"

I could tell she didn't really believe that I would tell anyone what she'd done. I left her alone and went for a walk in the garden to get my thoughts together. When I came back inside, Maisie was looking like her old self again. She'd even made me a nice cup of tea.

I told her that something had been eating the rhododendrons, and when she went to take a look at them, I called the police. Deputy Reynolds took her away a little while ago, after I'd told him everything.

Maisie didn't say a word the whole time I was talking. She looked at me, though, just as she was being led out of the door. I knew what she was thinking.

I might have forgiven her for Sam. After all, she is my sister, and Sam's death was an accident . . . in a way. No one need have known what really happened. But I knew. And I couldn't forgive her for Harry.

You see, my Harry died of food poisoning, too. It was the same day that Maisie had paid us a visit. I didn't think anything of it at the time, because we all ate the same thing for lunch and Maisie and I were just fine.

The doctor put it down to the crab Harry had caught himself. He'd eaten it the day before he died. I don't like crab so I hadn't touched any of it.

Now I know that it wasn't the crab. Maisie had made the tea that afternoon. I remember distinctly. She must have given Harry her special brew.

She was so lonely after she retired. She was always telling me that when Harry died she'd come and live with me and keep me company. I guess she decided to hurry that along a little bit.

Harry suffered terribly before he died. Sam must have suffered, too. Maisie had to pay for that. I'd loved only two men in my life, and she'd sent them both to the grave. She might have sent me there, too, if I hadn't poured that last cup of tea down the drain.

Letter to His Son

Simon Brett

Parkhurst
16th June, 1986

DEAR BOY,
I AM sorry to hear the Fourth of June celebrations was a trial. I've used that agency before and they never give me no trouble, but I will certainly withdraw my future custom after this lot and may indeed have to send the boys round. Honest, Son, I asked them to send along a couple what would really raise you in your fellow-Etonians' esteem when they saw who you got for parents. I had to get Blue Phil to draw quite a lot out of the old deposit account under the M23/M25 inter-section, and I just don't reckon I got value for my hard-earned oncers.

OK, the motor was all right. Vintage Lagonda must've raised a few eyebrows. Pity it was hot. Still, you can't have everything. But really . . . To send along Watchstrap Malone and Berwick Street Barbara as your mum and dad is the height of naffness so far as yours truly is concerned. I mean, doesn't no one have any finesse these days? No, it's not good enough. I'm afraid there's going to be a few broken fingers round that agency unless I get a strongly worded apology in folded form.

For a start, why did they send a villain to be *in loco parentis*? (See, I am not wasting my time down in the prison library.) Are they under new management? Always when I used them in the past, they sent along actors, people with no form. Using Watchstrap, whose record's as long as one of Barry Manilow's *sounds*, is taking unnecessary risks. OK, he looks the toff, got the plummy voice and all that, but he ISN'T THE GENUINE ARTICLE. Put him in a marquee with an authentic Eton dad and the other geezer's going to see he's not the business within thirty seconds. Remember, in matters of class, THERE'S NO WAY SOMEONE WHO ISN'T CAN EVER PASS HIMSELF OFF AS THE REAL THING (a point which I will return to later in this letter).

And, anyway, if they was going to send a villain, least they could have done was to send a good one. Watchstrap Malone, I'll have you know, got his cognomen (prison library again) from a case anyone would wish to draw a veil over, when he was in charge of hijacking a container-load of what was supposed to be watches from Heathrow. Trouble was, he only misread the invoice, didn't he? Wasn't the watches, just the blooming straps. Huh, not the kind of form suitable to someone who's going to pass themselves off as any son of mine's father.

And as for using Berwick Street Barbara, well, that's just a straight insult to your mother, isn't it? I mean, I know she's got the posh voice and the clothes, but she's not the real thing any more than Watchstrap is. She gets her business from nasty little common erks who think they're stepping up a few classes. But no genuine Hooray Henry'd be fooled by Barbara. Anyway, that lot don't want all the quacking vowels and the headscarves—get enough of that at home. What they're after in that line is some pert little scrubber dragged out of the gutters of Toxteth. But I digress.

Anyway, like I say, it's an insult to your mother and if she ever gets to hear about it, I wouldn't put money on the roof staying on Holloway.

No, I'm sorry, I feel like I've been done, and last time I felt like that, with Micky "The Cardinal" O'Riordhan, he ended up having a lot more difficulty in kneeling down than what he had had theretofore.

BUT NOW, SON, I come on to the more serious part of this letter. I was *not amused* to hear what your division master said about your work. If you've got the idea in your thick skull that being a toff has anything to do with sitting on your backside and doing buggerall, then it's an idea of which you'd better disabuse yourself sharpish.

I haven't put in all the time (inside and out) what I have to pay for your education with a view to you throwing it all away. It's all right for an authentic scion (prison library) of the aristocracy to drop out of the system; the system will cheerfully wait till he's ready to go back in. But someone in your shoes, Sonny, if you drop out, you stay out.

Let me clarify my position. Like all fathers, I want my kids to have things better than I did. Now, I done all right, I'm not complaining. I've got to the top of my particular tree. There's still a good few pubs round the East End what'll go quiet when my name's mentioned and, in purely material terms, with the houses in Tenerife and Jamaica and Friern Barnet (not to mention the stashes under various bits of the country's motorway network), I am, to put it modestly, comfortable.

But—and this is a big but—in spite of my career success, I remain an old-fashioned villain. My methods—and I'm not knocking them, because they work—are, in the ultimate analysis, crude. All right, most people give you what you want if you hit them hard enough, but that system of business has not changed since the beginning of time. Nowadays, there is no question, considerably more sophisticated methods are available to the aspiring professional.

Computers obviously have made a big difference. The advance of microtechnology has made possible that elusive goal, the perfect crime, in which you just help yourself without getting your hands dirty.

For this reason I was *particularly* distressed to hear that you haven't been paying attention in your computer studies classes. Listen, Son, I am paying a great deal to put you through Eton and (I think we can safely assume after the endowment for the new library block) Cambridge, but if at the end of all that you emerge unable to fiddle a computerized bank account, I am going to be less than chuffed. Got it?

However, what I'm doing for you is not just with a view to you getting *au fait* with the new technology. It's more than that.

OK, like I say, I been successful, and yet the fact remains that here I am writing to you from the nick. Because my kind of operation, being a straightforward villain against the system, will never be without its attendant risks. Of which risks the nick is the biggest one.

You know, being in prison does give you time for contemplation, and, while I been here, I done a lot of thinking about the inequalities of the society in which we live.

I mean, say I organize a security-van hijack, using a dozen heavies, with all the risks involved (bruises from the pickaxe handles, whiplash injuries from ramming the vehicle, being shopped by one of my own team, being traced through the serial numbers, to name but a few), what do I get at the end of it? I mean, after it's all been shared out, after I've paid everyone off, bribed a few, sorted out pensions for the ones who got hurt, all that, what do I get? Couple of hundred grand if I'm lucky.

Whereas some smartarse in the City can siphon off that many million in a morning without stirring from his desk (and in many cases without even technically breaking the law).

Then, if I'm caught, even with the most expensive solicitor in London acting for me, I get twelve years in Parkhurst.

And, if he's caught, what does he get? Maybe has to resign from the board. Maybe has to get out the business and retire to his country estate, where he lives on investment income and devotes himself to rural pursuits, shooting, fishing, being a JP, that sort of number.

Now, I ask myself, is that a fair system?

And the answer, of course, doesn't take long to come back. No.

Of course it isn't fair. It never has been. That's why I've always voted Tory. All that socialist rubbish about trying to 'change society' . . . huh. It's never going to change. The system is as it is. Which is why, to succeed you got to go *with* the system, rather than *against* it.

Which brings me, of course, to what I'm doing for you.

By the time you get through Eton and Cambridge, Son, the world will be your oyster. Your earning potential will be virtually unlimited.

Now don't get me wrong. I am not suggesting that you should go straight. Heaven forbid. No son of mine's going to throw away five generations of tradition just like that.

No, what I'm suggesting is, yes, you're still a villain, but you're a villain from *inside* the system. I mean, think of the opportunities you'll

have. You'll be able to go into the City, the Law . . . we could use a
bent solicitor in the family . . . even, if you got *really* lucky, into
Parliament. And let's face it, in any of those professions, you're going
to clean up in a way that'll make my pickaxe-and-bovver approach
look as old-fashioned as a slide-rule in the days of calculators.

Which is why it is so, so important that you take your education
seriously. You have got to come out the genuine article. Never relax.
You're not there just to do the academic business, you got to observe
your classmates, too. Follow their every move. Do as they do. You can
get to the top, Son (not just in the country, in the world—all big businesses are going multinational these days), but for you to get there you
got to be the real thing. No chinks in your armour—got that? Many
highly promising villains have come unstuck by inattention to detail
and I'm determined it shouldn't happen to you.

PERHAPS I CAN best clarify what I'm on about by telling you what happened to old Squiffy Yoxborough.

Squiffy was basically a con-merchant. Used to be an actor, specialized in upper-class parts. Hadn't got any real breeding, brought up
in Hackney as a matter of fact, but he could do the voice real well and,
you know, he'd studied the type. Made a kind of specialty of an
upper-class drunk act, pretending to be pissed, you know. Hence the
name, Squiffy. But times got hard, the acting parts wasn't there, so he
drifted into our business.

First of all, he never did anything big. Main specialty was borrowing the odd fifty at upper-class piss-ups. Henley, Ascot, hunt balls, that
kind of number, he'd turn up in the full fig and come the hard-luck
story when the guests had been hitting the champers for a while. He
sounded even more smashed than them, but of course he knew exactly where all his marbles was.

It was slow money, but fairly regular, and moving with that crowd
opened up other possibilities. Nicking the odd bit of jewellery, occasional blackmail, a bit of "winkling" old ladies out of their flats for
property developers, you know what I mean. Basically, just doing the

upper-classes' dirty work. There's always been a demand for people to do that, and I dare say there always will be.

Well, inevitably, this led pretty quick to drugs. When London's full of Hooray Henries wanting to stick stuff up their ancestral noses, there's bound to be a lot of openings for the pushers, and Squiffy took his chances when they come. He was never in the big league, mind, not controlling the business, just a courier and like point-of-sale merchant. But it was better money, and easier than sponging fifties.

Incidentally, Son, since the subject's come up, I don't want there to be any doubt in your mind about my views on drugs. You keep away from them.

Now, I am not a violent man—well, let's say I am not a violent man to my *family*, but if I hear you've been meddling with drugs, either as a user or a pusher, so help me I will somehow get out of this place and find you and give you such a tanning with my belt that you'll need a rubber ring for the rest of your natural. That sort of business attracts a really unpleasant class of criminal that I don't want any son of mine mixing with. Got that?

Anyway, getting back to Squiffy, obviously once he got into drugs, he was going to get deeper in and pretty soon he's involved with some villains who was organizing the smuggling of the stuff through a yacht-charter company. You know the sort of set-up, rich gits rent this boat and crew and swan round the West Indies for a couple of weeks, getting alternately smashed and stoned.

Needless to say, this company would keep their punters on the boat supplied with cocaine; but not only that, they also made a nice little business of taking the stuff back into England and flogging it to all the Sloane Rangers down the Chelsea discothèques.

I suppose it could have been a good little earner if you like that kind of thing, but these plonkers who was doing it hadn't got no sense of organization. The crew were usually as stoned as the punters, so it was only a matter of time before they come unstuck. Only third run they do, they moor in the harbour of this little island in the West Indies and, while they're all on shore getting well bobbled on the ethnic rum, local Bill goes and raids the yacht. Stuff's lying all over the place, like there's been a snowstorm blown through the cabins, and when the crew and punters come back, they all get nicked and shoved in the local slammer to unwind for a bit.

Not a nice place, the jail on this little island. They had to share their cells with a nasty lot of local fauna like cockroaches, snakes, and mosquitoes, not to mention assorted incendiaries, gunrunners, rapists, and axe-murderers.

Not at all what these merchant bankers and their Benenden-educated crumpet who had chartered the yacht was used to. So, because that's how things work at that level, pretty soon some British consular official gets contacted, and pretty soon a deal gets struck with the local authorities. No hassle, really, it comes down to a thousand quid per prisoner. All charges dropped, and home they go. Happened all the time, apparently. The prisons was one of the island's two most lucrative industries (the other being printing unperforated stamps). A yacht had only to come into the harbour to get raided. Squiffy's lot had just made it easy for the local police; usually the cocaine had to be planted.

Well, obviously, there was a lot of transatlantic telephoning, a lot of distraught daddies (barristers, MPs, what-have-you) cabling money across, but it gets sorted out pretty quick and all the Hoorays are flown back to England with a good story to tell at the next cocktail party.

They're all flown back, that is, except Squiffy.

And it wasn't that he couldn't raise the readies. He'd got a few stashes round about, and the odd blackmail victim who could be relied on to stump up a grand when needed.

No, he stayed because he'd met this bloke in the nick.

Don't get me wrong. I don't mean he fancied him. Nothing Leaning Tower of Pisa about Squiffy.

No, he stayed because he'd met someone he thought could lead to big money.

Bloke's name was Masters. Alex Masters. But, it didn't take Squiffy long to find out, geezer was also known as the Marquess of Gorsley.

Now, I don't know how it is, but some people always land on their feet in the nick. I mean, I do all right. I get all the snout I want and if I feel like a steak or a bottle of whiskey there's no problem. But I get that because I have a bit of reputation outside, and I have to work to keep those privileges. I mean, if there wasn't a good half-dozen heavies round the place who owe me the odd favour, I might find it more difficult.

But I tell you, I got nothing compared to what this marquess geezer'd got. Unlimited supplies of rum, so he's permanently smashed, quietly, and happily drinking himself to death. All the food he wants, very best of the local cuisine. Nice cell to himself, air conditioning, fridge, video, compact-disc player, interior-sprung bed. Pick of the local talent to share that bed with, all these slim, brown-legged beauties, different one every night, so Squiffy said (though apparently the old marquess was usually too pissed to do much about it).

Now, prisons work the same all over the world, so you take my word that I know what I'm talking about. Only one thing gets those kind of privileges.

Money.

But pretty soon even Squiffy realizes there's something not quite kosher with the set-up. I mean, this Gorsley bloke's not inside for anything particularly criminal. Just some fraud on a holiday villa development scheme. Even if the island's authorities take property fiddling more seriously than cocaine, there's still got to be a price to get him released. I mean, say it's five grand, it's still going to be considerably less than what he's paying per annum for these special privileges.

Besides, when Squiffy raises the subject, it's clear that the old marquess doesn't know a blind thing about this "buy-out" system. But he does go on about how grateful he is to his old man, the Duke of Glammerton, for shelling out so much per month "to make the life sentence bearable."

Now Squiffy's not the greatest intellect since Einstein, but even he's capable of putting two and two together. He checks out this Gorsley geezer's form and discovers the property fraud's not the first bit of bovver he's been in. In fact, the bloke is a walking disaster area, his past littered with bounced cheques, petty theft, convictions for drunkenness, you name it. (I don't, incidentally, mean *real* crimes, the ones that involve skill; I refer to the sort people get into by incompetence.)

Squiffy does a bit more research. He's still got some cocaine stashed away and for that the prison governor's more than ready to spill the odd bean. Turns out the marquess's dad pays up regular, never objects when the price goes up, encourages the governor to keep increasing the supply of rum, states quite categorically he's not interested in pardons, anything like that. Seems he's got a nephew who's a real Mr. Goody-Goody. And if the marquess dies in an alcoholic

stupor in some obscure foreign jail, it's all very handy. The prissy
nephew inherits the title, and the Family Name remains untarnished.
Duke's prepared to pay a lot to keep that untarnished.

So it's soon clear to Squiffy that the duke is not only paying a
monthly sum to keep his son in the style to which he's accustomed;
it's also to keep his son out of the country. In fact, he's paying the
island to let the Marquess of Gorsley die quietly in prison.

It's when he realizes this that Squiffy Yoxborough decides he'll
stick around for a while.

NOW, EXCEPT FOR the aforementioned incendiaries, gunrunners,
rapists, and axe-murderers . . . oh, and the local talent (not that that
talked much), the marquess has been a bit starved of civilized conversation, so he's pretty chuffed to be joined by someone who's English
and talks with the right sort of accent. He doesn't notice that Squiffy's
not the genuine article. Too smashed most of the time to notice anything and, since the marquess's idea of a conversation is him rambling
on and someone else listening, Squiffy doesn't get too much chance to
give himself away.

Anyway, he's quite content to listen, thank you very much. The
more he finds out about the Marquess of Gorsley's background, the
happier he is. It all ties in with a sort of plan that's slowly emerging in
his head.

Particularly he wants to know about the marquess's schooldays.
So, lots of warm, tropical evenings get whiled away over bottles of rum
while the marquess drunkenly reminisces and Squiffy listens hard. It's
really just an extension of how he started in the business, pretending
to get plastered with the Hoorays. But this time he's after considerably
more than the odd fifty.

The Marquess of Gorsley was, needless to say, at one of these really posh schools. Like his father before him, he had gone to Raspington
in Wiltshire (near where your grandfather was arrested for the first
time, Son). And as he listens, Squiffy learns all about it.

He learns that there was four houses: Thurrocks, Wilmington, Stuke, and Fothergill. He learns that the marquess was in Stuke, that kids just starting in Stuke was called "tads" and on their first night in the dorm they underwent "scrogging." He learns that prefects was called "whisks," that in their common room, called "the Treacle Tin," they was allowed to administer a punishment called "spluggers"; that they could wear the top buttons of their jackets undone, and was the only members of the school allowed to walk on "Straggler's Hump."

He learns that the teachers was called "dommies," that the sweet shop called the "Binn," that a cricket cap was a "skiplid," that the bogs was called "fruitbowls," that studies was called "nitboxes," that lunch was called "slops," and that a minor sports colours tie was called a "slagnoose."

He hears the marquess sing the school songs. After a time, he starts joining in with them. Eventually, he even gets a bit good at doing a solo on the School Cricket Song, traditionally sung in Big Hall on the evening after the Old Raspurian Match. It begins:

> Hark! the shout of a schoolboy at twilight
> Comes across from the far-distant pitch,
> Goads his team on to one final effort,
> "Make a stand at the ultimate ditch!"
> Hark! the voice of the umpiring master
> Rises over the white-flannelled strife,
> Tells his charges that life is like cricket,
> Tells them also that cricket's like life . . .

Don't think you have that one at Eton, do you, Son?

I tell you, after two months in that prison, Squiffy Yoxborough knows as much about being at Raspington as the Marquess of Gorsley does himself. He stays on a couple more weeks, to check there's nothing more, but by now the marquess is just rambling and repeating himself, sinking deeper and deeper into an alcoholic coma. So Squiffy quickly organizes his own thousand quid release money and scarpers back to England.

FIRST THING HE does when he gets back home, Squiffy forms a company. Well, he doesn't actually literally form a company, but he, like, gets all the papers forged so it looks like he's formed a company. He calls this company "Only Real Granite Hall-Building Construction Techniques" (ORGHBCT) and he gets enough forged paperwork for him to be able to open a bank account in that name.

Next thing he gets his clothes together. Moves carefully here. Got to get the right gear or the whole thing falls apart.

Dark blue pinstripe suit. Donegal tweed suit. Beale and Inmans corduroy trousers. Cavalry twills. Turnbull and Asser striped shirts. Viyella Tattersall checked shirts. Church's Oxford shoes. Barbour jacket. Herbert Johnson trilby.

He steals or borrows this lot. Can't just buy them in the shops. Got to look old, you see.

Has trouble with the Old Raspurian tie. Doesn't know anyone who went there—except of course for the marquess, and he's rather a long way away.

So he has to buy a tie new and distress it a bit. Washes it so's it shrinks. Rubs in a bit of grease. Looks all right.

(You may be wondering, Son, how I come to know all this detail. Not my usual special subject, I agree. Don't worry, all will be revealed.)

Right, so having got the gear, he packs it all in a battered old leather suitcase, rents a Volvo estate, and drives up to Scotland.

HE'S CHECKED OUT where the Duke of Glammerton's estate is, he's checked that the old boy's actually in residence, and he just drives up to the front of Glammerton House. Leaves the Volvo on the gravel, goes up to the main door, and pulls this great ring for the bell.

Door's opened by some flunkey.

"Hello," says Squiffy, doing the right voice of course. "I'm a chum of Alex's. Just happened to be in the area. Wondered if the old devil was about."

"Alex?" says the flunkey, bit suspicious.

"Yes. The Marquess of Gorsley. I was at school with him."

"Ah. I'm afraid the marquess is abroad."

"Oh, really? What a swiz," says Squiffy. "Still, I travel a lot. Whereabouts is the old devil?"

Flunkey hesitates a bit, then says he'll go off and try to find out. Comes back with the butler. Butler confirms the marquess is abroad. Cannot be certain where.

"What, hasn't left a forwarding address? Always was bloody inefficient. Never mind, I'm sure some of my chums could give me a lead. Don't worry, I'll track him down."

This makes the butler hesitate, too. "If you'll excuse me, sir, I'll just go and see if his Grace is available. He might have more information about the marquess's whereabouts than I have."

Few minutes later, Squiffy gets called into this big lounge-type room, you know, all deers' heads and gilt frames, and there's the Duke of Glammerton sitting over a tray of tea. Duke sees the tie straight away.

"Good Lord, are you an Old Raspurian?"

"Yes, your Grace," says Squiffy.

"Which house?"

"Stuke."

"So was I."

"Well, of course, Duke, I knew you must have been. That's where I met Alex, you see. Members of the same family in the same house, what?"

Duke doesn't look so happy now he knows Squiffy's a friend of his son. No doubt the old boy's met a few unsuitable ones in his time, so Squiffy says quickly, "Haven't seen Alex for yonks. Virtually since school."

"Oh." Duke looks relieved. "As Moulton said, I'm afraid he's abroad."

"Living there?"

"Yes. For the time being," Duke says carefully.

"Oh, dear. You don't by any chance have an address, do you?"

"Erm . . . Not at the moment, no."

Now all this is suiting Squiffy very nicely. The more the Duke's determined to keep quiet about his son's real circumstances, the better.

"That's a nuisance," says Squiffy. "Wanted to sting the old devil for a bit of money."

"Oh?" Duke looks careful again.

"Well, not for me, of course. For the old school."

"Oh, yes?" Duke looks interested.

"Absolutely." (Squiffy knows he should say this every now and then instead of "Yes.") "For my sins I've got involved in some fund-raising for the old place."

"Again? What are they up to this time?"

"Building a new Great Hall to replace Big Hall."

Duke's shocked by this. "They're not going to knock Big Hall down?"

"Good Lord, no. No, Big Hall'll still be used. The Great Hall will be for school plays, that sort of thing."

"Ah. Where are they going to build it?"

"Well, it'll be at right angles to Big Hall, sort of stretching past Thurrocks out towards 'Straggler's Hump.'"

"Really? Good Lord." The old geezer grins. "I remember walking along 'Straggler's Hump' many a time."

"You must've been a 'whisk' then."

He looks guilty. "Never was, actually."

"Doing it illegally, were you?"

Duke nods.

"But didn't that mean you got dragged into the 'Treacle Tin' for 'spluggers'?"

"Never caught." Duke giggles naughtily. "Remember, actually, I did it my second day as a 'tad.'"

"What, directly after you'd been 'scrogged'?"

"Absolutely."

"And none of the 'dommies' saw you?"

Duke shakes his head, really chuffed at what an old devil he used to be. "Tell me," he says, "where are you staying up here?"

"I was going to check into the . . . what is it in the village? The Glammerton Arms?"

"Well, don't do that, old boy. Stay here the night. I'll get Moulton to show you a room."

GETS A GOOD dinner, that night, Squiffy does. Pheasant, venison, vintage wines, all that. Just the two of them. Duchess had died a long time ago.

Get on really well, they do. Squiffy does his usual getting-plastered act, but, as usual, he's careful. Talks a lot about Raspington, doesn't talk too much about the marquess. But listens. And gets confirmation of his hunch that the duke never wants to see his son again. Also knows there's a very strong chance of this happening in the natural course of events. The amount of rum the marquess is putting away, his liver must be shrivelled down to like a dried pea.

Anyway, when they're giving the port and brandy and cigars a bash, the Duke, who's a bit the worse for wear, says, "What is all this about the old school? Trying to raise money, did you say?"

"Absolutely," says Squiffy. "Don't just want to raise money, though. Want to raise a monument."

"What—a monument to all the chaps who died from eating 'slops'?"

"Or the chaps who were poisoned in the 'Binn'?"

"Or everyone who got 'scrogged' in their own 'nitbox'!"

"Yes, or all those who had a 'down-the-loo-shampoo' in the 'fruit-bowls'!"

Duke finds this dead funny. Hasn't had such a good time for years.

"No, actually," says Squiffy, all serious now, "we want the new Great Hall to be a monument to a great Old Raspurian."

"Ah."

"So that every chap who walks into that hall will think of someone who was really a credit to the old school."

"Oh. Got anyone in mind?" asks the duke.

"Absolutely," says Squiffy. "We thought of Alex."

"What!"

"Well, he's such a great chap."

"Alex—great chap?"

"Yes. As I say, I've hardly seen him since school . . . nor have any of the other fellows on the fund-raising committee, actually, but we all thought he was such a terrific chap at school . . . I mean, I'm sure he's gone on to be just as successful in the outside world."

"Well . . . er . . ."

"So you see, Duke, we all thought, what a great idea to have the place named after Alex—I mean he'd have to put up most of the money, but that's a detail—and then everyone who went into the hall would be reminded of what a great Old Raspurian he was. Give the 'tads' something to aspire to, what?"

"Yes, yes." The Duke gets thoughtful. "But are you sure that Alex is the right one?"

"Oh. Well, if there's any doubt about his suitability, perhaps we should investigate a bit further into what he's been up to since he left Raspington . . ."

"No, that won't be necessary," says the Duke, sharpish. "What sort of sum of money are we talking about?"

"Oh . . ." Squiffy looks all casual like. "I don't know. Five hundred thousand, something like that."

"Five hundred thousand to ensure that Alex is always remembered as one of the greatest Old Raspurians . . . ?"

"I suppose you could think of it like that. Absolutely."

A light comes into the old Duke's eyes. He's had reports from the West Indies. He knows his son hasn't got long to go. And suddenly he's offered a way of . . . like *enshrining* the marquess's memory. With a great permanent monument at the old school, a little bit of adverse publicity in the past'll soon be forgotten. The Family Name will remain untarnished. Half a million's not much to pay for that.

He rings a bell and helps them both to some more pre-War port. Moulton comes in.

"My cheque book, please."

The butler geezer delivers it and goes off again.

"Who should I make this payable to?" asks the Duke.

"Well, in fact," says Squiffy, "the full name's the 'Old Raspurian Great Hall-Building Charitable Trust,' but you'll never get all that on the cheque. Just the initials will do."

With the cheque safely in his pocket, Squiffy starts humming the tune of the Raspington School Cricket Song.

"Great," says the Duke. "Terrific. I always used to do the solo on the second verse. Do you know the descant?"

"Absolutely," says Squiffy, and together they sing,

> See the schoolboy a soldier in khaki,
> Changed his bat for the Gatling and Bren.
> How his officer's uniform suits him,

How much better he speaks than his men.
Thank the school for his noble demeanour,
And his poise where vulgarity's rife,
Knowing always that life is like cricket,
Not forgetting that cricket's like life.

All right, Son. Obvious question is, how do I know all that? How do I know all that detail about Squiffy Yoxborough?

Answer is, he told me. And he'll tell me again every blooming night if he gets the chance.

Yes, he's inside here with me.

And why? Why did he get caught? Was it because the Duke woke up next morning and immediately realized it was a transparent con? Realized that he'd been pissed the night before and that it really was a bit unusual to give a complete stranger a cheque for half a million quid?

No, Duke's mind didn't work like that. So long as he thought he was dealing with a genuine Old Raspurian, he reckoned he'd got a good deal. OK, it'd cost him five hundred grand, but, as a price for covering up everything that his son'd done in the past, it was peanuts. The Family Name would remain untarnished—that was the important thing.

But, like I just said, that was only going to work *so long as he thought he was dealing with a genuine Old Raspurian.*

And something the butler told him the next morning stopped him thinking that he was.

So, when Squiffy goes to the bank to pay in his cheque to the "Only Real Granite Hall-Building Construction Techniques" account, he's asked to wait for a minute, and suddenly the cops are all over the shop.

So what was it? He got the voice right, he got the clothes right, he got all the Old Raspurian stuff right, he used the right knives and forks at dinner, he said "Absolutely" instead of "Yes" . . . where'd he go wrong?

I'll tell you—when he got up the next morning he made his own bed.

Well, butler sussed him straight away. Poor old Squiffy'd shown up his upbringing. Never occur to the sort of person he was pretending to be to make a bed. There was always servants around to do that for you.

See, there's some things you can learn from outside, and some you got to know from inside. And that making the bed thing, it takes generations of treating peasants like dirt to understand that.

I HOPE I'VE made my point. Stick at it, Son. Both the work and the social bit. You're going to get right to the top, like I said. You're not going to be an old-fashioned villain, you're going to do it through the system. And if you're going to succeed, you can't afford the risk of being let down by the sort of mistake that shopped Squiffy Yoxborough. Got that?

Once again, sorry about the Fourth of June. (Mind you, someone else is going to be even sorrier.) I'll see to it you get better parents for the Eton and Harrow Match.

This letter, with the customary greasy oncers, will go out through Blue Phil, as per usual. Look after yourself, Son, and remember—keep a straight bat.

Your loving father,
Nobby Chesterfield

The Poisoned Pen

Arthur B. Reeve

I

KENNEDY'S SUITCASE WAS lying open on the bed, and he was literally throwing things into it from his chiffonier, as I entered after a hurried trip uptown from the *Star* office in response to an urgent message from him.

"Come, Walter," he cried, hastily stuffing in a package of clean laundry without taking off the wrapping-paper, "I've got your suitcase out. Pack up whatever you can in five minutes. We must take the six o'clock train for Danbridge."

I did not wait to hear any more. The mere mention of the name of the quaint and quiet little Connecticut town was sufficient. For Danbridge was on everybody's lips at that time. It was the scene of the now famous Danbridge poisoning case—a brutal case in which the pretty little actress, Vera Lytton, had been the victim.

"I've been retained by Senator Adrian Willard," he called from his room, as I was busy packing in mine. "The Willard family believe that that young Dr. Dixon is the victim of a conspiracy—or at least Alma Willard does, which comes to the same thing, and—well, the senator called me up on long-distance and offered me anything I

161

would name in reason to take the case. Are you ready? Come on, then. We've simply got to make that train."

As we settled ourselves in the smoking compartment of the Pullman, which for some reason or other we had to ourselves, Kennedy spoke again for the first time since our frantic dash across the city to catch the train.

"Now let us see, Walter," he began. "We've both read a good deal about this case in the papers. Let's try to get our knowledge in an orderly shape before we tackle the actual case itself."

"Ever been in Danbridge?" I asked.

"Never," he replied. "What sort of place is it?"

"Mighty interesting," I answered; "a combination of old New England and new, of ancestors and factories, of wealth and poverty, and above all it is interesting for its colony of New Yorkers—what shall I call it?—a literary-artistic-musical combination, I guess."

"Yes," he resumed. "I thought as much. Vera Lytton belonged to the colony. A very talented girl, too—you remember her in *The Taming of the New Woman* last season? Well, to get back to the facts as we know them at present.

"Here is a girl with a brilliant future on the stage discovered by her friend, Mrs. Boncour, in convulsions—practically insensible—with a bottle of headache powder and a jar of ammonia on her dressing table. Mrs. Boncour sends the maid for the nearest doctor, who happens to be a Dr. Waterworth. Meanwhile she tries to restore Miss Lytton, but with no result. She smells the ammonia and then just tastes the headache powder, a very foolish thing to do, for by the time Dr. Waterworth arrives he has two patients."

"No," I corrected, "only one, for Miss Lytton was dead when he arrived, according to his latest statement."

"Very well, then—one. He arrives, Mrs. Boncour is ill, the maid knows nothing at all about it; and Vera Lytton is dead. He, too, smells the ammonia, tastes the headache powder—just the merest trace— and then he has two patients, one of them himself. We must see him, for his experience must have been appalling. How he ever did it I can't imagine, but he saved both himself and Mrs. Boncour from poisoning—cyanide, the papers say, but of course we can't accept that until we see. It seems to me, Walter, that lately the papers have made the rule in murder cases: When in doubt, call it cyanide."

Not relishing Kennedy in the humor of expressing his real opinion of the newspapers, I hastily turned the conversation back again by
asking, "How about the note from Dr. Dixon?"

"Ah, there is the crux of the whole case—that note from Dixon. Let
us see. Dr. Dixon is, if I am informed correctly, of a fine and aristocratic
family, though not wealthy. I believe it has been established that while
he was an intern in a city hospital he became acquainted with Vera
Lytton, after her divorce from that artist Thurston. Then comes his
removal to Danbridge and his meeting and later his engagement with
Miss Willard. On the whole, Walter, judging from the newspaper pictures, Alma Willard is quite the equal of Vera Lytton for looks, only of a
different style of beauty. Oh, well, we shall see. Vera decided to spend the
spring and summer at Danbridge in the bungalow of her friend,
Mrs. Boncour, the novelist. That's when things began to happen."

"Yes," I put it, "when you come to know Danbridge as I did after
that summer when you were abroad, you'll understand, too. Everybody
knows everybody else's business. It is the main occupation of a certain
set, and the per-capita output of gossip is a record that would stagger
the census bureau. Still, you can't get away from the note, Craig. There
it is, in Dixon's own handwriting, even if he does deny it: 'This will
cure your headache. Dr. Dixon.' That's a damning piece of evidence."

"Quite right," he agreed hastily; "the note was queer, though,
wasn't it? They found it crumpled up in the jar of ammonia. Oh,
there are lots of problems the newspapers have failed to see the significance of, let alone trying to follow up."

Our first visit in Danbridge was to the prosecuting attorney,
whose office was not far from the station on the main street. Craig
had wired him, and he had kindly waited to see us, for it was evident
that Danbridge respected Senator Willard and every one connected
with him.

"Would it be too much to ask just to see that note that was found
in the Boncour bungalow?" asked Craig.

The prosecutor, an energetic young man, pulled out of a document case a crumpled note which had been pressed flat again. On it
in clear, deep black letters were the words, just as reported:

This will cure your headache.
                                                                 DR. DIXON.

"How about the handwriting?" asked Kennedy.

The lawyer pulled out a number of letters. "I'm afraid they will have to admit it," he said with reluctance, as if down in his heart he hated to prosecute Dixon. "We have lots of these, and no handwriting expert could successfully deny the identity of the writing."

He stowed away the letters without letting Kennedy get a hint as to their contents. Kennedy was examining the note carefully.

"May I count on having this note for further examination, of course always at such times and under such conditions as you agree to?"

The attorney nodded. "I am perfectly willing to do anything not illegal to accommodate the senator," he said. "But, on the other hand, I am here to do my duty for the state, cost whom it may."

The Willard house was in a virtual state of siege. Newspaper reporters from Boston and New York were actually encamped at every gate, terrible as an army, with cameras. It was with some difficulty that we got in, even though we were expected, for some of the more enterprising had already fooled the family by posing as officers of the law and messengers from Dr. Dixon.

The house was a real old colonial mansion with tall white pillars, a door with a glittering brass knocker, which gleamed out severely at you as you approached through a hedge of faultlessly trimmed boxwoods.

Senator, or rather former Senator, Willard met us in the library, and a moment later his daughter Alma joined him. She was tall, like her father, a girl of poise and self-control. Yet even the schooling of twenty-two years in rigorous New England self-restraint could not hide the very human pallor of her face after the sleepless nights and nervous days since this trouble had broken on her placid existence. Yet there was a mark of strength and determination on her face that was fascinating. The man who would trifle with this girl, I felt, was playing fast and loose with her very life. I thought then, and I said to Kennedy afterward: "If this Dr. Dixon is guilty, you have no right to hide it from that girl. Anything less than the truth will only blacken the hideousness of the crime that has already been committed."

The senator greeted us gravely, and I could not but take it as a good omen when, in his pride of wealth and family and tradition, he laid bare everything to us, for the sake of Alma Willard. It was clear that in this family there was one word that stood above all others, "Duty."

As we were about to leave after an interview barren of new facts, a young man was announced, Mr. Halsey Post. He bowed politely to us, but it was evident why he had called, as his eye followed Alma about the room.

"The son of the late Halsey Post, of Post & Vance, silversmiths, who have the large factory in town, which you perhaps noticed," explained the senator. "My daughter has known him all her life. A very fine young man."

Later, we learned that the senator had bent every effort toward securing Halsey Post as a son-in-law, but his daughter had had views of her own on the subject.

Post waited until Alma had withdrawn before he disclosed the real object of his visit.

In almost a whisper, lest she should still be listening, he said, "There is a story about town that Vera Lytton's former husband—an artist named Thurston—was here just before her death."

Senator Willard leaned forward as if expecting to hear Dixon immediately acquitted. None of us was prepared for the next remark.

"And the story goes on to say that he threatened to make a scene over a wrong he says he has suffered from Dixon. I don't know anything more about it, and I tell you only because I think you ought to know what Danbridge is saying under its breath."

We shook off the last of the reporters who affixed themselves to us, and for a moment Kennedy dropped in at the little bungalow to see Mrs. Boncour. She was much better, though she had suffered much. She had taken only a pinhead of the poison, but it had proved very nearly fatal.

"Had Miss Lytton any enemies whom you think of, people who were jealous of her professionally or personally?" asked Craig.

"I should not even have said Dr. Dixon was an enemy," she replied evasively.

"But this Mr. Thurston," put in Kennedy quickly. "One is not usually visited in perfect friendship by a husband who has been divorced."

She regarded him keenly for a moment. "Halsey Post told you that," she said. "No one else knew he was here. But Halsey Post was an old friend of both Vera and Mr. Thurston before they separated. By chance he happened to drop in the day Mr. Thurston was here, and later in the day I gave him a letter to forward to Mr. Thurston, which had come after the artist left. I'm sure no one else knew the artist. He was there the morning of the day she died, and—and—that's every bit I'm going to tell you about him, so there. I don't know why he came or where he went."

"That's a thing we must follow up later," remarked Kennedy as we made our adieus. "Just now I want to get the facts in hand. The next thing on my programme is to see this Dr. Waterworth."

We found the doctor still in bed; in fact, a wreck as the result of his adventure. He had little to correct in the facts of the story which had been published so far. But there were many other details of the poisoning he was quite willing to discuss frankly.

"It was true about the jar of ammonia?" asked Kennedy.

"Yes," he answered. "It was standing on her dressing table with the note crumpled up in it, just as the papers said."

"And you have no idea why it was there?"

"I didn't say that. I can guess. Fumes of ammonia are one of the antidotes for poisoning of that kind."

"But Vera Lytton could hardly have known that," objected Kennedy.

"No, of course not. But she probably did know that ammonia is good for just that sort of faintness which she must have experienced after taking the powder. Perhaps she thought of sal volatile, I don't know. But most people know that ammonia in some form is good for faintness of this sort, even if they don't know anything about cyanides and—"

"Then it was cyanide?" interrupted Craig.

"Yes," he replied slowly. It was evident that he was suffering great physical and nervous anguish as the result of his too-intimate acquaintance with the poisons in question. "I will tell you precisely how it was, Professor Kennedy. When I was called in to see Miss Lytton, I found her on the bed. I pried open her jaws and smelled the sweetish odor of the cyanogen gas. I knew then what she had taken, and at the moment she was dead. In the next room I heard someone moaning. The maid said that it was Mrs. Boncour, and that she was deathly sick. I ran into her room, and though she was beside herself with pain I managed to control her, though she struggled desperately against me. I was rushing her to the bathroom, passing through Miss Lytton's room. 'What's wrong?' I asked as I carried her along. 'I took some of that,' she replied, pointing to the bottle on the dressing-table.

"I put a small quantity of its crystal contents on my tongue. Then I realized the most tragic truth of my life. I had taken one of the deadliest poisons in the world. The odor of the released gas of cyanogen was strong. But more than that, the metallic taste and the horrible burning sensation told of the presence of some form of mercury, too. In that terrible moment my brain worked with the incredible swiftness of light. In a flash I knew that if I added malic acid to the mercury—perchloride of mercury or corrosive sublimate—I would have calomel or subchloride of mercury, the only thing that would switch the poison out of my system and Mrs. Boncour's.

"Seizing her about the waist, I hurried into the dining room. On a sideboard was a dish of fruit. I took two apples. I made her eat one, core and all. I ate the other. The fruit contained the malic acid I needed to manufacture the calomel, and I made it right there in nature's own laboratory. But there was no time to stop. I had to act just as quickly to neutralize that cyanide, too. Remembering the ammonia, I rushed back with Mrs. Boncour, and we inhaled the fumes. Then I found a bottle of hydrogen peroxide. I washed out her stomach with it, and then my own. Then I injected some of the peroxide into various parts of her body. The hydrogen peroxide and hydrocyanic acid, you know, make oxamide, which is a harmless compound.

"The maid put Mrs. Boncour to bed, saved. I went to my house a wreck. Since then I have not left this bed. With my legs paralyzed I lie here, expecting each hour to be my last!"

"Would you taste an unknown drug again to discover the nature of a probable poison?" asked Craig.

"I don't know," he answered slowly, "but I suppose I would. In such a case a conscientious doctor has no thought of self. He is there to do things, and he does them, according to the best that is in him. In spite of the fact that I haven't had one hour of unbroken sleep since that fatal day, I suppose I would do it again."

When we were leaving, I remarked: "That is a martyr to science. Could anything be more dramatic than his willing penalty for his devotion to medicine?"

We walked along in silence. "Walter, did you notice he said not a word of condemnation of Dixon, though the note was before his eyes? Surely Dixon has some strong supporters in Danbridge, as well as enemies."

The next morning we continued our investigation. We found Dixon's lawyer, Leland, in consultation with his client in the bare cell of the county jail. Dixon proved to be a clear-eyed, clean-cut young man. The thing that impressed me most about him, aside from the prepossession in his favor due to the faith of Alma Willard, was the nerve he displayed, whether guilty or innocent. Even an innocent man might well have been staggered by the circumstantial evidence against him and the high tide of public feeling, in spite of the support that he was receiving. Leland, we learned, had been very active. By prompt work at the time of the young doctor's arrest, he had managed to secure the greater part of Dr. Dixon's personal letters, though the prosecutor secured some, the contents of which had not been disclosed.

Kennedy spent most of the day in tracing out the movements of Thurston. Nothing that proved important was turned up and even visits to nearby towns failed to show any sales of cyanide or sublimate to anyone not entitled to buy them. Meanwhile, in turning over the gossip of the town, one of the newspapermen ran across the fact that the Boncour bungalow was owned by the Posts, and that Halsey Post, as the executor of the estate, was a more frequent visitor than the mere collection of the rent would warrant. Mrs. Boncour maintained a stolid silence that covered a seething internal fury when the newspaperman in question hinted that the landlord and tenant were on exceptionally good terms.

It was after a fruitless day of such search that we were sitting in the reading room of the Fairfield Hotel. Leland entered. His face was positively white. Without a word he took us by the arm and led us across Main Street and up a flight of stairs to his office. Then he locked the door.

"What's the matter?" asked Kennedy.

"When I took this case," he said, "I believed down in my heart that Dixon was innocent. I still believe it, but my faith has been rudely shaken. I feel that you should know about what I have just found. As I told you, we secured nearly all of Dr. Dixon's letters. I had not read them all then. But I have been going through them tonight. Here is a letter from Vera Lytton herself. You will notice it is dated the day of her death."

He laid the letter before us. It was written in a curious grayish-black ink in a woman's hand, and read:

DEAR HARRIS:

Since we agreed to disagree we have at least been good friends, if no longer lovers. I am not writing in anger to reproach you with your new love, so soon after the old. I suppose Alma Willard is far better suited to be your wife than is a poor little actress—rather looked down on in this Puritan society here. But there is something I wish to warn you about, for it concerns us all intimately.

We are in danger of an awful mix-up if we don't look out. Mr. Thurston—I had almost said my husband, though I don't know whether that is the truth or not—who has just come over from New York, tells me that there is some doubt about the validity of our divorce. You recall he was in the South at the time I sued him, and the papers were served on him in Georgia. He now says the proof of service was fraudulent and that he can set aside the divorce. In that case you might figure in a suit for alienating my affections.

I do not write this with ill will, but simply to let you know how things stand. If we had married, I suppose I would be guilty of bigamy. At any rate, if he were disposed he could make a terrible scandal.

Oh, Harris, can't you settle with him if he asks anything? Don't forget so soon that we once thought we were going to be the happiest of mortals—at least I did. Don't desert me, or the very earth will cry out against you. I am frantic and hardly know what I am writing. My head aches, but it is my heart that is breaking. Harris, I am yours still, down in my heart, but not to be cast off like an old suit for a new one. You know the old saying about a woman scorned. I beg you not to go back on

Your poor little deserted

VERA.

As we finished reading, Leland exclaimed, "That never must come before the jury."

Kennedy was examining the letter carefully. "Strange," he muttered. "See how it was folded. It was written on the wrong side of the sheet, or rather folded up with the writing outside. Where have these letters been?"

"Part of the time in my safe, part of the time this afternoon on my desk by the window."

"The office was locked, I suppose?" asked Kennedy. "There was no way to slip this letter in among the others since you obtained them?"

"None. The office has been locked, and there is no evidence of anyone having entered or disturbed a thing."

He was hastily running over the pile of letters as if looking to see whether they were all there. Suddenly he stopped.

"Yes," he exclaimed excitedly, "one of them is gone." Nervously he fumbled through them, again. "One is gone," he repeated, looking at us, startled.

"What was it about?" asked Craig.

"It was a note from an artist, Thurston, who gave the address of Mrs. Boncour's bungalow—ah, I see you have heard of him. He asked Dixon's recommendation of a certain patent headache medicine. I thought it possibly evidential, and I asked Dixon about it. He explained it by saying that he did not have a copy of his reply, but as near as he could recall, he wrote that the compound would not cure a headache except at the expense of reducing heart action dangerously. He says he sent no prescription. Indeed, he thought it a scheme to extract advice without incurring the charge for an office call and answered it only because he thought Vera had become reconciled to Thurston again. I can't find that letter of Thurston's. It is gone."

We looked at each other in amazement.

"Why, if Dixon contemplated anything against Miss Lytton, should he preserve this letter from her?" mused Kennedy. "Why didn't he destroy it?"

"That's what puzzles me," remarked Leland. "Do you suppose someone has broken in and substituted this Lytton letter for the Thurston letter?"

Kennedy was scrutinizing the letter, saying nothing. "I may keep it?" he asked at length. Leland was quite willing and even undertook to obtain some specimens of the writing of Vera Lytton. With these and the letter Kennedy was working far into the night and long after

I had passed into a land troubled with many wild dreams of deadly poisons and secret intrigues of artists.

The next morning a message from our old friend First Deputy O'Connor in New York told briefly of locating the rooms of an artist named Thurston in one of the cooperative studio apartments. Thurston himself had not been there for several days and was reported to have gone to Maine to sketch. He had had a number of debts, but before he left they had all been paid—strange to say, by a notorious firm of shyster lawyers, Kerr & Kimmel. Kennedy wired back to find out the facts from Kerr & Kimmel and to locate Thurston at any cost.

Even the discovery of the new letter did not shake the wonderful self-possession of Dr. Dixon. He denied ever having received it and repeated his story of a letter from Thurston to which he had replied by sending an answer, care of Mrs. Boncour, as requested. He insisted that the engagement between Miss Lytton and himself had been broken before the announcement of his engagement with Miss Willard. As for Thurston, he said the man was little more than a name to him. He had known perfectly all the circumstances of the divorce, but had had no dealings with Thurston and no fear of him. Again and again he denied ever receiving the letter from Vera Lytton.

Kennedy did not tell the Willards of the new letter. The strain had begun to tell on Alma, and her father had had her quietly taken to a farm of his up in the country. To escape the curious eyes of reporters, Halsey Post had driven up one night in his closed car. She had entered it quickly with her father, and the journey had been made in the car, while Halsey Post had quietly dropped off on the outskirts of the town, where another car was waiting to take him back. It was evident that the Willard family relied implicitly on Halsey, and his assistance to them was most considerate. While he never forced himself forward, he kept in close touch with the progress of the case, and now that Alma was away his watchfulness increased proportionately, and twice a day he wrote a long report which was sent to her.

Kennedy was now bending every effort to locate the missing artist. When he left Danbridge, he seemed to have dropped out of sight completely. However, with O'Connor's aid, the police of all New England were on the lookout.

The Thurstons had been friends of Halsey's before Vera Lytton had ever met Dr. Dixon, we discovered from the Danbridge gossips, and I, at least, jumped to the conclusion that Halsey was shielding the artist, perhaps through a sense of friendship when he found that Kennedy was interested in Thurston's movement. I must say I rather liked Halsey, for he seemed very thoughtful of the Willards, and was never too busy to give an hour or so to any commission they wished carried out without publicity.

Two days passed with not a word from Thurston. Kennedy was obviously getting impatient. One day a rumor was received that he was in Bar Harbor; the next it was a report from Nova Scotia. At last, however, came the welcome news that he had been located in New Hampshire, arrested, and might be expected the next day.

At once Kennedy became all energy. He arranged for a secret conference in Senator Willard's house, the moment the artist was to arrive. The senator and his daughter made a flying trip back to town. Nothing was said to anyone about Thurston, but Kennedy quietly arranged with the district attorney to be present with the note and the jar of ammonia properly safeguarded. Leland of course came, although his client could not. Halsey Post seemed only too glad to be with Miss Willard, though he seemed to have lost interest in the case as soon as the Willards returned to look after it themselves. Mrs. Boncour was well enough to attend, and even Dr. Waterworth insisted on coming in a private ambulance which drove over from a nearby city especially for him. The time was fixed just before the arrival of the train that was to bring Thurston.

It was an anxious gathering of friends and foes of Dr. Dixon who sat impatiently waiting for Kennedy to begin this momentous exposition that was to establish the guilt or innocence of the calm young physician who sat impassively in the jail not half a mile from the room where his life and death were being debated.

"In many respects this is the most remarkable case that it has ever been my lot to handle," began Kennedy. "Never before have I felt so keenly my sense of responsibility. Therefore, though this is a somewhat irregular proceeding, let me begin by setting forth the facts as I see them.

"First, let us consider the dead woman. The question that arises here is, Was she murdered or did she commit suicide? I think you will discover the answer as I proceed. Miss Lytton, as you know, was, two years ago, Mrs. Burgess Thurston. The Thurstons had temperament, and temperament is quite often the highway to the divorce court. It was so in this case. Mrs. Thurston discovered that her husband was paying much attention to other women. She sued for divorce in New York, and he accepted service in the South, where he happened to be. At least it was so testified by Mrs. Thurston's lawyer.

"Now here comes the remarkable feature of the case. The law firm of Kerr & Kimmel, I find, not long ago began to investigate the legality of this divorce. Before a notary Thurston made an affidavit that he had never been served by the lawyer for Miss Lytton, as she was now known. Her lawyer is dead, but his representative in the South who served the papers is alive. He was brought to New York and asserted squarely that he had served the papers properly.

"Here is where the shrewdness of Mose Kimmel, the shyster lawyer, came in. He arranged to have the Southern attorney identify the man he had served the paper on. For this purpose he was engaged in conversation with one of his own clerks when the lawyer was due to appear. Kimmel appeared to act confused, as if he had been caught napping. The Southern lawyer, who had seen Thurston only once, fell squarely into the trap and identified the clerk as Thurston. There were plenty of witnesses to it, and it was point number two for the great Mose Kimmel. Papers were drawn up to set aside the divorce decree.

"In the meantime, Miss Lytton, or Mrs. Thurston, had become acquainted with a young doctor in a New York hospital, and had become engaged to him. It matters not that the engagement was later broken. The fact remains that if the divorce were set aside all action would lie against Dr. Dixon for alienating Mrs. Thurston's affections, and a grave scandal would result. I need not add that in this quiet little town of Danbridge the most could be made of such a suit."

Kennedy was unfolding a piece of paper. As he laid it down, Leland, who was sitting next to me, exclaimed under his breath:

"My God, he's going to let the prosecutor know about that letter. Can't you stop him?"

It was too late. Kennedy had already begun to read Vera's letter. It was damning to Dixon, added to the other note found in the ammonia jar.

When he had finished reading, you could almost hear the throbbing in the room. A scowl overspread Senator Willard's features. Alma Willard was pale and staring wildly at Kennedy. Halsey Post, ever solicitous for her, handed her a glass of water from the table. Dr. Waterworth had forgotten his pain in his intense attention, and Mrs. Boncour seemed stunned with astonishment. The prosecuting attorney was eagerly taking notes.

"In some way," pursued Kennedy in an even voice, "this letter was either overlooked in the original correspondence of Dr. Dixon or it was added to it later. I shall come back to that presently. My next point is that Dr. Dixon says he received a letter from Thurston on the day the artist visited the Boncour bungalow. It asked about a certain headache compound, and his reply was brief and, as nearly as I can find out, read, 'This compound will not cure your headache except at the expense of reducing heart action dangerously.'

"Next comes the tragedy. On the evening of the day that Thurston left, after presumably telling Miss Lytton about what Kerr & Kimmel had discovered, Miss Lytton is found dying with a bottle containing cyanide and sublimate beside her. You are all familiar with the circumstances and with the note discovered in the jar of ammonia. Now, if the prosecutor will be so kind as to let me see that note— thank you, sir. This is the identical note. You have all heard the various theories of the jar and have read the note. Here it is in plain, cold black and white—in Dr. Dixon's own handwriting, as you know, and read: 'This will cure your headache, Dr. Dixon.'"

Alma Willard seemed as one paralyzed. Was Kennedy, who had been engaged by her father to defend her fiancé, about to convict him?

"Before we draw the final conclusion," continued Kennedy gravely, "there are one or two points I wish to elaborate. Walter, will you open that door into the main hall?"

I did so, and two policemen stepped in with a prisoner. It was Thurston, but changed almost beyond recognition. His clothes were worn, his beard shaved off, and he had a generally hunted appearance.

Thurston was visibly nervous. Apparently he had heard all that Kennedy had said and intended he should hear, for as he entered he almost broke away from the police officers in his eagerness to speak.

"Before God," he cried dramatically, "I am as innocent as you are of this crime, Professor Kennedy."

"Are you prepared to swear before *me*," almost shouted Kennedy, his eyes blazing, "that you were never served properly by your wife's lawyers in that suit?"

The man cringed back as if a stinging blow had been delivered between his eyes. As he met Craig's fixed glare, he knew there was no hope. Slowly, as if the words were being wrung from him syllable by syllable, he said in a muffled voice:

"No, I perjured myself. I was served in that suit. But—"

"And you swore falsely before Kimmel that you were not?" persisted Kennedy.

"Yes," he murmured. "But—"

"And you are prepared now to make another affidavit to that effect?"

"Yes," he replied. "If—"

"No buts or ifs, Thurston," cried Kennedy sarcastically. "What did you make that affidavit for? What is *your* story?"

"Kimmel sent for me. I did not go to him. He offered to pay my debts if I would swear to such a statement. I did not ask why or for whom. I swore to it and gave him a list of my creditors. I waited until they were paid. Then my conscience"—I could not help revolting at the thought of conscience in such a wretch, and the word itself seemed to stick in his throat as he went on and saw how feeble an impression he was making on us—"my conscience began to trouble me. I determined to see Vera, tell her all, and find out whether it was she who wanted this statement. I saw her. When at last I told her, she scorned me. I can confirm that, for as I left a man entered. I now knew how grossly I had sinned in listening to Mose Kimmel. I fled. I disappeared in Maine. I travelled. Every day my money grew less. At last, I was overtaken, captured, and brought back here."

He stopped and sank wretchedly down in a chair and covered his face with his hands.

"A likely story," muttered Leland in my ear.

Kennedy was working quickly. Motioning the officers to be seated by Thurston, he uncovered a jar which he had placed on the table. The color had now appeared in Alma's cheeks, as if hope had again sprung in her heart, and I fancied that Halsey Post saw his claim on her favor declining correspondingly.

"I want you to examine the letters in this case with me," continued Kennedy. "Take the letter which I read from Miss Lytton, which was found following the strange disappearance of the note from Thurston."

He dipped a pen into a little bottle, and wrote on a piece of paper:

What is your opinion about Cross's Headache Cure? Would
you recommend it for a nervous headache?
                    BURGESS THURSTON,
                         c/o MRS. S. BONCOUR.

Craig held up the writing so that we could all see that he had written what Dixon declared Thurston wrote in the note that had disappeared. Then he dipped another pen into a second bottle, and for
some time he scrawled on another sheet of paper. He held it up, but it
was still perfectly blank.

"Now," he added, "I am going to give a little demonstration which
I expect to be successful only in a measure. Here in the open sunshine
by this window I am going to place these two sheets of paper side by
side. It will take longer than I care to wait to make my demonstration
complete, but I can do enough to convince you."

For a quarter of an hour we sat in silence, wondering what he
would do next. At last he beckoned us over to the window. As we
approached he said, "On sheet number one I have written with quinoline; on sheet number two I wrote with a solution of nitrate of silver."

We bent over. The writing signed "Thurston" on sheet number
one was faint, almost imperceptible, but on paper number two, in
black letters, appeared what Kennedy had written: "Dear Harris:
Since we agreed to disagree we have at least been good friends."

"It is like the start of the substituted letter, and the other is like
the missing note," gasped Leland in a daze.

"Yes," said Kennedy quickly. "Leland, no one entered your office.
No one stole the Thurston note. No one substituted the Lytton letter. According to your own story, you took them out of the safe and
left them in the sunlight all day. The process that had been started
earlier in ordinary light, slowly, was now quickly completed. In other
words, there was writing which would soon fade away on one side of
the paper and writing which was invisible but would soon appear on
the other.

"For instance, quinoline rapidly disappears in sunlight. Starch
with a slight trace of iodine writes a light blue, which disappears in
air. It was something like that used in the Thurston letter. Then,

too, silver nitrate dissolved in ammonia gradually turns black as it is acted on by light and air. Or magenta treated with a bleaching agent in just sufficient quantity to decolorise it is invisible when used for writing. But the original color reappears as the oxygen of the air acts upon the pigment. I haven't a doubt but that my analyses of the inks are correct and on one side quinoline was used and on the other nitrate of silver. This explains the inexplicable disappearance of evidence incriminating one person, Thurston, and the sudden appearance of evidence incriminating another, Dr. Dixon. Sympathetic ink also accounts for the curious circumstance that the Lytton letter was folded up with the writing apparently outside. It was outside and unseen until the sunlight brought it out and destroyed the other, inside, writing—a chance, I suspect, that was intended for the police to see after it was completed, not for the defence to witness as it was taking place."

We looked at each other aghast. Thurston was nervously opening and shutting his lips and moistening them as if he wanted to say something but could not find the words.

"Lastly," went on Craig, utterly regardless of Thurston's frantic efforts to speak, "we come to the note that was discovered so queerly crumpled up in the jar of ammonia on Vera Lytton's dressing table. I have here a cylindrical glass jar in which I place some sal-ammoniac and quicklime. I will wet it and beat it a little. That produces the pungent gas of ammonia.

"On one side of this third piece of paper I myself write with this mercurous nitrate solution. You see, I leave no mark on the paper as I write. I fold it up and drop it into the jar—and in a few seconds withdraw it. Here is a very quick way of producing something like the slow result of sunlight with silver nitrate. The fumes of ammonia have formed the precipitate of black mercurous nitrate, a very distinct black writing which is almost indelible. That is what is technically called invisible rather than sympathetic ink."

We leaned over to read what he had written. It was the same as the note incriminating Dixon:

This will cure your headache.

DR. DIXON.

A servant entered with a telegram from New York. Scarcely stopping in his exposure, Kennedy tore it open, read it hastily, stuffed it into his pocket, and went on.

"Here in this fourth bottle I have an acid solution of iron chloride, diluted until the writing is invisible when dry," he hurried on. "I will just make a few scratches on this fourth sheet of paper—so. It leaves no mark. But it has the remarkable property of becoming red in vapor of sulpho-cyanide. Here is a long-necked flask of the gas, made by sulphuric acid acting on potassium sulpho-cyanide. Keep back, Dr. Waterworth, for it would be very dangerous for you to get even a whiff of this in your condition. Ah! See—the scratches I made on the paper are red."

Then hardly giving us more than a moment to let the fact impress itself on our minds, he seized the piece of paper and dashed it into the jar of ammonia. When he withdrew it, it was just a plain sheet of white paper again. The red marks which the gas in the flask had brought out of nothingness had been effaced by the ammonia. They had gone and left no trace.

"In this way I can alternately make the marks appear and disappear by using the sulpho-cyanide and the ammonia. Whoever wrote this note with Dr. Dixon's name on it must have had the doctor's reply to the Thurston letter containing the words, 'This will not cure your headache.' He carefully traced the words, holding the genuine note up to the light with a piece of paper over it, leaving out the word *not* and using only such words as he needed. This note was then destroyed.

"But he forgot that after he had brought out the red writing by the use of the sulpho-cyanide, and though he could count on Vera Lytton's placing the note in the jar of ammonia and hence obliterating the writing, while at the same time the invisible writing in the mercurous nitrate involving Dr. Dixon's name would be brought out by the ammonia indelibly on the other side of the note—he forgot"— Kennedy was now speaking eagerly and loudly—"that the sulpho-cyanide vapors could always be made to bring back to accuse him the words that the ammonia had blotted out."

Before the prosecutor could interfere, Kennedy had picked up the note found in the ammonia jar beside the dying girl and had jammed the state's evidence into the long-necked flask of sulpho-cyanide vapor.

"Don't fear," he said, trying to pacify the now furious prosecutor, "it will do nothing to the Dixon writing. That is permanent now, even if it is only a tracing."

When he withdrew the note, there was writing on both sides, the black of the original note and something in red on the other side.

We crowded around, and Craig read it with as much interest as any of us:

> Before taking the headache powder, be sure to place the con-
> tents of this paper in a jar with a little warm water.

"Hum," commented Craig, "this was apparently written on the outside wrapper of a paper folded about some sal-ammoniac and quicklime. It goes on:

> Just drop the whole thing in, *paper and all*. Then if you feel a
> faintness from the medicine the ammonia will quickly restore
> you. One spoonful of the headache powder swallowed quickly
> is enough.

No name was signed to the directions, but they were plainly written, and "*paper and all*" was underscored heavily.

Craig pulled out some letters. "I have here specimens of writing of many persons connected with this case, but I can see at a glance which one corresponds to the writing on this red death warrant by an almost inhuman fiend. I shall, however, leave that part of it to the handwriting experts to determine at the trial. Thurston, who was the man whom you saw enter the Boncour bungalow as you left—the constant visitor?"

Thurston had not yet regained his self-control, but with trembling forefinger he turned and pointed to Halsey Post.

"Yes, ladies and gentlemen," cried Kennedy as he slapped the telegram that had just come from New York down on the table decisively, "yes, the real client of Kerr & Kimmel, who bent Thurston to his purposes, was Halsey Post, once secret lover of Vera Lytton till threatened by scandal in Danbridge—Halsey Post, graduate in technology, student of sympathetic inks, forger of the Vera Lytton letter and the other notes, and dealer in cyanides in the silversmithing business, fortune hunter for the Willard millions with which to recoup the Post & Vance losses, and hence rival of Dr. Dixon for the love of Alma Willard. That is the man who wielded the poisoned pen. Dr. Dixon is innocent."

A Literary Death

Martin Harry Greenberg

Dear Isaac:

THINGS HAVE settled down here sufficiently for me to try to answer your questions about the tragic death of Eddie Advent. As you know (perhaps too well), Eddie was a writer of ambition—he had a firmer grip on where he wanted to go and how he was going to get there than any SF writer I have ever met (and he would hate me, if he could see me categorizing him in any way), and it may have been ambition which finally killed him.

Anyway, here are the "facts" as best I can reconstruct them: Eddie had worked for years on what he thought was his masterpiece—a 900-page manuscript with the working title of *The Political Geography of the Promised World*, and like almost all his work, it was difficult to classify—perhaps "science fantasy" would be the closest, but it doesn't matter now. I read the manuscript and liked it—it was the best thing he had ever done (will ever do), but I had serious reservations about who, if anyone, would publish it, given present commercial realities. I suggested a university press, but Eddie flatly refused my offer of contacts in those places—he wanted a major publisher, one who would give it maximum exposure and support. Well, the first big houses he tried all said no, several after holding it for quite a while. It was at this point that he approached old Doc Greenston at W & W. Now W & W is a medium-to-small New York house, with a distinguished past but with its best days definitely behind it.

But Doc really liked the manuscript, fought it through a very skeptical editorial board, and made Eddie a decent offer (I know, because Eddie told me about it). After much thought and discussion—he talked about this with at least seven authors and two agents—he told Doc he would take their offer subject to a few minor changes. I thought that everything was set, and so did everybody who knew about the project. It was at this point that the trouble began—Peter Dean of Solomon and Solomon (who had just been promoted from senior editor in charge of who knows what to editor-in-chief of their trade books division) told Eddie that his new position made it possible for him to take the book at four times the advance that Doc had offered and with a guaranteed ad budget of $45,000 to boot. But Eddie had already verbally accepted Doc's offer. Well, this didn't stop Eddie—he told me that he had worked too long and too hard to let his word stand in the way of his destiny (or words to that effect), and he said he was going to tell Doc the same thing. Doc (rest his soul) always believed that the only important thing in life was honor (how he lasted so long in publishing must remain one of the Great Mysteries of the Western World), and he was mad as hell at Eddie.

Now things become grim—Doc saw Eddie at the SFWA Party in New York, and in front of several witnesses (including yours truly) put a curse on him, telling him that he "would die a literary death" by 2:00 P.M., November 20, some two weeks away at the time. Eddie laughed in his face and no more words were spoken between them (as far as I know).

Now, I spoke with Eddie (remember that we were working on that big anthology during this period) at least six times after that night, so I have a pretty good idea of what he was thinking. You may or may not know that Eddie was a great admirer of Cornell Woolrich, and of course was familiar with that great and sadly neglected author's *Night Has a Thousand Eyes*, in which a man is told by a mystic (as I recall the story—I'm actually afraid to go back and read it again) that he will "die by the jaws of a lion." The guy carefully avoids zoos, cats, and anything feline until just before his death by the jaws of the lion that sits in front of the New York Public Library at Forty-second and Fifth. I mention this because Eddie did—as time went by, he got more and more nervous, even desperate. He told me on the phone that he found himself avoiding bookstores, libraries, publishers, other writers, etc. (remember, the curse said he would die a *literary death*). This finally became an obsession by the time of my last two conversations with him (especially after poor Doc had committed suicide). I told him that the right thing to do was to honor his word to Doc, but he steadfastly refused—ole devil ambition, I guess, or maybe he just thought it was too late for the curse to be removed, now that Doc was dead.

As best as I can piece things together (and I talked with everyone, including the state police—you should see my phone bill for November), Eddie's concern turned into panic a few days before November 20 (you might recall that week because it was the week of the first big snowstorm in the Northeast), and he holed up in his apartment (he had apparently *given away* his typewriter and all his books by this time). On the morning of the twentieth, another tenant in his building saw him getting into his car—he had told me that he felt totally vulnerable in New York, the center of this country's literary world. Eddie had decided to flee the city on that fateful day. I don't know his exact route, but he was obviously (since that is where they found the body and car) heading out on the Garden State Parkway, making his way slowly (since the traffic was heavy and the melting snow made driving hazardous), and for all I know, watching out for bookmobiles! The last details are somewhat fuzzy, but his car apparently skidded on the melting snow, went into a spin and off the road just before 2:00 P.M. (the clock in the car was smashed and read 1:58). He died instantly of a broken neck, and with his car half buried—in a pile of slush.

All best wishes,
Marty the Other

The Adventure of the Penny Magenta

August Derleth

FROM HIS PLACE AT the window one summer morning, Solar Pons said, "Ah, we are about to have a visitor and, I trust, a client. London has been oppressively dull this week, and some diversion is long past due."

I stepped over to his side and looked down.

Our prospective visitor was just in the act of stepping out of his cab. He was a man somewhat past middle-age, of medium height, and spare almost to thinness. He affected a greying Van Dyke and eye-glasses in old-fashioned square frames. He wore a greening black bowler and a scuffed smoking jacket, beneath which showed a waistcoat of some flowered material, and he carried a cane, though he did not walk with any pronounced impediment.

"A tradesman," I ventured.

"The keeper of a small shop," said Pons.

"Dry goods?"

"You observed his clothing, Parker. His square spectacles and his walking stick are both old-fashioned. I submit he is in antiques or something of that sort. The nature of his business is such as to permit the casual, since he evidently wears his smoking jacket at his work."

"Perhaps he came from his home?"

"On the contrary. It is now ten o'clock. Some time after he arrived at his shop this morning something occurred that has brought him to us."

But our caller was now at the threshold, and in a moment our good landlady, Mrs. Johnson, had ushered him into our quarters. He bowed to her, and, his glance passing over me, he bowed to Pons.

"Mr. Solar Pons?"

"I am at your service. Pray sit down."

Our visitor sat down to face Pons, who was now leaning against the mantel, his eyes twinkling with anticipation.

"My name is Athos Humphreys," said our client. "I have a small shop for antiques, old books, and stamps near Hampstead Heath. Other than that I doubt your need to know."

"Save that you are a member of the Masonic order, a bachelor or widower accustomed to living alone, without an assistant at your shop and with insufficient business to demand your unremitting attendance there," said Pons. "Pray continue, Mr. Humphreys."

Our client betrayed neither astonishment nor displeasure at Pon's little deductions. His glance fell to his Masonic ring, then to the torn and worn cuffs of his smoking jacket, which no self-respecting woman would have permitted to go unmended, and finally to the lone key depending over the pocket into which he had hastily thrust his chain of keys after locking his shop.

"I'm glad to see I've made no mistake in coming to you, Mr. Pons," he continued. "The problem doesn't concern me personally, however, as far as I can determine, but my shop. I must tell you that for the past three mornings I have had indisputable evidence that my shop has been entered. Yet nothing has been taken."

A small sound of satisfaction escaped Pons. "And what was the nature of your evidence that the shop had been entered, if nothing was taken, Mr. Humphreys?" he asked.

"Well, sir, I am a most methodical man. I maintain a certain order in my shop, no matter how careless it looks—that is by design, of course, for an antique shop ought to have an appearance of careful disorder. For the past three mornings I have noticed—sometimes not at once on my arrival—that some object has been moved and put back not quite where it stood before. I have never discovered any way of entry; all else, save for one or two objects, remains as I left it; so I can only suppose that whoever entered my shop did so by means of the door, to which, I ought to say, I have the only key."

"You are fully aware of your inventory, Mr. Humphreys?"

"Positively, sir. I know every item in my shop, and there is nothing there of sufficient value to tempt anyone but a sneak thief content with small reward for his pains."

"Yet it is patent that someone is going to considerable pains to search your shop night after night," said Pons. "A man in your business must lead a relatively sedentary life, Mr. Humphreys. Did you, immediately prior to this sequence of events, do anything at all to attract attention to yourself?"

"No, sir."

"Or your business?"

"No, sir." But here our client hesitated, as if he were about to speak otherwise, yet thought better of it.

"Something caused you to hesitate, Mr. Humphreys. What was it?"

"Nothing of any consequence. It is true that a week ago I was forced to post a small personal asking that relatives of the late Arthur Benefield come forward and call on me at the shop."

"Who was Arthur Benefield?"

"A patron of mine."

"Surely an unusual patron if you knew neither his address nor his heirs," said Pons. "For if you did, you would hardly have had to extend an invitation to his heirs through the columns of the papers."

"That is correct, Mr. Pons. He left no address. He appeared at my shop for the first time about a month ago, and brought with him a manila envelope filled with loose stamps. He had posted the envelope to me—apparently at a branch post office—but had then immediately retrieved it from the clerk, evidently someone whose acquaintance he had made—and brought it in person. He appeared to be an American gentleman, and asked me to keep the stamps for him. He paid a 'rental' fee of five pounds for that service during the month following his visit. He also bought several stamps from my collection and added them to his own.

"Mr. Benefield was run down and killed in an automobile accident ten days ago. I saw his picture in one of the papers, together with a request for relatives to come forward. Let me hasten to assure you, Mr. Pons, if you are thinking that the entry to my shop has anything to do with Mr. Benefield, I'm afraid you're very much mistaken. I took the liberty of examining the contents of Mr. Benefield's envelope as soon as I learned of his death. It contains no stamp worth more than a few shillings. Indeed, I doubt very much if the entire lot of mixed stamps would command more than ten pounds."

Pons stood for a moment in an attitude of deep thought. Then he said, "I fancy a look at the premises would not be amiss. Are you prepared to take us to your shop, Mr. Humphreys?"

"I would be honored to do so, Mr. Pons. I have a cab waiting below, if you care to return with me."

OUR CLIENT'S WAS indeed a little shop. It was one of those charming, old-fashioned places not uncommon in London and its environs, standing as if untouched by time from 1780 onward. A pleasant, tinkling bell announced our entrance, Mr. Humphreys having thrown the door wide and stood aside to permit us to pass. Then he in turn passed us, hanging his bowler on a little rack not far from the door, and throwing his keys carelessly to his counter. His shop was crowded, and wore just that air of planned carelessness which would intrigue the searcher after curios or unusual pieces for the household. Shelves, floors, tables—all were filled with bric-a-brac, knickknacks, and period pieces. One wall was given over to books of all kinds, neatly arranged on shelves which reached from floor to ceiling. At the far end of the shop—next to a curtained-off alcove which was evidently a small place in which our client could brew himself tea, if he liked, for the sound of boiling water came from it—stood Mr. Humphreys' desk, a secretary of Chippendale design.

Our client was eager to show us how he had discovered that his shop had been entered in the night. He went directly to a Chinese vase which stood on top of a lacquered box on a table not far from the counter.

"If you will look carefully, Mr. Pons, you will see that the position of this vase varies by a quarter of an inch from the faint circle of lint and dust which indicates where it stood before it was moved. I have not had occasion to move this piece for at least a week. Of itself, it has no value, being an imitation Han Dynasty piece. Nor has the lacquer box on which it stands. The box, I have reason to believe, has been opened. Of course, it is empty."

Pons, however, was not particularly interested in our client's demonstration. "And where do you keep Mr. Benefield's stamps?" he asked.

Our client went around his counter and placed his right hand on a letter rack which stood on his desk. "Right here, Mr. Pons."

"Dear me!" exclaimed Pons, with an ill-concealed smile twitching his lips, "is that not an unorthodox place for it?"

"It was where Mr. Benefield asked me to keep it. Indeed, he enjoined me to keep it here, in this envelope, in this place."

"So that anyone whose eye chanced to fall upon it would think it part of your correspondence, Mr. Humphreys?"

"I had not thought of it so, but I suppose it would be true," said Humphreys thoughtfully.

"Let us just have a look at Mr. Benefield's collection of stamps."

"Very well, Mr. Pons. It can do no harm, now the poor fellow is dead."

He handed the manila envelope to Pons. It was not a large envelope—perhaps four and a half inches by six and a half or thereabouts, but it bulged with its contents, and it had been stamped heavily with British commemorative issues of larger-than-common size. It had been addressed to Mr. Humphreys, and the stamps on its face had been duly cancelled; manifestly, if Mr. Humphreys' story were true, Mr. Benefield had had to apply to someone in the post office for its return to his hand, so that he could bring it in person to our client's shop. Pons studied the envelope thoughtfully.

"It did not seem to you strange that Mr. Benefield should make such a request of you, Mr. Humphreys?"

"Mr. Pons, I am accustomed to dealing with all manner of strange people. I suppose the collector is always rather more extraordinary in his habits and conduct than ordinary people."

"Perhaps that is true," pursued Pons. "Still, the circumstances of your possession of this envelope suggest that it contains something of value—of such value, indeed, that its owner was extremely reluctant to let it out of his sight long enough for the postman to deliver it, and left it here only because of dire necessity."

"But if that were true," objected our client reasonably, "what had he to gain by leaving it here?"

"In such plain sight, too, Mr. Humphreys," said Pons, chuckling. "I submit he had to gain what he most wanted—effective conceal-ment. There is a story by the American, Poe, which suggests the gam-bit—a letter hidden in a torn envelope on a rack in sight of anyone who might walk into the room. What better place of concealment for an object—let us say, a stamp—than in the letter rack of a man who does a small philatelic business?"

"Mr. Pons, your theory is sound, but in fact it doesn't apply. I have gone over the stamps in that envelope with the greatest care. I assure you, on my word as a modest authority in philately, that there is not a stamp in that collection worth a second glance from a serious collec-tor of any standing. There is most certainly nothing there to tempt a thief to make such elaborate forays into my humble establishment."

"I believe you, Mr. Humphreys," said Pons, still smiling. "Yet I put it to you that this is the object of your malefactor's search."

"Mr. Pons, I would willingly surrender it to him—if he could prove he had a right to it, of course."

"Let us not be hasty," said Pons dryly.

So saying, he calmly opened the envelope and unceremoniously emptied its contents to the counter before us. Then, much to our client's amazement, he bestowed not a glance at the stamps but gave his attention again to the envelope, which he now took over to the window and held up against the sunlight. The manila, however, was too thick to permit him any vision through it.

"It would seem to be an ordinary envelope," he said. "And these stamps which were to have paid its way here?"

"They are only British Empire Exhibition adhesives, issue of 1924, not very old, and not worth much more than their face value."

Pons lowered the envelope and turned to look toward the cur-tained alcove. "Is that not a teakettle, Mr. Humphreys?"

"Yes, sir. I keep hot water always ready for tea."

"Let us just repair to that room, if you please."

"It is hardly large enough for us all."

"Very well, then. I will take the liberty of using it, and you and Parker may guard the door."

Our client flashed a puzzled glance at me, but I could not relieve his dubiety nor inform him of Pons's purpose. That, however, was soon clear, for Pons went directly to the teapot on Mr. Humphreys' electric plate, and proceeded without a qualm to hold the stamped corner of the envelope over the steam.

"What are you doing, Mr. Pons?" cried our client in alarm.

"I trust I am about to find the solution to the initial part of our little problem, Mr. Humphreys," said Pons.

Our client suppressed the indignation he must have felt, and watched in fascinated interest as Pons finally peeled back the stamps.

"Aha!" exclaimed Pons, "what have we here?"

Beneath the stamps lay revealed, carefully protected by a thin square of cellophane, a shabby-looking stamp of a faded magenta color. Indeed, it was such a stamp that, were I a philatelist, I would have cast aside, for not only was it crudely printed, but it had also been clipped at the corners. Pons, however, handled it with the greatest care.

"I daresay this is the object of the search which has been conducted of your premises, Mr. Humphreys," said Pons. "Unless I am very much mistaken, this is the famous one-penny magenta rarity, printed in British Guiana in 1856, discovered by a boy of fifteen here in our country, and originally sold for six shillings. After being in the collection of Philippe Ferrari for many years, it was sold to a rich American at auction for the fabulous price of seventy-five hundred pounds. Correct me if I am wrong, Mr. Humphreys."

Our client, who had been staring at the stamp in awe and fascination, found his voice. "You have made no error of fact, Mr. Pons, but one of assumption. There is only one penny magenta known to exist, despite the most intensive search for others. That stamp is still in the collection of the widow of the American millionaire who bought it at the Ferrari auction in 1925. This one can be only a forgery—a very clever, most deceptive counterfeit—but still, Mr. Pons, a forgery, with only the value of a curiosity. The original would now be worth close to ten thousand pounds; but this copy is scarcely worth the labor and care it took to make it."

Pons carefully replaced the stamps on the envelope, keeping the penny magenta to one side. Then he returned to the counter and put the loose stamps back into the envelope.

"If you have another, larger envelope, Mr. Humphreys, put this into it, and label it 'Property of Arthur Benefield,'" instructed Pons. "I am somewhat curious now to know more of your late customer. Was he a young man?"

"Mr. Pons, I can only show you the clipping from the *News of the World*. It conveys all I can tell you," replied Humphreys.

He went back to his desk, opened a drawer, and took out the clipping.

Pons bent to it, and I looked over his shoulder.

The photograph was that of a young man, certainly not over thirty-five. He was not ill-favored in looks, and wore a short moustache. He appeared to be of medium weight. The story beneath it indicated that the photograph had been found in his billfold, but that no address had been discovered. From the presence of American currency in the billfold, the authorities had concluded that Benefield was an American tourist in London. They had had no response to official inquiries at the usual sources, however.

Benefield had been found in the street one night. Evidence indicated that he had been struck and killed by a fast-traveling car; police were looking for one which must have been severely damaged by the force of the impact. Car and driver had vanished, as was to be expected.

Pons read this in silence and handed it back to our client.

"Our next step," he said, "will be to catch the intruder. I have no question but that he will return tonight."

Athos Humphreys paled a little. "I should say, Mr. Pons, I am not a wealthy man. I had not inquired about your fee . . ."

"Say no more, Mr. Humphreys," replied Pons with animation. "If you will permit me to retain this little stamp for its curiosity value, I shall feel amply repaid."

"By all means, Mr. Pons."

"Very well, then. Parker and I will return here late this afternoon prepared to spend the night in your shop, if that is agreeable to you."

"It is indeed, sir."

We bade our client farewell and repaired to our lodgings.

WE RETURNED TO Athos Humphreys' antique shop just before his closing hour that evening. It was not without some patent misgivings that
our client locked us into his shop and departed. Clearly he was doubtful of our success and perhaps concerned lest our venture result in a
scuffle in the narrow confines of his premises, and concomitant damage to his stock.

Pons had insisted that both of us be armed. In addition, he carried
a powerful electric torch. So protected, we took up a cramped position
concealed behind the curtain in the little alcove leading off the shop.
Once we were alone, Pons warned again that our quarry was likely to
be more desperate than I had imagined, and adjured me to keep my
eyes on the door of the shop.

"You are so positive he'll come by the door," I said. "Suppose he
opens a window and drops in from behind?"

"No, Parker, he will not. He has a key," replied Pons. "Surely you
observed how careless Humphreys was with his keys when he came in
with us this morning! He simply threw them to the counter and left
them in plain sight. Anyone prepared to do so could have made wax
impressions of the lot. I have no doubt that is what took place, as soon
as our client's advertisement appeared and apprised our quarry that
Humphreys undoubtedly possessed something belonging to Benefield,
and what, more likely, than the very object of his search? I see him as
a patient and dangerous man, unwilling to be caught, but determined
to have what he is after."

"The penny magenta? But why would anyone take the trouble to
conceal a forgery so carefully?"

"Why, indeed!" answered Pons enigmatically. "It suggests nothing
to you?"

"Only that the man who wants it is deceived as to its actual
value."

"Nothing other?"

"I can think of nothing."

"Very well, then. Let us just look at the problem anew. Mr. Athos Humphreys, a comparatively obscure dealer in antiques, is sought out by an American as a repository for a packet of stamps, all of no great value. Mr. Benefield has gone to the trouble of achieving a cancellation of his stamps, and then to the even greater trouble of recovering the packet to bring it in person—a considerable achievement, considering the rigidity of our post office. He pays at least half what his packet of stamps is manifestly worth to make sure that Humphreys keeps it where he directs. And where does he direct that it be kept? In plain sight in Humphreys' own letter rack, after Benefield has made certain that it bears every appearance of having been posted to Humphreys. Does all this still suggest nothing further to you, Parker?"

"Only that Benefield seemed certain someone wanted the packet."

"Capital! You are making progress."

"So he made sure it wouldn't attract attention, and, if seen, would be mistaken for other than what it was. The envelope bore no return address, and the name of Humphreys was hurriedly printed in blocks. That, I presume, was so the man who wanted it wouldn't recognize Benefield's handwriting, which very probably he knew."

"It gives me pleasure to discover how handsomely your capacity for observation has grown, Parker. But—no more?"

"I fear I have shot my bolt, Pons."

"Well, then, let us just say a few words about Mr. Benefield. It does not seem to you strange that he should have so conveniently met with a fatal accident after reaching London?"

"Accidents happen every day. It is a well-known fact that the accident toll exceeds the mortality rate in wartime."

"I submit that the late Benefield and his pursuer were in this matter together. I put it to you further that Benefield slipped away from his partner in the venture and came to London by himself to offer the penny magenta for sale without the necessity of dividing the spoils with his partner, who followed and found him but has not yet found the stamp. It is not too much to conclude that it was his hand at the wheel of the car that caused Benefield's death."

"Ingenious," I said dubiously.

"Elementary, my dear Parker," said Pons.

"Except for the fact that the penny magenta is a forgery," I finished.

"Ah, Parker, you put my poor powers to shame," he answered with a dry chuckle. "But now I think we had better keep quiet. I should tell you I have notified Inspector Taylor, who will be within earshot waiting upon our signal."

I HAD BEGUN to drowse, when Pons's light touch on my arm woke me. The hour was close to midnight, and the sound of a key in the lock came distinctly to ear. In a moment the outer door opened, and, from my position behind the curtain, I saw a dark figure slip into the shop. In but a moment more, the shade of a dark lantern was drawn cautiously a little to one side. Its light fell squarely upon the counter and there, framed in it, was the envelope on which our client had written Arthur Benefield's name.

The light held to the counter.

Then, in four rapid and silent strides, the intruder was at the counter. I saw his hand reach down and take up the envelope.

At that moment Pons turned on his electric torch and silhouetted a well-dressed, thin-faced young man whose startled glance gave him a distinctly foxlike look. He stood for but a split second in the light; then he dropped, spun around, and leaped for the door.

Pons was too quick for him. He caught up a heavy iron and threw it with all his force. It struck our quarry cruelly on the side of one knee; he went down and stayed down.

"Keep your hands out of your pockets; we are armed," said Pons, advancing toward him. "Parker, just open the door and fire a shot into the air. That will bring Taylor."

Our quarry sat up, one hand gripping his knee painfully, the other still clinging to the envelope of stamps. "The most you can charge me with," he said in a cultured voice, "is breaking and entering. Perhaps theft. This is as much my property as it was Arthur's."

"I fancy the charge will be murder," said Pons, as Inspector Taylor's pounding footsteps waxed in the night.

BACK IN OUR quarters at 7B Praed Street, Pons lingered over a pipe of shag. I, too, hesitated to go to bed.

"You do not seem one whit puzzled over this matter, Pons," I said at last. "Yet I confess that its entire motivation seems far too slight to justify its events."

"You are certainly right, Parker," he answered with maddening gravity. "It does not then suggest anything further to you?"

"No, I am clear as to the picture."

"But not as to its interpretation, eh?"

"No."

"I submit there is a basic error in your reasoning, Parker. It has occurred to you to realize that one would hardly go to such lengths, even to commit murder, for a counterfeit stamp worth five pounds at best. Yet it does not seem to have occurred to you that the penny magenta I have here as a gift from our client may indeed be worth, as he estimated, ten thousand pounds?"

"We know that the single copy of that stamp exists in an American collection."

"Say, rather, we believe it does. I submit that this is the only genuine British Guiana penny magenta rarity, and that the copy in the America collection is a counterfeit. I took the liberty of sending a cable this afternoon, and I fancy we shall have a visitor from America just as fast as an aeroplane will make it possible from New York to Croydon."

PONS WAS NOT in error.

Three days later, a representative of the American collector presented himself at our quarters and paid Pons a handsome reward for the recovery of the penny magenta. Both Benefield and his partner, who had been identified as a man named Watt Clark, had been in the collector's service. They had manufactured the false penny magenta and exchanged it for the genuine stamp, after which they had left their positions. The substitution had not been noticed until Pons's cable sent the collector to the experts, whose verification of Pons's suspicion had resulted in the dispatching of the collector's representative to bear the fabulously valuable penny magenta home in person.

Letter from a Very Worried Man

Henry Slesar

Here, within a thousand words, is a vignette—a portrait of our disturbing times . . .

ABBY HAD SPENT THE past four days with her parents in Springfield. So as soon as she got back to Chicago, she anxiously examined the accumulated mail in her mailbox. She shuffled hurriedly through the envelopes, magazines, and leaflets until she saw the familiar scrawl of Richard's handwriting. She wanted this letter above all, because it was from her fiancé, all the way from New York where he was attending a physicists' conference.

She waited until she was settled in a lounge chair, with a fresh cigarette between her lips. Then she tore open the envelope and extracted the folded sheet.

Dear Abby,
I love you. We're in the fourth day of the Conference now, and nobody's gotten drunk yet. What a convention! You'll be

happy to hear that there are only four women physicists in the crowd, and they're all strictly from Lower Slobbovia, so you can stop worrying about my dubious virtue. Did I mention that I love you?

There was a seminar yesterday on the Physicist's Responsibility in the Modern World, or some such jawbreaking title. The yawn might have come up like thunder in the audience, except that there were some pretty scary headlines on the hotel newsstand that morning, so everybody was a bit edgy. I got up and did some talking myself, but maybe I should have kept my mouth shut. You know how I am when I get started on Topic A.

I know what you're thinking now: Old guilt-ridden Richard's off the deep end again, blaming himself for helping to make the H-bomb. Well, I've been thinking about it, sure. How can you help it in this atmosphere? And when I look at the headlines, and remember that we're getting married in two weeks—how can you blame me for a slight case of jitters? We're walking down the aisle under the most menacing shadow that ever fell across this cockeyed world. We're going to have children (in due course, or didn't you know?) that will have to live, and maybe die, with the H-bomb in their backyard. You can't stop these thoughts, Abby, not even by trying. I thought about it all last night, and not sleeping much, if you want the truth. Wondering how a guy like me, a guy who helped put the thing together, who feels like a criminal, has a right to such happy prospects. Marrying you, settling down, raising kids, just like everybody else, just like Joe Normal. But then I think, well, I'm Joe Normal, too, and if the bomb hits, I go to pieces like everyone else; if the Strontium 90 starts filling up the water, and the milk, and the green vegetables, well, I'll get just as sick and dead as the next man. I'm not so special, honey. I don't feel guilty any more; just scared.

But you know something? I learned something out here. Sitting around with the guys, meeting up with the science boys from England, and France, and Yugoslavia (yep, they're here, too). I began to realize something. I began to think that maybe the problems of getting along with each other aren't

much worse than math problems. Even the big political problems, the ones which end up *Bang!* if the answers come out
wrong, they can be licked, too. Sure, we'll be depending on a
lot of people whose actions we can't predict or control—but
we put our trust in strangers every day. The guy who drives the
bus. The airline pilot. The elevator operator. The short-order
cook. One wrong step, and these guys could end our short,
worried lives, too. So why not have faith? Why not trust a little bit? Maybe there won't be any big boom to put an end to
our plans. Maybe there'll be sweetness and light for a change.
Peace on Earth, good will to men, and all that jazz.

I don't know what started me feeling this way. (No, I haven't
touched a drop.) But all of a sudden, I'm hopeful. I feel good
about you, and about us, and about our wedding day. I feel
good about how we're going to live, and how the kids are
going to grow up, and how we're going to sit in front of the
fireplace for the next fifty years until we run out of things to
say. The truth is, honey, all of a sudden I'm an optimist. I think
we're going to lick our problems, all of them. I think the
patient's really and truly going to live.

Well, that's all the ink in this pen. I'm going to take a walk
around this town now, and see how it looks for a honeymoon.
I'll let you know if it measures up to our high standards.

I love you, by the way.

Yours,

Richard.

Abby sighed happily at the conclusion of the letter, and ground
out her cigarette in an ashtray. Then she looked at the next envelope
in the pile of mail. It appeared to be official and had a local postmark,
so she opened it curiously.
The contents were brief.

Dear Miss Butler:

We have been unable to reach you for the past few days, to inform you that the New York Police Department has contacted us regarding a man identified as Mr. Richard Cole. Mr. Cole was killed on the night of September 4 by a street gang of young hoodlums, and your name and address were discovered among his effects. We would appreciate it if you would contact Lieutenant Frank Kowlanski, Precinct 63, Chicago Police Department.

Pure Rotten

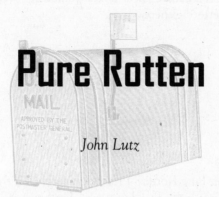

John Lutz

M AY 25, 7:00 A.M. TELEPHONE call to Clark Forthcue, Forthcue Mansion, Long Island:

"Mr. Forthcue, don't talk, listen. Telephone calls can be traced easy, letters can't be. This will be the only telephone call, and it will be short. We have your stepdaughter Imogene, who will be referred to in typed correspondence as Pure Rotten, a name that fits a ten-year-old spoiled rich brat like this one. For more information check the old rusty mailbox in front of the deserted Garver farm at the end of Wood Road near your property. Check it tonight. Check it every night. Tell the police or anyone else besides your wife about this and the kid dies. We'll know. We mean business."

Click.

Buzz.

May 25

Dear Mr. Forthcue:
Re our previous discussion on Pure Rotten: It will cost you
exactly one million dollars for the return of the merchandise
unharmed. We have researched and we know this is well within your capabilities. End the agony you and your wife are going
through. Give us your answer by letter. We will check the
Garver mailbox sometime after ten tomorrow evening. Your
letter had better be there.

Sincerely,
A. Snatcher

Snatchers, Inc.
May 26

Mr. Snatcher:
Do not harm Pure Rotten. I have not contacted the authorities and do not intend to do so. Mrs. Forthcue and I will follow your instructions faithfully. But your researchers have
made an error. I do not know if one million dollars is within
my capabilities, and it will take me some time to find out. Be
assured that you have my complete cooperation in this matter.
Of course if some harm should come to Pure Rotten, this
cooperation would abruptly cease.

Anxiously,
Clark Forthcue

Dear Mr. Forthcue:
Come off it. We know you can come up with the million. But
in the interest of that cooperation you mentioned we are willing to come down to $750,000 for the return of Pure Rotten.
It will be a pleasure to get this item off our hands, *one way or
the other*.

Determinedly,
A. Snatcher

Snatchers, Inc.
May 27

Dear Mr. Snatcher:
I write this letter in the quietude of my veranda, where for the first time in years it is tranquil enough for me to think clearly, so I trust I am dealing with this matter correctly. By lowering your original figure by 25 percent you have shown yourselves to be reasonable men, with whom an equally reasonable man might negotiate. Three quarters of a million is, as I am sure you are aware, a substantial sum of money. Even one in my position does not raise that much on short notice without also raising a few eyebrows and some suspicion. Might you consider a lower sum?

Reasonably,
Clark Forthcue

Dear Mr. Forthcue:
Pure Rotten is a perishable item and a great inconvenience to store. In fact, live explosives might be a more manageable commodity for our company to handle. In light of this we accede to your request for a lower figure by dropping our fee to $500,000 delivered immediately. This is our final figure. It would be easier, in fact a pleasure, for us to dispose of this commodity and do business elsewhere.

Still determinedly,
A. Snatcher

Snatchers, Inc.
May 29

Dear Mr. Snatcher:
This latest lowering of your company's demands is further proof that I am dealing with intelligent and realistic individuals.

Of course my wife has been grieving greatly over the loss, however temporary, of Pure Rotten, though with the aid of new furs and jewelry she has recovered from similar griefs.

When one marries a woman, as in acquiring a company, one must accept the liabilities along with the assets. With my rapidly improving nervous condition, and as my own initial grief and anxiety subside somewhat, I find myself at odds with my wife and of the opinion that your $ 500,000 figure is outrageously high. Think more in terms of tens of thousands.

Regards,

Clark Forthcue

⌒

Forthcue:

Ninety thousand is *it! Final!* By midnight tomorrow in the Garver mailbox, or Pure Rotten will be disposed of. You are keeping us in an uncomfortable position and we don't like it. We are not killers, but we can be.

A. Snatcher

⌒

Snatchers, Inc.
May 30

Dear Mr. Snatcher:

Free after many years of the agonizing pain of my ulcer, I can think quite objectively on this matter. Though my wife demands that I pay some ransom, ninety thousand dollars is out of the question. I suggest you dispose of the commodity under discussion as you earlier intimated you might. After proof of this action, twenty thousand dollars will accompany my next letter in the Garver mailbox. Since I have been honest with you and have not contacted the authorities, no one, including my wife, need know the final arrangements of our transaction.

Cordially,

Clark Forthcue

⌒

Forthcue:

Are you crazy? This is a human life. We are not killers. But you are right about one thing—no amount of money is worth more

than your health. Suppose we return Pure Rotten unharmed
tomorrow night? Five thousand dollars for our trouble and
silence will be plenty.

A. Snatcher

Snatchers, Inc.
May 31

Dear Mr. Snatcher:
After due reflection I must unequivocally reject your last suggestion and repeat my own suggestion that you dispose of the
matter at hand in your own fashion. I see no need for further
correspondence in this matter.

Clark Forthcue

June 1

Clark Forthcue:
There has been a take over of the bord of Snatchers, Inc. and
my too vise presidents who haven't got a choice agree with
me, the new president. I have all the carbon copys of
Snatchers, Inc. letters to you and all your letters back to us.
The law is very seveer with kidnappers and even more seveer
with people who want to kill kids.

But the law is not so seveer with kids, in fact will forgive
them for almost anything if it is there first ofense. If you don't
want these letters given to the police you will leave 500,000
dollars tomorrow night in Garvers old mailbox. I meen it.
Small bils is what we want but some fiftys and hundreds will
be o.k.

Sinseerly,
Pure Rotten

Computers Don't Argue

Gordon R. Dickson

TREASURE BOOK CLUB
PLEASE DO NOT FOLD,
SPINDLE, OR MUTILATE
THIS CARD

MR WALTER A. CHILD   Balance: $4.98
Dear Customer: Enclosed in your latest book selection,
Kidnapped, by Robert Louis Stevenson.

437 Woodlawn Drive
Panduk, Michigan
Nov. 16, 198–

Treasure Book Club
1823 Mandy Street
Chicago, Illinois

Dear Sirs:

I wrote you recently about the computer punch card you sent, billing me for *Kim*, by Rudyard Kipling. I did not open the package containing it until I had already mailed you my check for the amount on the card. On opening the package, I found the book missing half its pages. I sent it back to you, requesting either another copy or my money back, Instead, you have sent me a copy of *Kidnapped*, by Robert Louis Stevenson. Will you please straighten this out?

I hereby return the copy of *Kidnapped*.

Sincerely yours,
Walter A. Child

TREASURE BOOK CLUB
SECOND NOTICE
PLEASE DO NOT FOLD,
SPINDLE, OR MUTILATE THIS CARD

Mr. Walter A. Child   Balance: $4.98
For *Kidnapped*, by Robert Louis Stevenson
(If remittance has been made for the above, please disregard this notice)

437 Woodlawn Drive
Panduk, Michigan
Jan. 21, 198–

Treasure Book Club
1823 Mandy Street
Chicago, Illinois

Dear Sirs:

May I direct your attention to my letter of November 16, 198–? You are still continuing to dun me with computer punch cards for a book I did not order. Whereas, actually, it is your company that owes me money.

> Sincerely yours,
> Walter A. Child

～

> Treasure Book Club
> 1823 Mandy Street
> Chicago, Illinois
> Feb. 1, 198–

Mr. Walter A. Child
437 Woodlawn Drive
Panduk, Michigan

Dear Mr. Child:

We have sent you a number of reminders concerning an amount owing to us as a result of book purchases you have made from us. This amount, which is $4.98, is now long overdue.

This situation is disappointing to us, particularly since there was no hesitation on our part in extending you credit at the time original arrangements for these purchases were made by you. If we do not receive payment in full by return mail, we will be forced to turn the matter over to a collection agency.

> Very truly yours,
> Samuel P. Grimes
> Collection Mgr.

～

> 437 Woodlawn Drive
> Panduk, Michigan
> Feb. 5, 198–

Dear Mr. Grimes:

Will you stop sending me punch cards and form letters and make me some kind of a direct answer from a human being?

I don't owe you money. *You* owe me money. Maybe I should turn your company over to a collection agency.

> Walter A. Child

～

FEDERAL COLLECTION OUTFIT
88 Prince Street
Chicago, Illinois
Feb. 28, 198–

Mr. Walter A. Child
437 Woodlawn Drive
Panduk, Michigan

Dear Mr. Child:
Your account with the Treasure Book Club, of $4.98 plus interest and charges, has been turned over to our agency for collection. The amount due is now $6.83. Please send your check for this amount or we shall be forced to take immediate action.

Jacob N. Harshe
Vice President

FEDERAL COLLECTION OUTFIT
88 Prince Street
Chicago, Illinois
April 8, 198–

Mr. Walter A. Child
437 Woodlawn Drive
Panduk, Michigan

Dear Mr. Child:
You have seen fit to ignore our courteous requests to settle your long overdue account with Treasure Book Club, which is now, with accumulated interest and charges, in the amount of $7.51.
If payment in full is not forthcoming by April 11, 198–, we will be forced to turn the matter over to our attorneys for immediate court action.

Ezekiel B. Harshe
President

MALONEY, MAHONEY, MacNAMARA and PRUITT
Attorneys

89 Prince Street
Chicago, Illinois
April 29, 198–

Mr. Walter A. Child
437 Woodlawn Drive
Panduk, Michigan

Dear Mr. Child:

Your indebtedness to the Treasure Book Club has been referred to us for legal action to collect.

This indebtedness is now in the amount of $10.01. If you will send us this amount so that we may receive it before May 5, 198–, the matter may be satisfied. However, if we do not receive satisfaction in full by that date, we will take steps to collect through the courts.

I am sure you will see the advantage of avoiding a judgment against you, which as a matter of record would do lasting harm to your credit rating.

Very truly yours,
Hagthorpe M. Pruitt Jr.
Attorney at Law

~

437 Woodlawn Drive
Panduk, Michigan
May 4, 198–

Mr. Hagthorpe M. Pruitt Jr.
Maloney, Mahoney, MacNamara and Pruitt
89 Prince Street
Chicago, Illinois

Dear Mr. Pruitt:

You don't know what a pleasure it is to me in this matter to get a letter from a live human being to whom I can explain the situation.

This whole matter is silly. I explained it fully in my letters to the Treasure Book Company. But I might as well have been trying to explain to the computer that puts out their punch cards, for all the good it seemed to do. Briefly, what happened was I ordered a copy of *Kim*, by Rudyard Kipling, for $4.98. When I opened the package they sent me, I found the book had only half its pages, but I'd previously mailed a check to pay them for the book.

I sent the book back to them, asking either for a whole copy or my money back. Instead, they sent me a copy of *Kidnapped*, by Robert Louis Stevenson—which I had not ordered; and for which they have been trying to collect from me.

Meanwhile, I am still waiting for the money back that they owe me for the copy of *Kim* that I didn't get. That's the whole story. Maybe you can help me straighten them out.

Relievedly yours,
Walter A. Child

P.S.: I also sent them back their copy of *Kidnapped*, as soon as I got it, but it hasn't seemed to help. They have never even acknowledged getting it back.

⌒

MALONEY, MAHONEY, MacNAMARA and PRUITT
Attorneys

89 Prince Street
Chicago, Illinois
May 9, 198–

Mr. Walter A. Child
437 Woodlawn Drive
Panduk, Michigan

Dear Mr. Child:

I am in possession of no information indicating that any item purchased by you from the Treasure Book Club has been returned.

I would hardly think that, if the case had been as you stated, the Treasure Book Club would have retained us to collect the amount owing from you.

If I do not receive payment in full within three days, by May 12, 198–, we will be forced to take legal action.

Very truly yours,
Hagthorpe M. Pruitt, Jr.

~

COURT OF MINOR CLAIMS
Chicago, Illinois

Mr. Walter A. Child:
437 Woodlawn Drive
Panduk, Michigan

Be informed that a judgment was taken and entered against you in this court this day of May 26, 198–, in the amount of $15.66 including court costs.

Payment in satisfaction of this judgment may be made to this court or to the adjudged creditor. In the case of payment being made to the creditor, a release should be obtained from the creditor and filed with this court in order to free you of legal obligation in connection with this judgment. Under the recent Reciprocal Claims Act, if you are a citizen of a different state, a duplicate claim may be automatically entered and judged against you in your own state so that collection may be made there as well as in the State of Illinois.

~

COURT OF MINOR CLAIMS
Chicago, Illinois
PLEASE DO NOT FOLD,
SPINDLE, OR MUTILATE
THIS CARD

Judgment was passed this day of May 27, 198–, under Statute 941.

Against: Child, Walter A. of 437 Woodlawn Drive, Panduk, Michigan. Pray to enter a duplicate claim for judgment.

In: Picayune Court—Panduk, Michigan

For Amount: $15.66

~

437 Woodlawn Drive
Panduk, Michigan
May 31, 198–

Samuel P. Grimes
Vice President, Treasure Book Club
1823 Mandy Street
Chicago, Illinois

Grimes:

   This business has gone far enough. I've got to come down
to Chicago on business of my own tomorrow. I'll see you then
and we'll get this straightened out once and for all, about who
owes what to whom, and how much!

Yours,
Walter A. Child

From the desk of the Clerk
Picayune Court

June 1, 198–

Harry:

   The attached computer card from Chicago's Minor Claims
Court against A. Walter has a 1500-series Statute number on
it. That puts it over in criminal with you, rather than civil,
with me. So I herewith submit it for your computer instead of
mine. How's business?

Joe

CRIMINAL RECORDS
Panduk, Michigan
PLEASE DO NOT FOLD,
SPINDLE, OR MUTILATE
THIS CARD
Convicted: (Child) A. Walter
On: May 26,198–
Address: 437 Woodlawn Drive,
Panduk, Mich.

Statute: 1566 (Corrected) 1567
Crime: Kidnap
Date: Nov. 16, 198–
Notes: At large. To be picked up at once.
POLICE DEPARTMENT, PANDUK, MICHIGAN. TO POLICE DEPART-
MENT, CHICAGO, ILLINOIS. CONVICTED SUBJECT A. (COMPLETE
FIRST NAME UNKNOWN) WALTER, SOUGHT HERE IN CONNECTION
REF. YOUR NOTIFICATION OF JUDGMENT FOR KIDNAP OF CHILD
NAMED ROBERT LOUIS STEVENSON, ON NOV. 16, 198–. INFORMA-
TION HERE INDICATES SUBJECT FLED HIS RESIDENCE, AT 437
WOODLAWN DRIVE, PANDUK, AND MAY BE AGAIN IN YOUR AREA.
POSSIBLE CONTACT IN YOUR AREA: THE TREASURE BOOK CLUB,
1823 MANDY STREET, CHICAGO, ILLINOIS. SUBJECT NOT KNOWN
TO BE ARMED, BUT PRESUMED DANGEROUS. PICK UP AND HOLD,
ADVISING US OF CAPTURE . . .

TO POLICE DEPARTMENT, PANDUK, MICHIGAN. REFERENCE, YOUR
REQUEST TO PICK UP AND HOLD A. (COMPLETE FIRST NAME
UNKNOWN) WALTER, WANTED IN PANDUK ON STATUTE 1567,
CRIME OF KIDNAPPING.
SUBJECT ARRESTED AT OFFICES OF TREASURE BOOK CLUB, OPER-
ATING THERE UNDER ALIAS WALTER ANTHONY CHILD AND
ATTEMPTING TO COLLECT $4.98 FROM ONE SAMUEL P. GRIMES,
EMPLOYEE OF THAT COMPANY.
DISPOSAL: HOLDING FOR YOUR ADVICE.

POLICE DEPARTMENT, PANDUK, MICHIGAN, TO POLICE DEPART-
MENT CHICAGO, ILLINOIS
REF: A. WALTER (ALIAS WALTER ANTHONY CHILD) SUBJECT
WANTED FOR CRIME OF KIDNAP, YOUR AREA, REF: YOUR COM-
PUTER PUNCH CARD NOTIFICATION OF JUDGMENT, DATED MAY
27, 198–. COPY OUR CRIMINAL RECORDS PUNCH CARD HERE-
WITH FORWARDED TO YOUR COMPUTER SECTION.

⁓

CRIMINAL RECORDS
Panduk, Michigan
PLEASE DO NOT FOLD,
SPINDLE, OR MUTILATE
THIS CARD

SUBJECT (CORRECTION—OMITTED RECORD SUPPLIED)
APPLICABLE STATUTE NO. 1567
JUDGMENT NO. 456789
TRIAL RECORD: APPARENTLY MISFILED AND UNAVAILABLE
DIRECTION: TO APPEAR FOR SENTENCING BEFORE JUDGE JOHN
ALEXANDER MCDIVOT, COURTROOM A, JUNE 9, 198–

~

From the Desk of
Judge Alexander J. McDivot

June 2, 198–

Dear Tony:

I've got an adjudged criminal coming up before me for sentencing Thursday morning—but the trial transcript is apparently misfiled.

I need some kind of information (Ref. A. Walter—Judgment No. 456789, Criminal). For example, what about the victim of the kidnapping? Was victim harmed?

Jack McDivot

~

June 3, 198–

Records Search Unit
Re: Ref. Judgment No. 456789—was victim harmed?

Tonio Malagasi
Records Division

~

June 3, 198–

To: United States Statistics Office
Attn: Information Section
Subject: Robert Louis Stevenson
Query: Information concerning

Records Search Unit
Criminal Records Division
Police Department
Chicago, Ill.

June 5, 198–

To: Records Search Unit
Criminal Records Division
Police Department
Chicago, Illinois
Subject: Your query re Robert Louis Stevenson (File no. 189623)
Action: Subject deceased. Age at death, 44 yrs. Further information requested?

A. K.
Information Section
U.S. Statistics Office

June 6, 198–

To: United States Statistics Office
Attn: Information Division
Subject: Re: File no. 189623
   No further information required.

Thank you.
Records Search Unit
Criminal Records Division
Police Department
Chicago, Illinois

June 7, 198–

To: Tonio Malagasi
Records Division
Re: Ref: judgment No. 456789—victim is dead.
Records Search Unit

June 7, 198–

To: Judge Alexander J. McDivot's Chambers
Dear Jack:
Ref: Judgment No. 456789. The victim in this kidnap case was apparently slain.

From the strange lack of background information on the killer and his victim, as well as the victim's age, this smells to me like a gangland killing. This for your information. Don't quote me. It seems to me, though, that Stevenson—the victim—has a name that rings a faint bell with me. Possibly, one of the East Coast Mob, since the association comes back to me as something about pirates—possibly New York dockage hijackers—and something about buried loot.

As I say, above is only speculation for your private guidance. Any time I can help . . .

Best,
Tony Malagasi
Records Division

MICHAEL R. REYNOLDS
Attorney at Law

49 Water Street
Chicago, Illinois
June 8, 198–

Dear Tim:
Regrets: I can't make the fishing trip. I've been court-appointed here to represent a man about to be sentenced tomorrow on a kidnapping charge.

Ordinarily, I might have tried to beg off, and McDivot, who is doing the sentencing, would probably have turned me loose. But this is the damndest thing you ever heard of.

The man being sentenced has apparently been not only charged, but adjudged guilty as a result of a comedy of errors too long to go into here. He not only isn't guilty—he's got the best case I ever heard of for damages against one of the larger book clubs headquartered here in Chicago. And that's a case I wouldn't mind taking on.

It's inconceivable—but damnably possible, once you stop to think of it in this day and age of machine-made records—that a completely innocent man could be put in this position.

There shouldn't be much to it. I've asked to see McDivot tomorrow before the time of sentencing, and it'll just be a matter of explaining to him. Then I can discuss the damage suit with my freed client at his leisure.

Fishing next weekend?

Yours,
Mike

~

MICHAEL R. REYNOLDS
Attorney at Law

49 Water Street
Chicago, Illinois
June 10

Dear Tim:

In haste—

No fishing this coming week either. Sorry.

You won't believe it. My innocent-as-a-lamb-and-I'm-not-kidding client has just been sentenced to death for first-degree murder in connection with the death of his kidnap victim.

Yes, I explained the whole thing to McDivot. And when he explained his situation to me, I nearly fell out of my chair.

It wasn't a matter of my not convincing him. It took less than three minutes to show him that my client should never have been within the walls of the County Jail for a second. But—get this—McDivot couldn't do a thing about it.

The point is, my man had already been judged guilty according to the computerized records. In the absence of a trial record—of course there never was one (but that's something I'm not free to explain to you now)—the judge has to go by what records are available. And in the case of an adjudged prisoner, McDivot's only legal choice was whether to sentence to life imprisonment, or execution.

The death of the kidnap victim, according to the statute, made the death penalty mandatory. Under the new laws governing length of time for appeal, which has been shortened because of the new system of computerizing records, to force an elimination of unfair delay and mental anguish to those condemned, I have five days in which to file an appeal, and ten to have it acted on.

Needless to say, I am not going to monkey with an appeal. I'm going directly to the governor for a pardon—after which we will get this farce reversed. McDivot has already written the governor, also, explaining that his sentence was ridiculous, but that he had no choice. Between the two of us, we ought to have a pardon in short order.

Then, I'll make the fur fly . . .

And we'll get in some fishing.

Best,
Mike

⌒

OFFICE OF THE
GOVERNOR OF ILLINOIS

June 17, 198–

Mr. Michael R. Reynolds
49 Water Street
Chicago, Illinois

Dear Mr. Reynolds:

In reply to your query about the request for pardon for Walter A. Child (A. Walter), may I inform you that the governor is still on his trip with the Midwest Governors Committee, examining the Wall in Berlin. He should be back next Friday.

I will bring your request and letters to his attention the minute he returns.

Very truly yours,
Clara B. Jilks
Secretary to the Governor

⌒

June 27, 198–

Michael R. Reynolds
49 Water Street
Chicago, Illinois

Dear Mike:

Where is that pardon?

My execution date is only five days from now!

Walt

⌒

June 29, 198–

Walter A. Child (A. Walter)
Cell Block E
Illinois State Penitentiary
Joliet, Illinois

Dear Walt:

The governor returned, but was called away immediately to the White House in Washington to give his views on inter-state sewage.

I am camping on his doorstep and will be on him the moment he arrives here.

Meanwhile, I agree with you about the seriousness of the situation. The warden at the prison there, Mr. Allen Magruder, will bring this letter to you and have a private talk with you. I urge you to listen to what he has to say; and I enclose letters from your family also urging you to listen to Warden Magruder.

Yours,
Mike

June 30, 198–

Michael R. Reynolds
49 Water Street
Chicago, Illinois

Dear Mike: (This letter being smuggled out by Warden Magruder)

As I was talking to Warden Magruder in my cell here, news was brought to him that the governor has at last returned for a while to Illinois, and will be in his office early tomorrow morning, Friday. So you will have time to get the pardon signed by him and delivered to the prison in time to stop my execution on Saturday.

Accordingly, I have turned down the warden's kind offer of a chance to escape; since he told me he could by no means guarantee to have all the guards out of my way when I tried it; and there was a chance of my being killed escaping.

But now everything will straighten itself out. Actually, an experience as fantastic as this had to break down sometime under its own weight.

Best,
Walt

~

FOR THE SOVEREIGN STATE OF ILLINOIS, I Hubert Daniel Willikens, Governor of the State of Illinois, and invested with the authority and powers appertaining thereto, including the power to pardon those in my judgment wrongfully convicted or otherwise deserving of executive mercy, this day of July 1, 198–, do announce and proclaim that Walter A. Child (A. Walter), now in custody as a consequence of erroneous conviction upon a crime of which he is entirely innocent, is fully and freely pardoned of said crime. And I do direct the necessary authorities having custody of the said Walter A. Child (A. Walter) in whatever place or places he may be held, to immediately free, release, and allow unhindered departure to him . . .

Interdepartmental Routing Service
PLEASE DO NOT FOLD,
MUTILATE, OR SPINDLE
THIS CARD

Failure to route Document properly.
To: Governor Hubert Daniel Willikens
Re: Pardon issued to Walter A. Child, July 1, 198–
Dear State Employee:

You have failed to attach your Routing Number.

PLEASE: Resubmit document with this card and Form 876, explaining your authority for placing a TOP RUSH category on this document. Form 876 must be signed by your Departmental Superior.

RESUBMIT ON: Earliest possible date ROUTING SER-VICE office is open. In this case, Tuesday, July 5, 198–.

WARNING: Failure to submit Form 876 WITH THE SIGNATURE OF YOUR SUPERIOR may make you liable to prosecution for misusing a Service of the State Government. A warrant may be issued for your arrest.

There are NO exceptions. YOU have been WARNED.

A Letter to Amy

Joyce Harrington

DEAR AMY,
DID YOU get my last letter? Why don't you write? Just a note saying Hi, Pop, would be nice. The circus is in town. I'm not planning to go, but it reminds me of the time you and me went. Remember the clown who kept tripping over the little white dog? Every time he fell down, you laughed and laughed. I guess you're too big for circuses now. Why don't you send me a picture? I don't have even one. I guess maybe your mother is taking these letters and not letting you have them. If that's what she's doing, I just want to tell her it's not right. No matter what I did or didn't do, you're still my little girl and I love you. And I miss you."

Gene-Boy signed the letter "Love, Daddy," and folded it up. It wasn't much of a letter, he knew, but he'd worn himself out struggling to write long letters to both of them about how much he'd changed and what he was doing and how Jesus had come into his life and made a new man of him. Letters that just seemed to disappear into the blue and never brought back an answer.

No, he wasn't planning to go to the circus. He wasn't planning to go anywhere, just to the machine shop and back again, listen to the preacher on Sunday, in between read the Bible after supper and sometimes the

225

newspaper. That's where he'd seen the ad for the circus. It reminded him so much of the old days, and Amy's little fingers digging into his wrist while she squirmed and giggled and tried not to miss a single thing going on in the dinky little ring spread out before them. He could feel those little fingers on his wrist like burning tips of cigarettes.

Gene-Boy didn't smoke anymore, and that was a blessing. He didn't drink, either, but he didn't have much choice about that, so it didn't count as a full-fledged blessing. It was a good thing, though. If you counted it all up, it was probably drink that got him where he was today. Drink and his own evil ways. Preacher made him see that. Praise the Lord.

He wrote Amy's name and address on the envelope, slid the letter inside, and stuck his last red, white, and blue stamp up in the corner. Lying down on his bunk, he tried to tune out the sounds around him so he could think about Georgina. How pretty she was back when he first caught sight of her. Wild, too. She'd do any crazy thing on a dare. Like the time she climbed out on the courthouse flagpole and stayed there until the Fire Department came and got her down. Got her picture in the paper for that one. Asked why she did it, she said, "Just wanted to liven things up a bit."

That was Georgina, always livening things up. Singing in the morning, dancing all night. Laughing all day long, at everything and everybody. They were quite a pair in those days, Gene-Boy and Georgina, always doing something outrageous.

And when the black mood came on him, it was only Georgina who could travel the road with him and bring him back alive. He was always sorry later for the things he did to her those times. The black eyes and fat lips, the scar where she had to have her hand stitched up, the names he called her and the things he blamed on her. She always seemed to know that he didn't mean them, that it was his own self he was fighting with, the part of him that had no hope and nothing to live for. Three times she'd kept him from killing himself.

All that was over now.

Gene-Boy reached for his Bible but didn't open it. The lights would be going out soon. He didn't need the lights to read what he wanted to read. He knew it by heart. "The heart of the sons of men is full of evil, and madness is in their heart while they live, and after that they go to the dead." Hard words, but true. Too true.

Preacher had told him about that one, old Ecclesiastes, and made him see what it meant—to him, Gene-Boy, personally. Preacher said that all the time he was walking around the earth hell-raising and being bad, he was filling up his heart with evil and turning himself into a living dead man. And the black mood was just the stored-up evil in his heart tempting him toward the greatest sin of all, turning himself into a *dead* dead man. Preacher was right: Without hope, a man might just as well be dead. Although Gene-Boy still thought that the drink and the war and no decent job went a long ways toward bringing on the gloom. Or at least bringing on the hell-raising that brought on the gloom.

He picked up his letter to Amy and ran his finger along the unsealed flap of the envelope. Maybe he wouldn't send it after all. None of the others had done any good. Amy would be what now, twelve or thirteen? Old enough to write to him if she wanted to, even without Georgina knowing about it. Old enough to find out where he was if Georgina wouldn't tell her. Did she ever ask about him? Did she remember him at all? All these years and no word.

The lights went out as they always did, without warning. And as always the men on either side of him groaned and some of them stamped their feet. Gene-Boy welcomed the darkness, even though it wasn't completely dark—there was always a light on in the corridor so the guards could see into the cellblock in case there was any mischief or trouble. In the darkness, Gene-Boy could rest his eyes and his mind from the gray plainness of day-after-day and conjure up pictures that were more pleasing.

He made a picture of himself getting off the Greyhound bus, still in his uniform, so glad to see home again even though there wasn't anybody there to meet him. He hadn't let anybody know he was coming—he didn't want any fuss made over him, even though he had medals and wound scars and papers that said he was a hero. Still and all, he was a trifle disappointed that no one took any notice of him when he stepped off that bus right in the middle of the town's suppertime. He'd been proud to go to Vietnam and wanted to be proud of coming back. Georgina would have been proud of him.

But he didn't even know Georgina on that day—didn't know she was working in that cocktail lounge catty-corner across from the bus depot, just waiting on the day when he would come staggering through the door and order up a beer for himself. That day wouldn't come for some little while yet. In the picture in his mind of the day of his homecoming, Georgina wasn't in it yet and the town was ordinary—changed but still the same, with the streetlights just coming on in the late purple dusk. It was summer and hot, with the smell of car exhaust hanging heavy over the street. Fifteen years later, he could still smell that evening air.

He had decided to treat himself to a taxi. The driver was a black man—young, about his own age—with a thick neck and big shoulders like a football player. The neck and shoulders made Gene-Boy feel he had to come on strong.

"Boy, you know the way out to the Watkins place?"

"Never heard of it."

"You know Twelve Mile Road?"

"I know it."

"Well, just keep going out it till I tell you to stop."

"How far?"

"Till we get there."

"Five miles? Ten miles? Two hundred miles?"

"What the hell difference does it make?"

"More than ten miles, I got to charge you double."

"You shouldn't charge me at all. See this uniform? Last week this uniform was all covered up with jungle slime and gook blood. This uniform's seen action."

"Was you in it at the time?"

"Now what kind of remark is that?" Gene-Boy recalled the feeling of hurt that made him want to haul out the picture he had of himself standing over that dead Vietcong who'd tried to sneak up on him and his buddies. He'd saved his buddies' lives and he wasn't ashamed of the fact. "You some kind of peace freak?"

"Easy, man. I been there. It don't buy free taxi rides or free nothing else. Now how far you be wanting to go?"

Gene-Boy scrunched down in the back seat and muttered, "Nine and a half miles."

The driver laughed. "All right," he said, "I won't be charging you double, you being a fellow victim. But you understand I got to come back empty and that uses up gas."

"I ain't no victim," Gene-Boy muttered.

Skip over the ride out of town, past scenes Gene-Boy remembered as if they'd been part of someone else's life—gas stations, drive-ins, the bowling alley, car lots—thinning out into patchy fields and junk yards. It wasn't pretty, not in the way he'd remembered it as pretty while he was over in the heat and the stink. Driving past it, looking at it, seeing the pale, beefy people moving about in it, he yearned for the dense green he'd left behind and the thin, brown women who'd giggled at his jokes. It was peculiar. He didn't understand what was going on, except that he didn't seem to belong in either place. Skip over that part.

The house, when they pulled up in front of it, looked small and mean. Even in the gathering darkness, he could see that it needed paint. The lights were on and Gene-Boy was grateful for that. What if nobody'd been home? He paid the driver and gave him a good tip. The driver got out to help him with his duffel bag.

"Don't bother," said Gene-Boy. "I hauled it half across the world. I guess I can haul it into my own house."

"You ever want to talk about things," the driver said, "you mostly can find me by the bus station."

"Don't guess I will," said Gene-Boy. "What's there to talk about?"

The driver shrugged. "Some guys have trouble fitting themselves back in. Sometimes we get together and just talk about it. It helps."

"I won't be needing any help," said Gene-Boy, and he stomped up onto the porch, deliberately making noise so they'd know he'd arrived.

The taxi drove away.

Gene-Boy tried to open the front door. It was locked. That made him mad. Since when did they lock the door against him? He kicked at the door and rattled the knob. Inside the house, a dog started up. Since when did they get a dog? They hadn't written to him much. His mother had sometimes, mostly about the weather and the operations she was always having. She'd never mentioned a dog. He hadn't had a letter in about six months. He hadn't written a letter in longer than that.

The dog was barking on the other side of the door now, scraping at it with hard, quick claws. He heard his father's voice yell, "Shut up! I'm coming!"

Gene-Boy waited, trying on a smile, feeling silly and changing it to a stern, serious look. Save the smile for his mother. She'd be glad to

see him. She'd have fun coaxing him to eat. He wasn't sure how his
father would be. The old man hadn't thought much of his going into
the army. He never did think much of anything Gene-Boy thought of
on his own. Always had to be one-up on him.

The door opened and the dog shot out onto the porch, a
medium-sized yellow dog, fat and bare-looking. It yipped and growled,
making nervous, feinting lunges at his shoes. His father stood looking at
him. Despite himself, Gene-Boy felt a smile spreading his lips. He
couldn't help it, even though it made him feel lower than the nasty yellow dog.

His father said, "Oh, it's you. I might have known. I had a dream
the other night."

"Can I come in?" Gene-Boy asked.

"I guess you better. Don't plan on staying, though."

Gene-Boy edged past his father and dumped his duffel bag in the
hall. Here again, everything looked the same but different. Smaller.
He peered into the front room. Same furniture, same rug, same picture
of a sad-eyed clown hanging over the couch—everything worn and
dusty, newspapers and stuff all over everything. His mother would
never let things get that way.

"Where's Ma?" he asked.

"Gone."

"Gone? Gone where?" Surely she would have written to him if she
was going somewhere. People like his mother and father didn't get
divorced. They'd put in too many years together. His mother'd been
born again. Born-again Christians stuck it out, even if it got hairy.
And sometimes it did. Gene-Boy'd seen his father smack his mother
around ever since he was a little kid. But she'd never leave him.
"Where's she gone to?" he asked again.

"She died. I guess nobody told you."

Gene-Boy just stood there. The yellow dog trotted across the front
room and jumped up onto the couch as if he belonged there. His
mother wouldn't have allowed that.

From the kitchen, a voice called out, "Who is that, Eugene?"

His father shouted back, "Just my son. I told you about him."

Gene-Boy heard slippers slapping against the hall floor. He looked
up and saw a youngish woman ambling toward him. Long yellow hair
same color as the dog's hanging down around a fat, pale face; big green

eyes, bulgy like a frog's, staring at him; baggy jeans and a billowing flowered smock. Was she just fat or was she pregnant?

"This my wife," his father said. "Sandra."

"How-do," Sandra said. "Stay for supper? I'll throw in another TV dinner."

"Thanks," said Gene-Boy. "Pleased to meet you."

Sandra smiled. "Your daddy didn't tell me you was so good-looking. But he's a handsome man himself, so it makes sense."

Gene-Boy looked at his father. The old man was grinning fit to burst. The old fool. Him, handsome? Some people'll believe anything. Sandra slip-slopped back toward the kitchen.

"See why you can't plan on staying?" his father said. "We'll be needing your room. Already got a crib in there."

"When did my mother die?" Gene-Boy asked.

"Oh, four, five months ago. It was real quick. She didn't suffer much."

"When's the baby due?"

"Any minute now." His father smirked. "Never thought I'd be a daddy again. Your poor mother was too sickly for much of that."

"When did you and Sandra get married?"

"Matter of fact, it was just last week. Thought we better do it before the baby came. If we'd known you was coming, we could've held off. You could've been best man."

"How long have you and Sandra—?"

"Couple or three years now. Oh, don't go getting upset. Your mother never knew anything about it. But even if she did, she wouldn't have minded. After all those operations, all she wanted was me to leave her alone. There wasn't much left of her there at the end."

"What if she hadn't died? What would you and Sandra have done?"

"Nothing, I guess. I mean, she would still be having the baby and I would be going out to see her just like I been doing. It's a lot better this way."

"I guess so," said Gene-Boy. "Well, is it okay if I sleep here tonight? I sent the taxi back to town."

"You'll have to bed down on the couch. I sold your bed."

"I've slept in worse places."

His father laughed, false hearty. "I bet you have. I just bet you have. That army life ain't no picnic, I guess you found out."

"No picnic," Gene-Boy echoed.

GENE-BOY GOT himself a room in town up over the Tulip Tree Cafe, next to the newspaper office. The room smelt of all the home-cooking that had ever been done in the Tulip Tree, fifty years' worth of chicken grease and boiled greens. Just breathing it, Gene-Boy hardly had to eat, but he went down to the cafe every evening and ate what he'd been smelling. Looked up some of his old buddies and found out that one of them, Roy Blanchard, was working for the newspaper, writing up house fires and automobile accidents on the interchange, once in a while a murder or a suicide. Roy took Gene-Boy home to meet his wife and little boy. It was a pretty life, safe and comfortable, and it made Gene-Boy mad. While he'd been off in the jungle, his good old buddy Roy Blanchard was living the good life and making a place for himself. And now Gene-Boy couldn't get any kind of job that was worth having.

Not that he didn't try. He took it into his mind that after all the filth and mud he'd been through, he wanted a clean job. He wanted to wear a suit and a tie. He bought himself a Sears, Roebuck outfit, shoes and all, and wore it into two banks, one insurance office, the town's only travel agency, a bunch of real-estate sales offices, and a place that sold cemetery plots. He got the impression that the people he saw couldn't wait for him to leave so they could bust out laughing at him, although one sweet-faced old lady advised him to get himself into the community college and learn something. "To make yourself more marketable," she'd said. But what would he do in college with a bunch of kids when he was a man and had been doing a man's work in Vietnam?

Roy Blanchard offered to put in a word for him at the newspaper. He could drive a truck, couldn't he? But Gene-Boy knew he couldn't stand that, Roy writing the stories on the front page and him trucking the bundled newspapers all over town and out into the countryside. He was any man's equal and certainly Roy's, and he wouldn't be beholden for crumbs.

The more he got turned down, the madder Gene-Boy got. His money was running out. His old car—at least his father hadn't sold *that*—needed new tires. And to top it all off, Sandra had popped out a pair of twins, blond-haired little boys, and he was expected to act like a big brother to them. Presents and such. Say how cute they were. Otherwise, he wouldn't be welcome to visit his own old home. He stopped going out there. Couldn't stand to see the old man behaving like a frisky young stallion, couldn't stand the way he googled and gaggled over them babies. Nothing was turning out the way Gene-Boy thought it would.

Long about that time, he met Georgina. Just when he was thinking about leaving town and trying his luck someplace else, Texas or California, he found himself outside the bus depot one evening and there was that same taxi waiting for a passenger. The driver spotted him and called out.

"Hey, man. How's it going?"

Gene-Boy's first instinct was to tell a glowing tale of opportunity about to strike and great wealth about to fall into his lap. But the taxi driver's brown eyes took in his cheap polyester finery and the scuff marks on his shoes, and Gene-Boy knew he couldn't carry off the lie.

"Not so hot," Gene-Boy said, leaning on the door of the taxi. "Seems like nobody cares."

"Having yourself a little pity party?" the driver inquired.

Gene-Boy's anger, never very far from the surface these days, flared. "I don't have to listen to that. You wasn't in that cab, I'd punch you right through the sidewalk."

"Hold on," the driver said. "No call to get righteous. What makes you think anybody's supposed to care about you?"

"Huh?" Gene-Boy hadn't thought about that. He'd just assumed that people would be falling all over themselves to give him, the returned hero, a fine job. When it didn't happen, he didn't ask himself why not. He just got madder and madder.

"I need another driver," the black man said. "You got a driver's license?"

"Well, sure," Gene-Boy said. "What do you think?"

"Well, how about it?"

"You mean me work for you?"

"What I mean."

"You own this cab?"

"This and four others. One of them's sitting back in the garage 'cause one of my drivers quit on me. So how about it?"

"Well, I don't know," said Gene-Boy, confused over certain feelings he didn't want to look at too closely.

"Bother you to work for a black man?" the driver asked.

"No, not a bit," Gene-Boy said too quickly. But that was part of it. The other part was that driving a taxi wasn't exactly his idea of a fine, clean job. It wasn't dirty work, like road-paving or trash-hauling, but it sure didn't require a suit and tie. Still and all—"I'll think it over," Gene-Boy said.

"Well, don't think too long." The driver handed him a printed card. "If you want the job, show up here in the morning. I need somebody right away."

Gene-Boy read the card. "Is that you?" he asked. "Harlan W. Harrison?"

The driver nodded. "Everybody calls me Harry."

Gene-Boy stuck his hand through the cab's open window. "Eugene P. Watkins Jr.," he said, shaking hands. "Everybody calls me Gene-Boy. Could be I'll see you in the A.M."

"I hope so, Gene-Boy."

"Thanks, Harry."

Gene-Boy walked away from the taxi shaking and dry-mouthed, and wondering why he should be so. He couldn't be mad at Harry for offering him a job. He could be mad at himself for even thinking of taking it. And he knew he would take it. He wasn't fit for anything else. He crossed the street, and as soon as he saw the cocktail lounge he knew that he craved a cold beer more than anything else in the world.

Inside the darkened room, a jukebox wailed an old Hank Williams tune. It suited his mood. Old Hank Williams knew all about the demons that bedeviled men in their souls. Not caring much for the easy companionship of the bar, Gene-Boy sprawled into the first empty booth he saw and blinked his eyes to accustom them to the gloom. Pretty soon a waitress came up to him and said, "Yes, sir?"

Her face floated above him, pale and angelic and sort of misty. He saw black hair, sleek and shiny, and dark eyes that sprang out at him and pinned him to the crumbly leatherette of the booth.

"A beer," he said. "Draft."

She went away, and he watched her go. She was small and trim. Her rear end, in tight jeans, was taut and smooth, but she didn't wiggle the way some girls thought was sexy. Her back was straight and her shoulders looked strong and proud. Gene-Boy sighed.

She brought his beer and a small plastic bowl of pretzel sticks. He said, "Thank you." She smiled.

He nodded toward the jukebox and said, "You like Hank Williams?"

"Oh, yeah," she said. "And I like the Beatles and Bob Dylan and vanilla ice cream and skinny-dipping and a lot of things I haven't even tried yet."

Gene-Boy took a swig of his beer, so cold it made his teeth ache. "How do you know you like them if you haven't tried them yet?"

"How do I know I won't?" she said. "I haven't seen you in here before."

"Could be because I never been in here before. But now I think I might be coming in here a lot."

She smiled and went away to tend to other customers.

Later, when Gene-Boy was ordering up his third beer, he asked the waitress her name.

"What you want to know that for?" she asked, not in a flirty way but kind of mean and edgy.

"Well," said Gene-Boy, feeling like fooling around and having a good time, "if I'm gonna marry you, I got to know what to call you."

"Huh!" she said. "Will you just listen to that!" But when she brought him the beer, she said, "My name's Georgina. What's yours?"

And that was how it all began. He woke up the next morning in Georgina's bed with the smell of fresh coffee nudging him to get up. She lived in a little cottage not far from the railroad station where no trains came any more. Gene-Boy had no recollection of how he'd got there, but peering out the bedroom window he saw his old car parked beside the house and in the near distance the abandoned redbrick station building. He remembered that he was supposed to turn up at Harry's garage.

In the kitchen, he found Georgina frying up sausage. "How come you let me sleep so late?" he asked. "I got a job to go to."

"I know," she said. "You told me. It's not late. I was planning to bring you breakfast in bed."

Gene-Boy didn't know what to say. Nobody'd been nice to him in so long, he didn't know how to behave when it happened. "I got to go," he said and, looking for an excuse, he brushed at his rumpled suit. "I got to go change my clothes."

"Well, take a sausage sandwich with you," she said. And she began slapping the fried sausage patties between two hunks of bread.

The last thing Gene-Boy heard as he left the house was her sweet voice singing "Careless Love."

HARLAN W. HARRISON put him to work that very morning. He showed him how to work the car radio and the taximeter, and told him the best places to wait for fares: the mall outside town, the two movie theaters when the pictures let out, the hospital. He introduced him to his tall, skinny wife who operated the dispatcher's radio from the living room in their house next to the garage.

"Job pays two dollars an hour," Harry said.

Gene-Boy frowned.

"Plus you get to keep all tips."

Gene-Boy remembered that he'd tipped Harry real well the night he'd taken the taxi out to his father's house. If everybody tipped as well as that, he'd do all right.

But everybody didn't. Gene-Boy found that out on his very first call—a feeble old lady from one of the big houses on the hill who had to go to her doctor. Even though he helped her into the cab and out of it and was polite when she complained about the bumps in the road, all she gave him was a measly dime. That first day, Gene-Boy figured he got a good close look at human nature, and he didn't like what he saw. The women were the worst, expecting him to help them with their kids and their packages and then trying to cheat him on the fare. But the men weren't much better, accusing him of taking the long way around, or carrying on with a girl in the back seat as if he wasn't there at all. When he'd put in his eight hours, he drove back to Harry's garage in a foul temper. Mrs. Harry silently collected his money and paid him sixteen dollars out of it. That plus the tips he'd been grudgingly given made twenty dollars and change, more than he'd had in the morning. It was sure as hell no way to get rich.

"See you tomorrow," said Mrs. Harry.

"Yeah. Maybe."

He drove in his own car back downtown straight to the cocktail lounge, where he hoped to find Georgina. She wasn't there. Another girl with big wobbly bosoms and a beehive hairdo came to wait on him. He ordered a whiskey with a beer chaser. When she brought it, he asked her where Georgina was.

"Her day off," she said.

Gene-Boy felt betrayed. After last night, she could have at least told him. But he couldn't even remember what they'd done last night. All he could remember was waking up in her bed, and if he woke up there they must have done *something*. After his third or fourth whiskey, he realized that Georgina was sitting across from him in the booth.

"Where you been?" she demanded.

"Sitting right here," he said. "Where *you* been?"

"Waiting for you. I thought we had a date. You said we'd go dancing."

Gene-Boy couldn't bear to admit that he'd forgotten. "Well, let's go," he said. "I had a rough day. I needed to get a little fortified."

"Well, how about you buy me a drink? Unless you like drinking alone."

She drank her vodka and Seven-Up in little ladylike sips, but it disappeared fast enough. When she finished it, she stood up and twirled around in her high heels, sending her short skirt ballooning out like a parachute. "Let's go," she said. "I could dance all night."

Gene-Boy wasn't sure he could. The black mood was on him and all he wanted to do was smash things. People. But Georgina looked so pretty and happy. She was the only one in the world who didn't treat him mean and he wanted to please her. He crawled out of the booth and stood up, swaying and grinning.

"Pretty little thing," he said. "Let's go get married."

"Not tonight," she said. "Maybe tomorrow."

THEY DIDN'T GET married the next day or the next. They drifted through the fall and the winter, drinking, dancing, quarreling, making up. Gene-Boy moved out of his little room over the Tulip Tree Cafe and into Georgina's house. He got in fights now and then if he thought some guy was looking the wrong way at Georgina. He knew Georgina didn't invite the looks—she wasn't like that—but he blamed her for them anyway. They went ice-skating on a little pond out in the middle of nowhere and fell through the ice, but only landed knee-deep in muck that stank up their clothes like a dead squirrel when they got warmed up. Georgina laughed at everything, good times and bad times alike. Sometimes Gene-Boy wondered why she liked him so much, but he never dared to ask her. He was afraid he wouldn't like the answer. It could be she felt sorry for him.

Especially after he lost his job driving taxi for Harry Harrison for decking a drunk who was trying to pick a fight with him from the back seat. Left him sprawled in the road—with a broken jaw, as it turned out. But the guy had it coming to him. He had no call to bring the police into it and sue the cab company. Gene-Boy thought Harry should've stuck by him, but instead he turned cold and mean.

"I can't afford to keep you on," he said. "I've had complaints about you before this. You got some hell of a chip on your shoulder."

"I don't need your stinking job," Gene-Boy muttered.

"You got some unlearning to do, boy. You go around acting like you're still in the jungle."

"Seems like it to me," said Gene-Boy. "I don't let nobody crap on me."

"Live and learn," Harry said. "You got a lot of it to do."

After that, the black mood descended and wouldn't let up. He was only happy when he was with Georgina, but even that was only a glimmer of what he believed was rightfully his. He wanted a new car to drive Georgina around in. He wanted to give her a color TV in place of the old black-and-white number she had. He wanted to take her on a trip to Las Vegas with money to burn.

Not that she was asking for any of those things. Georgina never asked for anything. She always said, "If I can't get it for myself, I don't guess I need it."

She said, "You're the only thing I'll ever need."

But she still wouldn't marry him, no matter how many times he asked her. Not even after Amy was born. "I know who her daddy is," she would say, "and so does her daddy. So what do I need with a piece of legal paper?"

It hurt Gene-Boy a whole lot the day Georgina went down and got food stamps. She'd given up her waitressing job and he was glad of that. No more guys looking at her and trying to get their hands on her. But all he was ever able to do was now-and-then laboring work, the dirty jobs he'd started out sneering at. After a day's work, he could smell the dirt on himself and he despised himself for it. Georgina would make him get in the bathtub and scrub his back and tickle him and work up a big lather of sweet-smelling shampoo on his head. But the dirt smell never left his nostrils. The smell of the jungle. The smell of blood.

Amy made him happy, too, once she got past the smelly diaper, spit-up, and sour-milk stage and started walking and talking like a little lady. She would climb into his lap, unbutton and button his shirt, and whisper her breathy secrets in his ear. Sometimes it was "I love you best." Sometimes it was "Mommy is a sillyhead." And if she whispered, "Can I have a pogo stick?" or a tricycle or a Tony the Pony or a doll with real nylon hair, he'd go right off and get it for her even if he had to give up his whiskey for a week.

When Amy started kindergarten, Georgina went back to work, this time doing the breakfast and lunch shift at a nearby truckstop so she could pick up Amy after school. Gene-Boy wasn't well pleased. "Truckers are a horny bunch," he said. "You just watch your step."

"I can take care of myself," Georgina told him.

It seemed to Gene-Boy that she didn't laugh so much anymore. She didn't sing around the house. He couldn't remember when they had gone dancing. And when did all that start happening?

He said, "It's been six years, going on seven. Ain't it time we got married?" He knew he'd feel better if he was surer.

She just looked at him and went on out the door.

GENE-BOY BROODED. He drank—at home alone when he wasn't working, in his car that was practically falling apart and couldn't go as fast as he wanted it to, even when he was working from a thermos bottle he pretended was full of coffee. His only joy was Amy.

Pretty little Amy, with her black hair like Georgina's and her blue eyes like his own, climbed into his lap every night and wiggled her little butt around like a bird settling into its nest. She told him about school and the silly old teacher and the mean boys who pinched her.

One night she whispered, "Danny says I'm pretty."

Gene-Boy laughed. "Well, you sure are, honey," he said. "And who's this Danny? Is he your boyfriend?"

"Oh, no," Amy whispered. "He's Mommy's."

Gene-Boy stopped laughing. He got very quiet. Georgina was making an angry-sounding racket in the kitchen. He held Amy hard by her small shoulders and said, "He's Mommy's what?"

"What you said." Amy's voice slid into a loud whine. "Boyfriend, boyfriend, boyfriend. That hurts." She tried to wriggle out of his grip.

Gene-Boy held onto her, slapped her once to make her quiet down. "How do you know that?" he demanded.

Amy's blue eyes stared shock at him before she began blubbering. "He kisses her," she sobbed. "In the car. He gives me M&M's."

Georgina came into the room. "What's going on in here?" she asked.

Gene-Boy got up, dumping Amy to the floor. She started howling. Gene-Boy stood over her, weaving back and forth, the blackness descending blacker than ever before. "Who's this Danny?" he shouted.

Georgina looked at Amy writhing and screaming on the floor. "What did you do to her?" she shouted back.

"What have *you* been doing with her? Taking her in the car with you while you're out acting the tramp? Who's this Danny?"

Georgina's eyes shot scorn at him. She picked up Amy and crooned in her ear, "Hush, now, baby. Don't cry. Supper's ready soon and then you can have a Twinkie."

And off she went back to the kitchen without giving Gene-Boy any kind of answer.

Gene-Boy followed her, his hands tingling with the need to make things right. He found her sitting in a kitchen chair, cuddling Amy and singing to her about Mr. Frog and Miss Mousie. She heard him coming up behind her and stopped her song.

She said, "I think you better pack up your things and shift along someplace else."

She wouldn't even look at him.

"You're crazy," he said. "We're gonna get married. You been putting it off long enough."

"You're the crazy one," she said, "if you think I'd marry you. I've stood it as long as I can. It was okay when it was fun, but it hasn't been fun for a long time."

"I suppose you think you could have fun with this Danny?" he shouted at her.

But she didn't answer, just went back to her song. Amy peered up at him out of tearful blue eyes, and then stuck her tongue out.

Gene-Boy stalked off to the bedroom. The whiskey in him roiled in his stomach and fumed in his head. Okay, she wanted him to leave, he'd go. He didn't stick around where he wasn't wanted. She'd be sorry, though. She wasn't so young anymore and who'd be interested in a worn-out bag with a brat. Not even this Danny. She'd find out, and then she'd be begging him to come back. He hauled his old army duffel bag down from the top shelf of the closet. There was something in it but he didn't even look to see what it was, just started stuffing his clothes into it.

But what about Amy? If he left, he wouldn't see Amy every night. She'd be climbing into this Danny's lap and he'd be giving her M&M's. Pretty soon she'd be calling *him* Daddy. No way could Gene-Boy let that happen.

He remembered what it was that had been hiding down in the bottom of his duffel bag all these years. He up-ended the bag and dumped everything he'd packed out onto the bed. The gun plopped out last, on top of the pile of clothes. His old Colt .45, the one he'd carried all the way from Vietnam, the one that had saved his life more times than he could count. It was just as nice-looking now as it was then. He picked it up and hefted it. It felt good in his hand, just like old times. He couldn't remember if it was loaded, though. Probably not.

Gene-Boy was amazed to find three bullets in the magazine. It was like a sign. An omen. They wouldn't be there if he wasn't supposed to do what he was supposed to do. He started back to the kitchen.

GENE-BOY LICKED the flap of the envelope of his letter to Amy. The picture show was over for the night. He always stopped it just right there.

Somewhere in his mind he knew what had happened, but he never let the picture of it rise up and take him over. He knew it was the cause of his being where he was and never likely to get out. And he knew that Danny was only Georgina's brother who'd come back to town after a long while away and talked her into believing Gene-Boy was nothing but a deadbeat drunk and she'd be well rid of him. Danny'd come to visit him once and cried for his sister and his little niece, the only family he had left. All gone. Gene-Boy'd cried, too.

He lifted up his thin mattress and slid his letter to Amy underneath it along with all the others, the hundreds of others, all addressed and sealed and stamped. They made his bed rustle in the night.

The Adventure of the One-Penny Black

Ellery Queen

AH," SAID OLD UNEKER. "It iss a terrible t'ing, Mr. Quveen, a terrible t'ing, like I vass saying. Vat iss New York coming to? Dey come into my store—*polizei*, undt bleedings, undt whackings on de headt. . . . Diss iss vunuff my oldest customers, Mr. Quveen. He too hass hadt exberiences. . . . Mr. Hazlitt, Mr. Quveen. . . . Mr. Quveen iss dot famous detectiff feller you read aboudt in de papers, Mr. Hazlitt. Inspector Richardt Quveen's son."

Ellery Queen laughed, uncoiled his length from old Uneker's counter, and shook the man's hand. "Another victim of our crime wave, Mr. Hazlitt? Unky's been regaling me with a feast of a whopping bloody tale."

"So you're Ellery Queen," said the frail little fellow; he wore a pair of thick-lensed goggles and there was a smell of suburbs about him. "This *is* luck! Yes, I've been robbed."

Ellery looked incredulously about old Uneker's bookshop. "Not *here?*" Uneker was tucked away on a side street in mid-Manhattan, squeezed between the British Bootery and Mme. Carolyne's, and it was just about the last place in the world you would have expected thieves to choose as the scene of a crime.

"Nah," said Hazlitt. "Might have saved the price of a book if it had. No, it happened last night about ten o'clock. I'd just left my office on Forty-fifth Street—I'd worked late—and I was walking crosstown. Chap stopped me on the street and asked for a light. The street was pretty dark and deserted, and I didn't like the fellow's manner, but I saw no harm in lending him a packet of matches. While I was digging it out, though, I noticed he was eyeing the book under my arm. Sort of trying to read the title."

"What book was it?" asked Ellery eagerly. Books were his private passion.

Hazlitt shrugged. "Nothing remarkable. That best-selling nonfiction thing, *Europe in Chaos*; I'm in the export line and I like to keep up to date on international conditions. Anyway, this chap lit his cigarette, returned the matches, mumbled his thanks, and I began to walk on. Next thing I knew something walloped me on the back of my head and everything went black. I seem to remember falling. When I came to, I was lying in the gutter, my hat and glasses were on the stones, and my head felt like a baked potato. Naturally thought I'd been robbed; I had a lot of cash about me, and I was wearing a pair of diamond cuff links. But—"

"But, of course," said Ellery with a grin, "the only thing that was taken was *Europe in Chaos*. Perfect, Mr. Hazlitt! A fascinating little problem. Can you describe your assailant?"

"He had a heavy mustache and dark-tinted glasses of some kind. That's all. I—"

"He? He can describe not'ing," said old Uneker sourly. "He iss like all you Americans—blindt, a *dummkopf*. But de book, Mr. Quveen—de book! Vhy should any von vant to steal a book like dot?"

"And that isn't all," said Hazlitt. "When I got home last night—I live in East Orange, New Jersey—I found my house broken into! And what do you think had been stolen, Mr. Queen?"

Ellery's lean face beamed. "I'm no crystal-gazer, but if there's any consistency in crime, I should imagine another book had been stolen."

"Right! And it was my second copy of *Europe in Chaos!*"

"Now you do interest me," said Ellery, in quite a different tone. "How did you come to have two, Mr. Hazlitt?"

"I bought another copy from Uneker two days ago to give to a friend of mine. I'd left it on top of my bookcase. It was gone. Window was open—it had been forced; and there were smudges of hands on the sill. Plain case of housebreaking. And although there's plenty of valuable stuff in my place—silver and things—nothing else had been taken. I reported it at once to the East Orange police, but they just tramped about the place, gave me funny looks, and finally went away. I suppose they thought I was crazy."

"Were any other books missing?"

"No, just that one."

"I really don't see . . . ." Ellery took off his *pince-nez* eyeglasses and began to polish the lenses thoughtfully. "Could it have been the same man? Would he have had time to get out to East Orange and burglarize your house before you got there last night?"

"Yes. When I picked myself out of the gutter, I reported the assault to a cop, and he took me down to a nearby stationhouse, and they asked me a lot of questions. He would have had plenty of time—I didn't get home until one o'clock in the morning."

"I think, Unky," said Ellery, "that the story *you* told me begins to have point. If you'll excuse me, Mr. Hazlitt, I'll be on my way. *Auf wiedersehen!*"

Ellery left old Uneker's little shop and went downtown to Center Street. He climbed the steps of police headquarters, nodded amiably to a desk lieutenant, and made for his father's office. The Inspector was out. Ellery twiddled with an ebony figurine of Bertillon on his father's desk, mused deeply, then went out and began to hunt for Sergeant Velie, the Inspector's chief of operations. He found the mammoth in the Press Room, bawling curses at a reporter.

"Velie," said Ellery, "stop playing bad man and get me some information. Two days ago there was an unsuccessful manhunt on Forty-ninth Street, between Fifth and Sixth Avenues. The chase ended in a little bookshop owned by a friend of mine named Uneker. Local officer was in on it. Uneker told me the story, but I want less colored details. Get me the precinct report like a good fellow, will you?"

Sergeant Velie waggled his big black jaws, glared at the reporter, and thundered off. Ten minutes later he came back with a sheet of paper, and Ellery read it with absorption.

The facts seemed bald enough. Two days before, at the noon hour, a hatless, coatless man with a bloody face had rushed out of the office building three doors from old Uneker's bookshop, shouting: "Help! Police!" Patrolman McCallum had run up, and the man yelled that he had been robbed of a valuable postage stamp—"My one-penny black!" he kept shouting. "My one-penny black!"—and that the thief, black-mustached and wearing heavy blue-tinted spectacles, had just escaped. McCallum had noticed a man of this description a few minutes before, acting peculiarly, enter the nearby bookshop. Followed by the screaming stamp dealer, he dashed into old Uneker's place with drawn revolver. Had a man with black mustache and blue-tinted spectacles come into the shop within the past few minutes? "Ja—he?" said old Uneker. "Sure, he iss still here." Where? In the back room looking at some books. McCallum and the bleeding man rushed into Uneker's back room; it was empty. A door leading to the alley from the back room was open; the man had escaped, apparently having been scared off by the noisy entrance of the policeman and the victim a moment before. McCallum had immediately searched the neighborhood; the thief had vanished.

The officer then took the complainant's statement. He was, he said, Friederich Ulm, dealer in rare postage stamps. His office was in a tenth-floor room in the building three doors away—the office of his brother Albert, his partner, and himself. He had been exhibiting some valuable items to an invited group of three stamp collectors. Two of them had gone away. Ulm happened to turn his back; and the third, the man with the black mustache and blue-tinted glasses, who had introduced himself as Avery Beninson, had swooped on him swiftly from behind and struck at his head with a short iron bar as Ulm twisted back. The blow had cut open Ulm's cheekbone and felled him, half-stunned; and then with the utmost coolness the thief had used the same iron bar (which, said the report, from its description was probably a "jimmy") to pry open the lid of a glass-topped cabinet in which a choice collection of stamps was kept. He had snatched from a leather box in the cabinet an extremely high-priced item—"the Queen Victoria one-penny black"—and had then dashed out, locking the door behind him. It had taken the assaulted dealer several minutes to open the door and follow. McCallum went with Ulm to the office, examined the rifled cabinet, took the names and addresses of the three collectors who had been present that morning—with particular note of "Avery Beninson"—scribbled his report, and departed.

The names of the other two collectors were John Hinchman and J. S. Peters. A detective attached to the precinct had visited each in turn and had then gone to the address of Beninson. Beninson, who presumably had been the man with a black mustache and blue-tinted spectacles, was ignorant of the entire affair; and his physical appearance did not tally with the description of Ulm's assailant. He had received no invitation from the Ulm brothers, he said, to attend the private sale. Yes, he had had an employee, a man with a black mustache and tinted glasses, for two weeks—this man answered Beninson's advertisement for an assistant to take charge of the collector's private stamp albums, had proved satisfactory, and had suddenly, without explanation or notice, disappeared after two weeks' service. He had disappeared, the detective noted, on the morning of the Ulms' sale.

All attempts to trace this mysterious assistant, who had called himself William Planck, were unsuccessful. The man had vanished among New York City's millions.

Nor was this the end of the story. For the day after the theft old Uneker himself had reported to the precinct detective a queer tale. The previous night—the night of the Ulm theft—said Uneker, he had left his shop for a late dinner; his night clerk had remained on duty. A man had entered the shop, had asked to see *Europe in Chaos*, and had then to the night clerk's astonishment purchased all copies of the book in stock—seven. The man who had made this extraordinary purchase wore a black mustache and blue-tinted spectacles!

"Sort of nuts, ain't it?" growled Sergeant Velie.

"Not at all," smiled Ellery. "In fact, I believe it has a very simple explanation."

"And that ain't the half of it. One of the boys told me just now of a new angle on the case. Two minor robberies were reported from local precincts last night. One was uptown in the Bronx; a man named Hornell said his apartment was broken into during the night, and what do you think? Copy of *Europe in Chaos* which Hornell had bought in this guy Uneker's store was stolen! Nothing else. Bought it two days ago. Then a dame named Janet Meakins from Greenwich Village had *her* flat robbed the same night. Thief had taken her copy of *Europe in Chaos*—she'd bought it from Uneker the afternoon before. Screwy, hey?"

"Not at all, Velie. Use your wits." Ellery clapped his hat on his head. "Come along, you Colossus; I want to speak to old Unky again."

They left Headquarters and went uptown.

"Unky," said Ellery, patting the little old bookseller's bald pate affectionately, "how many copies of *Europe in Chaos* did you have in stock at the time the thief escaped from your back room?"

"Eleffen."

"Yet only seven were in stock that same evening when the thief returned to buy them," murmured Ellery. Therefore, four copies had been sold between the noon hour two days ago and the dinner hour. So! Unky, do you keep a record of your customers?"

"*Ach*, yes! De few who buy," said old Uneker sadly. "I add to my mailing lisdt. You vant to see?"

"There is nothing I crave more ardently at the moment."

Uneker led them to the rear of the shop and through a door into the musty back room from whose alley door the thief had escaped two days before. Off this room there was a partitioned cubicle littered with papers, files, and old books. The old bookseller opened a ponderous ledger and, wetting his ancient forefinger, began to slap pages over. "You vant to know de four who boughdt *Europe in Chaos* dot afternoon?"

"Ja."

Uneker hooked a pair of greenish-silver spectacles over his ears and began to read in a singsong voice. "Mr. Hazlitt—dot's the gentleman you met, Mr. Quveen. *He* bought his second copy, de vun dot vass robbed from his house . . . Den dere vass Mr. Hornell, an oldt customer. Den a Miss Janet Meakins—*ach*! dese Anglo-Saxon names. *Schrecklich*! Undt de fourt' vun vass Mr. Chester Singermann, uff t'ree-tvelf East Siggsty-fift' Street. Und dot's all."

"Bless your orderly old Teutonic soul," said Ellery. "Velie, cast those Cyclopean peepers of yours this way." There was a door from the cubicle which, from its location, led out into the alley at the rear, like the door in the back room. Ellery bent over the lock; it was splintered away from the wood. He opened the door; the outer piece was scratched and mutilated. Velie nodded. "Forced," he growled. "This guy's a regular Houdini."

Old Uneker was goggle-eyed. "Broken!" he shrilled. "Budt dot door is neffer used! I didn't notice not'ing, undt de detectiff—"

"Shocking work, Velie, on the part of the local man," said Ellery. "Unky, has anything been stolen?" Old Uneker flew to an antiquated bookcase; it was neatly tiered with volumes. He unlocked the case with anguished fingers, rummaging like an aged terrier. Then he heaved a vast sigh. "*Nein*," he said. "Dose rare vons . . . Not'ing stole."

"I congratulate you. One thing more," said Ellery briskly. "Your mailing list—does it have the business as well as private addresses of your customers?" Uneker nodded. "Better and better. Ta-ta, Unky. You may have a finished story to relate to your other customers after all. Come along, Velie; we're going to visit Mr. Chester Singermann."

They left the bookshop, walked over to Fifth Avenue, and turned north, heading uptown. "Plain as the nose on your face," said Ellery, stretching his long stride to match Velie's. "And that's pretty plain, Sergeant."

"Still looks nutty to me, Mr. Queen."

"On the contrary, we are faced with a strictly logical set of facts. Our thief stole a valuable stamp. He dodged into Uneker's bookshop, contrived to get into the back room. He heard the officer and Friederich Ulm enter and got busy thinking. If he were caught with the stamp on his person . . . You see, Velie, the only explanation that will make consistent the business of the subsequent thefts of the same book—a book not valuable in itself—is that the thief, Planck, slipped the stamp between the pages of one of the volumes on a shelf while he was in the back room—it happened by accident to be a copy of *Europe in Chaos*, one of a number kept in stock on the shelf—and made his escape immediately thereafter. But he still had the problem of regaining possession of the stamp—what did Ulm call it?—the 'one-penny black,' whatever that may be. So that night he came back, watched for old Uneker to leave the shop, then went in and bought from the clerk all copies of *Europe in Chaos* in the place. He got seven. The stamp was not in any one of the seven he purchased, otherwise why did he later steal others which had been bought that afternoon? So far, so good. Not finding the stamp in any of the seven, then, he returned, broke into Unky's little office during the night—witness the shattered lock—from the alley, and looked up in Unky's Dickensian ledger the names and addresses of those who had bought copies of the book during that afternoon. The next night he robbed Hazlitt; Planck evidently followed him from his office. Planck saw at once that he had made a mistake; the condition of the weeks-old book would have told him that this wasn't a book purchased only the day before. So he hurried out to East Orange, knowing Hazlitt's private as well as business address, and stole Hazlitt's recently purchased copy. No luck there either, so he feloniously visited Hornell and Janet Meakins, stealing their copies. Now, there is still one purchaser unaccounted for, which is why we are calling upon Singermann. For if Planck was unsuccessful in his theft of Hornell's and Miss Meakins's books, he will inevitably visit Singermann, and we want to beat our wily thief to it if possible."

Chester Singermann, they found, was a young student living with his parents in a battered old apartment-house flat. Yes, he still had his copy of *Europe in Chaos*—needed it for supplementary reading in political economy—and he produced it. Ellery went through it carefully, page for page; there was no trace of the missing stamp.

"Mr. Singermann, did you find an old postage stamp between the leaves of this volume?" asked Ellery.

The student shook his head. "I haven't even opened it, sir. Stamp? What issue? I've got a little collection of my own, you know."

"It doesn't matter," said Ellery hastily, who had heard of the maniacal enthusiasm of stamp collectors, and he and Velie beat a precipitate retreat.

"It's quite evident," explained Ellery to the sergeant, "that our slippery Planck found the stamp in either Hornell's copy or Miss Meakins's. Which robbery was first in point of time, Velie?"

"Seem to remember that this Meakins woman was robbed second."

"Then the one-penny black was in her copy . . . Here's that office building. Let's pay a little visit to Mr. Friederich Ulm."

Number 1026 on the tenth floor of the building bore a black legend on its frosted-glass door:

ULM
Dealers in
Old & Rare Stamps

Ellery and Sergeant Velie went in and found themselves in a large office. The walls were covered with glass cases in which, separately mounted, could be seen hundreds of canceled and uncanceled postage stamps. Several special cabinets on tables contained, evidently, more valuable items. The place was cluttered; it had a musty air astonishingly like that of Uneker's bookshop.

Three men looked up. One, from a crisscrossed plaster on his cheekbone, was apparently Friederich Ulm himself, a tall gaunt old German with sparse hair and the fanatic look of the confirmed collector. The second man was just as tall and gaunt and old; he wore a green eyeshade and bore a striking resemblance to Ulm, although from his nervous movements and shaky hands he must have been much older. The third man was a little fellow, quite stout, with an expressionless face.

Ellery introduced himself and Sergeant Velie; and the third man picked up his ears. "Not *the* Ellery Queen?" he said, waddling forward. "I'm Heffley, investigator for the insurance people. Glad to meet you." He pumped Ellery's hand with vigor. "These gentlemen are the Ulm brothers, who own this place. Friederich and Albert. Mr. Albert Ulm was out of the office at the time of the sale and robbery. Too bad; might have nabbed the thief."

Friederich Ulm broke into an excited gabble of German. Ellery listened with a smile, nodding at every fourth word. "I see, Mr. Ulm. The situation, then, was this: you sent invitations by mail to three well-known collectors to attend a special exhibition of rare stamps—object, sale. Three men called on you two mornings ago, purporting to be Messrs. Hinchman, Peters, and Beninson. Hinchman and Peters you knew by sight, but Beninson you did not. Very well. Several items were purchased by the first two collectors. The man you thought was Beninson lingered behind, struck you—yes, yes, I know all that. Let me see the rifled cabinet, please." The brothers led him to a table in the center of the office. On it there was a flat cabinet, with a lid of ordinary thin glass framed by a narrow rectangle of wood. Under the glass reposed a number of mounted stamps, lying nakedly on a field of black satin. In the center of the satin lay a leather case, open; its white lining had been denuded of its stamp. Where the lid of the cabinet had been wrenched open there were the unmistakable marks of a "jimmy," four in number. The catch was snapped and broken.

"Amatchoor," said Sergeant Velie with a snort. "You could damn near force that locked lid up with your fingers."

Ellery's sharp eyes were absorbed in what lay before him. "Mr. Ulm," he said, turning to the wounded dealer, "the stamp you call 'the one-penny black' was in this open leather box?"

"Yes, Mr. Queen. But the leather box was closed when the thief forced open the cabinet."

"Then how did he know so unerringly what to steal?" Friederich Ulm touched his check tenderly. "The stamps in this cabinet were not for sale; they're the cream of our collection; every stamp in this case is worth hundreds. But when the three men were here we naturally talked about the rarer items, and I opened this cabinet to show them our very valuable stamps. So the thief saw the one-penny black. He was a collector, Mr. Queen, or he wouldn't have chosen that particular stamp to steal. It has a funny history."

"Heavens!" said Ellery. "Do these things have histories?"

Heffley, the man from the insurance company, laughed. "And how! Mr. Friederich and Mr. Albert Ulm are well known to the trade for owning two of the most unique stamps ever issued, both identical. The one-penny black, as it is called by collectors, is a British stamp first issued in 1840; there are lots of them around, and even an uncanceled one is worth only seventeen and a half dollars in American money. But the two in the possession of these gentlemen are worth thirty thousand dollars apiece. Mr. Queen—that's what makes the theft so doggone serious. In fact, my company is heavily involved, since the stamps are both insured for their full value."

"Thirty thousand dollars!" groaned Ellery. "That's a lot of money for a little piece of dirty paper. Why are they so valuable?"

Albert Ulm nervously pulled his green shade lower over his eyes. "Because both of ours were actually initialed by Queen Victoria, that's why. Sir Rowland Hill, the man who created and founded the standard penny-postage system in England in 1839, was responsible for the issue of the one-penny black. Her majesty was so delighted—England, like other countries, had had a great deal of trouble working out a successful postage system—that she autographed the first two stamps off the press and gave them to the designer—I don't recall his name. Her autograph made them immensely valuable. My brother and I were lucky to get our hands on the only two in existence."

"Where's the twin? I'd like to take a peep at a stamp worth a queen's ransom."

The brothers bustled to a large safe looming in a corner of the office. They came back, Albert carrying a leather case as if it were a consignment of golden bullion, and Friederich anxiously holding his elbow, as if he were a squad of armed guards detailed to protect the consignment. Ellery turned the thing over in his fingers; it felt thick and stiff. It was an average-sized stamp rectangle, imperforate, bordered with a black design, and containing an engraving in profile view of Queen Victoria's head—all done in tones of black. On the lighter portion of the face appeared two tiny initials in faded black ink—V. R.

"They're both exactly alike," said Friederich Ulm, "even to the initials."

"Very interesting," said Ellery, returning the case. The brothers scurried back, placed the stamp in a drawer of the safe, and locked the safe with painful care. "You closed the cabinet, of course, after your three visitors looked over the stamps inside?"

"Oh, yes," said Friederich Ulm. "I closed the case of the one-penny black itself, and then I locked the cabinet."

"And did you send the three invitations yourself? I noticed you have no typewriter here."

"We use a public stenographer in Room 1102 for all our correspondence, Mr. Queen."

Ellery thanked the dealers gravely, waved to the insurance man, nudged Sergeant Velie's meaty ribs, and the two men left the office. In Room 1102 they found a sharp-featured young woman. Sergeant Velie flashed his badge, and Ellery was soon reading carbon copies of the three Ulm invitations. He took note of the names and addresses, and the two men left.

THEY VISITED THE collector named John Hinchman first. Hinchman was a thickset old man with white hair and gimlet eyes. He was brusque and uncommunicative. Yes, he had been present in the Ulms' office two mornings before. Yes, he knew Peters. No, he'd never met

Beninson before. The one-penny black? Of course. Every collector knew of the valuable twin stamps owned by the Ulm brothers; those little scraps of paper bearing the initials of a queen were famous in stampdom. The theft? Bosh! He, Hinchman, knew nothing of Beninson or whoever it was that impersonated Beninson. He, Hinchman, had left before the thief. He, Hinchman, furthermore didn't care two raps in Hades who stole the stamp; all he wanted was to be let strictly alone.

Sergeant Velie exhibited certain animal signs of hostility; but Ellery grinned, sank his strong fingers into the muscle of the sergeant's arm, and herded him out of Hinchman's house. They took the subway uptown.

J. S. Peters, they found, was a middle-aged man, tall and thin and yellow as Chinese sealing wax. He seemed anxious to be of assistance. Yes, he and Hinchman had left the Ulms' office together, before the third man. He had never seen the third man before, although he had heard of Beninson from other collectors. Yes, he knew all about the one-penny blacks, had even tried to buy one of them from Friederich Ulm two years before; but the Ulms had refused to sell.

"Philately," said Ellery outside to Sergeant Velie, whose honest face looked pained at the word, "is a curious hobby. It seems to afflict its victims with a species of mania. I don't doubt these stamp-collecting fellows would murder each other for one of the things."

The sergeant was wrinkling his nose. "How's she look now?" he asked rather anxiously.

"Velie," replied Ellery, "she looks swell—and different."

They found Avery Beninson in an old brownstone house near the River; he was a mild-mannered and courteous host.

"No, I never did see that invitation," Beninson said. "You see, I hired this man who called himself William Planck, and he took care of my collection and the bulky mail all serious collectors have. The man knew stamps, all right. For two weeks he was invaluable to me. He must have intercepted the Ulms' invitation. He saw his chance to get into their office, went there, said he was Avery Beninson . . ." The collector shrugged. "It was quite simple, I suppose, for an unscrupulous man."

"Of course, you haven't had word from him since the morning of the theft?"

"Naturally not. He made his haul and lit out."

"Just what did he do for you, Mr. Beninson?"

"The ordinary routine of the philatelic assistant—assorting, cataloguing, mounting, answering correspondence. He lived here with me for the two weeks he was in my employ." Beninson grinned deprecatingly. "You see, I'm a bachelor—live in this big shack all alone. I was really glad of his company, although he was a queer one."

"A queer one?"

"Well," said Beninson, "he was a retiring sort of creature. Had very few personal belongings, and I found those gone two days ago. He didn't seem to like people, either. He always went to his own room when friends of mine or collectors called, as if he didn't want to mix with company."

"Then there isn't anyone else who might be able to supplement your description of him?"

"Unfortunately, no. He was a fairly tall man, well advanced in age, I should say. But then his dark glasses and heavy black mustache would make him stand out anywhere."

Ellery sprawled his long figure over the chair, slumping on his spine. "I'm most interested in the man's habits, Mr. Beninson. Individual idiosyncrasies are often the innocent means by which criminals are apprehended, as the good sergeant here will tell you. Please think hard. Didn't the man exhibit any oddities of habit?"

Beninson pursed his lips with anxious concentration. His face brightened. "By George, yes! He was a snuff taker."

Ellery and Sergeant Velie looked at each other. "That's interesting," said Ellery with a smile. "So is my father—Inspector Queen, you know—and I've had the dubious pleasure of watching a snuff taker's gyrations ever since my childhood. Planck inhaled snuff regularly?"

"I shouldn't say that exactly, Mr. Queen," replied Beninson with a frown. "In fact, in the two weeks he was with me I saw him take snuff only once, and I invariably spent all day with him working in this room. It was last week; I happened to go out for a few moments, and when I returned I saw him holding a carved little box, sniffing from a pinch of something between his fingers. He put the box away quickly, as if he didn't want me to see it—although I didn't care, Lord knows, so long as he didn't smoke in here. I've had one fire from a careless assistant's cigarette, and I don't want another."

Ellery's face had come alive. He sat up straight and began to finger his *pince-nez* eyeglasses studiously. "You didn't know the man's address, I suppose?" he asked slowly.

"No, I did not. I'm afraid I took him on without the proper precautions." The collector sighed. "I'm fortunate that he didn't steal anything from me. My collection is worth a lot of money."

"No doubt," said Ellery in a pleasant voice. He rose. "May I use your telephone, Mr. Beninson?"

"Surely.

Ellery consulted a telephone directory and made several calls, speaking in tones so low that neither Beninson nor Sergeant Velie could hear what he was saying. When he put down the instrument he said: "If you can spare a half hour, Mr. Beninson, I'd like to have you take a little jaunt with us downtown."

Beninson seemed astonished; but he smiled, said: "I'd be delighted," and reached for his coat.

Ellery commandeered a taxicab outside, and the three men were driven to Forty-ninth Street. He excused himself when they got out before the little bookshop, hurried inside, and came out after a moment with old Uneker, who locked his door with shaking fingers.

In the Ulm brothers' office they found Heffley, the insurance man, and Hazlitt, Uneker's customer, waiting for them. "Glad you could come," said Ellery cheerfully to both men. "Good afternoon, Mr. Ulm. A little conference, and I think we'll have this business cleared up to the Queen's taste. Ha, ha!"

Friederich Ulm scratched his head; Albert Ulm, sitting in a corner with his hatchet knees jackknifed, his green shades over his eyes, nodded.

"We'll have to wait," said Ellery. "I've asked Mr. Peters and Mr. Hinchman to come, too. Suppose we sit down?"

They were silent for the most part, and not a little uneasy. No one spoke as Ellery strolled about the office, examining the rare stamps in their wall cases with open curiosity, whistling softly to himself. Sergeant Velie eyed him doubtfully. Then the door opened, and Hinchman and Peters appeared together. They stopped short at the threshold, looked at each other, shrugged, and walked in. Hinchman was scowling.

"What's the idea, Mr. Queen?" he said. "I'm a busy man."

"A not unique condition," smiled Ellery. "Ah, Mr. Peters, good day. Introductions, I think, are not entirely called for . . . Sit down, gentlemen!" he said in a sharper voice, and they sat down.

The door opened and a small, gray, birdlike little man peered in at them. Sergeant Velie looked astounded, and Ellery nodded gaily. "Come in, Dad, come in! You're just in time for the first act."

Inspector Richard Queen cocked his little squirrel's head, looked at the assembled company shrewdly, and closed the door behind him. "What the devil is the idea of the call, son?"

"Nothing very exciting. Not a murder, or anything in your line. But it may interest you. Gentlemen, Inspector Queen."

The Inspector grunted, sat down, took out his old brown snuff box; and inhaled with the voluptuous gasp of long practice.

Ellery stood serenely in the hub of the circle of chairs, looking down at curious faces. "The theft of the one-penny black, as you inveterate stamp fiends call it," he began, "presented a not uninteresting problem. I say 'presented' advisedly. For the case is solved."

"Is this that business of the stamp robbery I was hearing about down at Headquarters?" asked the Inspector.

"Yes."

"Solved?" asked Beninson. "I don't think I understand, Mr. Queen. Have you found Planck?"

Ellery waved his arm negligently. "I was never too sanguine of catching Mr. William Planck, as such. You see, he wore tinted spectacles and a black mustachio. Now, anyone familiar with the science of crime detection will tell you that the average person identifies faces by superficial details. A black mustache catches the eye. Tinted glasses impress the memory. In fact, Mr. Hazlitt here, who from Uneker's description is a man of poor observational powers, recalled even after seeing his assailant in dim street light that the man wore a black mustache and tinted glasses. But this is all fundamental and not even particularly smart. It was reasonable to assume that Planck wanted these special facial characteristics to be remembered. I was convinced that he had disguised himself, that the mustache was probably a false one, and that ordinarily he does not wear tinted glasses."

They all nodded.

"This was the first and simplest of the three psychological signposts to the culprit." Ellery smiled and turned suddenly to the Inspector.

"Dad, you're an old snuff addict. How many times a day do you stuff that unholy brown dust up your nostrils?"

The Inspector blinked. "Oh, every half hour or so. Sometimes as often as you smoke cigarettes."

"Precisely. Now, Mr. Beninson told me that in the two weeks during which Planck stayed at his house, and despite the fact that Mr. Beninson worked side by side with the man every day, he saw Planck take snuff only *once*. Please observe that here we have a most enlightening and suggestive fact."

From the blankness of their faces it was apparent that, far from seeing light, their minds on this point were in total darkness. There was one exception—the Inspector; he nodded, shifted in his chair, and coolly began to study the faces about him.

Ellery lit a cigarette. "Very well," he said, expelling little puffs of smoke, "there you have the second psychological factor. The third was this: Planck, in a fairly public place, bashes Mr. Friederich Ulm over the face with the robust intention of stealing a valuable stamp. Any thief under the circumstances would desire speed above all things. Mr. Ulm was only half-stunned—he might come to and make an outcry; a customer might walk in; Mr. Albert Ulm might return unexpectedly—"

"Just a moment, son," said the Inspector. "I understand there are two of the stamp thingamajigs in existence. I'd like to see the one that's still here."

Ellery nodded. "Would one of you gentlemen please get the stamp?"

Friederich Ulm rose, pottered over to the safe, tinkered with the dials, opened the steel door, fussed about the interior a moment, and came back with the leather case containing the second one-penny black. The Inspector examined the thick little scrap curiously; a thirty-thousand-dollar bit of old paper was as awesome to him as to Ellery.

He almost dropped it when he heard Ellery say to Sergeant Velie: "Sergeant, may I borrow your revolver?"

Velie's massive jaw seesawed as he fumbled in his hip pocket and produced a long-barreled police revolver. Ellery took it and hefted it thoughtfully. Then his fingers closed about the butt and he walked over to the rifled cabinet in the middle of the room.

"Please observe, gentlemen—to expand my third point—that in order to open this cabinet Planck used an iron bar; and that in prying up the lid he found it necessary to insert the bar between the lid and the front wall four times, as the four marks under the lid indicate.

"Now, as you can see, the cabinet is covered with thin glass. Moreover, it was locked, and the one-penny black was in this closed leather case inside. Planck stood about here, I should judge, and mark that the iron bar was in his hand. What would you gentlemen expect a thief, working against time, to do under these circumstances?"

They stared. The Inspector's mouth tightened, and a grin began to spread over the expanse of Sergeant Velie's face.

"But it's so clear," said Ellery. "Visualize it. I'm Planck. The revolver in my hand is an iron 'Jimmy.' I'm standing over the cabinet . . ." His eyes gleamed behind the *pince-nez*, and he raised the revolver high over his head. And then, deliberately, he began to bring the steel barrel down on the thin sheeting of glass atop the cabinet. There was a scream from Albert Ulm, and Friederich Ulm half-rose, glaring. Ellery's hand stopped a half inch from the glass.

"Don't break that glass, you fool!" shouted the green-shaded dealer. "You'll only—"

He leaped forward and stood before the cabinet, trembling arms outspread as if to protect the case and its contents. Ellery grinned and prodded the man's palpitating belly with the muzzle of the revolver. "I'm glad you stopped me, Mr. Ulm. Put your hands up. Quickly!"

"Why—why, what do you mean?" gasped Albert Ulm, raising his arms with frantic rapidity.

"I mean," said Ellery gently, "that you're William Planck, and that brother Friederich is your accomplice!"

The brothers Ulm sat trembling in their chairs, and Sergeant Velie stood over them with a nasty smile. Albert Ulm had gone to pieces; he was quivering like an aspen leaf in high wind.

"A very simple, almost an elementary, series of deductions," Ellery was saying. "Point three first. Why did the thief, instead of taking the most logical course of smashing the glass with the iron bar, choose to waste precious minutes using a 'Jimmy' four times to force open the lid? *Obviously to protect the other stamps in the cabinet which lay open to possible injury*, as Mr. Albert Ulm has just graphically pointed out. And

who had the greatest concern in protecting these other stamps—
Hinchman, Peter, Beninson, even the mythical Planck himself? Of
course not. Only the Ulm brothers, owners of the stamps."

Old Uneker began to chuckle; he nudged the Inspector. "See?
Didn't I say he vass smardt? Now me—me, I'd neffer t'ink of dot."

"And why didn't Planck steal these other stamps in the cabinet?
You would expect a thief to do that? Planck did not. But if the *Herren*
Ulm were the thieves, the theft of the other stamps became pointless."

"How about that snuff business, Mr. Queen?" asked Peters.

"Yes. The conclusion is plain from the fact that Planck apparently
indulged only once during the days he worked with Mr. Beninson.
Since snuff addicts partake freely and often, Planck wasn't a snuff
addict. Then it wasn't snuff he inhaled that day. What else is sniffed in
a similar manner? Well—drugs in powder form—heroin! What are the
characteristics of a heroin addict? Nervous, drawn appearance; gauntness, almost emaciation; and most important, telltale eyes, the pupils of
which contract under influence of the drug. Then here was another
explanation for the tinted glasses Planck wore. They served a double
purpose—as an easily recognizable disguise and also to conceal his eyes,
which would give his vice addiction away! But when I observed that
Mr. Albert Ulm"—Ellery went over to the cowering man and ripped the
green eyeshade away, revealing two stark, pinpoint pupils—"wore this
shade, it was a psychological confirmation of his identity as Planck."

"Yes, but that business of stealing all those books," said Hazlitt.

"Part of a very pretty and rather farfetched plot," said Ellery.
"With Albert Ulm the disguised thief, Friederich Ulm, who exhibited
the wound on his cheek, must have been an accomplice. Then with
the Ulm brothers the thieves, the entire business of the books was a
blind. The attack on Friederich, the ruse of the bookstore escape, the
trail of the minor robberies of copies of *Europe in Chaos*—a cleverly
planned series of incidents to authenticate the fact that there was an
outside thief, to convince the police and the insurance company that
the stamp actually was stolen when it was not. Object, of course, to
collect the insurance without parting with the stamp. These men are
fanatical collectors."

Heffley wriggled his fat little body uncomfortably. "That's all very
nice, Mr. Queen, but where the deuce is that stamp they stole from
themselves? Where'd they hide it?"

"I thought long and earnestly about that, Heffley. For while my trio of deductions were psychological indications of guilt, the discovery of the stolen stamp in the Ulms' possession would be evidential proof." The Inspector was turning the second stamp over mechanically. "I said to myself," Ellery went on, "in a reconsideration of the problem: What would be the most likely hiding place for the stamp? And then I remembered that the two stamps were identical, even the initials of the good Queen being in the same place. So I said to myself: If I were Messrs Ulm, I should hide that stamp—like the character in Edgar Allan Poe's famous tale—in the most obvious place. And what is the most obvious place?"

Ellery sighed and returned the unused revolver to Sergeant Velie. "Dad," he remarked to the Inspector, who started guiltily, "I think that if you allow one of the philatelists in our company to examine the second one-penny black in your fingers, you'll find that the *first* has been pasted with noninjurious rubber cement precisely over the second!"

Make Yourselves
at Home

Joan Hess

IT WAS THE SUMMER of her discontent. This particular moment on this particular morning had just become its zenith; its epiphany, if you will; its culmination of simmering animosity and precariously constrained urges to scream curses at the heavens while flinging herself off a precipice, presuming there was such a thing within five hundred miles. There was not. Florida is many things; one of them is flat.

Thus thwarted by geographical realities, Wilma Chadley could do no more than gaze sullenly out the kitchen window at the bleached grass and limp, dying shrubs. Fierce white sunlight baked the concrete patio. In one corner of the yard remained the stubbles of what had never been a flourishing vegetable garden, but merely an impotent endeavor to economize on groceries. Beyond the fence, tractor-trailers blustered down the interstate. Cars topped with luggage racks darted between them like brightly colored cockroaches. The motionless air was laden with noxious exhaust fumes and the miasma from the swampy expanse on the far side of the highway.

Wilma poured a glass of iced tea and sat down at the dinette to reread the letter for the fifth time since she'd taken it from the mailbox only half an hour ago. When she finished, her bony body quivered with resentment. Her breath came out in ragged grunts. A bead of sweat formed on the tip of her narrow nose, hung delicately, and then splattered on the page. More sweat trickled down the harshly angular creases of her face as the words blurred before her eyes.

From the living room she could hear the drone of the announcer's voice as he listed a batter's statistics. As usual, her husband, George, was sprawled on the recliner, drifting between the game and damp, uneasy naps, the fan whirring at his face, his sparse white hair plastered to his head. If she were to step between him and his precious game in order to read the letter, he would wait woodenly until she was done, then ask her to get him another beer. She had no doubt his response would be identical if she announced the house was on fire (although she was decidedly not in the mood to conduct whimsical experiments in behavioral psychology).

Finally, when she could no longer suffer in silence, she snatched the leash from a hook behind the door and tracked Popsie down in the bathroom, where he lay behind the toilet. "It's time for Popsie's lunchie walk," she said in a wheedling voice, aware that the obese and grizzled basset hound resented attempts to drag him away from the cool porcelain. "Come on, my sweetums," she continued, "and we'll have a nice walk and then a nice visit with our neighbor next door. Maybe she'll have a doggie biscuit just for you."

Popsie expressed his skepticism with a growl before wiggling further into the recess. Sighing, Wilma left him and went through the living room. George had not moved in over an hour, but she felt no optimism that she might be cashing a check from the life insurance company any time soon. Since his retirement from an insignificant managerial position at a factory five years ago, he had perfected the art of inertia. He could go for hours without saying a word, without turning his head when she entered the room, without so much as flickering when she spoke to him. He bathed irregularly, at best. In the infrequent instances in which she failed to harangue him, he donned sweat-stained clothes from the previous day. Only that morning he'd made a futile attempt to leave his dentures in the glass beside the bed, citing swollen gums. Wilma had made it clear that was not acceptable.

She headed for the house next door. It was indistinguishable from its neighbors, each being a flimsy box with three small bedrooms, one bathroom, a poorly arranged kitchen, and an airless living room. At some point in the distant past the houses had been painted in an array of pastels, but by now the paint was gone and the weathered wood was uniformly drab. Some carports were empty, others filled with cartons of yellowed newspapers and broken appliances. There were no bicycles in the carports or toys scattered in the yards. Silver Beach was a retirement community. The nearest beach was twenty miles away. There may have been silverfish and silver fillings, but everything else was gray. During the day, the streets were empty. Cemetery salesmen stalked the side-walks each evening, armed with glossy brochures and trustworthy faces.

Polly Simps was struggling with a warped screen as Wilma cut across the yard. She wore a housedress and slippers, and her brassy orange hair was wrapped around pink foam curlers. There was little reason to dress properly in Silver Beach since the air conditioner had broken down at the so-called clubhouse. For the last three years the building had been used solely by drug dealers and shaky old alcoholics with unshaven cheeks and unfocused eyes. Only a month ago a man of indeterminate age had been found in the empty swimming pool behind the clubhouse. The bloodstains were still visible on the cracked concrete.

"Damn this thing," Polly muttered in greeting. "I don't know why I bother. The mosquitoes get in all the same." She dropped the screen to scratch at one of the welts on her flabby, freckled arm. "Every year they seem to get bigger and hungrier. One of these days they're gonna carry me off to the swamp."

Wilma had no interest in anyone else's problems. "Listen to this," she said as she unfolded the letter. When she was done, she wadded it up, stuffed it in her pocket, and waited for a response from one of the very few residents of Silver Beach with whom she was on speaking terms. Back in Brooklyn, she wouldn't have bothered to share the time of day with the likes of someone as ignorant and opinionated as Polly Simps. That was then.

"I never heard of such a thing," Polly said at last. "The idea of allowing strangers into your own home is appalling. The fact that they're foreigners makes it all the worse. Who knows what kind of germs they might carry? I'd be obliged to boil the sheets and towels, and I'd feel funny every time I used my silverware."

"The point is that Jewel Jacoby and her sister spent three weeks in an apartment in Paris. Jewel was a bookkeeper just like I was, and I know for a fact her social security and pension checks can't add up to more than mine. Her husband passed away at least ten years ago. Whatever she gets as a widow can't be near as much as we get from George's retirement." Wilma rumbled in frustration as she considered Jewel's limited financial resources. "And she went to Paris in April for three weeks! You know where George and I went on vacation last year? Do you?"

Polly blinked nervously as she tried to think. "Did you and George take a vacation last year?"

"No," Wilma snapped, "and that's the issue. We talked about driving across the country to visit Louisa and her loutish husband in Oregon, but George was afraid that the car wouldn't make it and we'd end up stranded in a Kansas cornfield. He's perfectly happy to sit in his chair and stare at that infernal television set. We've never once had a proper vacation. Now I get this letter from Jewel Jacoby about how she went to France and saw museums and cathedrals and drank coffee at sidewalk cafes. All it cost her was airfare and whatever she and her sister spent on groceries. It's not fair."

"But the French people stayed in her apartment," Polly countered. "They slept in her bed and used her things just like they owned them."

"While she slept in their bed and sat on their balcony, watching the boats on the Seine! I've never set foot in Europe, but Jewel had the time of her life—all because the French people agreed to this foolish exchange. I'll bet they were sorry. I've never been in Jewel's apartment, but she was the worst slob in the entire office. I'd be real surprised if her apartment wasn't filthier than a pigsty."

Polly held her peace while Wilma made further derogatory remarks about her ex-coworker back in Brooklyn. Wilma's tirades were infamous throughout Silver Beach. She'd been kicked out of the Wednesday bridge club after an especially eloquent one and was rarely included in the occasional coffee-and-gossip sessions in someone's kitchen. It was just as well, since she was often the topic.

Wilma finally ran out of venom. Polly took a breath and said, "I still don't like the idea of foreigners in my house. What was the name of the organization?"

"Traveler's Vacation Exchange or something like that." Wilma took out the letter and forced herself to scan the pertinent paragraph. "She paid fifty dollars and sent in her ad in the fall. Then in January she got a catalog filled with other people's ads and letters started coming from all over Europe, and even one from Hawaii. She says she picked Paris because she'd taken French in high school forty years ago. What a stupid reason to make such an important decision! I must say I'm not surprised, though. Jewel was a very stupid woman, and no doubt still is."

Wilma went home and dedicated herself to making George utterly and totally miserable for the rest of the summer. Since she had had more than forty years of practice, this was not challenging.

FLORIDA/ORLANDO	X	3-6wks	O
George & Wilma Chadley 2/0		A, 4, 2	GB
122 Palmetto Rd, Silver Beach, FL 34101			
(407) 521-7357			
ac bb bc cf cl cs dr fi fn gd gg go hh mk ns o pk pl			
pv ro rt sba se sk ss tv uz wa wf wm wv yd			

"Here's one," Wilma said, jabbing her finger at an ad. "They live in a village called Cobbet, but it's only an hour away from London by train. They have three children and want to come to Florida in July or August for a month."

"I reckon they don't know how hot it gets," Polly said, shaking her head. "I'd sooner spend the summer in Hades than in Silver Beach."

"That's their problem, not mine." Wilma consulted the list of abbreviations, although by this time she'd memorized most of them. "No air conditioning, but a washer and dryer, modern kitchen with dishwasher and microwave, garden, domestic help, and a quiet neighborhood. They want to exchange cars, too. I do believe I'll write them first."

"What does George think about this?"

Wilma carefully copied the name and address, then closed the catalog and gave Polly a beady look. "Not that it's any of your business, but I haven't discussed it with him. I don't see any reason to do it until

I've reached an agreement and found out exactly how much the air-fare will be."

Polly decided it was too risky to ask about the finances of this crazy scheme. "Let me see your ad."

Wilma flipped open the catalog and pointed to the appropriate box. While Polly tried to make sense of the abbreviations, she sat back and dreamily imagined herself in a lush garden, sipping tea and enjoying a cool, British breeze.

Polly looked up in bewilderment. "According to what this says, the nearest airport is Orlando. Isn't Miami a sight closer?"

"The main reason people with children come to Florida is to go to Disney World. I want them to think it's convenient."

"Oh," Polly murmured. She consulted the list several more times. "This says you have four bedrooms and two bathrooms, Wilma. I haven't been out in your backyard lately, but last time I was there I didn't notice any swimming pool or deck with a barbecue grill. We ain't on the beach, either. The nearest one is a half-hour's drive and it's been closed for two years because of the pollution. It takes a good two hours to get to an open beach."

"The couch in the living room makes into a bed, so they can consider it a bedroom. One bathroom's plenty. I'll be the one paying the water bill at the end of the month, after all."

"Your air conditioner doesn't work any more than mine, and if you've got a microwave and a clothes dryer, you sure hide 'em well. I suppose there's golf and skiing and playgrounds and scuba diving and boating and hiking, but not anywhere around these parts. You got one thing right, though. It's a quiet neighborhood now that everyone's afraid to set foot outside because of those hoodlums. Mr. Hodkins heard gunfire just the other night."

Wilma did not respond, having returned to her fantasy. It was now replete with crumpets.

122 Palmetto Road
Silver Beach, FL 34101

Dear Sandra,

I received your letter this morning and I don't want to waste a single minute in responding. You and your husband sound like a charming couple. I shall always treasure the photograph of you and your three beautiful children. I was particularly taken with little Dorothy's dimples and angelic smile.

As I mentioned in my earlier letter, you will find our home quite comfortable and adequate for your needs. Our car is somewhat older than yours, but it will get you to Disneyworld in no time at all.

You have voiced concern about your children and the swimming pool, but you need not worry. The ad was set incorrectly. The pool is a block away at our neighborhood club house. There is no lifeguard, however.

I fully intended to enclose photographs of ourselves and our house, but my husband forgot to pick up the prints at the drug store on his way home from the golf course. I'll do my best to remember to put them in the next letter.

I believe we'll follow your advice and take the train from Gatwick to Cobbet. Train travel is much more limited here, so we will leave our car at the Orlando airport for your convenience. In the meantime, start stocking up on suntan oil for your wonderful days on the beach. I wouldn't want Dorothy's dimples to turn red.

Your dear friend in Florida,
Wilma

"Have you told George?" Polly whispered, glancing at the doorway: Noises from the television set indicated that basketball had been replaced with baseball, although it was impossible to determine if George had noticed. His only concession to the blistering resurgence of summer was a pair of stained plaid shorts.

Wilma snorted. "Yes, Polly, I have told George. Did you think I crept into the living room and took his passport photographs without him noticing?"

"Is he excited?"

"He will be when the time comes," she said firmly. "In any case, it really doesn't matter. The Millingfords are coming on the first of

July whether he likes it or not. I find it hard to imagine he would enjoy sharing this house with three snotty-nosed children. Look at the photograph if you don't believe me. They look like gargoyles, especially the baby. The two older ones have the same squinty eyes as their father."

"The house looks nice."

"It does, doesn't it? If it's half as decent as that insufferably smug woman claims, we should be comfortable. The flowerbeds are pretentious, but I'm not surprised. She made a point of mentioning that they have a gardener twice a week. I was tempted to write back and say ours comes three times a week, but I let it go." She tapped the photograph. "Look at that structure near the garden wall. It's a hutch, of all things. It seems that Lucinda and Charles keep pet rabbits. Because little Dorothy has asthma and all kinds of allergies, the rabbits are not allowed in the house. The idea of stepping on a dropping makes my stomach turn."

"Will that cause a problem with Popsie?"

Wilma leaned down to stroke Popsie's satiny ears. He'd been lured away from the toilet with chocolate-chip cookies, and now crumb-flecked droplets of saliva were sprinkled beneath the table. She felt a prick of remorse at the idea of leaving him for a month, but it couldn't be helped, not if she was to have a vacation that would outshine Jewel Jacoby's. "I haven't mentioned Popsie in my letters. The boarding kennel wants twenty-five dollars a day. I've had to set aside every penny for our airfare, which is why the washing machine is still leaking. The tires on the car are bald and the engine makes such a terrible rattle that I literally hold my breath every time I drive to the store. There's absolutely no way I can get anything repaired until we build up some cash in the fall. Besides that, my Popsie is very delicate and would be miserable in a strange place. If there are any disruptions in his schedule, he begins piddling on the floor and passing wind." She looked thoughtfully at Polly and decided not to even hint that Popsie would enjoy a lengthy visit in his neighbor's home. Not after what Popsie had done to Polly's cat.

"I do want to ask a small favor of you," she continued with a conspiratorial wink. "I'm worried about the children damaging the house. I'm going to lock away all the good dinnerware, but they're quite capable of leaving muddy footprints all over the furniture and handprints on the walls. I'm hoping you'll drop by at least once a day. Just ask if they're having a pleasant vacation or something."

Polly flinched. "Won't they think I'm spying on them?"

"That's exactly what I want them to think. They need to be reminded they're guests in my home."

"Is there anything else?"

"One other favor. I'm going to leave a note in the car for them to come by your house to pick up the house key and a letter regarding their stay. If you don't mind, of course?"

As dim as she was, Polly suspected the British family might be disgruntled by the time they arrived in Silver Beach. However, nothing interesting had taken place since the knifing by the clubhouse several weeks ago. Shrugging, she said, "I'll make a point of being here when they arrive."

Dear Sandra,

Welcome to Florida! I'm writing this while we pack, but I'll try very hard not to forget anything. I hope you and the family enjoyed the flight to Orlando. I was a tiny bit muddled about the distance from the airport to the house, but George insisted that it was no more than an hour's drive. How embarrassing to have discovered only the other day that it's nearly three times that far! In any case, I shall assume my map and directions were clear and you successfully arrived at my dear friend Polly Simps's house. She is excited about your visit, and will come by often to check on you.

I must apologize for the air conditioner. The repairman has assured me that the part will arrive within a matter of days and he will be there to put it in working order. Please be very careful with the washing machine. Last night I received a nasty shock that flung me across the room and left my body throbbing most painfully. I was almost convinced my heart had received enough of a jolt to kill me! You might prefer to use the launderette in town. I had a similar experience with the dishwasher—why do these things go haywire on such short notice???

I am so sorry to tell you that our cleaning woman was diagnosed with terminal liver cancer three days ago. She immediately left to spend her last few weeks with her family in Atlanta. Her son, who works as our gardener, went with her. I was so stricken that all I could do was offer her a generous sum and wish them both the best. The lawn mower is in the carport storage area. It's balky, but will start with encouragement. You can buy gas (or petrol, as you say) for it at any service station.

And now I must mention dearest Popsie, whom you've surely discovered by now. We've had him for twelve years and he's become as beloved to us as a child. I had a long and unpleasant conversation with the brutes at the boarding kennel. They made it clear that Popsie would be treated with nothing short of cruelty. He is much too delicate to withstand such abuse and estrangement from his familiar surroundings. You will find him to be only the most minor nuisance, and I implore you to behave like decent Christians and treat him with kindness.

He must be taken for a walk (in order to do his duty) three times a day, at eight in the morning, noon, and five in the afternoon. His feeding instructions, along with those for the vitamin and mineral supplements and details regarding his eye drops and insulin shots, are taped on the refrigerator. Once he becomes accustomed to the children, he will stop snapping and allow them to enter the bathroom. Until he does so, I strongly suggest that he be approached with caution. I should feel dreadful if dear little Dorothy's rosy cheeks were savaged. The Silverado Community Beach is closed because of an overflow from a sewage disposal facility. You'll find Miami Beach, although a bit farther, to be lovely. The presence of a lifeguard should be reassuring, in that you've obviously neglected to teach your children how to swim. You might consider lessons in the future.

The refrigerator has been emptied for your convenience. I left bread and eggs for your first night's supper. Milk would have spoiled, but you'll find a packet of powdered lemonade mix for the children. Polly will give you directions to the supermarket. The car started making a curious clanking sound only yesterday. I would have taken it to the garage had time permitted, but it was impossible to schedule an appointment. George suspects a problem with the transmission. I will leave the telephone numbers of several towing services should you experience any problems. All of them accept credit cards.

But above all, make yourselves at home!

Wilma

⌒

Ferncliffe House
Willow Springs Lane
Cobbet, Lincs LN2 3AB
15 July (as they say)

Dear Polly,

We're having an absolutely wonderful time. The house is much nicer than I expected. Everything works properly, and even the children's room were left tidy.

I spend a great deal of time in the garden with a cup of tea and a novel, while George pops over to the pub to shoot billiards and play darts with his cronies. Last Sunday our lovely neighbors invited us to a picnic at the local cricket field. The game itself is incredibly stupid, but I suffered through it for the sake of cucumber sandwiches and cakes with clotted cream and jam.

I must say things are primitive. The washing machine is so small that our cleaning woman has to run it continually all three mornings every week when she's here. Her accent is droll, to put it kindly, and she is forever fixing us mysterious yet tasty casseroles. If I knew what was in them, I doubt I could choke down a single bite. The village shops are pathetically small, poorly stocked, and close at odd hours of the day. I don't know how these people have survived without a decent supermarket. And as for their spelling, you'd think the whole population was illiterate. I wonder if I'm the first person who's mentioned that they drive on the wrong side of the road.

I had reservations about the lack of air conditioning, but the days are mild and the nights cool. Sandra "conveniently" forgot to mention how often it rains; I suppose she was willing to lie simply to trick us into the exchange. She was certainly less than honest about the train ride from London. It takes a good seventy minutes.

I've searched every drawer and closet in the entire house and have yet to find a Bible. It does make one wonder what kind of people they really are. In the note I left, I begged them to treat Popsie with a Christian attitude, but now I wonder if they're even familiar with the term. Everyone is so backward in this country. For all I know, the Millingfords are Catholics—or Druids!

I must stop now. Tonight we're being treated to dinner at a local restaurant, where I shall become queasy just reading the menu. And I'm dreading tomorrow morning. Someone failed to shut the door of the hutch and the rabbits have escaped. No doubt the gardener will be upset in his amusing guttural way, since they were his responsibility. I honestly think it's for the best. The animals are filthy and one of them scratched my arm so viciously that I can still see a mark. What kind of parents would allow their children to have pets like those? Dogs are so much cleaner and more intelligent. I do believe I shall leave a note to that effect for Sandra to read when the family returns home.

Wilma

Polly was waiting on her porch when George and Wilma pulled into the driveway. She would have preferred to cower inside her house, blinds drawn and doors locked, but she knew this would only add to Wilma's impending fury. "Welcome home," she called bravely.

Wilma told George to unload the luggage, then crossed into the adjoining yard. "I feel like we've been traveling for days and days. It would have been so much easier to fly into the Miami airport, but the Millingfords had to go to Disney World, didn't they?"

"And they did," Polly began, then faltered as the words seemed to stick in her mouth like cotton balls (or, perhaps, clumps of rabbit fur similar to the ones the gardener had found in the meadow behind Ferncliffe House).

"So what?"

"They left two weeks ago."

"Just what are you saying, Polly Simps? I'm exhausted from the trip, and I have no desire to stand here while you make cryptic remarks about these whiny people. I'm not the least bit interested at the moment, although I suppose in a day or two when I'm rested you can tell me about them." She looked back at George, who was struggling toward the house with suitcases. "Be careful! I have several jars of jam in that bag."

Florida was still flat, so Polly's desperate desire to disappear into a gaping hole in the yard was foiled. "I think you'd better listen to me, Wilma. There were . . . some problems."

"I'm beginning to feel faint. If there's something you need to say, spit it out so I can go into my own home and give Popsie the very expensive milk biscuits I bought for him in England."

"Come inside and I'll fix you a glass of iced tea."

Wilma's nostrils flared as if she were a winded racehorse. "All I can say is this had better be good," she muttered as she followed her neighbor across the porch and through the living room. "Did the Millingfords snivel about everything? Are you going to present me with a list of all their petty complaints?"

"They didn't complain," Polly said as she put glasses on the table. "They were a little disappointed when they arrived, I think. Five minutes after I'd given them the key and your letter, Sandra came back to ask if it was indeed the right house. I said it was. Later that afternoon David came over and asked if I could take him to the grocery store, since your car wouldn't start."

"What colossal nerve! Did he think you were the local taxi service?"

Polly shrugged. "I told him I didn't have one, but I arranged for him to borrow Mr. Hodkins's car for an hour. The next morning a tow truck came for the car, and within a week or so it was repaired. During that time, they stayed inside the house for the most part. At one point the two older children came to ask me about the swimming pool, but that was the last time any of them knocked on my door."

"I'd like to think they were brought up not to pester people all the time. But as I hinted in my letter to you, they seem to be growing up in a heathen environment. You did go over there every day, didn't you?"

"I tried, Wilma, but I finally stopped. I'd ring the bell and ask how they were enjoying their visit, but whichever parent opened the door just stared at me and then closed the door without saying a word. Once I heard the baby wailing in one of the bedrooms, but other than that it was so quiet over there that I wondered what on earth they were doing."

Wilma entertained images of primitive rituals, embellishing them with her limited knowledge of Druids and gleanings from Errol Flynn movies. "Poor Popsie," she said at last. "How hideous for him. Did they walk him three times a day?"

"For the few days. Then the baby had an asthma attack and had to be taken to the hospital in an ambulance. After that, they left Popsie in the backyard, where he howled all night. The misery in that dog's voice was almost more than I could bear."

"Those barbarians! I'm going to write a letter to Mrs. Snooty Millingford and remind her that she was supposed to treat poor Popsie in a civilized, if not Christian, fashion. Your instincts were right, Polly. It's very dangerous to allow foreigners in your home."

"There's more. Once they got the car back, they took some day trips, but then two weeks ago they upped and left. It must have been late at night, because I never saw them loading the car and I made sure I kept an eye on them from my bedroom window during the day. Anyway, the key was in my mailbox one morning. I rushed over, but their luggage was gone. Everything was nice and neat, and they put a letter addressed to you on the kitchen counter."

Wilma started to comment on the unreliability of foreigners, then realized Polly was so nervous that her eyelid was twitching and her chin trembling. "What about Popsie?" she asked shrewdly, if also anxiously.

"Gone."

"Gone? What do you mean?"

"I organized a search party and we hunted for him for three days straight. I put an ad in that shopping circular and called the dog pound so many times that they promised they'd call me if they picked him up."

Wilma clasped the edge of the table and bared her teeth in a comical (at least from Polly's perspective) parody of a wild beast. "They must have stolen Popsie! What did the police say? You did call the police, didn't you? All they'd have to do is stop the car and drag those wicked Millingfords off to jail."

"They wouldn't have taken him, Wilma. When the ambulance men came to the house, I heard the father say that the baby's asthma attack was brought on by dog hairs. The last thing they'd do is put Popsie right there in the car with them and risk another attack."

"Well, I'm calling the police now," Wilma snarled as she shoved back her chair and started for the front door. "And you can forget about your jar of jam, Polly Simps. I asked you to do one little favor for me. Look what I get in return!"

George was sound asleep on the recliner as she marched through the living room, intent on the telephone in the kitchen. Of course it was too late for the police to take action. The Millingfords had safely escaped across the Atlantic Ocean, where they could ignore official demands concerning Popsie's disappearance. She could imagine the smugness on Sandra's face and her syrupy avowals of innocence. Perhaps she would feel differently when her children discovered the empty hutch.

The envelope was on the counter. Wilma ripped it open, and with an unsteady hand, took out the letter.

Dear Mrs. Chadley,

Thank you so very much for making your home available to us this last fortnight. It was not precisely what we'd anticipated, but after a bit we accepted your invitation to "make ourselves at home."

Tucked under the telephone you will find invoices from the towing service, auto repair shop, and tire shop. They were all quite gracious about awaiting your payment. The chap from the air conditioner service never came. My husband called all shops listed in the back pages of the telephone directory, but none seemed to have been the one with which you trade. He tried to have a look at it himself, but became leery that he inadvertently might damage some of the rustier parts.

After he checked the wiring, I had a go at the washing machine, but I must have done something improperly because water gushed everywhere. It made for quite a mopping.

We've changed our plans and have decided to spend the remaining fortnight touring the northern part of the state. Lucinda and Charles are frightfully keen about space technology and are exceedingly eager to visit the Kennedy Center. Dorothy adores building sand castles on the beach. Also, this will make it easier for us to leave your car at the Orlando airport as we'd arranged.

I hope you enjoyed your stay in Cobbet. Our neighbors are quite friendly in an unobtrusive way, and several of them promised to entertain you. I also hope you enjoyed Mrs. Bitney's cooking. She is such a treasure.

In honour of your return, I adapted one of Mrs. Bitney's family recipes for steak and kidney pie. It's in the freezer in an oblong pan. When you and your husband eat it, I do so hope you'll remember our exchange.

Yours truly,
Sandra Millingford

Wilma numbly put down the letter and went to the back door. Popsie's water and food bowls were aligned neatly in one corner of the patio. A gnawed rubber ball lay in the grass. The three pages of instructions were no longer taped to the door of the refrigerator, but several cans of dog food were lined up beside the toaster.

She went into the bathroom and peered behind the toilet as if Popsie had been hiding there all this time, too wily to show himself to Polly while he awaited their return. Not so much as a hair marred the vinyl.

At last, when she could no longer avoid it, she returned to the kitchen and sat down. As her eyes were drawn toward the door of the freezer, they began to fill with tears.

Sandra Millingford had made herself at home. What else had she made?

Deadlier Than the Mail

There were toys and Santas and Christmas carols, even on the Bowery. There was also a frightened, desperate killer . . .

(A Matt Cordell Story)

Evan Hunter

THERE WERE SANTA CLAUSES along Third Avenue, and the promise of snow greyed the sky over the blackened el structure. The Santas had straggly, dirty white beards and they pounded their hands against the cold. Their uniforms were ill-fitting. The crimson and white bagged over the pillows wrapped around their middles. The black oil-cloth boots over their shoes told the world they were imitations, and there wasn't a kid alive who'd believe in Santa ever again. Not after seeing these phonies behind their phonier beards.

I walked up Third, and the Santas tinkled their bells and stood behind their wooden chimneys or their cast-iron pots. I walked past them with my head bent and the collar of my jacket high. The air was knife-cold. It slashed at the skin, reached into the bones, put an edge on the tongue for a good, warming shot of bourbon.

Wassail, wassail . . .

I'd been here before. Long, long ago when I'd been a kid they all called Matty. More recently when a guy named Charlie Dagerra woke up with his throat slit because he'd refused to pay protection money to a local punk. And now it was a Monday in December, and the calendar said it was the 21st, four days to Christmas. The store windows huddled against the cold, lighted like potbellied stoves, looking warm and cheerful, overflowing with things to give and tinsel and cotton snow and toy trains and small plaster statues of Saint Nick.

The call had come from Kit O'Donnell, the girl I used to call Katie in the old days. I wouldn't have made the trip for anyone else, not in this weather, but there'd been something in her voice that made me forget the cold. I cut down 119th Street and kept walking toward First Avenue. The grocery shop was on First, between 118th and 119th. I opened the door, and a bell tinkled, and then Kit rushed from the back room.

She'd let her black hair grow longer, pulled it back from the oval of her face into a saucy ponytail. Her brown eyes opened wide, and then she smiled and said, "Matt, you came."

"I said I would."

She came out from behind the counter and took both my hands in hers. Her hands were warm, and she looked up into my face and for some reason I thought she would start bawling.

"You're cold, Matt," she said.

"A little brisk out there."

"Can I get you something to drink? My father keeps a bot . . ."

"Just a little," I said. "To take off the chill."

She went into the back room and came out front again with a bottle of Schenley's and a water glass. She poured the glass half-full and then handed it to me. I smiled, threw it off, and then put the glass down on the counter.

"Now," I said, "what's all the trouble about?"

"I guess I shouldn't have called you, Matt. I mean, you did so much for us last time, you . . ."

"What is it, Kit?"

"Do you remember Andy Traconni?"

"I remember. What about him?"

"He hasn't been doing too well, Matt. He was a bricklayer until he had an accident with his hands, and he's been out of work since. He gets checks from the Welfare Department. He's got a wife and a kid, Matt, and the checks don't stretch too far."

"I don't understand, Kit."

"Matt, someone's been stealing his checks. You know the mailboxes in these old buildings. You can open them with a bad breath. Someone's been taking the checks from his box."

"How long has this been going on?"

"A month, two months."

"Well for Christ's sake, why hasn't he reported it?"

"He's afraid to, Matt."

"Afraid to? Honey, tampering with the mails is a government offense. He'd be sensible to . . ."

"And suppose the thief has friends, Matt? What happens then? Who's going to protect Andy and his family?"

I shook my head. "Kit . . ."

"I know, Matt. I shouldn't have asked you. Only I thought . . . well, it's getting close to Christmas. I thought if we could find whoever is doing it, we might at least get the money back."

"Fat chance of that. This is an old racket, Kit, and not likely to be run by an amateur. Getting the checks is only half of it. They still have to be cashed after that, and that entails a phony driver's license or some other forged identification." I shook my head again. "I'd like to help, but honestly . . ."

"It isn't only Andy, Matt. There are others in the neighborhood, too. You knew Andy, so I mentioned him."

"How many others?"

"Ten, twelve. Won't you help, Matt?"

"You put me on a spot, Kit."

"I want to. Will you help?"

I sighed heavily. "I'll try. Let me have another drink, will you?"

She poured, and I drank, and then I asked her for the names of the people who'd been hit so far. She scribbled them on a sheet of paper, together with the addresses, and I left her and told her I'd get on it first thing in the morning.

DECEMBER 22ND, AND it still hadn't snowed. It was colder, if anything, and I tried to walk fast because the soles of my shoes were worn through and there's nothing icier than a winter pavement. When I got to Andy Traconni's building, there was a lot of excitement. Three patrol cars were parked at an angle to the curb, and cops and photographers were swarming all over the place. I stopped an old man in a mackinaw and I asked him what had happened.

"Andy," he said in broken English. "Som'body kill him."

"What!"

"In the hall," he said, nodding his head emphatically. "Andy come down for the mail . . ." He broke off here, held both hands in front of him and then squeezed them together in pantomime of someone being strangled. He nodded his head again and repeated, "Andy."

It was impossible to get into the hallway, so I walked away from the building and hung around until the reporters began to thin out. I spotted the bulls when they came out of the building and piled into a Mercury sedan across the street. Then they pulled away and the uniformed cops followed them, and the crowd broke. Two internes came out with a stretcher, the sheet pulled up over what was left of Andy Traconni. The crowd disappeared entirely after the ambulance left, and I had the building to myself. I walked into the hallway and looked at the mailboxes.

The one marked Traconni was battered and dented near the lock. It was a cinch it had been forced once, and never been repaired after that. A pile of square envelopes sat in the box, and I figured them to be Christmas cards. A merry Christmas it would be for Mrs. Traconni and her kid this year. The numeral 35 was stamped into the metal of the box, so I took the narrow steps up to the third-floor landing and found the apartment without even looking at the number. I stood outside the door and listened to the sobbing behind it, and finally I knocked.

A kid of about eight answered the door. His face was streaked with dirt and tears, and he looked as if he were ready to start crying all over again.

"I want to talk to your mother," I said.

He looked at me suspiciously. He looked at my wrinkled suit and my bearded face. He studied my bloodshot eyes, the flabbiness of my flesh. He was thinking *This is a bum*, and he was wondering if I'd had anything to do with his father's death.

"I knew your father when we were kids, son," I told him. "I want to help."

"Come in," he said, as if I'd whispered the magic words.

He led me into a small living room dominated by a TV set in one corner. The blinds were drawn, and a frail woman in a print house-dress sat in one of the easy chairs, a handkerchief to her face.

"Mrs. Traconni," I said, "my name is Matt Cordell. I knew Andy well a long time ago."

"I've heard of you," she said softly.

"Do you have any idea who killed him?"

"Yes," she said without hesitation. "The one who's been stealing our checks."

"How do you know?"

"Because Andy watched last week, and he found out something. He didn't tell me what it was, but he said he would wait until the next check was due and find out for sure then. When he saw the mailman coming down the street this morning, he went down to watch. I think he hid himself while he watched. Then this . . . this happened. He should have left it alone. He should have forgot it. You can't buck them, Mr. Cordell."

"What did the police say?"

"They said Andy was hit first, they don't know with what. It hit him on the side of his face, and they figured it stunned him. Then . . . then he was strangled."

"And you think he knew who was stealing the checks?"

"I'm sure of it," she said.

"I'll look around," I told her. "Maybe I'll come up with some-thing."

"Thank you," she said, and then she went back to her handker-chief, and she was crying when I left the apartment. I met a guy with a Christmas tree in the hallway. He was a fat guy, and he struggled with the tree, and sweat poured down his face, but there was a healthy smile on his face. The tree had made him forget the grubbiness of the tenement he lived in, and the cheapness of the coat on his back. When he passed me, he nodded his head happily and said, "A real big one this year," and I nodded back and said nothing.

In the street, it was bitter cold. I clenched my eyes against the sud-den onslaught, and I thought of a Christmas long ago. She'd done the

tree with popcorn, Trina, popcorn and tinsel, and there'd been a fire
going on the hearth. It was our first Christmas together, and the presents were piled under the tree, bright ribbons glistening in the light
of the fire. There was a white tablecloth on the table, and she'd placed
two candles on it, one for each plate. I'd come into the apartment
with my face cold from the raw wind outside.

She cupped my face with her slender hands, and her mouth had
found mine, her lips full and moist, her body alive with the warmth of
the room.

Four months. Four months of marriage. Part autumn and part winter, and then Garth. Trina in his arms, with the thin stuff of her gown
caught in his grasping fingers, his lips buried in her flesh. And the .45
snaking out of the holster under my armpit, the walnut stock reaching
out for his head, hitting him again and again and again. And then it was
all over, and there was an Assault-With-A-Deadly-Weapon charge, and
no more Trina. They dropped the ADW, and they went to Mexico for
a divorce, but the police decided it was time to lift my license.

And this was the Matt Cordell they'd left. Carrying a torch a mile
high, feeding the flames with alcohol, huddling against the cold and
looking for a guy who lifted checks from broken mailboxes.

I caught up with the mailman about six blocks from Andy's house.
His bag was packed with Christmas cards, and he was sweating in spite
of the cold. He was a big man with wiry black hair that spilled onto
his forehead from beneath his tilted cap. His hands curled with the
same wiry hair, and I watched the swift, sure way his fingers dropped
letters into the open row of boxes. I watched him for a few minutes,
and then I asked, "Did you see Andy Traconni this morning?"

He didn't turn from the boxes. He kept dumping the letters in,
and he spoke without looking up. "Who'd you say?"

"Andy Traconni."

"Oh. No, missed him today."

"He was killed today."

His hands paused for a moment. "What?"

"In the hallway. Did you happen to see anyone hanging around
when you made your delivery?"

"No, Jesus. Killed, you say. Jesus!"

"Lot of people getting welfare checks on this route?"

He regarded me suspiciously. "Why? Why do you ask?"

"I'm just curious. Andy's checks have been stolen for the past few months."

"No kidding? Hell, why didn't he say something about it? No kidding?"

"He never mentioned it to you?"

"No. He asked me if I'd delivered them a few times, and I told him sure. But I never suspected . . ."

"Anyone in this building get checks?" I asked.

"Lemme see. Yeah, Riley does. Apartment 4C. He gets 'em every week."

"Thanks," I said. "Keep your eyes open."

The mailman blinked. "I will."

I left him stuffing cards into the boxes, and I took the steps up to the fourth floor and then knocked on the door to 4C. I waited for a few moments until a woman's voice called, "Come in. It's open."

I opened the door and walked directly into the kitchen. A small Christmas tree stood on an end table at the far corner of the room. Chimney paper had been wrapped around the end table, and cotton had been used to cover the stand. The tree had no ornaments and no lights. It was sprinkled with aluminum foil, and someone with energy had swabbed the branches with Rinso for a snow-laden effect.

"Anybody home?" I called.

"Just a second."

I waited, looking at the chipping paint on the wall, the dulled, blackened area over the four-burner stove. I heard a door behind me open, and a girl stepped into the room. She was wearing a full slip, and the slip ended just above her knees. It was cut low in the front, and her full breasts bunched against the silken fabric. One strap dangled over a pale white shoulder. The girl was a redhead, that natural carroty red that goes with a name like Riley. Her eyes were blue, and there were deep pockets under them. Her skin was pale. I stared at her for a moment, and she said, "Sorry to keep you waiting."

She took a step closer to me, soundlessly moving on the worn linoleum that covered the floor.

I looked down and saw that she was barefoot.

"You got a cigarette, or are you in a hurry?"

"I've got one," I said. I fished into my pocket and pulled out a rumpled package of Pall Malls. The girl took one, and I lighted it for her.

She sucked in the smoke gratefully, and then said, "Busy day, by Christ. The bastards are starting the holiday early."

"Are you Mrs. Riley?" I asked.

"Me? Hell no, Mac. *Miss* Riley, if you please. Christ, do I look like that old bag?"

"I don't know your mother," I said.

"You ain't missing nothing, Mac. She's a lush from 'way back. You'll find her souped to the ears in the local pub." She took a close look at me and said, "Hey, don't I know you?"

"I don't think so."

"Sure, ain't you Matt Cordell? Weren't you the guy who wiped up the street with those punks who were shaking down the neighborhood? Sure, I recognize you."

I didn't answer her.

"You got a yearning, huh, Matt boy?" she said. "Well, little Fran will take care of you."

She took a step closer to me, and I said, "Your father gets welfare checks, they tell me."

"What's that got to do with the price of fish?"

"That's why I'm here."

"That's a good one," she said. She took my hand and started leading me across the room. I watched the way her flesh wiggled tautly beneath the tightness of her slip. I pulled my hand away and she turned, surprised.

"What is it, boy?"

"How old are you, Fran? Sixteen?"

"Nineteen, if you're worried about Quentin Quail. Hey, boy, what is it with you? You still got eyes for that bitchy wife of yours?"

"Can it, honey."

"Sure. So carry the torch, who cares? Let me help you burn it brighter, boy. I need the dough."

"Because your old man's checks have been lifted?"

"Sure, but that don't cut my ice, boy. The old man never gave me a cent anyway. The holidays are coming, and I use what I've got to get what I want." She cupped her breasts suddenly, reaching forward toward me. "Come on, boy, it's good stuff."

"I'm on the wagon." I paused. "Besides, I'm broke."

"Mmm. Well, I ain't Santa Claus. What's on your mind, Cordell?"

"When was the first check missing?"

"About a month ago, I guess."

"Lifted from the box?"

"Yeah. I saw the postman delivering that check on my way out in the morning. When the old man went down later in the day, the lock was snapped. Goodbye check."

"And the others?"

"Boy, we never even get a look at them. This hijacker must be Speedy Gonzalez." She laughed abruptly and said, "Hey, Cordell, you know the one about Speedy Gonzalez?"

"Did your father report these thefts?"

"My old man? Cordell, he's afraid to eat Rice Krispies. The explosions scare him."

"What have you been living on?"

Fran Riley shrugged. "I make out. Times have been pretty good." She smiled, and I saw something of the nineteen-year-old in her face for just an instant. "And, it's all tax-free," she said.

"You should marry a straight man," I told her.

"Any offers, Cordell?"

"I was in the club once," I said. "My membership expired."

She smiled again. "Besides, you're no straight man." The smile dropped from her face. "What do you say, Cordell? This is the slow time of day. You won't be sorry."

"I appreciate it," I said. "But I've got a dead man on my mind."

I left her to puzzle that one out, and when I got down to the street it was snowing. The flakes were big and wet at first, and then they got smaller and sharper, biting at the skin, crusting the hair. I fished the list Kit had given me out of my pocket and scanned it quickly. Then I began making the rounds.

The story was the same at each stop I made. The checks had begun disappearing a while back. The locks on the mailboxes had been broken. After that, the owners of the checks never got a look at them. By the time they went down to pick up the mail, the checks were gone.

I asked why they didn't keep a closer watch on the boxes, and they all told me the checks never came on the same days. It would have been close to impossible to keep a steady vigil. When I'd finished with the last name on the list, I began wondering just who the hell would commit murder for a pile of checks that couldn't amount to more than a couple of hundred a week.

And then I began wondering about the people in the neighborhood whose checks *weren't* missing. It was a poor neighborhood, and there were certainly more than ten or twelve people who were getting financial aid. I started looking around for the postman again, and I found him going into a tailor shop on First Avenue. I waited until he came out, and then I pulled up alongside him.

"Hi," I said.

He looked at me and said, "Oh, hi."

"I suppose you know the names of most everyone on the route, don't you?"

"Oh, sure," he said. He reached into the leather bag on his shoulder and pulled out a stack of Christmas cards. "Bitch of a time, Christmas," he said. "And the tips in this neighborhood are from hunger."

"Do you know the names of everyone getting welfare checks?"

"Yeah, sure," he said. "Why?"

I followed him up the steps into the building next to the tailor shop. He stuck his key in the box lock and pulled down the row of boxes. Then he began tossing the letters into the open row.

"I'm checking up on the thefts," I said.

He stopped dropping mail for a moment, and he looked at me steadily. "You?" he asked.

"Yeah, me."

He shrugged. "Okay. I know the people getting checks."

"Have you got a pencil?"

The postman sighed, and then reached into his pocket. "Here," he said.

I took a scrap of paper from the inside pocket of my jacket, and then said, "Shoot."

He reeled off the names and addresses, and I wrote them down. He glanced at his watch occasionally, and I realized I was holding him up at the busiest time of the year, but I didn't let him off the hook until he'd given me all the names. He was not happy when he left me. He glanced at his watch again, grunted, then shouldered his heavy bag and stomped out into the snow.

I stood in the hallway, and I compared the postman's list with the one Kit had given me. There weren't as many names as I'd thought there would be. I picked out two that were on the postman's list and not on Kit's, and I went to look them up.

GEORGE KASAIRUS WAS a thin man with angular black brows and a soiled undershirt. He had a can of beer in his hand when he opened the door to his apartment, and he glared at me belligerently.

"What are you selling?" he asked.

"Christmas cheer," I said.

He snorted and then took a long drag at the beer can. "I got no time for jokes," he said.

"I'm looking into the stolen welfare checks," I told him. "You want to help?"

"My checks ain't been stolen," Kasairus said.

"Then you should be willing to cooperate."

"Agh, come on in," he said.

I followed him into the dingy flat, and he opened a fresh can of beer for himself, not bothering to offer me one. "I don't know how the hell I can help," he said.

"Have any of your checks ever been missing?" I asked.

"Yeah, one. A long while back."

"And none since?"

"No, sir. I'm too smart for that bastard."

"How so?"

"My check comes on either Wednesday, Thursday, or Friday. I'm down by that box early on every one of those mornings. I get the check straight from Frankie."

"Who's Frankie?"

"Our postman. He puts it right into the palm of my hand. I eliminate the middleman that way. There's no bastard who's going to out-shrewd me when it comes to dough. No, sir."

"Do you know that a lot of people in the neighborhood are missing checks?"

"Sure, I know."

"Why haven't you let them on to your system of beating the game?"

"Screw 'em. It's every man for himself. They're too dumb to figure it out, that's tough. I worry about George Kasairus, and that's all, and you can bet nobody else is worryin' about me."

"You're a nice guy, Georgie," I said.

"Sure," he answered quickly. "What are you, a goddamn Good Samaritan or something?"

"I'm the ghost of Christmas Past, Georgie."

"Who?"

"Skip it."

"Just don't get smart with me, Mac."

"I won't, Georgie. But I'll wonder why you're one of the few guys whose checks haven't been lifted. I'll wonder that, Georgie. You won't mind, will you?"

Kasairus banged his beer can down on the tabletop and then took a fast step toward me. He threw a fist before I realized what was happening, and it caught on my jaw and sent me flying back against the wall.

"Don't call me no crook!" he shouted. "Don't call me no goddamn crook!"

He came at me again, and this time I shoved out against his chest and sent him sprawling onto the floor. He seemed ready to get up, but he changed his mind when he saw my cocked fists.

"I may be back, Georgie."

"Drop dead," he said.

I walked out, and I thought *Drop dead, a few days before Christmas.* A great goddamn world. Peace on earth. Silent night. Drop dead.

I went to the nearest bar, and I drank a few warm-up beers. Then I found a liquor store and I bought a gallon of wine. I found a hallway, and I drank straight from the bottle.

I toasted Trina first, and I wished her a bloody Merry Christmas and a Happy New Year. Then I toasted Garth, and I wished him the same thing. I toasted Kit O'Donnell and all her troubles, and all the poor bastards whose piddling checks were being stolen. And then I toasted Santa Claus and the State of New York, and Washington, D. C., and President Eisenhower.

The super of the building kicked me out of the hallway, but I held onto the jug of wine, and I reeled down the street and I sang *"Deck the halls with boughs of holly, fa-la-la-la-la, la-la, la-la . . ."*

I passed a Santa Claus with an iron pot, and I poured a little of the wine into the pot and said, "Drink up, Nick. Put some goddamn color back into your beard."

I stopped everyone I saw and offered them a drink, and they all laughed in that slightly patronizing way and patted me on the back.

I sang four choruses of "Deck the Halls," and then I batted out a few refrains of "God Rest Ye Merry, Gentlemen." I kept thinking of George Kasairus all the way. A Good Samaritan, he'd called me, and then he'd ordered me to drop dead.

That was the trouble with this little old goddamn world. Too many Good Samaritans dropping dead. The meek inherited the earth, all right, six feet of it, and all underground.

Like poor Andy Traconni who got the breath squeezed out of him because he wanted to protect the lousy little check he got each week.

Well, the hell with Andy, and the hell with Kasairus, and all the rest. It was almost Christmas, and it was no time to be chasing checks around the city. Nobody gives a damn about poor George Kasairus, and nobody gives a damn about goddamn Matt Cordell, either, that's for sure. So I drank the gallon, and goddamn it, I really felt in a holiday mood. I scrounged some more dimes from the people in the street, and it was easy because hell, it was Christmas time. Then I bought another gallon and I started on that one, singing all the way, and the last song I sang was "Jingle Bells," and then I was lying in the snow with the empty jug beside me, and all was well with the world.

JINGLE BELLS, JINGLE *bells, jingle all the way*
    Oh what fun it is to ride
    In a one-horse open slay-eigh . . .

The singing was somewhere near me. I pried open my eyes and looked for it, and the song went on and on, and the bells jingled inside my head. The snow under me had melted, and the front of my shirt and jacket were soaking wet. My feet were cold, and my face was cold, and I sat up and began thumping my hands against my sides. Where the hell was I, and what the hell day was it?

I got to my feet, and I stopped the first guy who passed.

"What day is it?" I asked.

"Christmas Eve," he said, and then he hurried off, his arms full of Christmas packages.

I washed a hand over my face, and I thought, *Christmas Eve. And no checks for Andy Traconni.*

I reached into my pocket and found the list the postman had given me, and then I looked for the nearest clock. I found it in a bar. I had a shot of bourbon to wash off the taste, and when I left the bar, it was three-thirty in the afternoon. I headed directly for a man named Juan Diaz, a man who still received his checks in spite of the wholesale thefts.

Juan Diaz was small, with dark black hair and friendly brown eyes. There was a Christmas tree on top of the radio cabinet in his living room. The apartment was shabby, but it smelled warm, and I could hear the excited babble of children's voices coming from the kitchen.

"Hello," Diaz said, "Hello. Merr' Chreestmas. Come in."

I walked into the apartment, and a smile formed on my face unconsciously. There weren't many presents around the tree, nor was the tree expensively decorated. But a big picture of Santa had been hung on the wall mirror, and small figures depicting the birth at Bethlehem were under the tree. The radiators whistled piping hot, and the smell of popcorn and baked apples drifted from the kitchen.

"You get welfare checks, Mr. Diaz?" I asked.

"*Si*," he said. "Yes, I do."

"Have any been stolen?"

"One," he said. "Only one. Then I smart up. Thees crook, he ees fast, but Juan Diaz, he be faster. I meet Frankie don'stairs when I theenk check should come. Sometime I go down every day, so not to miss it. I get heem, all right. Evr' week." Diaz paused. "Man, you got to live!"

"This first one that was stolen," I said. "How?"

"The lock. He snap heem. But no more."

"Now Frankie gives you the check, huh?"

"Good boy, Frankie. I geeve him dreenk for Chreestmas. Good boy, Frankie." Diaz grinned, showing bright white teeth. "You want dreenk, hey?"

"No," I said. "Thanks a lot."

"Well, Merr' Chreestmas," Diaz said.

"Same to you."

He closed the door behind me, and I stood in the warmth of the hallway for a moment, listening to the voices of the kids behind the doors. Well, two of them had learned how to beat the system. Just get to the check before the thief did. The rest were either too lazy or too stupid or too drunk to realize that was the only way to beat it. So the thief swiped the checks each week, and through fear, they kept their mouths shut. And now, with Andy Traconni dead, they'd never report the thefts in a million years.

I went down into the street. The snow had turned black with the churning of automobile tires and shoe soles. I walked, with the wind sharp, and the cold a living thing that gnawed and bit, and I thought it all over. Then I got my idea, and I started looking in earnest.

I found him in another hallway. The hallway was hot. The radiators sang their torrid songs, and he worked with the sweat pouring down his face.

"Hello, Frankie," I said.

The mailman looked up. "You again," he answered. "Look, mister, I got enough headaches. This is Christmas Eve, and I want to get home, you know? Let me work in peace, will you?"

"The missing checks, Frankie."

"Yeah, what about them?"

"Have you cashed them yet?"

Frankie turned, his hands on the leather strap of his bag. "What!"

"Nobody else, Frankie. Couldn't be. You snapped the locks the first time to make it look like an outsider was rifling the boxes *after* the checks were delivered. After that, smooth sailing. When the suckers asked you if you'd delivered the checks, you said sure. But those checks never reached the boxes. Except where the sucker was smart enough to wait for the check. Then you had to deliver."

"Go away, bum," Frankie said. "You're drunk."

"Andy Traconni was a sucker who woke up, Frankie. He began watching your deliveries. He watched, and he saw that you damn well never delivered his checks. He probably asked you if you had, and you said yes. Last week, he was fairly certain. This week, he made sure. He watched again, and when the check didn't come, he accused you."

"Listen . . ."

I expected him to say more, but he cut himself short and swung the leather bag up by the strap, swinging it at my head, in the same way he'd probably swung it when Andy accused him. I dodged the bag, and I leaped forward, grabbing his throat in my hands and ramming him against the wall.

"Did you cash the checks, you bastard?" I yelled.

"I needed the dough. Jesus, there are guys make eight, nine hundred dollars on a route during Christmas. I needed the dough, I tell you. I figured . . ."

"Did you cash the checks yet?"

"I ain't figured how to do that yet. I . . . look, Mac, let's forget this. Let's forget all about it. I'll split the dough with you. I'll . . ."

I slammed the back of my hand across his mouth. "Take me to the checks," I said.

Frankie spit blood, and then shook his head. "Sure," he said.

I GOT THE checks, and then I delivered him to the police. I bought a pint of bourbon, and then I delivered the checks personally, and each time I delivered one, I said, "Merry Christmas."

I felt good when I was finished. I felt good because all the faces that greeted those checks were smiling and happy. I went out into the street, and I wondered if I should drop in on Kit O'Donnell, say hello maybe, exchange greetings. And then it started snowing again, so I drank the bourbon a few nips at a time, and I watched the flakes, and when I finally boarded the Third Avenue El heading for the Bowery, the conductor said, "Merry Christmas, fella," and I just smiled and didn't say anything.

Contributors

Look up **Lawrence Block** in any work on American writers and you'll find it packed with accolades. Author of Leo Haig, Bernie Rhodenbarr, Matthew Scudder, Evan Tanner, and, most recently, the John Keller series. He's a fixture in the mystery field, writing hard-edged mysteries, such as *A Ticket to the Boneyard*, lighthearted comedy capers, like *Burglars Can't be Choosers*, to tongue-in-cheek adventure novels, including *The Thief Who Couldn't Sleep*, and his excellent stand-alone books, including *After the First Death* and *Random Walk*. Honored with the Nero Wolfe award (1979), Private Eye Writers of America Shamus award (1983, 1985), Mystery Writers of America Edgar Allan Poe award (1985), and the MWA Grand Master award in 1994—you get the point. Block is deservedly one of the most acclaimed and celebrated writers of our time.

In 1957 the poet W. H. Auden scolded American literary critics for teaching **Edgar Allen Poe** (1809–1849) as "a respectable rival to the pulps." Poe was, Auden insisted, a serious literary artist. If longevity is a measure of seriousness, then Poe has certainly proved his worth. If anything, he is more widely read, filmed, recorded, and illustrated worldwide than ever before. And such poems as "The Raven" and tales such as "The Murders in the Rue Morgue," "The Fall of the House of Usher," and "The Tell-Tale Heart," each a staggering example of psychological suspense, are all staples in modern American literature textbooks. Auden, one surmises, was right.

Though **William F. Nolan** is known for his great science-fiction trilogy *Logan's Run*, *Logan's World*, and *Logan's Search*, he has distinguished himself in the crime, mystery, and western genres as well—as a glance at his awards tell you. He has received the American Library Association citation (1960), Mystery Writers of America award (1970, 1972), the Academy of Science Fiction and Fantasy award for fiction and film (1976), the Maltese Falcon award (1977), and an honorary doctorate from American River College in Sacramento, California (1975). He has written major dramas for both television and movies. And he is considered a master at both the crime and horror short story, a popular opinion that is more than supported with this short story.

A pro's pro is somebody who can work in a variety of styles and forms with equal skill. One such man is **Peter Lovesey**. Whether he's writing about Victorian times (his Cribb and Thackery novels), early Hollywood (*Keystone*), or World War II (*On the Edge*), Lovesey is always in artful command of his material. His humor is genuinely funny and his dramatics genuinely moving, especially in the elegiac *Rough Cider*. Many of his novels and stories have been adapted to film and television.

Edward Marston is a busy man. He writes radio and theatrical drama, contemporary and historical mysteries, and young-adult novels as well. He was nominated for the Edgar award in 1986. What is remarkable about his work is that he finds a style appropriate to each subject, and each style is polished and always eminently readable. His stock is definitely rising as a creator of mystery fiction.

Barry N. Malzberg is a seminal figure in contemporary commercial fiction and not just because he's written so much of it. In addition to his fiction, he's also written some of the most perceptive and engaging commentary on the craft of fiction and how it's practiced in these turbulent times. Though known primarily as a science-fiction author, Malzberg's best novel is a powerful, unforgettable book about a hack writer's mental and spiritual breakdown titled *Herovit's World*. It proves that commercial fiction can also be true art. *Night Screams, Acts of Mercy*, and *The Running of Beasts* (all with Bill Pronzini) are just a few of his other titles. He has been honored with the John Campbell Memorial award (1973) and Locus award (1983).

Richard Christian Matheson is the author of the popular novel *Created By*, a truly horrifying tale of trendy Hollywood. He's even better known for his short stories in the fields of crime and dark suspense. Winner of the Bram Stoker award for best novel, Matheson has written many hours of television and movies. His style is both unique and startling. Nobody else approaches fiction in quite the same way.

Matthew Costello was known primarily as a horror writer and author of the best-selling computer games The 7th Guest and The 11th Hour until the late 1990s, when he began to collaborate with F. Paul Wilson on best-selling mainstream science fiction. Costello is primarily a character-driven writer. Whatever else is going on in the story, Costello is letting you know about his people. *Beneath Still Waters* and *Darkborn* are good (early) examples of Costello at his powerful best.

Morris Hershman is a pro's pro. He's done it all—mysteries, westerns, gothics, erotica, war—virtually every category of modern commercial fiction. During his decades-spanning career, he's written a couple dozen especially remarkable short stories that other writers constantly "borrow" from for both content and structure. He manages to find the human element in each of his pieces, and that makes the novelty of his plots just all that much more enjoyable.

Ralph McInerny's Father Dowling series has been a hit in both print and on television where, after several successful seasons on network television, it now runs on cable. He writes many other books—and types of books—as well. He has been honored with a Fulbright Fellowship (1959), a National Endowment for the Humanities

Fellowship (1977), and a National Endowment for the Arts Fellowship (1982). He has taught philosophy and medieval studies at Creighton University in Omaha, Nebraska and currently teaches at the University of Notre Dame in Indiana. He is the rare scholar who can also hold his own with the best writers of popular fiction.

Kate Kingsbury has written well and presented workshops about writing well and selling your material in publishing's most difficult time—today. Her novels include *Room with a Clue*, *Check-Out Time*, and *Maid to Murder*. She's honed her observations about life in a hotel to a sharp, witty style that pleases her ever-growing audience.

Simon Brett's Charles Paris, the alcoholic actor who frequently stumbles across murder in his pursuit of extremely modest success in British show business, is one of the most unique and endearing characters in contemporary crime fiction. The wry melancholy of the writing lifts the Paris novels far above most genre fiction. Not that Brett is satisfied with creating only one memorable character. There is also the Mrs. Pargeter series. And a number of first-rate, stand-alone suspense novels. Brett has received the Writer's Guild of Great Britain radio award (1973) and Broadcasting Press Guild award (1987). He was also chairman of the Crime Writers Association in 1986–87.

Though largely forgotten now, **Arthur B. Reeve** (1880–1936) was one of the first detective writers to use scientific methodology for catching criminals. This was around the time of World War I, when he was asked to set up a scientific crime lab. He then went on to have a long, prosperous, and extremely varied career in pulp magazines and books. He was probably best known, in the pulps, for his stories featuring Professor Craig Kennedy, often called "The American Sherlock Holmes." The Kennedy stories ran for many years, and his best cases were collected in the anthology *The Silent Bullet* in 1912. He was also an editor of great renown in the nonfiction field, as well as writing journalistic articles and producing radio programs on crime and criminology.

Martin H. Greenberg is the world's most successful anthologist and book packager, with nearly a thousand titles to his credit. He has worked with worldwide best-selling authors ranging from Tom Clancy to Tony Hillerman to Mary Higgins Clark, and from Dean Koontz to Father Andrew Greely. In addition to being his best friend, the late Isaac Asimov also did more than fifty books with Martin Greenberg. What's little known about Mr. Greenberg is that he's also a fine writer, as you'll learn when you read his contribution to this anthology.

August Derleth is associated with the H. P. Lovecraft circle of the 1930s, young authors who corresponded with Lovecraft, and frequently imitated him in their own fiction. The best of that circle—such as Robert Bloch—went on to find their own voices and do their own work. Derleth was also his own man. While he wrote various kinds of pastiche in both science fiction and mystery over the course of his career—his character Solar Pons was his unique take on Sherlock Holmes—as both writer and editor he brought passionate gifts to the horror field. It would not exist today as it does without his various contributions.

Henry Slesar was a mainstay of the fiction magazines of the late 1950s and early 1960s, the last big boom of the digests, which were just the pulps in more convenient size. He did it all and he did it well. A collection of his crime work is long overdue. In the course of his career he has won the Mystery Writers of America Edgar Allan Poe award for novel (1960) and for a TV series (1977), and an Emmy award for a continuing daytime series (1974). He has written for many TV series such as *Alfred Hitchcock Presents* and *Twilight Zone*. And he survived many years as the writer-producer of a long-running soap opera.

John Lutz is the author of the Fred Carver and Alo Nudger series, with *Oops*, *Hot*, and *Kiss* being just a few of his titles. He has received the Private Eye Writers of America Shamus award for short story (1982) and for novel (1988), and the Mystery Writers of America Edgar Allan Poe award for short story (1986). His short story "SWF

Seeks Same" was the basis for the film *Single White Female*, and his novel *The Ex*, was recently made into a cable-television movie. Lutz is another original, his own voice, his own take on everyday and not so everyday life in our times.

Gordon R. Dickson is a science-fiction writer of such reach and accomplishment one isn't quite sure how to start listing the accolades. From his celebrated Dorsai series to his humorous Dragon novels, he writes the kind of science fiction and fantasy that is equally rich with ideas and humanity. His work has been lauded in those communities as well, awarding him two Hugo awards, a Nebula, a Derleth, and a Jupiter award. And he sure knows how to pull off a thigh-slapper of an ending—as in the story published here—when the need arises.

Joyce Harrington has been awarded the Mystery Writers of America Edgar Allan Poe award for short story (1973) and has long been regarded as an original and important voice in the mystery field. Though her career in public relations and advertising hasn't always allowed her the time she'd like to spend on stories, she's created a formidable and imposing body of work.

Ellery Queen—the name has resounded on radio, in movies and television, and in many, many books and magazines. A pseudonym for cousins and authors Frederic Dannay and Manfred B. Lee, creators of the Ellery Queen and Inspector Richard Queen series—which includes *Calamity Town*, *The Roman Hat Mystery*, and *A Fine and Private Place* among many, many others—Queen is one of the seminal figures in the crime fiction of the past century. Whether as writer, editor, or scenarist, the name Ellery Queen stood for the best in mystery and detective fiction and helped found the Mystery Writers of America.

Joan Hess, on or off the page, is funny. Off the page that's great. On the page, that's not always so good. At least not when reviewers, trained to look for "deep meanings," look over her books. Nothing this enjoyable, they seem to think, can possibly have real merit. Not true, as she continues to demonstrate in novel after novel. Hess's spirited takes on her home state of Arkansas combines the cozy form with her own version of black comedy–domestic comedy that is set down with the same neurotic glee one finds in the stories of Anne Beatty. Whether she's writing about Clare Malloy, her young widow who runs a bookstore; or Arly Hanks, who is police chief of Maggody, Arkansas, Hess's two series are engaging but quite serious takes on relationships, middle age, parental duties, and life in small-town America.

Evan Hunter wrote the screenplay for Hitchcock's suspense film *The Birds*. He also wrote one of the great novels of juvenile delinquency, *The Blackboard Jungle*. And, under the name Ed McBain, he created the immortal 87th Precinct novels. He has been honored with the Mystery Writers of America Edgar Allan Poe award (1957) and Grand Master award (1985). And it's certainly easy to see why. He has brought to the American crime story a breathtaking new approach to both form and substance. A good deal of contemporary crime fiction bears his mark. He is probably the single-most influential crime novelist of the past two generations, and he's still going strong, with another 87th Precinct novel, *The Last Dance*, out recently. Virtually everybody has learned from and imitated him.

Copyrights and Permissions

Murder Most Delectable

Savory Tales of Culinary Crimes

Contents

Introduction

"Let the stoics say what they please, we do not eat for the good of living, but because the meat is savory and the appetite is keen."

Ralph Waldo Emerson

"When the wine goes in, the murder comes out."

The Talmud

Of all the various kinds of romance throughout the world, there is one that cultures and peoples from America to Europe to Asia indulge in freely and, for the most part, without remorse. Ever since the first man speared a chunk of mammoth or bison and held it over a roaring fire, we have indulged in our passion for food.

And what a grand love affair it is, for food is the only thing that can delight all five of our senses at once. The sound of a porterhouse steak as it sears on the grill . . . the sight of a golden brown turkey roasting in the oven . . . the cool feel of watermelon on a hot day . . . the smell of an apple pie as it bakes to perfection . . . I'm sorry, I think I lost my train of thought for a moment.

When all is said and done, the final, most glorious sense is sated with that first delectable bite . . . taste. For no matter how beautifully it is prepared or how mouthwatering it smells, that first bite will reveal if the chef has created a triumph or a tragedy. From a simple backyard barbecue to the most elegant seven-course meal, there are as many ways to prepare a meal as there are people on this planet. Each person has his or her own favorite dish and a method for preparing it that they consider to be the best, for when it all comes down to it, the ideal meal is truly a matter of personal taste.

Of course, some peoples' appetite for food is exceeded only by their appetite for crime. As our demand for most flavorful and intricate dishes has increased, so has the opportunity for these evil epicureans to combine their talent for wickedness and their love for good food in one fell swoop to lay another low, the device for the crime nothing more than a well-cooked meal. With that in mind, we've collected these eighteen stories of culinary crimes and deaths by dinner party. Joyce Carol Oates explores a relationship between two brothers that leaves a sour taste in one's mouth. Peter Crowther invites us to a gourmet dinner party where murder is a crucial ingredient in every course. Gillian Linscott visits a nineteenth-century manor house where the fruit flies aren't the only pests exterminated in the orchard. And Rex Stout's incomparable gourmand and sleuth, Nero Wolfe, turns his talents to his own dining club, where one member gives up his membership permanently after a meal prepared by Wolfe's own private chef.

Make sure all your hunger pangs have been quieted before turning the page, for even though many of these crimes involve food, the meals described are often worth dying for. As an extra bonus, we've added recipes for many of the dishes or ingredients mentioned here, with special thanks going to Denise Little for providing the majority of these recipes. So tuck in your napkin, pick up your knife and fork, and dive into this eighteen-course feast of *Murder Most Delectable.*

Murder Most Delectable

The Last Bottle
in the World

Stanley Ellin

I t was a bad moment. The café on the rue de Rivoli near the
Meurice had looked tempting. I had taken a chair at one of its
sidewalk tables, and then, glancing casually across at the next
table, had found myself staring into the eyes of a young woman
who was looking at me with startled recognition. It was Madame
Sophia Kassoulas. Suddenly, the past towered over me like a monstrous genie released from a bottle. The shock was so great that I
could actually feel the blood draining from my face.

Madame Kassoulas was instantly at my side.

"Monsieur Drummond, what is it? You look so ill. Is there anything I can do?"

"No, no. A drink, that's all. Cognac, please."

She ordered me one, then sat down to solicitously undo the
buttons of my jacket. "Oh, you men. The way you dress in this
summer heat."

This might have been pleasant under other conditions, but I
realized with embarrassment that the picture we offered the
other patrons of the café must certainly be that of a pitiful, white-
haired old grandpa being attended to by his softhearted grand-
daughter.

"Madame, I assure you—"

She pressed a finger firmly against my lips. "Please. Not another word until you've had your cognac and feel like yourself again. Not one little word."

I yielded the point. Besides, turnabout was fair play. During that nightmarish scene six months before when we were last in each other's company, she had been the one to show weakness and I had been the one to apply the restoratives. Meeting me now, the woman must have been as hard hit by cruel memory as I was. I had to admire her for bearing up so well under the blow.

My cognac was brought to me, and even *in extremis*, so to speak, I automatically held it up to the sunlight to see its color. Madame Kassoulas's lips quirked in a faint smile.

"Dear Monsieur Drummond," she murmured. "Always the connoisseur."

Which, indeed, I was. And which, I saw on grim reflection, was how the whole thing had started on a sunny Parisian day like this the year before. . . .

THE WAS THE DAY a man named Max de Marechal sought me out in the offices of my company, Broulet and Drummond, wine merchants, on the rue de Berri. I vaguely knew of de Marechal as the editor of a glossy little magazine, *La Cave*, published solely for the enlightenment of wine connoisseurs. Not a trade publication, but a sort of house organ for *La Société de la Cave*, a select little circle of amateur wine fanciers. Since I generally approved of the magazine's judgments, I was pleased to meet its editor.

Face to face with him, however, I found myself disliking him intensely. In his middle forties, he was one of those dapper, florid types who resemble superannuated leading men. And there was a feverish volatility about him which put me on edge. I tend to be low-geared and phlegmatic myself. People who are always bouncing about on top of their emotions like a Ping-Pong ball on a jet of water make me acutely uncomfortable.

The purpose of his visit, he said, was to obtain an interview from me. In preparation for a series of articles to be run in his magazine, he was asking various authorities on wine to express their opinions about the greatest vintage they had ever sampled. This way, perhaps, a consensus could be made and placed on record. If—

"If," I cut in, "you ever get agreement on the greatest vintage. Ask a dozen experts about it and you'll get a dozen different opinions."

"It did look like that at the start. By now, however, I have found some small agreement on the supremacy of two vintages."

"Which two?"

"Both are Burgundies. One is the Richebourg 1923. The other is the Romanée-Conti 1934. And both, of course, indisputably rank among the noblest wines."

"Indisputably."

"Would one of these be your own choice as the vintage without peer?"

"I refuse to make any choice, Monsieur de Marechal. When it comes to wines like these, comparisons are not merely odious, they are impossible."

"Then you do not believe any one vintage stands by itself beyond comparison?"

"No, it's possible there is one. I've never tasted it, but the descriptions written of it praise it without restraint. A Burgundy, of course, from an estate which never again produced anything like it. A very small estate. Have you any idea which vintage I'm referring to?"

"I believe I do." De Marechal's eyes gleamed with fervor. "The glorious Nuits Saint-Oen 1929. Am I right?"

"You are."

He shrugged helplessly "But what good is knowing about it when I've never yet met anyone who has actually tasted it? I want my series of articles to be backed by living authorities. Those I've questioned all know about this legendary Saint-Oen, but not one has even seen a bottle of it. What a disaster when all that remains of such a vintage—possibly the greatest of all—should only be a legend. If there were only one wretched bottle left on the face of the earth—"

"Why are you so sure there isn't?" I said.

"Why?" De Marechal gave me a pitying smile. "Because, my dear Drummond, there can't be. I was at the Saint-Oen estate myself not long ago. The *vigneron*'s records there attest that only forty dozen cases of the 1929 were produced altogether. Consider. A scant forty dozen cases spread over all the years from then to now, and with thousands of connoisseurs thirsting for them. I assure you, the last bottle was emptied a generation ago."

I had not intended to come off with it, but that superior smile of his got under my skin.

"I'm afraid your calculations are a bit off, my dear de Marechal." It was going to be a pleasure setting him back on his heels. "You see, a bottle of Nuits Saint-Oen 1929 is, at this very moment, resting in my company's cellars."

The revelation jarred him as hard as I thought it would. His jaw fell. He gaped at me in speechless wonderment. Then his face darkened with suspicion.

"You're joking," he said. "You must be. You just told me you've never tasted the vintage. Now you tell me—"

"Only the truth. After my partner's death last year I found the bottle among his private stock."

"And you haven't been tempted to open it?"

"I resist the temptation. The wine is dangerously old. It would be extremely painful to open it and find it has already died."

"Ah, no!" De Marechal clapped a hand to his brow. "You're an American, monsieur, that's your trouble. Only an American could talk this way, someone who's inherited the obscene Puritan pleasure in self-denial. And for the last existing bottle of Nuits Saint-Oen 1929 to have such an owner! It won't do. It absolutely will not do. Monsieur Drummond, we must come to terms. What price do you ask for this Saint-Oen?"

"None. It is not for sale."

"It must be for sale!" de Marechal said explosively. With an effort he got himself under control. "Look, I'll be frank with you. I am not a rich man. You could get at least a thousand francs—possibly as much as two thousand—for that bottle of wine, and I'm in no position to lay out that kind of money. But I am close to someone who can meet any terms you set. Monsieur Kyros Kassoulas. Perhaps you know of him?"

Since Kyros Kassoulas was one of the richest men on the Continent, someone other magnates approached with their hats off, it would be hard not to know of him despite his well-publicized efforts to live in close seclusion.

"Of course," I said.

"And do you know of the one great interest in his life?"

"I can't say I do. According to the newspapers, he seems to be quite the man of mystery."

"A phrase concocted by journalists to describe anyone of such wealth who chooses to be reticent about his private affairs. Not that there is anything scandalous about them. You see, Monsieur Kassoulas is a fanatic connoisseur of wines." De Marechal gave me a meaningful wink. "That's how I interested him in founding our *Société de la Cave* and in establishing its magazine."

"And in making you its editor."

"So he did," said de Marechal calmly. "Naturally, I'm grateful to him for that. He, in turn, is grateful to me for giving him sound instruction on the great vintages. Strictly between us, he was a sad case when I first met him. A man without any appetite for vice, without any capacity to enjoy literature or music or art, he was being driven to distraction by the emptiness of his life. I filled that emptiness the day I pointed out to him that he must cultivate his extraordinarily true palate for fine wine. The exploration of the worthier vintages since then has been for him a journey through a wonderland. By now, as I have said, he is a fanatic connoisseur. He would know without being told that your bottle of Nuits Saint-Oen 1929 is to other wines what the Mona Lisa is to other paintings. Do you see what that means to you in a business way? He's a tough man to bargain with, but in the end he'll pay two thousand francs for that bottle. You have my word on it."

I shook my head. "I can only repeat, Monsieur de Marechal, the wine is not for sale. There is no price on it."

"And I insist you set a price on it!"

That was too much.

"All right," I said, "then the price is one hundred thousand francs. And without any guarantee the wine isn't dead. One hundred thousand francs exactly."

"Ah," de Marechal said furiously, "so you really don't intend to sell it! But to play dog in the manger—!"

Suddenly, he went rigid. His features contorted, his hands clutched convulsively at his chest. As crimson with passion as his face had been the moment before, it was now ghastly pale and bloodless. He lowered himself heavily into a chair.

"My heart," he gasped in agonized explanation. "It's all right. I have pills—"

The pill he slipped under his tongue was nitroglycerine, I was sure. I had once seen my late partner Broulet undergo a seizure like this.

"I'll call a doctor," I said, but when I went to the phone de Marechal made a violent gesture of protest.

"No, don't bother. I'm used to this. It's an old story with me."

He was, in fact, looking better now.

"If it's an old story you should know better," I told him. "For a man with a heart condition you allow yourself to become much too emotional."

"Do I? And how would you feel, my friend, if you saw a legendary vintage suddenly appear before you and then found it remained just out of reach? No, forgive me for that. It's your privilege not to sell your goods if you don't choose to."

"It is."

"But one small favor. Would you, at least, allow me to see the bottle of Saint-Oen? I'm not questioning its existence. It's only that the pleasure of viewing it, of holding it in my hands—"

It was a small enough favor to grant him. The cellars of Broulet and Drummond were near the Halles au Vin, a short trip by car from the office. There I conducted him through the cool, stony labyrinth bordering the Seine, led him to the Nuits Saint-Oen racks where, apart from all the lesser vintages of later years, the one remaining bottle of 1929 rested in solitary grandeur. I carefully took it down and handed it to de Marechal, who received it with reverence.

He examined the label with an expert eye, delicately ran a fingertip over the cork. "The cork is in good condition."

"What of it? That can't save the wine if its time has already come."

"Naturally. But it's an encouraging sign." He held the bottle up to peer through it. "And there seems to be only a normal sediment. Bear in mind, Monsieur Drummond, that some great Burgundies have lived for fifty years. Some even longer."

He surrendered the bottle to me with reluctance. His eyes remained fixed on it so intensely as I replaced it in the rack that he looked like a man under hypnosis. I had to nudge him out of the spell before I could lead him upstairs to the sunlit outer world.

We parted there.

"I'll keep in touch with you," he said as we shook hands. "Perhaps we can get together for lunch later this week."

"I'm sorry," I said without regret, "but later this week I'm leaving for New York to look in on my office there."

"Too bad. But of course you'll let me know as soon as you
return to Paris."

"Of course," I lied.

HOWEVER, THERE WAS NO putting off Max de Marechal now that he
had that vision of the Nuits Saint-Oen 1929 before his eyes. He must
have bribed one of the help in my Paris office to tell him when I was
back from the States, because no sooner was I again at my desk on
the rue de Berri than he was on the phone. He greeted me with
fervor. What luck he had timed his call so perfectly! My luck, as well
as his. Why? Because *La Société de la Cave* was to have a dinner the
coming weekend, a positive orgy of wine sampling, and its presiding
officer, Kyros Kassoulas himself, had requested my presence at it!

My first impulse was to refuse the invitation. For one thing, I
knew its motive. Kassoulas had been told about the Nuits Saint-
Oen 1929 and wanted to get me where he could personally bargain for it without losing face. For another thing, these
wine-tasting sessions held by various societies of connoisseurs were
not for me. Sampling a rare and excellent vintage is certainly
among life's most rewarding experiences, but, for some reason I
could never fathom, doing it in the company of one's fellow *afi-
cionados* seems to bring out all the fakery hidden away in the soul
of even the most honest citizen. And to sit there, watching ordinarily sensible men vie with each other in their portrayals of ecstasy
over a glass of wine, rolling their eyes, flaring their nostrils, straining to find the most incongruous adjectives with which to describe
it, has always been a trial to me.

Weighed against all this was simple curiosity. Kyros Kassoulas
was a remote and awesome figure, and here I was being handed
the chance to actually meet him. In the end, curiosity won. I
attended the dinner. I met Kassoulas there and I quickly realized,
with gratification, that we were striking it off perfectly.

It was easy to understand why. As de Marechal had put it, Kyros
Kassoulas was a fanatic on wines, a man with a single-minded interest

in their qualities, their history, and their lore; and I could offer him more information on the subject than anyone else he knew. More, he pointed out to me, than even the knowledgeable Max de Marechal.

As the dinner progressed, it intrigued me to observe that where everyone else in the room deferred to Kassoulas—especially de Marechal, a shameless sycophant—Kassoulas himself deferred to me. I enjoyed that. Before long I found myself really liking the man instead of merely being impressed by him.

He was impressive, of course. About fifty, short, and barrel-chested, with a swarthy, deeply lined face and almost simian ears, he was ugly in a way that some clever women would find fascinating. Somehow, he suggested an ancient idol rough-hewn out of a block of mahogany. His habitual expression was a granite impassivity, relieved at times by a light of interest in those veiled, ever-watchful eyes. That light became intense when he finally touched on the matter of my bottle of Saint-Oen.

He had been told its price, he remarked with wry humor, and felt that a hundred thousand francs—twenty thousand hard American dollars—was, perhaps, a little excessive. Now if I would settle for two thousand francs—

I smilingly shook my head.

"It's a handsome offer," Kassoulas said. "It happens to be more than I've paid for any half dozen bottles of wine in my cellar."

"I won't dispute that, Monsieur Kassoulas."

"But you won't sell, either. What are the chances of the wine's being fit to drink?"

"Who can tell? The 1929 vintage at Saint-Oen was late to mature, so it may live longer than most. Or it may already be dead. That's why I won't open the bottle myself or sell anyone else the privilege of opening it. This way, it's a unique and magnificent treasure. Once its secret is out, it may simply be another bottle of wine gone bad."

To his credit, he understood that. And, when he invited me to be a guest at his estate near Saint-Cloud the next weekend, it was with the blunt assurance that it was only my company he sought, not the opportunity to further dicker for the bottle of Saint-Oen. In fact, said he, he would never again broach the matter. All he wanted was my word that if I ever decided to sell the bottle, he would be given first chance to make an offer for it. And to that I cheerfully agreed.

The weekend at his estate was a pleasant time for me, the first of many I spent there. It was an enormous place but smoothly run by a host of efficient help under the authority of a burly, grizzled majordomo named Joseph. Joseph was evidently Kassoulas's devoted slave. It came as no surprise to learn he had been a sergeant in the Foreign Legion. He responded to orders as if his master was the colonel of his regiment.

What did come as a surprise was the lady of the house, Sophia Kassoulas. I don't know exactly what I expected Kassoulas's wife to be like, but certainly not a girl young enough to be his daughter, a gentle, timid creature whose voice was hardly more than a whisper. By today's standards which require a young woman to be a lank-haired rack of bones she was, perhaps, a little too voluptuous, a little too ripely curved, but I am an old-fashioned sort of man who believes women should be ripely curved. And if, like Sophia Kassoulas, they are pale, dark-eyed, blushing beauties, so much the better.

As time passed and I became more and more a friend of the family, I was able to draw from her the story of her marriage, now approaching its fifth anniversary. Sophia Kassoulas was a distant cousin of her husband. Born to poor parents in a mountain village of Greece, convent bred, she had met Kassoulas for the first time at a gathering of the family in Athens, and, hardly out of her girlhood, had married him soon afterward. She was, she assured me in that soft little voice, the most fortunate of women. Yes, to have been chosen by a man like Kyros to be his wife, surely the most fortunate of women—

But she said it as if she were desperately trying to convince herself of it. In fact, she seemed frightened to death of Kassoulas. When he addressed the most commonplace remark to her she shrank away from him. It became a familiar scene, watching this happen, and watching him respond to it by then treating her with an icily polite disregard that only intimidated her the more.

It made an unhealthy situation in that household because, as I saw from the corner of my eye, the engaging Max de Marechal was always right there to soothe Madame's fears away. It struck me after a while how very often an evening at Saint-Cloud wound up with Kassoulas and myself holding a discussion over our brandy at one end of the room while Madame Kassoulas and Max de Marechal were head to head in conversation at the other end. There was nothing indecorous about those *tête-à-têtes*, but still I didn't like the look of them. The girl appeared to be as wide-eyed and ingenuous as a doe, and de Marechal bore all the earmarks of the trained predator.

Kassoulas himself was either unaware of this or remarkably indifferent to it. Certainly, his regard for de Marechal was genuine. He mentioned it to me several times, and once, when de Marechal got himself dangerously heated up in an argument with me over the merits of some vintage or other, Kassoulas said to him with real concern, "Gently, Max, gently. Remember your heart. How many times has the doctor warned you against becoming overexcited?"—which, for Kassoulas, was an unusual show of feeling. Generally, like so many men of his type, he seemed wholly incapable of expressing any depth of emotion.

Indeed, the only time he ever let slip any show of his feelings about his troublesome marriage was once when I was inspecting his wine cellar with him and pointed out that a dozen Volnay-Caillerets 1955 he had just laid in were likely to prove extremely uneven. It had been a mistake to buy it. One never knew, in uncorking a bottle, whether or not he would find it sound.

Kassoulas shook his head.

"It was a calculated risk, Monsieur Drummond, not a mistake. I don't make mistakes." Then he gave an almost imperceptible little shrug. "Well, one perhaps. When a man marries a mere child—"

He cut it short at that. It was the first and last time he ever touched on the subject. What he wanted to talk about was wine, although sometimes under my prodding and because I was a good listener, he would recount stories about his past. My own life has been humdrum. It fascinated me to learn, in bits and pieces, about the life of Kyros Kassoulas, a Piraeus wharf rat who was a thief in his childhood, a smuggler in his youth, and a multimillionaire before he was thirty. It gave me the same sense of drama Kassoulas appeared to feel when I would recount to him stories about some of the great vintages which, like the Nuits Saint-Oen 1929, had been cranky and uncertain in the barrel until, by some miracle of nature, they had suddenly blossomed into their full greatness.

It was at such times that Max de Marechal himself was at his best. Watching him grow emotional in such discussions, I had to smile inwardly at the way he had once condescendingly described Kassoulas as a fanatic about wines. It was a description which fitted him even better. Whatever else might be false about Max de Marechal, his feelings about any great vintage were genuine.

During the months that passed, Kassoulas proved to be as good as his word. He had said he wouldn't again bargain with me for the precious bottle of Saint-Oen, and he didn't. We discussed the Saint-Oen often enough—it was an obsession with de Marechal—but no matter how much Kassoulas was tempted to renew the effort to buy it, he kept his word.

Then, one dismally cold and rainy day in early December, my secretary opened my office door to announce in awestruck tones that Monsieur Kyros Kassoulas was outside waiting to see me. This was a surprise. Although Sophia Kassoulas, who seemed to have no friends in the world apart from de Marechal and myself, had several times been persuaded to have lunch with me when she was in town to do shopping, her husband had never before deigned to visit me in my domain, and I was not expecting him now.

He came in accompanied by the ever dapper de Marechal who, I saw with increased mystification, was in a state of feverish excitement.

We had barely exchanged greetings when de Marechal leaped directly to the point.

"The bottle of Nuits Saint-Oen 1929, Monsieur Drummond," he said. "You'll remember you once set a price on it. One hundred thousand francs."

"Only because it won't be bought at any such price."

"Would you sell it for less?"

"I've already made clear I wouldn't."

"You drive a hard bargain, Monsieur Drummond. But you'll be pleased to know that Monsieur Kassoulas is now prepared to pay your price."

I turned incredulously to Kassoulas. Before I could recover my voice, he drew a check from his pocket and, impassive as ever, handed it to me. Involuntarily, I glanced at it. It was for one hundred thousand francs. It was worth, by the going rate of exchange, twenty thousand dollars.

"This is ridiculous," I finally managed to say. "I can't take it."

"But you must!" de Marechal said in alarm.

"I'm sorry. No wine is worth a fraction of this. Especially a wine that may be dead in the bottle."

"Ah," said Kassoulas, lightly, "then perhaps that's what I'm paying for—the chance to see whether it is or not."

"If that's your reason—" I protested, and Kassoulas shook his head.

"It isn't. The truth is, my friend, this wine solves a difficult problem for me. A great occasion is coming soon, the fifth anniversary of my marriage, and I've been wondering how Madame and I could properly celebrate it. Then inspiration struck me. What better way of celebrating it than to open the Saint-Oen and discover it is still in the flush of perfect health, still in its flawless maturity? What could be more deeply moving and significant on such an occasion?"

"That makes it all the worse if the wine is dead," I pointed out. The check was growing warm in my hand. I wanted to tear it up but couldn't bring myself to do it.

"No matter. The risk is all mine," said Kassoulas. "Of course, you'll be there to judge the wine for yourself. I insist on that. It will be a memorable experience, no matter how it goes. A small dinner with just the four of us at the table, and the Saint-Oen as climax to the occasion."

"The *pièce de résistance* must be an *entrecôte*," breathed de Marechal. "Beef, of course. It will suit the wine perfectly."

I had somehow been pushed past the point of no return. Slowly, I folded the check for the hundred thousand francs and placed it in my wallet. After all, I was in the business of selling wine for a profit.

"When is this dinner to be held?" I asked. "Remember that the wine must stand a few days before it's decanted."

"Naturally, I'm allowing for that," said Kassoulas. "Today is Monday; the dinner will be held Saturday. That means more than enough time to prepare every detail perfectly. On Wednesday I'll see that the temperature of the dining room is properly adjusted, the table set, and the bottle of Saint-Oen placed upright on it for the sediment to clear properly. The room will then be locked to avoid any mishap. By Saturday the last of the sediment should have settled completely. But I don't plan to decant the wine. I intend to serve it directly from the bottle."

"Risky," I said.

"Not if it's poured with a steady hand. One like this." Kassoulas held out a stubby-fingered, powerful-looking hand which showed not a sign of tremor. "Yes, this supreme vintage deserves the honor of being poured from its own bottle, risky as that may be. Surely you now have evidence, Monsieur Drummond, that I'm a man to take any risk if it's worthwhile to me."

I HAD GOOD CAUSE to remember those concluding words at a meeting I had with Sophia Kassoulas later in the week. That day she phoned early in the morning to ask if I could meet her for lunch at an hour when we might have privacy in the restaurant, and, thinking this had something to do with her own plans for the anniversary dinner, I cheerfully accepted the invitation. All the cheerfulness was washed out of me as soon as I joined her at our table in a far corner of the dimly lit, almost deserted room. She was obviously terrified.

"Something is very wrong," I said to her. "What is it?"

"Everything," she said piteously. "And you're the only one I can turn to for help, Monsieur Drummond. You've always been so kind to me. Will you help me now?"

"Gladly. If you tell me what's wrong and what I can do about it."

"Yes, there's no way around that. You must be told everything." Madame Kassoulas drew a shuddering breath. "It can be told very simply. I had an affair with Max de Marechal. Now Kyros has found out about it."

My heart sank. The last thing in the world I wanted was to get involved in anything like this.

"Madame," I said unhappily, "this is a matter to be settled between you and your husband. You must see that it's not my business at all."

"Oh, please! If you only understood—"

"I don't see what there is to understand."

"A great deal. About Kyros, about me, about my marriage. I didn't want to marry Kyros, I didn't want to marry anybody. But my family arranged it, so what could I do? And it's been dreadful from the start. All I am to Kyros is a pretty little decoration for his house. He has no feeling for me. He cares more about that bottle of wine he bought from you than he does for me. Where I'm concerned, he's like stone. But Max—"

"I know," I said wearily. "You found that Max was different. Max cared very much for you. Or, at least, he told you he did."

"Yes, he told me he did," Madame Kassoulas said with defiance. "And whether he meant it or not, I needed that. A woman must have some man to tell her he cares for her or she has nothing. But it was wicked of me to put Max in danger. And now that Kyros knows about us, Max is in terrible danger."

"What makes you think so? Has your husband made any threats?"

"No, he hasn't even said he knows about the affair. But he does. I can swear he does. It's in the way he's been behaving toward me these past few days, in the remarks he makes to me, as if he were enjoying a joke that only he understood. And it all seems to have something to do with that bottle of Saint-Oen locked up in the dining room. That's why I came to you for help. You know about these things."

"Madame, all I know is that the Saint-Oen is being made ready for your dinner party Saturday."

"Yes, that's what Kyros said. But the way he said it—" Madame Kassoulas leaned toward me intently. "Tell me one thing. Is it possible for a bottle of wine to be poisoned without its cork being drawn? Is there any way of doing that?"

"Oh, come now. Do you seriously believe for a moment that your husband intends to poison Max?"

"You don't know Kyros the way I do. You don't know what he's capable of."

"Even murder?"

"Even murder, if he was sure he could get away with it. They tell a story in my family about how, when he was very young, he killed a man who had cheated him out of a little money. Only it was done so cleverly that the police never found out who the murderer was."

That was when I suddenly recalled Kassoulas's words about taking any risk if it were worthwhile to him and felt a chill go through me. All too vividly, I had a mental picture of a hypodermic needle sliding through the cork in that bottle of Saint-Oen, of drops of deadly poison trickling into the wine. Then it struck me how wildly preposterous the picture was.

"Madame," I said, "I'll answer your question this way. Your husband does not intend to poison anyone at your dinner party unless he intends to poison us all, which I am sure he does not. Remember that I've also been invited to enjoy my share of the Saint-Oen."

"What if something were put into Max's glass alone?"

"It won't be. Your husband has too much respect for Max's palate for any such clumsy trick. If the wine is dead, Max will know it at once and won't drink it. If it's still good, he'd detect anything foreign in it with the first sip and not touch the rest. Anyhow, why not discuss it with Max? He's the one most concerned."

"I did try to talk to him about it, but he only laughed at me. He said it was all in my imagination. I know why. He's so insanely eager to try that wine that he won't let anything stop him from doing it."

"I can appreciate his feelings about that." Even with my equanimity restored I was anxious to get away from this unpleasant topic. "And he's right about your imagination. If you really want my advice, the best thing you can do is to behave with your husband as if nothing has happened and to steer clear of Monsieur de Marechal after this."

It was the only advice I could give her under the circumstances. I only hoped she wasn't too panic-stricken to follow it. Or too infatuated with Max de Marechal.

KNOWING TOO MUCH FOR my own comfort, I was ill at ease the evening of the party, so when I joined the company it was a relief to see that Madame Kassoulas had herself well in hand. As for Kassoulas, I could detect no change at all in his manner toward her or de Marechal. It was convincing evidence that Madame's guilty conscience had indeed been working overtime on her imagination, and that Kassoulas knew nothing at all about her *affaire*. He was hardly the man to take being cuckolded with composure, and he was wholly composed. As we sat down to dinner, it was plain that his only concern was about its menu, and, above all, about the bottle of Nuits Saint-Oen 1929 standing before him.

The bottle had been standing there three days, and everything that could be done to ensure the condition of its contents had been done. The temperature of the room was moderate; it had not been allowed to vary once the bottle was brought into the room, and, as Max de Marechal assured me, he had checked this at regular intervals every day. And, I was sure, had taken time to stare rapturously at the bottle, marking off the hours until it would be opened.

Furthermore, since the table at which our little company sat down was of a size to seat eighteen or twenty, it meant long distances between our places, but it provided room for the bottle to stand in lonely splendor clear of any careless hand that might upset it. It was noticeable that the servants waiting on us all gave it a wide berth. Joseph, the burly, hard-bitten majordomo who was supervising them with a dangerous look in his eye, must have put them in fear of death if they laid a hand near it.

Now, Kassoulas had to undertake two dangerous procedures as preludes to the wine-tasting ritual. Ordinarily, a great vintage like the Nuits Saint-Oen 1929 stands until all its sediment has collected in the base of the bottle, and is then decanted. This business of transferring it from bottle to decanter not only ensures that sediment and cork crumbs are left behind, but it also means that the wine is being properly aired. The older a wine, the more it needs to breathe the open air to rid itself of mustiness accumulated in the bottle.

But Kassoulas, in his determination to honor the Saint-Oen by serving it directly from its original bottle, had imposed on himself the delicate task of uncorking it at the table so skillfully that no bits of cork would filter into the liquid. Then, after the wine had stood open until the entrée was served, he would have to pour it with such control that none of the sediment in its base would roil up. It had taken three days for that sediment to settle. The least slip in uncorking the bottle or pouring from it, and it would be another three days before it was again fit to drink.

As soon as we were at the table, Kassoulas set to work on the first task. We all watched with bated breath as he grasped the neck of the bottle firmly and centered the point of the corkscrew in the cork. Then, with the concentration of a demolitions expert defusing a live bomb, he slowly, very slowly, turned the corkscrew, bearing down so lightly that the corkscrew almost had to take hold by itself. His object was to penetrate deep enough to get a grip on the cork so that it could be drawn, yet not to pierce the cork through; it was the one sure way of keeping specks of cork from filtering into the wine.

It takes enormous strength to draw a cork which has not been pierced through from a bottle of wine which it has sealed for decades. The bottle must be kept upright and immobile, the pull must be straight up and steady without any of the twisting and turning that will tear a cork apart. The old-fashioned corkscrew which exerts no artificial leverage is the instrument for this because it allows one to feel the exact working of the cork in the bottleneck.

The hand Kassoulas had around the bottle clamped it so hard that his knuckles gleamed white. His shoulders hunched, the muscles of his neck grew taut. Strong as he appeared to be, it seemed impossible for him to start the cork. But he would not give way, and in the end it was the cork that gave way. Slowly and smoothly it was pulled clear of the bottle-mouth, and for the first time since the wine had been drawn from its barrel long years before, it was now free to breathe the open air.

Kassoulas waved the cork back and forth under his nose, sampling its bouquet. He shrugged as he handed it to me.

"Impossible to tell anything this way," he said, and of course he was right. The fumes of fine Burgundy emanating from the cork meant nothing, since even dead wine may have a good bouquet.

De Marechal would not even bother to look at the cork.

"It's only the wine that matters," he said fervently. "Only the wine. And in an hour we'll know its secret for better or worse. It will seem like a long hour, I'm afraid."

I didn't agree with that at first. The dinner we were served was more than sufficient distraction for me. Its menu, in tribute to the Nuits Saint-Oen 1929, had been arranged the way a symphony conductor might arrange a short program of lighter composers in preparation for the playing of a Beethoven masterwork. Artichoke hearts in a butter sauce, *langouste* in mushrooms, and, to clear the palate, a lemon ice unusually tart. Simple dishes flawlessly prepared.

And the wines Kassoulas had selected to go with them were, I was intrigued to note, obviously chosen as settings for his diamond. A sound Chablis, a respectable Muscadet. Both were good, neither was calculated to do more than draw a small nod of approval from the connoisseur. It was Kassoulas's way of telling us that nothing would be allowed to dim the glorious promise of that open bottle of Nuits Saint-Oen standing before us.

Then my nerves began to get the better of me. Old as I was at the game, I found myself more and more filled with tension and as the dinner progressed I found the bottle of Saint-Oen a magnet for my eyes. It soon became an agony, waiting until the entrée would be served and the Saint-Oen poured.

Who, I wondered, would be given the honor of testing the first few drops? Kassoulas, the host, was entitled to that honor, but as a

mark of respect he could assign it to anyone he chose. I wasn't sure
whether or not I wanted to be chosen. I was braced for the worst,
but I knew that being the first at the table to discover the wine was
dead would be like stepping from an airplane above the clouds
without a parachute. Yet, to be the first to discover that this greatest
of vintages had survived the years—! Watching Max de Marechal,
crimson with mounting excitement, sweating so that he had to constantly mop his brow, I suspected he was sharing my every thought.

The entrée was brought in at last, the *entrecôte* of beef that de
Marechal had suggested. Only a salver of *petits pois* accompanied it.
The *entrecôte* and peas were served. Then Kassoulas gestured at
Joseph, and the majordomo cleared the room of the help. There
must be no chance of disturbance while the wine was being
poured, no possible distraction.

When the servants were gone and the massive doors of the
dining room were closed behind them, Joseph returned to the
table and took up his position near Kassoulas, ready for anything
that might be required of him.

The time had come.

Kassoulas took hold of the bottle of Nuits Saint-Oen 1929. He
lifted it slowly, with infinite care, making sure not to disturb the
treacherous sediment. A ruby light flickered from it as he held it at
arm's length, staring at it with brooding eyes.

"Monsieur Drummond, you were right," he said abruptly.

"I was?" I said, taken aback. "About what?"

"About your refusal to unlock the secret of this bottle. You once
said that as long as the bottle kept its secret it was an extraordinary
treasure, but that once it was opened it might prove to be nothing
but another bottle of bad wine. A disaster. Worse than a disaster, a
joke. That was the truth. And in the face of it I now find I haven't
the courage to learn whether or not what I am holding here is a
treasure or a joke."

De Marechal almost writhed with impatience.

"It's too late for that!" he protested violently. "The bottle is
already open!"

"But there's a solution to my dilemma," Kassoulas said to him.
"Now watch it. Watch it very closely."

His arm moved, carrying the bottle clear of the table. The bottle
slowly tilted. Stupefied, I saw wine spurt from it, pour over the polished boards of the floor. Drops of wine spattered Kassoulas's shoes,

stained the cuffs of his trousers. The puddle on the floor grew larger. Trickles of it crept out in thin red strings between the boards.

It was an unearthly choking sound from de Marechal which tore me free of the spell I was in. A wild cry of anguish from Sophia Kassoulas.

"Max!" she screamed. "Kyros, stop! For God's sake, stop! Don't you see what you're doing to him?"

She had reason to be terrified. I was terrified myself when I saw de Marechal's condition. His face was ashen, his mouth gaped wide open, his eyes, fixed on the stream of wine relentlessly gushing out of the bottle in Kassoulas's unwavering hand, were starting out of his head with horror.

Sophia Kassoulas ran to his side but he feebly thrust her away and tried to struggle to his feet. His hands reached out in supplication to the fast-emptying bottle of Nuits Saint-Oen 1929.

"Joseph," Kassoulas said dispassionately, "see to Monsieur de Marechal. The doctor warned that he must not move during these attacks."

The iron grasp Joseph clamped on de Marechal's shoulder prevented him from moving, but I saw his pallid hand fumbling into a pocket, and at last regained my wits.

"In his pocket!" I pleaded. "He has pills!"

It was too late. De Marechal suddenly clutched at his chest in that familiar gesture of unbearable pain, then his entire body went limp, his head lolling back against the chair, his eyes turning up in his head to glare sightlessly at the ceiling. The last thing they must have seen was the stream of Nuits Saint-Oen 1929 become a trickle, the trickle become an ooze of sediment clotting on the floor in the middle of the vast puddle there.

Too late to do anything for de Marechal, but Sophia Kassoulas stood swaying on her feet ready to faint. Weak-kneed myself, I helped her to her chair, saw to it that she downed the remains of the Chablis in her glass.

The wine penetrated her stupor. She sat there breathing hard, staring at her husband until she found the strength to utter words.

"You knew it would kill him," she whispered. "That's why you bought the wine. That's why you wasted it all."

"Enough, madame," Kassoulas said frigidly. "You don't know what you're saying. And you're embarrassing our guest with this

emotionalism." He turned to me. "It's sad that our little party had
to end this way, monsieur, but these things do happen. Poor Max.
He invited disaster with his temperament. Now I think you had
better go. The doctor must be called in to make an examination
and fill out the necessary papers, and these medical matters can be
distressing to witness. There's no need for you to be put out by
them. I'll see you to the door."

I got away from there without knowing how. All I knew was that
I had seen a murder committed and there was nothing I could do
about it. Absolutely nothing. Merely to say aloud that what I had
seen take place was murder would be enough to convict me of
slander in any court. Kyros Kassoulas had planned and executed
his revenge flawlessly, and all it would cost him, by my bitter calculations, were one hundred thousand francs and the loss of a faith-
less wife. It was unlikely that Sophia Kassoulas would spend
another night in his house even if she had to leave it with only the
clothes on her back.

I never heard from Kassoulas again after that night. For that
much, at least, I was grateful . . .

NOW, SIX MONTHS LATER, here I was at a café table on the rue de
Rivoli with Sophia Kassoulas, a second witness to the murder and as
helplessly bound to silence about it as I was. Considering the shock
given me by our meeting, I had to admire her own composure as
she hovered over me solicitously, saw to it that I took down a cognac
and then another, chattered brightly about inconsequential things
as if that could blot the recollection of the past from our minds.

She had changed since I had last seen her. Changed all for the
better. The timid girl had become a lovely woman who glowed with
self-assurance. The signs were easy to read. Somewhere, I was sure,
she had found the right man for her and this time not a brute like
Kassoulas or a shoddy Casanova like Max de Marechal.

The second cognac made me feel almost myself again, and
when I saw my Samaritan glance at the small, brilliantly jeweled
watch on her wrist I apologized for keeping her and thanked her
for her kindness.

"Small kindness for such a friend," she said reproachfully. She rose and gathered up her gloves and purse. "But I did tell Kyros I would meet him at—"

"Kyros!"

"But of course. Kyros. My husband." Madame Kassoulas looked at me with puzzlement.

"Then you're still living with him?"

"Very happily." Then her face cleared. "You must forgive me for being so slow-witted. It took a moment to realize why you should ask such a question."

"Madame, I'm the one who should apologize. After all—"

"No, no, you had every right to ask it." Madame Kassoulas smiled at me. "But it's sometimes hard to remember I was ever unhappy with Kyros, the way everything changed so completely for me that night—

"But you were there, Monsieur Drummond. You saw for yourself how Kyros emptied the bottle of Saint-Oen on the floor, all because of me. What a revelation that was! What an awakening! And when it dawned on me that I really did mean more to him than even the last bottle of Nuits Saint-Oen 1929 in the whole world, when I found the courage to go to his room that night and tell him how this made me feel—oh, my dear Monsieur Drummond, it's been heaven for us ever since!"

Roast of Beef in Burgundy Wine Sauce with Roasted Garlic

3- to 4-lb. beef shoulder, chuck, blade, strip, or rump roast
1 head of garlic, peeled, separated into cloves, and sliced into thin slices
½ cup flour
3 Tbsp. olive oil
2 cups beef stock, canned or homemade
2 cups Burgundy wine
1 cup water
2 Tbsp. cornstarch

PREHEAT OVEN TO 300 degrees F.

DREDGE ROAST IN flour on all sides. Place olive oil in a big skillet. Heat. Sauté garlic slices in the olive oil until soft and slightly clear. Brown roast on all sides in the hot skillet. Place roast and garlic and oil in a roasting pan. Add beef stock, wine, and water to the roasting pan. Place in oven and bake at 300 degrees F. for two to three hours, turning roast over in pan every 30 minutes. Add additional water to the roasting pan, if needed, to keep it from drying out.

REMOVE ROAST FROM oven when the meat is done to your satisfaction. Pull meat from roasting pan and set on platter. Place roasting pan on stove burner set for low to medium heat, or, if this is not possible, transfer contents of roast pan to a saucepan. Place cornstarch in an empty cup or bowl. Add hot liquid from the roast pan, one tablespoon at a time, to the cornstarch, stirring carefully to prevent lumps from forming. Continue adding liquid into cornstarch until it is fully dissolved. Add the liquid in the cup to contents of roasting pan, adding water if necessary to bring total volume of liquid to a cup and a half. Cook, stirring constantly, until the liquid takes on a glossy sheen and thickens. Remove sauce from stove. Slice roast. Serve with warm sauce drizzled over the slices or on the side.

Takeout

Joyce Christmas

Lady Margaret Priam, in spite of a fine aristocratic upbringing in England at the hands of her mother, the Countess of Brayfield, and her father, the earl, plus a select group of proper nannies, still harbored a dark secret that was allowed to surface now that she lived in Manhattan, rather than in London or at Priam's Priory, the family estate in England.

The secret—well, it was more of a shameful quirk—was that Margaret Priam, a woman of the upper classes, now in her midthirties and welcomed out and about in Manhattan society, possessed, indeed treasured, an extensive and wide-ranging collection of Chinese takeout menus for restaurants in her part of the fashionable Upper East Side of New York City.

Margaret was accustomed to being served, and she liked Chinese food, preferably eaten at home in the comfort of her well-appointed apartment on the twentieth floor of a fairly expensive high rise. Takeout food represented a workable solution, and the menus were the medium that made it possible.

She assumed, perhaps incorrectly, that deliverymen from New York City's Chinese restaurants received large bonuses based on the number of menus they were able to stuff under apartment doors when making deliveries. In any case, Margaret acquired every one she saw, and delighted in the grand names and flowery descriptions: "Three Kings of the Sea—shrimp, lobster meat, and scallops fit only for the connoisseur" . . . "Crispy Whole Fish

339

Hunan Style—fresh whole fish lightly battered and seared until
golden brown, then smothered in a hot, pungent, homemade rice
wine sauce. Delightful!" . . . "Special Garden—splendiferous array
of vegetables enhanced by a bed of lotus stems, tasty wood-ear
mushrooms, shredded dried bean curd, bamboo shoots, baby
corn, snow pea pods, broccoli, and tomatoes in chef's special hot
sauce." Tomatoes? Perhaps, although their wide distribution in
China was somewhat doubtful.

She liked reading about the "delicious gentle sauces" and the
creations "originally served to royal families, now brought to you."
And, of course, there were the many "Triple Delights," "Lover's
Nests," and General Tso dishes, and, finally, "Happy Family,"
which she remembered dining on long ago on first meeting her
gentleman friend, Sam De Vere of the New York police. De Vere
especially liked the many variations of Happy Family.

Mr. Davidson, the strict concierge on the ground floor, who was
one step up in the building's hierarchy from the pleasant young
man who actually opened the door, had strictly forbidden deliverymen to leave piles of menus in the semi-ornate lobby. They were
also discouraged from shoving menus under the doors on the
upper floors as they made their deliveries. Mr. Davidson, at his discretion and with tenant permission, did allow deliverymen he recognized to ascend alone with their plastic shopping bags of
takeout food up to the tenants' floors and doors. If, however, they
were found scattering menus about (and sometimes they did), he
banned them from the upper floors, causing them and those who
ordered food no end of inconvenience. Those of whom Mr. Davidson disapproved were required to be accompanied by a member of
the building's staff. Since such a person was not always readily
available, food got cold, and the restaurant lost future business.

She wasn't sure the other tenants were as dedicated to the concept of dinner packed in cardboard containers and rushed on
bicycles or in little vans through the streets of New York to fill
empty stomachs.

For herself, she was never happier than when she was leafing
through her pile of Chinese menus, pencil in hand, deciding
which restaurant to call and devising just the right combination of
dishes to order in. Who had the best pan-fried noodles, the best
orange-flavored beef, the puffiest roast pork buns, the crispiest
spring roll? Whose shrimp was not old and recently unfrozen?

Whose fortune cookies not only gave fortunes but lucky numbers—enough to fill out one game of Lotto, surely leading to winnings in the millions of dollars?

She had many places to choose from, but she usually called Pearl of the Orient, only a couple of blocks away, and she never hesitated to call when a trip to the grocery store or deli was more than she could handle in the rain, snow, sleet, or simply the cold of a New York night.

Mr. Arrigo, whose apartment was two doors from hers, apparently had a taste for pizza, since she had several times seen a handsome youth with a large padded pizza delivery box standing at Mr. Arrigo's door and then be admitted.

Indeed, once or twice in the elevator she'd been engaged in conversation by Mr. Arrigo, who actually discussed the pleasures of a large pie with pepperoni, and a big order of hot mussels with good Italian bread to soak up the sauce. She did not admit that she was unfamiliar with hot mussels, nor did she comment that it seemed a great deal of food for one man to consume. Maybe Mr. Arrigo liked leftovers. It seemed that he rather liked her, but she had long ago learned that men of any age—Mr. Arrigo was perhaps in his fifties—found it hard to resist a well-put-together blonde with an English accent. Italian blood seemed to be especially stirred by blonde hair and blue eyes. Her young friend Prince Paul Castrocani was similarly bowled over by blondes, although he preferred to have an idea of the woman's financial status before proceeding. Paul was undeniably nice, but he was also something of a gold digger. He had never, however, to the best of her knowledge, used hot mussels to open a conversation with a pretty wench.

As genial as Mr. Arrigo appeared to be in the close confines of the elevator, she was wary of him. He had cold eyes, and the aura of a man always keeping control of his temper. She remembered times when that control slipped. The elevator door did not close quickly enough to suit him, and he jabbed furiously at the buttons, purpling slightly, his mouth tight with anger. She'd heard angry shouts as she passed his apartment door; and she'd seen him become enraged when the doorman was not quick to open the door—and the door of his long black town car purring at the curb. She'd prefer not to be the object of Mr. Arrigo's anger.

Tonight—rainy and blustery—was perfect for ordering takeout, and she had additional justification. Sam De Vere, when released from his duties as a police detective, had half promised to make his way later to her place. On that expectation, she'd turned down an invitation to dine at the showplace apartment of a prominent woman Realtor to the well known and well heeled. Her legendary dinner parties drew the celebrated and the social from both coasts, as well as Washington's seats of power. Margaret preferred a quiet evening at home with De Vere, and she'd have something for him to eat when he arrived.

Margaret phoned Pearl of the Orient with her order, with the total cost precalculated from the menu prices, including the tax and, of course, the tip for Mr. Feng, the regular deliveryman.

Within fifteen minutes Mr. Davidson rang her intercom to announce the arrival of Mr. Feng, who was already on his way up. The concierge knew him well, and Mr. Feng knew his way around the corner from the elevators, along the corridor to her apartment.

The doorbell buzzed. Mr. Feng was outside the door, grinning and offering with a polite bob of his head a shopping bag crammed with brown paper bags holding white cardboard containers and aluminum foil dishes with cardboard covers, which were invariably splashed with soy and sweet and sour sauce from someone else's order.

No matter how horrid the weather, Mr. Feng was always cheerful, as though he had personally cooked Margaret's meal (perhaps he had) prior to delivering it on his beat-up bicycle through the inclemencies outside. He worked long hours. Margaret had seen him from time to time during the day careening through traffic on his rounds to deliver lunches to offices in the area, the bag of takeout food hooked over the handlebars. He did not seem to take particular heed of the traffic, but then, not many people did.

"Bad night," Mr. Feng said as he handed her a double order of wonton soup, stir-fried spinach with garlic, and prawns with black bean sauce.

A large drop of water made its way slowly down his nose. After a moment's suspension at the tip, it dropped to the carpet outside her apartment door. "You always calling on a bad night." He spoke it not as a complaint, but as a simple truth.

"Yes," Margaret said, "I do." She really didn't mind a bit that it was Mr. Feng rather than she out on a night like this.

She handed Mr. Feng the exact amount she'd calculated, a modest enough sum for her evening meal, with leftovers for De Vere or even breakfast. She stepped into the hall to take the bag from Mr. Feng and saw from the corner of her eye that the pizza delivery boy was entering Mr. Arrigo's apartment, laden with bags and a big white pizza box.

Mr. Feng looked at the money she'd handed him. "Ah, miss," he said, "is not enough. Look . . . lobster . . . eleven dollar, fifty cents . . ." He showed her the bill, with three items neatly printed in Chinese characters. "Lobster very expensive."

"Lobster! Then there's been a mistake! I ordered shrimp. I cannot eat lobster. I am allergic. It makes me very ill."

Mr. Feng looked concerned, and then suddenly alarmed, as though she might topple over from her doorway into his arms.

"You'll have to go back and bring me the right thing," Margaret said. "I simply can't eat lobster. I'll call the Pearl right away and have them fix the shrimp, so it will be waiting when you get there. You can bring it right back to me." The aroma of the dishes in the white bag seeped into the hall. She was hungry, but she handed the bag back to him.

"Ah," Mr. Feng said again, and brushed away another enormous drop of rain from the end of his nose. He looked so disconcerted that she felt sorry for him, since it couldn't have been his fault but rather that of the abrupt woman who took telephone orders. Mr. Feng was a nice, gentle man, shorter than she by several inches, with smooth, tannish skin and floppy, black hair, very badly cut. Tonight it was plastered down damply because of the rain. The poor man was wearing nothing in the way of rain gear, and he had a large white bandage affixed to the side of his head.

"Did you have an accident?" Margaret indicated the bandage with her chin.

Mr. Feng thought for a moment. "Car hit bicycle," he said. "Happens all the time. Is nothing."

"I'm so sorry," she said. "You must be more careful. Now let me just call the restaurant and tell them about the mistake."

She left him at the door and called the Pearl of the Orient. She had the number on speed dial. The explanation took some time, and then she agreed to examine the dish to be sure it was lobster.

She fetched the bag from Mr. Feng, who was lounging against the wall in the hallway. He seemed distracted as he peered down the corridor. She looked at the food he'd brought her. It was definitely lobster and not shrimp.

As she spoke to the restaurant again, she could hear the rain lashing the window that overlooked Third Avenue. The woman at the Pearl of the Orient sounded quite put-out, but finally agreed to correct the error. In the competitive takeout business, it paid to humor a good customer.

"All right," she said to Mr. Feng. "If you go back to the restaurant, they'll have the shrimp ready for you to bring back to me. I'll just keep the other things, so you don't have to carry them back and forth."

Mr. Feng appeared to be thinking hard, and seemed not even to be listening to her. She wondered if he understood, since she wasn't sure how strong his English was.

"Have to hurry, miss," he said. "Very bad night." He seemed anxious to depart. Then she wondered if she ought to tip him again when he returned. She probably should, since he was the one braving the bad weather, when it could so easily have been her.

"I'll be seeing you in just a few minutes," she said. As she closed the door, she remembered that De Vere loved fried dumplings. Mr. Feng could bring some back with the shrimp. She opened the door again. "Mr. Feng—"

She stopped abruptly. Mr. Feng was edging along the corridor, close to the wall, and was now opposite Mr. Arrigo's apartment door. He stopped and stared, with that look of alarm she recognized. The door was certainly open, because she heard it being slammed shut. Mr. Feng hesitated, and suddenly he ran—toward the branching hallway that led to the bank of elevators.

Mr. Arrigo, an impressive figure in a finely tailored charcoal business suit, stepped from his apartment and shouted after Mr. Feng, "Hey, you!"

Mr. Feng had disappeared around the corner. Mr. Arrigo sighed heavily and muttered to himself. Then he noticed Margaret. "Well, Lady Margaret . . ." He took a step in her direction. She was surprised to note that he was wearing a witty Nicole Miller necktie. "Who was that fellow? Know him? I saw him hanging around outside your door."

"Oh, it's only Mr. Feng, the deliveryman."

"Delivery?" Mr. Arrigo's tone was not warm.

"You know, Chinese takeout. Like your pizza boy."

Mr. Arrigo looked quickly back at his apartment door. "Izzat right? Like Tony? I don't think so. Tony knows to mind his own business. Where's your guy from?"

"I don't think . . ." She didn't like the look on Mr. Arrigo's face. "Pearl of the Orient," she said quickly. "The restaurant just up the avenue a few blocks. They made a mistake with my order, so he's gone off to bring back the right thing."

"Yeah, well, you can't get reliable service nowadays," Mr. Arrigo said. "Say, I'd have you over tonight for some of those hot mussels Tony just brought, but I got business associates in. You know how it is. We'll do it sometime, though, one of these days. Tony'll deliver 'em to us right off the stove, practically right out of the ocean."

"Lovely," Margaret said. "I'd like that. Sometime." She wasn't terribly keen on a *tête-à-tête* with Mr. Arrigo, since as far as she knew there was no Mrs. Arrigo, although any number of times she'd noticed sexy, well-dressed women coming and going from his place. Professionals, perhaps, who for a fee would agree to enjoy hot mussels and pizza with pepperoni.

"It's a deal," he said, and in an instant he had disappeared back into his apartment, calling, "Hey, Tony! On your feet!"

Margaret pondered Mr. Feng's hasty departure as she took from a cabinet a beautiful antique Chinese bowl of considerable value that her former employer, Bedros Kasparian, the Oriental art dealer, had given her when he closed his shop. He would be horrified—or maybe not—to know that she used it for the purpose for which it had been created. She dumped the wonton soup into the bowl and delicately placed some spinach on top, using her prized ebony chopsticks with tops of Baccarat crystal banded in gold.

She ate a little, but slowly, watching the news and the weather on television. The bad weather was due to continue all week.

It was quite a long time after Mr. Feng had left that Mr. Davidson rang to announce, "Delivery."

Poor Mr. Feng, she thought, *wet through again*. She found a few more dollars for a bigger tip.

"Oh!" She was startled when she opened the door at the doorbell's ring. It wasn't Mr. Feng at all but a different Chinese man she didn't recognize. He held out the white plastic bag to her.

"Shrimp, black bean sauce," he said. "No charge."

"Where is Mr. Feng?"

The deliveryman looked serious, shook his head. "Gone home," he said quickly. "Sick."

"Well, yes. He was soaked." She gave him a couple of dollars, not the whole amount she'd planned to tip Mr. Feng for his second trip.

"Bad sick," the man said. "Hit by car on Third Avenue." He started back in the direction of the elevators.

"Wait!" He stopped. "Tell me what happened. Please."

The deliveryman shrugged. "Little van from . . ." He gestured, making a wide circle with his arms.

"Pizza!"

The man smiled and nodded agreement. "Mr. Feng coming back with your order, van goes right at him. Don't worry, chef cooks more shrimp for you." He hurried back toward the elevator.

She found she was no longer very hungry.

Margaret put the shrimp aside in the kitchen, along with the spinach and the remains of the wonton soup. She was restless, remembering Mr. Feng's widened eyes as he looked into Mr. Arrigo's apartment, Mr. Arrigo's questions about Feng and the restaurant, and his shout for Tony.

Then Mr. Feng had been hit by a pizza delivery van as he bicycled back to her.

Ridiculous. There could be no possible connection, but she couldn't stop imagining things. What could Mr. Feng have seen through the open door or while he stood in the corridor? Something that would have caused him to be silenced on Mr. Arrigo's orders?

Which pizza restaurant did Tony deliver for? She couldn't, under the circumstances, ask Mr. Arrigo, even if she confessed an irresistible longing for her own order of hot mussels.

She remained as uncertain as ever as to the exact nature of hot mussels. She glanced at her shelf of cookbooks, but instead of leafing through an index or two, she suddenly remembered *moules marinere*, mussels cooked in white wine, vegetables, and herbs. That was a French dish, of course, but then she realized that it was an easy step linguistically from French *marinere* to Italian *marinara*. Aha! Hot mussels were certainly mussels cooked in marinara sauce, spiced with red pepper. She was rather proud of herself for figuring it out.

Again she thought how difficult it would be for one man to eat a large pizza and a large order of hot mussels—with bread to dip up the spicy red sauce—but Mr. Arrigo had said he had business associates visiting. No doubt all hearty eaters.

She didn't enjoy harboring suspicions about Mr. Arrigo. True, he was invariably polite, well dressed, quite distinguished-looking, but she had no idea what he did for a living, and certainly no idea what he might have been doing in his apartment—with the door open—that had alarmed Mr. Feng, and perhaps had led to his "accident." Or maybe it was something his "business associates" were doing. What was the worst thing she could imagine seeing? She made a mental list:

. . . The expression on Princess Margaret's face when she was told that she was not allowed to smoke.

. . . Getting off a subway train late at night at an empty station and seeing that the exit was at the far end.

She also imagined the look on people's faces if she showed up at the Metropolitan Museum of Art's Costume Institute Winter Gala in old jeans and a plaid man's shirt—without having had her hair or nails done.

. . . Finding a dead body, possibly murdered. A terrible sight.

The choice was easy. She'd found bodies, and the sight had been quite unnerving.

Now she was convinced that Mr. Feng must have seen something awful, like a body. What could be worse? Well, she'd once cautioned Princess Margaret about smoking, and that had been pretty awful, too.

She pushed the speed dial button for Pearl of the Orient.

"I . . . this is Lady Margaret Priam," she said to the woman who answered. It sounded like the woman who usually took phone orders.

"Boy is on the way," the woman said with some irritation. "No more trouble. Food is right this time."

"Yes, yes, it is," Margaret said hastily. "The deliveryman has been here. I wanted to ask about Mr. Feng."

The silence was so long she eventually said, "Hello? Are you there?"

"You want to order?"

"No. I mean, I wanted to know how Mr. Feng is. The deliveryman said he was hit by a car."

"No," the woman said firmly. "Everything is good. Mr. Feng fall off bicycle. Gone home. No car."

"But the deliveryman said—"

"No car," the woman said even more firmly, and hung up. Surely, if the substitute deliveryman saw what happened, someone else must have. The temptation to call De Vere was very strong. If a man had been hit by a car, even a lowly deliveryman who paid little heed to traffic, the police would know about it. But then she would have to explain why she wanted to know, and she had repeatedly promised De Vere that she wouldn't involve herself with mysterious deaths. She had encountered murders once or twice too often for De Vere's taste. Maybe Mr. Feng wasn't dead, but she was now certain that someone was, in Mr. Arrigo's apartment.

There were always the hospital emergency rooms, but she suspected that if Mr. Feng were able to make his way from such an accident, he would indeed have gone home.

By the time the local ten o'clock television news came on, De Vere had not yet appeared at her apartment. Margaret was still wondering what to do about Mr. Feng, when she heard a brief report of a hit-and-run accident on a street corner on the east side of Third Avenue. A victim, dead at the scene. A small van seen by witnesses speeding from the accident. The name was not given, but Margaret felt a sudden pang of sorrow for Mr. Feng, whose smiling face and punctilious courtesy had often softened the harsh realities of New York life. He was a kind of friend, the way the old servants at Priam's Priory were her friends. And her responsibility. She had to know the truth.

But what could she do tonight? Advancing on Mr. Arrigo to demand an explanation was considered. Very briefly. Affable, distinguished Mr. Arrigo might chat easily about trivialities in the elevator, he might find her attractive, but he did not appear to be a man who could be manipulated by a proper Brit lady into confessing a crime against his will. Given what she now suspected, crime could very well be his business, and murder—either of a "business associate" or a harmless deliveryman—only a minor blip on his screen of life.

She remembered with sadness the huge raindrops plopping from Mr. Feng's nose.

Then she remembered Tony. She got out the classified pages of the phone book and turned to the section on restaurants. On the page listing restaurants by type and location, there were lots of Italian restaurants, lots of pizzerias. And lots of them were in her general neighborhood. She picked up the phone.

"Hello? Do you have hot mussels and a delivery boy named Tony?"

"Lady, everybody's got a delivery boy named Tony." This was the fifth place she'd called. "Yeah, we got mussels . . ." The man sounded wary.

"Aren't you the place that delivers to Mr. Arrigo at . . . ?" She gave the building's address.

"Hey, yeah. Enzo Arrigo. You know him?" The man sounded impressed, and wavered between truculence and a desire to ingratiate himself with someone who was a friend of Enzo Arrigo's.

"My neighbor," Margaret said brightly. "He's so terribly enthusiastic about your food."

"Arrigo said that? Hey, it's only pizza and calzone, some pretty good lasagne, the usual stuff . . ."

"And Tony."

"Lady, Tony's only a kid, you know? Give him a break."

"I have no . . . no designs on Tony," Margaret said primly. "I just want . . ."

"So, what *do* you want?"

"Mussels. Hot mussels. Umm . . . Do you have a car for deliveries? I'll need them fast, I have a guest coming."

"Tony's just gone off," the man said quickly. "You'll like Sal just as good. He's a little older, you know? More of a man of the world. Yeah, we got a delivery truck for bad nights like this. I'll put your order in now. Fifteen, twenty, maybe twenty-five minutes at the outside, it'll be there. Apartment?"

Margaret was too impatient to wait quietly for Sal's arrival. If she took a stroll down the hall, past Mr. Arrigo's apartment, she might get an idea. . . .

Outside Mr. Arrigo's door, she looked down and froze.

On the deep-pile hall carpet was a splotch of red. Several splotches.

It can't be blood, she thought. *It can't. Things involving blood don't happen in my apartment building.*

Hesitantly, she touched one of the splotches with her finger, and retreated rapidly to her apartment. Inside, she looked at her finger, then sniffed it, but refused to taste it. It didn't look like blood, but still . . . There was a very faint scent of garlic and fennel, Italian herbs and spices.

Margaret relaxed with a sigh. Marinara sauce. It had to be. Not that it explained anything, unless some of the other splotches were not marinara, but something else.

Where was De Vere? He'd know what to do. She wiped the red substance from her finger, then wondered if she should collect more samples, just in case.

What if Mr. Feng had seen a body covered in blood in Mr. Arrigo's apartment? Or even one covered in marinara sauce? Something must have happened in or just outside of Mr. Arrigo's apartment that put Mr. Feng in danger. Someone had taken note of Mr. Feng.

The sharp ring of her doorbell startled her. Mr. Davidson rarely failed to advise her from downstairs of a delivery.

She took a deep breath and prepared to meet Sal, the man with the hot mussels.

Sal was outside her door, all right, but so was Mr. Arrigo, looking as grim as she'd ever seen him. He entered her apartment without waiting to be asked. "Come on in, kid," he said to Sal. "This here's a real lady, even if no lady I know pokes her nose into other people's private business."

Margaret heard herself babbling, "How nice of you to drop by. I kept thinking of how good those mussels you like sounded, so I ordered some. Have you eaten? Well, you must have, since Tony brought in all that food. What do I owe you, Sal?"

Mr. Arrigo cut her off. "It's been taken care of. So, you didn't like the Chinese takeout you got before?"

"I . . . I rather lost my appetite for it," Margaret said, and took a deep breath, "after what happened to the deliveryman."

"Yeah? So what did happen? Put that stuff down, Sal, and get lost." Sal obeyed promptly, closing the apartment door behind him.

"He was killed in a hit-and-run accident. Silly man, he paid no attention to traffic. I liked him."

"Did you, now? He's another one who poked his nose into things he shouldn't. It can be dangerous."

"Look, Mr. Arrigo . . . Enzo . . ." Margaret attempted wide-eyed winsomeness, but it didn't seem to work with Mr. Arrigo.

"No problem," Mr. Arrigo said. "He's dead." He stood in front of Margaret. "Now, what do I do about you?"

"Me?" Margaret said. "Whatever do you mean?"

"Hey, if that little Chinese guy saw my . . . associate, who was . . . seriously indisposed, he mighta told you, since you're such big pals." Arrigo ignored her vigorous denying headshake. "Anyhow, next I hear you're calling around about Tony and then I see you prowling around outside my door . . ."

"Someone was terribly careless," Margaret said. "The building people will be very cross about the marinara stains on the carpeting."

Mr. Arrigo stared at her. Then he laughed a loud, rumbling laugh. "Marinara! Geez! I bet you thought it was, like, blood. Well, so did I. We took this guy away. I was going to clean it up later. Hey, the joke's on me."

"Mr. Feng is dead," Margaret said. "That's no joke."

Mr. Arrigo grinned. "He was taken out by Tony, with his dinky delivery van." He rumbled again. "Taken out by the takeout guy! Now *that's* a joke. Get it?"

Margaret looked away. Yes, she got it, but she was rather more worried about herself, now that Mr. Arrigo had confirmed her suspicions.

"Sweetheart, you know a little too much." Mr. Arrigo frowned.

"I don't know anything," Margaret said firmly, "except that you spilled sauce from the hot mussels on the carpet when you were taking the trash to the trash room."

Mr. Arrigo chuckled. He seemed to be in high spirits. "Yeah, the trash. Right. Still . . ."

The buzzer from the concierge in the lobby sounded.

"What's that?"

"More takeout," Margaret said, and hoped he would believe her. "I've got to answer, or Mr. Davidson will send someone up to check."

"Okay, then. Just say, 'Yes.' No yelling for somebody. I mean it."

Margaret was sure he did. She said into the intercom phone, "Yes?"

Mr. Davidson said, "Your boyfriend's here. He's on his way up."

"That's good," Margaret said evenly. "Thank you." She hated the idea of being rescued by De Vere, but consider the alternative. She faced Mr. Arrigo. "Could I put the mussels away? I'll heat them up later." Was she being optimistic about there being a "later" for her?

"Go ahead." Arrigo followed her into the kitchen and watched her remove the aluminum container from the bag. The metal was very hot. Sal must have raced to the apartment.

The doorbell rang. De Vere at last.

"Could you get the door, please? My hands are full." She was busy dumping the container of mussels and sauce into the big cast-iron pot she always used for simmering pasta sauce.

Surprisingly, Mr. Arrigo went obediently to the door. He opened it to reveal Sam De Vere, who was definitely startled to be facing Mr. Arrigo and not Lady Margaret Priam. Margaret edged out of the kitchen, carrying the heavy pot full of mussels. Raising it to her shoulder, she hurled it at Mr. Arrigo's back.

Her aim was perfect. A spray of shiny blue-black mussels and bright red sauce exploded over Mr. Arrigo's handsome charcoal jacket, the iron pot striking the back of his head. He staggered, and was perhaps too stunned by the blow to think to reach for the gun she imagined he carried.

Nevertheless, she shouted, "He has a gun!"

De Vere merely endured the surprise of his life and a few splashes of marinara sauce on his sport jacket and jeans. But then, he was not what one would call a cutting-edge dresser. As Mr. Arrigo, awash in red marinara, lurched against the doorjamb, De Vere managed to gain control of him. No gun was drawn, although there was in fact a gun, which De Vere managed to liberate from Mr. Arrigo's person.

"Margaret," De Vere said sternly, "exactly what is the meaning of this?"

"It's about ordering takeout," Margaret said. "Come on in, and I'll explain."

"Yes," DeVere said, "you will." Mussel shells crunched under the men's shoes as De Vere prodded Mr. Arrigo into the apartment.

"For heaven's sake, put him in the leather chair, I don't need marinara all over my chintz cushions," Margaret said.

De Vere said, "Now, how did you know that this gentleman would have a gun?" Mr. Arrigo looked a little the worse for wear as he sat heavily in the leather chair and rubbed the back of his head.

Margaret shrugged. "The thought just occurred to me. Because he arranged to have a friend of mine killed tonight. He's my neighbor, Enzo Arrigo. He might have had someone else killed, too." She gestured at the sauce and mussels on her floor. "He likes Italian stuff, like hot mussels, so I called for takeout. Not that I was planning on entertaining him . . . Sam, I'm so glad you came in time, even if the mussels are gone."

"Margaret." De Vere was stern again, but he reached out and squeezed her shoulder. "You know I prefer Chinese."

Chinese Takeout

CONSULT YELLOW PAGES under "Restaurants." Pick a Chinese restaurant that delivers in your neighborhood. If you already have a favorite Chinese restaurant, consult the wrinkled menu you've got stashed by the phone. Remove money from wallet. Call restaurant. Order what you like, ask for total with tax, and set aside appropriate money to pay the delivery person. Wait until delivery person arrives, and pay up. If food is hot, tip profusely. Close door, open cardboard containers. Break apart the chopsticks, and make sure all splinters are gone from them by rubbing the rough bits together. Dig in and enjoy!

The Case of the Shaggy Caps

Ruth Rendell

Blewits," said Inspector Burden, "Parasols, Horns of Plenty, Morels, and Boletus. Mean anything to you?"

Chief Inspector Wexford shrugged. "Sounds like one of those magazine quizzes. What have these in common? I'll make a guess and say they're crustacea. Or sea anemones. How about that?"

"They are edible fungi," said Burden.

"Are they now? And what have edible fungi to do with Mrs. Hannah Kingman's throwing herself off, or being pushed off, a balcony?"

The two men were sitting in Wexford's office at the police station, Kingsmarkham, in the County of Sussex. The month was November, but Wexford had only just returned from his holiday. And while he had been away, enjoying two weeks of Italian autumn, Hannah Kingman had committed suicide. Or so Burden had thought at first. Now he was in a dilemma, and as soon as Wexford had walked in that Monday morning, Burden had begun to tell the whole story to his chief.

Wexford, getting on for sixty, was a tall, ungainly, rather ugly man who had once been fat to the point of obesity but had slimmed to gauntness for reasons of health. Nearly twenty years his junior, Burden had the slenderness of a man who has always been thin. His face was ascetic, handsome in a frosty way. The older man, who had a good wife who looked after him devotedly, nevertheless always looked as if his clothes came off the peg from the War on Want shop, while the younger, a widower, was sartorially immaculate. A tramp and a Beau Brummell, they seemed to be, but the dandy relied on the tramp, trusted him, understood his powers and his perception. In secret he almost worshiped him.

Without his chief he had felt a little at sea in this case. Everything had pointed at first to Hannah Kingman's having killed herself. She had been a manic-depressive, with a strong sense of her own inadequacy; apparently her marriage, though not of long duration, had been unhappy, and her previous marriage had failed. Even in the absence of a suicide note or suicide threats, Burden would have taken her death for self-destruction—if her brother hadn't come along and told him about the edible fungi. And Wexford hadn't been there to do what he always could do—sort out sheep from goats and wheat from chaff.

"The thing is," Burden said across the desk, "we're not looking for proof of murder so much as proof of *attempted* murder. Axel Kingman could have pushed his wife off that balcony—he has no alibi for the time in question—but I had no reason to think he had done so until I was told of an attempt to murder her some two weeks before."

"Which attempt has something to do with edible fungi?"

Burden nodded. "Say with administering to her some noxious substance in a stew made from edible fungi. Though if he did it, God knows how he did it, because three other people, including himself, ate the stew without ill effects. I think I'd better tell you about it from the beginning."

"I think you had," said Wexford.

"The facts," Burden began, very like a prosecuting counsel, "are as follows. Axel Kingman is thirty-five years old and he keeps a health-food shop here in the High Street called Harvest Home. Know it?" When Wexford signified by a nod that he did, Burden went on, "He used to be a teacher in Myringham, and for about seven years before he came here he'd been living with a woman named Corinne Last. He left her, gave up his job, put all the capital he had into his shop, and married a Mrs. Hannah Nicholson."

"He's some sort of food freak, I take it," said Wexford.

Burden wrinkled his nose. "Lot of affected nonsense," he said. "Have you ever noticed what thin pale weeds these health-food people are? While the folks who live on roast beef and suet and whiskey and plum cake are full of beans and rarin' to go."

"Is Kingman a thin pale weed?"

"A feeble—what's the word?—aesthete, if you ask me. Anyway, he and Hannah opened this shop and took a flat in the high-rise tower our planning geniuses have been pleased to raise over the top of it. The fifth floor. Corinne Last, according to her and according to Kingman, accepted it after a while and they all remained friends."

"Tell me about them," Wexford said. "Leave the facts for a bit and tell me about them."

Burden never found this easy. He was inclined to describe people as "just ordinary" or "just like anyone else," a negative attitude, which exasperated Wexford. So he made an effort. "Kingman looks the sort who wouldn't hurt a fly. The fact is, I'd apply the word *gentle* to him if I wasn't coming round to thinking he's a cold-blooded wife killer. He's a total abstainer with a bee in his bonnet about drink. His father went bankrupt and finally died of a coronary as a result of alcoholism, and our Kingman is an antibooze fanatic.

"The dead woman was twenty-nine. Her first husband left her after six months of marriage and went off with some girlfriend of hers. Hannah went back to live with her parents and had a part-time job helping out with the meals at the school where Kingman was a teacher. That was where they met."

"And the other woman?" said Wexford.

Burden's face took on a repressive expression. Sex outside marriage, however sanctioned by custom and general approval, was always distasteful to him. That, in the course of his work, he almost daily came across illicit sex had done nothing to mitigate his disapproval. As Wexford sometimes derisively put it, you would think that in Burden's eyes all the suffering in the world, and certainly all the crime, somehow derived from men and women going to bed together outside the bonds of wedlock. "God knows why he didn't marry her," Burden now said. "Personally, I think things were a lot better in the days when education authorities put their foot down about immorality among teachers."

"Let's not have your views on that now, Mike," said Wexford. "Presumably, Hannah Kingman didn't die because her husband didn't come to her a pure virgin."

Burden flushed slightly. "I'll tell you about this Corinne Last. She's very good-looking, if you like the dark sort of intense type. Her father left her some money and the house where she and Kingman lived, and she still lives in it. She's one of those women who seem to be good at everything they put their hands to. She paints and sells her paintings. She makes her own clothes, she's more or less the star in the local dramatic society, she's a violinist and plays in some string trio. Also she writes for health magazines and she's the author of a cookbook."

"It would look then," Wexford put in, "as if Kingman split up with her because all this was more than he could take. And hence he took up with the dull little schoolmeals lady. No competition from her, I fancy."

"I daresay you're right. As a matter of fact, that theory has already been put to me."

"By whom?" said Wexford. "Just where did you get all this information, Mike?"

"From an angry young man, the fourth member of the quartet, who happens to be Hannah's brother. His name is John Hood, and I think he's got a lot more to tell. But it's time I left off describing the people and got on with the story.

"No one saw Hannah fall from the balcony. It happened last Thursday afternoon at about four. According to her husband, he was in a sort of office behind the shop doing what he always did on early closing day—stock-taking and sticking labels on various bottles and packets.

"She fell onto a hard-top parking area at the back of the flats, and her body was found by a neighbor a couple of hours later between two parked cars. We were sent for, and Kingman seemed to be distraught. I asked him if he had had any idea that his wife would have wished to take her own life, and he said she had never threatened to do so but had lately been very depressed and there had been quarrels, principally about money. Her doctor had put her on tranquilizers—of which, by the way, Kingman disapproved—and the doctor himself, old Dr. Castle, told me Mrs. Kingman had been to him for depression and because she felt her life wasn't worth living and she was a drag on her husband. He wasn't surprised that she had killed herself and neither, by that time, was I. We were all set for an inquest verdict of suicide while the balance of the mind was disturbed when John Hood walked in here and told me Kingman had attempted to murder his wife on a previous occasion."

"He told you just like that?"

"Pretty well. It's plain he doesn't like Kingman, and no doubt he was fond of his sister. He also seems to like and admire Corinne Last. He told me that on a Saturday night at the end of October the four of them had a meal together in the Kingmans' flat. It was a lot of vegetarian stuff cooked by Kingman—he always did the cooking—and one of the dishes was made out of what I'm old-fashioned enough, or maybe narrow-minded enough, to call toadstools. They all ate it and they were all okay but for Hannah, who got up from the table, vomited for hours, and apparently was quite seriously ill."

Wexford's eyebrows went up. "Elucidate, please," he said.

Burden sat back, put his elbows on the arms of the chair, and pressed the tips of his fingers together. "A few days before this meal was eaten, Kingman and Hood met at the squash club of which they are both members. Kingman told Hood that Corinne Last had promised to get him some edible fungi called Shaggy Caps from her own garden, the garden of the house which they had at one time shared. A crop of these things show themselves every autumn under a tree in this garden. I've seen them myself, but we'll come to that in a minute.

"Kingman's got a thing about using weeds and whatnot for cooking, makes salads out of dandelions and sorrel, and he swears by this fungi rubbish, says they've got far more flavor than mushrooms. Give me something that comes in a plastic bag from the supermarket every time, but no doubt it takes all sorts to make a world. By the way, this cookbook of Corinne Last's is called *Cooking for Nothing*, and all the recipes are for making dishes out of stuff you pull up by the wayside or pluck from the hedgerow."

"These Warty Blobs or Spotted Puffets or whatever, had he cooked them before?"

"Shaggy Caps," said Burden, grinning, "or *Coprinus comatus*. Oh, yes, every year, and every year he and Corinne had eaten the resulting stew. He told Hood he was going to cook them again this time, and Hood says he seemed very grateful to Corinne for being so—well, magnanimous."

"Yes, I can see it would have been a wrench for her. Like hearing 'our tune' in the company of your ex-lover and your supplanter."

Wexford put on a vibrant growl. " 'Can you bear the sight of me eating our toadstools with another'?"

"As a matter of fact," said Burden seriously, "it could have been just like that. Anyway, the upshot of it was that Hood was invited round for the following Saturday to taste these delicacies and was told that Corinne would be there. Perhaps it was that fact which made him accept. Well, the day came. Hood looked in on his sister at lunchtime. She showed him the pot containing the stew, which Kingman had already made, and she said *she had tasted it* and it was delicious. She also showed Hood half a dozen specimens of Shaggy Caps, which she said Kingman hadn't needed and which they would fry for their breakfast. This is what she showed him."

Burden opened a drawer in the desk and produced one of those plastic bags which he had said so inspired him with confidence. But the contents of this one hadn't come from a supermarket. He removed the wire fastener and tipped out four whitish, scaly objects. They were egg-shaped, or rather elongated ovals, each with a short fleshy stalk.

"I picked them myself this morning," he said, "from Corinne Last's garden. When they get bigger, the egg-shaped bit opens like an umbrella, or a pagoda really, and there are sort of black gills underneath. You're supposed to eat them when they're in the stage these are."

"I suppose you've got a book on fungi?" said Wexford.

"Here." This also was produced from the drawer. *British Fungi, Edible and Poisonous.* "And here we are—Shaggy Caps."

Burden opened it at the "Edible" section and at a line and wash drawing of the species he held in his hand. He handed it to the chief inspector.

"'*Coprinus comatus,*'" Wexford read aloud. "'A common species, attaining when full grown a height of nine inches. The fungus is frequently to be found, during late summer and autumn, growing in fields, hedgerows, and often in gardens. It should be eaten before the cap opens and disgorges its inky fluid, but is at all times quite harmless.'" He put the book down but didn't close it. "Go on, please, Mike," he said.

"Hood called for Corinne and they arrived together. They got there just after eight. At about eight fifteen they all sat down to table and began the meal with avocado *vinaigrette*. The next course was to be the stew, followed by nut cutlets with a salad and then an applecake. Very obviously, there was no wine or any liquor on account of Kingman's prejudices. They drank grape juice from the shop.

"The kitchen opens directly out of the living-dining room. Kingman brought in the stew in a large tureen and served it himself at the table, beginning, of course, with Corinne. Each one of those Shaggy Caps had been sliced in half lengthwise, and the pieces were floating in a thickish gravy to which carrots, onions, and other vegetables had been added. Now, ever since he had been invited to this meal, Hood had been feeling uneasy about eating fungi, but Corinne had reassured him, and once he began to eat it and saw the others were eating it quite happily, he stopped worrying for the time being. In fact, he had a second helping.

"Kingman took the plates out and the empty tureen and immediately *rinsed them under the tap*. Both Hood and Corinne Last have told me this, though Kingman says it was something he always did, being fastidious about things of that sort."

"Surely his ex-girlfriend could confirm or deny that," Wexford put in, "since they lived together for so long."

"We must ask her. All traces of the stew were rinsed away. Kingman then brought in the nut concoction and the salad, but before he could begin to serve them, Hannah jumped up, covered her mouth with her napkin, and rushed to the bathroom.

"After a while Corinne went to her. Hood could hear a violent vomiting from the bathroom. He remained in the living room while Kingman and Corinne were both in the bathroom with Hannah. No one ate any more. Kingman eventually came back, said that Hannah must have picked up some 'bug' and that he had put her to bed. Hood went into the bedroom where Hannah was lying on the bed with Corinne sitting beside her. Her face was greenish and covered with sweat and she was evidently in great pain, because while he was there she doubled up and groaned. She had to go to the bathroom again and that time Kingman had to carry her back.

"Hood suggested Dr. Castle should be sent for, but this was strenuously opposed by Kingman, who dislikes doctors and is one of those people who go in for herbal remedies—raspberry-leaf tablets and camomile tea and that sort of thing. Also he told Hood, rather absurdly, that Hannah had had quite enough to do with doctors and that if this wasn't some gastric germ it was the result of her taking 'dangerous' tranquilizers.

"Hood thought Hannah was seriously ill and the argument got heated, with Hood trying to make Kingman either call a doctor or take her to a hospital. Kingman wouldn't do it, and Corinne took his part. Hood is one of those angry but weak people who are all bluster, and although he might have called a doctor himself, he didn't. The effect on him of Corinne again, I suppose. What he did do was tell Kingman he was a fool to mess about cooking things everyone knew weren't safe, to which Kingman replied that if the Shaggy Caps were dangerous, how was it they weren't all ill? Eventually, at about midnight, Hannah stopped retching, seemed to have no more pain, and fell asleep. Hood drove Corinne home, returned to the Kingmans', and remained there for the rest of the night, sleeping on their sofa.

"In the morning Hannah seemed perfectly well, though weak, which rather upset Kingman's theory about the gastric bug. Relations between the brothers-in-law were strained. Kingman said he hadn't liked Hood's suggestions and that when he wanted to see his sister he, Kingman, would rather he came there when he was out or in the shop. Hood went off home, and since that day he hasn't seen Kingman.

"The day after his sister's death he stormed in here, told me what I've told you, and accused Kingman of trying to poison Hannah. He was wild and nearly hysterical, but I felt I couldn't dismiss this allegation as—well, the ravings of a bereaved person. There were too many peculiar circumstances—the unhappiness of the marriage, the fact of Kingman's rinsing those plates, his refusal to call a doctor. Was I right?"

Burden stopped and sat waiting for approval. It came in the form of a not very enthusiastic nod.

After a moment Wexford spoke. "Could Kingman have pushed her off that balcony, Mike?"

"She was a small, fragile woman. It was physically possible. The back of the flats isn't overlooked. There's nothing behind but the parking area and then open fields. Kingman could have gone up by the stairs instead of using the lift and come down by the stairs. Two of the flats on the lower floors are empty. Below the Kingmans lives a bedridden woman whose husband was at work. Below that the tenant, a young married woman, was in but she saw and heard nothing. The invalid says she thinks she heard a scream during the afternoon but she did nothing about it, and if she did hear it, so what? It seems to me that a suicide, in those circumstances, is as likely to cry out as a murder victim."

"Okay," said Wexford. "Now to return to the curious business of this meal. The idea would presumably be that Kingman intended to kill her that night but that his plan misfired because whatever he gave her wasn't toxic enough. She was very ill but she didn't die. He chose those means and that company so that he would have witnesses to his innocence. They all ate the stew out of the same tureen, but only Hannah was affected by it. How then are you suggesting he gave her whatever poison he did give her?"

"I'm not," said Burden, frankly, "but others are making suggestions. Hood's a bit of a fool, and first of all he would only keep on about all fungi being dangerous and the whole dish being poisonous. When I pointed out that this was obviously not so, he said Kingman must have slipped something into Hannah's plate, or else it was the salt."

"What salt?"

"He remembered that no one but Hannah took salt with the stew. But that's absurd because Kingman couldn't have known that would happen. He wouldn't have dared put, say, arsenic in the saltcellar on the thin chance that only she would take salt. Besides, she recovered far too quickly for it to have been arsenic. Corinne Last, however, has a more feasible suggestion.

"Not that she goes along with Hood. She refuses to consider the possibility that Kingman might be guilty. But when I pressed her she said she was not actually sitting at the table while the stew was served. She had got up and gone into the hall to fetch her handbag. So she didn't see Kingman serve Hannah." Burden reached across and picked up the book Wexford had left open at the description and drawing of the Shaggy Caps. He flicked over to the "Poisonous" section and pushed the book back to the chief inspector. "Have a look at some of these."

"Ah, yes," said Wexford. "Our old friend, the Fly Agaric. A nicelooking little red job with white spots, much favored by illustrators of children's books. They usually stick a frog on top of it and a gnome underneath. I see that when ingested it causes nausea, vomiting, tetanic convulsions, coma, and death. Lots of these Agarics, aren't there? Purple, Crested, Warty, Verdigris—all more or less lethal. Aha! The Death Cap, *Amanita phalloides*. How very unpleasant. The most dangerous fungus known, it says here. Very small quantities will cause intense suffering and often death. So where does all that get us?"

"Corinne Last says that the Death Cap is quite common round here. What she doesn't say, but what I infer, is that Kingman could have got hold of it easily. Now, suppose he cooked just one specimen separately and dropped it into the stew just before he brought it in from the kitchen? When he comes to serve Hannah he spoons up for her this specimen, or the pieces of it, in the same way as someone might select a special piece of chicken for someone out of a casserole. The gravy was thick, it wasn't like a thin soup."

Wexford looked dubious. "Well, we won't dismiss it as a theory. If he had contaminated the rest of the stew and others had been ill, that would have made it look even more like an accident, which was presumably what he wanted. But there's one drawback to that, Mike. If he meant Hannah to die, and was unscrupulous enough not to mind about Corinne and Hood being made ill, why did he rinse the plates? To *prove* that it was an accident, he would have wanted above all to keep some of that stew for analysis when the time came, for analysis would have shown the presence of poisonous as well as nonpoisonous fungi, and it would have seemed that he had merely been careless.

"But let's go and talk to these people, shall we?"

THE SHOP CALLED HARVEST Home was closed. Wexford and Burden went down an alley at the side of the block, passed the glass-doored main entrance, and went to the back to a door that was labeled "Stairs and Emergency Exit." They entered a small tiled vestibule and began to mount a steepish flight of stairs.

On each floor was a front door and a door to the lift. There was no one about. If there had been and they had had no wish to be seen, it would only have been necessary to wait behind the bend in the stairs until whoever it was had got into the lift. The bell by the front door on the fifth floor was marked "A. and H. Kingman." Wexford rang it.

The man who admitted them was smallish and mild-looking, and he looked sad. He showed Wexford the balcony from which his wife had fallen. It was one of two in the flat, the other being larger and extending outside the living-room windows. This one was outside a glazed kitchen door, a place for hanging washing and for gardening of the window-box variety. Herbs grew in pots, and in a long trough there still remained frostbitten tomato vines. The wall surrounding the balcony was about three feet high, the drop sheer to the hard-top below.

"Were you surprised that your wife committed suicide, Mr. Kingman?" said Wexford.

Kingman didn't answer directly "My wife set a very low valuation on herself. When we got married, I thought she was like me, a simple sort of person who doesn't ask much from life but has quite a capacity for contentment. It wasn't like that. She expected more support and more comfort and encouragement than I could give. That was especially so for the first three months of our marriage. Then she seemed to turn against me. She was very moody, always up and down. My business isn't doing very well, and she was spending more money than we could afford. I don't know where all the money was going, and we quarreled about it. Then she'd become depressed and say she was no use to me, she'd be better dead."

He had given, Wexford thought, rather a long explanation, for which he hadn't been asked. But it could be that these thoughts, defensive yet self-reproachful, were at the moment uppermost in his mind. "Mr. Kingman," he said, "we have reason to believe, as you know, that foul play may have been involved here. I should like to ask you a few questions about a meal you cooked on October 29, after which your wife was ill."

"I can guess who's been telling you about that."

Wexford took no notice. "When did Miss Last bring you these—er, Shaggy Caps?"

"On the evening of the twenty-eighth. I made the stew from them in the morning, according to Miss Last's own recipe."

"Was there any other type of fungus in the flat at the time?"

"Mushrooms, probably."

"Did you at any time add any noxious object or substance to that stew, Mr. Kingman?"

Kingman said quietly, wearily, "Of course not. My brother-in-law has a lot of ignorant prejudices. He refused to understand that that stew, which I have made dozens of times before in exactly the

same way, was as wholesome as, say, a chicken casserole. More
wholesome, in my view."

"Very well. Nevertheless, your wife was very ill. Why didn't you
call a doctor?"

"Because my wife was not 'very' ill. She had pains and diarrhea,
that's all. Perhaps you aren't aware of what the symptoms of fungus
poisoning are. The victim doesn't just have pain and sickness. His
vision is impaired, he very likely blacks out, or has convulsions of
the kind associated with tetanus. There was nothing like that with
Hannah."

"It was unfortunate that you rinsed those plates. Had you not
done so and called a doctor, the remains of that stew would almost
certainly have been sent for analysis, and if it was as harmless as
you say, all this investigation could have been avoided."

"It was harmless," Kingman said stonily.

Out in the car Wexford said, "I'm inclined to believe him, Mike.
And unless Hood or Corinne Last has something really positive to
tell us, I'd let it rest. Shall we go and see her next?"

THE COTTAGE SHE HAD shared with Axel Kingman was on a lonely
stretch of road outside the village of Myfleet. It was a stone cottage
with a slate roof, surrounded by a well-tended pretty garden. A
green Ford Escort stood on the drive in front of a weatherboard
garage. Under a big old apple tree, from which the yellow leaves
were falling, the Shaggy Caps, immediately recognizable, grew in
three thick clumps.

She was a tall woman, the owner of this house, with a beautiful
square-jawed, high-cheekboned face and a mass of dark hair. Wexford was at once reminded of the Klimt painting of a languorous
red-lipped woman, gold-neckleted, half covered in gold draperies,
though Corinne Last wore a sweater and a denim smock. Her voice
was low and measured. He had the impression she could never be
flustered or caught off her guard.

"You're the author of a cookbook, I believe?" he said.

She made no answer but handed him a paperback which she
took down from a bookshelf. *Cooking for Nothing: Dishes from
Hedgerow and Pasture* by Corinne Last. He looked through the

index and found the recipe he wanted. Opposite it was a colored photograph of six people eating what looked like brown soup. The recipe included carrots, onions, herbs, cream, and a number of other harmless ingredients. The last lines read: "Stewed Shaggy Caps are best served piping hot with whole-wheat bread. For drinkables, see page 171." He glanced at page 171, then handed the book to Burden.

"This was the dish Mr. Kingman made that night?"

"Yes." She had a way of leaning back when she spoke and of half lowering her heavy, glossy eyelids. It was serpentine and a little repellent. "I picked the Shaggy Caps myself out of this garden. I don't understand how they could have made Hannah ill, but they must have, because she was fine when we first arrived. She hadn't got any sort of gastric infection, that's nonsense. And there was nothing wrong with the avocados or the dressing."

Burden put the book aside. "But you were all served stew out of the same tureen."

"I didn't see Axel actually serve Hannah. I was out of the room." The eyelids flickered and almost closed.

"Was it usual for Mr. Kingman to rinse plates as soon as they were removed?"

"Don't ask me." She moved her shoulders. "I don't know. I do know that Hannah was very ill just after eating that stew. Axel doesn't like doctors, of course, and perhaps it would have—well, embarrassed him to call Dr. Castle in the circumstances. Hannah had black spots in front of her eyes, she was getting double vision. I was extremely concerned for her."

"But you didn't take it on yourself to get a doctor, Miss Last? Or even support Mr. Hood in his allegations?"

"Whatever John Hood said, I knew it couldn't be the Shaggy Caps." There was a note of scorn when she spoke Hood's name. "And I was rather frightened. I couldn't help thinking it would be terrible if Axel got into some sort of trouble, if there was an inquiry or something."

"There's an inquiry now, Miss Last."

"Well, it's different now, isn't it? Hannah's dead. I mean, it's not just suspicion or conjecture anymore."

She saw them out and closed the front door before they had reached the garden gate. Farther along the roadside and under the hedges more Shaggy Caps could be seen as well as other kinds of fungi that Wexford couldn't identify—little mushroom-like things with pinkish gills, a cluster of small yellow umbrellas, and from the trunk of an oak tree, bulbous smoke-colored swellings that Burden said were Oyster Mushrooms.

"That woman," said Wexford, "is a mistress of the artless insinuation. She damned Kingman with almost every word, but she never came out with a direct insinuation." He shook his head. "I suppose Hood will be at work?"

"Presumably," said Burden, but Hood was not at work. He was waiting for them at the police station, fuming at the delay, and threatening "if something wasn't done at once" to take his grievances to the chief constable, even to the Home Office.

"Something is being done," said Wexford quietly. "I'm glad you've come here, Mr. Hood. But try to keep calm, will you, please?"

It was apparent to Wexford from the first that John Hood was in a different category of intelligence from that of Kingman and Corinne Last. He was a thickset man of perhaps no more than twenty-seven or twenty-eight, with bewildered, resentful blue eyes in a puffy, flushed face. *A man*, Wexford thought, *who would fling out rash accusations he couldn't substantiate, who would be driven to bombast and bluster in the company of the ex-teacher and that clever, subtle woman.*

He began to talk now, not wildly, but still without restraint, repeating what he had said to Burden, reiterating, without putting forward any real evidence, that his brother-in-law had meant to kill his sister that night. It was only by luck that she had survived. Kingman was a ruthless man who would have stopped at nothing to be rid of her. He, Hood, would never forgive himself that he hadn't made a stand and called the doctor.

"Yes, yes, Mr. Hood, but what exactly were your sister's symptoms?"

"Vomiting and stomach pains, violent pains," said Hood.

"She complained of nothing else?"

"Wasn't that enough? That's what you get when someone feeds you poisonous rubbish."

Wexford merely raised his eyebrows. Abruptly, he left the events of that evening and said, "What had gone wrong with your sister's marriage?"

Before Hood replied, Wexford could sense he was keeping something back. A wariness came into his eyes and then was gone. "Axel wasn't the right person for her," he began. "She had problems, she needed understanding, she wasn't . . ." His voice trailed away.

"Wasn't what, Mr. Hood? What problems?"

"It's got nothing to do with all this," Hood muttered.

"I'll be the judge of that. You made this accusation, you started this business off. It's not for you now to keep anything back." On a sudden inspiration Wexford said, "Had these problems anything to do with the money she was spending?"

Hood was silent and sullen. Wexford thought rapidly over the things he had been told—Axel Kingman's fanaticism on one particular subject, Hannah's desperate need of an unspecified kind of support during the early days of her marriage, and later on, her alternating moods, then the money, the weekly sums of money spent and unaccounted for.

He looked up and said baldly, "Was your sister an alcoholic, Mr. Hood?"

Hood hadn't liked his directness. He flushed and looked affronted. He skirted round a frank answer. Well, yes, she drank. She was at pains to conceal her drinking. It had been going on more or less consistently since her first marriage broke up.

"In fact, she was an alcoholic," said Wexford.

"I suppose so."

"Your brother-in-law didn't know?"

"Good God, no. Axel would have killed her!" He realized what he had said. "Maybe that's why, maybe he found out."

"I don't think so, Mr. Hood. Now, I imagine that in the first few months of her marriage she made an effort to give up drinking. She needed a good deal of support during this time, but she couldn't or wouldn't tell Mr. Kingman why she needed it. Her efforts failed, and slowly, because she couldn't manage without it, she began drinking again."

"She wasn't as bad as she used to be," Hood said with pathetic eagerness. "And only in the evenings. She told me she never had a drink before six, and then she'd have a few more, gulping them down on the quiet so Axel wouldn't know."

Burden said suddenly, "Had your sister been drinking that evening?"

"I expect so. She wouldn't have been able to face company, not even just Corinne and me, without a drink."

"Did anyone besides yourself know that your sister drank?"

"My mother did. My mother and I had a sort of pact to keep it dark from everyone so that Axel wouldn't find out." He hesitated, then said rather defiantly, "I did tell Corinne. She's a wonderful person, she's very clever. I was worried about it and I didn't know what I ought to do. She promised she wouldn't tell Axel."

"I see." Wexford had his own reasons for thinking that hadn't happened. Deep in thought, he got up and walked to the other end of the room, where he stood gazing out the window. Burden's continuing questions, Hood's answers, reached him only as a confused murmur of voices. Then he heard Burden say more loudly, "That's all for now, Mr. Hood, unless the chief inspector has anything more to ask you."

"No, no," said Wexford abstractedly, and when Hood had somewhat truculently departed, "Time for lunch. It's past two. Personally, I shall avoid any dishes containing fungi, even *Psalliota campestris.*"

After Burden had looked that one up and identified it as the Common Mushroom, they lunched and then made a round of such wineshops in Kingsmarkham as were open at that hour. At the Wine Basket they drew a blank, but the assistant in the Vineyard told them that a woman answering Hannah Kingman's description had been a regular customer, and that on the previous Wednesday, the day before her death, she had called in and bought a bottle of Courvoisier cognac.

"There was no liquor of any kind in Kingman's flat," said Burden. "Might have been an empty bottle in the rubbish, I suppose." He made a rueful face. "We didn't look, didn't think we had any reason to. But she couldn't have drunk a whole bottleful on the Wednesday, could she?"

"Why are you so interested in this drinking business, Mike? You don't seriously see it as a motive for murder, do you? That Kingman killed her because he'd found out, or been told, that she was a secret drinker?"

"It was a means, not a motive," said Burden. "I know how it was done. I know how Kingman tried to kill her that first time." He grinned. "Makes a change for me to find the answer before you, doesn't it? I'm going to follow in your footsteps and make a mystery of it for the time being, if you don't mind. With your permission we'll go back to the station, pick up those Shaggy Caps, and conduct a little experiment."

MICHAEL BURDEN LIVED IN a neat bungalow in Tabard Road, Kingsmarkham. He had lived there with his wife until her untimely and tragic death and continued to live there still with his sixteen-year-old daughter, his son being away at a university. But that evening Pat Burden was out with her boyfriend, and there was a note left for her father on the refrigerator. "Dad, I ate the cold beef from yesterday. Can you open a tin for yourself? Back by eleven. Love, P."

"I'm glad she hasn't cooked anything," said Burden with what Wexford called his sloppy look, the expression that came over his face whenever he thought his children might be inconvenienced or made to lift a finger on his account. "I shouldn't be able to eat it, and I'd hate her to take it as criticism."

Wexford made the sound that used to be written "Pshaw!" "You've got sensible kids and you treat them like paranoiacs. While you're deciding just how much I'm to be told about this experiment of yours, d'you mind if I phone my wife?"

"Be my guest."

It was nearly six. Wexford came back to find Burden peeling carrots and onions. The four specimens of *Coprinus comatus*, beginning now to look a little wizened, lay on a chopping board. On the stove a saucepanful of bone stock was heating up.

"What the hell are you doing?"

"Making Shaggy Cap stew. My theory is that the stew is harmless when eaten by nondrinkers, and toxic, or toxic to some extent, when taken by those with alcohol in the stomach. How about that? In a minute, when this lot's cooking, I'm going to take a moderate quantity of alcohol, then I'm going to eat the stew. Now say I'm a damned fool if you like."

Wexford shrugged. He grinned. "I'm overcome by so much courage and selfless devotion to the duty you owe the taxpayers. But wait a minute. Are you sure only Hannah had been drinking that night? We know Kingman hadn't. What about those other two?"

"I asked Hood that while you were off in your daydream. He called for Corinne Last at six, at her request. They picked some apples for his mother, then she made him coffee. He did suggest they call in at a pub for a drink on their way to the Kingmans', but apparently she took so long getting ready that they didn't have time."

"Okay. Go ahead then. But wouldn't it be easier to call in an expert? There must be such people. Very likely someone holds a chair of fungology at the University of the South."

"Very likely. We can do that after I've tried it. I want to know for sure *now*. Are you willing, too?"

"Certainly not. I'm not your guest to that extent. Since I've told my wife I won't be home for dinner, I'll take it as a kindness if you'll make me some innocent scrambled eggs."

He followed Burden into the living room, where the inspector opened a door in the sideboard. "What'll you drink?"

"White wine, if you've got any, or vermouth if you haven't. You know how abstemious I have to be."

Burden poured vermouth and soda. "Ice?"

"No, thanks. What are you going to have? Brandy? That was Hannah Kingman's favorite, apparently."

"Haven't got any," said Burden. "It'll have to be whiskey. I think we can reckon she had two double brandies before that meal, don't you? I'm not so brave I want to be as ill as she was." He caught Wexford's eye. "You don't think some people could be more sensitive to it than others, do you?"

"Bound to be," said Wexford breezily. "Cheers!"

Burden sipped his heavily watered whiskey, then tossed it down. "I'll just have a look at my stew. You sit down. Put the television on."

Wexford obeyed him. The big colored picture was of a wood in autumn, pale blue sky, golden beech leaves. Then the camera closed in on a cluster of red-and-white-spotted Fly Agaric. Chuckling, Wexford turned it off as Burden put his head round the door.

"I think it's more or less ready."

"Better have another whiskey."

"I suppose I had." Burden came in and refilled his glass. "That ought to do it."

"Oh, God, I forgot. I'm not much of a cook, you know. Don't know how women manage to get a whole lot of different things brewing and make them synchronize."

"It is a mystery, isn't it? I'll get myself some bread and cheese, if I may."

The brownish mixture was in a soup bowl. In the gravy floated four Shaggy Caps, cut lengthwise. Burden finished his whiskey at a gulp.

"What was it the Christians in the arena used to say to the Roman emperor before they went to the lions?"

"*Morituri te salutamus,*" said Wexford. " 'We who are about to die salute thee.' "

"Well . . ." Burden made an effort with the Latin he had culled from his son's homework. "*Moriturus te saluto.* Would that be right?"

"I daresay. You won't die, though."

Burden made no answer. He picked up his spoon and began to eat. "Can I have some more soda?" said Wexford.

There are perhaps few stabs harder to bear than derision directed at one's heroism. Burden gave him a sour look. "Help yourself. I'm busy."

The chief inspector did so. "What's it like?" he said.

"All right. It's quite nice, like mushrooms."

Doggedly, he ate. He didn't once gag on it. He finished the lot and wiped the bowl round with a piece of bread. Then he sat up, holding himself rather tensely.

"May as well have your telly on now," said Wexford. "Pass the time." He switched it on again. No Fly Agaric this time, but a dog fox moving across a meadow with Vivaldi playing. "How d'you feel?"

"Fine," said Burden gloomily.

"Cheer up. It may not last."

But it did. After fifteen minutes had passed, Burden still felt perfectly well. He looked bewildered. "I was so damned positive. I *knew* I was going to be retching and vomiting by now. I didn't put the car away because I was certain you'd have to run me down to the hospital."

Wexford only raised his eyebrows.

"You were pretty casual about it, I must say. Didn't say a word to stop me, did you? Didn't it occur to you it might have been a bit awkward for you if anything had happened to me?"

"I knew it wouldn't. I said to get a fungologist." And then Wexford, faced by Burden's aggrieved stare, burst out laughing. "Dear old Mike, you'll have to forgive me. But you know me, d'you honestly think I'd have let you risk your life eating that stuff? I knew you were safe."

"May one ask how?"

"One may. And you'd have known, too, if you'd bothered to take a proper look at that book of Corinne Last's. Under the recipe for

Shaggy Cap Stew it said, 'For drinkables, see page 171.' Well, I looked at page 171, and there Miss Last gave a recipe for cowslip wine and another for sloe gin, both highly intoxicating drinks. Would she have recommended a wine and a spirit to drink with those fungi if there'd been the slightest risk? Not if she wanted to sell her book, she wouldn't. Not unless she was risking hundreds of furious letters and expensive lawsuits from her readers."

Burden had flushed a little. Then he too began to roar with laughter.

After a little while Burden made coffee.

"A little logical thinking would be in order, I fancy," said Wexford. "You said this morning that we were not so much seeking to prove murder as attempted murder. Axel Kingman could have pushed her off that balcony, but no one saw her fall and no one heard him or anyone else go up to that flat during the afternoon. If, however, an attempt was made to murder her two weeks before, the presumption that she was eventually murdered is enormously strengthened."

Burden said impatiently, "We've been through all that. We know that."

"Wait a minute. The attempt failed. Now, just how seriously ill was she? According to Kingman and Hood, she had severe stomach pains and she vomited. By midnight she was peacefully sleeping, and by the following day she was all right."

"I don't see where this is getting us."

"To a point which is very important and which may be the crux of the whole case. You say that Axel Kingman attempted to murder her. In order to do so he must have made very elaborate plans—the arranging of the meal, the inviting of two witnesses, the ensuring that his wife tasted the stew earlier in the day, and preparing for some very nifty sleight of hand at the time the meal was served. Isn't it odd that the actual method used should so signally have failed? That Hannah's *life* never seems to have been in danger? And what if the method had succeeded? At postmortem some noxious agent would have been found in her body, or the effects of such. How could he have hoped to get away with that, since, as we know, neither of his witnesses actually watched him serve Hannah and one of them was even out of the room?

"So what I am postulating is that no one *attempted* to murder her, but someone attempted to make her ill so that, taken in conjunction with the sinister reputation of nonmushroom fungi and Hood's admitted suspicion of them, taken in conjunction with the known unhappiness of the marriage, it *would look as if there had been a murder attempt.*"

Burden stared at him. "Kingman would never have done that. He would either have wanted his attempt to succeed or not to have looked like an attempt at all."

"Exactly. And where does that get us?"

Instead of answering him Burden said on a note of triumph, his humiliation still rankling, "You're wrong about one thing. She *was* seriously ill, she didn't just have nausea and vomiting. Kingman and Hood may not have mentioned it, but Corinne Last said she had double vision and black spots before her eyes and . . ." His voice faltered. "My God, you mean—?"

Wexford nodded. "Corinne Last only of the three says she had those symptoms. Only Corrine Last is in a position to say, because she lived with him, if Kingman was in the habit of rinsing plates as soon as he removed them from the table. What does she say? That she doesn't know. Isn't that rather odd? Isn't it rather odd, too, that she chose that precise moment to leave the table and go out into the hall for her handbag?

"She knew that Hannah drank, because Hood had told her so. On the evening that meal was eaten, you say Hood called for her at her own request. Why? She has her own car, and I don't for a moment believe a woman like her would feel anything much but contempt for Hood."

"She told him there was something wrong with her car."

"I see. She asked him to come at six, although they were not due at the Kingmans' till eight. She gave him *coffee.* A funny thing to drink at that hour, wasn't it, and before a meal? So what happens when he suggests calling in at a pub on the way? She doesn't say no or say it isn't a good idea to drink and drive. She takes so long getting ready that they don't have time.

"She didn't want Hood to drink any alcohol, Mike, and she was determined to prevent it. She, of course, would take no alcohol, and she knew Kingman never drank. But she also knew Hannah's habit of having her first drink of the day at about six.

"Now, look at her motive, far stronger than Kingman's. She strikes me as a violent, passionate, and determined woman. Hannah had taken Kingman away from her. Kingman had rejected her. Why not revenge herself on both of them by killing Hannah and seeing to it that Kingman was convicted of the crime? If she simply killed Hannah, she had no way of ensuring that Kingman would come under suspicion. But if she made it look as if he had previously attempted her life, the case against him would become very strong indeed.

"Where was she last Thursday afternoon? She could just as easily have gone up those stairs as Kingman could. Hannah would have admitted her to the flat. If she, known to be interested in gardening, had suggested that Hannah take her onto that balcony and show her the pot herbs, Hannah would willingly have done so. And then we have the mystery of the missing brandy bottle with some of its contents surely remaining. If Kingman had killed her, he would have left that there, as it would greatly have strengthened the case for suicide. Imagine how he might have used it. 'Heavy drinking made my wife ill that night. She knew I had lost respect for her because of her drinking. She killed herself because her mind was unbalanced by drink.'

"Corinne Last took that bottle away because she didn't want it known that Hannah drank, and she was banking on Hood's keeping it dark from us as he had kept it from so many people in the past. And she didn't want it known because the fake murder attempt that *she* staged depended on her victim having alcohol present in her body."

Burden sighed, poured the last dregs of coffee into Wexford's cup. "But we tried that out," he said. "Or I tried it out, and it doesn't work. You knew it wouldn't work from her book. True, she brought the Shaggy Caps from her own garden, but she couldn't have mixed up poisonous fungi with them because Axel Kingman would have realized at once. Or if he hadn't, they'd all have been ill, alcohol or no alcohol. She was never alone with Hannah before the meal, and while the stew was served she was out of the room."

"I know. But we'll see her in the morning and ask her a few sharp questions. I'm going home now, Mike. It's been a long day."

"Shall I run you home?"

"I'll walk," said Wexford. "Don't forget to put your car away, will you? You won't be making any emergency trips to the hospital tonight."

With a shamefaced grin Burden saw him out.

THEY WERE UNABLE TO puncture her self-possession. The languorous Klimt face was carefully painted this morning, and she was dressed as befitted the violinist or the actress or the author. She had been forewarned of their coming, and the gardener image had been laid aside. Her long, smooth hands looked as if they had never touched the earth or pulled up a weed.

Where had she been on the afternoon of Hannah Kingman's death? Her thick, shapely eyebrows went up. At home, indoors, painting. Alone?

"Painters don't work with an audience," she said rather insolently, and she leaned back, dropping her eyelids in that way of hers. She lit a cigarette and flicked her fingers at Burden for an ashtray as if he were a waiter.

Wexford said, "On Saturday, October 29, Miss Last, I believe you had something wrong with your car?"

She nodded lazily.

In asking what was wrong with it, he thought he might catch her. He didn't.

"The glass in the offside front headlight was broken while the car was parked," she said, and although he thought how easily she could have broken that glass herself, he could hardly say so. In the same smooth voice she added, "Would you like to see the bill I had from the garage for repairing it?"

"That won't be necessary." *She wouldn't have offered to show it to him if she hadn't possessed it,* he thought. "You asked Mr. Hood to call for you here at six, I understand."

"Yes. He's not my idea of the best company in the world, but I'd promised him some apples for his mother, and we had to pick them before it got dark."

"You gave him coffee but no alcohol. You had no drinks on the way to Mr. and Mrs. Kingman's flat. Weren't you a little disconcerted at the idea of going out to dinner at a place where there wouldn't even be a glass of wine?"

"I was used to Mr. Kingman's ways." *But not so used,* thought Wexford, *that you can tell me whether it was normal or abnormal for him to have rinsed those plates.* Her mouth curled a little, betraying her a little. "It didn't bother me. I'm not a slave to liquor."

"I should like to return to these—er, Shaggy Caps. You picked them from here on October 28 and took them to Mr. Kingman that evening. I think you said that?"

"I did. I picked them from this garden."

She enunciated the words precisely, her eyes wide open and gazing sincerely at him. The words, or perhaps her unusual straightforwardness, stirred in him a glimmer of an idea. But if she had said nothing more, that idea might have died as quickly as it had been born.

"If you want to have them analyzed or examined or whatever, you're getting a bit late. Their season's practically over." She looked at Burden and gave him a gracious smile. "But you took the last of them yesterday, didn't you? So that's all right."

Wexford, of course, said nothing about Burden's experiment. "We'll have a look in your garden, if you don't mind."

She didn't seem to mind, but she had been wrong. Most of the fungi had grown into black-gilled pagodas in the twenty-four hours that had elapsed. Two new ones, however, had thrust their white oval caps up through the wet grass. Wexford picked them, and still she didn't seem to mind. Why, then, had she seemed to want their season to be over? He thanked her, and she went back into the cottage. The door closed. Wexford and Burden went out into the road.

The fungus season was far from over. From the abundant array on the roadside it looked as if the season would last weeks longer. Shaggy Caps were everywhere, some of them smaller and grayer than the clump that grew out of Corinne Last's well-fed lawn; green and purple Agarics, horn-shaped toadstools, and tiny mushrooms growing in fairy rings.

"She doesn't exactly mind us having them analyzed," Wexford said thoughtfully, "but it seems she'd prefer the analysis to be done on the ones you picked yesterday than on those I picked today. Can that be so or am I just imagining it?"

"If you're imagining it, I'm imagining it too. But it's no good, that line of reasoning. We know they're not potentiated—or whatever the word is—by alcohol."

"I shall pick some more all the same," said Wexford. "Haven't got a paper bag, have you?"

"I've got a clean handkerchief. Will that do?"

"Have to," said Wexford, who never had a clean one. He picked a dozen more young Shaggy Caps, big and small, white and gray, immature and fully grown. They got back into the car, and Wexford told the driver to stop at the public library. He went in and emerged a few minutes later with three books under his arm.

"When we get back," he said to Burden, "I want you to get on to the university and see what they can offer us in the way of an expert in fungology."

He closeted himself in his office with the three books and a pot of coffee. When it was nearly lunchtime, Burden knocked on the door.

"Come in," said Wexford. "How did you get on?"

"They don't have a fungologist. But there's a man on the faculty who's a toxicologist and who's just published one of those popular science books. This one's about poisoning by wild plants and fungi."

Wexford grinned. "What's it called? *Killing for Nothing*? He sounds as if he'd do fine."

"I said we'd see him at six. Let's hope something will come of it."

"No doubt it will." Wexford slammed shut the thickest of his books. "We need confirmation," he said, "but I've found the answer."

"For God's sake! Why didn't you say?"

"You didn't ask. Sit down." Wexford motioned him to the chair on the other side of the desk. "I said you'd done your homework, Mike, and so you had, only your textbook wasn't quite comprehensive enough. It's got a section on edible fungi and a section on poisonous fungi—*but nothing in between*. What I mean by that is, there's nothing in your book about fungi which aren't wholesome yet which don't cause death or intense suffering. There's nothing about the kind which can make a person ill under certain circumstances."

"But we know they ate Shaggy Caps," Burden protested. "And if by 'circumstances' you mean the intake of alcohol, we know Shaggy Caps aren't affected by alcohol."

"Mike," said Wexford quietly, "*do* we know they ate Shaggy Caps?" He spread out on the desk the haul he had made from the roadside and from Corinne Last's garden. "Look closely at these, will you?"

Quite bewildered now, Burden looked at and fingered the dozen or so specimens of fungi. "What am I to look *for*?"

"Differences," said Wexford laconically.

"Some of them are smaller than the others, and the smaller ones are grayish. Is that what you mean? But, look here, think of the differences between mushrooms. You get big flat ones and small button ones and—"

"Nevertheless, in this case it is that small difference that makes all the difference." Wexford sorted the fungi into two groups. "All the small grayer ones," he said, "came from the roadside. Some of the larger white ones came from Corinne Last's garden and some from the roadside."

He picked up between forefinger and thumb a specimen of the former. "This is not a Shaggy Cap, it is an Ink Cap. Now listen." The thick book fell open where he had placed a marker. Slowly and clearly he read: " 'The Ink Cap. *Coprinus atramentarius*, is not to be confused with the Shaggy Cap, *Coprinus comatus*. It is smaller and grayer in color, but otherwise the resemblance between them is strong. While *Coprinus atramentarius* is usually harmless, when cooked, it contains, however, a chemical similar to the active principle in Antabuse, a drug used in the treatment of alcoholics, and if eaten in conjunction with alcohol, would cause nausea and vomiting.' "

"We'll never prove it," Burden gasped.

"I don't know about that," said Wexford. "We can begin by concentrating on the *one lie* we know Corinne Last told, when she said she picked the fungi she gave Axel Kingman from *her own garden*."

Mushroom and Onion Frittata

¼ **cup olive oil (divided use)**
8 oz. mushrooms, sliced
1 small bunch green onions, roots removed
6 room-temperature eggs, beaten just until the yolks
    and whites are blended
Salt and pepper to taste

TWO 10-INCH SKILLETS are needed for this dish, and the serving plate for the frittata should be warmed and ready.

CAREFULLY WASH THE green onions and remove any bruised or unsavory-looking areas. Slice the green onions into roughly one-inch-long bits.

PUT HALF THE olive oil into each 10-inch skillet. Place both oiled skillets on the stove on low to medium heat. Put the green onion bits into one skillet. Sauté until onion is slightly limp, about one minute, then add the mushrooms. Sauté until the mushrooms are brown and limp, about another two minutes. Pour the onions and mushrooms from the skillet into the beaten eggs. Set greasy skillet aside back on its burner for later. Stir eggs. Pick up the unused heated skillet and roll the olive oil around in the pan until the entire surface has been covered in olive oil. Return skillet to burner. Pour egg mixture into it. Rotate the pan slightly to spread the egg mixture evenly across the skillet surface. If the eggs are not cooking evenly, gently lift the cooked eggs up and move them to the center of the pan, and swirl the pan again until the remaining liquid eggs once again cover the surface. When the bottom of the eggs are set and the top is still glossy and creamy, place the other warm skillet, the greasy one used to cook the mushrooms and onions, upside down over the skillet containing the eggs, and flip the two skillets. The egg mixture should fall out of the pan it is in, its less-cooked side facedown on the onion and mushroom pan. Place the pan back on the stove until the eggs are cooked through, usually one to two minutes.

SERVE IMMEDIATELY ON a warmed platter.

The Cassoulet

Walter Satterthwait

I must speak with you," says Pascal, "regarding a matter of great importance."

"And which matter," I ask him, "might that be?"

Thoughtfully, using forefinger and thumb, he strokes his moustache. "The cassoulet," he says.

"Ah," I say, and within my chest my heart dips a few melancholy millimeters.

We are drinking Pascal's passable filtered coffee in his somewhat too elaborate dining room. The room is situated in a corner of his apartment, and the apartment itself on the top floor of a portly old building along the Quai de Gesvres. A pair of wide windows, running from ceiling to floor, affords us an uninterrupted view of the Île de la Cité and of Notre Dame with its many fine and graceful buttresses. The view no doubt is often charming; but today a gaudy sun is shining, and the river is perfectly reflecting the flawless blue of sky, as though posing for a tourist postcard; and I cannot help but find it all, as I find Pascal's dining room, a trifle overdone.

"You know, of course," says Pascal, "that I have always experienced a certain difficulty with the cassoulet."

"Yes, of course," I say. Pascal's failure with the cassoulet is renowned.

"I have never understood it," he says. As usual, Pascal is wearing black—a silk shirt, a pair of linen slacks—on the mistaken

assumption that black makes him appear at once more intellectual and less corpulent.

"I believe," he says, "that I am in all other respects a tolerable
cook. The cassoulet, however . . ." he shakes his head ". . . invariably the cassoulet has eluded me. At the market I have purchased
the most delectable of beans, the most savory of sausages, the
most succulent of pork. When I used fresh duck, I obtained the
plumpest of these, and I plucked their feathers myself, with the
utmost care. Always, before the final cooking, I rubbed the casserole scrupulously with garlic, like a painter preparing a canvas.
Always, as the dish bubbled in the oven, I broke the gratin crust
many times—"

"Seven times," I ask him, curious, "as they do in Castelnaudary?"

"On occasion. And on occasion eight times, as they do in
Toulouse."

He sits back in his chair and shrugs. "Yet no matter what I
assayed, always my cassoulet lacked . . ." Frowning, he holds up his
hand and delicately moves his fingers, as though attempting to
pluck a thought, like a feather, carefully from the air.

"That certain something?" I offer.

"Exactly, yes," he nods. "That certain something." He smiles
sadly. "You recall the party last year, on Bastille Day."

"Only with reluctance," I say. For a moment that evening, after
each guest had taken a small tentative taste of the cassoulet, no
one could look at anyone else. Silence fell across the table like the
blade of a guillotine. Poor Pascal, who had been so embarrassingly
hopeful before the presentation, suddenly became quite embarrassingly, quite volubly, apologetic.

"Yes," he nods ruefully. "A disaster."

"I have always," I say, "accounted it rather intrepid of you, this
endless combat with the cassoulet."

He wags a finger at me. "Intrepid, yes, perhaps—but confess it,
my friend, also rather foolish."

"Ah well," I say, and I shrug. "In this life we are all of us permitted a certain amount of foolishness, no?"

He inclines his head and smiles. "You are, as always, too kind."
But then he frowns again. "You know," he says, "it was largely
because of this Bastille cassoulet that Sylvie wandered out of my life."

"Come now, Pascal." I smile. "You know very well that Sylvie was
wandering long before Bastille Day."

"Certainly. Sylvie was a free spirit and, I agree, a prodigious wanderer. Yet despite our many difficulties, after her wanderings it was to our life here that she invariably returned. Until the day of that fatal cassoulet. The embarrassment was too much for her. The cassoulet was the ultimate of straws."

Pascal's way with a cliché can best be described as unfortunate.

"Nonsense," I tell him. "By her very nature Sylvie was utterly incapable of fidelity."

He smiles sadly. "As you learned yourself, my friend, isn't it so?"

I return his smile, replacing its sadness with curiosity. "Surely, Pascal, you cannot hold that against me, my little incident with Sylvie?"

He lowers his eyebrows and raises his hand, showing me his pale scrubbed palm. "But of course not," he says. "It is inevitable, the attraction between one's friend and one's lover. It is, in a way, a confirmation of one's high regard for both." He shakes his head. "No, my friend, all that is history now. Water far beneath the bridge. But I speak of Sylvie. A few weeks ago, I saw her in the Café de la Paix. She was sitting with her American."

"The American is still in Paris, then?"

"Astounding, is it not? Almost ten months now, and the two of them are as inseparable as ever. You've met the man?"

"I've heard stories only. There are boots, I understand."

"The boots of the cowboy, yes. Constructed from the skin of some unfortunate bird. A turkey, I believe."

"Not a turkey, surely?"

He shrugs. "A bird of some sort. And with them, inevitably, a ridiculous pair of denim trousers. *Gray*. Sitting beside Sylvie, he looked like a circus clown."

"What was Sylvie wearing?" I ask in passing.

"A lovely little sleeveless Versace, red silk, and around her neck a red Hermes scarf."

I smile. "Sylvie and her endless scarves."

"Yes. She saw me, from across the room, and waved to me to join them. I could hardly refuse, not without causing a scene. Not in the Café de la Paix. So I crossed the room, and the American stood to greet me. He's quite excessively tall, you know. He *looms*."

"It is something they all do, the Americans. Even the women. Even the short ones. They learn it from John Wayne films."

"Doubtless. In any event, we shook hands, the American and I, and naturally he squeezed mine as though it were a grapefruit."

"Naturally."

"His name is Zeke." Frowning, he cocks his head. "That cannot be a common name, can it, even among Americans?"

"I shouldn't think so." I glance at my watch. Eleven thirty now, and I have a one o'clock rendezvous at La Coupole. "So you joined them?" I say. "Sylvie and her Cowboy?"

"What choice had I? The American sat back and crossed his legs, perching his horizontal boot along his knee, so we might all admire the elegant stitchery in the dead turkey."

"I hardly think turkey, Pascal."

"Whatever. The point is the *flamboyance* of the gesture. Why not simply rip the thing from his foot and hurl it, *plonk*, to the center of the table?" Pascal shudders elaborately. "And then he hooked his thumbs over his belt, as they do, these American cowboys, and he said, *'Sylvie tells me you're in chemicals.'*

"I said, 'Not in them, exactly.' "

"*Touché*," I say. "In French, this was, or in English?"

Pascal smiles. "He believed himself to be speaking French. It was execrable, of course. In simple self-defense, I replied in English. 'I have an interest in a small pharmaceutical company,' I told him. 'But naturally I leave the running of it to others.'

"And here Sylvie leaned forward and she said, 'Pascal's primary interest is the kitchen.'

" '*Is that right?*' said the Cowboy. I cannot duplicate the accent. You recall Robert Duvall as Jesse James?"

"Vividly. *The Great Northfield Minnesota Raid*. A Philip Kaufman film."

"Something like Duvall. A combination of Duvall and Marlon Brando in Kazan's *Streetcar*. '*Is that right?*' he said. '*I purely do admire the way you French people cook up your food.*' "

"Pascal," I say. "You exaggerate."

Indignant, he raises his chins. "Indeed I do not."

"And what did you reply?"

"I said, 'We French people are filled with awe at your Big Mac.' " I smile.

"And then he grinned at me, one of those lunatic American grins that reach around behind the ears, and he said, '*Ain't all that big on burgers myself—*' "

"Pascal!"

"I do not invent this. '*Me*,' he said, '*I like to chow down on a real fine home-cooked meal.*'

"'Perhaps,' I said, 'one day you will permit me to prepare something for you.'

"'*That'd tickle me*,' he said, '*like all get-out.*'"

"Pascal—"

"Wait, wait! Sylvie had been sitting in silence, leaning forward, her elbows on the table, her arms upraised, her fingers locked to form a kind of saddle for her chin. You recall how she nestles her chin against the backs of her fingers? How she watches, with those shrewd blue eyes darting back and forth from beneath that glossy black fringe of hair?"

"I recall, yes," I tell him.

"Suddenly, she spoke. Blinking sweetly, with a perfectly innocent expression, she said, 'Zeke's favorite dish is the cassoulet.'"

"Ah," I say. "I was wondering if we should ever return to the cassoulet."

"I was, of course, stunned," says Pascal. "I had believed us to be friends still, Sylvie and I."

"Possibly your comment about the Big Mac . . . ?"

"Possibly. I was stunned nonetheless. And then the Cowboy, this Zeke creature, said, '*I reckon there ain't no food I like better than a good cassoulet.*'

"And at that point Sylvie, still the picture of innocence, sat up and blinked again and said, 'Why, Pascal would love to prepare a cassoulet, wouldn't you, Pascal?'"

"Clearly," I say, "it was your comment about the Big Mac."

"Very likely. But what could I do?"

"You had no choice, obviously, but to accept."

"None. I invited them to dinner on the following Saturday. As I said goodbye to them both, I could not help but notice in Sylvie's eye that little twinkle she gets when she is anticipating some devilment. You recall that twinkle?"

"I recall it."

"Well. This occurred on a Thursday. That afternoon, and throughout most of Friday, I pored over the literature. Brillat-Savarin. Prosper Montagné. The Larousse. On Friday evening I bought the *lingot* beans, the finest, the most expensive in Paris, and I carried them home—in a taxi, on my lap, so as not to bruise them—and I set them to soak. Early on Saturday morning I purchased the rest of the ingredients. Again, all the finest and the most expensive. And then, when the beans had soaked for exactly twelve hours, I began."

He strokes his mustache, remembering. "First I drained the beans. Then I cooked them in just enough water for them to swim comfortably, along with some pork rinds, a carrot, a clove-studded onion, and a bouquet garni containing three cloves of garlic."

"So far," I say, "the method is unimpeachable."

"Using another pan," he goes on, "in some goose fat I browned a few pork spareribs and a small boned shoulder of mutton—"

"Mutton? Pascal, this sounds ominously like the cassoulet you prepared for Jean Claude's birthday."

"The very same recipe." He nods. "I know, I know. A catastrophe."

"You are a brave man, Pascal."

"A desperate man, my friend. But to continue. When the meats were nicely browned, I transferred them gently to a large skillet, and I cooked them, covered, with some chopped onion, another bouquet garni, and two *additional* cloves of garlic—"

"Bravo."

"—as well as three tomatoes, chopped, seeded, and crushed. Then, when the beans in their separate pan were just approaching tenderness, I removed all the vegetables from them and I added the pork, mutton, onions, and a fat garlic sausage. And the preserved goose. It was while I was adding the goose that the accident occurred."

"The accident?"

"Yes." He glances at my empty cup. "Some more coffee, my friend?"

I look at my watch. Twelve o'clock. "Only a bit," I tell him.

He pours the coffee and sits back, sighing, and then with a ruminative look he stares out the tall window at the buttresses of Notre Dame.

"The accident?" I say.

He turns back to me. He smiles. "The accident, yes. It was extraordinary. Really quite extraordinary, in light of what followed. As I was cutting the leg of preserved goose, my knife slipped, and the blade went sliding along my left hand. You see?"

He holds out his left hand. Along the base of the thumb is the clear mark of a recent scar, nearly two inches long, still pink against Pascal's plump pallor.

"Impressive," I say. "Was it painful?"

"I barely noticed it at the time," he says, "so intent was I upon the cassoulet. And then suddenly I realized that I was bleeding. *Into* the beans."

"Goodness."

"I had bled rather a lot into the beans as it happens. As soon as I understood what had happened, I wrapped my thumb in a dish towel to staunch the flow, and with a spoon I attempted to remove the blood from the beans. This was impossible, of course. Already it had mixed with the liquid in the pot. I had no choice but to mix it in more thoroughly and continue. You understand?"

"Certainly. It was too late in the day for you to begin anew. But still, Pascal . . ."

He raises his brows. "Yes?"

"It is . . . a tad macabre, don't you think?"

"Not at all. Think of blood sausage. Think of civet of hare. Think of sanguette."

"Yes, but human blood. Your own blood."

Dismissively, he shrugs. "I could not afford to be squeamish. As you say, it was late in the day. So, after having mixed everything, I simmered it for another hour, then removed the meat from the beans. I cut the meat, and I arranged all the ingredients in the casserole. A layer of beans, a sprinkling of pepper, a layer of meat, a sprinkling of pepper, a layer of beans—"

"I am familiar with the procedure."

"—and so on. Over the top I sprinkled melted goose fat and bread crumbs—"

"Naturally."

"—and then I placed it in the oven. During the next hour and a half, I broke the gratin crust eight times, at regular intervals. By the time Sylvie and her Cowboy arrived, it was ready."

"And?" I say.

He smiles slyly. "And what?"

"You toy with me, Pascal. The cassoulet. It was a success?"

"Not a success," he says. "A *triumph*. Sylvie took a single bite and closed her eyes—you recall how she closes her eyes when she savors the taste of something, how that little smile spreads across—"

"Yes, yes," I say. "I recall." I had been recalling Sylvie rather more often than I liked. "And the Cowboy?"

"In raptures. He consumed three enormous portions. It was, and I quote, '*the best goldarned cassoulet*' he ever ate."

I sit back and shake my head. "You astound me, Pascal. A remarkable story."

"But no, there is more. Over the weekend, Sylvie and her Cowboy mentioned the cassoulet to everyone they knew. It became a *cause célèbre*. You were gone from Paris at the time."

"In Provence," I say. "I returned, as I told you, only last week."

"I began to receive telephone calls from people—occasionally from people whom I myself had never met—importuning me to prepare for them a cassoulet. You can imagine how gratifying this was to me, after my long and notorious history of failure."

"Certainly. But, Pascal. You could hardly repeat the accident which brought about your one success. The *contretemps* with the knife."

"Ah, but I could, you see."

"Pardon?"

Smiling, he unbuttons the cuff of his left sleeve. With a magician's flourish, he pulls the sleeve up along his thick arm.

Stuck everywhere along the pallid flesh are pink adhesive bandages, eight or nine of them.

For a moment I do not comprehend. And then I do.

"Pascal!" I exclaim. "But this is madness!"

Lowering the arm, he nods sadly. "I agree. I cannot continue. In the morning, I can barely climb from the bed. And yet everyone in Paris, it seems, hungers for my cassoulet."

I pick up my coffee cup, and very much to my surprise I drop it. It falls to my lap, spattering me with warm coffee, then rolls off and tumbles to the floor, shattering against the polished parquet. I look up at Pascal. "How very odd," I say.

He smiles. "The drug begins to take effect." He looks at his watch. "Precisely on time. It requires an hour. It was in your first cup of coffee."

"The drug?" Strangely, this emerges from my throat as a croak.

"A rather interesting variant of curare. A chemist at my pharmaceutical company developed it. Unlike curare, which paralyzes the body's involuntary muscles, this one leaves certain muscles untouched. One can breathe, one can blink one's eyes, one can chew, one can swallow. But one cannot otherwise move."

I open my mouth, attempt to say, "You are joking," but only a shrill sibilant hiss escapes me.

"Nor can one speak," says Pascal, and smiles. Paternally. At me, or at the drug and its effects.

I attempt standing. None of my muscles respond. Suddenly, without my willing it, my body slumps back against the chair. My head topples forward as though it might snap off at the neck, roll down my legs, and go rattling across the floor. I can feel my heart pounding against my ribs like an animal trying, frantically, to escape a trap.

"Relax, my friend," says Pascal. "You will only excite yourself."

With my head lowered, I can see of Pascal only his feet. They move as he stands up. I feel him clap me in a friendly manner upon the shoulder. Then the feet and legs disappear off to my right.

My mind, like my heart, is racing. The rest of me is frozen.

A few moments later I feel myself being lifted into the air. My head flops to the side. Pascal, for all his corpulence, is surprisingly strong. I am placed in what I recognize as a wheelchair. My head lolls back, and I have a view of Pascal's ceiling, and then of Pascal's face as he leans into my line of vision.

"Believe me," he says with an upside-down smile, "this will all go better for you if you simply accept it."

His face vanishes, and the ceiling unscrolls above me as he wheels me from the dining room.

"Perhaps you are asking yourself," I hear him say, "why I should choose you as the source of my—well, let us call it my *special seasoning*.

"First of all," he says, "you commend yourself to this purpose by the sheer emptiness of your life. No one will miss you. No one will ever even suspect that you are gone. Oh, here and there, I imagine, some poor benighted secretary, some simpleminded shopgirl, may wonder why you never telephone. But she will survive this."

We are in another room now. I feel Pascal lift me once again. The ceiling lurches, sways, and then I am lying on a bed. I feel Pascal's hand on my head as he swivels it, gently, to face him.

He stands back, pursing his lips. "And second," he says, "I confess that I have never been terribly fond of you. Your condescension, your arrogance. That metabolism of yours that permits you to eat whatever you like without gaining a gram. Insufferable. And, of course, there is your seduction of Sylvie. Her relationship with me was never the same afterward. You are as much responsible for her leaving me as that cassoulet of Bastille Day."

I want to cry out that it had *not* been a seduction, that Sylvie had been as willing as I, which is very possibly true. But no sound comes.

Smiling again, Pascal leans forward and pats me on the shoulder once more. "Please," he says. "Relax. We shall have a splendid time together, you and I. Like two beans in a pod. We shall have enormous amounts of time to discuss Sylvie. We can analyze her reasons for leaving us both, endlessly. And during the day, before I set off to gather the other ingredients of the cassoulet, I shall prop you up against the pillows, and you can watch the television. Game shows, soap operas. Not your usual fare, I suspect, but it will be great fun, eh?"

He stands upright. "And you need have no fear. I will never take more from you than you can afford to give. A pint here, a pint there. I am not a barbarian. And naturally, to keep up your strength, I shall provide you with the most nutritious and the richest of foods. Tonight you will be enjoying a lovely duckling in orange sauce. With American wild rice and baby peas. A vinaigrette salad of lettuce and arugula. And, I think, a nice Saint Emilion. Until then I bid you adieu."

I watch him walk from the room, pull the door shut behind him.

I stare at the door. I have no choice but to stare at the door. Inside me, horror boils.

Boils and boils and goes screaming through my brain like steam from kettle. And then, finally, like that steam, it exhausts itself. I continue to stare at the door. And all at once it occurs to me that Pascal is, as he says, a tolerable cook. And that his duckling with orange sauce is famous. His wine cellar, of course, is legendary.

Feed the Hungry Hordes Cassoulet

THIS WILL FEED an army, with plenty of leftovers—which is great, because it tastes better the second day. It's also what I call a weekend food. It doesn't take much prep time in the kitchen to fix, but the dish needs to be started the night before you plan to serve it for dinner (put your beans on to soak), and it takes roughly six to seven hours—with excursions into the kitchen on roughly an hourly basis—from the time you start the roast cooking to the earliest possible time you can eat the dish. In other words, you need to be home most of the day to make it. But trust me, the house will smell fabulous.

    1 lb. dried white beans, soaked overnight in the
        refrigerator in 4 quarts water
    1 small bunch fresh parsley
    1 bay leaf
    1 small bunch green onions, washed, cleaned, and
        with the roots chopped off
    2 carrots, scrubbed and with the green tops chopped
        off
    4 large celery stalks, cleaned and rinsed, cut to a
        length that will fit in your stockpot
    Leafy bit from the middle of the celery head
    White cotton string—kitchen quality
    Optional—unbleached cotton cheesecloth, kitchen
        quality
    3 lbs. pork loin
    1 tsp. salt
    1 shoulder of lamb
    ¼ cup butter
    1 medium ham shank
    1 lb. bacon
    Water

½ lb. hard Italian sausage or other heavily flavored
   sausage (I've used browned Jimmy Dean Sage
   Sausage when I can't find authentic Italian hard
   sausage)
Peeled and separated cloves of garlic to taste (I use
   anything from 3 cloves to a whole head, depending
   on who's coming to dinner)
6 white onions, peeled and quartered
1 can tomato sauce
2 cups seasoned bread crumbs

PREHEAT OVEN TO 350 degrees F.

MAKE A BOUQUET garni. First take several sprigs of parsley (reserve
some of the bunch to use as a garnish later) and the bay leaf in
hand. Put them inside the leafy bit from the middle of the celery.
Take the prepared leafy celery bit, the carrots, the green onions,
and set them longwise on two stalks of celery. Top off with two
more celery stalks. Tie the whole thing up with a couple lengths of
string. This will be cooked in your beans to add flavor, then
retrieved and thrown out before the dish is served, so you want to
make the bundle tight and secure enough that you can grab it and
get it out of there. If you want to be absolutely sure it won't fall to
bits and vanish, wrap the whole thing in cheesecloth before tying it
up with string. Set the bouquet garni aside.

RUB THE PORK loin with the salt. Bake in oven for two hours, or until
tender. Meanwhile, put the ham and the bacon in a pan on the
stove. Cover them with cold water. Bring the water to a boil, then
turn it off. This will blanch the ham and bacon. Set the pot aside.

TAKE THE SOAKED beans from the refrigerator. Pour the water the
beans soaked in into a big bowl and reserve for later. Rinse the
soaked beans, drain them, and set the beans aside.

PUT THE WATER the beans soaked in into a stockpot (I soak my
beans in the stockpot—this isn't necessarily the best solution
because it stains the stainless steel. But it does cut down on one
more large dish needed for a dish-intensive meal). Add enough

chicken stock to the pot to make four quarts of liquid. Add the soaked beans. Bring the water to a boil and skim it. Add the blanched ham, the bacon, the bouquet garni, and the garlic, and cover. Simmer for about an hour and a half.

MEANWHILE, BROWN THE lamb shoulder in the butter. Remove the meat from the bone. Place the lamb meat and its bone in the pan with the pork loin. Put the roasts back into the oven and continue cooking them for another hour.

MEANWHILE, ADD THE quartered white onions and the sausage to the beans, simmer for one more hour. Take the roasts from the oven and pour the tomato sauce over them. Return the meat to the oven for about another half an hour. Lower oven temperature to 300 degrees F.

PULL THE MEAT from the oven. Move the roasts from the pan to a platter or cutting board and slice them on the diagonal into individual serving-size slices. Drain the roast pan, reserving the drippings. Pull the ham shank out of the beans and slice the meat, placing it with the sliced pork loin and sliced roast lamb. Pull the sausage out of the beans, and slice it into coin-sized pieces that can be put with the other sliced meats. Discard the lamb bone and ham shank bone. Drain the beans and pull the bouquet garni out of the mixture. Throw the bouquet garni away. Add the roast pan drippings to the drained beans and stir gently. Set aside to let some of the fat pool on the surface. Skim the fat off the bean mixture.

LAYER THE VARIOUS sliced meats into a casserole, alternating layers of meat with the bean mixture. Top the casserole with dried bread crumbs. Place casserole in the oven and cook for about an hour.

REMOVE FROM THE oven when the bread crumbs are a nice golden brown, top with a sprinkling of chopped fresh parsley, and serve.

Tea for Two

M. D. Lake

T he door opens and a tall, elegantly clad woman with sleek
black hair strides into the restaurant. She glances around,
spots Jane already seated at a table against the front window,
and marches over to her. Other guests, mostly middle-aged women
having late-afternoon tea, glance up at her as she passes and comment in undertones that she looks familiar.

"It's remarkable," she exclaims as she slides into the chair opposite Jane. "I recognized you the moment I came in. You haven't
changed at all." She shrugs out of her mink stole, letting it fall over
the back of her chair. "You should exercise more, though, Jane—as
much for health reasons as for appearance. I exercise an hour
every day—even have my own personal masseuse now, an
absolutely adorable man!"

She peers into Jane's cup, sniffs. "What're you drinking? Herbal
tea!" She shakes her head in mock disbelief. "Same old Jane! You
were the first person I ever knew who drank the stuff—you grew
the herbs yourself, didn't you? Not for me, thanks. Oh, well, since
you've poured it anyway, I suppose I can drink a cup of it for old
times' sake. But when the waiter gets here, I want coffee. What are
these? Tea cakes? I shouldn't, but I'll take a few. It's my special day,
after all."

She puts some on her plate and one in her mouth. "Um, delicious! Did you make them yourself? Of course you did! It's just
amazing what a clever cook can do with butter and sugar and—

cardamom? A hint of anise? What else?" She laughs gaily. "You're not going to tell me, are you? Oh, you gourmet cooks and your secret recipes! Well, it would be safe with me, since I don't even know how to turn on the stove in either of my homes."

She eats another cookie, washes it down with a swallow of tea, and then makes a face. "Needs sugar. Oh, look! I haven't seen sugar bowls like this on a restaurant table in years. Nowadays all you see are those hideous little sugar packets that are so wasteful of our natural resources." She spoons sugar into her cup, tastes the result. "That's better," she says.

She looks at her jeweled watch. "Unfortunately, Jane, I don't have a lot of time. I told the escort to be back to pick me up in an hour—one of those damned receptions before the awards banquet tonight, you know. I don't know why I bother going to those things anymore. Vanity, I suppose, but this one is special, after all."

She glances around the room, an amused smile on her lips.

"So this is your little restaurant! Such a cozy place, just like you—and I mean that in the kindest possible way! You started out as a waitress here, didn't you? Then you became the cook, and finally, when you inherited some money and the owner died, you bought the place. See, I didn't cut *all* ties with you when you suddenly dropped out of my life, Jane. I've kept myself informed through our mutual friends."

She smiles. "It's ironic, isn't it? The author of cozy little mysteries featuring the owner of a cozy little restaurant quits writing and becomes the owner of a cozy little restaurant of her own! You've turned fiction into reality, Jane, haven't you? It's usually the other way around."

Becoming more serious, she goes on: "Oh, Jane, I've wanted so much to see you again, to try to clear the air and restore the trust that was lost twenty years ago through misunderstandings—but I wasn't sure you would want to, or that you were ready for it. I was afraid that your wounds, real and imagined, might never heal. But they have, haven't they?

"I can't tell you how happy I was when my secretary told me you'd called and wanted to get together while I'm in New York. 'My cup runneth over,' I thought—isn't that what they say? To get a lifetime achievement award from my peers and, on top of that, to see you again—all on the same day!"

She swallows a cookie, chokes on it, and tries to wash it down with tea.

"It came as such a shock," she continues when she's recovered, "when you threw your writing career away and went to work as a waitress! I mean, over just one little rejection!"

She laughs. "If I'd known it was going to do that to you, I might have accepted the manuscript. I mean, you should have talked to me about it before doing anything so drastic—we could have worked something out. Our relationship, after all, was more than just editor-slash-author. Much more—we were *friends*!

"Your manuscript *was* bad, of course, but your track record was good enough that you could have survived one weak effort like that. Not that I don't think I was right to reject it! As an editor, I had an obligation to my company, and I couldn't let friendship cloud my professional judgment. I did what I thought was right, without considering the consequences. And damn, Jane, there wouldn't have been any consequences if you'd been strong! You could have taken the rejection as a challenge to rise to another plateau. And I thought you were strong—everybody did. 'Strong Jane' we all called you. Quiet, unassuming—maybe even a little dull and drab—but strong. How wrong we were!"

She wags a long, slim finger playfully in Jane's face. "And I don't feel a single twinge of guilt. Don't think for a moment I do, Jane! I'm sure that the rejection couldn't have been the sole reason you gave up writing! Admit it! Doing something that drastic is a lot like suicide. Something had been building up in you for a long time, and my rejection of the manuscript was just the last, but not the only, straw that broke the camel's back. Am I right? Of course I am! You were burned out, or burning out, weren't you? I could sense it in the manuscript. No—no more tea for me or I'll be spending most of the evening in the Ladies, instead of at the head table as guest of honor! Besides, it's a little too bitter, even with the sugar. Well, half a cup, then, since my throat's so dry—probably because I've been doing most of the talking, haven't I? Well, you always were the quiet type, weren't you?"

She spoons sugar into the cup and stirs it, sips tea and scrutinizes Jane across the table, a look of concern on her face. "Are you happy, Jane?"

She rolls her eyes and shakes her head in resignation. "Why do I ask! I don't think you were ever happy, were you? You always went around with a frown on your face, you were always concerned that you weren't writing enough, you were afraid you'd run out of ideas. You once told me you died a little every time you sent in a manuscript, wondering if I'd like it enough to buy it. Well, you look happy now—not happy, exactly, but content—even pleased with yourself, it seems to me. God, I'd give anything to be content! Well, not anything—I don't know any successful author who's content, do you? But you know what I mean. Here I am, about to receive a lifetime achievement award—a *lifetime* achievement award, Jane, after only twenty years, isn't that funny!—and I'm still not content. I don't think I'm writing enough, or good enough, and except for that first book, none of my books have been successfully translated into film. And I'm afraid I'm going to run out of ideas! I've pretty well taken up where you left off in the worry department, haven't I?"

Suddenly, she leans across the table, rests one hand lightly on one of Jane's. "Look, Jane, I accepted your invitation this afternoon because on this, what should be the happiest day of my life, I don't like the thought that you might blame me for your career going into the toilet the way it did. I don't want that shadow over my happiness. I'm here because I want us to be friends again—you do see that, don't you?

"Don't frown at me like that! I know what you're thinking, but you're wrong! When I rejected the manuscript, I didn't have any intention of—of appropriating your plot! I rejected it on its own merits—its own *lack* of merits, I should say."

She lowers her voice. "But then the plot began to haunt me, you see. It was so original, so clever—and you hadn't known what to do with it! You'd played it out with such small people—your heroine, that drab little owner of a cozy little restaurant, for Chrissakes! Her friends, the kitchen help, and her dreary little husband—not to speak of her poodle and her parakeet!"

She laughs harshly. "And all those suspects, the sort of people who patronize restaurants like that—cozy people with cozy middle-class lives and cares and secrets! Who's going to pay good money to read books about characters like that?

"I saw immediately that your plot could be applied to talented and successful characters—characters who were larger than life, the kind that most people want to read about. Characters who own horses and big, expensive cars—not poodles and parakeets! And I took it from there, and it was successful beyond my wildest dreams— and beyond anything you could ever have achieved, Jane!"

She laughs a little wildly. "My God—even I'll admit I've been living off that book ever since. One critic actually went so far as to say that I haven't written seventeen books, I've written the same book seventeen times! That hurt, but there's some truth in it. Even I'll admit it—as I laugh all the way to the bank!"

"Oh, I know, I can see that you've caught me in a little contradiction. First I said I didn't have any intention of appropriating your plot and then I said I saw immediately that it could be put to so much better use than you'd put it to. But there's really no contradiction, Jane. Once I'd read your manuscript, I couldn't get the plot out of my head! It haunted me day and night. I couldn't sleep, couldn't think of anything else. I'd been trying to write a mystery for years—God knows, as an editor, I'd read enough of them to know how to do it—but after reading your manuscript my own seemed to turn to ash."

She arranges her mink stole around her shoulders, shivers. "It's cold in here. And where's the damned waiter? I'd like coffee. You'd think he'd be dancing attendance on us, Jane, considering he works for you."

She lowers her voice. "Was what I did so wrong? Your plot was like a succubus, eating away at my creativity. And since your creativity destroyed mine, didn't I have a right to steal from you? But I didn't think it would end your career! I assumed you'd go on writing those miserable little mysteries featuring Maggie O'Hare—or whatever her name was—forever, earning tidy little advances, a steady dribble of royalties, and tepid reviews. Damn it, Jane, I wasn't stealing *everything* from you—just that one brilliant little plot!"

A sheen of perspiration glistens on her forehead and upper lip, and she glances quickly around the room. "Sorry! I didn't mean to raise my voice like that. But you can see how aggravated it still makes me when I think of how you were going to waste it. I thought of you as a bad parent, Jane, and I felt it was my moral obligation to take your child from you to save it. You should have thanked me for that, not quit writing and disappeared without so much as a by-your-leave."

She picks up the teapot and starts to pour tea into Jane's cup, but, when she sees it's full, refills her own instead.

"And when your apartment burned down," she goes on after a moment, "and with it your computer and all the diskettes, it seemed to me that that was a sign from God—or whoever it is who watches over the really creative people in this world—that I should seize the moment! I mean, after the fire your plot was in the air, so to speak, wasn't it—just ashes floating in the air for anybody to grab who had the moral courage to grab it. And I did. I grabbed it, since I was left with the only copy of your manuscript still in existence!"

She dabs at her forehead with the napkin bunched in her hand. "Don't you think it's too hot in here?" she asks, shrugging out of her mink stole again.

"Even then," she continues after a moment, "I'm not sure I would have done it—taken your plot, I mean, changing the names and occupations of the characters—if it hadn't been for your husband. In fact, I'm not sure it wasn't Brad's idea in the first place! You see, he'd grown tired of being the husband of a plump, rather drab, lower midlist mystery author, and one afternoon when we were lying in bed idly chatting about this and that, I happened to mention how possessed I was by the plot of your latest manuscript and how I thought it was bigger, much bigger, than your abilities to do anything with it. It needed larger characters and a larger milieu, I told him—perhaps a strikingly beautiful gourmet cook who has studied with some of the best chefs in France or Italy and is married to a remarkably handsome stockbroker—strong, self-possessed characters who move with casual grace in a world of money, power, and elegance!"

She smiles at a memory. "And you know how it goes when you're lying in bed after sex with your lover. Brad remarked—in all innocence, I'm sure—that unfortunately you weren't equipped to write about such a world. You didn't know it. You only knew the world of the middle class.

"And then I said that, well, *I* knew the world of the beautiful people very well! After all, as an editor I'd had to attend the kind of literary soirees that now, as one of the world's best-selling authors of romantic suspense, I'm forced to attend all the time.

"And that's how it happened, you see, Jane. I rejected your book because it wasn't up to your usual standards. Brad and I discussed what I could do with its marvelous plot—and the next thing I knew, your apartment burned down with all your records! You were lucky to get out with your life, if I remember correctly—

although you did lose the poodle and the parakeet you'd loved so much. I remember that because Brad hated them both and was glad they were gone, although he did feel badly about everything else you lost."

She nibbles a cookie. "And your miscarriage, of course," she adds. "Brad was very, *very* sad about that, as was I. Brad had ceased to love you by that time, of course, but he still *cared* about you. *Deeply.*"

She smiles compassionately across the table at Jane. "If you need money, Jane—for expansion or to get more help—and God knows you could use another waiter!—I'd be glad to give you some. I've got more than I know what to do with now. I'll even give you a little monthly stipend if you want it, even though I don't have to and I certainly don't feel any moral qualms about what I did."

She picks up her cup and brings it to her lips, pauses suddenly, and then puts it down and stares at it thoughtfully for a long moment. Then she laughs uneasily, shrugs, and picks it up again and takes a big swallow.

"Funny," she says, "in your manuscript it's in a pot of tea that Nora Smith puts the poison that kills first her husband and then her husband's lover in Maggie—Margie?—O'Hare's restaurant. Do you remember, or has it been too long ago for you? I'd probably have forgotten about it myself except I had a big quarrel with my editor, who wanted me to make the poison a faster-acting one, cyanide or strychnine. I pointed out that if it acted that fast, the police would have no trouble tracing where the victims ingested it, but by making it take several days, nobody would know—until Maggie or Margie figures it out in the end, that is. Of course, by the time I rewrote it my way, it wasn't Maggie's—Megan's?—drab little restaurant anymore, it was the elegant bistro belonging to my heroine, Titania Oakes, a culinary artist, which attracted only the beautiful people—the trendsetters, the movers and the shakers. And the victims weren't a dowdy schoolteacher and an insurance salesman either—they were famous Broadway stars! That's how I made your wretched little story into a blockbuster, Jane! But I kept the poison the same as yours, except in my book it wasn't in tea, it was in a lovely risotto, for which Titania's restaurant was famous."

She frowns in thought, her eyes moving involuntarily to the teapot. "What was the name of that poison, anyway—do you remember? Something odorless and tasteless that leaves no trace, unless the medical examiner knows what to look for. I remember asking you where you got the idea for it and you said you'd had mushrooms like that growing in your backyard when you were a kid. Your mother had warned you against eating them. Once they got into your system, she said, you were done for—nothing could save you."

She shudders, picks up her teacup, and starts to take another swallow, then changes her mind and puts the cup down with a clatter.

"God, how you must hate me!" she whispers. "First I steal your husband and then your novel. Then you lose your poodle, your parakeet, and your baby—and finally your career. It sounds awful now, in the cold light of a gray autumn day in this cozy Godawful place—but it seemed so right at the time! And I didn't mean to hurt you, Jane! I expected you to bounce back stronger than ever. And probably meaner, too."

She tries to laugh but coughs instead. "I even imagined you'd write a novel in which you murdered me in the most horrible possible way! Isn't that ridiculous? Instead, you just dried up and blew away, didn't you?

"But you did get Brad back! When it didn't work out between us and I was forced to show him the door, right around the time my novel hit the *New York Times* best-seller list, he crawled back to you, didn't he? I seem to recall hearing that somewhere. As I said, I've kept track of you all these years, Jane. I don't know why. I guess I just don't know how to let go of a friend, even one who's turned her back on me the way you did. Call me a fool, but at least I'm a *loyal* fool!"

She frowns at a sudden memory. "But then Brad died, didn't he? I recall hearing that, too. First, you got remarried, and then, a year or so later, he came into some money. And then he died—suddenly, although he wasn't very old."

She's pale and breathing hard now, but she manages a ghastly smile. "Did you have him cremated, Jane?" she asks with forced humor. "So they'd never be able to find out if you'd put something in his food?"

Her voice rising, she asks, "What was it called again—the poison? There's no known antidote for it, is there? And a little goes a long way. Isn't that what your Megan or Maggie or Margie told the homicide inspector? 'No known antidote, Inspector—and a little goes a long way.' " She laughs. "How much better that line sounded in my Titania's mouth than in—in your dreary little protagonist's!

"But once you've got it in your system," she goes on slowly, ominously, "it doesn't do any good to pump your stomach, does it? It doesn't do any good at all! Isn't that right, Jane?"

She jumps up and stares down at Jane in horror. "How long before you begin to feel the effects?" she shouts. "Do you remember? Of course you do—how could you forget? And the symptoms—chills and fever that mimic the flu, aren't they?" She wipes her forehead with her soggy napkin, stares at her shaking hand.

"And then, shortly after Brad died, the owner of this place died too, didn't he, Jane? Suddenly. And you bought the restaurant from his heirs with the money you'd inherited from Brad!"

She looks around the room wildly. "Why hasn't the waiter come over to our table? It's because you told him to leave us alone, didn't you? The tea and cookies were already here, waiting for me. It was in the tea, wasn't it? You never touched a drop of it. Or was it the cookies, or the sugar? Damn you, Jane, tell me!"

Without waiting for an answer, she turns to the others in the room and shouts, "She's killed me! As sure as if she'd pointed a pistol at me and pulled the trigger, she's killed me because I stole her plot, her story, her husband—everything—and she's never forgiven me! And I won't die quickly, either. No—it'll be tomorrow or the next day and I have to live with that knowledge and with the knowledge that it's going to be a slow and painful death. And I'll be conscious every moment of the hideous ordeal!"

She rushes around the table and throws herself on Jane. "Monster!" she screams. "Mass murderer! First your husband, then the owner of the restaurant, now me!"

The waiter runs over and pulls her off Jane. She struggles violently for a moment, then collapses onto the floor.

"Oh, God!" she whispers. "This was supposed to be the happiest day of my life, and now look what you've done! How cleverly you've plotted your revenge, Jane!"

Her face lights up briefly when something occurs to her. "But you won't get away with it this time. They'll do an autopsy! After my long, slow, agonizing death, they'll open me up and find what you murdered me with—and then you'll spend the rest of your life in prison—or worse!"

She chuckles madly and closes her eyes. "Will somebody please cover me with my mink stole?" she says plaintively. "But try not to let it touch the floor. Oh, how like you, Jane, to add insult to

injury—poisoning me in such a grubby little place, among such
drab people!"

She pulls the stole up over her face, after which her muffled voice
can still be heard complaining that the pains have already begun, the
poison is acting faster than Ms. Know-It-All thought it would.

As Jane waits for the ambulance and the police to arrive, she
stirs sugar into her cold tea (she likes cold tea), helps herself to a
couple of the remaining cookies, and begins planning tomorrow's
menu. She remembers to turn off the tape recorder in her purse,
too. That goes without saying.

𝒞hocolate 𝒮urprise 𝒮ugar 𝒯ea 𝒞akes

---

3 cups flour
1½ tsp. baking powder
1 tsp. salt
1 cup sugar
¾ cup canola oil
2 eggs, beaten
1 tsp. vanilla
½ tsp. almond extract
12-oz. bag of wrapped chocolate miniatures (Her-
shey's Dark Chocolate Almond are a favorite),
unwrapped
½ cup sugar

PREHEAT OVEN TO 375 degrees F.

BLEND FLOUR, BAKING powder, and salt, and set aside. In a large
bowl, mix together sugar, oil, eggs, vanilla, and almond extract.
Add the flour mixture all at once and stir until blended. Take a
miniature chocolate bar and wrap it completely in cookie dough.
Roll resulting ball in sugar, set on cookie sheet. Continue until
cookie dough and/or candy bars are gone. Bake for 10-15 minutes,
until cookie is brown on the bottom and cooked through. Serve
warm (the chocolate is nicely melted) or at room temperature.

The Second-Oldest Profession

Linda Grant

*N*o one in their right mind goes to the market at five o'clock, Bianca Diamante thought as she surveyed the crowded parking lot. *Unless, of course, they've spent the entire day waiting for the repairman to come fix the dishwasher.*

At four-thirty she had called Angeli's Appliances for the third time to check on Mario's progress toward her home.

"Oh, Mrs. Diamante," an apologetic female voice had said, "he's so sorry. He was really trying to get to you, but this last job has just lasted much longer than he expected. He said to tell you he'd be at your house first thing tomorrow."

I've heard that before, Bianca had thought. Yesterday, in fact. Mario himself had promised to be there "first thing."

She'd felt genuine sympathy for the young woman at the other end of the phone. They both knew that in all likelihood Mario's last job had been performed in the bedroom of some bored housewife. It was too much to wish that the cuckolded husband might arrive home early and armed, but the possibility cheered Bianca.

She knew the repairman well enough to recognize how he prioritized his work orders. Attractive, horny women first, less attractive, horny women second, old ladies last. If she didn't keep after him, it could take weeks to get her dishwasher fixed.

In the parking lot ahead of her a tan station wagon was backing out, but before she could pull forward, a red Miata zipped around her, pulled in front, and took the place.

Bianca honked, then pulled up behind the Miata and got out. "I beg your pardon," she said, "that was my parking place."

A young woman with a shaved skull and a skirt up to her crotch stepped out of the Miata with a snippy smile on her face. "Too bad, Grandma," she said. "Slow folks suck."

The girl turned and headed for the store, and Bianca steamed. She allowed herself a moment to visualize the back of the shaved head in the sights of a rifle, then climbed into her car. The world was producing far too many overindulged, undersocialized young people these days.

It took several turns through the parking lot to find a place and Bianca had thought of at least three nasty ways that the shaved one might meet an early end by the time she pulled her Plymouth into a slot made too narrow by the monstrous sports utility vehicle hulking over the white line. SUV drivers were another category of people the world could do without.

The light on the supermarket's glass door had turned it into a mirror. As she approached it, an old woman walked to meet her. Bianca studied the image with satisfaction. Gray hair framed a wrinkled face, a shapeless dark dress shrouded a short, plump body. Up close she could even see the dark eyebrow pencil that stood in for thinning brows and the lipstick that went slightly outside the line of the lips. The eternal grandma. Harmless and invisible.

Another woman might have regretted the signs of age, maybe considered a visit to the hairdresser or a trip to the mall. Not Bianca. She'd worked hard for that look, plucked her luxurious brows down to next to nothing, and fought off every suggestion of a tint or a more modern hairstyle. No actor had spent more time perfecting the stooped posture and halting movements of old age than Bianca had.

But today she had no need for the stoop or shuffling walk as she pushed the door open and hurried inside. Today, she wasn't working.

The store was as crowded as the parking lot, and half the women had small, whiny children attached to their legs. Bianca was glad she didn't have a lot to buy, just a few things for dinner and apples for the pie.

She headed for the meat counter to get some lamb chops. As she was reaching for the only package that had two chops, a woman in a charcoal power suit stepped forward and grabbed it. She bumped Bianca's arm as she did and gave her a quick look, mumbled "Sorry," and hustled off.

You would be sorry if you knew who you were pushing, Bianca thought. That was the downside of being invisible: You had to put up with people treating you poorly. And you never got the satisfaction of seeing the look on their faces when they realized they'd just insulted someone who killed people for a living.

But it was worth it. Being a harmless old woman was the best possible cover for a hit person. Who else could get close to a powerful Mafia leader without being noticed, or remembered? No man certainly, even an old one. And a young woman would attract notice. But an old woman could go anywhere, and even the most alert bodyguard wouldn't push her out of the way if she passed too close and stumbled.

That's how she'd gotten Johnny the Clam, number three man in the Detroit family. She'd devised a special ring, a gaudy stone on the top, a sharp tack on the back of the band. A tack that she'd dipped in a poison that certain primitive people used on the tips of their arrows. Then it had been a matter of finding the right time and place where she could pass Johnny close enough to grasp his hand when she stumbled. He'd winced when she cut him, but a man like Johnny didn't make a fuss over a cut. In fact, Johnny never made a fuss again.

She'd used a sharp-tipped umbrella with the same poison, and it might have become her favorite weapon if the Bulgarians hadn't used it to assassinate a mark in England and botched the hit. Now everyone knew about umbrellas.

She picked up a quart of milk, a loaf of bread, two tomatoes, and some green beans for dinner, then remembered she'd come for apples.

As she surveyed the neatly stacked pyramids of bright green to deep red apples, a familiar, too-loud voice said, "McIntoshes are the best for pies."

It was Isabel Brasi, she who knew all and couldn't wait to share it. Bianca sighed, then came as close to a smile as she could manage as she turned to greet her neighbor.

Isabel was a constant trial. A bird fanatic, she called at least once a day to complain that Bianca's cats were stalking the birds at her feeders, digging in her garden, or doing something "nasty" in her yard. When she wasn't fussing over the cats, she was gossiping about the other neighbors. Her nosiness knew no bounds, and while Bianca was careful never to have clients come to her house, she didn't like the idea that someone was watching her every move.

Bianca's husband, Tony, had taught her that the first rule of a professional was never to let your personal feelings get involved. "We're probably the world's second-oldest profession," he'd said with a smile. "And we follow the same rules as the oldest profession. Never give it away." No whacking your enemies or those you found intolerably annoying. Isabel was a real test of Bianca's professionalism.

"Of course, the Gravesteins are very nice, too," Isabel said in her annoyingly chirpy voice, "but you can always count on the McIntoshes for flavor. My apple pie has won first place at the church bazaar for the last four years."

Bianca's smile was genuine as she congratulated Isabel; she was thinking of the apple pie she was going to bake. It was a safe bet no one had ever paid $10,000 for one of Isabel's pies.

"The children coming for Mother's Day?" Isabel asked.

Mother's Day! Bianca stared at Isabel in horror. "Mother's Day?" she said. "This Sunday is Mother's Day?"

Sympathy pulled Isabel's face into a somber expression. Poor Bianca. Obviously, her children had forgotten all about Mother's Day.

Jesus, Mary, and Joseph, Bianca thought, *how could I miss that? I must be slipping.* She prided herself on her attention to detail, never leaving any loose ends, and here she was three days from the job and she'd missed completely that Sunday was Mother's Day.

"They get so busy," Isabel was saying. "So many things to remember when you're young. They don't realize how we look forward to their visits."

Speak for yourself, Bianca thought. Cara and Sophia visited quite often enough, thank you. She loved them dearly, but they fussed over her like mother hens. Lately Cara'd started interrogating her about whether she was taking her medicine, how well she was eating, every little thing. You'd think she was an errant teenager the way her daughter fussed. Even her social life was an object of scrutiny. She should get out more, join the bridge club or the garden society, maybe think of moving into one of those nice adult communities.

And Sophia had suggested on two occasions that her friendship with certain members of the Gianni family should be terminated. "You don't know what kind of people they are," she'd said, her lips stretched tight with disapproval.

Bianca knew exactly what kind of people they were. They were the kind of people whose money had bought shoes and put food on the table. Her husband Tony had never been a member of the Gianni family, but favors had been exchanged from time to time, and the Don had been particularly helpful after Tony's cancer had left her a widow with children to support. It was Gianni money that had sent Cara, Sophia, and their brother Robert to college. And her family's connection to the Gianni family had meant that the wild boys stayed away from Cara and Sophia and never challenged Robert.

She and Tony had been careful to shield the children from the realities of Tony's profession. They thought he worked for a company that sold office machines and that his frequent trips were to distant business sites. You couldn't have your kid bringing his father's gun to show-and-tell.

"Maybe Cara's planning to surprise you?" Isabel said, trying to put a good face on things.

Bianca hated surprises, always had. Especially now.

She'd told the client the hit was scheduled for Sunday so that he could arrange an airtight alibi, and she was always careful to deliver exactly what she promised. It hadn't been easy making it as a woman in this field, even with Tony's training and his contacts. Clients were hesitant to trust a woman. For years after Tony's death she'd maintained the fiction that she was just a go-between who set things up with his "brother." At least half her clients still believed that. A hit man could reschedule; a hit woman could not.

She made as quick an escape as possible from Isabel, who was anxious to discuss at length her own children's plans for Mother's Day, and hurried to the checkout counter. There were only four registers open, and long lines of carts were stacked up at each one.

The line at the nine-items-or-less counter was the shortest of the four, an encouraging bit of luck until she realized that the man at the head of it had piled at least twice that many items on the belt. The clerk rolled his eyes at the pile but rang up the goods. It was only as he announced the total that the man pulled out his checkbook.

A ripple of irritation ran up the line. "I could kill him," the woman in front of Bianca muttered.

Bianca nodded agreement. Lucky for him she was a professional.

The checker was pleasant and efficient. The bagger looked to be about fourteen and dropped the tomatoes into the bag first, where they would have been smashed by the milk if Bianca hadn't made him retrieve them.

I'd be doing the world a favor to take that one out of the gene pool, Bianca thought.

"Would you like help to the car with that, ma'am?" the kid asked, indicating the small bag of groceries. She detected a slight smirk on his face.

"I think I can manage, thank you," she said.

Sunday's target was a sleazy lawyer who'd cheated the wrong person once too often. Bianca demanded a fair amount of background on her jobs. She'd developed her own rather quirky code. Abusive husbands were fair game; inconvenient witnesses were not. She needed to know about the marks so she could devise an appropriate exit strategy for them.

You didn't need to know a lot about a guy's habits if you were going to pick him off with a rifle, but Bianca specialized in deaths from natural causes, and for that, you needed background. Sometimes the client supplied it; sometimes she did the research herself. Always, there was a premium for a method that wouldn't attract police attention.

The roads were crammed with cranky drivers working themselves into a frenzy to get home quickly so they could relax. Bianca was deep in thought as she stopped at a traffic light and didn't notice when it changed to green. A loud horn blasted her awake, and a man's angry voice yelled, "Get a move on, Granny. We don't have all day."

At home, she decided the best solution to her problem was to find out what, if anything, her daughters had in mind for Sunday. She called Cara, who was more likely to be home than her sister.

"Mother, I'm so glad you called," Cara said. *She sounded a bit guilty,* Bianca thought. "I've been meaning to call you, but things have been crazy at the office."

"How's your wrist?" Bianca asked. Cara had sprained her wrist when she tripped on the stairs.

"Much better, thanks," Cara said, then launched into a long description of a problem involving a secretary at her office. Bianca made comforting sounds. There was always some problem at the office; she could never keep all the players straight. It was enough to make her glad she worked alone.

"So how are you doing?" Cara asked as she finished her lament.

"The dishwasher's broken," Bianca said. "It stopped midway through the cycle last night. I've been waiting for Mario to come fix it."

"Mario? Is he still fixing appliances? He's such a creep." Cara had gone to school with Mario. They had even dated briefly, until Cara found out he was also dating one of her close friends. No one had ever accused Mario of being long on brains.

"He fixes appliances when he gets around to it," Bianca said. "He's not very reliable."

"Never was," Cara said. "He still have an eye for the ladies?"

"More than an eye," Bianca said. "He's married, but he hasn't let that slow him down."

"He's a creep," Cara repeated. "I don't think he even lives with Sarah—that's his wife. I heard he has a place on Rose Street."

"You mean he's divorced?"

"Oh, no. Mario doesn't believe in divorce; that'd mean child support, and he's not big on sharing his money with his wife and children. Sarah had to take a job, just to get by."

"Why doesn't she file for divorce? She certainly has grounds."

"She won't talk about it," Cara said. "I don't know if she's scared of him or still hopes he'll come back. She just refuses to discuss it. She's one of those women who can't stand up for herself."

Cara told her about another friend who'd filed for divorce only to end up with crushing legal bills and no way to collect child support, then about a colleague who was continuing to date a man who broke her nose. It was all very depressing. Finally, just when Bianca had decided she'd have to bring up the issue of Mother's Day herself, Cara said, "Oh, Sophia and I would like to take you to dinner on Sunday."

"How sweet of you," Bianca said, then added quickly, "How about four o'clock?"

"Uh, fine, four o'clock would be fine."

"Would you like to meet somewhere?"

"No, no. We'll pick you up at the house," Cara said.

As she hung up, Bianca realized they hadn't discussed where they'd go. That meant the girls had already chosen a place, no doubt one that prided itself on combining unlikely ingredients into minuscule servings on gigantic plates. You couldn't even trust the pasta in such places.

But at least she'd gotten the time schedule right. That meant she would be able to use the poisoned pie.

The lawyer was the perfect candidate for a pie. There weren't that many people who were. First off, you couldn't give a poisoned pie to a family man—too much chance of unintended victims. And you couldn't give it to someone who'd take it to a sick friend or ask a buddy over for dinner. Or a gentleman of the old school who'd feel obliged to invite her to have a piece. No, a pie only worked with the selfish loner, the kind of guy who as a kid would have rather eaten lunch by himself than risk having to share his dessert.

The lawyer was just such a guy. Bianca could count on him to keep every bite for himself.

She could drop by with the pie around eleven. She'd already introduced herself as a new neighbor and told him she'd just moved in with her daughter up the block. As she'd expected, he wasn't interested enough to ask the name of her "daughter." He probably didn't know his neighbors' names.

She'd played the lonely widow checking out the prospects. He wasn't bad-looking and had plenty of money, so he'd probably been through that routine before. Sunday, she'd pay a second visit and give him the pie, then scurry off shyly. Just after dark she'd come back to check on him. If the car was there and the lights were out, she'd know she'd succeeded. A call from a phone booth late that night would confirm it.

BIANCA MADE THE APPLE pie Saturday morning so she could bake it before the day heated up. If she'd believed Mario's promise to come by "first thing," she'd have waited, but she knew better than that. In fact, she didn't expect him until Monday. He only worked a half-day on Saturday, and she figured it'd take more than four hours for him to get around to her, so she was surprised when the doorbell rang at eleven o'clock, just as she was taking the pie from the oven.

"Hear the dishwasher's on the fritz," he said. "I got a cancellation so I hurried right over."

"I thought you were coming yesterday," Bianca said sternly.

"I got held up. It's not like a busted dishwasher is an emergency," he said in a tone that suggested *he* was the wronged party.

"No, not like a freezer that's not working," Bianca said, remembering the time she'd had to throw everything out because he'd been "held up."

"Right," he said, no memory of the freezer incident clouding his smile.

Mario spotted the pie as soon as he entered the kitchen. "Boy, that pie sure smells good," he said. "I love apple pie."

"I baked that one for a friend," Bianca said, knowing that Mario was on his way to asking for a piece.

"Aren't I your friend? Come out on a Saturday to fix your dishwasher?"

Bianca smiled thinly and resisted mentioning that he wouldn't have been there at all if he'd come when he was supposed to. Instead, she explained what was wrong with the dishwasher.

Mario dumped his tools on her clean floor and studied the appliance.

"Aw, you got a Kitchen-Aid. I tried to warn you about them. You shoulda bought the GE I tried to sell you. It was a good machine."

Bianca was fairly sure that the "good machine" had fallen off a truck somewhere. Mario had been much too anxious to sell it. "Yes, well, this is the machine I have, so it's the one you'll have to fix."

Mario bent down to pry the front off the dishwasher and continued his complaints about it.

Bianca decided it was time to find something to do in another room before she gave in to the temptation to tap Mario on the head with a cast-iron skillet. "Don't you touch that pie, Mario Angeli," she ordered.

"No need to get overheated," Mario said. He said something else as she was leaving, but he lowered his voice so she couldn't hear it.

When she came back to the kitchen fifteen minutes later, Mario had parts of the motor spread all over the floor and was talking on her phone.

"Tell him you're going to a movie with a girlfriend," he said in a wheedling tone. "Come on, just a couple of hours."

"Mario," Bianca said sternly. "I'm not paying you to arrange your social calendar."

"Gotta go," he said. "Meet me at eight at Phinny's." He gave her his best aw-shucks smile and said, "Sorry, Mrs. D. I won't charge you for the time I was on the phone."

"Very generous of you," Bianca said.

"Speaking of generous, how about a piece of that pie?" Mario moved toward the counter where the pie was cooling.

"No," Bianca said, loudly enough to stop him in his tracks. "Stay away from that pie."

"Just one piece. Your friend wouldn't miss one piece."

Only Mario would imagine it was proper to give a friend a pie with one piece missing. She almost wished she could give it to him, but she was a professional and Tony's second cardinal rule of professionalism was: You never hit someone you know. Tony used to say that anger was one emotion a pro couldn't afford.

"I said no," Bianca said sternly, "and I meant it. You are to stay away from that pie. Do you understand?"

But, of course, he didn't. He only understood what he wanted to understand. Bianca put on the oven mitts, picked up the still-hot pie, and carried it into the study where she could keep an eye on it.

She was going over her plans for Sunday a second time when the phone rang. It was Cara.

"Sophia can't make it at four," she said. "So we had this great idea. She'll take you to brunch at around ten or so, and I'll take you to dinner at four. How's that?"

Dreadful, Bianca thought. *It's just dreadful.* It was hard to imagine a worse schedule.

"Oh, now, you're making much too much of a fuss over me," she said. "Why don't we all just go to brunch?"

"We *want* to make a fuss," Cara said. "We want your Mother's Day to be special."

"Just being with you will be special," Bianca said. "I'd really rather just do the brunch. After all, I get tired easily these days."

"Is something wrong?" Cara asked anxiously. "Aren't you feeling well?"

"I'm fine," Bianca said quickly. "Really. It's just that you don't have as much energy at my age."

"Maybe you should see the doctor."

"Cara, don't be such a worrywart. I'm in excellent health."

"How's your shoulder? Is it still bothering you?"

"It's much better." Bianca had hurt her shoulder six months ago when she'd had to rearrange the body of a minor mob figure who'd lurched the wrong way in his final moments. Cara and Sophia had assumed it was arthritis.

"I really think you should see the doctor. Fatigue can be a symptom of more serious problems."

Bianca sighed. She should have known better than to plead anything remotely connected to poor health. Now she'd have to prove how fit she was or they'd drive her crazy with their fussing. "I'm fine," she said. "And your plans for Mother's Day sound lovely."

"You're sure? We don't want to tire you."

"I'm sure," Bianca said.

As she hung up the phone, she could hear Mario whistling tunelessly in the kitchen. She looked at her watch. He'd been at work for over an hour. At this rate she could have bought a new dishwasher and saved herself a lot of aggravation.

She couldn't use the pie. The timing was too tight. She'd just have to find another way. Aggravating, but not too difficult. Still, it was a shame she'd gone to the work of baking the pie.

For just a moment, she considered offering the pie to Mario.

There was no danger of him sharing it with anyone—he was selfish enough to keep it all for himself. She doubted that the woman he'd been cajoling on the phone would go looking for him when he stood her up, and the poison she'd carefully mixed into the pie filling produced symptoms close enough to food poisoning to confuse all but the most sophisticated autopsy.

She could get away with it, and no one would be the wiser, but it violated the code. No personal hits. It was an indulgence she couldn't afford. Whack Mario and next week it'd be Isabel or the bimbo with the shaved head. One simply had to have standards in this business.

The whole problem with Sunday's job was the deadline. She hated deadlines; they made things so much more difficult. Poisons acted differently on different bodies, even when you tried to adjust the dose to size.

With enough time, she could always come up with a means that would slip by most coroners. The trick was to give them a set of symptoms that looked like a natural cause they recognized. As long as you weren't dealing with a high-profile mark and didn't leave any glaring evidence, you could rely on them to see what they expected.

To ensure that the lawyer was dead by Sunday night, she'd need a fairly fast-acting poison. The ring with the spring-loaded injector was the best bet for a delivery device. She was particularly proud of her latest invention; it was a big step beyond the old ring with the tack on the back. That had been a crude device with no way to measure the dose and too much risk of nicking herself.

She'd found the injector in a medical supply book, another benefit of her volunteer work for the Poison Control Center, and designed the device herself. A hollow glass stone served as the reservoir for the poison; the injector extended down from it, fitting between her fingers. It remained safely sheathed until triggered by the pressure of her hand against a solid surface.

She glanced in the kitchen on her way upstairs to get the ring. Mario seemed to be finishing up—at least there were fewer tools on the floor.

In her bedroom, she carefully removed the ring from its hiding place in the lovely antique bureau with the secret drawer. A note on a yellow Post-it in the box reminded her that it still contained a deadly dose of brown recluse spider venom.

It was a nearly ideal weapon for a local hit. The spider was indigenous to this area, and the venom caused so little pain on injection that by the time the first symptoms appeared a couple of hours later, the victim might not even remember being stuck.

But would it do for this job? She decided it wouldn't. Death usually took more than a day, and the victim could sometimes be saved if he got to a doctor in time.

She slipped the ring on her finger. The safest means to release the venom was to shoot it into an apple or an orange. That wouldn't damage the needle, and the flesh of the fruit would absorb the poison.

As she headed down to the kitchen, the phone summoned her back.

"Mrs. D? This is Jason." Jason, her "social secretary."

"Hello, Jason. How's your daughter?" The question was her signal that it was all right to talk.

"She's fine, thank you. I just learned that my client would like to reschedule the package you were to deliver tomorrow. If you could take care of it today, there'd be a 20-percent bonus."

Bianca considered. She hated changes in plan, but this time it worked to her advantage. She checked her watch. There was still time to deliver the pie.

"I think that would be possible," she said. She didn't ask why the change in plans. She didn't care.

"Excellent. I'll inform my client."

Bianca replaced the receiver and smiled. Everything was working out after all. Now all she had to do was get Mario out of her kitchen, put on her old-lady clothes, and drive the pie across town.

She hurried to the kitchen to tell Mario he had fifteen minutes to finish fixing her dishwasher, but the room was empty. The dishwasher had been reassembled and the tools were back in their box, but the repairman was nowhere to be seen.

Bianca rushed to the study. There, she found Mario by the desk, carefully lifting a fat piece of pie from the pan. She dashed across the room and smacked his hand, knocking the pie from it. The pie landed with a splat on the blotter, spewing crust and filling across the desk. Mario yelped. "Jeeze, Mrs. Diamante," he protested, "don't get so excited. I didn't mean no harm."

He launched into a string of excuses, while Bianca stared at the tiny bright red spot of blood on his hand.

German Apple Cake

Cake:
1 cup sugar
1 cup unsifted, unbleached flour
4 Tbsp. butter, cut into pieces
1 tsp. baking powder
1 tsp. vanilla extract
1 large egg
4 large pippin or Granny Smith apples

Topping:
3 Tbsp. sugar
3 Tbsp. melted butter
1 tsp. cinnamon
1 large egg

IF YOU'RE USING a food processor, put all the cake ingredients, except the apples, into the bowl, and process until the mixture is the consistency of cornmeal. Spread the mixture in the bottom of a well-buttered, 9-inch springform pan. (If you don't have a food processor, mix the dry ingredients together, then cut in the butter, and when the mixture is like cornmeal, add the vanilla and egg.)

PEEL THE APPLES and remove the cores, then slice them.

ARRANGE THE APPLES in layers on top of the crumb mixture. Bake in a pre-heated 350-degree oven for 45 minutes.

MEANWHILE, MIX TOGETHER the topping ingredients. Spoon the mixture over the apples and bake 25 to 30 minutes more or until the top is firm.

Connoisseur

Bill Pronzini

Norman Tolliver was a connoisseur of many things: art, music, literature, gourmet cuisine, sports cars, beautiful women. But above all else, he was a connoisseur of fine wine.

Nothing gave him quite so much pleasure as the bouquet and delicate taste of a claret from the Médoc region of Bordeaux—a 1924 Mouton-Rothschild, perhaps, or a 1929 Haut-Brion; or a brilliant Burgundy such as a Clos de Vougeot 1915. His memory was still vivid of the night in Paris when an acquaintance of his father's had presented him with a glass of the *impériale* claret, the 1878 Latour Pauillac. It was Norman's opinion that a man could experience no greater moment of ecstasy than his first sip of that venerable Latour.

Norman resided in an elegant penthouse in New York that commanded a view of the city best described as lordly. That is, he resided there for six months of the year; the remaining six months were divided among Europe and the pleasure islands of the Caribbean and the Mediterranean. During his travels he expended an appreciable amount of time and money in seeking out new varieties and rare vintages of wine, most of which he arranged to have shipped to New York for placement in his private cellar.

It was his custom every Friday evening, no matter where he might happen to be, to sample an exceptional bottle of claret or Burgundy. (He enjoyed fine whites, of course—the French

Sauterne, the German Moselle—but his palate and his temperament were more suited to the classic reds.) These weekly indul-
gences were always of a solitary nature; as a connoisseur he
found the communion between him and great wine too intimate
to share with anyone, too poignant to be blunted by even polite
conversation.

On this particular Friday Norman happened to be in New York
and the wine he happened to select was a reputedly splendid
claret: the Château Margaux 1900. It had been given to him by a
man named Roger Hume, whom Norman rather detested.
Whereas he himself was the fourth-generation progeny in a family
of wealth and breeding, Hume was *nouveau riche*—a large, grace-
less individual who had compiled an overnight fortune in textiles
or some such and who had retired at the age of forty to, as he put
it in his vulgar way, "find out how the upper crust lives."

Norman found the man to be boorish, dull-witted, and incredibly ignorant concerning any number of matters, including an
understanding and appreciation of wine. Nevertheless, Hume
had presented him with the Margaux—on the day after a small
social gathering that they had both attended and at which
Norman chanced to mention that he had never had the pleasure
of tasting that difficult-to-obtain vintage. The man's generosity
was crassly motivated, to be sure, designed only to impress; but
that could be overlooked and even forgiven. A bottle of Margaux
1900 was too fine a prize to be received with any feeling other
than gratitude.

At three o'clock Norman drew his study drapes against the
afternoon sun and placed one of Chopin's nocturnes on his
quadraphonic record changer. Then, with a keen sense of anticipation, he carefully removed the Margaux's cork and prepared to
decant the wine so that it could breathe. It was his considered
judgment that an aged claret should be allowed no less than five
hours of contact with new air and no more than six. A healthy,
living wine must be given time to breathe in order for it to express
its character, release its bouquet, become *more* alive; but too much
breathing causes a dulling of its subtle edge.

He lighted the candle that he had set on the Duncan Phyfe
table, waited until the flame was steady, then began to slowly pour
the Margaux, holding the shoulder of the bottle just above the
light so that he could observe the flow of the wine as it passed

through the neck. There was very little age-crust or sediment. The color, however, did not look quite right; it had a faint cloudiness, a pale brown twinge, as wine does when it has grown old too quickly.

Norman felt a sharp twinge of apprehension. He raised the decanter and sniffed the bouquet. Not good, not good at all. He swirled the wine lightly to let air mix with it and sniffed again. Oh, Lord—a definite taint of sourness.

He poured a small amount into a crystal glass, prepared himself, and took a sip. Let the wine flood over and under his tongue, around his gums.

And then spat the mouthful back into the glass.

The Margaux was dead.

Sour, unpalatable—*dead.*

White-faced, Norman sank onto a chair. His first feelings were of sorrow and despair, but these soon gave way to a sense of outrage focused on Roger Hume. It was Hume who had given him not a living, breathing 1900 Margaux but a desiccated *corpse*; it was Hume who had tantalized him and then left him unfulfilled, Hume who had caused him this pain and anguish, Hume who might even have been responsible for the death of the Margaux through careless mishandling. Damn the man. Damn him!

The more Norman thought about Roger Hume, the more enraged he became. Heat rose in his checks until they flamed scarlet. Minutes passed before he remembered his high blood pressure and his doctor's warning about undue stress; he made a conscious effort to calm himself.

When he had his emotions under control he stood, went to the telephone, found a listing for Hume in the Manhattan directory, and dialed the number. Hume's loud, coarse voice answered on the third ring.

"This is Norman Tolliver, Hume," Norman said.

"Well, Norm, it's been awhile. What's the good word?"

Norm. A muscle fluttered on Norman's cheek. "If you plan to be in this afternoon, I would like a word with you."

"Oh? Something up?"

"I prefer not to discuss it on the telephone."

"Suit yourself," Hume said. "Sure, come on over. Give me a chance to show off my digs to you." He paused. "You shoot pool, by any chance?"

"No, I do not 'shoot pool.' "

"Too bad. Got a new table and I've been practicing. Hell of a good game, Norm, you should try it."

The man was a bloody Philistine. Norman said, "I'll be by directly," and cradled the handset with considerable force.

He recorked the bottle of dead Margaux and wrapped it in a towel. After which he blew out the candle, switched off his quadraphonic unit, and took the penthouse elevator to the street. Fifteen minutes later a taxi delivered him to the East Side block on which Hume's townhouse was situated.

Hume admitted him, allowed as how it was good to see him again, swatted him on the back (Norman shuddered and ground his teeth), and ushered him into a spacious living room. There were shelves filled with rare first editions, walls adorned with originals by Degas and Monet and Sisley, fine Kerman Orientals on the floor. *But all of these works of art,* Norman thought, *could mean nothing to Hume; they would merely be possessions, visible evidence of his wealth.* He had certainly never read any of the books or spent a moment appreciating any of the paintings. And there were cigarette burns (Norman ground his teeth again) in one of the Kerman carpets.

Hume himself was fifty pounds overweight and such a plebeian type that he looked out of place in these genteel surroundings. He wore expensive but ill-fitting clothes, much too heavy for the season because of a professed hypersensitivity to cold; his glasses were rimmed in gold and onyx and quite thick because of a professed astigmatism in one eye; he carried an English walking stick because of a slight limp that was the professed result of a sports car accident. He pretended to be an eccentric, but did not have the breeding, intelligence, or flair to manage even the *pose* of eccentricity. Looking at him now, Norman revised his previous estimate: The man was not a Philistine; he was a Neanderthal.

"How about a drink, Norman?"

"This is not a social call," Norman said.

"No?" Hume peered at him. "So what can I do for you?"

Norman unwrapped the bottle of Margaux and extended it accusingly. "*This* is what you can do for me, as you put it."

"I don't get it," Hume said.

"You gave me this Margaux last month. I trust you remember the occasion."

"Sure, I remember. But I still don't see the point—"

"The point, Hume, is that it's dead."

"Huh?"

"The wine is undrinkable. It's *dead*, Hume."

Hume threw back his head and made a sound like the braying of a jackass. "You hand me a laugh sometimes, Norm," he said, "you really do. The way you talk about wine, like it was alive or human or something."

Norman's hands had begun to tremble. "The Margaux *was* alive. Now it is nothing but seventy-nine-year-old vinegar."

"So what?" Hume said.

"So what?" A reddish haze seemed to be forming behind Norman's eyes. "So what! You insensitive idiot, don't you have any conception of what tragedy this is?"

"Hey," Hume said, "who you calling an idiot?"

"You, you idiot. If you have another Margaux 1900, I demand it in replacement. I demand a *living* wine."

"I don't give a damn what you demand," Hume said. He was miffed too, now. "You got no right to call me an idiot, Norm; I won't stand for it. Suppose you just get on out of my house. And take your lousy bottle of wine with you."

"*My* lousy bottle of wine?" Norman said through the reddish haze. "Oh no, Hume, it's *your* lousy bottle of wine, and I'm going to let *you* have it!"

Then he did exactly that: he let Hume have it. On top of the head with all his strength.

There were several confused moments that Norman could not recall afterward. When the reddish haze dissipated, he discovered that all of his anger had drained away, leaving him flushed and shaken. He also discovered Hume lying quite messily dead on the cigarette-scarred Kerman, the unbroken bottle of Margaux beside him.

It was not in Norman's nature to panic in a crisis. He marshaled his emotions instead and forced himself to approach the problem at hand with cold logic.

Hume was as dead as the Margaux; there was nothing to be done about that. He could, of course, telephone the police and claim self-defense. But there was no guarantee that he would be believed, considering that this was Hume's house, and in any case he had an old-fashioned gentleman's abhorrence of adverse and sensational publicity. No, reporting Hume's demise was out of the question.

Which left the reasonable alternative of removing all traces of his presence and stealing away as if he had never come. It was unlikely that anyone had seen him entering; if he was careful his departure would be unobserved as well. And even if someone *did* happen to notice him in a casual way, he was not known in this neighborhood and there was nothing about his physical appearance that would remain fixed in a person's memory. An added point in his favor was that Hume had few friends and by self-admission preferred his own company. The body, therefore, might well go undiscovered for several days.

Norman used the towel to wipe the unbloodied surfaces of the Margaux bottle—a distasteful but necessary task—and left the bottle where it lay beside the body. Had he touched anything in the house that might also retain a fingerprint? He was certain he had not. He *had* pressed the doorbell button on the porch outside, but it would be simple enough to brush that clean before leaving. Was there anything else, anything he might have overlooked? He concluded that there wasn't.

With the towel folded inside his coat pocket, he went down the hallway to the front door. There was a magnifying-glass peephole in the center of it; he put his eye to the glass and peered out. Damn. Two women were standing on the street in front, conversing in the amiable and animated fashion of neighbors. They might decide to part company in ten seconds, but they might also decide to remain there for ten minutes.

Norman debated the advisability of exiting through the rear. But a man slipping out the back door of someone's house was much more likely to be seen and remembered than a man who departed the front. And there was still the matter of the doorbell button to be dealt with. His only intelligent choice was to wait for the street in front to become clear.

As he stood there he found himself thinking again of the tragedy of the Margaux 1900 (a far greater tragedy to his connoisseur's mind than the unlamented death of Roger Hume). It was considered by many experts to be one of the most superlative vintages in history; and the fact remained that he had yet to taste it. To have come so close and then to be denied as he had was intolerable.

It occurred to him again that perhaps Hume *did* have another bottle on the premises. While presenting the first bottle last month Hume had boasted that he maintained a "pretty well-stocked" wine cellar, though he confided that he had never had "much of a taste for the grape" and seldom availed himself of its contents. Neanderthal, indeed. But a Neanderthal with a good deal of money who had managed, through luck or wise advice, to obtain at least one bottle of an uncommon and classic wine—

Was there another Margaux 1900 in his blasted cellar?

Norman debated a second time. On the one hand it would behoove him to make as rapid an escape as possible from the scene of his impulsive crime; but on the other hand the 1900 Margaux was virtually impossible to find today, and if he passed up this opportunity to secure a bottle for himself he might never taste it. It would be a decision he might well rue for the rest of his days.

He looked once more through the peephole; the two women were still talking together outside. Which only served to cement a decision already made. He was, first and foremost, a connoisseur: he simply *had* to know if Hume had another bottle of the Margaux.

Norman located the wine cellar without difficulty. It was off the kitchen, with access through a door and down a short flight of steps. It was also adequate, he noticed in a distracted way as he descended—a smallish single room, walled and floored in concrete, containing several storage bins filled with at least two hundred bottles of wine.

But no, not just wine; remarkably *fine* wine. Reds from Châteaux Lafite, Haut-Brion, Lascombes, Cos D'Estournel, Mouton-D'Armailhacq, La Tâche, Romanée Saint-Vivant; whites from the Bommes and Barsac communes of France, from the Rhine Hessen of Germany, from Alsace and Italy and the Napa Valley of California. Norman resisted the impulse to stop and more closely examine each of the labels. He had no time to search out anything except the Margaux 1900.

He found two different Château Margaux clarets in the last row of bins, but neither of them was the 1900 vintage. Then, when he was about to abandon hope, he knelt in front of the final section of bins and there they were, a pair of dusty bottles whose labels matched that on the spoiled bottle upstairs.

Norman expelled a breath and removed one of them with care. Should he take the second as well? Yes: if he left it here there was no telling into whose unappreciative hands it might fall. There would doubtless be a paper sack in the kitchen in which to carry both. He withdrew the second bottle, straightened, and started to the stairs.

The door at the top was closed. Blinking, Norman paused. He could not recall having shut the door; in fact he was quite certain he had left it standing wide open. He frowned, went up the steps, set the two living Margaux 1900s down carefully at his feet, and rotated the knob.

It was locked.

It took a moment of futile shaking and rattling before he realized that the top of the door was outfitted with one of those silent pneumatic door closers. He stared at it in disbelief. Only an idiot would put such a device on the door to a wine cellar! But that was, of course, what Hume had been. For whatever incredible reason he had had the thing installed—and it seemed obvious now that he carried on his person the key to the door latch.

There was no other way out of the cellar, no second door and no window; Norman determined that with a single sweep of his gaze. And the door looked to be fashioned of heavy solid wood, which made the task of forcing it or battering it down an insurmountable one.

He was trapped.

The irony was as bitter as the taste of the dead Margaux: trapped in Roger Hume's wine cellar with the man's murdered corpse in the living room upstairs. He had been a fool to come down here, a fool to have listened to the connoisseur in him. He could have been on his way home to his penthouse by now. Instead, here he was, locked away awaiting the eventual arrival of the police . . .

As he had done earlier, Norman made an effort to gather his wits. Perhaps all was *not* lost, despite the circumstances. He could claim to have been visiting Hume when two burly masked men entered the house; and he could claim that these men had locked him in the cellar and taken Hume away to an unknown fate. Yes, that was plausible. After all, he was a respected and influential man. Why shouldn't he be believed?

Norman began to feel a bit better. There remained the problem of survival until Hume's body was found; but as long as that did not take more than a week—an unlikely prospect—the problem was not really a serious one. He was surrounded by scores of bottles of vintage wine, and there *was* a certain amount of nourishment to be had from the product of the vintner's art. At least enough to keep him alive and in passable health.

Meanwhile, he would have to find ways to keep himself and his mind occupied. He could begin, he thought, by examining and making a mental catalogue of Hume's collection of vintages and varieties.

He turned from the door and surveyed the cellar again. And for the first time, something struck him as vaguely odd about it. He had not noticed it before in his haste and purpose, but now that he was locked in here with nothing to distract him—

A faint sound reached his ears and made him scowl. He could not quite identify it or its source at first; he descended the stairs again and stood at the bottom, listening. It seemed to be coming from both sides of the cellar. Norman moved to his left—and when the sound became clear the hackles rose on the back of his neck.

What it was, was a soft hissing.

ROGER HUME'S BODY WAS discovered three days later by his twice-weekly cleaning lady. But when the police arrived at her summons, it was not Hume's death which interested them quite so much as that of the second man, whose corpse was found during a routine search of the premises.

This second "victim" lay on the floor of the wine cellar, amid a rather astonishing carnage of broken wine bottles and spilled wine. His wallet identified him as Norman Tolliver, whose name and standing were recognized by the cleaning lady, if not by the homicide detectives. The assistant medical examiner determined probable cause of death to be an apoplectic seizure, a fact which only added to the consternation of the police. Why was Tolliver locked inside Roger Hume's wine cellar? Why had he evidently smashed dozens of bottles of expensive wine? Why was he dead of natural causes and Hume dead of foul play?

They were, in a word, baffled.

One other puzzling aspect came to their attention. A plain-clothes officer noticed the faint hissing sound and verified it as forced air coming through a pair of wall ducts; he mentioned this to his lieutenant, saying that it seemed odd for a wine cellar to have heater vents like the rest of the rooms in the house. Neither detective bothered to pursue the matter, however. It struck them as unrelated to the deaths of the two men.

But it was, of course, the exact opposite: it was the key to everything. Along with several facts of which they were not yet aware: Norman's passion for wine and his high blood pressure, Roger Hume's ignorance in the finer arts and *his* hypersensitivity to cold—and the tragic effect on certain wines caused by exposure to temperatures above 60 degrees Fahrenheit.

No wonder Norman, poor fellow, suffered an apoplectic seizure. Can there be any greater horror for the true connoisseur than to find himself trapped in a cellar full of rare, aged, and irreplaceable wines that have been stupidly turned to vinegar?

Mulled Wine

⅔ **cup sugar**
⅓ **cup water**
1 dozen whole cloves
2 cinnamon sticks
1 crushed nutmeg
1 orange
1 lemon
1 cup lime or lemon juice, heated
1 bottle red wine, heated

CUT THE ORANGE and lemon in half. Juice one half of the orange and one half of the lemon. Add juice to the lime or lemon juice.

SLICE THE REMAINING half of the lemon and orange, and set aside. The citrus slices will be used to garnish the final product.

PUT THE SUGAR, water, cloves, cinnamon sticks, nutmeg, and the peels of the juiced halves of the lemon and orange in a saucepan. Bring to a boil over low to medium heat and boil for about five minutes, until the sugar melts and forms a syrup. Let cool slightly and strain. Return the strained syrup to the pan. Add the hot lemon or lime juice slowly to the syrup while stirring. Add the heated wine and stir. Serve hot, garnished with citrus slices.

Gored

Bill Crider

No one ever invited Sheriff Dan Rhodes to the annual Blacklin County Stag BBQ. It wasn't that no one liked him. The truth was that the Stag BBQ was something of a scandal, and everyone wanted to be sure that the sheriff ignored it.

And he did. He would never have been there if it hadn't been for the dead man.

THE STAG BBQ WAS held at a different location every year. This year's site was the camphouse on George Newberry's ranch, about ten miles out of Clearview and just off a paved two-lane highway that ran practically straight as an arrow thanks to the fact that it was built on an old narrow-gauge railroad bed.

Rhodes pulled the county car up to a lightweight metal gate. There was a blue-and-white metal sign on the gate to let the world know that George Newberry was a member of the ABBA, the American Brahman Breeders Association.

Newberry himself got out of a red-and-cream-colored Ford pickup and opened the gate. Rhodes drove through. Newberry closed the gate and got in the car beside Rhodes.

"I'll just ride down with you," he said. "I'll come back for the truck later."

Newberry was a big man, over two hundred pounds, very little of which appeared to be muscle. The car sagged slightly to the side when he sat down.

"I'll show you where to go," he said. He pointed to the barn. "It's around that way."

He sounded nervous, and Rhodes didn't blame him. It wasn't every day that someone found a dead man on your property.

The road they were following wasn't much of a road after it passed by the dilapidated sheet-metal barn. It was really just a pair of ruts through a pasture blooming with yellow bitterweed and goldenrod.

Every now and then the county car hit a bump, and Newberry had to take off his Western-style straw hat to keep it from being crushed against the roof. He wiped the sweat off his forehead with his blue bandanna and stuck the bandanna in his pocket.

"It's Gabe Tolliver," he said.

So it wasn't just any dead man, not some homeless drifter that just happened to turn up on Newberry's property looking for a place to rest for a day or so and praising his luck at finding the empty camphouse. No, it was a Somebody. It was Gabe Tolliver, who had been a loan officer at the larger of Clearview's two banks.

"What happened?" Rhodes asked.

"I'll let you be the judge of that," Newberry said. Though the car's air conditioner was running full blast, Newberry was still sweating. His western shirt had dark circles under the armpits. "All I know for sure's that Ben Locklin found him lyin' by a brush pile, and Bo Peevehouse called you on that cellular phone of his that he's so proud of."

Ben Locklin was a vice president of the bank where Tolliver worked. Or *had* worked. He wouldn't be reporting in on Monday. Peevehouse sold life and accident insurance. Newberry was also a big man in Clearview. He owned three of the most prosperous businesses in town: two convenience stores and a video store.

In fact, that was what the Stag BBQ was all about. It was a chance for the movers and shakers to get together and drink a lot of beer, eat some BBQ and homemade ice cream, tell a few dirty jokes, and do a little gambling.

It was the gambling that no one wanted the sheriff to know about, though it was an open secret. If the men wanted to lose a few dollars to one another shooting craps or playing jacks-or-better-to-open, Rhodes didn't really see the harm in it.

But it seemed that this year there had been some harm after all, at least for Gabe Tolliver.

The BBQ was the social event of the year for the men in Blacklin County, and everyone who was anyone got invited. Everyone who was anyone and male, that is. Women weren't allowed. Blacklin County was becoming more conscious of women's rights every day, but Blacklin County was, after all, in Texas, where a great many men still believed that some activities just weren't appropriate for women. Maybe they were okay in Las Vegas, but that was different.

Rhodes looked over at Newberry, who was holding his hat in his lap. The businessman was wearing jeans and a pair of expensive-looking boots that were covered with dust. It hadn't rained in Blacklin County for nearly a month.

"Don't worry," Newberry said, noticing Rhodes's glance. "I haven't stepped in anything."

"I didn't think you had," Rhodes told him.

Rhodes figured he'd be the only man at the ranch without a pair of boots. He was pretty certain that he was the only sheriff in Texas who didn't wear them. But they hurt his toes and he couldn't walk in them very well, so he was wearing an old pair of scuffed Rockports.

The car went up over a low rise, and Rhodes could see New-berry's camphouse, painted dark green and sitting on top of a hill not far from a big stock tank and in front of a thickly wooded area that began about thirty yards away and ran down the hill. There was a four-strand barbed-wire fence around the camphouse.

"Any fish in the tank?" Rhodes asked.

"Bass," Newberry said. "A couple of the guys have tried it today, but nobody's caught anything. I caught a five-pounder last spring, though."

Rhodes wished that he'd brought his rod and reel along, but it wouldn't have been very professional to go fishing while he was supposed to be conducting a murder investigation.

There were white Brahman cattle scattered out over the pasture, crunching the grass with their heads down or looking at whatever it was that cows looked at. Rhodes couldn't tell whether they were purebred or not. They paid no attention to his car.

"Nice-looking herd," he said.

"Yeah," Newberry said, sounding a little distracted. "Kind of wild, though."

"Wild?"

"You'll see," Newberry said.

RHODES SAW WHEN THEY got to the body, which was located just inside the woods. Gabe Tolliver was lying on his back, and there was a terrible wound in his stomach, as if a horn had twisted his insides. Black flies buzzed around the wound, and a couple of them were crawling on it, near a curling brown leaf that stuck to the torn skin. Rhodes hadn't known Tolliver well, and what he'd heard about, he didn't much like. Tolliver was said to be a womanizer and a bully, and that might have been true. But even if it was, Tolliver hadn't deserved to die like this.

"Did you call a doctor?" Rhodes asked Newberry.

They were standing over the body. Everyone else was in the fenced yard of the house, and Rhodes could almost feel their eyes boring into his back.

"Didn't see any need of a doctor," Newberry said. His face was white. "Not much doubt that Gabe's dead. But listen, Sheriff, as wild as those braymahs are, I don't think any of them did this. What about you?"

Rhodes didn't think so either. He knelt down by the body and shooed the flies away with his hand. There were wood splinters in the twisted flesh, and there was a sliver of bark on Tolliver's blue western shirt.

There was a dark stain by the back of Tolliver's head, and his hair was wet with blood. He'd been hit, probably before the goring.

Rhodes stood up. The trees were native hardwoods, oak and elm mostly, with a few pecan trees thrown in. There were several dead tree limbs lying near where Rhodes was standing and more in the brush pile near the body, but nothing that looked as if it had been used to kill Tolliver.

"Cows didn't do this," Rhodes said.

He looked around the area carefully. There was a place nearby where the ground was gouged up as if an armadillo had been rooting around, though Rhodes suspected that no animal was responsible. He'd have to get soil samples to be sure.

He turned to Newberry. "Let's get back to your camphouse."

Newberry looked glad of the chance to leave the body. They walked up a little cattle trail, and Newberry sidestepped a cow pie, the same one he had avoided on their way down to see the body. Someone had stepped in the manure earlier, but not Rhodes, which was surprising to the sheriff. Whenever he visited a pasture, he generally stepped in something within ten seconds of getting out of his car.

He stopped and looked down at the cow pie. There was another one just to the side of it, and that one had been kicked to pieces. Both were fairly fresh, and the one that had been shattered wasn't yet entirely dry.

"What was Tolliver doing in the woods, anyway?" Rhodes asked Newberry.

Newberry turned around. "I don't know. There's not any bathroom up there at the camphouse, so nearly ever'body's goin' to come to the woods once or twice."

Rhodes hadn't seen any signs of that kind of activity, and said so.

"Well, mostly people just go behind the tank dam. But I know some of 'em have come down here to get wood for the fire. Maybe that's what Gabe was after."

"Who's the cook?"

"Jerry Foster."

Foster ran a discount auto parts store. He was the one Rhodes wanted to talk to.

Just before they got back to the house, an armadillo shot out of the weeds beside the trail and charged through the goldenrods and bitterweeds. Little puffs of dust flew from its feet. Rhodes had never understood how something with such short legs could go so fast. He wondered if he could have been wrong about the gouges in the earth near Tolliver's body, but he didn't think so. No armadillo had done that.

IT WAS NEARLY FIVE o'clock, but because it was the first week in October it wouldn't be dark for more than two hours. The shadows in the woods were beginning to deepen, but there was a pleasant glow to the light that belied the circumstances. Newberry's cattle grazed peacefully in the pasture, unable to get near the house thanks to the barbed-wire fence.

Rhodes didn't have time to enjoy the deceptive peacefulness of the scene. He went to the county car, which was parked outside the fence. He opened the car door, got in, and called the jail on the radio. Then he told Hack Jensen, the dispatcher, to send the justice of the peace to Newberry's ranch. And an ambulance.

"You think an ambulance can make it up to that camphouse?" Hack asked.

Rhodes said that he hoped so. He didn't want to have to haul Tolliver's body out in the back of someone's pickup.

"I'll tell 'em then," Hack said. "You gonna solve this and be home in time for supper, or do you want me to call Ivy for you?"

Rhodes thought about the barbecue that Jerry Foster was cooking. He thought about bread soaked in barbecue sauce and about potato salad and pinto beans and cool, thick slices of white onion. He thought about homemade ice cream. And he thought about the low-fat diet he was on at home.

"You better call her," he said. "This might take a while."

THE GIANT BARBECUE GRILL was made from three fifty-five-gallon drums split in half and welded together end to end. There was a stovepipe on one end. Rhodes could smell the mesquite smoke as he walked over to talk to Jerry Foster, who stood by the grill.

Foster was taller than Rhodes's six feet, and he was wearing a chef's hat that had once been white but which was now mostly gray and stained with smoke and grease. He was also wearing an equally stained apron that had "Kiss the Cook" printed on it in red. Someone had used a black marking pen to add the word "Don't" to the front of the sentence and an exclamation mark at the end.

Foster opened the grill as Rhodes walked up. Smoke billowed out, enveloping them and stinging the sheriff's eyes. Rhodes waved a hand in front of his face to push the smoke away.

Coals glowed under the slow-cooked meat. Rhodes looked hungrily at the juicy pork ribs while Foster poked a brisket with a long fork. Satisfied that everything was all right, Foster lowered the lid.

"Still planning to eat?" Rhodes asked.

"I expect we will, but Gabe's dyin' has pretty much put a damper on the festivities." Foster had a raspy smoker's voice. "There's no need to let the meat burn up even if we don't eat it today, though."

Foster was right about the festivities. There weren't any that Rhodes could see. He looked over at a big oak tree by the camphouse. The ground beneath it was worn smooth and packed hard, but there were no crapshooters gathered there. Everyone was standing around in small groups, whispering and looking over at Rhodes and Foster.

The shaded tables under the other trees were clear of cards and poker chips, but Rhodes wasn't entirely sure whether the gambling had come to a stop because he was there or because of Tolliver's murder.

Also in the shade of the oak were three washtubs covered with thick quilts. Rhodes knew that the tubs would be full of ice and that under the quilts were hand-cranked wooden ice cream freezers. Rhodes hadn't had any homemade ice cream in years. The thought of its cold smoothness made his mouth water.

"What kind of ice cream in the freezers?" he asked.

"Peach," Foster said. "Last of the Elbertas came in back in August, and my wife put some up in the freezer for us to use for the barbecue."

Peach was Rhodes's favorite.

"Did Ben Locklin bring you any firewood?" Rhodes asked.

"Nope." Foster pushed up his chef's hat and wiped his forehead. "Who did?"

"I brought the mesquite myself, in my truck. Got it from my place. Newberry doesn't have any mesquite trees, or if he does you can't see 'em from here. You need some mesquite for the flavor."

"I wasn't talking about the mesquite," Rhodes said, thinking how the smoked ribs would taste. "I was talking about wood from the trees down the hill."

Foster gave it some thought. "Bo Peevehouse. Brian Colby. Hal Janes. Ben Locklin was goin' to, but he got a little sidetracked, what with findin' Gabe dead like that. There might've been a few more. I didn't try to keep up. They just dumped it on the pile and left it. I didn't look to see who brought it."

There was a little stack of twigs at one end of the grill.

"Looks like you're about out of wood," Rhodes said.

"Yeah. I've used most of it. But the brisket's about done. We won't need any more."

Rhodes supposed that was good, but it was too bad that all the wood had been burned, not that he'd expected to find anything.

"Any idea who'd want to kill Gabe?" he asked.

Foster readjusted his chef's hat. "Sheriff, you know as well as I do that half the people here've known each other since they were kids. They've got reasons to kill each other that go all the way back to high school, if not before. And the other half didn't like Gabe all that much. He wasn't bein' any too lenient with his loans these days."

Rhodes had heard the same thing. He left Foster and went looking for Newberry, whom he found talking to Bo Peevehouse.

"I need to talk to a few people," Rhodes told Newberry. "I'll do it inside if that's all right."

"Don't see any reason why not," Newberry said. "Who did you want to see?"

"I'll start with Bo," Rhodes said.

Bo Peevehouse, who had the cellular phone, also had the biggest TV set in Blacklin County, or so Rhodes had heard. He'd never seen it, himself. Bo had done very well in insurance, which Rhodes knew about in the same way he knew about the TV set: through Ivy, Rhodes's wife, who worked at a rival insurance agency.

Peevehouse had red hair that he wore in a spiky crew cut that Rhodes thought looked pretty strange with his western garb. Bo's boots were dusty but otherwise clean. His hands were smooth and white. Not the hands of a cowboy.

"Did you see the body?" Rhodes asked him.

They were sitting at a small wooden table in the camphouse, which had only one big room with a concrete floor. The rafters were covered with antlers, some of them small, some of them having five or six points, and the walls held pictures of wolves, deer, mountain lions, and Rocky Mountain sheep. There was a cot in one corner, a fireplace with more antlers nailed to the rough wooden mantel, and some metal folding chairs.

"Nope," Peevehouse said. "I didn't see it, and I sure didn't want to. Ben Locklin threw up, they told me, and I would've done the same thing. I don't need to see any bodies. All I did was call your office on my phone."

He patted his shirt pocket, where Rhodes could see the slim outline of the telephone.

"Flip model," Peevehouse said. "You wanta have a look?"

Rhodes didn't. "You brought some wood for the fire?"

"Sure did. Somebody gotta do it, and I figured it might as well be me. I don't mind working for my dinner."

"Who else brought wood up?"

Peevehouse didn't know. "I was busy shootin' di—I mean, I was doin' somethin' else."

"Who do you know that might want to kill Gabe Tolliver?"

Peevehouse didn't want to talk about it. He looked at the antlers, at the pictures, and at the concrete floor. Finally, he said, "Sheriff, you know what it's been like in this county for the last ten years? People haven't had much money, and when the bank was sold to that holdin' company, a lot of the old guys who'd been there for years lost their jobs. Gabe held onto his, but he had to be tough to do it. He couldn't do business the way he had before. You might say he was foreclosin' on the widows and orphans, and the only people who could get a loan were the folks who didn't need one. There were plenty of people who didn't like Gabe."

Rhodes knew Tolliver's reputation. But the word was that Gabe *liked* being tough. Foster had already hinted at it, and Rhodes had been hearing it for a long time before that. That wasn't really what he was interested in.

"Anybody here today get turned down for money he needed to keep his doors open?" he asked. "Anybody here today lose a house or a car because of Gabe?"

Peevehouse shook his head. "Not that I know of."

"I didn't think so. Now, what about other things? The kind of things that people get really upset about."

"I don't like to gossip, Sheriff," Peevehouse said. "When you sell insurance, you meet a lot of people and you hear a lot of stories. I don't pay 'em much attention."

He was looking at the fireplace while he talked. Rhodes figured he was lying.

"I think you should tell me if you've heard anything," Rhodes said. "I'll just find out from someone else."

"I guess you're right," Peevehouse said. He looked away from the fireplace and sighed. And then he told Rhodes what he'd heard.

BEN LOCKLIN WAS FIVE inches over six feet, but his hands were as small and soft as those of a teenage girl.

"It was a hell of a shock," he said. "Seeing Gabe lying there, like that, his stomach ripped open. I don't mind telling you I lost my lunch. It was a hell of a mess. Looked like he got gored by a bull to me, but I hadn't seen any bull down there in the woods, or any cows either. That's why I told Bo he'd better call you."

"You thought somebody had a reason to kill him?" Rhodes asked.

"Gabe was a good man," Locklin said, folding his arms across his wide chest. "I know what people think about him, but they think worse of me. I'm his boss, after all. I could tell him to do different if I wanted to."

Rhodes didn't really believe that. Locklin had been with the bank for twenty years, but everyone knew that didn't make a bit of difference to the new owners, who were probably planning to get rid of him as soon as they got more of their own men in place.

"I wasn't wondering about his business practices," Rhodes said. "I wanted to hear about his troubles with women."

Locklin looked at him.

"You know what I mean," Rhodes said. "He had a wandering eye, from what I hear."

"I don't know about that," Locklin said. "What my employees do on their own time is their own business."

"In a town the size of Clearview it isn't. I've already heard about it from Bo."

Ben waved a dismissive hand. "Gutter talk."

"Maybe. You've heard about it too, though, haven't you?"

"I've heard. That doesn't mean I believe it."

"That kind of talk gets under people's skin," Rhodes said. "Whether it's true or not." He told Locklin what he'd heard.

Locklin thought for a second or two and then admitted that he'd heard more or less the same things. Rhodes asked if he'd mentioned the talk to Gabe.

"Yeah, I said something. He told me to mind my own damn business, not that I blame him. Whatever he was doing, it didn't affect his work at the bank."

"And those men I mentioned, they had loans they'd missed a payment or two on?"

Locklin shrugged. "Yeah, I guess that's right."

That was all Rhodes wanted to know.

GEORGE NEWBERRY WAS JUST as reluctant to talk as Peevehouse and Locklin had been, but when Rhodes told him that he'd already heard the gossip, Newberry gave in. He confirmed everything that Peevehouse and Locklin had said.

"But it's just gossip," he said. "Stuff you hear if you hang around a convenience store all day like I do. I don't know that a word of it's true. You know what it is like when stories get started."

Rhodes knew. But there was generally a factual basis for things, even if the facts weren't as juicy as the story that finally made the rounds of the entire community.

"Both those men went down for firewood, according to Foster," Rhodes said.

"Maybe so," Newberry agreed, "but that doesn't make them killers."

That was true enough, but it put them in the vicinity of the murder. Right now that was about all Rhodes had to go on, that and the gossip.

"Send them in," he told Newberry. "I'll talk to them together."

"You think that's a good idea?"

"Maybe not," Rhodes said. "But it's the only one I have."

NEITHER HAL JANES NOR Brian Colby looked like a killer. They were young and skinny, and in their tight jeans and western hats, they looked as if they were just about to go to a rodeo and ride a bronc or maybe enter the calf-roping event. Colby had a red-and-white bandanna tied around his neck.

They came into the camphouse and stood awkwardly until Rhodes told them to sit at the table. He stood by the fireplace and watched them.

Janes was a little taller than Colby, but Colby was a lot wider through the shoulders. Either one of them looked big enough to have killed Gabe without too much trouble. Colby's boots were dirty, but Janes's were spotless.

Both men were nervous. Colby fidgeted in the folding chair, and Janes rubbed his hands together as if he were washing them.

Rhodes gave them a few seconds to wonder about what he was going to ask them. Then he said, "I know that you both went down to bring in some wood for the fire, and I know that one of you killed Gabe Tolliver. What I don't know is which one of you did it."

"Jesus Christ," Colby said, standin, up and knocking over his chair. It clanged on the hard floor. "You must be crazy, Sheriff."

"Lots of people think so," Rhodes said. "What about you, Hal?"

Janes was still sitting at the table, still dry-washing his hands.

"I wouldn't know about that," he said. "I think you're makin' a big mistake, though, accusin' two innocent men without any evidence."

"How would you know I don't have any evidence?" Rhodes asked.

Colby picked up his chair and sat back down. He looked at Janes and seemed as interested in his answer to the question as Rhodes did.

Janes gripped the edge of the table with his fingers, looking down at his nails. "The way I heard it, Gabe's just lyin' down there dead. Nobody saw him get killed, so there's no witnesses." He looked up at Rhodes. "Ben Locklin found the body, and he said it looked like a cow did it, or a bull. Said Gabe looked like he'd been gored."

"So there must not be any evidence of any murder," Colby said, more relaxed now and tipping back his chair. "Ben would've seen it if there was."

"Ben's not a trained lawman," Rhodes said. "He works in a bank."

"So did Gabe," Janes pointed out. "The same bank. Maybe they had a fight and Ben killed Gabe."

"Ben found the body, all right," Rhodes said. "He didn't kill anybody, though."

"Did you ask him?"

"I didn't have to," Rhodes said. "Now, let me tell you what I think happened."

"It won't do you any good," Colby told him. "I didn't kill anybody, and I don't have to listen to you."

"Me neither," Janes said. "I don't see why you're pickin' on us."

"Because of your wives," Rhodes said.

"You son of a bitch," Janes said.

Colby didn't say anything. He just sat there and looked as if he'd like to be somewhere else.

"Tolliver was after both of them," Rhodes went on, ignoring Janes. He'd been called worse. "You were both behind on loans, and he was using that to get at your wives. That's the way he was. He'd promise a little leeway if the woman would meet him somewhere for a drink."

"I think you'd better shut up, Sheriff," Colby said.

Rhodes ignored him the way he'd ignored Janes and leaned an elbow on the mantel in a space that was free of antlers.

"I think it happened this way," he said. "One of you saw Tolliver going for wood and followed him down there. Maybe you already had in mind what you were going to do, but I don't know about that. Maybe you just wanted to talk to him, tell him to stay away from your wife."

"So what?" Colby said. "What'd be wrong with that? If he was messin' where he shouldn't have been, he needed tellin'."

Rhodes agreed. "There's nothing wrong with telling. But that's not what happened. Whoever followed Gabe got so mad that he killed him. Maybe there was an argument first, and maybe Gabe said a few things he shouldn't have said. I don't know about that, either. I do know that somebody took a tree limb and clubbed Gabe in the back of the head."

"That wouldn't look like a bull gored him," Colby pointed out.

"No, so someone tried to cover up. Not that it did any good. That mark on the back of the head couldn't be hidden."

"Maybe he hit his head when he fell," Janes said. "After he got gored."

"That's a good argument, but it's not what happened. If he hadn't been hit first, he would have screamed. Somebody hit

Tolliver and then gored him with a tree limb. Maybe with the same one he hit him with."

"Where's the limb, then?" Colby asked.

"Burned up," Rhodes said. "The killer broke it up and took it to Jerry for firewood."

Colby didn't believe it. "Wouldn't Jerry have noticed the blood on the pieces of the limb when he put it in the fire?"

"Whoever killed Gabe jammed the limb in the dirt to clean the blood off," Rhodes said. "If there was any blood still on it, the dirt covered it up. Foster wouldn't have been looking for it."

"Sounds like you don't have any evidence, then, Sheriff," Janes said.

"Maybe not. But I know who killed Gabe Tolliver."

"Who?" Janes asked.

"You did," Rhodes said, stepping toward the table.

Janes shoved back his chair, kicked over the table, and threw Brian Colby at Rhodes.

Colby and Rhodes went down in a heap on the floor. Rhodes banged his elbow, and Janes ran out the door.

NO ONE IN THE yard tried to stop Janes. They didn't even know for sure what was going on until Rhodes came running out after him.

By that time Janes had vaulted the fence and headed across the pasture. Rhodes knew that if Janes made it to the river bottoms, about a mile away, they might never catch him. The bottom land was thick with trees and if a man was careful and knew the woods, he could stay hidden in the trees most of the way across the state.

Rhodes knew better than to try vaulting the fence. He valued the more delicate parts of his anatomy too much for that. He went through the gate, but that put him even farther behind Janes.

He probably wouldn't have caught him if it hadn't been for the armadillo. The armored mammal, frightened by Janes's approach, sprang up out of nowhere and shot across Janes's path.

It was too late for Janes to try to avoid the armadillo. He kicked it, tripped, and went sprawling in the bitterweed. The armadillo rolled a few feet and then it was on its way again.

Janes got to his knees, but Rhodes reached him before he could get up, put an armlock on him, and then slapped on the cuffs. After that it was easy to march him back to the camphouse.

They got there at the same time that the ambulance arrived, followed closely by the J. P., another county car carrying Deputy Ruth Grady, and Red Rogers, a reporter for the local radio station who was looking for a good story. Rhodes figured he would get one.

IT WAS NEARLY DARK before things were straightened out, but no one left. They were all too curious to know the story, and besides, there was all that barbecue to eat, not to mention peach ice cream.

They were so eager to hear the story that they even invited Rhodes to stay.

Red Rogers tried to get Rhodes on tape, but Rhodes didn't want to talk for the radio. He wanted to eat ribs and ice cream.

"You owe it to the community," Rogers said. "You have to tell us how you knew that Hal Janes was the killer."

Rhodes could smell the barbecue and he looked longingly at the ice cream freezers under their quilt covers.

"We'll save you some cream," Newberry assured him. "You go on and talk."

"Great," Rogers said. "So how did you know it was Janes?"

"His boots were too clean," Rhodes said. "He was the only one here with clean boots. Which meant that he'd cleaned them off. I think he stepped in a cow patty on the trail and left a boot print in it. But he noticed the print and kicked the patty to pieces, so naturally he had to clean his boots. Deputy Grady is looking around for his bandanna right now. I think she'll find it."

Rogers was incredulous. "And that's it? You know he did it because his boots were clean?"

"That and his hands," Rhodes said. "You look at all these men here, they're dressed up in cowboy clothes, but they're not cowboys. They're bankers and salesmen and store owners. There's not a callused hand in the bunch. Janes didn't want me to see his hands because he'd scratched them up on the limb he used to kill Tolliver with. You can't fool with that rough bark like that, not without marking your hands."

"But what about hard evidence?" Rogers asked.

"We'll find that bandanna," Rhodes said. "And we'll find traces of bark in the scratches on Janes's hands. We'll find cow manure on his boots, too, in the cracks and crevices. He couldn't get it all off."

"But will that prove he killed Gabe Tolliver?"

"He had a motive, the means, and the opportunity," Rhodes said. "We'll see what a jury thinks."

There was more that Rogers wanted to say, but Rhodes didn't listen. Everyone was eating from paper plates heaped with ribs and brisket, beans and potato salad, and the covers were off the ice cream freezers. Rhodes wanted to get his share.

It turned out to be even better than he'd thought. The ribs were smoky and spicy, and the ice cream was so smooth and sweet and cold that he could have eaten a whole gallon.

It was too bad, he thought, that Hal Janes and Gabe Tolliver weren't there to enjoy it.

Peach Ice Cream

Makes one gallon

5 eggs
2 cups sugar
Pinch of salt
3 tsp. vanilla
1 can sweetened condensed milk
1 large can evaporated milk (13 ounces)
1 quart mashed peaches
Enough whole milk to fill freezer can within 2 inches
   of top (about 3 cups)

BEAT EGGS UNTIL thick, adding sugar gradually. Add remaining ingredients and pour into freezer can. Put dasher in freezer can. Put freezer can in bucket and fill bucket with ice (add salt to ice about every six inches). Attach freezer crank, and turn until mixture is hard. Remove dasher and keep the freezer can iced down until serving.

USE A WOODEN freezer with a hand crank. Whoever turns the crank gets to lick the dasher.

Day for a Picnic

Edward D. Hoch

I suppose I remember it better than the other, countless other, picnics of my childhood, and I suppose the reason for that is the murder. But perhaps this day in mid-July would have stood out in my mind without the violence of sudden death. Perhaps it would have stood out simply because it was the first time I'd ever been out alone without the ever-watching eyes of my mother and father to protect me. True, my grandfather was watching over me that month while my parents vacationed in Europe, but he was more a friend than a parent—a great old man with white hair and tobacco-stained teeth who never ceased the relating of fascinating tales of his own youth out West. There were stories of Indians and warfare, tales of violence in the youthful days of our nation, and at that youthful age I was fully content in believing that my grandfather was easily old enough to have fought in all those wars as he so claimed.

It was not the custom in the thirties, as it is today, for parents to take their children along when making their first tour of Europe, and so as I've said I was left behind in Grandfather's care. It was really a month of fun for me, because the life of the rural New York town is far different from the hustle of the city, even for a boy of nine or ten, and I was to spend endless days running barefoot along dusty roads in the company of boys who never—hardly ever—viewed me strangely because of my city background. The days were sunny with warmth, because it had been a warm summer

447

even here on the shores of a cooling lake. Almost from the beginning of the month my grandfather had spoken with obvious relish
of the approach of the annual picnic, and by mid-month I was
looking forward to it also, thinking that here would be a new
opportunity of exploring the byways of the town and meeting
other boys as wild and free as I myself felt. Then too, I never
seemed to mind at that time the company of adults. They were
good people for the most part, and I viewed them with a proper
amount of childish wonder.

There were no sidewalks in the town then, and nothing that
you'd really call a street. The big touring cars and occasional late-
model roadsters raised endless clouds of dust as they roared
(seemingly to a boy of ten) through the town at fantastic speeds
unheard of in the city. This day especially, I remember the cars
churning up the dust. I remember Grandfather getting ready for
the picnic, preparing himself with great care because this was to be
a political picnic, and Grandfather was a very important political
figure in the little town.

I remember standing in the doorway of his bedroom (leaning,
really, because boys of ten never stood when they could lean),
watching him knot the black string tie that made him look so
much like that man in the funny movies. For a long time I watched
in silence, seeing him scoop up coins for his pockets and the solid
gold watch I never tired of seeing, and the little bottle he said was
cough medicine even in the summer, and, of course, his important
speech.

"You're goin' to speak, Gramps?"

"Sure am, boy. Every year I speak. Give the town's humanitarian
award. It's voted on by secret ballot of all the townspeople."

"Who won it?"

"That's something no one knows but me, boy. And I don't tell
till this afternoon."

"Are you like the mayor here, Gramps?"

"Sort of, boy," he said with a chuckle. "I'm what you call a select-
man, and since I'm the oldest of them here I guess I have quite a
lot to say about the town."

"Are you in charge of the picnic?"

"I'm in charge of the awards."

"Can we get free Coke and hot dogs?"

He chuckled at that. "We'll see, boy. We'll see."

Grandfather didn't drive, and as a result we were picked up for the picnic by Miss Pinkney and Miss Hazel, two old schoolteachers who drove a white Ford with a certain misplaced pride. Since they were already in front, the two of us piled in back, a bit crowded but happy. On the way to the picnic grounds we passed others going on foot, and Grandfather waved like a prince might wave.

"What a day for a picnic!" Miss Hazel exclaimed. "Remember how it rained last year?"

The sun was indeed bright and the weather warm, but with the contrariness of the very young I remember wishing that I'd been at the rainy picnic instead. I'd never been at a rainy picnic for the very simple reason that my parents always called them off if it rained.

"It's a good day," my grandfather said. "It'll bring out the voters. They should hold elections in the summertime, and we'd win by a landslide every time."

The Fourth of July was not yet two weeks past, and as we neared the old picnic grounds we could hear the belated occasional crackling of leftover fireworks being set off by the other kids. I was more than ever anxious to join them, though I did wonder vaguely what kind of kids would ever have firecrackers unexploded and left over after the big day.

We traveled down a long and dusty road to the picnic property, running winding down a hillside to a sort of cove by the water where brown sandy bluffs rose on three sides. There was room here for some five hundred people, which is the number that might be attracted by the perfect weather, and already a few cars were parked in the makeshift parking area, disgorging there the loads of children and adults. Miss Pinkney and Miss Hazel parked next to the big touring car that belonged to Dr. Stout, and my grandfather immediately cornered the doctor on some political subject. They stood talking for some minutes about—as I remember—the forthcoming primary election, and all the while I shifted from one foot to the other, watching the other kids at play down by the water, watching the waves of the lake whitened by a brisk warming breeze that fanned through the trees and tall uncut grass of the bluffs.

Finally, with a nod of permission from my grandfather, I took off on the run, searching out a few of the boys I'd come to know best in these weeks of my visit. I found them finally, playing in a

sort of cave on the hillside. Looking back now I realize it was probably no more than a lovers' trysting place, but at the time it held
for us all the excitement and mystery of a smuggler's den. I played
there with the others for nearly an hour, until I heard my grandfather calling me from down near the speakers' platform.

Already as I ran back down the hill I saw that the campaign
posters and patriotic bunting were in place. The picnic crowd was
gradually drifting down to the platform, clutching hot dogs and
bottles of soda pop and foaming mugs of beer. Over near the cars I
could see the men tapping another keg of beer, and I watched as a
sudden miscalculation on the part of the men sent the liquid
shooting up into a fizzing fountain. "It's raining beer," shouted
one of the men, standing beneath the descending stream with his
mouth open. "This must be heaven!"

Frank Coons, the town's handyman and occasional black sheep,
had cornered my grandfather and was asking him something.
"Come on, how about some of your gin cough medicine? I been
waitin' all afternoon for it!"

But my grandfather was having none of it. "None today, Frank."

"Why not? Just a drop."

"Have some beer instead. It's just as good." He moved off, away
from Frank, and I followed him. There were hands to be shaken,
words to be spoken, and in all of it Grandfather was a past master.

"When's your speech, Gramps?" I asked him.

"Soon now, boy. Want a soda pop?"

"Sure!"

He picked a bottle of cherry-colored liquid from the red and
white cooler and opened it for me. It tasted good after my running
and playing in the hot dirt of the hillside. Now Grandfather saw
someone else he knew, a tall handsome man named Jim Tweller,
whom I'd seen at the house on occasion. He had business dealings
with my grandfather, and I understood that he owned much of the
property in the town.

"Stay close to the platform, Jim," Grandfather was saying.

"Don't tell me I won that foolish award!"

"Can't say yet, Jim. Just stay close."

I saw Miss Pinkney and Miss Hazel pass by, casting admiring
glances at Jim Tweller. "Doesn't he have such a *mannish* smell about
him!" Miss Pinkney whispered loudly. Tweller, I gathered even at
that tender age, was much admired by the women of the town.

"Come, boy," Grandfather was saying. "Bring your soda and I'll find you a seat right up in front. You can listen to my speech."

I saw that the mayor, a Mr. Myerton, was already on the platform, flanked by two men and a woman I didn't know. In the very center was a big microphone hooked up to an overhead loudspeaker system borrowed from the sole local radio station. Empty beer mugs stood in front of each place. My grandfather's chair was over on the end, but right now he strode to the speaker's position, between Mayor Myerton and the woman.

"Ladies and gentlemen," he began, speaking in his best political voice. "And children, too, of course. I see a lot of you little ones here today, and that always makes me happy. It makes me aware of the fact that another generation is on the rise, a generation that will carry on the fine principles of our party in the decades to come. As many of you know, I have devoted the years since the death of my wife almost exclusively to party activities. The party has been my lifeblood, as I hope it will be the lifeblood of other, future generations. But enough of that for the moment. Mayor Myerton and Mrs. Finch of the school board will speak to you in due time about the battle that lies ahead of us this November. Right now, it's my always pleasant duty to announce the annual winner of the party's great humanitarian award, given to the man who has done the most for this community and its people. I should say the man or woman, because we've had a number of charming lady winners in past years. But this year it's a man, a man who has perhaps done more than any other to develop the real estate of our town to its full potential, a man who during this past year donated—yes, I said donated—the land for our new hospital building. You all know who I mean, the winner by popular vote of this year's humanitarian award—Mr. Jim Tweller!"

Tweller had stayed near the speakers' stand and now he hopped up, waving to a crowd that was cheering him with some visible restraint. Young as I was, I wondered about this, wondered even as I watched Grandfather yield the honored speaker's position to Tweller and take his chair at the end of the platform. Tweller waited until the scattered cheers had played themselves out in the afternoon breeze and then cheerfully cleared his throat. I noticed Frank Coons standing near the platform and saw Grandfather call him over. "Get a pitcher of beer for us, Frank," he asked. "Speeches make us thirsty."

While Frank went off on his mission, Jim Tweller adjusted the wobbly microphone and began his speech of thanks and acceptance. I was just then more interested in two boys wrestling along the water's edge, tussling, kicking sand at each other. But Tweller's speech was not altogether lost on me. I remember scattered words and phrases, and even then to me they seemed the words and phrases of a political candidate rather than simply an award winner. ". . . Thank you from the bottom of my heart for this great honor . . . I realize, I think, more than anyone else the fact that our party needs a rebirth with new blood if it is to win again in November . . . loyal old horses turned out to pasture while the political colts run the race . . ." I saw Mayor Myerton, a man in his sixties, flinch at these words, and I realized that the simple acceptance speech was taking a most unexpected turn.

But now my attention was caught by the sight of Frank Coons returning with the foaming pitcher of beer. He'd been gone some minutes and I figured he'd stopped long enough to have one himself, or perhaps he'd found someone else who carried gin in a cough medicine bottle. Anyway, he passed the pitcher up to the man at the end of the platform, the opposite end from my grandfather. I wondered if this was his revenge for being refused that drink earlier. The man on the end filled his glass with beer and then passed it on to the mayor who did likewise. Jim Tweller interrupted his speech a moment to accept the pitcher and fill his glass, then pass it to Mrs. Finch of the school board who was on his right. She shook her head with a temperant vigor and let it go on to the man I didn't know, sitting next to Grandfather at the end of the platform.

Tweller had taken a drink of his beer and shook his head violently as if it were castor oil. "Got a bad barrel here," he told the people with a laugh. "I'm going to stick to the hard stuff after this. Or else drink milk. Anyway, before I finish I want to tell you about my plans for our community. I want to tell you a little about how . . ." He paused for another drink of the beer ". . . about how we can push back the final remains of the depression and surge ahead into the forties with a new prosperity, a new ve . . . agh . . ."

Something was wrong. Tweller had suddenly stopped speaking and was gripping the microphone before him. Mayor Myerton put down his own beer and started to get up. "What's wrong, man?" he whispered too near the microphone. "Are you sick?"

"I . . . gnugh . . . can't breathe . . . help me . . ." Then he toppled backward, dragging the microphone with him, upsetting his
glass of beer as he fell screaming and gasping to the ground.

Somewhere behind me a woman's voice took up the scream, and
I thought it might have been Miss Hazel. Already Dr. Stout had
appeared at the platform and was hurrying around to comfort the
stricken man. As I ran forward myself I caught a funny odor in the air
near the platform, near where the beer had spilled from Tweller's
overturned glass. It was a new smell to me, one I couldn't identify.

Behind the platform, Dr. Stout was loosening the collar of the
convulsed man as Grandfather and the mayor tried to assist him.
But after a moment the thrashing of arms and legs ceased, and the
doctor straightened up. The bright overhead sun caught his
glasses as he did so, reflecting for an instant a glare of brilliance.
"There's nothing I can do," he said quietly, almost sadly. "The man
is dead."

SUDDENLY, I WAS BUNDLED off with the other children to play where
we would, while the adults moved in to form a solid ring of curiosity about the platform. The children were curious too, of course,
but after a few minutes of playing many of the younger ones had
forgotten the events with wonder at their newly found freedom.
They ran and romped along the water's edge, setting off what few
firecrackers still remained, wrestling and chasing each other up
the brilliant brown dunes to some imagined summit. But all at
once I was too old for their games of childhood and longed to be
back with the adults, back around the body of this man whom I
hadn't even known a few weeks earlier.

Finally, I did break away, and hurried back to the edges thinning now as women pulled their husbands away. I crept under the
wooden crossbeams of the platform, became momentarily entan-
gled in the wiles of the loudspeaker system, and finally freed
myself to creep even closer to the center of the excitement. A big
man wearing a pistol on his belt like a cowboy had joined them
now, and he appeared to be the sheriff.

"Just tell me what happened," he was saying. "One at a time, not
all it once."

Mayor Myerton grunted. "If you'd been at the picnic, Gene, instead of chasing around town, you'd know what happened."

"Do you pay me to be the sheriff or to drink beer and listen to speeches?" He turned to one of the other men. "What happened, Sam?"

Sam was the man who'd been on the end of the platform, the opposite end from Grandfather. "Hell, Gene, you know as much about it as I do. He was talkin' and all of a sudden he just toppled over and died."

At this point Dr. Stout interrupted. "There's no doubt in my mind that the man was poisoned. The odor of bitter almonds was very strong by the body."

"Bitter almonds?" This from Mayor Myerton. He was wiping the sweat from his forehead, though it didn't seem that hot to me.

Dr. Stout nodded. "I think someone put prussic acid in Tweller's beer. Prussic acid solution or maybe bitter almond water."

"That's impossible," the mayor insisted. "I was sitting right next to him."

Grandfather joined in the discussion now, and I ducked low to the ground so he wouldn't see me. "Maybe the whole pitcher was poisoned. I didn't get around to drinking mine."

But the mayor had drunk some of his without ill effects, as had the man on the end named Sam. Someone went for the pitcher of beer, now almost empty, and Dr. Stout sniffed it suspiciously. "Nothing here. But the odor was on the body, and up there where his glass spilled."

"Maybe he killed himself," Frank Coons suggested, and they seemed to notice him for the first time. Frank seemed to be a sort of town character, lacking the stature of the others, an outsider within the party. And—I knew they were thinking it—after all, he was the one who went for the pitcher of beer in the first place.

"Frank," the sheriff said a little too kindly, "did you have any reason to dislike Jim Tweller?"

"Who, me?"

"Don't I remember hearing something a few years back about a house he sold you? A bum deal on a house he sold you?"

Frank Coons waved his hands airily. "That was nothing, a misunderstanding. I've always liked Jim. You don't think I could have killed him, do you?"

The sheriff named Gene said, "I think we'd all better go down to my office. Maybe I can get to the bottom of things there."

Some of them moved off then, and I saw that the undertaker's ambulance had come for Jim Tweller's body. The undertaker discussed the details of the autopsy with the sheriff, and the two of them proceeded to lift the body onto a stretcher. At that time and that place, no one worried about taking pictures of the death scene or measuring critical distances.

But I noticed that the woman from the school board, Mrs. Finch, pulled Grandfather back from the rest of the group. They paused just above me, and she said, "You know what he was trying to do as well as I do. He was using the acceptance of the award to launch a political campaign of his own. All this talk about rebirth and new blood meant just one thing—he was getting to the point where he was going to run against Mayor Myerton."

"Perhaps," my grandfather said.

"Do you think it's possible that the mayor slipped the poison into his beer?"

"Let me answer that with another question, Mrs. Finch. Do you think the mayor would be carrying a fatal dose of prussic acid in his pocket for such an occasion?"

"I don't know. He was sitting next to Tweller, that's all I know."

"So were you, though, Mrs. Finch," my grandfather reminded her.

They moved off with that, and separated, and I crawled back out to mingle with the children once more. Over by the beer barrel, the man named Sam was helping himself to a drink, and I saw a couple of others still eating their lunch. But for the most part the picnic had ended with Tweller's death. Even the weather seemed suddenly to have turned coolish, and the breeze blowing off the water had an uncomfortable chill to it. Families were folding up their chairs and loading picnic baskets into the cars, and one group of boys was helpfully ripping down the big colored banners and campaign posters. Nobody stopped them, because it was no longer a very good day for a picnic.

THE TWO REMAINING WEEKS of my visit were a blur of comings and goings and frequent phone calls at my grandfather's house. I

remember the first few days after the killing, when the excitement of
the thing was still on everybody's lips, when one hardly noticed the
children of the town and we ran free as birds for hours on end.
Frank Coons was jailed by the sheriff when they learned for certain
that the beer had been poisoned, but after a few days of questioning
they were forced to release him. No one could demonstrate just how
he would have been able to poison only the beer poured into Jim
Tweller's glass while leaving the mayor and the others unharmed.

I knew that Mrs. Finch still harbored her suspicion of the mayor,
and it was very possible that he suspected her as well. All of them
came to Grandfather's house, and the conversations went on by the
hour. The fact that no one much regretted the death of Tweller did
little to pacify things in those first two weeks. The man still had his
supporters outside of the political high command, all the little
people of the town who'd known him not as a rising politician but
only as the donor of land for a hospital. These were the people
who'd voted him his humanitarian award, and these were the
people who publicly mourned him now, while the top-level conferences at Grandfather's house continued long into the night.

At the end of two weeks I departed, and Grandfather took me
down to the railroad station with what seemed a genuine sadness
at my going. I stood in the back of the train waving at him as we
pulled out of the station, and he seemed at that moment as always
to be a man of untried greatness. His white hair caught the afternoon sunlight as he waved, and I felt a tear of genuine feeling
trickle down my cheek.

If this had been a detective novel instead of a simple memoir of
youth, I would have provided a neat and simple solution to the poisoning of Jim Tweller. But no such solution was ever forthcoming.
I heard from my mother and father that the excitement died down
within a few weeks, and the life of the town went on as it had
before. That November, the mayor and my grandfather and the
other town officials were reelected.

I saw my grandfather only briefly after that, at annual family
reunions and his occasional visits to our home. When I was sixteen
he died quietly in his sleep, and we went up to the town once
more. It hadn't changed much, really, and the people seemed
much the same as I remembered them. In the cemetery, I stood
between Father and Mrs. Finch, who commented on how much I'd
grown. The mayor was there, of course, and Dr. Stout, and even

Miss Pinkney and Miss Hazel. I understood from the talk that
Frank Coons no longer lived in town. He'd moved south shortly
after the murder investigation.

So I said good-bye to my grandfather and his town forever, and
went back to the city to grow into manhood.

I SAID A MOMENT ago that this was a memoir and not a mystery and
as such would offer no solution to the death of Jim Tweller. And
yet—I would not be honest either as a writer or a man if I failed to
set down here some thoughts that came to me one evening not
long ago, as I sat sipping a cocktail in the company of a particularly
boring group of friends.

I suppose it was the sight of cocktails being poured from an
icy pitcher that made me remember that other occasion, when
the beer had passed down the line of speakers. And remembering it, as the conversation about me droned on, I went over the
details of that day once more. I remembered especially that
pitcher of beer, and the pouring of Tweller's drink from it. I
remembered how he drank from the glass almost immediately,
and commented on the bad taste. Certainly, no poison was
dropped into the glass *after* the beer had been poured. And yet it
was just as impossible to believe that the poison had gone into
the glass *with* the beer, when others had drunk unharmed from
the same pitcher. No, there was only one possibility—the poison
had been in the glass before the beer was poured in.

I imagined a liquid, colorless as water, lying in the bottom of
the glass. Just a few drops perhaps, or half an ounce at most. The
chances were that Jim Tweller never noticed it, or if he did he
imagined it to be only water left from washing out the glass. He
would pour the beer in over the waiting poison, in all likelihood,
or at worst empty the glass onto the grass first. In any event, there
was no danger for the poisoner, and the odds for success were in
his favor.

And I remembered then who had occupied the speaker's position immediately before Tweller. I remembered Grandfather with
the empty glass before him, the empty beer mug with its thickness
of glass to hide the few drops of liquid. I remembered Grandfather

with his little bottle of cough medicine, clear cough medicine that usually was gin. Remembered his reluctance that day to give Frank Coons a drink from it. Remembered that I hadn't seen the bottle again later. Remembered most of all Grandfather's devotion to the party, his friendship with Tweller that must have warned him earlier than most of the man's political ambitions. Remembered, finally, that of all the people at the picnic, only Grandfather had known that Tweller was the winner of the award, that Tweller would be on the speaker's platform that day. Grandfather, who called out to Coons for the pitcher of beer. Grandfather, the only person with the motive and the knowledge and the opportunity. And the weapon, in a bottle that might have been cough medicine or gin—or prussic acid.

But that was a long time ago, a generation ago. And I remember him best standing at the station, waving good-bye. . . .

Home-Brewed Beer

THIS IS NOT a recipe. Given that those of you who wish to brew your own beer are going to need specialized ingredients (just try buying malted hops at your grocery store!), as well as equipment, it's best to get both from a reputable home-brewing shop, which will happily bury you in recipes for home-brewed beer and ales. After all, the better the recipes, the more supplies you'll buy. You can check the Yellow Pages for a nearby supplier, but many towns don't have access to a local shop. But, thanks to the magic of the Internet and decent mail service, everybody with access to a computer also has access to all the resources they could possibly want to brew their own beer. Just type home-brew beer into your search engine and have fun!

Guardian Angel

Caroline Benton

P eople react to death in various ways. Me, I stare through a window. I've always done it, even when I was a small girl. I stare out at the view, sometimes for hours at a time, thinking, adapting, willing myself to cope. Like when I was eight and my father died. I spent whole days in my bedroom then, staring out across cold, January fields. Shortly after his death we moved.

The view from my next bedroom was less exciting—vegetable gardens, allotments, the back of the row of houses in the next street. I felt squeezed and hemmed in. So I cast my eyes upward and watched the sky. It was constantly changing. From my encyclopedia I learned the names of clouds—cirrus, nimbostratus, cumulonimbus. Such wonderful names. They were cumulonimbus some nine years later on the day of my mother's funeral.

The clouds that afternoon were spectacular, rising in vast towering peaks like snowcapped mountains. I pretended they were mountains. I stared out through my window, imagining myself in Switzerland, Austria, the Himalayas—anywhere rather than that gloomy house which overnight had become so empty.

Shortly after her death I moved.

For the next few years the sky was my salvation, drawing my eyes from dismal streets beneath countless bed-sitting rooms. Then I married and once again had a view. It was my husband who found the small house overlooking the town.

As soon as I walked in I made a beeline for the window. You could see the cathedral, Saint Mary's, the bend in the river where the boats are moored. I turned to him and grinned.

"I think she likes it," he told the agent before coming over and putting his arm around my shoulder, giving me a hug.

Like it? I loved it. From the day we moved in, the view was a constant source of delight. In the evenings we would sit side by side watching the darkness gather, the lights come on in the city spread out below. Holding hands, touching. We became so close. It was *our* view, a symbol of our togetherness. We even had our special view-watching music—Pink Floyd, "Dark Side of the Moon."

WHEN I HEARD HE'D been killed in a road accident I was numbed. It couldn't be happening, not to me. Hadn't I already suffered enough?

Instinctively, I turned to the window. But the view just mocked me, reminding me of what had been and would never be again, and I knew I couldn't stay in the house. It seemed that every time someone died, I had to move.

IT WAS AFTER HIS death that I bought this cottage. It's not much to look at, but its setting is superb, tucked into a hillside overlooking pasture fields and beyond that the moor. When I moved in—emotionally drained, desperately trying to adjust—it never occurred to me that I would ever share it with anyone, let alone another man. Three years later I met Marcus.

I was out walking in nearby woods and had stopped to look at a strange fungus growth on a fallen tree, when a dog came rushing up.

"It's okay, she's friendly," called a voice from farther up the track. "But don't let her jump up, she's been in the water."

The bedraggled mass of hair at my feet belonged to a springer spaniel, the voice to a man dressed in jeans and a Barbour. He came striding up, six-foot-one in his Wellingtons, smiling broadly.

"She hasn't made you muddy? Good. She loves the water. Can't keep her out, can I, Tess?"

He looked from me to the fungus. "Know what it is?"

I shook my head. "The only mushrooms I know are the ones I buy in the supermarket."

"Me, too. I keep meaning to buy a book, but . . ." He broke off, squinted. "I've seen you before. That cottage on the hill. You were outside trimming the hedge."

It turned out he lived in the next village and regularly drove past the gate. Not that I discovered that then. I had to wait till the next evening when I answered my doorbell and found him standing on the step.

"*Clitocybe flaccida*," he said, holding out a book.

"I'm sorry?"

"*Clitocybe flaccida*—that fungus you were looking at. At least I think it is. A lot of them look the same."

I took the book, flipped absently through the pages.

"It's for you," he added. "I thought you might like it."

It seemed rude not to invite him in.

HE STAYED ABOUT TWO hours. I found him easy to talk to, relaxed, perhaps because of what we had in common. He was thirty-six, a lecturer, a divorcé; I was twenty-seven and a widow. We both preferred the country. We both loved a house with a view. When he left he suggested we return to the woods with the newly acquired book to make an accurate identification, and before I knew it I'd agreed. We went on the Saturday.

The weather was perfect for fungi (though we didn't know that at the time), a warm autumnal day following rain, and once we started looking we found a whole host of them. Many were beautiful, others grotesque, one or two smelled disgusting. Some, like the Fly Agaric with its white-spotted scarlet cap, we could identify immediately, but most were less distinctive. We were amazed at how many were edible.

"Perhaps we should buy a recipe book," he said jokingly, and a few days later he did.

And that's how it started. On a fungus foray. God knows I didn't intend to get involved, but these things happen, creeping up on us unawares until it's too late. Even so, it was more than a year before I allowed him to move in.

Marcus loved the cottage as much as I did, especially the view, the way it constantly changes. On rainy days the moor is obscured by mist, but on clear days you can make out sheep grazing the lower slopes. And the skies! Have you ever noticed the proportion of sky to land? About eighty-twenty if you get really close to the window. And we did get close—to the window and to each other. Often we would pick out patterns in the clouds, the way some people find faces in a fire. "That looks like my aunt," he once said, and I laughed. "It does," he insisted, tracing the outline on the glass with his finger. "See the nose and the hair?"

One day I came in from shopping and found him playing Pink Floyd. I stopped dead in my tracks. I'd no idea he had it in his collection. I'd thrown my own copy away. "What's wrong?" he asked when he saw my face. "Nothing," I assured him. And there wasn't; truly, there wasn't. As time went on I even began to play it myself.

I could hardly believe it when Marcus said he thought we should move, though his reason was perfectly valid. This was *my* cottage, and he wanted a home we could share, one he could feel a part of. He had my sympathy. Yet it seemed silly to move when we were both so happy here. Adding his name to the deeds seemed like the obvious solution.

We never lost our interest in fungi. Every year, spring and autumn, we tramped the fields and woods, searching them out. Last year we found morels for the first time, but we've yet to find an Earth Star. I know they're around somewhere.

It was with extreme caution that we first began to cook and eat our finds. Some proved edible but disappointing; others were delicious. Parasols *à la Jane Grigson* are a culinary delight. Our friends regard our eating habits mistrustfully and I suspect are wary of accepting invitations to dinner. The timid amongst them still refuse to taste my exciting side dishes, and even the more adventurous usually wait for us to eat the first mouthful. "It's perfectly safe," I assure them. "The most important thing is knowing which ones to avoid."

And it's true. Most so-called poisonous mushrooms are merely indigestible and will cause, at worst, a bad attack of stomachache. Only a few are deadly, like the Death Cap and the aptly named Destroying Angel, where one mouthful can be fatal. Both are *amanitas*; *amanita phalloides* and *amanita virosa*. The Destroying Angel is pure white. It's quite rare in this part of the country, but I know where it can be found. I discovered it on one of my forays.

It was his attitude to the forays that first made me realize something was wrong. Normally, we look forward to autumn, to the new season's crop, but this year he seemed indifferent.

"You go," he said, when I suggested an expedition.

"But we might find an Earth Star."

"I've work to do. Can't you go alone?"

So I did—me and Tess together. How convenient!

LAST WEEK HE TOLD me the reason for his indifference. Her name's Laura. She's one of his students, just twenty-one years old. He'll need money, he told me, to start a new life, so regretfully—he knows how much it means to me—the cottage will have to be sold. I went to the window.

The clouds were extraordinary, cirrocumulus, lit from behind by the setting sun. Above the horizon their formation resembled an angel with outspread wings. True, the wings were different sizes, the halo tilted to one side, but it was undoubtedly an angel, of the purest white. The edges of the wings were silver.

I'M AT THE WINDOW now, listening to Pink Floyd, waiting for Marcus to arrive. He's not moving out until the end of the week. He's so relieved at the way I've taken the news, he'd been afraid I wouldn't understand.

Me? Not understand?

I'm cooking us a risotto of wild mushrooms for supper, with lots of garlic and herbs. It smells delicious. The Destroying Angel is already sautéed and waiting in the microwave. I couldn't cook it with the others; there would be no way of separating it out.

Today's clouds are truly remarkable. They're stratified, in three distinct layers, all traveling at different speeds. The uppermost layer is white but slow, the middle one grayer and faster. But it's the bottom layer that is most beautiful, sheer and ethereal, forming and re-forming into delicate wispy patterns as it races across the sky. Like dark gray widow's lace.

It's all about patterns, you see . . . I really must break the pattern. I'm damned if I'll let it happen again. This time death will mean I *don't* have to move.

Mushroom Risotto

2 14.5-oz. cans chicken stock, or 5 cups homemade
  stock
½ tsp. saffron threads
1 clove garlic, peeled and smashed
¼ cup olive oil
1 small white onion, finely chopped
1 bunch olives, diced (about ½ cup, divided use)
8 oz. mushrooms, sliced
1½ cups Aborio rice
2 cups dry white wine (divided use)
Water as needed
¼ cup Parmesan cheese, grated
Salt and pepper to taste

HEAT THE CHICKEN stock, and add the saffron. Steep the saffron until the stock is a deep golden color. Strain and reserve the stock. In a large skillet, heat the olive oil, add the garlic and onions, and sauté until the onions are clear and soft, about two minutes. Add the mushrooms and the chives, reserving two tablespoons of the chives to be used as a garnish on the finished dish. Sauté the vegetables until the mushrooms are limp and brown, about a minute. Add the rice to the pan, and sauté until the rice is coated evenly with oil. Add two cups chicken stock and one cup of the wine. Reserve the remaining liquids for now. Stirring constantly, simmer until almost all of the liquid has been absorbed. Taste the rice. Continue stirring. Add chicken stock as needed until the rice grains are softened and chewy and yet distinct and firm. Don't let the rice dry out. Because the moisture content of rice differs dramatically from bag to bag, it is impossible to give exact quantities of liquid needed to make a good risotto. Simply keep adding chicken stock until it runs out, then water, stirring all the while, until the rice feels and tastes the way you like it. Typically, you should add about two-thirds of the liquid in about 10 minutes, and the remainder over about eight more minutes, at which point the rice should be done. Once the rice is cooked to your liking, add the reserved cup of white wine. Bring the dish to a simmer, stirring constantly, until the rice has absorbed most of the liquid. Add cheese, stirring, until the risotto has a creamy texture. Adjust seasoning with salt and pepper. Serve immediately.

The Main Event

Peter Crowther

We gonna go bed now, baby?" Dolores trilled sleepily as she slouched around the table and lifted the Calvados from the after-dinner wreckage. "Dosie tired."

Vince watched her pour two fingers into a goblet that still held traces of claret, then he turned around to the window. Listening to his wife slurp and hiccup, Vince pulled the corner of the curtain aside and watched the Cadillac's taillights move off down the drive. The tension in his stomach subsided only when he saw the car pull out into the street and disappear. The sharp sound of breaking glass made him spin around in time to see Dolores, having staggered against the table, picking pieces of cut glass out of the Roquefort cheese. "Jesus, Dolores!" he snapped.

Dolores straightened up and pouted. "Hey, no need to get spikey, honey," she said, slurring the words. "Just a little accident." She dropped the shards of glass onto a side plate and giggled, lifting a hand to cover her mouth. Vince saw that she had smudged her lipstick, and he was annoyed to find that it aroused him. Despite the effects of the alcohol, Dolores noticed it, saw it in his eyes. She leaned against the table and ran her hand through her hair. "We gonna go up and make Buster warm, huh? We gonna have, you know, the main event now? Are we, honey?"

Buster was Vince's penis. Making Buster warm entailed jamming it inside Dolores as far as it would go. And then some. That was Dolores's main event. Vince sometimes thought that she had some kind of dimensional warp up there, the same way that the inside of Doctor Who's phonebox looked like the Cape Canaveral operations room. Maybe you could ram a broom handle up inside her, right to the bristles, and still not encounter any obstacles, and even if he stared down her throat there would be no trace of the end.

Dolores ran a hand down her camel-colored cashmere rib-knit dress until she reached the outside of her thigh, then she moved it over to her crotch and started to rub between her legs, pushing the material in and out, in and out. Vince moved away from the window and brushed past her. "You're sick, you know that?" he said. "And you said you needed oysters."

"Hey, I di'n't say I *needed* the oysters, honey, I said I *wanted* them. I still can't understand why you wouldn't let me have none." She took another drink of brandy, swallowed hard, and asked, "Why was that, honey? Why di'n't you let me have no oysters? Why'd we haveta have chowder insteada oysters, like Jerry an' Estelle did, bull?"

"There weren't enough." Vince shook a Marlboro out of the packet and tossed it back onto the table, leaned over, and lit the cigarette from the burning candle. "I told you that."

"Yeah, I heard you say there wasn't enough, and that you knew how much they liked oysters so they should just eat and enjoy. 'Eat and enjoy, Jer,' you said." Dolores swept her arm expansively as she mimicked Vince. " 'Cept I know there was enough. I saw them when you were preparing them. You threw a whole bunch out with the trash."

Blowing a thick column of smoke across the table, Vince looked at his watch and said, "They were bad. I threw them out because they were bad."

Dolores thought about that for a moment. "How'd you know they was bad?"

Vince looked at her and narrowed his eyes. "I just knew, okay? I know these things. It's what I used to do for a living, remember?"

The truth of the matter was there was nothing wrong with the oysters. None of them. At least, not the ones that Vince had thrown out. He'd just wanted only Jerry and Estelle to eat those he'd saved. Those were the ones with the small capsules inside. Vince couldn't take the chance of his guests getting the wrong ones—the safe ones—if Dolores screwed up the portions. Worse than that, he couldn't take the chance of getting one of the capsules himself. Taken alone, they probably wouldn't do much harm, just an upset stomach or maybe a bad dose of the runs. But if he and Dolores had eaten them then Jerry and Estelle wouldn't have. And it was important—crucial—that the guests ate all the ingredients.

"Mmm." Dolores plopped onto a chair and hoisted her dress up above the tops of her hose, wafting the pale flesh at the tops of her legs with her free hand. "It was a nice meal though, honey. I meant to tell you that."

Vince nodded.

"Real nice meal."

"So you said," he snapped, glancing at the clock on the wall. "Thanks for the compliment, okay? I appreciate it."

Dolores shook her head and pulled down her dress. "That salad—what was the name of that salad again? Nishsomethin' or other?"

"Niçoise. Salad Niçoise."

"I liked that," Dolores slurred.

"Good," Vince said. He stubbed out his cigarette and adjusted his tie.

"Maybe it was just a little salty, though."

"You just said you liked it."

"I did too like it. All I said was that maybe it was just a little bit salty. That's all." She stood up from the table and walked to the bar and the bourbon.

Vince shook his head as he watched her stagger across the room. "You're drunk."

"I'm getting there," she said, unscrewing the cap. "If we ain't gonna have no main event, then I just might as well have a few drinks." Pouring whiskey into a shot glass, Dolores said, "The cheese tasted the same way."

"Like salad?"

Dolores glared at him. "Like salty," she said. "Salty like the fucking nishwahrs salad."

"Go to bed, will you?"

Dolores shook the liquid in her glass from side to side, watching it climb and fall, climb and fall. "The curry was good."

"You liked the curry. I'm glad. I feel whole again."

She pulled a face. "Smelly, though."

"It was a Korma."

"Not a curry?"

Vince sighed and reached for the Marlboros. "A Korma is a kind of curry, okay? Cream, coconut, lampasander, buttered chicken. Curry. Korma. All the same." He lit a cigarette with a match and shook out the flame.

Dolores looked into her drink some more.

Vince said, "Smelled how?"

"Huh?"

"You said it smelled. You said it was smelly, the Korma. How was it smelly?"

For a moment Dolores looked blank, like someone had reached into her head and turned off the generator. Then she started to laugh.

"What?"

She kept on laughing.

Vince ruffled his hair in frustration and marched across to the window. "Suddenly I'm—what am I? Woody Allen? I ask you—"

"Like a fart," Dolores said amidst chuckles. "It smelled a little like a fart."

Vince turned around and looked at her.

"I'm sorry, hon—"

"Did anybody else think it smelled?"

"Oh, hey, I—"

"Look! I'm fucking asking you if anybody else thought the Korma smelled funny, okay?"

Her smile faded. "Okay," she said. "There's no need—"

"And the answer is? I'm waiting for the answer, Dolores."

She shrugged. "Nobody said nothin'."

He nodded and took a pull on the Marlboro. "Good," he said, around a mouthful of smoke. "That's good."

Silence again.

"He's funny isn't he, you know . . . Jerry."

"How is Jerry funny?"

Dolores drained her glass and reached for the bottle. "His ways, you know."

"He's a very busy, very important man, Dolores."

Dolores laughed as she swallowed, spraying liquor in a fine mist. "He's a crook."

"Look, we've been through all this a dozen times. Maybe a hundred times. Jerry is a businessman."

"In a pig's eye." She hiccuped, and then added, disdainfully, "Businessman! Hmph!"

"I'm not going to argue, Dolores, I'm—"

"Why d'you keep looking at your watch?"

Vince lowered his arm and shook it until his shirtsleeve slid down over his wrist. "I'm not looking at my watch."

"You were too. I saw—"

"Okay, I was looking at my watch. I wanted to know what time it was, for crissakes."

Dolores took a slug of bourbon and swallowed hard. "It's about thirty seconds later than it was when you last looked at it," she said.

"What are you? My—" He was going to say "timekeeper" but realized immediately that it sounded stupid. The same with "watchman." Instead, he pulled on his cigarette and shook his head some more. Then he looked out of the window.

"He's a crook, Vinny. You know it and I know it." She swirled the liquor around the glass and then threw it into her mouth. "And you're a crook, too."

Vince looked around at her and smiled. "Hey, we both enjoy the fruits of my labor. I don't see you complaining any about where the money comes from."

She poured some more bourbon into her glass silently.

"He's a businessman. Got a lot of contacts, sees a lot of people, makes a lot of deals. That's how he makes his money. That's how I make my money. I'm not ashamed of it."

"He know a lot of people?"

"A *lot* of people. He knows everybody. And I mean *every*body."

"They all crooks, too?"

"Dolores, not everybody is a crook." Vince pulled one of the chairs away from the table and sat down, loosening his tie. He was starting to feel a little easier. This one was the one. He'd thought about every way he could do it—shooting, knifing, even poison—but each of those methods could have led back to him. But not this way. This way there would be nothing left to lead anyone anywhere. He smiled across the table at his wife, watched her backside stretch the clinging material of her dress, saw the small metal clips of her garters outlined against her thighs.

"He keep all their names in his goddamned book?"

Vince shrugged. "It's his way, okay? He calls it his memory bank." He blew smoke out in small rings and watched them swirl up to the ceiling. "Takes it everywhere he goes. I never seen him without that book. It's like it's attached to him surgically, you know what I'm saying?"

"Yeah, I hear you."

Vince softened his voice. "Hey."

"What?"

"C'm'ere. "

"What?"

"I said, c'm'ere." A little harder now.

Dolores stood up and walked across to him. She was trying to look disinterested but the first faint signs of a smile were pulling at her mouth. When Dolores had reached him, Vince patted his knees and shuffled the chair farther from the table. "Siddown."

"I'm fine standing right here," she said petulantly, swaying her body from side to side, legs stretched wide. Vince looked at her, allowing his eyes to travel up and down the curves and bulges. He liked what he saw. Buster liked it, too, uncoiling himself from Vince's Calvin Klein briefs and fighting off the effects of the booze.

He felt good, suddenly. A good evening. He remembered the dessert, remembered thinking it tasted fine and wondering—as he watched Jerry and Estelle gorge themselves on two pieces—if they noticed anything unusually gritty about it. He reached out to trace a finger across Dolores's lower stomach, and said, "My, how'd you like the chocolate gateau?"

She stopped swaying and said, "You still wanna talk about the food? I thought we was getting ready for the main event . . . getting ready to warm up li'l Buster, honey."

"We are, we are. I just wondered how you liked the dessert is all."

"I liked it, okay?"

She started swaying again, moving her body closer to him with each pass.

"You didn't think . . . you didn't think that maybe it tasted a little gritty?"

Dolores placed her glass on the table and pulled up her dress, slowly, inch by loving inch, until she exposed the tops of her hose, then the pale flesh of her upper thighs, and then, last but by no means least, the soft blue of her panties. Vince could see thin, spindly hairs curling their way out of the crotch, could see the first faint traces of wet on it, could smell the deodorant she used down there, could smell it wafting across at him. Buster could smell it too, apparently, and he stretched against Vince's trousers wanting to be out. Out and in. "Gritty?" she said. The word came out as a whisper.

Without watching what he was doing, but rather keeping his eyes focused on the endless sky of those briefest of bikini panties, Vince reached out his right hand to lower his glass to the floor beside the large wing chair. As he removed his hand from the glass, he heard it topple over with a dull thud. He turned around to see if there was much of a mess on the carpet, and saw the polished black of Jerry's memory bank half-covered by the chair.

At first
takes it everywhere he goes
it didn't register
never seen him without that book
and then
it's like it's attached to him surgically
he looked up at Dolores. She was turning around to look at the window, shuffling her dress back down her legs. "A car, Vinny," she said, simply. "Now who the hell—"

Vince grabbed the book and jumped off his chair. "It's Jerry," he said, "come for his damned book."

"Jesus H. Christ on a fucking bicycle," Dolores snarled, spitting out the words like bad food.

Vince ran into the hall, heading for the door, trying to beat Jerry's having to get out of the car, having to walk up to the house, having to ring the bell, having to waste all that time . . . precious time. As he ran, seeming to take forever, every step like running in slow motion or through water, his life flashed before him. Not his whole life, just the afternoon. One afternoon.

He saw himself working tiny lumps of elemental sodium into small gelatin capsules of oil and then inserting them almost lovingly into the oysters.

He saw himself sprinkling potassium and more sodium onto the anchovies, eggs, and olives. And then more—just to be safe— smeared inside the Roquefort cheese.

He saw himself mixing liberal quantities of sulphur into the buttered chicken.

He saw himself grinding up lumps of charcoal for the chocolate gateau.

Reaching for the key to the front door, he shook his head, trying to convince himself it had all been a stupid idea. It wouldn't work. Why the hell was he panicking?

He saw his arm reach out in front of him, reach out toward the door, the key held in his hand, reaching to the small lock.

He heard the footsteps on the steps, someone coming to the front door. "With you in a second, Jer," he shouted. "Forgot your fucking book, didn't you?"

He heard Jerry laugh. And then the laugh stopped. Abruptly. Jerry gasped. The sound was a mixture of pain and surprise.

Vince's hand had reached the door, inserted the key. He began to turn his hand and reach for the handle. Then the world turned bright white . . .

The

and somewhere, far off in the distance but getting closer with every millionth of a second . . .

Main

a shuddering growl of thunder sounded, traveling toward him at ten times the speed of light . . .

Event!

traveling with the shards of door and lumps of masonry and a billion tiny spears of glass.

Vince didn't hear the second explosion. Nor did he notice the small pieces of perfumed meat, leather upholstery, and blackened metal that rained on the burning ruins of his house.

The Menu

PRE-DINNER: CHAMPAGNE
Dom Perignon, 1970

Appetizer: Oysters Rockefeller

2 dozen fresh oysters in shells
½ small onion, minced
3 Tbsp. parsley, finely chopped
½ stick celery
¼ cup butter
2 oz. fresh raw spinach, finely chopped
2 oz. fine dry bread crumbs
¼ tsp. salt
4 Tbsp. butter
Paprika
Olive oil
8 oz. gelatin, heated

PRY OPEN THE oyster shells with a sharp knife, remove oysters, and drain them. Wash the deep halves of the shells and place an oyster on each.

Fry onion, parsley, and celery in ¼ cup butter until tender. Add spinach, bread crumbs, and salt, and cook, stirring constantly for one minute. Place a spoonful of spinach mixture on each oyster, top with ½ teaspoon of butter, and sprinkle lightly with paprika. Bake in a hot oven (450 degrees F.) for 10 minutes or until browned.

Serve in shells.

Wine: A chablis
(Vince provided two bottles of Le Montrachet, 1971.)

Main Course: Chicken Korma (Moorgee Korma)

CUT UP A fair-sized chicken and marinade it for one hour in a mixture of two or three tablespoons of Dhye (sour curds), one heaped teaspoon of ground turmeric, and one clove of garlic (either ground into a paste or finely mixed).

USING A STEW pan, combine:
> 2 oz. ghee or other fat
> 1 large onion, halved and finely sliced
> 1 clove garlic, finely sliced lengthwise
> Several 1-inch pieces of fresh or pickled ginger, finely sliced
> 6 whole cloves
> 6 whole cardamom pods
> One 2-inch stick of cinnamon

COOK UNTIL THE onions are half-done, then add one heaped tablespoon of Korma mixture. Stir well and cook on a low flame for three or four minutes longer.

Now add the chicken and marinade. Mix lightly but thoroughly. Cover the pan tightly and simmer until the chicken is done. Add salt and lemon juice to taste . . . and to try to minimize the smell of the sulphur.

Serve with a Salad Niçoise:
Rub your salad bowl with garlic and then place in it:

> 2 tomatoes, peeled and quartered
> 1 cucumber, peeled and finely cut
> 6 fillets of anchovy, coarsely chopped
> 12 pitted black olives, coarsely chopped
> 1 cup bibb lettuce
> 1 cup romaine

Now toss in a store-bought French dressing.

Wine: A fine claret
(Vince served Chateau Lafite-Rothschild, 1962.)

Dessert: Chocolate Gateau

3 large eggs
3 oz. caster sugar
3 oz. all-purpose flour
1 Tbsp. cocoa
3 oz. flaked almonds
3 oz. butter cream or ½ pint fresh cream, whipped
Chocolate icing
8-oz. can finely chopped fruit in syrup

WHISK THE EGGS and sugar until thick and creamy. Fold in the sieved flour and cocoa. Divide the mixture into three greased six-inch cake tins. Bake in a hot oven (400 degrees) for about 10 minutes and then turn out onto a cooling tray.

When cold, sandwich two cakes together with cream. Cut a circle one-inch wide around the edge of the third cake and sandwich the "circle" to the other two cakes. Spread cream around the outside edge of the cake and roll in flaked almonds. Pipe whirls of cream around the edge, strain the canned fruit, and pile in the center. Cover the remaining sponge with chocolate icing, pipe whirls of cream around the edge, and place on top of the fruit.

Wine: A good sauterne
(Vince served Chateau Yquem [pronounced *Dick-emm*] 1955.)

Cheese: Roquefort

Wine: A vintage red sherry
(Vince's choice was Manzanilla from San Lucar de Barrameda.)

The Deadly Egg

Janwillem van de Wetering

T he siren of the tiny dented Volkswagen shrieked forlornly between the naked trees of the Amsterdam Forest, the city's largest park, set on its southern edge: several square miles of willows, poplars, and wild-growing alders, surrounding ponds and lining paths. The paths were restricted to pedestrians and cyclists, but the Volkswagen had ignored the many No Entry signs, quite legally, for the vehicle belonged to the Municipal Police and more especially to its Criminal Investigation Department, or the Murder Brigade. Even so, it looked lost, and its howl seemed defensive.

It was Easter Sunday and it rained, and the car's two occupants, Detective Adjutant Grijpstra and Detective Sergeant de Gier, sat hunched in their overcoats, watching the squeaky, rusted wipers trying to deal with the steady drizzle. The car should have been junked some years before, but the adjutant had lost the form that would have done away with his aging transport, lost it on purpose and with the sergeant's consent. They had grown fond of the Volkswagen, of its shabbiness and its ability to melt away in traffic.

But they weren't fond of the car now. The heater didn't work, it was cold, and it was early. Not yet nine o'clock on a Sunday is early, especially when the Sunday is Easter. Technically they were both off duty, but they had been telephoned out of warm beds by headquarters' radio room. A dead man dangling from a branch in the forest; please, would they care to have a look at the dead man?

Grijpstra's stubby index finger silenced the siren. They had followed several miles of winding paths so far and hadn't come across anything alive except tall blue herons, fishing in the ponds and moats and flapping away slowly when the car came too close for their comfort.

"You know who reported the corpse? I wasn't awake when the radio room talked to me."

De Gier had been smoking silently. His handsome head with the perfect curls turned obediently to face his superior. "Yes, a gentleman jogger. He said he jogged right into the body's feet. Gave him a start. He ran all the way to the nearest telephone booth, phoned headquarters, then headquarters phoned us, and that's why we are here, I suppose. I am a little asleep myself—we are here, aren't we?"

They could hear another siren, and another. Two limousines came roaring toward the Volkswagen, and Grijpstra cursed and made the little car turn off the path and slide into a soggy lawn; they could feel its wheel sink into the mud.

The limousines stopped and men poured out of them; the men pushed the Volkswagen back on the path.

"Morning, Adjutant, morning, Sergeant. Where is the corpse?"

"Shouldn't you know, too?"

"No, Adjutant," several men said simultaneously, "but we thought maybe you know. All we know is that the corpse is in the Amsterdam Forest and that this is the Amsterdam Forest."

Grijpstra addressed the sergeant. "You know?"

De Gier's well-modulated baritone chanted the instructions. "Turn right after the big pond, right again, then left. Or the other way round. I think I have it right, we should be close."

The three cars drove about for a few minutes more until they were waved down by a man dressed in what seemed to be long blue underwear. The jogger ran ahead, bouncing energetically, and led them to their destination. The men from the limousines brought out their boxes and suitcases, then cameras clicked and a video recorder hummed. The corpse hung on and the two detectives watched it hang.

"Neat," Grijpstra said, "very neat. Don't you think it is neat?"

The sergeant grunted.

"Here. Brought a folding campstool and some nice new rope, made a perfect noose, slipped it around his neck, kicked the stool. Anything suspicious, gentlemen?"

The men from the limousines said there was not. They had found footprints—the prints of the corpse's boots. There were no other prints, except the jogger's. The jogger's statement was taken, he was thanked and sent on his sporting way. A police ambulance arrived and the corpse was cut loose, examined by doctor and detectives, and carried off. The detectives saluted the corpse quietly by inclining their heads.

"In his sixties," the sergeant said, "well dressed in old but expensive clothes. Clean shirt. Tie. Short gray beard, clipped. Man who took care of himself. A faint smell of liquor—he must have had a few to give him courage. Absolutely nothing in his pockets. I looked in the collar of his shirt—no laundry mark. He went to some trouble to be nameless. Maybe something will turn up when they strip him at the mortuary; we should phone in an hour's time."

Grijpstra looked hopeful. "Suicide?"

"I would think so. Came here by himself, no traces of anybody else. No signs of a struggle. The man knew what he wanted to do, and did it, all by himself. But he didn't leave a note; that wasn't very thoughtful."

"Right," Grijpstra said. "Time for breakfast, Sergeant! We'll have it at the airport—that's close and convenient. We can show our police cards and get through the customs barrier; the restaurant on the far side is better than the coffee shop on the near side."

De Gier activated the radio when they got back to the car.

"Male corpse, balding but with short gray beard. Dentures. Blue eyes. Sixty-odd years old. Three-piece blue suit, elegant dark gray overcoat, no hat. No identification."

"Thank you," the radio said.

"Looks very much like suicide. Do you have any missing persons of that description in your files?"

"No, not so far."

"We'll be off for breakfast and will call in again on our way back."

"Echrem," the radio said sadly, "there's something else. Sorry."

De Gier stared at a duck waddling across the path and trailing seven furry ducklings. He began to mumble. Adjutant Grijpstra mumbled with him. The mumbled four-letter words interspersed with mild curses formed a background for the radio's well-articulated message. They were given an address on the other side of the city. "The lady was poisoned, presumably by a chocolate Easter egg. The ambulance that answered the distress call just radioed in. They are taking her to hospital. The ambulance driver thought the poison was either parathion, something used in agriculture, or arsenic. His assistant is pumping out the patient's stomach. She is in a bad way but not dead yet."

Grijpstra grabbed the microphone from de Gier's limp hand. "So if the lady is on her way to hospital, who is left in the house you want us to go to?"

"Her husband, man by the name of Moozen, a lawyer, I believe."

"What hospital is Mrs. Moozen being taken to?"

"The Wilhelmina."

"And you have no one else on call? Sergeant de Gier and I are supposed to be off duty for Easter, you know!"

"No," the radio's female voice said, "no, Adjutant. We never have much crime on Easter day, especially not in the morning. There are only two detectives on duty, and they are out on a case too—some boys have derailed a streetcar with matches."

"Right," Grijpstra said coldly, "we are on our way."

The old Volkswagen made an effort to jump away, protesting feebly. De Gier was still muttering but had stopped cursing. "Streetcar? Matches?"

"Yes. They take an empty cartridge, fill it with matchheads, then close the open end with a hammer. Very simple. All you have to do is insert the cartridge into the streetcar's rail and when the old tram comes clanging along, the sudden impact makes the cartridge explode. If you use two or three cartridges the explosion may be strong enough to lift the wheel out of the rail. Didn't you ever try that? I used to do it as a boy. The only problem was to get the cartridges. We had to sneak around on the rifle range with the chance of getting shot at."

"No," de Gier said. "Pity. Never thought of it, and it sounds like a good game."

He looked out of the window. The car had left the park and was racing toward the city's center through long empty avenues. There was no life in the huge apartment buildings lining the old city—nobody had bothered to get up yet. Ten o'clock and the citizenry wasn't even considering the possibility of slouching into the kitchen for a first cup of coffee.

But one man had bothered to get up early and had strolled into the park, carrying his folding chair and a piece of rope to break off the painful course of his life, once and for all. An elderly man in good but old clothes. De Gier saw the man's beard again, a nicely cared-for growth. The police doctor had said that he hadn't been dead long. A man alone in the night that would have led him to Easter, a man by himself in a deserted park, testing the strength of his rope, fitting his head into the noose, kicking the campstool.

"Bah!" he said aloud.

Grijpstra had steered the car through a red light and was turning the wheel.

"What's that?"

"Nothing. Just bah."

"Bah is right," Grijpstra said.

They found the house, a bungalow, on the luxurious extreme north side of the city. Spring was trying to revive the small lawn and a magnolia tree was in hesitant bloom. Bright yellow crocuses off the path. Grijpstra looked at the crocuses. He didn't seem pleased.

"Crocuses," de Gier said, "very nice. Jolly little flowers."

"No. Unimaginative plants, manufactured, not grown. Computer plants. They make the bulbs in a machine and program them to took stupid. Go ahead; Sergeant, press the bell."

"Really?" the sergeant asked.

Grijpstra's jowls sagged. "Yes. They are like mass-manufactured cheese, tasteless; cheese is probably made with the same machines."

"Cheese," de Gier said moistly, "there's nothing wrong with cheese either, apart from not having any right now. Breakfast has slipped by, you know." He glanced at his watch.

They read the nameplate while the bell rang. *H. F. Moozen, Attorney at Law.* The door opened. A man in a housecoat made out of brightly striped towel material said good morning. The detectives showed their identifications. The man nodded and stepped back. A pleasant man, still young, thirty years or a bit more. The ideal model for an ad in a ladies' magazine. A background man, showing off a modern house, or a minicar, or expensive furniture. The sort of man ladies would like to have around. Quiet, secure, mildly good-looking. Not a passionate man, but lawyers seldom are. Lawyers practice detachment; they identify with their clients, but only up to a point.

"You won't take long, I hope," Mr. Moozen said. "I wanted to go with the ambulance, but the driver said you were on the way, and that I wouldn't be of any help if I stayed with my wife."

"Was your wife conscious when she left here, sir?"

"Barely. She couldn't speak."

"She ate an egg, a chocolate egg?"

"Yes. I don't care for chocolate myself. It was a gift, we thought, from friends. I had to let the dog out early this morning, an hour ago, and there was an Easter bunny sitting on the path. He held an egg wrapped up in silver paper. I took him in, woke up my wife, and showed the bunny to her, and she took the egg and ate it, then became ill. I telephoned for the ambulance and they came almost immediately. I would like to go to hospital now."

"Come in our car, sir. Can I see the bunny?"

Mr. Moozen took off the housecoat and put on a jacket. He opened the door leading to the kitchen and a small dog jumped around the detectives, yapping greetings. The bunny stood on the kitchen counter; it was almost a foot high. Grijpstra tapped its back with his knuckles; it sounded solid.

"Hey," de Gier said. He turned the bunny around and showed it to Grijpstra.

"Brwah!" Grijpstra said.

The rabbit's toothless mouth gaped. The beast's eyes were close together and deeply sunk into the skull. Its ears stood up aggressively. The bunny leered at them, its torso crouched; the paws that had held the deadly egg seemed ready to punch.

"It's roaring," de Gier said. "See? A roaring rabbit. Easter bunnies are supposed to smile."

"Shall we go?" Mr. Moozen asked.

They used the siren, and the trip to hospital didn't take ten minutes. The city was still quiet. But there proved to be no hurry. An energetic, bright young nurse led them to a waiting room. Mrs. Moozen was being worked on; her condition was still critical. The nurse would let them know if there was any change.

"Can we smoke?" Grijpstra asked.

"If you must." The nurse smiled coldly, appraised de Gier's tall, wide-shouldered body with a possessive feminist glance, swung her hips, and turned to the door.

"Any coffee?"

"There's a machine in the hall. Don't smoke in the hall, please."

There were several posters in the waiting room. A picture of a cigarette pointing to a skull with crossed bones. A picture of a happy child biting into an apple. A picture of a drunken driver (bubbles surrounding his head proved he was drunk) followed by an ambulance. The caption read: "Not *if* you have an accident, but *when* you have an accident."

De Gier fetched coffee and Grijpstra offered cigars. Mr. Moozen said he didn't smoke.

"Well," Grijpstra said patiently and puffed out a ragged dark cloud, "now who would want to poison your wife, sir? Has there been any recent trouble in her life?"

The question hung in the small white room while Moozen thought. The detectives waited. De Gier stared at the floor, Grijpstra observed the ceiling. A full minute passed.

"Yes," Mr. Moozen said, "some trouble. With me. We contemplated a divorce."

"I see."

"But then we decided to stay together. The trouble passed."

"Any particular reason why you considered a divorce, sir?"

"My wife had a lover." Mr. Moozen's words were clipped and precise.

"*Had*," de Gier said. "The affair came to an end?"

"Yes. We had some problems with our central heating, something the mechanics couldn't fix. An engineer came out, and my wife fell in love with him. She told me—she doesn't like to be secretive. They met each other in motels for a while."

"You were upset?"

"Yes. It was a serious affair. The engineer's wife is a mental patient; he divorced her and was awarded custody of his two children. I thought he was looking for a new wife. My wife has no children of her own—we have been married some six years and would like to have children. My wife and the engineer seemed well matched. I waited a month and then told her to make up her mind—either him or me, not both, I couldn't stand it."

"And she chose you?"

"Yes."

"Do you know the engineer?"

A vague pained smile floated briefly on Moozen's face. "Not personally. We did meet once and discussed central heating systems. Any further contact with him was through my wife."

"And when did all this happen, sir?"

"Recently. She only made her decision a week ago. I don't think she has met him since. She told me it was all over."

"His name and address, please, sir."

De Gier closed his notebook and got up. "Shall we go, Adjutant?"

Grijpstra sighed and got up, too. They shook hands with Moozen and wished him luck. Grijpstra stopped at the desk. The nurse wasn't helpful, but Grijpstra insisted and de Gier smiled, and eventually they were taken to a doctor who accompanied them to the next floor. Mrs. Moozen seemed comfortable. Her arms were stretched out on the blanket. The face was calm. The detectives were led out of the room again.

"Bad," the doctor said. "Parathion is a strong poison. Her stomach is ripped to shreds. We'll have to operate and remove part of it, but I think she will live. The silly woman ate the whole egg, a normal-size egg. Perhaps she was still too sleepy to notice the taste."

"Her husband is downstairs. Perhaps you should call him up, especially if you think she will live." Grijpstra sounded concerned. *He probably was*, de Gier thought. He felt concerned himself. The woman was beautiful, with a finely curved nose, very thin in the bridge, and large eyes and a soft and sensitive mouth. He looked at her long delicate hands.

"Husbands," the doctor said. "Prime suspects in my experience. Husbands are supposed to love their wives, but usually they don't. It's the same the other way around. Marriage seems to breed violence—it's one of the impossible situations we humans have to put up with."

Grijpstra's pale blue eyes twinkled. "Are you married, Doctor?"

The doctor grinned back. "Very. Oh, yes."

"A long time?"

"Long enough."

Grijpstra's grin faded. "So am I. Too long. But poison is nasty. Thank you, Doctor."

There wasn't much conversation in the car when they drove to the engineer's address. The city's streets had filled up. People were stirring about on the sidewalks and cars crowded each other, honking occasionally. The engineer lived in a block of apartments, and Grijpstra switched off the engine and lit another small black cigar.

"A family drama. What do you think, Sergeant?"

"I don't think. But that rabbit was most extraordinary. Not bought in a shop. A specially made rabbit, and well made, not by an amateur."

"Are we looking for a sculptor? Some arty person? Would Mr. Moozen or the engineer be an artist in his spare time? How does one make a chocolate rabbit, anyway?"

De Gier tried to stretch, but didn't succeed in his cramped quarters. He yawned instead. "You make a mold, I suppose, out of plaster of Paris or something, and then you pour hot chocolate into the mold and wait for it to harden. That rabbit was solid chocolate, several kilos of it. Our artistic friend went to a lot of trouble."

"A baker? A pastry man?"

"Or an engineer—engineers design forms sometimes, I believe. Let's meet this lover man."

The engineer was a small nimble man with a shock of black hair and dark lively eyes, a nervous man, nervous in a pleasant childlike manner. De Gier remembered that Mrs. Moozen was a small woman, too. They were ushered into a four-room apartment, They had to be careful not to step on a large number of toys, spread about evenly. Two little boys played on the floor; the eldest ran out of the room to fetch his Easter present to show it to the uncles. It was a basketful of eggs, homemade, out of chocolate. The other boy came to show his basket, identical but a size smaller.

"My sister and I made them last night," the engineer said. "She came to live here after my wife left and she looks after the kids, but she is spending the Easter weekend with my parents in the country. We couldn't go because Tom here had measles, hadn't you, Tom?"

"Yes," Tom said. "Big measles. Little Klaas here hasn't had them yet."

Klaas looked sorry. Grijpstra took a plastic truck off a chair and sat down heavily after having looked at the engineer, who waved him on. "Please, make yourself at home." De Gier had found himself a chair, too, and was rolling a cigarette. The engineer provided coffee and shooed the children into another room.

"Any trouble?"

"Yes," Grijpstra said. "I am afraid we usually bring trouble. A Mrs. Moozen has been taken to hospital. An attempt was made on her life. I believe you are acquainted with Mrs. Moozen?"

"Ann," the engineer said. "My God! Is she all right?"

De Gier had stopped rolling his cigarette. He was watching the man carefully; his large brown eyes gleamed, but not with pleasure or anticipation. The sergeant felt sorrow, a feeling that often accompanied his intrusions into the private lives of his fellow citizens. He shifted, and the automatic pistol in his shoulder holster nuzzled into his armpit. He impatiently pushed the weapon back. This was no time to be reminded that he carried death with him, legal death.

"What happened?" the engineer was asking. "Did anybody hurt her?"

"A question," Grijpstra said gently. "A question first, sir. You said your sister and you were making chocolate Easter eggs last night. Did you happen to make any bunnies, too?"

The engineer sucked noisily on his cigarette. Grijpstra repeated his question.

"Bunnies? Yes, or no. We tried, but it was too much for us. The eggs were easy—my sister is good at that. We have a pudding form for a bunny, but all we could manage was a pudding. It is still in the kitchen, a surprise for the kids later on today. Chocolate pudding—they like it."

"Can we see the kitchen, please?"

The engineer didn't get up. "My God," he said again, "so she was poisoned, was she? How horrible! Where is she now?"

"In the hospital, sir."

"Bad?"

Grijpstra nodded. "The doctor said she will live. Some sort of pesticide was mixed into chocolate, which she ate."

The engineer got up; he seemed dazed. They found the kitchen. Leftover chocolate mix was still on the counter. Grijpstra brought out an envelope and scooped some of the hardened chips into it.

"Do you know that Ann and I had an affair?"

"Yes, sir."

"Were you told that she finished the affair, that she decided to stay with her husband?"

"Yes, sir."

The engineer was tidying up the counter mechanically. "I see. So I could be a suspect. Tried to get at her out of spite or something. But I am not a spiteful man. You wouldn't know that. I don't mind being a suspect, but I would like to see Ann. She is in the hospital, you said. What hospital?"

"The Wilhelmina, sir."

"Can't leave the kids here, can I? Maybe the neighbors will take them for an hour or so. Ann. This is terrible."

Grijpstra marched to the front door with de Gier trailing behind him. "Don't move from the house today if you please, sir, not until we telephone or come again. We'll try and be as quick as we can."

"Nice chap," de Gier said when the car found its parking place in the vast courtyard of headquarters. "That engineer, I mean. I rather liked Mr. Moozen, too, and Mrs. Moozen is a lovely lady. Now what?"

"Go back to the Moozen house, Sergeant, and get a sample of the roaring bunny. Bring it to the laboratory together with this envelope. If they check we have a heavy point against the engineer."

De Gier restarted the engine. "Maybe he is not so nice, eh? He could have driven his wife crazy and now he tries to murder his girlfriend, his ex-girlfriend. Lovely Ann Moozen, who dared to stand him up. Could be, do you think so?"

Grijpstra leaned his bulk against the car and addressed his words to the emptiness of the yard. "No. But that could be the obvious solution. He was distressed, genuinely distressed, I would say. If he hadn't been and if he hadn't had those kids in the house, I might have brought him in for further questioning."

"And Mr. Moozen?"

"Could be. Maybe he didn't find the bunny on the garden path; maybe he put it there, or maybe he had it ready in the cupboard and brought it to his wandering wife. He is a lawyer—lawyers can be devious at times. True?"

De Gier said, "Yes, yes, yes . . ." and kept on saying so until Grijpstra squeezed the elbow sticking out of the car's window. "You are saying *yes*, but you don't sound convinced."

"I thought Moozen was suffering, too."

"Murderers usually suffer, don't they?"

De Gier started his "Yes, yes," and Grijpstra marched off.

They met an hour later, in the canteen in headquarters. They munched rolls stuffed with sliced liver and roast beef and muttered diligently at each other.

"So it is the same chocolate?"

"Yes, but that doesn't mean much. One of the lab's assistants has a father who owns a pastry shop. He said that there are only three mixes on the market and our stuff is the most popular make. No, not much of a clue there."

"So?"

"We may have a full case on our hands. We should go back to Mr. Moozen, I think, and find out about friends and relatives. Perhaps his wife had other lovers, or jealous lady friends."

"Why her?"

Grijpstra munched on. "Hmm?"

"Why *her*?" de Gier repeated. "Why not him?"

Grijpstra swallowed. "Him? What about him?"

De Gier reached for the plate, but Grijpstra restrained the sergeant's hand. "Wait, you are hard to understand when you have your mouth full. What about him?"

De Gier looked at the roll. Grijpstra picked it up and ate it.

"Him," de Gier said unhappily. "He found the bunny on the garden path, the ferocious bunny holding the pernicious egg. A gift, how nice. But he doesn't eat chocolate, so he runs inside and shows the gift to his wife and his wife grabs the egg and eats it. She may have thought *he* was giving it to her, she was still half asleep. Maybe she noticed the taste, but she ate on to please her husband. She became ill at once and he telephoned for an ambulance. Now, if he had wanted to kill her he might have waited an hour or so, to give the poison a chance to do its job. But he grabbed his phone, fortunately. What I am trying to say is, the egg may have been intended for him, from an enemy who didn't even know Moozen had a wife, who didn't care about killing the wife."

"Ah," Grijpstra said, and swallowed the last of the roll. "Could be. We'll ask Mr. Moozen about the enemies. But not just now. There is the dead man we found in the park—a message came in while you were away. A missing person has been reported and the description fits our corpse. According to the radio room a woman phoned to say that a man who is renting a room in her house has been behaving strangely lately and has now disappeared. She traced him to the corner bar, where he spent last evening until 2:00 A.M., when they closed.

"He was a little drunk, according to the barkeeper, but not blind drunk. She always takes him tea in the morning, but this morning he wasn't there and the bed was still made. But she does think he's been home, for she heard the front door at a little after 2:00 A.M., opening and closing twice. He probably fetched the rope and his campstool then."

"And the man was fairly old and has a short gray beard?"

"Right."

"So we go and see the landlady. I'll get a photograph—they took dozens this morning and they should be developed by now. Was anything found in his clothes?"

"Nothing." Grijpstra looked guiltily at the empty plate. "Want another roll?"

"You ate it."

"That's true, and the canteen is out of rolls; we got the last batch. Never mind, Sergeant. Let's go out and do some work. Work will take your mind off food."

"That's him," the landlady with the plastic curlers said. Her glasses had slipped to the tip of her blunt nose while she studied the photograph. "Oh, how horrible! His tongue is sticking out. Poor Mr. Marchant, is he dead?"

"Yes, ma'am."

"For shame, and such a nice gentleman. He has been staying here for nearly five years now, and he was always so polite."

Grijpstra tried to look away from the glaring pink curlers pointing at his forehead from the woman's thinning hair.

"Did he have any troubles, ma'am? Anything that may have led him to take his own life?"

The curlers bobbed frantically. "Yes. Money troubles. Nothing to pay the tax man with. He always paid the rent, but he hadn't been paying his taxes. And his business wasn't doing well. He has a shop in the next street; he makes things—ornaments, he calls them, out of brass. But there was some trouble with the neighbors. Too much noise, and something about the zoning, too; this is a residential area now, they say. The neighbors wanted him to move, but he had nowhere to move to, and he was getting nasty letters, lawyers' letters. He would have had to close down, and he had to make money to pay the tax man. It was driving him crazy. I could hear him walk around in his room at night, round and round, until I had to switch off my hearing aid."

"Thank you, ma'am."

"He was alone," the woman said and shuffled with them to the door. "All alone, like me. And he was always so nice." She was crying.

"Happy Easter," de Gier said, and opened the Volkswagen's door for the adjutant.

"The same to you. Back to Mr. Moozen again—we are driving about this morning. I could use some coffee again. Maybe Mr. Moozen will oblige."

"He won't be so happy either. We aren't making anybody happy today," the sergeant said, and tried to put the Volkswagen into first gear. The gear slipped and the car took off in second.

They found Mr. Moozen in his garden. It had begun to rain again, but the lawyer didn't seem to notice that he was getting wet. He was staring at the bright yellow crocuses, touching them with his foot. He had trampled a few of them into the grass.

"How is your wife, sir?"

"Conscious and in pain. The doctors think they can save her, but she will have to be on a stringent diet for years and she'll be very weak for months. I won't have her back for a while."

Grijpstra coughed. "We visited your wife's, ah, previous lover, sir." The word *previous* came out awkwardly, and he coughed again to take away the bad taste.

"Did you arrest him?"

"No, sir."

"Any strong reasons to suspect the man?"

"Are you a criminal lawyer, sir?"

Moozen kicked the last surviving crocus, turned on his heels, and led his visitors into the house. "No, I specialize in civil cases. Sometimes I do divorces, but I don't have enough experience to point a finger in this personal case. Divorce is a messy business, but with a little tact and patience reason usually prevails. To try and poison somebody is unreasonable behavior. I can't visualize Ann provoking that type of action—she is a gentle woman, sensuous but gentle. If she did break her relationship with the engineer she would have done it diplomatically."

"He seemed upset, sir, genuinely upset."

"Quite. I had hoped as much. So where are we now?"

"With you, sir. Do you have any enemies? Anybody who hated you so badly that he wanted you to die a grotesque death, handed to you by a roaring rabbit? You did find the rabbit on the garden path this morning, didn't you, sir?"

Moozen pointed. "Yes, out there, sitting in between the crocuses, leering and, as you say, roaring. Giving me the egg."

"Now, which demented mind might have thought of shaping that apparition, sir? Are you dealing with any particularly unpleasant cases at this moment? Any cases that have a badly twisted undercurrent? Is anyone blaming you for something bad that is happening to them?"

Moozen brushed his hair with both hands. "No. I am working on a bad case having to do with a truckdriver who got involved in a complicated accident; his truck caught fire and it was loaded with expensive cargo. Both his legs were crushed. His firm is suing the firm that owned the other truck. A lot of money in claims is involved and the parties are becoming impatient, with me mostly. The case is dragging on and on. But if they kill me the case will become even more complicated, with no hope of settlement in sight."

"Anything else, sir?"

"The usual. I collect bad debts, so sometimes I have to get nasty. I write threatening letters, sometimes I telephone people or even visit them. I act tough—it's got to be done in my profession. Usually they pay, but they don't like me for bothering them."

"Any pastry shops?"

"I beg your pardon?"

"Pastry shops," Grijpstra said, "people who make and sell confectionery. That rabbit was a work of art in a way, made by a professional. Are you suing anybody who would have the ability to create the roaring rabbit?"

"*Ornaments!*" de Gier shouted. His shout tore at the quiet room. Moozen and Grijpstra looked up, startled.

"Ornaments! Brass ornaments. Ornaments are made from molds. We've got to check his shop."

"Whose shop?" Grijpstra frowned irritably. "Keep your voice down, Sergeant. What shop? What ornaments?"

"Marchant!" de Gier shouted. "Marchant's shop."

"Marchant?" Moozen was shouting too. "Where did you get that name? *Emil* Marchant."

Grijpstra's cigar fell on the carpet. He tried to pick it up and it burned his hand, sparks finding their way into the carpet's strands. He stamped them out roughly.

"You know a Mr. Marchant, sir?" de Gier asked quietly.

"No, I haven't met him. But I have written several letters to a man named Emil Marchant. On behalf of clients who are hindered by the noise he makes in his shop. He works with brass, and it isn't only the noise, but there seems to be a stink as well. My clients want him to move out and are prepared to take him to court if necessary. Mr. Marchant telephoned me a few times, pleading for mercy. He said he owed money to the tax department and wanted time to make the money, that he would move out later; but my clients have lost patience. I didn't give in to him—in fact, I just pushed harder. He will have to go to court next week, and he is sure to lose out."

"Do you know what line of business he is in, sir?"

"Doorknobs, I believe, and knockers for doors, in the shape of lions' heads—that sort of thing. And weather vanes. He told me on the phone. All handmade. He is a craftsman."

Grijpstra got up. "We'll be on our way, sir. We found Mr. Marchant this morning, dead, hanging from a tree in the Amsterdam Forest. He probably hanged himself around 7:00 A.M., and at some time before he must have delivered the rabbit and its egg. According to his landlady he has been behaving strangely lately. He must have blamed you for his troubles and tried to take his revenge. He didn't mean to kill your wife, he meant to kill you. He didn't know that you don't eat chocolate, and he probably didn't even know you were married. We'll check further and make a report. The rabbit's mold is probably still in his shop, and if not we'll find traces of the chocolate. We'll have the rabbit checked for fingerprints. It won't be difficult to come up with irrefutable proof. If we do, we'll let you know, sir, a little later today. I am very sorry all this has happened."

"Nothing ever happens in Amsterdam," de Gier said as he yanked the door of the Volkswagen open, "and when it does it all fits in immediately."

But Grijpstra didn't agree.

"We would never have solved the case, or rather *I* wouldn't have, if you hadn't thought of the rabbit as an ornament."

"No, Grijpstra, we would have found Marchant's name in Moozen's files."

The adjutant shook his heavy grizzled head. "No, we wouldn't have checked the files. If he had kept on saying that he wasn't working on any bad cases I wouldn't have pursued that line of thought. I'd have reverted to trying to find an enemy of his wife. We might have worked for weeks and called in all sorts of help and wasted everybody's time. You are clever, Sergeant."

De Gier was studying a redheaded girl waiting for a streetcar.

"Am I?"

"Yes. But not as clever as I am," Grijpstra said and grinned. "You work for me. I personally selected you as my assistant. You are a tool in my expert hands."

De Gier winked at the redheaded girl and the girl smiled back. The traffic had jammed up ahead and the car was blocked. De Gier opened his door.

"Hey! Where are you going?"

"It's a holiday, Adjutant, and you can drive this wreck for a change. I am going home. That girl is waiting for a streetcar that goes to my side of the city. Maybe she hasn't had lunch yet. I am going to invite her to go to a Chinese restaurant."

"But we have reports to make, and we've got to check out Marchant's shop; it'll be locked, we have to find the key in his room, and we have to telephone the engineer to let him off the hook."

"I am taking the streetcar," de Gier said. "You do all that. You ate my roll."

Chocolate Cherry Truffles

⅓ cup whipping cream
12 oz. good milk chocolate, broken or chopped into small pieces (Milk chocolate chips will work, but get the best available. The better the chocolate, the better the truffle!)
3 Tbsp. kirsch
½ cup maraschino cherries, drained and finely chopped
Large cookie sheet lined with waxed paper
½ cup of something—cocoa, or confectioner's sugar, or shredded coconut, or finely chopped nuts, or chocolate sprinkles—as desired, to coat completed truffles
Paper candy cups—paper mini-muffin cups work well if you can't find candy cups

PLACE CREAM IN small saucepan over low to medium heat. Bring just to boiling, stirring constantly. Turn off burner and remove pan from heat. Mix chopped chocolate in the hot cream. Cover and set aside for three to four minutes, just until chocolate is melted. Stir the mixture until smooth. Stir in kirsch and chopped cherries. Refrigerate for an hour. Remove mixture from refrigerator and beat until fluffy. (Using a hand mixer on high speed for about three minutes will do the job, as will beating for four to five minutes by hand.) Refrigerate until firm. Using a melon baller or a rounded measuring spoon or a teaspoon, scoop tablespoon-sized rounded balls of the chocolate mixture onto the waxed paper. Roll the chocolate balls in the chosen coating material and place completed truffles in the paper candy cups.

TRUFFLES WILL KEEP for up to three weeks in the refrigerator if placed in a tightly sealed container. But the container must be absolutely sealed, otherwise the truffles will absorb any stray odors floating around your fridge (I discovered this when I accidentally served garlic and onion-flavored truffles to guests right after the nice lasagna that tainted the chocolate.)

Dead and Breakfast

Barbara Collins

Laura sat in the front on the passenger's side of the white Transport minivan in the Holiday Inn parking lot, waiting for her husband to come out of the lobby.

In the back seat, their son, Andy, a dark-haired, round-faced, eleven-year-old boy with glasses, was hunched over, peering into the small screen of his Turbo Express, moving the expensive video game back and forth in his hands to catch the last fading rays of the sun.

Even with the volume turned down, Laura could hear the frantic tune of the game he was playing, "Splatterhouse": a particularly violent one she didn't approve of (and wouldn't have allowed her husband to buy for the boy, if *she'd* been along on that shopping trip). She mentally blocked the sound out, gazing toward the horizon at the picture-postcard sunset descending on lush green trees.

Wisconsin was a beautiful state, and the weather had been perfect; but now, dark, threatening clouds were moving quickly in, bringing to an end a memorable summer-vacation day.

She spotted her husband, Pete, coming out of the lobby. He'd only been in there a minute or so . . . not very long.

It wasn't a good sign.

"We're in trouble," he said, after opening the van's door and sliding in behind the wheel. The brow of his ruggedly handsome face was furrowed.

"No room?" she asked.

"No room."

"Let's try another."

Pete turned toward her. "Honey," he said, his expression grave, "according to the desk clerk, there's not a vacancy between Milwaukee and Minneapolis."

"But that's impossible!" Laura said, astounded. "What's going on?"

Pete started the van. "A country festival, for one thing," he replied. "And this *is* the tourist season . . ."

"Aren't we staying here?" Andy asked from the back seat.

"No, son," his dad answered, as he wheeled the van out of the packed hotel parking lot and toward the Interstate ramp. "We have to go on."

"But I'm tired," the boy whined, "and there's not enough light anymore to play my game!"

Annoyed—more with their current predicament than with her son—Laura picked up a small white sack on the seat next to her and threw it to Andy, hitting him on the arm. "Here . . . have some fudge," she said flatly.

"I don't *like* fudge!" the boy retorted, and threw the sack back at his mom, smacking her on the head.

"Andy!" Pete said sharply, looking at his son in the rearview mirror. "That's five points! When you get to ten, you lose your Turbo Express for a week, remember?"

"Well, *she* started it!" he protested.

"Six," his father said.

The van fell silent, the air tense and heavy with more than the humidity of the oncoming storm. Big drops of rain splattered on the windshield. The sky was crying, and suddenly Laura felt like crying, too. She stared at the dark highway before her, upset that their wonderful day had turned sour.

"We shouldn't have stopped at the Dells," she sighed.

It had to be said, and it might as well be said by her, because she was the one who first suggested the detour to the expensive touristy playground . . .

A sign on the road advertising the Oak Street Antiques Mall had caught her attention, but Pete and Andy had just groaned.

Then Andy saw the gigantic 3-D billboard for Pirate's Cove—a seventy-two-hole miniature golf course set in tiers of sandstone and waterfalls that overlooked the Wisconsin River. Quickly, he defected to his mother's side.

Pete, reminding them both of their agreement to make it from Illinois to Minnesota by nightfall, where a coveted condominium at Kavanaugh's Resort in Brainerd awaited them, held firm . . . until he drove over the next hill on the highway.

There, among the trees, was a pretty blonde, braided billboard *Fräulein* wearing an alluring peasant dress; she beckoned to him with her wooden finger, teasingly, tempting him to taste the homemade fudge (sixteen flavors) at the German Candy Shoppe.

"Well," Pete had said, slowly, "maybe we can stop for just a little while."

But "just a little while" had turned into all afternoon, because there was much more to the Wisconsin Dells than antiquing and golfing and rich gooey fudge, like river rides and go-carts, wax museums and haunted houses . . .

"Let's try that one," Laura suggested, as a roadside motel materialized in the mist. Three hours earlier, she wouldn't have dreamed of ever stopping at such a scuzzy place; but now they were desperate, and *any* bed looked good, even this biker's haven.

Pete pulled off the highway and into the motel—a long, single-story, rundown succession of tiny rooms. The lot was full of pickup trucks and motorcycles, so he parked in front of the entrance and got out of the van, leaving the engine running.

Laura locked the doors behind him and waited. Rain pelted the windshield. The van's huge wipers moved back and forth spastically, like gigantic grasshopper legs, grating on her nerves. She leaned over and shut the engine off.

Behind her, Andy sighed wearily.

Please, dear God, she thought, *let there be a room so we don't have to sleep in the car.*

She strained to see through the rain-streaked window, trying to spot Pete. He'd been gone a long time this time . . . too long.

That wasn't a good sign, either.

Suddenly, Laura saw him dart in front of the van, and quickly she unlocked the doors. He jumped inside. His clothes were soaked, hair matted, but he wore a grin.

"You got us a room!" Laura cried, elated.

Pete nodded, wiping wetness from his face with the back of one hand. "But not here."

"Then where?"

He looked at her. "When I went in," he explained, "the desk clerk was telling another family they had no rooms. So naturally, I turned around to leave. Then a maintenance man gave me a tip on a place . . . a *bed and breakfast*."

"Oh, really?" They'd never stayed at one.

"I used the pay phone and called," Pete continued. "The woman sounded very nice. They had one room left and promised to save it for us. I got the directions right here."

He fished around in his pocket and drew out a piece of paper.

"We gotta go back about forty miles, and it's a little out of our way, but—"

"But it's a *bed*." She smiled, relieved, throwing her arms around Pete, hugging him.

"And *breakfast*." He smiled back, and kissed her.

"What's a bed and breakfast?" Andy asked.

Laura looked at her son. "A bed and breakfast is not really a hotel," she answered. "It's somebody's home." She paused. "It'll be like staying at your Aunt Millie's house."

"Oh," the boy said sullenly, "then I gotta be good."

"You've got to be *especially* good," Pete said, "because these people don't usually take children, but they're going to make an exception for us. Okay, son?"

"I'll try," he said, but not very convincingly.

An hour later, as the storm began to die down, the little family drove into the small quaint town of Tranquillity, its old cobblestone streets shiny from the rain.

At a big County Market grocery store, Pete turned left, down an avenue lined with sprawling oak trees and old homes set back from the street.

They pulled up in front of a many-gabled house. An outside light was on, illuminating the large porch, which wrapped around the front of the home. On either side of the steps sat twin lions, their mouths open in a fierce frozen roar as they guarded the front door.

Laura clasped her hands together, gazing at the house. "Oh, isn't it *charming*? This will be such fun!"

Pete nodded, then read the wooden sign attached to the sharp spears at the wrought-iron gate. "*Die Gasthaus*?"

"That's German for 'the inn,' " Laura said, utilizing her high school foreign language class for the very first time.

"So let's go in," smiled Pete.

"What's German for 'Splatterhouse'?" said a small sarcastic voice from the back seat.

Anger ignited in Laura—why did the boy have to ruin things? And after all they had done for him today! She turned to reprimand Andy, but her husband beat her to it.

"*Shape up,*" Pete shouted at the boy. "You already have six points—wanna try for seven?"

"No."

"It's going to be a mighty long trip without your Turbo Express," his father threatened.

"I'm sorry," Andy said. "It's not *my* fault this place looks like a spook house."

Pete wagged a finger at his son. "Now we're going to go in, and you're going to behave, and, goddamnit, we're all going to have a *good time!*"

There was a long silence.

Laura couldn't stand it, so she reached back and patted Andy on the knee. "Now gather up your things, honey," she said cheerfully. "Don't you know how lucky we are to be here?"

IN THE PARLOR OF Die Gasthaus Bed and Breakfast, Marvin Butz sipped his tea from a china cup as he sat in a Queen Anne needlepoint chair in front of a crackling fireplace.

A bachelor, pushing fifty, slightly overweight, with thinning gray hair and a goatee, the regional sales manager of Midwest Wholesale Grocery Distributors was enjoying the solitude of the rainy evening.

Whenever he went on the road, Marvin always stayed at bed and breakfasts, avoiding the noisy, crowded, kid-infested chain hotels. The last thing he needed in his high-pressure job was being kept awake all night by a drunken wedding reception, or rowdy class reunion, or loud bar band.

Besides, he delighted in being surrounded by the finer things in life—rare antiques, crisply starched linens, delicate bone china—which reminded him of his mother's home, before the family went bankrupt and had to sell everything.

He couldn't find these "finer things in life" in a regular hotel, where lamps and pictures and clock radios were bolted down, like he might be some common thief. (Besides which, who would want such *bourgeois* kitch, anyway?) And he could *never* get any satisfaction—or compensation—for the many inconveniences that always happened to him in the usual hotels. Whenever he complained, all he ever got was rude behavior from arrogant desk clerks.

But at most bed and breakfasts, even the smallest complaint, Marvin found, almost guaranteed a reduction in his bill. Why, half the time, he stayed for free! (Charging his expense account the full amount, of course.)

"More tea, Mr. Butz?"

Mrs. Hilger, who owned and ran the establishment with her husband, stood next to Marvin, a Royal Hanover green teapot in her hand, a white linen napkin held under its spout to catch any drip. She was a large women, not fat, just big. Marvin guessed her age to be about sixty, and at one time she must have been a looker, but now her skin was wrinkled and spotted with old-age marks, her hair coarse and gray and pulled back in a bun.

He nodded and held out his cup. "With sugar."

"I'll bring you some."

He watched her walk away. She was nice enough, he thought, but the woman would talk his ear off if he let her. When he first arrived around 6:00 P.M., she started in lecturing him about how everybody should be nice to one another and do what they could to make the world a better place to live. If he had known he was going to be staying with a religious fanatic, he never would have come here!

He frankly told her *his* world would be a better place to live if she would leave him alone while he unpacked.

She had acted hurt and scurried off, and he hadn't seen her until about eight o'clock, when she had offered him tea.

Mrs. Hilger came back into the parlor, carrying a silver sugar bowl. She handed Marvin an unusual sterling sugar spoon with what appeared to be real rubies set into the handle.

He took the spoon and looked at it closely. "I've never seen anything like this before," he mused.

"That's because it's one of a kind," she replied.

He used the spoon to sugar his tea, then set it on the side of his saucer.

"There'll be another party coming in this evening," the woman informed him. "A couple with their young son."

About to take a sip of tea, Marvin looked at her sharply. "But you advertised 'no children,' " he complained.

"Yes, I know," the woman said, "but this poor family is caught out in the storm without hotel accommodations."

"So *I'm* to be inconvenienced because some dumb hicks didn't have the common sense to make reservations?"

There was a brief silence. Then Mrs. Hilger said, "If that's how you feel, Mr. Butz, your stay with us will be complimentary."

Marvin smiled.

And Mrs. Hilger smiled back, but he wasn't at all sure that the smile was friendly.

Mr. Hilger's large form filled the doorway to the parlor. He looked more like a handyman than the proprietor of a bed and breakfast, in his plaid shirt and overalls.

Marvin had had a brief conversation with the bald, bespectacled man earlier, when Marvin had gone into the kitchen to admire an old butcher's block. Mr. Hilger had come up from the basement.

"It's from our store," Mr. Hilger had said. "We had a little corner grocery before County Market came in and put us out of business."

"What a pity," Marvin had said, shrugging. "But personally, I don't believe anybody gets 'put out of business' by anybody else."

"Oh?"

"Yes. You do it yourself, by not keeping up. Survival of the fittest."

"You're probably right," Mr. Hilger had said, getting a butcher's apron out of a narrow closet by the pantry. The big man slipped it on and went back down into the basement.

Marvin had frowned—was food preparation going on down there? If so, he hoped conditions were sanitary.

"Those folks with the child are here," Mr. Hilger was saying to his wife. The apron was gone now. "I'm going to help them with their luggage."

"Thank you, dear," Mrs. Hilger replied.

Marvin quickly finished the last of his tea and stood up. "I'll be retiring now," he informed her. He'd rather die than spend one minute in boring, pointless small talk with these new people. "Please inform that family I will be using the bathroom at six in the morning. And I'd like my breakfast served promptly at seven, out in the garden."

"Yes, Mr. Butz." Mrs. Hilger nodded. "Good night."

Marvin left the parlor, through the main foyer and past a large, hand-carved grandfather clock. He climbed the grand oak staircase to the second floor.

To the left was the Gold Room, where an elderly couple from Iowa was staying. They had gone to bed already, the little woman not feeling well, and so their door was shut. But behind the door was a grandiose three-piece Victorian bedroom set of butternut and walnut, with a carved fruit cluster at the top of the headboard and dresser. (He had peeked in, earlier, when they were momentarily out.) He wished he had that room, because it had its own bath . . . but the old farts had gotten there first.

At the end of the hall on the left was the White Room. The bridal suite. Everything in it was white—from the painted four-poster bed with lace canopy to the white marble-topped dresser. It also had its own bathroom. He'd gotten to see the exquisite room when he first arrived and wouldn't have minded his company paying a little extra for such fine accommodations. But some newlyweds on a cross-country honeymoon were in there right now—doing God only knows what behind their closed door.

Across the hall from the White Room was the Blue Room, the least impressive (or so he thought). It was decorated in wicker, with a Battenburg lace comforter, and a collection of old cast-iron toys showcased on the ledges of the beveled glass windows. Mrs. Hilger had tried to put him in there, but he protested. (The furnishings were so informal, it would have been like sleeping on a porch!) He demanded a different room.

The door to the Blue Room stood open, awaiting the inconsiderate family that would soon be clomping nosily up the steps.

To the immediate right was the Red Room, his room, which had a massive oak bedroom set with eight-inch columns and carved capitals, and a beautiful red oriental rug on the floor. It was satisfactory.

Marvin used an old skeleton key to open his door: he had locked it to protect his belongings, even though the other skeleton room keys could also open his door. He would have to speak to Mrs. Hilger, later, about this little breach in security.

He entered the room, leaving the door open. He was planning on getting his shaving kit and using the bathroom, which he shared with the Blue Room, before turning in for the night, but he stopped at a small mahogany table next to the door. On the table was a lovely cranberry lamp with thumbprint shade and dropped crystals.

Marvin dug into his jacket pocket and pulled out the sweet little sugar spoon, leaned over, and turned on the lamp to examine the spoon better. Its red ruby handle sparkled in the light.

A nice addition to his spoon collection.

Suddenly, something caught his attention in the hallway. Flustered, caught off guard, Marvin shoved the spoon back into his pocket and looked up from the light.

A young boy stood in the hall, not six feet away. How long the kid had been there, watching, Marvin didn't know.

Marvin reached out with one hand and slammed his door in the boy's face.

How he hated children! They were a bunch of sneaky, snooping, immature brats.

Marvin yawned, aware for the first time of how tired he was. He got his toiletries and went off to the bathroom, then came back and got into a pair of burgundy silk pajamas.

He crawled under the beige crocheted bedspread and lace-trimmed sheets. He wanted to read awhile, but his eyes were too heavy. He got out of bed and turned off the push-button light switch on the wall by the door.

Then he went back to bed.

Soon, Marvin was fast asleep.

It was a deep sleep. So deep he didn't hear the skeleton key working in the keyhole of his door. Or see the dark form of Mr. Hilger poised over him, large hands outstretched.

But not so deep that he didn't feel those hands tighten around his neck like a vise, slowly squeezing him into the deepest of all deep sleeps.

A NOISE WOKE ANDY. It was a bump, or a thump, or *something*. He lay quietly in the dark on the cot Mrs. Hilger fixed up for him, and listened.

All was silent now, except for the soft breathing of his parents across the room in that great big bed. Whatever the noise had been, Andy was glad it woke him. He'd been having a nightmare. A bad dream where he'd been sucked into the video game, "Splatterhouse," he'd been playing. And ghouls and monsters were chasing him with butcher knives and stuff.

Andy reached under the cot, got his glasses, and put them on. A fancy clock on a table read a quarter to three in the morning. He sat up farther and looked at the window next to him. On the ledge was a row of small toys—little cars, and airplanes and trains. His mother had told him they were antiques and not to touch them.

Andy's favorite was the train. You could actually see the conductor standing inside! He picked the heavy toy up and held it in his hand. It was so much cooler than anything you ever saw in a toy store today! He reached under the cot again, opened his suitcase, and tucked the train inside. Then he lay back down.

There were so many of the toys—thirty-two, he'd counted—that he was sure the Hilgers wouldn't miss it. Besides, the boy thought, wasn't his mom always saying to his dad when they stayed in hotels, "Honey, take the soap, take the shampoo, get the Kleenex . . ."? This wasn't exactly soap, or shampoo, or Kleenex, but then this wasn't exactly a hotel. So it had to be kind of the same.

And if that nasty, mean man in the room next to them could cop a spoon, why couldn't he have the train? Andy *knew* the man had stolen it, because of the look on his face—there was guilt written all over it!

Andy had to pee. He remembered his mother telling him that if he woke up in the night to be sure and go, because someone else might be in the bathroom in the morning.

The boy got up from the cot and quietly slipped out of the room. He tiptoed down the dark hallway to the bathroom.

Inside, he used the toilet, which had a funny chain he had to pull to flush it. Then he washed his hands at a neat faucet where the water came out of a fish's head. He turned out the bathroom light, opened the door, and stepped into the hallway.

That's when he saw Mrs. Hilger coming out of the crabby man's room. She had some wadded-up sheets in her arms.

The woman didn't see him, because she had her back to the boy, heading toward the stairs with her bundle.

Andy stood frozen for a moment, and when the woman was gone, he walked down to that mean man's room.

The door was wide open. And even though the only light came from the moon that shone in through the windows, he could see that the bed had been made. There was no sign of that man *or* his things.

Andy tiptoed to the top of the stairs which yawned down into the blackness. Below, somewhere, he could hear noises—faint pounding and the sound of something electrical, something sawing, maybe, like his father sometimes used in the garage.

Quietly, he crept down the stairs, staying close to the railing, until he reached the bottom.

Suddenly, the big clock by the stairs bonged three times, scaring Andy nearly out of his skin. He waited until he'd calmed down, then moved silently along, toward the back of the dark house, through the dining room with its big, long table. He bumped into a chair, and its legs went *screech* on the wooden floor.

Andy froze. The faint noises below him stopped. He held his breath. Seconds felt like minutes. Then the sounds started up again.

He went into the kitchen.

There was a light coming from under the door that led to the basement. That's where the noises were coming from.

Andy thought about a movie he had seen last year with his father. At one point a kid—a boy a lot like himself—was going to go down in a basement where bad, evil people lived. Andy had turned to his dad and said, "Why's he going down there?" And Andy's father had said, "Because it's a story, and he just has to *know*."

And now, just like the boy in that scary movie, Andy reached his hand out for the doorknob. He didn't know why—he was certainly frightened—but he couldn't seem to stop himself.

Slowly, he opened the door to the basement, and the sound of sawing increased as the crack of bright light widened until Andy was washed in illumination. *What am I doing?* he thought, *I don't have to know!* And as he was starting to ease the door shut again, a hand settled on his shoulder.

He jumped. Someone was beside him! Shaking, he looked back at the shape of a figure with a knife in its hand, and gasped.

"What are you doing, young man?" the figure demanded.

The voice was low and cold—but a lady's voice.

Then there was a click and he saw her, one hand on the light switch, the other holding the butcher knife: Mrs. Hilger. The face that had been so friendly before was now very cross.

Even though Andy was trembling badly, he managed to say, "Wh-where am I? I . . . I must be sleepwalking again."

There was a long, horrible moment.

Then the knife disappeared behind Mrs. Hilger's back and she said sweetly, "You're in the kitchen, my boy. I'll see that you get back to your room."

"Th-that's all right, now I know where I am."

He backed away from her, and turned, and hurried through the dining room, and when he got to the stairs, he bolted up them, and dashed down the hallway, past the man's room who had stolen the spoon, to his parents' room, where he opened the door, then slammed it shut, ran to their bed, and jumped in between them.

"Andy!" his mother moaned. "What in the world . . . ?"

"Can I please sleep here, Mom?" he pleaded. "I had a terrible nightmare."

She sighed. "Well, all right, get under the covers."

Andy started to crawl beneath the sheets, but stopped.

"Wait," he said. "There's something I gotta do first."

He climbed out of the bed and went over to the cot, dug beneath it, and got into his suitcase.

He put the toy train back on the ledge of the window.

PETE WOKE TO A sunny morning, the smell of freshly brewed coffee, and the unmistakable aroma of breakfast. He breathed deeply, taking in the wonderful smells.

He looked over at Laura, still sleeping soundly in the big bed next to him, her hair spread out on the lace pillowcase like a fan. She was so beautiful—even snoring, with her mouth open.

He propped himself up with both elbows and noticed his son sitting on the cot across the room, fully dressed, his little suitcase, packed, by his feet. The boy was staring at him.

"Hey, partner," Pete said, still a little groggy, "what's the hurry?"

Andy didn't respond.

Now Pete realized something was wrong with the boy, and vaguely remembered his son sleeping with them in the night.

Pete sat up farther in the bed, letting the bedspread fall down around his waist. "Did you have a bad dream?" he asked.

The boy nodded. "Sort of."

"Well, why don't you come over here and tell me about it?" Pete patted a place on the bed next to himself. "Most bad dreams sound pretty silly in the light of day."

Andy stood up slowly, went to the bed, and sat on it. The springs made a little squeak.

Pete gazed at his son's face—his large brown eyes, made larger by the glasses, his little pug nose, the tiny black mole on the side of his cheek—the depth of Pete's love for the child was sometimes frightening.

"You know that man in the room next to us?" Andy said almost in a whisper, looking at his hands in his lap.

"The one who had dibs on the bathroom from six to seven this morning?"

Andy nodded.

Pete waited.

"When I went to the bathroom in the middle of the night," Andy said, "he was *gone*."

"Gone?"

Now the boy looked at his father. "His room was all made up, Dad . . . like he'd never been there!"

"Soooo," Pete said slowly, "what do you think happened?"

"I don't know," Andy said softly.

Pete looked toward the door of their room, and then back at his son. "Do you think somebody chopped him up with a meat cleaver," Pete said with a tiny smile, "and buried him in the garden, like in that movie we saw?"

Andy's eyes went wide, but then he smiled. "No," he said. "I guess not." He paused. "But where *did* he go?"

Pete put an arm around the boy. "Son, Mrs. Hilger told me about that man. He was very unhappy. And unhappy adults sometimes do unpredictable things. He just packed up and left."

"Really?"

"Sure." Pete hugged his son. "Now do you feel better?"

"Uh-huh."

"Okay." Pete slapped Andy's knee with one hand. "Let's wake up your mom and get down to breakfast, so we can get on the road!"

Breakfast at Die Gasthaus was offered in either the formal dining room, outside on the patio, or in the privacy of the rooms.

The elderly couple staying in the Gold Room had decided to
eat in the dining room; the wife was feeling much better this
morning after a good night's sleep.

The newlyweds, not surprisingly, were being served in their
room.

Pete let Laura decide where they would eat—that was the kind
of decision she always made, anyway—and she wanted to go out on
the patio.

The three sat at a white wrought-iron table, with comfortable
floral cushions on their chairs, surrounded by a variety of flowers.

Pete leaned toward Andy, and whispered that there didn't
appear to be any new additions in the garden today.

Andy smiled. Laura asked what the two of them were talking
about, and they both said, "Nothing."

Then Mrs. Hilger appeared in a starched white apron, carrying
a casserole dish which she placed in the center of the table. Pete
leaned forward.

It was an egg dish, a soufflé or something, and looked delicious—white and yellow cheeses baked over golden eggs with
crispy bits of meat. Pete's mouth began to water.

"Oh, Mrs. Hilger," Laura said, "our stay here has been so wonderful!"

"I'm glad, dear," Mrs. Hilger replied, as she gave each of them a
serving on a china plate. "My husband and I enjoy making other
people happy . . . people who are appreciative, that is. And we try,
in our small way, to do what we can to make this world a better
place to live."

Pete, wolfing down the eggs, said, in between bites, "What's in
this, Mrs. Hilger? Is it ham?"

"No," Mrs. Hilger said.

"Well, it's not sausage," Pete insisted.

Mrs. Hilger shook her head.

"Then, what is it?"

Mrs. Hilger smiled. "I'm sorry, but we never give out our
recipes," she said. "Our unique dishes are one of the reasons
people come back. Most of them, that is."

Mrs. Hilger reached for the silver coffee pot on the table.
"More coffee?" she asked Laura.

"Please," Laura said. "With sugar."

The woman reached into the pocket of her apron and pulled out a spoon—a silver one with red stones on the handle. She handed the spoon to Laura.

"Oh, how beautiful," Laura said, looking at the spoon.

"There's not another like it," Mrs. Hilger said.

Suddenly, Andy began to gag and cough, and the boy leaned over his plate and spit out a mouthful of food.

"Andrew!" Laura cried, shocked.

"Son, what's the matter?" Pete asked, alarmed. The boy must have choked on his breakfast.

"I . . . I'm not hungry," Andy said, his face ashen as he pushed his plate away from himself.

"Andy!" Laura said, sternly. "You're being rude!"

But Pete stepped in to defend the boy. "He had kind of a rough night, Laura. That's probably why he doesn't have an appetite. Let's just forget it."

Laura smiled. "Well, *I* certainly have an appetite! Mrs. Hilger, I'd love some more of your delicious eggs, but I don't want to trouble you, I can get it myself." Laura started to reach for the dish, but Mrs. Hilger picked it up.

"Nonsense, my dear," the woman said with a tiny smile, and she put another huge spoonful of eggs with cheeses and succulent meat on Laura's plate. "It's no trouble. We at Die Gasthaus just love to serve our guests!"

Die Gasthaus Breakfast Eggs

---

8 to 10 slices white bread
1 lb. meat (optional)
6 to 8 eggs, slightly beaten
½ cup sharp cheddar cheese
½ cup Swiss cheese
½ cup mushrooms, drained
¾ cup Half & Half
1¼ cup milk
1 tsp. Worcestershire sauce
1 tsp. prepared mustard
Salt & pepper to taste

BUTTER A 9" X 13" PAN. Cube bread, removing crusts, and line the bottom of the pan. Cook meat until done; crumble over bread. Add the remaining ingredients to the slightly beaten eggs. Pour into pan. Bake at 350 degrees F. for 35 to 40 minutes.

Recipe for a Happy Marriage

Nedra Tyre

Today is just not my day.
And it's not even noon.
Maybe it will take a turn for the better.
Anyway, it's foolish to be upset.

That girl from the *Bulletin* who came to interview me a little while ago was nice enough. I just wasn't expecting her. And I surely wasn't expecting Eliza McIntyre to trip into my bedroom early this morning and set her roses down on my bedside table with such an air about her as if I'd broken my foot for the one and only purpose of having her arrive at 7:30 to bring me a bouquet. She's been coming often enough since I broke my foot, but never before eleven or twelve in the morning.

That young woman from the *Bulletin* sat right down, and before she even smoothed her skirt or crossed her legs she looked straight at me and asked if I had a recipe for a happy marriage. I think she should at least have started off by saying it was a nice day or asking how I felt, especially as it was perfectly obvious that I had a broken foot.

I told her that I certainly didn't have any recipe for a happy marriage, but I'd like to know why I was being asked, and she said it was almost Saint Valentine's Day and she had been assigned to write a feature article on love, and since I must know more about love than anybody else in town she and her editor thought that my opinions should have a prominent place in the article.

Her explanation put me more out of sorts than her question. But whatever else I may or may not be, I'm a good-natured woman. I suppose it was my broken foot that made me feel irritable.

At that very moment Eliza's giggle came way up the back stairwell from the kitchen, and it was followed by my husband's laughter, and I heard dishes rattle and pans clank, and all that added fire to my irritability.

The one thing I can't abide, never have been able to stand, is to have somebody in my kitchen. Stay out of my kitchen and my pantry, that's my motto. People always seem to think they're putting things back in the right place, but they never do. How well I remember Aunt Mary Ellen saying she just wanted to make us a cup of tea and to cut some slices of lemon to go with it. I could have made that tea as well as she did, but she wouldn't let me. I couldn't tell a bit of difference between her tea and mine, yet she put my favorite paring knife some place or other and it didn't turn up until eight months later, underneath a stack of cheese graters. That was a good twenty years ago and poor Aunt Mary Ellen has been in her grave for ten, and yet I still think about that paring knife and get uneasy when someone is in my kitchen.

Well, that young woman leaned forward and had an equally dumbfounding question. She asked me just which husband I had now.

I don't look at things—at husbands—like that. So I didn't answer her. I was too aghast. And then again from the kitchen came the sound of Eliza's giggle and Lewis's whoop.

I've known Eliza Moore, now Eliza McIntyre, all my life. In school she was two grades ahead of me from the very beginning, but the way she tells it now she was three grades behind me; but those school records are somewhere, however yellowed and crumbled they may be, and there's no need for Eliza to try to pretend she's younger than I am when she's two years older. Not that it matters. I just don't want her in my kitchen.

That young woman was mistaking my silence. She leaned close as if I were either deaf or a very young child who hadn't paid attention. How many times have you been married? she asked in a very loud voice.

When she put it like that, how could I answer her? Husbands aren't like teacups. I can't count them off and gloat over them the way Cousin Lutie used to stand in front of her china cabinets, saying she had so many of this pattern and so many of that.

For goodness sake, I had them one at a time, a husband at a time, and perfectly legally. They all just died on me. I couldn't stay the hand of fate. I was always a sod widow—there weren't any grass widows in our family. As Mama said, it runs in our family to be with our husbands till death us do part. The way that girl put her question, it sounded as if I had a whole bunch of husbands at one time like a line of chorus men in a musical show.

I didn't know how to answer her. I lay back on my pillows with not a word to say, as if the cat had run off with my tongue.

It's sheer accident that I ever married to begin with. I didn't want to. Not that I had anything against marriage or had anything else special to do. But Mama talked me into it. Baby, she said, other women look down on women who don't marry. Besides, you don't have any particular talent and Aunt Sallie Mae, for all her talk, may not leave you a penny. I don't think she ever forgave me for not naming you after her, and all her hinting about leaving you her money may just be her spiteful way of getting back at me.

Besides, Mama said, the way she's held on to her money, even if she did leave it to you, there would be so many strings attached you'd have to have a corps of Philadelphia lawyers to read the fine print before you could withdraw as much as a twenty-five-cent piece. If I were you, Baby, Mama said, I'd go and get married. If you don't marry you won't get invited any place except as a last resort, when they need somebody at the last minute to keep from having thirteen at table. And it's nice to have somebody to open the door for you and carry your packages. A husband can be handy.

So I married Ray.

Well, Ray and I hadn't been married six months when along came Mama with a handkerchief in her hand and dabbing at her eyes. Baby, she said, the wife is always the last one to know. I've just got to tell you what everyone is talking about. I know how good you are and how lacking in suspicion, but the whole town is buzzing. It's Ray and Marjorie Brown.

Ray was nice and I was fond of him. He called me Lucyhoney, exactly as if it were one word. Sometimes for short he called me

Lucyhon. He didn't have much stamina or backbone—how could he when he was the only child and spoiled rotten by his mother and grandma and three maiden aunts?

Baby, Mama said, and her tears had dried and she was now using her handkerchief to fan herself with, don't you be gullible. I can't stand for you to be mistreated or betrayed. Should I go to the rector and tell him to talk to Ray and point out where his duty lies? Or should I ask your uncle Jonathan to talk to Ray man-to-man?

I said, Mama, it's nobody's fault but my own. For heaven's sake let Ray do what he wants to do. He doesn't need anyone to tell him when he can come and go and what persons he can see. It's his house and he's paying the bills. Besides, his taking up with Marjorie Brown is no discredit to me—she's a lot prettier than I am. I think it's romantic and spunky of Ray. Why, Marjorie Brown is a married woman. Her husband might shoot Ray.

I don't know exactly what it was that cooled Ray down. He was back penitent and sheep-eyed, begging forgiveness. I'm proud of you, Ray, I said. Why, until you married me you were so timid you wouldn't have said boo to a goose, and here you've been having an illicit affair. I think it's grand. Marjorie Brown's husband might have horsewhipped you.

Ray grinned and said, I really have picked me a wife.

And he never looked at another woman again as long as he lived. Which, unfortunately, wasn't very long.

I got to thinking about him feeling guilty and apologizing to me, when I was the one to blame—I hadn't done enough for him, and I wanted to do something real nice for him, so I thought of that cake recipe. Except we called it a receipt. It had been in the family for years—centuries, you might say, solemnly handed down from mother to daughter, time out of mind.

And so when that girl asked me whether I had a recipe for a happy marriage I didn't give the receipt a thought. Besides, I'm sure she didn't mean an actual recipe, but some kind of formula like let the husband know he's boss, or some such foolishness.

Anyway, there I was feeling penitent about not giving Ray the attention he should have had so that he was bored enough by me to go out and risk his life at the hands of Marjorie Brown's jealous husband.

So I thought, well, it's the hardest receipt I've ever studied and has more ingredients than I've ever heard of, but it's the least I can do for Ray. So I went here and there to the grocery stores, to drug-stores, to apothecaries, to people who said, good Lord, no, we don't carry that but if you've got to have it try so-and-so, who turned out to be somebody way out in the country that looked at me as if I asked for the element that would turn base metal into gold and finally came back with a little packet and a foolish question as to what on earth I needed that for.

Then I came on back home and began grinding and pounding and mixing and baking and sitting in the kitchen waiting for the mixture to rise. When it was done it was the prettiest thing I had ever baked.

I served it for dessert that night.

Ray began to eat the cake and to savor it and to say extravagant things to me, and when he finished the first slice he said, Lucyhon, may I have another piece, a big one, please.

Why, Ray, it's all yours to eat as you like, I said.

After a while he pushed the plate away and looked at me with a wonderful expression of gratitude on his face and he said, Oh, Lucyhoney, I could die happy. And as far as I know he did.

When I tapped on his door the next morning to give him his first cup of coffee and open the shutters and turn on his bathwater he was dead, and there was the sweetest smile on his face.

But that young woman was still looking at me while I had been reminiscing, and she was fluttering her notes and wetting her lips with her tongue like a speaker with lots of things to say. And she sort of bawled out at me as if I were an entire audience whose attention had strayed: Do you think that the way to a man's heart is through his stomach?

Excuse me, young lady, I wanted to say, but I never heard of Cleopatra saying to Mark Antony or any of the others she favored, Here, won't you taste some of my potato salad, and I may be wrong because my reading of history is skimpy, but it sounds a little unlikely that Madame de Pompadour ever whispered into the ear of Louis XV, I've baked the nicest casserole for you.

My not answering put the girl off, and I felt that I ought to apologize, yet I couldn't bring myself around to it.

She glanced at her notes to the next question and was almost beet-red from embarrassment when she asked: Did the financial situation of your husbands ever have anything to do with your marrying them?

I didn't even open my mouth. I was as silent as the tomb. Her questions kept getting more and more irrelevant. And I was getting more stupefied as her eyes kept running up and down her list of questions.

She tried another one: What do you think is the best way to get a husband?

Now that's a question I have never asked myself and about which I have nothing to offer anybody in a Saint Valentine's Day article or elsewhere. I have never gone out to *get* a husband. I haven't ever, as that old-fashioned expression has it, set my cap for anybody.

Take Lewis, who is this minute in the kitchen giggling with Eliza McIntyre. I certainly did not set out to get him. It was some months after Alton—no, Edward—had died, and people were trying to cheer me up, not that I needed any cheering up. I mean, after all the losses I've sustained, I've become philosophical. But my cousin Wanda's grandson had an exhibition of paintings. The poor deluded boy isn't talented, not a bit. All the same I bought two of his paintings, which are downstairs in the hall closet, shut off from all eyes.

Anyway, at the opening of the exhibition there was Lewis, looking all forlorn. He had come because the boy was a distant cousin of his dead wife. Lewis leaped up from a bench when he got a glimpse of me and said, Why, Lucy, I haven't seen you in donkey's years, and we stood there talking while everybody was going ooh and aah over the boy's paintings, and Lewis said he was hungry and I asked him to come on home with me and have a bite to eat.

I fixed a quick supper and Lewis ate like a starving man, and then we sat in the back parlor and talked about this and that, and about midnight he said, Lucy, I don't want to leave. This is the nicest feeling I've ever had, being here with you. I don't mean to be disrespectful to the dead, but there wasn't any love lost between Ramona and me. I'd like to stay on here forever.

Well, after that—after a man's revealed his innermost thoughts to you—you can't just show him the door. Besides, I couldn't put him out because it was beginning to snow, and in a little while the snow turned to sleet. He might have fallen and broken his neck going down the front steps, and I'd have had that on my conscience the rest of my life.

Lewis, I said, it seems foolish at this stage of the game for me to worry about my reputation, but thank heaven Cousin Alice came down from Washington for the exhibition and is staying with me, and she can chaperon us until we can make things perfectly legal and aboveboard.

That's how it happened.

You don't plan things like that, I wanted to tell the girl. They happen in spite of you. So it's silly of you to ask me what the best way is to get a husband.

My silence hadn't bothered her a bit. She sort of closed one eye like somebody about to take aim with a rifle and asked: Exactly how many times have you been married?

Well, she had backed up. She was repeating herself. That was practically the same question she had asked me earlier. It had been put a little differently this time, that was all.

I certainly had no intention of telling her the truth, which was that I wasn't exactly sure myself. Sometimes my husbands become a little blurred and blended. Sometimes I have to sit down with pencil and paper and figure it out.

Anyhow, that's certainly no way to look at husbands—the exact number or the exact sequence.

My husbands were an exceptional bunch of men, if I do say so. And fine-looking, too. Even Art, who had a harelip. And they were all good providers. Rich and didn't mind spending their money—not like some rich people. Not that I needed money. Because Aunt Sallie Mae, for all Mama's suspicions, left me hers, and there was nothing spiteful about her stipulations. I could have the money when, as, and how I wanted it.

Anyway, I never have cared about money or what it could buy for me.

There's nothing much I can spend it on for myself. Jewelry doesn't suit me. My fingers are short and stubby and my hands are square—no need to call attention to them by wearing rings. Besides, rings bother me. I like to cook and rings get in the way. Necklaces choke me and earrings pinch. As for fur coats, mink or chinchilla or just plain squirrel—well, I don't like the idea of anything that has lived ending up draped around me.

So money personally means little to me. But it's nice to pass along. Nothing gives me greater pleasure, and there's not a husband of mine who hasn't ended up without having a clinic or a college library or a hospital wing or a research laboratory or something of the sort founded in his honor and named after him.

Sometimes I've had to rob Peter to pay Paul. I mean, some of them have left more than others, and once in a while I've had to take some of what one left me to pay on the endowment for another. But it all evened itself out.

Except for Buster. There was certainly a nice surplus where Buster was concerned. He lived the shortest time and left me the most money of any of my husbands. For every month I lived with him I inherited a million dollars. Five.

My silent reminiscing like that wasn't helping the girl with her Saint Valentine's Day article. If I had been in anybody's house and the hostess was as taciturn as I was, I'd have excused myself and reached for the knob of the front door.

But, if anything, that young lady became even more impertinent.

Have you had a favorite among your husbands? she asked, and her tongue flicked out like a snake's.

I was silent even when my husbands asked that question. Sometimes they would show a little jealousy for their predecessors and make unkind remarks. But naturally I did everything in my power to reassure whoever made a disparaging remark about another.

All my husbands have been fine men, I would say in such a case, but I do believe you're the finest of the lot. I said it whether I really thought so or not.

But I had nothing at all to say to that girl on the subject.

Yet if I ever got to the point of being forced to rank my husbands, I guess Luther would be very nearly at the bottom of the list. He was the only teetotaler in the bunch. I hadn't noticed how he felt about drink until after we were married—that's when things you've overlooked during courtship can confront you like a slap in the face. Luther would squirm when wine was served to guests during a meal, and his eyes looked up prayerfully toward heaven when anybody took a second glass. At least he restrained himself to the extent of not saying any word of reproach to a guest, but Mama said she always expected him to hand around some of those tracts that warn against the pitfalls that lie in wait for drunkards.

Poor man. He was run over by a beer truck.

The irony of it, Mama said. There's a lesson in it for us all. And it was broad daylight, she said, shaking her head, not even dark, so that we can't comfort ourselves that Luther didn't know what hit him.

Not long after Luther's unfortunate accident Matthew appeared—on tiptoe, you might say. He was awfully short and always stretched himself to look taller. He was terribly apologetic about his height. I'd ask you to marry me, Lucy, he said, but all your husbands have been over six feet tall. Height didn't enter into it, I told him, and it wasn't very long before Matthew and I were married.

He seemed to walk on tiptoe and I scrunched down, and still there was an awful gap between us, and he would go on about Napoleon almost conquering the world in spite of being short. I started wearing low-heeled shoes and walking hunched over, and Mama said, For God's sake, Baby, you can push tact too far. You never were beautiful but you had an air about you and no reigning queen ever had a more elegant walk, and here you are slumping. Your aunt Francine was married to a midget, as you well know, but there wasn't any of this bending down and hunching over. She let him be his height and he let her be hers. So stop this foolishness.

But I couldn't. I still tried literally to meet Matthew more than halfway. And I had this feeling—well, why shouldn't I have it, seeing as how they had all died on me—that Matthew wasn't long for this world, and it was my duty to make him feel as important and as tall as I possibly could during the little time that was left to him.

Matthew died happy. I have every reason to believe it. But then, as Mama said, they all died happy.

Never again, Mama, I said. Never again. I feel like Typhoid Mary or somebody who brings doom on men's heads.

Never is a long time, Mama said.

And she was right. I married Hugh.

I think it was Hugh.

Two things I was proud of and am proud of. I never spoke a harsh word to any one of my husbands, and I never did call one of them by another's name, and that took a lot of doing because after a while they just all sort of melted together in my mind.

After every loss, Homer was the greatest solace and comfort to me. Until he retired last year, Homer was the medical examiner, and he was a childhood friend, though I never saw him except in his line of duty, you might say. It's the law here, and perhaps elsewhere, that if anyone dies unattended or from causes that aren't obvious, the medical examiner must be informed.

The first few times I had to call Homer I was chagrined. I felt
apologetic, a little like calling the doctor up in the middle of the
night when, however much the pain may be troubling you, you're
afraid it's a false alarm and the doctor will hold it against you for
disturbing his sleep.

But Homer always was jovial when I called him. I guess that's
not the right word. Homer was reassuring, not jovial. Anytime,
Lucy, anytime at all, he would say when I began to apologize for
having to call him.

I think it was right after Sam died. Or was it Carl? It could have
been George. Anyway, Homer was there reassuring me as always, and
then this look of sorrow or regret clouded his features. It's a damned
pity, Lucy, he said, you can't work me in somewhere or other. You
weren't the prettiest little girl in the third grade, or the smartest, but
damned if from the beginning there hasn't been something about
you. I remember, he said, that when we were in the fourth grade, I
got so worked up over you that I didn't pass a single subject but arith-
metic and had to take the whole term over. Of course you were promoted, so for the rest of my life you've been just out of my reach.

Why, Homer, I said, that's the sweetest thing anybody has ever
said to me.

I had it in the back of my mind once the funeral was over and
everything was on an even keel again that I'd ask Homer over for
supper one night. But it seemed so calculating, as if I was taking
him up on that sweet remark he had made about wishing I had
worked him in somewhere among my husbands. So I decided
against it.

Instead I married Beau Green.

There they go laughing again—Eliza and Lewis down in the
kitchen. My kitchen.

It's funny that Eliza has turned up in my kitchen, acting very
much at home, when she's the one and only person in this town I
never have felt very friendly toward—at least, not since word got
to me that she had said I snatched Beau Green right from under
her nose.

That wasn't a nice thing for her to say. Besides, there wasn't a
word of truth in it. I'd like to see the man that can be snatched
from under anybody's nose unless he wanted to be.

Eliza was surely welcome to Beau Green if she had wanted him
and if he had wanted her.

Why, I'd planned to take a trip around the world, already had my tickets and reservations, and had to put it off for good because Beau wouldn't budge any farther away from home than to go to Green River—named for his family—to fish. I really wanted to take that cruise—had my heart especially set on seeing the Taj Mahal by moonlight—but Beau kept on saying if I didn't marry him he would do something desperate, which I took to mean he'd kill himself or take to drink. So I canceled all those reservations and turned in all those tickets and married him.

Well, Eliza would certainly have been welcome to Beau.

I've already emphasized that I don't like to rank my husbands, but in many ways Beau was the least satisfactory one I ever had. It was his nature to be a killjoy—he had no sense of the joy of living, and once he set his mind on something he went ahead with it, no matter if it pleased anybody else or not.

He knew good and well I didn't care for jewelry. But my preference didn't matter to Beau Green, not one bit. Here he came with this package and I opened it. I tried to muster all my politeness when I saw that it was a diamond. Darling, I said, you're sweet to give me a present, but this is a little bit big, isn't it?

It's thirty-seven carats, he said.

I felt like I ought to take it around on a sofa pillow instead of wearing it, but I did wear it twice and felt as conspicuous and as much of a show-off as if I'd been waving a peacock fan around and about.

It was and is my habit when I get upset with someone to go to my room and write my grievances down and get myself back in a good humor, just as I'm doing now because of that girl's questions; but sometimes it seemed like there wasn't enough paper in the world on which to write down my complaints against Beau.

Then I would blame myself. Beau was just being Beau. Like all God's creatures he was behaving the way he was made, and I felt so guilty that I decided I ought to do something for him to show I really loved and respected him, as deep in my heart I did.

So I decided to make him a cake by that elaborate recipe that had been in our family nobody is sure for how long. I took all one day to do the shopping for it. The next day I got up at five and stayed in the kitchen until late afternoon.

Well, Beau was a bit peckish when it came to eating the cake. Yet he had the sweetest tooth of any of my husbands.

Listen, darling, I said when he was mulish about eating it, I made this special for you—it's taken the best part of two days. I smiled at him and asked wouldn't he please at least taste it to please me. Really, I was put out when I thought of all the work that had gone into it. For one terrible second I wished it were a custard pie and I could throw it right in his face, like in one of those old Keystone comedies; and then I remembered that we were sworn to cherish each other, so I just put one arm around his shoulder and with my free hand I pushed the cake a little closer and said, Belle wants Beau to eat at least one small bite. Belle was a foolish pet name he sometimes called me because he thought it was clever for him to be Beau and for me to be Belle.

He looked sheepish and picked up his fork and I knew he was trying to please me: the way I had tried to please him by wearing that thirty-seven-carat diamond twice.

Goodness, Belle, he said, when he swallowed his first mouthful, this is delicious.

Now, darling, you be careful, I said. That cake is rich.

Best thing I ever ate, he said, and groped around on the plate for the crumbs, and I said, Darling, wouldn't you like a little coffee to wash it down?

He didn't answer, just sat there smiling. Then after a little while he said he was feeling numb. I can't feel a thing in my feet, he said. I ran for the rubbing alcohol and pulled off his shoes and socks and started rubbing his feet, and there was a sort of spasm and his toes curled under, but nothing affected that smile on his face.

Homer, I said a little later—because of course I had to telephone him about Beau's death—what on earth is it? Could it be something he's eaten? And Homer said, What do you mean, something he's eaten? Of course not. You set the best table in the county. You're famous for your cooking. It couldn't be anything he's eaten. Don't be foolish, Lucy. He began to pat me on the shoulder and he said, I read a book about guilt and loss and it said the bereaved often hold themselves responsible for the deaths of their beloved ones. But I thought you had better sense than that, Lucy.

Homer was a little bit harsh with me that time.

Julius Babb settled Beau's estate. Beau left you a tidy sum, all right, he said, and I wanted to say right back at him but didn't: not as tidy as most of the others left me.

Right then that young woman from the *Bulletin* repeated her last question.

Have you had a favorite among your husbands? Her tone was that of a prosecuting attorney and had nothing to do with a reporter interested in writing about love for Saint Valentine's Day.

I had had enough of her and her questions. I dragged myself up to a sitting position in the bed. Listen here, young lady, I said. It looks as if I've gotten off on the wrong foot with you—and then we both laughed at the pun I had made.

The laughter put us both in a good humor and then I tried to explain that I had an unexpected caller downstairs who needed some attention, and that I really was willing to cooperate on the Saint Valentine's Day article, but all those questions at first hearing had sort of stunned me. It was like taking an examination and finding all the questions a surprise. I told her if she would leave her list with me I'd mull over it, and she could come back tomorrow and I'd be prepared with my answers and be a little more presentable than I was now, wearing a rumpled wrapper and with my hair uncombed.

Well, she was as sweet as apple pie and handed over the list of questions and said she hoped that ten o'clock tomorrow morning would be fine; and I said, Yes, it would.

There goes Eliza's laugh again. It's more of a caw than a laugh. I shouldn't think that. But it's been such a strange day, with that young reporter being here and Eliza showing up so early.

Come to think of it, Eliza has done very well for herself, as far as marrying goes. That reporter should ask Eliza some of those questions.

Mama was a charitable woman all her life and she lived to be eighty-nine, but Eliza always rubbed Mama's skin the wrong way. To tell the truth, Eliza rubbed the skin of all the women in this town the wrong way. It's not right, Baby, Mama said, when other women have skimped and saved and cut corners all their lives and then when they're in their last sickness here comes Eliza getting her foot in the door just because she's a trained nurse. Then the next thing you hear, Eliza has married the widower and gets in one fell swoop what it took the dead wife a lifetime to accumulate.

That wasn't the most generous way in the world for Mama to put it, but I've heard it put much harsher by others. Mrs. Perkerson across the street, for one. Eliza is like a vulture, Mrs. Perkerson

said. First she watches the wives die, then she marries, and then
she watches the husbands die. Pretty soon it's widow's weeds for
Eliza and a nice-sized bank account, not to mention some of the
most valuable real estate in town.

Why, Mrs. Perkerson said the last time I saw her, I know that
Lois Eubanks McIntyre is turning in her grave thinking of Eliza
inheriting that big estate, with gardens copied after the Villa
d'Este. And they tell you nursing is hard work.

I hadn't seen Eliza in some time. We were friendly enough, but
not real friends, never had been, and I was especially hurt after
hearing what she said about me taking Beau Green away from her.
But we would stop and chat when we bumped into each other
downtown, and then back off smiling and saying we must get
together. But nothing ever came of it.

And then three weeks ago Eliza telephoned and I thought for
sure somebody was dead. But, no, she was as sweet as magnolia
blossoms and cooing as if we saw each other every day, and she
invited me to come by that afternoon for a cup of tea or a glass of
sherry. I asked her if there was anything special, and she said she
didn't think there had to be any special reason for old friends to
meet, but, yes, there was something special. She wanted me to see
her gardens—of course they weren't her gardens, except by
default, they were Lois Eubanks McIntyre's gardens, which she had
opened for the Church Guild Benefit Tour and I hadn't come. So
she wanted me to see them that afternoon.

It was all so sudden that she caught me off guard. I didn't want
to go and there wasn't any reason for me to go, but for the life of
me I couldn't think of an excuse not to go. And so I went.

The gardens really were beautiful, and I'm crazy about flowers.

Eliza gave me a personally guided tour. There were lots of paths
and steep steps and unexpected turnings, and I was so delighted
by the flowers that I foolishly didn't pay attention to my footing. I
wasn't used to walking on so much gravel or going up and down
uneven stone steps and Eliza didn't give me any warning.

Then all of a sudden, it was the strangest feeling, not as if I'd
fallen but as if I'd been pushed, and there Eliza was leaning over
me saying she could never forgive herself for not telling me about
the broken step, and I was to lie right there and not move until the
doctor could come, and what a pity it was that what she had
wanted to be a treat for me had turned into a tragedy. Which was

making a whole lot more out of it than need be because it was only a broken foot—not that it hasn't been inconvenient.

But Eliza has been fluttering around for three weeks saying that I should sue her as she carried liability insurance, and anyway it was lucky she was a nurse and could see that I got devoted attention. I don't need a nurse, but she has insisted on coming every day, and on some days several times; she seems to be popping in and out of the house like a cuckoo clock.

I had better get on with that reporter's questions.

Do you have a recipe for a happy marriage?

I've already told her I don't, and of course there's no such thing as a recipe for a happy marriage; but I could tell her this practice I have of working through my grievances and dissatisfactions by writing down what bothers me and then tearing up what I've written. For all I know it might work for somebody else, too.

I didn't hear Eliza coming up the stairs. It startled me when I looked up and saw her at my bedside. What if she discovered I was writing about her? What if she grabbed the notebook out of my hands and started to read it? There isn't a thing I could do to stop her.

But she just smiled and asked if I was ready for lunch, and she hoped I'd worked up a good appetite. How on earth she thinks I could have worked up an appetite by lying in bed I don't know, but that's Eliza for you, and all she had fixed was canned soup and it wasn't hot.

All I wanted was just to blot everything out—that girl's questions, Eliza's presence in my home, my broken foot.

I would have thought that I couldn't have gone to sleep in a thousand years. But I was so drowsy that I couldn't even close the notebook, much less hide it under the covers.

I don't know what woke me up. It was pitch-dark, but dark comes so soon these winter days you can't tell whether it's early dark or midnight.

I felt refreshed after my long nap and equal to anything. I was ready to answer any question on that girl's list.

The notebook was still open beside me and I thought that if Eliza had been in here and had seen what I had written about her it served her right.

Then from the kitchen rose a wonderful smell and there was a lot of noise downstairs. Suddenly, the back stairway and hall were flooded with light, and then Eliza and Lewis were at my door and they were grinning and saying they had a surprise for me. Then Lewis turned and picked up something from a table in the hall and brought it proudly toward me. I couldn't tell what it was. It was red and heartshaped and had something white on top. At first I thought it might be a hat, and then I groped for my distance glasses, but even with them on I still couldn't tell what Lewis was carrying.

Lewis held out the tray. It's a Saint Valentine's Day cake, he said, and Eliza said, we iced it and decorated it for you; then Lewis tilted it gently and I saw *L U C Y* in wobbly letters spread all across the top.

I don't usually eat sweets. So their labor of love was lost on me. Then I thought how kind it was that they had gone to all that trouble, and I forgave them for messing up my kitchen and meddling with my recipes—or maybe they had just used a mix. Anyway, I felt I had to show my appreciation, and it certainly wouldn't kill me to eat some of their cake.

They watched me with such pride and delight as I ate the cake that I took a second piece. When I had finished they said it would be best for me to rest, and I asked them to take the cake and eat what they wanted, then wrap it in foil.

And now the whole house is quiet.

I never felt better in my life. I'm smiling a great big contented smile. It must look exactly like that last sweet smile on all my husbands' faces—except Luther, who was run over by a beer truck.

I feel wonderful and so relaxed.

But I can hardly hold this pencil.

Goodness, it's

f
  a
   l
    l
     l
      i
       n
        g

Valentine's Day Cake

2½ cups sugar
1 cup butter
6 eggs
3 cups cake flour
½ tsp. baking soda
½ tsp. salt
1 cup sour cream
½ tsp. orange extract
½ tsp. lemon extract
1 tsp. vanilla extract
1 Tbsp. fresh orange rind, finely chopped
3 pints fresh strawberries, washed, hulled, and sliced
  in half
1 cup whipping cream
3 Tbsp. confectioner's sugar
½ tsp. vanilla extract
½ cup chocolate syrup
mint sprigs to garnish (optional)

PREHEAT OVEN TO 350 degrees F.

GREASE AND FLOUR 10-inch tube pan. Set aside.

CREAM SUGAR AND butter until light and fluffy. Add eggs one at a time, beating well after each addition. Sift flour, soda, and salt together. Add dry ingredients in three additions to the creamed butter and sugar, alternating with the sour cream. Add extracts and orange rind, beat well for two minutes. Pour into prepared tube pan. Bake for roughly one hour and 20 minutes, until done (cake top springs back when gently pressed).

MAKE WHIPPING CREAM. Whip cream until soft peaks form. Stir in sugar and vanilla. Place in refrigerator until cake is cool enough to eat.

SERVE EACH SLICE of cake topped with strawberries and whipped cream, drizzled with chocolate sauce, and garnished with a sprig of mint.

Death Cup

Joyce Carol Oates

*A*manita phalloides he began to hear in no voice he could recognize.

Murmurous, only just audible—*Amanita phalloides.*

More distinctly that morning, a rain-chilled Saturday morning in June, at his uncle's funeral. In the austere old Congregationalist church he only entered, as an adult, for such ceremonies as weddings and funerals. As, seated beside his brother Alastor of whom he disapproved strongly, he leaned far forward in the cramped hardwood pew, framing his face with his fingers so that he was spared seeing his brother's profile in the corner of his eye. Feeling an almost physical repugnance for the man who was his brother. He tried to concentrate on the white-haired minister's solemn words yet was nervously distracted by *Amanita phalloides.* As if, beneath the man's familiar words of Christian forbearance and uplift, another voice, a contrary voice, strange, incantatory, was struggling to emerge. And during the interlude of organ music. The Bach Toccata and Fugue in D Minor which his uncle, an amateur musician and philanthropist, had requested be played at his funeral. Lyle was one who, though he claimed to love music, was often distracted during it; his mind drifting; his thoughts like flotsam, or froth; now hearing the whispered words, only just audible in his ears *Amanita phalloides, Amanita phalloides.* He realized he'd first heard these mysterious words the night before, in a dream. A sort of fever-dream. Brought on by his brother's sudden, unexpected return.

He did not hate his brother Alastor. Not here, in this sacred place. *Amanita phalloides. Amanita phalloides.*

How beautiful, the Bach organ music! Filling the spartan plain, dazzling white interior of the church with fierce cascades of sound pure and flashing as a waterfall. Such music argued for the essential dignity of the human spirit. The transcendence of physical pain, suffering, loss. All that's petty, ignoble. *The world is a beautiful place if you have the eyes to see it and the ears to hear it,* Lyle's uncle had often said, and had seemed to believe through his long life, apparently never dissuaded from the early idealism of his youth; yet how was such idealism possible, Lyle couldn't help but wonder, Lyle who wished to believe well of others yet had no wish to be a fool, how was such idealism possible after the evidence of catastrophic world wars, the unspeakable evil of the Holocaust, equally mad, barbaric mass slaughters in Stalin's Russia, Mao's China? Somehow, his uncle Gardner King had remained a vigorous, good-natured, and generous man despite such facts of history; there'd been in him, well into his seventies, a childlike simplicity which Lyle, his nephew, younger than he by decades, seemed never to have had. Lyle had loved his uncle, who'd been his father's eldest brother. Fatherless himself since the age of eleven, he'd been saddened by his uncle's gradual descent into death from cancer of the larynx, and had not wanted to think that he would probably be remembered, to some degree, in his uncle's will. The bulk of the King estate, many millions of dollars, would go into the King Foundation, which was nominally directed by his wife, now widow, Alida King; the rest of it would be divided among numerous relatives. Lyle was troubled by the anticipation of any bequest, however modest. The mere thought filled him with anxiety, almost a kind of dread. *I would not wish to benefit in any way from Uncle Gardner's death, I could not bear it.*

To which his brother Alastor would have replied in his glib, jocular way, as, when they were boys, he'd laughed at Lyle's over-scrupulous conscience: *What good's that attitude? Our uncle is dead and he isn't coming back, is he?*

Unfortunate that Alastor had returned home to Contracoeur on the very eve of their uncle's death, after an absence of six years.

Still, it could only have been coincidence. So Alastor claimed. He'd been in communication with none of the relatives, including his twin brother Lyle.

How murmurous, teasing in Lyle's ears—*Amanita phalloides.*

Intimate as a lover's caressing whisper, and mysterious—*Amanita phalloides.*

Lyle was baffled at the meaning of these words. Why, at such a time, his thoughts distracted by grief, they should assail him.

In the hardwood pew, unpleasantly crowded by Alastor on his left, not wanting to crowd himself against an elderly aunt on his right, Lyle felt his lean, angular body quiver with tension. His neck was beginning to ache from the strain of leaning forward. It annoyed him to realize that, in his unstylish matte-black gabardine suit that fitted him too tightly across the shoulders and too loosely elsewhere, with his ash-colored hair straggling past his collar, his face furrowed as if with pain, and the peculiar way he held his outstretched fingers against his face, he was making himself conspicuous among the rows of mourners in the King family pews. Staring at the gleaming ebony casket so prominently placed in the center aisle in front of the communion rail, that looked so forbidding; so gigantic; far larger than his uncle Gardner's earthly remains, diminutive at the end, would seem to require. *But of course death is larger than life. Death envelops life: the emptiness that precedes our brief span of time, the emptiness that follows.*

A shudder ran through him. Tears stung his cheeks like acid. How shaky, how emotional he'd become!

A nudge in his side—his brother Alastor pressed a handkerchief, white, cotton, freshly laundered, into his hand, which Lyle blindly took.

Managing, even then, not to glance at his brother. Not to upset himself seeing yet again his brother's mock-pious mock-grieving face. His watery eyes, in mimicry of Lyle's.

Now the organ interlude was over. The funeral service was ending so soon! Lyle felt a childish stab of dismay, that his uncle would be hurried out of the sanctuary of the church, out of the circle of the community, into the impersonal, final earth. Yet the white-haired minister was leading the congregation in a familiar litany of words beginning, "Our heavenly father . . ." Lyle wiped tears from his eyelashes, shut his eyes tightly in prayer. He hadn't been a practicing Christian since adolescence, he was impatient with unquestioned piety and superstition, yet there was solace in such a ritual, seemingly shared by an entire community. Beside him, his aunt Agnes prayed with timid urgency, as if God were in this church and needed only to be beseeched by the right formula of words, and in the right tone of voice. On his other side, his brother Alastor intoned the prayer, not ostentatiously but distinctly enough to be heard for several pews; Alastor's voice was a deep, rich baritone, the voice of a trained singer you might think, or an actor. A roaring in Lyle's ears like a waterfall—*Amanita phalloides! Amanita phalloides!* and suddenly he remembered what *Amanita phalloides* was: the death-cup mushroom. He'd been reading a pictorial article on edible and inedible fungi in one of his science magazines and the death-cup mushroom, more accurately a "toadstool," had been imprinted on his memory.

His month had gone dry, his heart was hammering against his ribs. With the congregation, he murmured, "Amen." All volition seemed to have drained from him. Calmly he thought, *I will kill my brother Alastor after all. After all these years.*

OF COURSE, THIS WOULD never happen. Alastor King was a hateful person who surely deserved to die, but Lyle, his twin brother, was not one to commit any act of violence; not even one to fantasize any act of violence. *Not me! Not me! Never.*

IN THE CEMETERY BEHIND the First Congregationalist Church of Contracoeur, the remainder of the melancholy funeral rite was enacted. There stood Lyle King, the dead man's nephew, in a daze in wet grass beneath a glaring opalescent sky, awakened by strong fingers gripping his elbow. "All right if I ride with you to Aunt Alida's, Lyle?" Alastor asked. There was an edge of impatience to his lowered voice, as if he'd had to repeat his question. And Lyle's twin brother had not been one, since the age of eighteen months, to wish to repeat questions. He was leaning close to Lyle as if hoping to read his thoughts; his eyes were steely blue, narrowed. His breath smelled of something sweetly chemical, mouthwash probably, to disguise the alcohol on his breath; Lyle knew he was carrying a pocket flask in an inside pocket. His handsome ruddy face showed near-invisible broken capillaries like exposed nerves. Lyle murmured, "Of course, Alastor. Come with me." His thoughts flew ahead swiftly—there was Cemetery Hill that was treacherously steep, and the High Street Bridge—opportunities for accidents? Somehow Lyle's car might swerve out of control, skid on the wet pavement, Alastor, who scorned to wear a seat belt, might be thrown against the windshield, might be injured, might die, while he, Lyle, buckled in safely, might escape with but minor injuries. And blameless. Was that possible? Would God watch over him?

Not possible. For Lyle would have to drive other relatives in his car, too. He couldn't risk their lives. And there was no vigilant God.

A SIMPLE SELF-EVIDENT FACT, though a secret to most of the credulous world: Alastor King, attractive, intelligent, and deathly "charming" as he surely was, was as purely hateful, vicious, and worthless an individual as ever lived. His brother Lyle had grown to contemplate him with horror the way a martyr of ancient times might have contemplated the engine of pain and destruction rushing at him. *How can so evil a person deserve to live?* Lyle had wondered, sick with loathing of him. (This was years ago when the brothers were twenty. Alastor had secretly seduced their seventeen-year-old cousin Susan, and within a week or two lost interest in her, causing the girl to attempt suicide and to suffer a breakdown from which she would never fully recover.) Yet, maddening, Alastor had continued to live, and live. Nothing in the normal course of events would stop him.

Except Lyle. His twin. Who alone of the earth's billions of inhabitants understood Alastor's heart.

And so how shocked Lyle had been, how sickened, having hurried to the hospital when word came that his uncle Gardner was dying, only to discover, like the materialization of one of his nightmares, his brother Alastor already there! Strikingly dressed as usual, with all expression of care, concern, solicitude, clasping their aunt Alida's frail hand and speaking softly and reassuringly to her, and to the others, most of them female relatives, in the visitors' waiting room outside the intensive care unit. As if Alastor had been mysteriously absent from Contracoeur for six years, not having returned even for their mother's funeral; as if he hadn't disappeared abruptly when he'd left, having been involved in a dubious business venture and owing certain of the relatives money, including Uncle Gardner (an undisclosed sum—Lyle didn't doubt it was many thousands of dollars) and Lyle himself (thirty-five hundred dollars).

Lyle had stood in the doorway, staring in disbelief. He had not seen his twin brother in so long, he'd come to imagine that Alastor no longer existed in any way hurtful to him.

Alastor cried, "Lyle, Brother, hello! Good to see you!—except this is such a tragic occasion."

Swiftly, Alastor came to Lyle, seizing his forearm, shaking his hand vigorously as if to disarm him. He was smiling broadly, with his old bad-boyish air, staring Lyle boldly in the face and daring him to wrench away. Lyle stammered a greeting, feeling his face burn. *He has come back like a bird of prey, now that Uncle Gardner is dying.* Alastor nudged Lyle in the ribs, saying in a chiding voice that he'd returned to Contracoeur just by chance, to learn the sad news about their uncle—"I'd have thought, Lyle, that you might have kept your own brother better informed. As when Mother died, too, so suddenly, and I didn't learn about it for months."

Lyle protested, "But you were traveling—in Europe, you said—out of communication with everyone. You—"

But Alastor was performing for Aunt Alida and the others, and so interrupted Lyle to cry, with a pretense of great affection, "How unchanged you are, Lyle! How happy I am to see you." It wasn't enough for Alastor to have gripped Lyle's hand so hard he'd nearly broken the fingers, now he had to embrace him; a rough bearlike hug that nearly cracked Lyle's ribs, calculated to suggest to those who looked on, *See how natural I am, how spontaneous and loving, and how stiff and unnatural my brother is, and has always been, though we're supposed to be twins.* Lyle had endured this performance in the past and had no stomach for it now, pushing Alastor away and saying in an angry undertone, "You! What are you doing here? I'd think you'd be damned ashamed, coming back like this." Not missing a beat, Alastor laughed and said, winking, one actor to another in a play performed for a credulous, foolish audience, "But why, Brother? When you can be ashamed for both of us?" And he squeezed Lyle's arm with deliberate force, making him wince; as he'd done repeatedly when they were boys, daring Lyle to

protest to their parents. *Daring me to respond with equal violence.*
Then slinging a heavy arm around Lyle's shoulders, and walking
him back to the women, as if Lyle were the reluctant visitor, and
he, Alastor, the self-appointed host. Lyle quickly grasped, to his disgust, that Alastor had already overcome their aunt Alida's distrust
of him and had made an excellent impression on everyone, brilliantly playing the role of the misunderstood prodigal son, tender-
hearted, grieved by his uncle's imminent death, and eager—so
eager—to give comfort to his well-to-do aunt.

How desperately Lyle wanted to take Aunt Alida aside, for she
was an intelligent woman, and warn her, *Take care! My brother is after
Uncle Gardner's fortune!* But of course he didn't dare; it wasn't in
Lyle King's nature to be manipulative.

IN THIS WAY, ALASTOR KING returned to Contracoeur.

And within a few days, to Lyle's disgust, he'd reestablished himself
with most of the relatives and certain of his old friends and acquaintances; probably, Lyle didn't doubt, with former women friends.
He'd overcome Alida King's distrust and this had set the tone for the
others. Though invited to stay with relatives, he'd graciously declined
and had taken up residence at the Black River Inn; Lyle knew that his
brother wanted privacy, no one spying on him, but others inter-
preted this gesture as a wish not to intrude, or impinge upon family
generosity. How thoughtful Alastor had become, how kind, how
mature. So Lyle was hearing on all sides. It was put to him repeatedly,
maddeningly: "You must be so happy, Lyle, that your brother has
returned. You must have missed him terribly."

And Lyle would smile warily, politely, and say, "Yes. Terribly."

The worst of it was, apart from the threat Alastor posed to Alida
King, that Lyle, who'd succeeded in pushing his brother out of his
thoughts for years, was forced to think of him again; to think
obsessively of him again; to recall the myriad hurts, insults, out-
rages he'd suffered from Alastor; and the numerous cruel and
even criminal acts Alastor had perpetrated, with seeming impunity.
And of course he was always being thrown into Alastor's company:
always the fraudulent, happy cry, "Lyle! Brother"—always the exuberant, rib-crushing embrace, a mockery of brotherly affection.

On one occasion, when he'd gone to pick up Alastor at the hotel, Lyle had staved Alastor off with an elbow, grimacing. "Damn you, Alastor, stop. We're not on stage, no one's watching." Alastor said, laughing, with a contemptuous glance around, "What do you mean, Brother? Someone is always watching."

It was true. Even on neutral ground, in the foyer of the Black River Inn, for instance, people often glanced at Alastor King. In particular, women were drawn to his energetic, boyish good looks and bearing.

As if they saw not the man himself but the incandescent, seductive image of the man's desire: his wish to deceive.

While, seeing Lyle, they saw merely—Lyle.

What particularly disgusted Lyle was that his brother's hypocrisy was so transparent. Yet so convincing. And he, the less demonstrative brother, was made to appear hesitant, shy, anemic by comparison. Lacking, somehow, manliness itself. Alastor was such a dazzling sight: his hair that should have been Lyle's identical shade of faded ashy-brown was a brassy russet-brown, lifting from his forehead in waves that appeared crimped, while Lyle's thinning hair was limp, straight. Alastor's sharply blue eyes were alert and watchful and flirtatious while Lyle's duller blue eyes were gently myopic and vague behind glasses that were invariably finger-smudged. Apart from a genial flush to his skin, from an excess of food and drink, Alastor radiated an exuberant sort of masculine health; if you didn't look closely, his face appeared youthful, animated, while Lyle's was beginning to show the inroads of time, small worried dents and creases, particularly at the corners of his eyes. Alastor was at least twenty pounds heavier than Lyle, thick in the torso, as if he'd been building up muscles, while Lyle, lean, rangy, with all unconscious tendency to slouch, looked by comparison wan and uncoordinated. (In fact, Lyle was a capable swimmer and an enthusiastic tennis player.) Since early adolescence Alastor had dressed with verve: At the hospital, he'd worn what appeared to be a suit of suede, honey-colored, with an elegantly cut jacket and a black silk shirt worn without a tie; after their uncle's death, he'd switched to theatrical mourning, in muted-gray fashionable clothes, a linen coat with exaggerated padded shoulders, trousers with prominent creases, shirts so pale a blue they appeared a grieving white, and a midnight-blue necktie of some beautiful glossy fabric. And he wore expensive black

leather shoes with soles that gave him an extra inch of height—so
that Lyle, who had always been Alastor's height exactly, was vexed
by being forced *to look up at him.* Lyle, who had no vanity, and
some might say not enough pride, wore the identical matte-black
gabardine suit in an outdated style he'd worn for years on special
occasions; often he shaved without really looking at himself in the
mirror, his mind turned inward; sometimes he rushed out of the
house without combing his hair. He was a sweet-natured, vague-
minded young-old man with the look of a perennial bachelor,
held in affectionate if bemused regard by those who knew him
well, largely ignored by others. After graduating summa cum
laude from Williams College—while Alastor had dropped out,
under suspicious circumstances, from Amherst—Lyle had
returned to Contracoeur to lead a quiet, civilized life: He lived in
an attractively converted carriage house on what had been his
parents' property, gave private music lessons, and designed books
for a small New England press specializing in limited editions distinguished within the trade, but little known elsewhere. He'd had
several moderately serious romances that had come to nothing yet
he harbored, still, a vague hope of marriage; friends were always
trying to match him with eligible young women, as in a stubborn
parlor game no one wished to give up. (In fact, Lyle had secretly
adored his cousin Susan, whom Alastor had seduced; after that
sorry episode, and Susan's subsequent marriage and move to
Boston, Lyle seemed to himself to have lost heart for the game.) It
amused Lyle to think that Alastor was considered a "world traveler"—an "explorer"—for he was certain that his brother had
spent time in prison, in the United States; in Europe, in his late
twenties, he'd traveled with a rich older woman who'd conveniently died and left him some money.

It wasn't possible to ask Alastor a direct question, and Lyle had
long since given up trying. He'd given up, in fact, making much
effort to communicate with Alastor at all. For Alastor only lied to
him, with a maddening habit of smiling and winking and sometimes nudging him in the ribs as if to say *I know you despise me,
Brother. And so what? You're too cowardly to do anything about it.*

AT THE FUNERAL LUNCHEON, Lyle noted glumly that Alastor was seated beside their aunt Alida and that the poor woman, her mind clearly weakened from the strain of her husband's death, was gazing up at Alastor as once she'd gazed at her husband Gardner: with infinite trust. Aunt Alida was one of those women who'd taken a special interest in Lyle from time to time, hoping to match him with a potential bride, and now, it seemed, she'd forgotten Lyle entirely. But then she was paying little attention to anyone except Alastor. Through the buzz and murmur of voices—Lyle winced to hear how frequently Alastor was spoken of, in the most laudatory way—he could make out fragments of their conversation; primarily Alastor's grave, unctuous voice. "And were Uncle Gardner's last days peaceful?—did he look back upon his life with joy?—that's all that matters." Seeing Lyle's glare of indignation, Alastor raised his glass of wine in a subtly mocking toast, smiling, just perceptibly winking, so that no one among the relatives could guess the message he was sending to his twin, as frequently he'd done when they were boys, in the company of their parents. *See? How clever I am? And what gullible fools these others are, to take me seriously?*

Lyle flushed angrily, so distracted he nearly overturned his water goblet.

Afterward, questioned about his travels, Alastor was intriguingly vague. Yet all his tales revolved around himself; always, Alastor King was the hero. Saving a young girl from drowning when a Greek steamer struck another boat, in the Mediterranean; establishing a medical trust fund for beggars, in Cairo; giving aid to a young black heroin addict, adrift in Amsterdam . . . Lyle listened with mounting disgust as the relatives plied Alastor with more questions, believing everything he said no matter how absurd; having forgotten, or wishing to forget, how he'd disappeared from Contracoeur owing some of them money. Alastor was, it seemed, now involved in the importing into the United States of "masterworks of European culture"; elliptically, he suggested that his business would flourish, and pay off investors handsomely, if only it might be infused with a little more capital. He was in partnership with a distinguished Italian artist of an "impoverished noble family." . . . As Alastor sipped wine, it seemed to Lyle that his features grew more vivid, as if he were an actor in a film, magnified many times. His artfully dyed brassy-brown hair framed his thuggish fox-face in crimped waves so that he looked like an animated doll. Lyle would have asked him skeptically who the distinguished artist was, what was the name of their business, but he knew that Alastor would give glib, convincing answers. Except for Lyle, everyone at the table was gazing at Alastor with interest, admiration, and, among the older women, yearning; you could imagine these aging women, shaken by the death of one of their contemporaries, looking upon Alastor as if he were a fairy prince, promising them their youth again, their lost innocence. They had only to believe in him unstintingly, to "invest" in his latest business scheme. "Life is a ceaseless pilgrimage up a mountain," Alastor was saying. "As long as you're in motion, your perspective is obscured. Only when you reach the summit and turn to look back, can you be at peace."

There was a hushed moment at the table, as if Alastor had uttered holy words. Aunt Alida had begun to weep, quietly. Yet there was a strange sort of elation in her weeping. Lyle, who rarely drank, and never during the day, found himself draining his second glass of white wine. *Amanita phalloides. Amanita . . .* he recalled how, years ago, when they were young children, Alastor had so tormented him that he'd lost control suddenly and screamed, flailing at his brother with his fists, knocking Alastor backward, astonished. Their mother had quickly intervened. But Lyle remembered vividly. *I wasn't a coward, once.*

LYLE DROVE ALASTOR BACK to the Black River Inn in silence. And Alastor himself was subdued, as if his performance had exhausted him. He said, musing aloud, "Aunt Alida has aged so, I was shocked. They all have. I don't see why you hadn't kept in closer touch with me, Lyle; you could have reached me care of American Express anytime you'd wanted in Rome, in Paris, in Amsterdam . . . Who will be overseeing the King Foundation now? Aunt Alida will need help. And that enormous English Tudor house. And all that property: thirty acres. Uncle Gardner refused even to consider selling to a developer, but it's futile to hold out much longer. All of the north section of Contracoeur is being developed; if Aunt Alida doesn't sell, she'll be surrounded by tract homes in a few years. It's the way of the future, obviously." Alastor paused, sighing with satisfaction. It seemed clear that the future was a warm beneficent breeze blowing in his direction. He gave Lyle, who was hunched behind the steering wheel of his nondescript automobile, a sly, sidelong glance. "And that magnificent Rolls Royce. I suppose, Brother, you have your eye on *that*?" Alastor laughed, as if nothing was more amusing than the association of Lyle with a Rolls Royce. He was dabbing at his flushed face, overheated from numerous glasses of wine.

Quietly, Lyle said, "I think you should leave the family alone, Alastor. You've already done enough damage to innocent people in your life."

"But—by what measure is 'enough'?" Alastor said, with mock seriousness. "By your measure, Brother, or mine?"

"There is only one measure—that of common decency."

"Oh well, then, if you're going to lapse into 'common' decency," Alistor said genially, "it's hopeless to try to talk to you."

At the Black River Inn, Alastor invited Lyle inside so that they could discuss "family matters" in more detail. Lyle, trembling with indignation, coolly declined. He had work to do, he said; he was in the midst of designing a book, a new limited edition with hand-sewn pages and letterpress printing, of Edgar Allan Poe's short story "William Wilson." Alastor shrugged, as if he thought little of this; not once had he shown the slightest interest in his brother's beautifully designed books, any more than he'd shown interest in his brother's life. "You'd be better off meeting a woman," he said. "I could introduce you to one."

Lyle said, startled, "But you've only just arrived back in Contra-coeur."

Alastor laughed, laying a heavy hand on Lyle's arm, and squeez-ing him with what seemed like affection. "God, Lyle! Are you seri-ous? Women are everywhere. And any time."

Lyle said disdainfully, "A certain kind of woman, you mean."

Alastor said, with equal disdain, "No. There is only one kind of woman."

Lyle turned his car into the drive of the Black River Inn, his heart pounding with loathing of his brother. He knew that Alastor spoke carelessly, meaning only to provoke; it was pointless to try to speak seriously with him, let alone reason with him. He had no conscience in small matters as in large. *What of our cousin Susan? Do you ever think of her, do you feel remorse for what you did to her?*—Lyle didn't dare ask. He would only be answered by a crude, flippant remark which would only upset him further.

The Black River Inn was a handsome "historic" hotel recently renovated, at considerable cost, now rather more a resort motel than an inn, with landscaped grounds, a luxurious swimming pool, tennis courts. It seemed appropriate that Alastor would be staying in such a place; though surely deep in debt, he was accustomed to first-rate accommodations. Lyle sat in his car watching his brother stride purposefully away without a backward glance. Already he'd forgotten his chauffeur.

Two attractive young women were emerging from the front entrance of the inn as Alastor approached. Their expressions when they saw him—alert, enlivened—the swift exchange of smiles, as if in a secret code—cut Lyle to the quick. *Don't you know that man is evil? How can you be so easily deceived by looks?* Lyle opened his car door, jumped from the car, stood breathless and staring at the young women as they continued on the walk in his direction; they were laughing together, one of them glancing over her shoulder after Alastor (who was glancing over his shoulder at her, as he pushed into the hotel's revolving door) but their smiles faded when they saw Lyle. He wanted to stammer—what? Words of warning, or apology? Apology for his own odd behavior? But without slowing their stride the women were past, their glances sliding over Lyle; taking him in, assessing him, and sliding over him. They seemed not to register that Alastor, who'd so caught their eye, and Lyle were twins; they seemed not to have seen Lyle at all.

RECALLING HOW YEARS AGO in circumstances long since forgotten he'd had the opportunity to observe his brother flirting with a cocktail waitress, a heavily made-up woman in her late thirties, still a glamorous woman yet no longer young, and Alastor had drawn her out, asking her name, teasing her, shamelessly flattering her, making her blush with pleasure; then drawing back with a look of offended surprise when the waitress asked him his name, saying, "Excuse me? I don't believe that's any of your business, miss." The hurt, baffled look on the woman's face! Lyle saw how, for a beat, she continued to smile, if only with her mouth; wanting to believe that this was part of Alastor's sophisticated banter. Alastor said, witheringly, "You don't seem to take your job seriously. I think I must have a conversation with the manager." Alastor was on his feet, incensed; the waitress immediately apologized, "Oh no, sir, please—I'm so sorry—I misunderstood—" Like an actor secure in his role since he has played it numberless times, Alastor walked away without a backward glance. It was left to Lyle (afterward, Lyle would realize how deliberately it had been left to him) to pay for his brother's drinks, and to apologize to the stunned waitress, who was still staring after Alastor. "My brother is only joking, he has a cruel sense of humor. Don't be upset, please!" But the woman seemed scarcely to hear Lyle, her eyes swimming with tears; nor did she do more than glance at him. There she stood, clutching her hands at her breasts as if she'd been stabbed, staring after Alastor, waiting for him to return.

IT WOULD BE CREAM of *Amanita phalloides* soup that Lyle served to his brother Alastor when, at last, Alastor found time to come to lunch.

An unpracticed cook, Lyle spent much of the morning preparing the elaborate meal. The soft, rather slimy, strangely cool pale-gray-pulpy fungi chopped with onions and moderately ground in a blender. Cooked slowly in a double boiler in chicken stock, seasoned with salt and pepper and grated nutmeg; just before Alastor was scheduled to arrive, laced with heavy cream and two egg yolks slightly beaten, and the heat on the stove turned down. How delicious the soup smelled! Lyle's mouth watered, even as a vein pounded dangerously in his forehead. When Alastor arrived in a taxi, a half-hour late, swaggering into Lyle's house without knocking, he drew a deep startled breath, savoring the rich cooking aroma, and rubbed his hands together in anticipation. "Lyle, wonderful! I didn't know you were a serious cook. I'm famished."

Nervously, Lyle said, "But you'll have a drink first, Alastor? And—relax?"

Of course Alastor would have a drink. Or two. Already he'd discovered, chilling in Lyle's refrigerator, the two bottles of good Italian chardonnay Lyle had purchased for this occasion. "May I help myself? You're busy."

Lyle had found the recipe for cream of mushroom soup in a battered Fanny Farmer cookbook in a secondhand bookshop in town. In the same shop he'd found an amateur's guide to fungi, edible and inedible, with pages of illustrations. Shabby mane, chanterelles, beefsteak mushrooms—these were famously edible. But there amid the inedible, the sinister lookalike toadstools, was *Amanita phalloides*. The death cup. A white-spored fungi, as the caption explained, with the volva separate from the cap. Highly poisonous. And strangely beautiful, like a vision from the deepest recesses of one's dreams brought suddenly into the light.

The "phallic" nature of the fungi was painfully self-evident. How ironic, Lyle thought, and appropriate. For a man like Alastor who sexually misused women.

It had taken Lyle several days of frantic searching in the woods back beyond his house before he located what appeared to be *Amanita phalloides*. He'd drawn in his breath at the sight—a malevolent little crop of toadstools luminous in the mist, amid the snaky gnarled roots of a gigantic beech tree. Almost, as Lyle quickly gathered them with his gloved hands, dropping them into a bag, the fungi exuded an air of sentient life. Lyle imagined he could hear faint cries of anguish as he plucked at them, in haste; he had an unreasonable fear of someone discovering him. *But those aren't edible mushrooms, those are death cups, why are you gathering those?*

Alastor was seated at the plain wooden table in Lyle's spartan dining room. Lyle brought his soup bowl in from the kitchen and set it, steaming, before him. At once Alastor picked up his soup spoon and began noisily to eat. He said he hadn't eaten yet that day; he'd had an arduous night—"well into the morning." He laughed, mysteriously. He sighed. "Brother, this *is* good. I think I can discern—chanterelles? My favorites."

Lyle served crusty French bread, butter, a chunk of goat's cheese, and set a second bottle of chardonnay close by Alastor's place. He watched, mesmerized, as Alastor lifted spoonfuls of soup to his mouth and sipped and swallowed hungrily, making sounds of satisfaction. How flattered Lyle felt, who could not recall ever having been praised by his twin brother before in his life. Lyle sat tentatively at his place, fumbling with icy fingers to pick up his soup spoon. He'd prepared for himself soup that closely resembled Alastor's but was in fact Campbell's cream of mushroom slightly altered. This had never been a favorite of Lyle's and he ate it now slowly, his eyes on his brother; he would have wished to match Alastor spoon for spoon, but Alastor as always ate too swiftly. The tiny, near-invisible capillaries in his cheeks glowed like incandescent wires; his steely blue eyes shone with pleasure. *A man who enjoys life, where's the harm in that?*

Within minutes Alastor finished his large deep bowl of streaming hot creamy soup, licking his lips. Lyle promptly served him another. "You have more talent, Brother, than you know," Alastor said with a wink. "We might open a restaurant together: I, the keeper of the books; you, the master of the kitchen." Lyle almost spilled a spoonful of soup as he lifted it tremendously to his lips. He was waiting for *Amanita phalloides* to take effect. He'd had the idea that the poison was nearly instantaneous, like cyanide. Evidently not. Or had—the possibility filled him with horror—boiling the chopped-up toadstool diluted its toxin? He was eating sloppily, continually wiping at his chin with a napkin. Fortunately, Alastor didn't notice. Alastor was absorbed in recounting, as he sipped soup, swallowed large mouthfuls of bread, butter, and cheese, and the tart white wine, a lengthy lewd tale of the woman, or women, with whom he'd spent his arduous night at the Black River Inn. He'd considered calling Lyle to insist that Lyle come join him—"As you'd done that other time, eh? To celebrate our twenty-first birthday?" Lyle blinked at him as if not comprehending his words, let alone his meaning. Alastor went on to speak of women generally. "They'll devour you alive if you allow it. They're vampires." Lyle said, fumblingly, "Yes, Alastor, I suppose so. If you say so." "Like Mother, who sucked life out of poor Father. To give birth to *us*—imagine!" Alastor shook his head, laughing. Lyle nodded gravely, numbly; yes, he would try to imagine. Alastor said, with an air almost of bitterness, though he was eating and drinking with as much appetite as before, "Yes, Brother, a man has to be vigilant. Has to make the first strike." He brooded, as if recalling more than one sorry episode. Lyle had a sudden unexpected sense of his brother with a history of true feeling, regret. Remorse? It was mildly astonishing, like seeing a figure on a playing card stir into life.

Lyle said, "But what of—Susan?"

"Susan?—who?" The steely blue eyes, lightly threaded with red, were fixed innocently upon Lyle.

"Our cousin Susan."

"Her? But I thought—" Alastor broke off in mid-sentence. His words simply ended. He was busying himself swiping at the inside of his soup bowl with a piece of crusty bread. A tinge of apparent pain made his jowls quiver and he pressed the heel of a hand against his midriff. A gas pain, perhaps.

Lyle said ironically, "Did you think Susan was dead, Alastor? Is that how you remember her?"

"I don't in fact remember her at all." Alastor spoke blithely, indifferently. A mottled flush had risen from his throat into his cheeks. "The girl was your friend, Brother. Not mine."

"No. Susan was never my friend again," Lyle said bitterly. "She never spoke to me, or answered any call or letter of mine, again. After . . . what happened."

Alistor snorted in derision. "Typical!"

" 'Typical'—?"

"Female fickleness. It's congenital."

"Our cousin Susan was not a fickle woman. You must know that, Alastor, damn you!"

"Why damn *me*? What have I to do with it? I was a boy then, hardly more than a boy, and you—so were *you*." Alastor spoke with his usual rapid ease, smiling, gesturing, as if what he said made perfect sense; he was accustomed to the company of uncritical admirers. Yet he'd begun to breathe audibly; perspiration had broken out on his unlined forehead in an oily glisten. His artfully dyed and crimped hair that looked so striking in other settings looked here, to Lyle's eye, like a wig set upon a mannequin's head. And there was an undertone of impatience, even anger, in Alastor's speech. "Look, she did get married and move away—didn't she? She did—I mean didn't—have a baby?"

Lyle stared at Alastor for a long somber moment.

"So far as I know, she did not. Have a baby."

"Well, then!" Alastor made an airy gesture of dismissal, and dabbed at his forehead with a napkin.

Seeing that Alastor's soup bowl was again empty, Lyle rose silently and carried it back into the kitchen and a third time ladled soup into it, nearly to the brim: This was the end of the cream of *Amanita phalloides* soup. Surely, now, within the next few minutes, the powerful poison would begin to act! When Lyle returned to the dining room with the bowl, he saw Alastor draining his second or third glass of the tart white wine and replenishing it without waiting for his host's invitation. His expression had turned mean, grim; as soon as Lyle reappeared, however, Alastor smiled up at him, and winked. "Thanks, Brother!" Yet there was an air of absolute complacency in Alastor as in one accustomed to being served by others.

Incredibly, considering all he'd already eaten, Alastor again picked up his spoon and enthusiastically ate.

So the luncheon, planned so obsessively by Lyle, passed in a blur, a confused dream. Lyle stared at his handsome, ruddy-faced twin, who spoke with patronizing affection of their aunt Alida—"A befuddled old woman who clearly needs guidance"; and of the King Foundation—"An anachronism that needs total restructuring, top to bottom"; and the thirty acres of prime real estate—"The strategy must be to pit developers against one another, I've tried to explain"; and of the vagaries of the international art market—"All that's required for 1,000-percent profits is a strong capital base to withstand dips in the economy." Lyle could scarcely hear for the roaring in his ears. What had gone wrong? He had mistaken an ordinary, harmless, edible mushroom for *Amanita phalloides*, the death cup? He'd been so eager and agitated out there in the woods, he hadn't been absolutely certain of the identification.

Numbed, in a trance, Lyle drove Alastor back to the Black River Inn. It was a brilliant summer day. A sky of blank blue, the scales of the dark river glittering. Alastor invited Lyle to visit him at the inn sometime soon, they could go swimming in the pool—"You meet extremely interesting people, sometimes, in such places." Lyle asked Alastor how long he intended to stay there and Alastor smiled enigmatically and said, "As long as required, Brother. You know me!"

At the inn, Alastor shook Lyle's hand vigorously, and, on all impulse, or with the pretense of acting on impulse, leaned over to kiss his cheek! Lyle was as startled as if he'd been slapped.

Driving away he felt mortified, yet in a way relieved. *It hasn't happened yet. I am not a fratricide, yet.*

GARDNER KING'S WILL WAS read. It was a massive document enumerating over one hundred beneficiaries, individuals and organizations.

Lyle, who hadn't wished to be present at the reading, heard of the bequest made to him from his brother Alastor, who had apparently escorted Aunt Alida to the attorney's office. Lyle was to receive several thousand dollars, plus a number of his uncle's rare first-edition books. With forced ebullience Alastor said, "Congratulations, Brother! You must have played your cards right, for once." Lyle wiped at his eyes; he'd genuinely loved their uncle Gardner, and was touched to be remembered by him in his will; even as he'd expected to be remembered, to about that degree. *Yes, and there's greater pleasure in the news, if Alastor has received nothing.* At the other end of the line Alastor waited, breathing into the receiver. Waiting for—what? For Lyle to ask him how he'd fared? For Lyle to offer to share the bequest with him? Alastor was saying dryly, "Uncle Gardner left me just a legal form, 'forgiving' me my debts." He went on to complain that he hadn't even remembered he owed their uncle money; you would think, wouldn't you, with his staff of financial advisors, Gardner King could have reminded him; it should have been his responsibility, to remind him; Alastor swore he'd never been reminded—not once in six years. Vividly, Lyle could imagine his brother's blue glaring eyes, his coarse, flushed face, and the clenched self-righteous set of his jaws. Alastor said, hurt, "I suppose I should be grateful for being 'forgiven,' Lyle, eh? It's so wonderfully Christian."

Lyle said coolly, "Yes. It is Christian. I would be grateful, in your place."

"In my place, Brother, how would you know what you would be? You're 'Lyle' not 'Alastor.' Don't give yourself airs."

Rudely, Alastor hung up. Lyle winced as if his brother had poked him in the chest as so frequently he'd done when they were growing up together, as a kind of exclamation mark to a belligerent statement of his.

Only afterward did Lyle realize, with a sick stab of resentment, that, in erasing Alastor's debt to him, which was surely beyond $10,000, their uncle had in fact given Alastor the money; and it was roughly the equivalent of the amount he'd left Lyle in his will. *As if, in his uncle's mind, Alastor and he were of equal merit after all.*

SHE CAME TO HIM when he summoned her. Knocking stealthily at his door in the still, private hour beyond midnight. And hearing him murmur *Come in!* and inside in the shadows he stood watching. How she trembled, how excited and flattered she was. Her girlish face, her rather too large hands and feet, a braid of golden-red hair wrapped around her head. In her uniform that fitted her young shapely body so becomingly. In a patch of caressing moonlight. Noiselessly, he came behind her to secure the door, lock and double-lock it. He made her shiver kissing her hand, and the soft flesh at the inside of her elbow. So she laughed, startled. He was European, she'd been led to believe. A European gentleman. Accepting the first drink from him, a toast to mutual happiness. Accepting the second drink, her head giddy. How flattered by his praise *Beautiful girl! Lovely girl!* And: *Remove your clothes please.* Fumbling with the tiny buttons of the violet rayon uniform. Wide lace collar, lace cuffs. He kissed her throat, a vein in her throat. Kissed the warm cleft between her breasts. *Lee Ann is it? Lynette?* In their loveplay on the king-sized bed he twisted her wrist just slightly. Just enough for her to laugh, startled; to register discomfort; yet not so emphatically she would realize he meant anything by it. *Here, Lynette. Give me a real kiss.* Boldly pressing her fleshy mouth against his and her heavy breasts against his chest and he bit her lips, hard; she recoiled from him, and still his teeth were clamped over her lips that were livid now with pain. When at last he released her she was sobbing and her lips were bleeding and he, the European gentleman, with genuine regret crying *Oh what did I do!—Forgive me, I was carried away by passion, my darling.* She cringed before him on her hands and knees, her breasts swinging. Her enormous eyes. Shining like a beast's. And wanting still to believe, how desperate to believe, so within a few minutes she allowed herself to be persuaded it had been an accident, an accident of passion, an accident for which she was herself to blame, being so lovely, so desirable she'd made him crazed. Kissing her hands, pleading for forgiveness, and at last forgiven and tenderly he arranged her arms and legs, her head at the edge of the bed, her long, wavy, somewhat coarse golden-red hair undone from its braid hanging over onto the carpet. She would have screamed except he provided a rag to shove into her mouth, one in fact used for previous visitors in Suite 181 of the Black River Inn.

"HOW CAN YOU BE so cruel, Alastor!"

Laughing, Alastor had recounted this lurid story for his brother Lyle as the two sat beside the hotel pool in the balmy dusk of an evening, in late June. Lyle had listened with mounting dismay and disgust and at last cried out.

Alastor said carelessly, " 'Cruel'?—why am I 'cruel'? The women love it, Brother. Believe me."

Lyle felt ill. Not knowing whether to believe Alastor or not— wondering if perhaps the entire story had been fabricated, to shock.

Yet there was something matter-of-fact in Alastor's tone that made Lyle think, yes, it's true. He wished he'd never dropped by the Black River Inn to visit with Alastor, as Alastor had insisted. And he would not have wished to acknowledge even to himself that Alastor's crude story had stirred him sexually.

I am falling into pieces, shreds. Like something brittle that has been cracked.

The day after the luncheon, Lyle had returned to the woods behind his house to look for the mysterious fungi; but he had no luck retracing his steps, and failed even to locate the gigantic beech tree with the snaky exposed roots. In a rage he'd thrown away *The Amateur's Guide to Fungi Edible & Inedible.* He'd thrown away *The Fanny Farmer Cookbook.*

Since the failure of the *Amanita phalloides* soup, Lyle found himself thinking obsessively of his brother. As soon as he woke in the morning he began to think of Alastor, and through the long day he thought of Alastor; at night his dreams were mocking, jeering, turbulent with emotion that left him enervated and depressed. It was no longer possible for him to work even on projects, like the book design for Poe's "William Wilson," that challenged his imagination. Though he loved his hometown, and his life here, he wondered despairingly if perhaps he should move away from Contracoeur, for hadn't Contracoeur been poisoned for him by Alastor's presence? Living here, with Alastor less than ten minutes away by car, Lyle had no freedom from thinking of his evil brother. For rumors circulated that Alastor was meeting with local real estate developers though Gardner King's widow was still insisting that her property would remain intact as her husband had wished; that Alastor was to be the next director of the King Foundation, though the present director was a highly capable man who'd had his position for years and was universally respected; that Alastor and his aunt Alida were to travel to Europe in the fall on an art-purchasing expedition, though Alida King had always expressed a nervous dislike, even a terror, of travel, and had grown frail since her husband's death. It had been recounted to Lyle by a cousin that poor Alida had said, wringing her hands, "Oh, I do hope I won't be traveling to Europe this fall, I know I won't survive away from Contracoeur!" and when the cousin asked why on earth she might be traveling to Europe if she didn't wish to, Alida had said, starting to cry, "But I may decide that I do wish to travel, that's what frightens me. I know I will never return alive."

Cocktail service at poolside had ended at 9:00 P.M.; the pool was officially closed, though its glimmering synthetic-aqua water was still illuminated from below; only boastful Alastor and his somber brother Lyle remained in deck chairs, as an eroded-looking but glaring bright moon rose in the night sky. Alastor, in swim trunks and a terry cloth shirt, trotted off barefoot for another drink, and Lyle, looking after him, felt a childish impulse to flee while his brother was in the cocktail lounge. He was sickened by the story he'd been told; knowing himself sullied as if he'd been present in Alastor's suite the previous night. As if, merely hearing such obscenities, he was an accomplice of Alastor's. *And perhaps somehow in fact he'd been there, helping to hold the struggling girl down, helping to thrust the gag into her mouth.*

Alastor returned with a fresh drink. He was eyeing Lyle with a look of bemusement as he'd done so often when they were boys, gauging to what extent he'd shocked Lyle or embarrassed him. After their father's death, for instance, when the brothers were eight years old, Lyle had wept for days; Alastor had ridiculed his grief, saying that if you believed in God (and weren't they all supposed to believe in God?) you believed that everything was ordained; if you were a good Christian, you believed that their father was safe and happy in heaven—"So why bawl like a baby?"

Why, indeed?

Alastor was drunker than Lyle had known. He said commandingly, his voice slurred, "Midnight swim. Brother, c'mon!"

Lyle merely laughed uneasily. He was fully dressed; hadn't brought swim trunks; couldn't imagine swimming companionably with his brother, even as adults; he who'd been so tormented by

Alastor when they were children, tugged and pummeled in the water, his head held under until he gasped and sputtered in panic. *Your brother's only playing, Lyle. Don't cry. Alastor, be good!*

Enlivened by drink, Alastor threw off his shirt and announced that he was going swimming, and no one could stop him. Lyle said, "But the pool is closed, Alastor"—as if that would make any difference. Alastor laughed, swaggering to the edge of the pool to dive. Lyle saw with reluctant admiration and a tinge of jealousy that his brother's body, unlike his own, was solid, hard-packed; though there was a loose bunch of flesh at his waist, and his stomach had begun to protrude, his shoulders and thighs were taut with muscle. A pelt of fine glistening hairs covered much of his body and curled across his chest; the nipples of his breasts were purply-dark, distinct as small staring eyes. Alastor's head, held high with exaggerated bravado as he flexed his knees, positioning himself to dive, was an undeniably handsome head; Alastor looked like a film star of another era, a man accustomed to the uncritical adoration of women and the envy of men. The thought flashed through Lyle like a knifeblade *It's my moral obligation to destroy this man, because he is evil; and because there is no one else to destroy him but me.*

With the showy ebullience of a twelve-year-old boy, Alastor dived into the pool at the deep end; a less-than-perfect dive that must have embarrassed him, with Lyle as a witness; Lyle who winced feeling the harsh slap of the water, like a retributive hand, against his own chest and stomach. Like a deranged seal, Alastor surfaced noisily, blowing water out of his nose, snorting; as he began to swim in short, choppy, angry-looking strokes, not nearly so coordinated as Lyle would have expected, Lyle felt his own arm and leg muscles strain in involuntary sympathy. How alone they were, Lyle and his twin brother Alastor! Overhead the marred moon glared like a light in an examination room.

Lyle thought *I could strike him on the head with—what?* One of the deck chairs, a small wrought-iron table caught his eye. And even as this thought struck Lyle, Alastor in the pool began to flail about; began coughing, choking; he must have inhaled water and swallowed it; drunker than he knew, in no condition to be swimming in water over his head. As Lyle stood at the edge of the pool staring he saw his brother begin to sink. And there was no one near! No witness save Lyle himself! Inside the inn, at a distance of perhaps one hundred feet, there was a murmur and buzz of voices, laughter, music; every hotel window facing the open courtyard and the pool area was veiled by a drape or a blind; most of the windows were probably shut tight, and the room air conditioners on. No one would hear Alastor cry for help even if Alastor could cry for help. Excited, clenching his fists, Lyle ran to the other side of the pool to more closely observe his brother, now a helpless, thrashing body sunk beneath the surface of the water like a weighted sack. A trail of bubbles lifted from his distorted mouth; his dyed hair too lifted, like seaweed. How silent was Alastor's deathly struggle, and how lurid the bright aqua water with its theatrical lights from beneath. Lyle was panting like a dog, crouched at the edge of the pool, muttering, "Die! Drown! Damn your soul to hell! You don't deserve to live!"

The next moment, Lyle had kicked off his shoes, torn his shirt off over his head, and dived into the water to save Alastor. With no time to think, he grabbed at the struggling man, overpowered him, hauled him to the surface; he managed to get Alastor's head in a hammerlock and swim with him into the shallow end of the pool; managed to lift him, a near-dead weight, a dense body streaming water, onto the tile. Alastor thrashed about like a beached seal, gasping for breath; he vomited, coughed, and choked, spitting up water and clots of food. Lyle crouched over him, panting, as Alastor rolled onto his back, his hair in absurd strings about his face and his face now bloated and puffy, no longer a handsome face, as if in fact he'd drowned. His breath was erratic, heaving. His eyes rolled in his head. Yet he saw Lyle, and must have recognized him. "Oh, God, Lyle, w-what happened?" he managed to say.

"You were drunk, drowning. I pulled you out."

Lyle spoke bitterly. He too was streaming water; his clothes were soaked; he felt like a fool, a dupe. Never, never would he comprehend what he'd done. Alastor, deathly pale, weak and stricken still with the terror of death, not hearing the tone of Lyle's voice or seeing the expression of impotent fury on Lyle's face, reached out with childlike pleading to clutch at Lyle's hand.

"Brother, thank you!"

THE WORLD IS A beautiful place if you have the eyes to see it and the ears to hear it.

Was this so? Could it be so? Lyle would have to live as if it were, for his brother Alastor could not be killed. Evidently. Or in any case, Lyle was not the man to kill him.

A WEEK AFTER HE'D saved Alastor from drowning, on a radiantly sunny July morning when Lyle was seated disconsolately at his workbench, a dozen rejected drawings for "William Wilson" scattered and crumpled before him, the telephone rang and it was Alastor announcing that he'd decided to move after all to Aunt Alida's house—"She insists. Poor woman, she's frightened of 'ghosts'—needs a man's presence in that enormous house. Brother, will you help me move? I have only a few things." Alastor's voice was buoyant and easy; the voice of a man perfectly at peace with himself. Lyle seemed to understand that his brother had forgotten about the near-drowning. His pride would not allow him to recall it, nor would Lyle ever bring up the subject. Lyle drew breath to say sharply, "No! Move yourself, damn you," but instead he said, "Oh, I suppose so. When?" Alastor said, "Within the hour, if possible. And, by the way, I have a surprise for you—it's for both of us, actually. A memento from our late beloved Uncle Gardner." Lyle was too demoralized to ask what the memento was.

When he arrived at the Black River Inn, there was Alastor proudly awaiting him at the front entrance, drawing a good deal of admiring attention. A tanned, good-looking, youthful man with a beaming smile, in a pale pinstriped seersucker suit, collarless white shirt, and straw hat, a dozen or more suitcases and valises on the sidewalk; and, in the drive beneath the canopy, a gleaming-black, chrome-glittering Rolls Royce. Alastor laughed heartily at the look on Lyle's face. "Some memento, eh, Brother? Aunt Alida was so sweet, she told me, 'Your uncle would want both you boys to have it. He loved you so—his favorite nephews.' "

Lyle stared at the Rolls Royce. The elegant car, vintage 1971, was as much a work of art, and culture, as a motor vehicle. Lyle had ridden in it numerous times, in his uncle's company, but he'd never driven it. Nor even fantasized driving it. "How—did it get here? How is this possible?" Lyle stammered. Alastor explained that their aunt's driver had brought the car over that morning and that Lyle should simply leave his car (so ordinary, dull, and plebeian a car—a compact American model Alastor merely glanced at, with a disdainful look) in the parking lot, for the time being. "Unfortunately, I lack a valid driving license in the United States at the present time," Alastor said, "or I would drive myself. But you know how scrupulous I am about obeying the law—technically." He laughed, rubbing his hands briskly together. Still Lyle was staring at the Rolls Royce. How like the hearse that had borne his uncle's body from the funeral home to the church it was; how magnificently black, and the flawless chrome and windows so glittering, polished to perfection. Alastor poked Lyle in the ribs to wake him from his trance and passed to him, with a wink, a silver pocket flask. Pure scotch whiskey at 11:00 A.M. of a weekday morning? Lyle raised his hand to shove the flask aside but instead took it from his brother's fingers, lifted it to his lips, and drank.

And a second time, drank. Flames darted in his throat and mouth, his eyes stung with tears.

"Oh! God."

"Good, eh? Just the cure for your ridiculous anemia, Brother," Alastor said teasingly.

While Alastor settled accounts in the Black River Inn, using their aunt's credit, Lyle and an awed, smiling doorman loaded the trunk and plush rear seat of the Rolls with Alastor's belongings. The sun was vertiginously warm and the scotch whiskey had gone to Lyle's head and he was perspiring inside his clothes, murmuring to himself and laughing. *The world is a beautiful place. Is a beautiful place. A beautiful place.* Among Alastor's belongings were several handsome new garment bags crammed, apparently, with clothing. There were suitcases of unusual heaviness that might have been crammed with—what? Statuary? There were several small canvases (oil paintings?) wrapped hastily in canvas and secured with adhesive tape; there was a heavy sports valise with a broken lock, inside which Lyle discovered, carelessly wrapped in what appeared to be women's silk underwear, loose jewelry of all kinds—gold chains, strings of pearls jumbled together, a silver pendant with a sparkling red ruby, bracelets and earrings and a single brass candlestick holder and even a woman's high-heeled slipper, stained (bloodstained?) white satin with a carved mother-of-pearl ornament. Lyle stared, breathless. What a treasure trove! Once, he would have been morbidly suspicious of his brother, suspecting him of theft—and worse. Now he merely smiled, and shrugged.

By the time Lyle and the doorman had loaded the Rolls, Alastor emerged from the inn, slipping on a pair of dark glasses. By chance—it must have been chance—a striking blond woman was walking with him, smiling, chatting, clearly quite impressed by him—a beautiful woman of about forty with a lynx face, a bold red mouth, and diamond earrings, who paused to scribble something (telephone number? address?) on a card and slip it into a pocket of Alastor's seersucker coat.

Exuberantly, Alastor cried, "Brother, let's go! Across the river and to Aunt Alida's—to our destiny."

Like a man in a dream Lyle took his place behind the wheel of the Rolls; Alastor climbed in beside him. Lyle's heart was beating painfully, with an almost erotic excitement. Neither brother troubled to fasten his seat belt; Lyle, who'd perhaps never once driven any vehicle without fastening his seat belt first, seemed not to think of doing so now as if, simply by sliding into this magnificent car, he'd entered a dimension in which old, tedious rules no longer applied. Lyle was grateful for Alastor passing him the silver flask, for he needed a spurt of strength and courage. He drank thirstily, in small choking swallows: how the whiskey burned, warmly glowed, going down! Lyle switched on the ignition, startled at how readily, how quietly, the engine turned over. Yes, this was magic. He was driving his uncle Gardner King's Rolls Royce is if it were his own; as he turned out of the hotel drive, he saw the driver of an incoming vehicle staring at the car, and at him, with frank envy.

And now on the road. In brilliant sunshine, and not much traffic. The Rolls resembled a small, perfect yacht; a yacht moving without evident exertion along a smooth, swiftly running stream. What a thrill, to be entrusted with this remarkable car; what sensuous delight in the sight, touch, smell of the Rolls! Why had he, Lyle King, been a puritan all of his life? What a blind, smug fool to be living in a world of luxury items and taking no interest in them; as if there were virtue in asceticism; in mere ignorance. Driving the Rolls on the highway in the direction of the High Street Bridge, where they would cross the Black River into the northern, affluent area of Contracoeur in which their aunt lived, Lyle felt intoxicated as one singled out for a special destiny. He wanted to shout out the car window *Look! Look, at me! This is the first morning of the first day of my new life.*

Not once since Alastor's call that morning had Lyle thought of—what? What had it been? The death-cup mushroom, what was its Latin name? At last, to Lyle's relief, he'd forgotten.

Alastor sipped from the pocket flask as he reminisced, tenderly, of the old Contracoeur world of their childhood. That world, that had seemed so stable, so permanent, was rapidly passing now, vanishing into a newer America. Soon, all of the older generation of Kings would be deceased. "Remember when we were boys, Lyle? What happy times we had? I admit, I was a bit of a bastard, sometimes—I apologize. Truly. It's just that I resented you, you know. My twin brother." His voice was caressing yet lightly ironic.

"Resented me? Why?" Lyle laughed, the possibility seemed so far-fetched.

"Because you were born on my birthday, of course. Obviously, I was cheated of presents."

Driving the daunting, unfamiliar car, that seemed to him higher built than he'd recalled, Lyle was sitting stiffly forward, gripping the elegant mahogany steering wheel and squinting through the windshield as if he were having difficulty seeing. The car's powerful engine vibrated almost imperceptibly, like the coursing of his own heated blood. Laughing, though slightly anxious, he said, "But, Alastor, you wouldn't have wished me not to have been born, would you? For the sake of some presents?"

An awkward silence ensued. Alastor was contemplating how to reply when the accident occurred.

Approaching the steep ramp of the High Street Bridge, Lyle seemed for a moment to lose the focus of his vision, and jammed down hard on the brake pedal; except it wasn't the brake pedal but the accelerator. A diesel truck crossing the bridge, belching smoke, seemed then to emerge out of nowhere as out of a tunnel. Lyle hadn't seen the truck until, with terrifying speed, the Rolls careened up the ramp and into the truck's oncoming grille. There was a sound of brakes, shouts, a scream, and as truck and car collided, a sickening wrenching of metal and a shattering of glass. Together the vehicles tumbled from the ramp, through a low guardrail, and onto an embankment; there was an explosion, flames; the last thing Lyle knew, he and his shrieking brother were being flung forward into a fiery-black oblivion.

THOUGH BADLY INJURED, THE driver of the diesel truck managed to crawl free of the flaming wreckage; the occupants of the Rolls Royce were trapped inside their smashed vehicle, and may have been killed on impact. After the fire was extinguished, emergency medical workers would discover in the wreckage the charred remains of two Caucasian males of approximately the same height and age; so badly mangled, crushed, burned, they were never to be precisely identified. As if the bodies had been flung together from a great height, or at a great speed, they seemed to be but a single body, hideously conjoined. It was known that the remains were those of the King brothers, Alastor and Lyle, fraternal twins who would have been thirty-eight years old on the following Sunday. But which body was which, whose charred organs, bones, blood had belonged to which brother, no forensic specialist would ever determine.

Cream of Mushroom Soup

¼ cup butter (divided use)
1 small onion, finely chopped
8 oz. fresh mushrooms, sliced
Two 14.5-oz. cans chicken stock (or 4 cups home-
    made)
2 Tbsp. flour or cornstarch
¾ tsp. salt (or to taste)
1 cup cream
¼ cup white wine or 2 Tbsp. light sherry
Fresh chives, finely chopped, to garnish (optional)

MELT TWO TABLESPOONS butter in large skillet. Add onion, sauté until clear and soft. Add mushrooms and sauté for about two minutes, until mushrooms are brown and limp. Add chicken stock and simmer on medium heat for 15 minutes, stirring occasionally. While the stock is simmering, melt remaining butter in a large saucepan. Slowly add flour or cornstarch, stirring constantly, and cook until thick and bubbly to make a roux. Add salt. Add chicken stock very slowly, stirring constantly, until liquid is smoothly incorporated into the mixture. Add cream slowly, stirring constantly. Add white wine or sherry, stir. Serve soup warm, topped with fresh chives.

Poison Peach

Gillian Linscott

". . . care must be taken not to bruise any part of the shoot; the wounds made by the knife heal quickly, but a bruise often proves incurable."
—*The Gardener's Monthly Volume*. "The Peach."
George W. Johnson and R. Errington. October 1847.

J anuary was the time for pruning. In the peach house the journeyman gardeners untied the branches from their wires on the whitewashed wall and spread them out as delicately as spiders spinning webs. The fruit-house foreman stepped among them with his bone-handled knife, trimming off the dead wood that had carried last year's fruit, choosing the shoots for this year's. Behind him an apprentice moved like an altar boy with a small basket, picking up every piece of branch as it fell. Few words were said, or needed to be said.

In the eighty years since the peach houses had been built by the grandfather of the present owner, this same ritual had gone on, winter after winter. Victoria ruled an empire and died, apprentices took root and grew into head gardeners, the nineteenth century turned the corner into the twentieth, and always, just after the turn of the year, with the solstice past but the days not yet perceptibly lengthening, the trees were pruned in the peach house at Briarley.

From the door between the peach house and the grape house, Henry Valance watched as his father and his grandfather had

watched before him, all of them decent, careful men, accepting
their role of guarding, cautiously improving, passing on to sons.
What was different this January was that Henry's wife, Edwina,
stood beside him, staring out through the sloping glass at the bras-
sicas and bare soil of the kitchen garden. In the five years they'd
been married, Edwina hadn't taken a great interest in the garden,
being more concerned with the house and the duties of a hostess—although not yet of a mother. She didn't seem very interested
now, but in the last few months had accepted her husband's timid
suggestions on how to spend her time as if they were commands,
following him dutifully but without the animation that had once
sparked in her every word or movement. Her hair under the
turban hat was still as glossy as the shoulder of a chestnut horse,
her tall figure graceful in the long astrakhan coat she wore
because it was cold, even inside the glass houses. But her hands,
smoothly gloved in silver-gray kid, were clasped tightly together
and her face was as blank as the winter sky.

HER HUSBAND MOVED CLOSER to her so that the men working on the
peaches couldn't hear them.

"I've had a letter from Stephen."

Over the past few months they'd fallen into the habit of talking
about the things that mattered in almost public places, with the
servants not far away. It limited the scope for damage. She moved
her head a little, still looking out at the vegetable garden, as if the
stiff rows of brussels sprouts might creep away if not watched.

"It seems he's written a book."

"What kind of book?"

"A novel."

"Why would he do that?"

Her voice had always been low. Now it was scarcely alive.

"He says he needs to make a career for himself." She said nothing. He glanced at her face, then away at the peach pruning. "I've
written offering to pay him. I've told him I'll double whatever he's
expecting to make from it, if he'll agree not to publish."

"He won't accept."

She said it with flat certainty. They stood for a while, then he gave her his arm and they walked away through the glass galleries of the grape house and the empty melon house scrubbed clean for winter, their feet echoing on the iron gratings. In the peach house, the foreman watched as two journeymen used strips of cloth to tie to the wall, fan-shaped, the tree he'd pruned back. He signaled them to stop, stepped forward with his pruning knife, hesitated over a fruiting spur, and then, without cutting, nodded to them to carry on. The shape was right after all and the shoot should live to carry its peach. Behind the fruit houses men were cleaning and riddling the great boiler that fed hot water into the pipes under the floor gratings. Soon, when the pruning was finished and the stopcock turned to start the artificial indoor spring, the sap would begin to rise up the narrow trunks, along the spread branches, and into that spur, along with the rest. For a day or two longer the peach trees could rest.

BY APRIL THE PEACH house was warm and full of pink blossoms, although the air outside hadn't lost the edge of winter. Amongst the petals, the gardeners fought their campaign against small pests that might threaten the setting of the fruit. An apprentice with a brass syringe walked the aisles between the trees, spraying the leaves with tobacco water to control the aphids. A journeyman with a paintbrush worked a mixture of sulfur and soft soap into every joint and crevice to kill off the eggs of red spiders and kept an eye on the apprentice at the same time.

"Careful with that bloody thing. You nearly knocked that spur clean off."

In fact, the apprentice's momentary carelessness had scarcely dislodged a petal, and the journeyman's attention was not wholly on the killing of spider eggs and aphids. Things were happening that even the apprentices knew about and the waves that had started in the family rooms of the house had spread out through the upper staff down to the kitchens, out through the scullery door to the gardeners who carried up baskets of vegetables every day. A collection had been organized among the journeyman gardeners and a discreet order placed at the bookshop in the nearest town. The groom was to collect the result of it when he went down to the station, along with the other copies ordered by the upstairs staff, the kitchen staff, and the stables. The butler, who had connections in London, was believed to have got his hands on a copy already but wasn't showing anybody. At lunchtime the journeyman gardeners gathered in their bothy behind the wall at the back of the fruit houses, made themselves as comfortable as possible on sacks and buckets, and elected a reader. His attempts to make an orderly start at the beginning of chapter 1 were immediately voted down.

"That's not what all the trouble's about. Start at the business between him and her, and we'll go back to the beginning later."

"If we want to."

Laughter, but muted. They were allowed half an hour in the bothy for their bread and cheese, but what they were doing was no part of their duties and could lead to trouble, and even dismissal for impudence, if discovered. The door had been firmly shut in the noses of the apprentices but was no protection against foreman or head gardener. The reader asked, plaintively, how he was supposed to know where the business was.

"They don't put it in the margins like they do with the Bible."

"I heard it was chapter 10."

The reader rustled pages, scanned silently, then whistled between his teeth.

Several voices told him to get on with it and not keep it to himself.

"It's where she calls him in to give him a piece of her mind because he's been getting too friendly with one of the maids."

"Is that how they put it—too friendly?"

"Oh, get on with it."

Now it had come to it, they were all a little embarrassed. The man trusted with the book read it in a fast mutter so that they had to crane forward to hear him. The lady calls the gentleman into her boudoir. She is stern. She does not usually listen to servants' gossip, but he must realize that the young housemaids are in her care and as employer she has a moral duty to them and to their parents. If the gentleman can assure her that these rumors are baseless then she will take severe action against the people spreading them. A sound outside. The men froze, but it was only two apprentices trying to listen and they were seen off, nursing cuffed ears.

"Go on."

The gentleman cannot give her that assurance. He compliments her instead on her good taste in employing such very attractive housemaids. She is unbelieving at first, then furious. He remains calm then asks her if she is not, perhaps, jealous, She loses control and actually tries to hit him. He grabs her by the wrist and she falls back across the sofa, her furious black eyes gazing up at him. He stands looking down at her, smiling a little inward smile.

"Well, what happens after that?"

"Nothing. It's the end of the chapter."

He turned the book toward them to show the blank half page.

"Well, go on to the next one then."

He turned the page.

"It doesn't go on. Not with that, anyway. It goes back to the husband at his club."

"Well, what does he—"

The bothy door opened suddenly. In the doorway was the square, bowler-hatted figure of the head gardener himself, who could dismiss all of them with a snap of his fingers, quick as pulling an earwig in half.

"What do you men think you're doing? You've been nearly an hour in here."

Then he saw the book and snatched it out of the reader's hand.

"I'm ashamed of you all. You should know where this filth belongs."

With the journeymen trailing shamefaced after him and the apprentices peering from behind the pot shed, he marched across the yard to the barrel that held liquid fertilizer, pats of cow dung seething in rainwater. He nodded to one of the men to remove the lid, tossed the book into it, and waited while it globbed into the viscous depths. Another nod, and the lid went back.

"If I catch anybody in my gardens dirtying his hands with that again, if I catch anybody even mentioning it or looking as if he's thinking about it, he'll be applying for a new post without a character. Now get back to your work, all of you."

Dispiritedly they went, two of them toward the fruit houses.

"Tell you what, though, he got one thing wrong."

"What's that?"

"Her eyes aren't black—they're brown."

They laughed at that but sobered up when they found Hobbes, the fruit foreman, waiting for them, and couldn't meet his eyes.

". . . neither peaches nor nectarines acquire perfection, either in richness or flavor, unless they be exposed to the full influence of the sun during their last swelling."

—*An Encyclopaedia of Gardening*
J. C. Loudon, 1835.

BY LATE JUNE THE peaches were close to perfection. Cosseted and watched over from the time the first green knobs formed behind the blossom, scrutinized and selected until there was just one fruit to every spur, all they waited for now was their final ripening. In case the midsummer sun should be too strong and scorch them through the glass, early every morning Hobbes would stand among the orderly rows of leaves, looking up, then say a few words, quietly as in church, to his assistant. The assistant would operate a wheel to open rows of ventilating panes, inch by inch, until they were at the exact angle to give a gentle circulation of air, and the process would be repeated every few hours as the sun climbed. Once the ventilators were open the peach house was tidied as carefully as a drawing room, every fragment of loam swept off the path, every tree checked for the slightest sign of insect damage, because by this time the season was at its height and the peaches were out in society. Briarley was famous for its fruit houses, and a stroll between breakfast and lunch past the swelling grapes, under green and golden melons hanging among their heavy leaves, was almost a social duty for guests. In fact, there'd not been many guests at Briarley that season, but the fruit houses were always kept ready for them, as they always had been. Today Henry Valance came on his morning visit alone. Alone, that is, apart from the train that followed at a respectful distance, first the head gardener, then Hobbes the foreman, then the two journeymen with particular responsibility for fruit.

Occasionally, he'd pause, palpate and sniff a melon, finger a grape. When this happened the head gardener would catch up with him and a few serious words would be exchanged. The procession made its slow way to the peach house and stopped between the rows of trees.

"Nearly ripe then, are they?"

A nod from the head gardener signaled to Hobbes to come closer. It was a sign of the respect he had for Hobbes as a master in his own field that he allowed the foreman to answer the employer's question directly. Hobbes stood there in his dark suit and hat in the green-dappled shade, gardening apron discarded for this formal visit, watch chain gleaming.

"The Hale's Early should be ripe by next Monday, sir, and the Early Beatrice not long after. Then the Rivers and the Mignonnes are coming on very nicely."

"Excellent. We'll look forward to that."

Henry's father and grandfather had stood in the same place and used much the same words. The difference was in the flatness of his voice that said everything he might have looked forward to was already in the past. Then, with an effort:

"You'll make sure we have plenty ripe for the second weekend in July, won't you? We have a lot of people coming, house quite full."

The two journeymen exchanged glances. It would be the first house party since it happened. The staff had been speculating that there wouldn't be any this year.

"We'll make sure, sir."

His question had not been necessary. It was the work of them all to see that there were ripe peaches all through the summer, whether there were guests to eat them or not. Still, there was no resentment that he'd asked it. He was, on the whole, liked by the gardening staff—and pitied.

"Nets . . . are perfectly useless in keeping off wasps and other insects, as they will alight on the outside and, folding their wings, pass through those of the smallest meshes."

—*An Encyclopaedia of Gardening*

THERE WAS THE SOUND of footsteps coming through the glass galleries from the direction of the house, too light and quick for a gardener's, too confident for a maid's. Hurrying steps. The man went tense.

"Henry."

His wife's voice with scarcely controlled panic in it. He met her in the doorway.

"A letter for you. It's just arrived."

She held it out to him. At first he'd looked simply puzzled. Dozens of letters arrived every day, and it was no part of Edwina's duties to chase him round the estate with them. Then he saw the handwriting. Took it from her and read.

"He's heard about the house party. He's inviting himself."

"No!"

The gardeners were in an impossible position. To eavesdrop on employers' private conversation was unthinkable. On the other hand, it was equally unthinkable to melt away through the door into the kitchen garden, since they'd been given no sign to go. They made a great business of scrutinizing the peach leaves, which they already knew were perfect.

"Write to him. Tell him he can't come."

"I can't do that. He is my brother, after all."

"He can't come if you don't let him."

"He'd come in any case, and what could I do then? Call the police to bring a van and drag him away? Tell the men to throw him in the lake, with the house full of visitors? It would mean that people would go on talking about it for years."

"That's what he wants."

"Yes, and the only way we can prevent him from getting it is facing it out, letting him come here."

"No."

But it was a different word now, numb and dispirited. He put out a hand to her, but she moved away and her slow steps back toward the house seemed to go on for a long time.

THE HEAD GARDENER SAID kindly: "The figs are doing very nicely, sir. Would you care to look at them?"

"Figs. Yes, certainly, figs."

As they were moving off, the head gardener stopped suddenly.

"Excuse me, sir, but look at that."

He pointed at one of the peaches. An intake of breath from the gardeners.

"A wasp. Early for them, isn't it?"

The insect was sitting, wings folded, on the down of a peach. Hobbes stepped forward, mortified.

"I'm sorry, sir."

One of the journeymen ventured, unasked: "The lad was saying he'd seen a nest of them at the back of the pot shed."

The head gardener glared at him.

"Well, why didn't you do something about it? See to it, will you, Hobbes." His instruction to the foreman was less brusque than it might have been, considering the shame of the wasp's invasion. Hobbes nodded and the party moved on.

"A gentle squeeze at the point where the stalk joins the fruit will soon determine whether it be ripe enough."
—*The Gardener's Monthly Volume:* "The Peach"

JULY, AND THE SCENT of ripe peaches hung on the air like a benignant gas. Every morning the foreman would pick the ripest and lay them gently onto a padded tray held by the apprentice, ready for the house party at lunch. All but a few. It was a custom at Briarley that some of the best fruit should be left on the trees for the look of it when the visitors walked round, glowing through green like the eyes of a sleepy animal. But the party hadn't reached the peach house yet, lingering on the way to admire the ripe purple clusters on the grapevine. Murmurs of admiration and white-gloved hands reaching out, almost touching but stopping just before making contact, unwilling to smudge a bloom on the fruit like the first morning in Eden. But one pair of hands, male and gloveless, kept moving, breached the invisible barrier, picked a grape. A little shiver, half shocked, half pleased, ran through the party. Relishing the attention, the picker put the grape in his mouth. His lips were full, for a man's, and as he munched he let the underside of his lower lip show, slick and smooth.

"Is it good?"

The woman guest who asked the question had dark piled hair and wide eyes. She smelt of carnations, and her dressmaker had been perhaps a shade too attentive in cutting her dress so exactly to the curve of her full breasts. Instead of answering in words, the man picked another grape and held it a half inch from her lips. Her eyes flickered sideways to where her host and hostess were standing, then she opened her lips in a little round pout just wide enough to let the grape in, dipped her head, and took it from his fingers like a bird.

"Yes, very good."

A silence, then from the side of the group, their host's voice: "Shall we go and look at the peaches?" But he couldn't stop himself adding: "If you've had enough, Stephen."

"Oh, enough for now, don't you think?"

The party moved on in silence.

"It is common practice to lay littery material beneath the trees to save from bruising the fruit which falls, and sometimes those which fall are extremely luscious."

— *The Gardener's Monthly Volume*. "The Peach"

ON SUNDAY MORNING THE day started later. Only a few guests came to the fruit houses between breakfast and lunch. Host and hostess went to church as usual. A few of the house party went with them, but it was a hot day and most preferred to stroll by the lake or in the lime avenue. After lunch, with the weekend drawing to its close, the strolls became lazier and polite slow-motion competition developed for places on rustic benches under the trees. Afterward, nobody knew who had proposed another tour of the fruit houses. It might have been a suggestion from the host—certainly not one from Edwina, because she had a headache and had retired to the drawing room after lunch, with an old friend in attendance. The suggestion might have come from Stephen, as he'd been the focus of the younger set in the part for most of the weekend. A stranger

might have taken him for the host instead of his brother, although
his behavior toward Henry and Edwina had been entirely correct
throughout. He'd let it be known that he enjoyed being back at the
old place so much that he thought he might stay for the week.
Whoever suggested it, the proposal collected a little following and
about a dozen people joined the tour, including the woman who
smelt of carnations. Some of the older guests felt that for a woman
whose husband was working abroad she'd been a little too eager for
Stephen's company over the weekend. Late at night, among some
of the men lingering in the billiard room after too much port,
there'd been jokes about Stephen doing research for his next
novel, only not in Henry's hearing. Only one more night to go and
she'd be leaving on Monday morning. The men in the billiard
room had even been placing bets.

SUN, FOOD, AND WINE swept away the touch of solemnity that usually
went with the fruit house tour. Stephen was triumphant, unstop-
pable. He ranged along the fruit-smelling avenues like a big child,
greedy to see, touch, taste. The younger element in the party had
caught his mood. The woman who'd eaten the grape had competition now as they all fingered, dared, ate. A melon was parted from
its stem and thrown from hand to hand until golden flesh and pips
splattered on the red-tiled floor. Henry watched, impassive. Farther
back, not part of the party, the head gardener watched, equally
impassive. He stayed ten yards behind them as they laughed and
pattered through the grape house, leaving the bunches blemished
with bare stems and torn tongues of purple skin.

WHEN THEY GOT TO the green-dappled shade of the peach house,
Hobbes was at work there, and it looked for a moment as if he
were going to commit the sackable sin of rudeness to his
employer's guests in defense of his cherished peaches. He actually
stood for a moment in the path of the party until the head gardener caught his eye, and he stood reluctantly aside. This little

stutter of opposition seemed to increase Stephen's pleasure. He
challenged one of the women to eat a peach without picking it.
She moved her lips toward a red and golden fruit that trembled on
its stem with ripeness. Hobbes started toward her, perhaps intending to hand it to her with proper respect for lady and peach. The
head gardener looked alarmed at the impending breach of eti-
quette and might have stopped him, but at the last minute the
woman drew her face away from the peach, giggling.

"You can't. It would fall. Nobody could."

"Yes, you can. All you need is a soft mouth. Look."

In silence, with them all watching him, Stephen advanced on
the largest peach in sight. It hung conveniently on a level with his
chin, standing out from the leaves on its spur. He bent a little at
the knees and turned his head back so that the fruit was almost
resting on his mouth. His teeth closed on it. Juice ran down his
chin, dribbled onto the lapel of his white jacket. A little gasp from
one of the women, hushed at once. The peach shifted a little,
rotating on its stem, but still didn't fall. His neck muscles tensed
and he took another, larger bite. Then there was a little cracking
sound and he was falling, falling backward with the peach
clenched in his jaws. This time the gasps weren't hushed but
turned to screams. Because of the way he'd been standing, the
back of his head hit the iron grating with a crash that sent every
leaf in the place quivering. Then voices.

"Choking. For heaven's sake, get it out of his mouth."

"Air. Get some air in here."

"Get the ladies out."

"Isn't there a doctor?"

Henry was at the front of the group, along with the head gardener and the foreman. They turned Stephen over, wrenched the
peach from his teeth. From the look of his contorted face it
seemed likely that he'd choked on the fruit before his head hit the
grating, but since he couldn't be dead twice over, that didn't seem
to matter. Henry got to his feet coughing, staggered backward
against the wall, then was violently sick.

"Get him outside. Get him into the air."

"Everybody, outside."

"A piece of cloth fastened to a stick, soaked in a saturated solution of cyanide of potassium, is immediate death to all wasps within or returning to the nest."

—*The Fruit Grower's Guide*
John Wright. 1892.

IT TOOK SOME TIME for the doctor to reach Briarley, and while they waited for him doubts were already setting in, mainly because of the smell. Several of the men besides Henry were coughing as they came out of the peach house, and a woman collapsed and had to be revived. When Henry and most of the party were on their way back to the house, the head gardener, Hobbes, and a few of the male guests covered the body with clean sacks. Then they shut the door firmly and waited on the other side of it in the grape house, the guests smoking, the two gardeners standing a little apart from them. When the doctor arrived at last they followed him in but stood at a safe distance although most of the smell had worn off by then. He peeled back the sack from the face.

"What did you say happened?"

"He was eating a peach and he choked."

He examined the body briefly, then told them they should cover it up again but not do anything else until the police arrived. He was a comparatively new doctor in the village, Scottish and conscientious. The old doctor might have managed things more tactfully.

THE VERDICT WAS NEVER in doubt: Stephen Valance had deserved what he got. If you seduce your brother's maidservant, then his wife, and—and for a profit—tell the world about it, you can't complain if your peach turns out to contain cyanide. Even those who had quite liked Stephen and watched his career with interest felt a kind of satisfaction that there was a limit after all, although there had been some sporting interest in seeing how far and fast a man could go before he hit it. Stephen had chosen to ride his course that way and by the natural law of things he was heading for a fall. No more needed to be done and very little said, except in private when the servants were out of the room.

THAT, AT ANY RATE, was the immediate verdict of society. The verdict of the country's system of justice was another matter and at first seemed likely to throw up more difficulties. That Stephen had died by cyanide poisoning and that the carrier of the poison had been the peach was never seriously in doubt. The hopeful theory of suicide in a moment of well-earned remorse was abandoned instantly by anybody who had the slightest acquaintance with Stephen or his reputation. Which left . . .

"Well, I suppose if it comes right down to it, it has to be murder."

The discussion was going on very late at night in the billiard room. Not that anybody had actually tried to play billiards, which would have been totally inappropriate on a Sunday, with the hostess prostrate upstairs, the host at her bedside, and the host's younger brother in the mortuary. The men who had influence had naturally congregated there—not the giddier sort who had followed Stephen but the more sober ones who had known Henry's father, who sat as magistrates and chose men to stand for Parliament.

"You can't blame him. I'd have done the same thing myself."

"Not very nice, poison."

"Quick, though. Practically painless, I'd have thought. Anyway, what can you do? I mean, you can't challenge a man to a duel in this day and age."

"I suppose the next thing's the inquest. They can bring in murder by person or persons unknown . . ."

"Or they can even name the person they think did it, if they think there's enough evidence."

Silence, while they considered it.

"Of course, there's always accidental death."

"There was a glass vial of cyanide in that peach. How does that get in there accidentally?"

"They use cyanide to kill wasp nests in glass houses. At any rate, my gardener does, and I don't suppose Henry's are any different. You get a lot of wasps after peaches."

More silence, finally broken by the oldest man amongst them.

"I think I'd better have a word with his head gardener in the morning."

"Only professional men can use it safely."
—*The Fruit Grower's Guide*

HOBBES STOOD IN A shaft of sunlight in the coroner's court, dark-suited in his Sunday best, new bowler hat on the table in front of him, and gave his evidence. By that point the court had already heard from the brother of the deceased, from two doctors, from a police officer, and from the head gardener, who clearly remembered telling the fruit foreman to do something about the wasps in the peach house. The coroner had been respectful to the brother's grief, businesslike with the doctors and the head gardener. To the fruit foreman his tone was colder, and Hobbes answered respectfully. He had been in Mr. Valance's employment for twenty years. Yes, he had used potassium cyanide on a wasp's nest; they kept a drum of it for the purpose in the pot shed. No, he did not know how it had come to contaminate a peach. Yes, he had been warned to be careful with it and knew that it was poisonous. If any of it had somehow come onto the fruit, from his gardening gloves or some tool, then that was very great carelessness. Could he think of any other way that the cyanide might have come onto the peach? No sir, he could think of no other way. There was a rustling and sighing in the court, like heavy leaves in a breeze. The coroner paused to let the answer sink in, then turned to another aspect of the matter. The doctor who had certified death and the police officer had noticed small fragments of glass in the peach.

"It was put on the floor, sir, by one of the gentlemen, when they took it out of his mouth."

"You're suggesting that was when the glass became attached to it?"

"Yes, sir."

"Are you accustomed to leaving glass fragments lying on the floor of your employer's fruit houses?"

"Not accustomed, no sir."

"And yet glass fragments were there?"

"Yes, sir."

"Should we assume that this was another example of carelessness?"

It took Hobbes some time to realize that an answer was required. When he did he said "Yes, sir" again in the same respectful voice. At last he was permitted to stand down. The head gardener—who would hardly allow a petal to settle on the floor of the glass houses for more than a second or two—looked straight ahead throughout the foreman's evidence, face expressionless. In his summing-up the coroner had some hard things to say about carelessness by men who should know better. Hobbes took them all, head bent over the bowler hat that rested on his knees. The verdict was accidental death.

OUTSIDE THE COURT, ONE of Henry Valance's friends went up to Hobbes as he stood on his own among departing cars and carriages.

"Well, Hobbes, always best to own up to things."

"Yes, sir."

"I gather Mr. Valance is letting you keep your position."

"Yes, sir."

"A very generous man, Mr. Valance. I'm sure you're grateful."

"Yes, sir."

And although he'd been one of the chief movers in arranging things so satisfactorily, the friend really did feel that Henry was acting generously. The coroner's rebuke had wrapped itself around Hobbes and his deplorable carelessness with cyanide was now a fact of history, officially recorded.

"Anyway, I don't suppose it will happen again."

"No, sir."

Both men took their hats off as the Valances' motor car drove slowly past, with Edwina sitting very upright beside her husband, pale under her heavy veil.

BY OCTOBER THE PEACH season was almost over. A few Prince of
Wales and Lady Palmerstons still gleamed among the leaves, but
there hadn't been much call for peaches from the household, or
many tours of the glass houses. Henry made his dutiful rounds
from time to time and exchanged a few words with Hobbes about
indifferent things, but that was all. One morning when there was
already a frosty feel to the air outside, the head gardener came in
while Hobbes was retying labels on wires. There was nobody else
within hearing.

"All well, Hobbes?"

"Yes."

The head gardener looked out through the panes to where the
men were digging over a potato plot.

"Some people are saying you got left with the dirty end of the
stick. Still, you said your piece very well and you didn't lose by it."

No response. The head gardener's attention seemed to be all
on the men outside, then he said: "Funny, the things you find
when you dig."

The wire under Hobbes's hand suddenly tightened and began
vibrating. He kept his head down.

"What are you thinking of?"

"End of July, I was in the herb garden and I noticed this little
freshly dug patch right at the back of the angelica. Now, I hadn't
told anyone to dig there. I went and got a spade from the shed and
turned it over to have a look. What do you suppose I found there?"

Hobbes's grip on the wire was now so tight that the tree branch
it supported was quivering too.

"Peaches, that's what I found. I backed off quickly, I can tell
you. There's a paving slab over them now, in case of any more accidents."

The tree branch was near to breaking when Hobbes released
his grip of the wire and straightened up. The head gardener took
his arm, not roughly.

"Of course, you couldn't be sure he'd take that one peach so
you'd have to do a few of them. And you were going to stop the
lady when she looked like biting into one of them instead."

Hobbes nodded. "How did you know?"

"That it was you? Well, Mr. Valance might have done the one of
them, but to do more than one like that you needed to be neat-
fingered and you needed to have time. Nobody has more time in

the peach house than you do, and nobody's got neater fingers. I've watched you grafting fruit trees."

Hobbes took the compliment with another nod.

"And another thing I know—I know why you did it, and I don't blame you."

The foreman looked at the head gardener's face, then the words surged out of him.

"They were all talking about what he'd done to her, to Mrs. Valance, as if my girl didn't matter. All this about the book, everybody reading about what he'd done to the housemaid, to my girl, and the lady calling him in to talk about it and then he . . . When I knew he had the face to come back here, laughing at us, I started thinking—supposing I did so and so. And, well, I did it."

The head gardener's hand stayed on his arm. Anybody looking into the peach house from outside would have seen nothing but two men enjoying the autumn sunshine on their employer's time.

"How is your girl?"

"Gone to her aunt in Wales. They've put it about that the father's a sailor lost at sea. She won't be coming back here."

Silence. They were two men used to patience, but Hobbes gave way first.

"Let's be going and get it over with."

"It *is* over. You've been careless. The coroner said so."

"But—"

"Be quiet. I'm thinking."

"I thought you'd already done the thinking."

"That space over there. Do you think another couple of Rivers or maybe Lord Napiers instead?"

Hobbes stared first at the blank white wall, then at him.

"You're asking me that—now?"

"Why not? None too soon for you to start planning for next year, is it?"

"For next year . . ."

It took him some time to understand. When he did he said thank you and turned back to the fruit trees. A spur, fruitless now, snagged at his cuff, but he freed it with a hand still shaking a little and went on with his work.

Perfect Peach Pie

CRUST FOR A 9-inch double-crust pie, either homemade or purchased (for the time-crunched cook, Pillsbury refrigerated piecrusts are excellent). In peach season, 2 pounds fresh peaches, blanched, peeled, pitted, and sliced. Out of season, two 12-oz. bags frozen unsweetened peach slices (prepared fruit should be about 4 to 5 cups)

> 2 Tbsp. lemon juice
> ¾ cup sugar
> 2 Tbsp. flour
> ½ tsp. cinnamon
> ½ tsp. salt
> 3 Tbsp. chilled butter, cut into small cubes
> 1 Tbsp. sugar
> ½ tsp. cinnamon

SET AN EMPTY cookie sheet on the bottom rack of your oven. This will save the oven bottom if the pie boils over and will keep the bottom crust from burning. Preheat oven to 400 degrees F.

PLACE PEACH SLICES in a large mixing bowl. Add lemon juice, toss to coat. In a smaller bowl, mix together ¾ cup sugar, flour, ½ teaspoon cinnamon, and salt. Pour dry mixture over peach slices, toss to coat. Put coated peach slices into bottom crust. Arrange them in a nice rounded pile. Sprinkle butter cubes on top of filling. Cover with top crust, and crimp and prick the top crust. Sprinkle one tablespoon sugar and ¼ teaspoon cinnamon over the top crust. Set the pie in the preheated oven on the middle rack. Bake the pie at 400 degrees F. for 15 minutes. Without opening the oven, reduce the heat to 300 degrees F. Bake about 50 more minutes, until crust is browned and flaky, and the filling is thick and bubbly. Serve warm or cold.

Of Course You Know That Chocolate Is a Vegetable

Barbara D'Amato

O f course you know that chocolate is a vegetable," I said. "Lovely! That means I can eat all I want," Ivor Sutcliffe burbled, reaching his fork toward the flourless double-fudge cake.

Eat more *than you want, you great tub of guts,* I thought. The tub-of-guts part was rather unfair of me; I could stand to lose a pound or two myself. What I said aloud was, "Of course it's a vegetable. Has to be. It's not animal or mineral, surely. It grows on a tree—a large bush, actually, I suppose. It's as much a vegetable as pecans or tomatoes. And aren't we told to have several servings of vegetables every day?"

We were seated at a round table covered with a crisp white cloth at Just Desserts, a scrumptious eatery in central Manhattan that specializes in chocolate desserts, handmade chocolate candy, and excellent coffees. Just Desserts was willing to serve salads and a few select entrees to keep themselves honest, but if you could eat chocolate, why would you order anything else?

"I must say, Ms. Grenfield, it's very handsome of you to invite me after my review of your last book," Ivor said, dropping a capsule on his tongue, which then took the medication inside, his mouth clos-ing like a file drawer. He washed the medication down with coffee.

I said, "No hard feelings. Reviewing books is your job."

"I may have been just a bit harsh."

Harsh? Like scrubbing your eyeball with a wire brush is harsh? I said, "Well, of course an author's feelings get hurt for a day or two. But we can't hold it against the critic. Not only is it his job, but, to be frank, it's in our best interests as writers to keep on pleasant terms. There are always future reviews to come, aren't there?"

"Very true."

Ivor's review had begun:

> In *Snuffed*, the victim, Rufus Crown, is dispatched with a gaseous fire extinguisher designed for use on fires in rooms with com-puter equipment and other such unpleasant hardware, though neither the reader nor the fictional detectives know this at the start when his dead but mysteriously unblemished body is found. The reader is treated to long efforts—quite incompatible with character development—on the part of the lab and medical examiner to establish what killed him.

"That's right; give away the ending," I had snarled to myself when I read this.

Snuffed had been universally praised by the critics and I thought I was a shoo-in for an award until the Ivor Sutcliffe review came out.

At the awards banquet, where I was not a nominee, fortune had seated me next to Sutcliffe. Just when the sorbet arrived, and I had happily pictured him, facedown, drowning in strawberry goo, he began to wheeze. My mind had quickly changed to picturing him suffocating. But he had popped a capsule in his greedy pink mouth and after a few minutes he quit wheezing.

Since one has to be moderately cordial at these events, or at least appear to be, I asked courteously, "Do you have a cold?"

"Asthma," he said.

"Sorry to hear that. My son had asthma. Seems to have out-grown it."

"Lucky for him. What did he take for it?"

I said, "Theophylline."

"Ah, yes. That's what my doctor gave me. So proud of his big words, just like you. Standard treatment, I believe. I have been taking it for several weeks." He said this as if conferring a great benediction upon the drug.

I was about to relate an anecdote about the time my husband, son, and I were on a camping trip, without the theophylline. We'd left it at home, since it had been many months since Teddy's last attack, and we weren't expecting trouble. Then Teddy had developed a wheeze. As evening came on, it got worse. And worse. There's nothing scarier than hearing your child struggle for breath. We were two hours away from civilization, and my husband and I panicked. We packed Teddy into the car, ready to race for the nearest country hospital; then I had called Teddy's doctor on my cell phone.

"Do you have any coffee?" he said. Well, of course we had. Who went camping without coffee?

"Give him some. Caffeine is chemically similar to theophylline. Then drive to the hospital."

All this I was about to tell Sutcliffe when something stopped me. It was not more than the faint aroma of an idea, a distant stirring of excitement. So—theophylline and caffeine were similar. Hmm.

Teddy had been warned to take his theophylline as directed, but never to overdose.

Then and there I invited Sutcliffe out to a "good will" snack the following week. He accepted. Well, my will was going to feel the better for it.

Sutcliffe's review had gone on:

> I deplore the substitution of technical detail for real plotting. One could amplify the question "Who cares who killed Roger Ackroyd?" by asking, "Who cares how Roger Ackroyd was killed?" No one cares what crime labs and pathologists really do.

"Agatha Christie cared," I had whispered as I read it, trying not to gnash my teeth. "And Dorothy Sayers and just about everybody then and just about everybody now on any best-seller list—Crichton, Clark, Cornwell, Grisham." In the first place, readers like to learn things. Second, technology is real and it's *now*. Third, it's exacting. Keeps a writer honest. You can't fake technical detail; it has to be right. You can't use the untraceable exotic poison these days. It has to be something people know about or even use every day. Or know they *should* know about. Then it's tantalizing.

But Ivor Sutcliffe wasn't scientific-minded. A know-it-all who knew nothing. A gross, hideous, undisciplined individual with bad table manners. I had once seen him, at a banquet, eat his own dinner and the dinners of three other guests who had failed to show.

So after the banquet I went home to my shelf of reference books, looking for something I almost knew about, or knew I should know about—just like a reader of fiction. I keep a large shelf of reference books. Having them at hand saves time, effort, and parking fees.

What would an overdose of theophylline do to a human being?

I turned first to the *Physician's Desk Reference.* This is a huge volume, twenty-eight hundred pages of medications, with their manufacturers, their brand names, their appearance shown in color pictures, their uses, their dosages, their effects, their adverse effects, and—overdosage.

An overdosage of theophylline was serious business. It said, "Contact a poison-control center." That was good. One didn't issue that kind of warning for minor side effects. I read on. One had to monitor the dose carefully. Apparently, the useful dose and dangerous dose were not far apart. I read on. Overdosage could produce restlessness, circulatory failure, convulsion, collapse, and coma. Or death.

Theophylline in normal use, it said, relaxed the smooth muscles of the bronchial airways and pulmonary blood vessels, acting as a bronchodilator and smooth-muscle relaxant. That was why it helped an asthma attack.

And then the punch line: "Theophylline should not be administered concurrently with other xanthines." And what were xanthines?

I turned to my unabridged dictionary. Why, xanthines included theophylline, caffeine (given Teddy's experience, this was no surprise), and the active ingredient of chocolate, theobromine. Aha!

Hmmm. Being similar, they would have an additive effect, wouldn't they? Synergistic, maybe? I turned to the *Merck Manual,* also huge, a twenty-seven-hundred-page volume, a bible of illnesses, their causes and treatments. In its section on poisons, caffeine poisoning was in the same sentence with theophylline poisoning. Among the symptoms of both were restlessness, circulatory-system collapse, and convulsions.

A medical text told me that 50 percent of theophylline convulsions result in death.

Isn't this fun? Research is so rewarding.

Well, I knew that theophylline was potentially deadly. Now, what about the caffeine?

My book on coffees from around the world told me that a cup of coffee, depending on how it's brewed, contains 70 to 150 milligrams of caffeine. Drip coffee is strongest. Well, what about the extra-thick specialty coffees at Just Desserts? Could I assume they might have 200 milligrams?

What the book didn't tell me was how much caffeine would kill.

I pulled out the *Merck Index*, a different publication from the *Merck Manual*, the *Index* being an encyclopedia of chemicals. Here I found that if you had a hundred mice and gave them all 137 milligrams of caffeine per kilogram of body weight, half would die. This was cheerfully called LD 50, or lethal dose for 50 percent. My dictionary said a kilogram is 2.2 pounds. So if a man reacted like a mouse (although to me Ivor was more like a rat), that would work out to 13.7 grams of caffeine per 220 pounds. Of course, getting 13 grams of caffeine into the 220-plus-pound Ivor was not going to happen, but then caffeine was not the only xanthine that was going to be going into Ivor.

A volume for the crime writer on poisons told me that one gram of caffeine could cause toxic symptoms, but it didn't tell me how much would kill. Well, if one gram was toxic, two grams ought to cause real trouble.

Now, what about theobromine, the xanthine in chocolate? The *Merck Index* informed me that theobromine, "the principal alkaloid of the cacao bean," was a smooth-muscle relaxant, diuretic, cardiac stimulant, and vasodilator. My, my! Sounded a lot like theophylline and caffeine. It said chocolate also contained some caffeine. That couldn't hurt.

How could I find out how much chocolate was dangerous? Certainly, people eat large amounts with no ill effects. But at some point, with the other two xanthines . . ?

I turned on my computer, thinking to get on the Net and ask how much theobromine there was in an average piece of dark bittersweet chocolate. But I held my hand back. This could be dangerous. I could be traced. Somewhere I had heard of people receiving catalogues from companies that sold items they had queried the Net about. Like travel brochures when they'd asked about tourist destinations or smoked salmon when they'd asked about where to get good fish. Webmasters could learn everything about you. I certainly didn't want anybody to know I was the person making queries about theobromine in chocolate. Could I ask anonymously? No. How could I be sure the query couldn't be traced?

Then I remembered the library at the local law school. If you looked like you belonged there, you could query databases at no charge, although there was a time limit. And there was a per-page charge if you wanted to print out what you found, but why should I want it in black and white? Now, if they just didn't ask for names. I grabbed my coat and ran out the door.

Two hours later I left the library highly pleased. I'd asked two databases to find articles that used "chocolate" within ten words of "theobromine" and got all kinds of good stuff. Chocolate, it seemed, frequently killed dogs. Dogs and cats didn't excrete the theobromine as well as humans. The poisoned animals would suffer rapid heart rates, muscle tremors, rapid respiration, convulsions, and even death.

Dark chocolate, I learned, contains ten times as much theobromine as milk chocolate. Bitter cooking chocolate contains four hundred milligrams in an ounce! And—oh, yes!—the amount in a moderate amount of chocolate is about the same as the amount of caffeine in a moderate amount of coffee.

In humans, theobromine is a heart stimulant, smooth-muscle relaxant, and dilates coronary arteries. So what if we eliminate it faster than Rover would? It still had to have an additive effect with the other two.

All three of my drugs caused low blood pressure, irregular heart rhythm, sweating, convulsions, and, potentially, cardiac arrest. What's not to like? Ha! *Take that!* I thought. Hoist with your own petard.

The *PDR* had said that oral theophylline acted almost as swiftly as intravenous theophylline. But I knew I would need time to get a lot of coffee and chocolate into Ivor. He'd better not feel sick right away and just stop eating. Well, the desserts themselves should slow the absorption.

At this point in my research I phoned Sutcliffe and suggested we hold our rendezvous at Just Desserts.

When the day came and we sat down like two friends at Just Desserts, I encouraged Ivor to try the dense "flourless chocolate cake" first.

"It's excellent," I said. "Like a huge slice of dark chocolate. I'll have a piece myself." The waiter brought the cake promptly and filled our coffee cups with mocha-java.

We tasted, nodded in appreciation, ate in companionable silence for a few minutes. Then I suggested he try the Turkish coffee, just for comparison, along with an almond-chocolate confection, for the blend of flavors. He agreed readily.

Now, since he was eating at my expense, he found the need to be borderline pleasant. "You know, I did say in the review that I've liked much of your past work."

Actually, no, you clot. His review of my first book, graven on my heart, said, "This novel is obviously the work of a beginner." And his review of my second book, also etched somewhere in my guts, said, "Ms. Grenfield has not yet got her sea legs for the mystery genre." The most recent review had, in fact, damned with faint praise: *This effort,* Snuffed, *is not up to her former standard.*

"Thank you," I said mildly.

"I suppose I should be frightened of eating with you, Ms. Grenfield. I've read so many novels where the central character, feeling wronged, invites his nemesis to dinner and poisons him."

"Well, Ivor, I was actually aware you might worry about that. I had thought of inviting you to my home. But it occurred to me that you might find it intimidating to be at the mercy of my cooking. Hence—Just Desserts."

Disarmed and possibly a little abashed, Sutcliffe said, "Well—you could hardly have found a more competent kitchen than this."

I nodded agreeably as Ivor finished his third cup of coffee—one regular, two Turkish so far—and pushed his cup within reach of the waiter. The calculator in my brain said that was six hundred milligrams of caffeine now, give or take, and another two hundred on the way as the hot brew filled the cup.

Let's see. Add the capsule of theophylline just half an hour ago when he arrived. Didn't dare ask him the dosage, but it had to be either the standard 300 or the 400-milligram dose. Plus he had taken his morning dose, I supposed.

Ha! Well, me fine beauty, we'll just see how inartistic technology is. And we'll give you every chance to save yourself. Just a little paying of attention, Ivor. A morsel of humility.

Lord! That man could eat! *Schokoladenpudding*, which was a German chocolate-coffee-almond pudding served warm with whipped cream. *Rigo Jancsi* squares, dense Viennese cake that was more like frosting, which the waiter explained was named after a Gypsy violinist. And a slice of Sacher torte, a Viennese chocolate cake glazed with dark chocolate. *Shokoladno mindalnyi tort*, a Russian chocolate-almond torte made with rum, cinnamon, and, of all things, potato. Then just to be fair to the United States, he agreed to a simple fudge brownie with chocolate frosting, à la mode, as he put it, with coffee ice cream on the side. I had cherry strudel.

With each dessert he tried a different coffee. Ethiopian *sidamo*, Kenyan *brune*, a Ugandan dark roast. In my coffee reading I had noted that the *robusta* coffees have more than twice as much caffeine as the *arabica* species, and smiled indulgently as he drank some.

Two grams of caffeine by now, minimum. Clever of me to suggest he switch to the demitasses of various strong coffees. Just as strong and less filling. He could drink more of them.

Plus two to maybe four or five grams of theobromine from the chocolate.

"What are you working on these days, Ms. Grenfield?" Ivor said in his plummy voice. Could I detect a slight restless, hyper edge in his tone now?

"A mystery with historical elements," I answered, and almost giddy with delight, lobbed him a clue. "About Balzac, and the discovery of some unknown, unpublished, very valuable manuscript." Balzac, of course, an avid, indeed compulsive coffee drinker, died of caffeine poisoning. Let's see if this self-important arbiter, this poseur, was any better at literature than he was at science.

"Oh, interesting," he drawled in boredom. "You know, I *could* just manage another dessert."

"Of course!" I caroled in glee. "How about a chocolate mousse? And another Turkish coffee to go with it." The waiter appeared, beaming. "And I'll have a vanilla cream horn."

"This is very pleasant," he said, chuckling as be plunged a spoon into his new dessert and gobbled the glob. "Actually, I'm rather surprised."

"Why?"

He became distracted, watching as another waiter passed with a silver tray of various chocolate candies on a lace doily—the house specialty, glossy dark bittersweet chocolates with various fillings, handmade in their own kitchens. I raised a finger, said, "One of each for the gentleman," and pointed at Ivor. The waiter tenderly lifted the little beauties from the tray with silver tongs and placed them on a white china dish near Ivor's hand.

"Why surprised?" I reminded him.

He said, "I'd always thought of you as lacking in appreciation of the finer things."

"Oh, surely not."

"All those bloody and explicit murders, or poisons with their effects lovingly detailed. Hardly the work of a subtle mind."

"*Au contraire*, Ivor. I am very subtle."

"Well, I suppose it does require a certain amount of delicacy to keep the knowledge of whodunit from a reader until the end." He fidgeted as if nervous.

"Yes. Until the end."

Ivor began to cram the candies into his chunky, piggy cheeks. The pitch of his voice was rising, not louder but more shrill. Satiated, he pushed the dish away.

"Come on. Have another chocolate."

"I shouldn't."

"Oh, you only live once."

"Well, maybe just a taste or two." His fat hand, as he reached for the morsels, showed a faint tremor. He shifted his bulk. Restlessness.

Time for another clue, Ivor. Last chance, Ivor.

"Did you know that the botanical name for the cacao tree is Greek and that it translates to 'food of the gods'? *Theobroma*," I said, trying not to chortle. Last chance, Ivor, you who know so much.

"Nope. Didn't know that. Rather apt, actually," he said without interest. He didn't care about this detail, either, didn't care how close to theophylline it sounded. His flushed face was a bit sweaty, seen in the subdued restaurant light. In fact, he looked as if he had been lightly buttered. He cleared his throat, took another swallow of coffee, and said, "Odd. I'm feeling a little short of breath."

"Your asthma?"

"Could be."

"That's too bad. Well, you know how to deal with it, anyhow."

"Ah—whew." Puff. "Yes."

"Well, shouldn't you do something? Don't you think you should take one of your pills?"

"I already did when I got here. The doc says don't exceed two per day."

"But that's a preventative dose, isn't it? If you have an attack coming on—?"

"Probably right." He groaned as he leaned his heavy bulk sideways to claw in his pocket for the pill vial. Wheezing harder, he drew it out. He tipped a capsule into his hand.

"Here," I said helpfully, and I pushed his cup of *robusta* coffee toward him. The waiter topped it up again.

"Hmmmp," was all the thanks he managed as he popped the pill and swallowed the java.

For another minute or so, Ivor sat still, catching his breath or whatever. His face was flushed, and he moved his head back and forth as if confused.

"Are you feeling all right, Ivor?"

"I may have eaten just a tad too much."

"Well, let's just sit awhile, then."

"Yes. Yes, we'll do that."

Ivor sat, but his hands twitched, then his fingers started to pleat and smooth the tablecloth. He took in deep breaths and let them out. His face was pinker still, almost the color of rare roast beef.

"I'm not sure about that tie you're wearing, Ivor," I said. "It's not up to your former standard."

Ivor goggled at me, but his bulging eyes were unfocused. He blew his cheeks out, let them sag back, then blew them out again. His head began to bob up and down in a kind of tremor.

"And that suit," I said. "A fine, well-bred wool. Quite incompatible with your character."

No answer. I said, "But perhaps that's a bit harsh."

He leaned forward, holding onto the table. Very slowly he drifted sideways, then faster and faster, until he fell off his chair, pulling the snowy white tablecloth, silver forks and spoons, a china cup, the remains of brownie à la mode, and the dregs of *robusta* coffee with him.

"Oh, my goodness!" I shouted.

The waiter came running. I fanned Ivor with a menu. "Stand back. Give him air," I said. The waiter stepped back obediently.

The manager came running also. He tried the Heimlich maneuver. No luck. Several diners stood up and gawked. Ivor was making bubbling, gasping sounds.

"That's not a fainting fit," the manager said, obviously a more analytical chap than the waiter.

"I guess not," I said.

The manager wrung his hands. "What should we do? What should we do?"

"Maybe it's an asthma attack. He carries some pills for it. They're in his pocket, I think."

The manager felt in Ivor's pocket. He read the label. A genuine doctor's prescription in a real pharmacy container. "Yes. Here they are. At least they can't hurt."

"This coffee is cool enough," I said. "Wash it down with this." He did, even though Ivor choked a lot and showed no awareness of what was going on.

"Call the paramedics," the manager told the waiter, who bustled away. The manager slapped Ivor's cheek. I envied the man this role, but had to stand by. Ivor produced no reaction to being slapped, now well and truly in a coma.

The paramedics arrived with reasonable promptness. The one with the box of medical supplies knelt by Ivor to take vital signs. The second said, "What can you tell us about this? What happened?"

I shook my head. "I can't imagine. He was just eating a perfectly delicious chocolate dessert."

Ivor gasped, but did not rouse. His cheeks were taking on a purplish hue, the color of a fine old burgundy.

I thought of the last line of Ivor Sutcliffe's review:

In Snuffed, *the only thing deader than Rufus Crown is Ms. Grenfield's plot.*

French Silk Pie

Prepared crust for single-crust 9-inch pie, either
   homemade or purchased
3 oz. dark chocolate, broken into small pieces
2 sticks butter, slightly softened
1 cup sugar
1 cup egg substitute (4 whole eggs can be used, but
   since the filling isn't cooked, be absolutely sure
   they are Pasteurized)
2 cups sweetened whipped cream, or 1 small container whipped topping, thawed
1 oz. dark chocolate, shredded into curls to garnish
   (optional)

PREHEAT OVEN TO 450 degrees F. Prick and weight piecrust (pie
weights work best, but lining the piecrust with heavy-duty foil and
filling the foil with either dried beans or coins will do the job, too.)
Bake piecrust for 9 to 11 minutes, until brown and flaky. Remove
from oven and remove pie weights as soon as they are cool enough
to handle. Set piecrust aside to cool completely (usually about an
hour from the time it was removed from the oven).

MELT CHOCOLATE OVER very low heat in a small saucepan. Set aside
to cool. (Chocolate can also be melted in a microwave with 10-
second bursts at medium power, stirring after each burst until the
chocolate is smooth and fully melted, if preferred, but this is
riskier. Be very careful not to burn or scorch the chocolate. It takes
longer on the stove, but the risk of destroying the chocolate is
much lower than in the microwave.)

CREAM (MIX UNTIL light and fluffy, and sugar grains can't be felt)
butter and sugar in mixing bowl. Add melted chocolate and blend.
Add vanilla, blend. Slowly add egg substitute, beating until mixture
is light, smooth, and fluffy. Pour mixture into cooked piecrust.
Refrigerate for at least three hours.

TO SERVE, TOP with whipped cream or whipped topping and garnish with chocolate curls.

Poison à la Carte

Rex Stout

I slanted my eyes down to meet her big brown ones, which were slanted up. "No," I said, "I'm neither a producer nor an agent. My name's Archie Goodwin, and I'm here because I'm a friend of the cook. My reason for wanting it is purely personal."

"I know," she said, "it's my dimples. Men often swoon."

I shook my head. "It's your earrings. They remind me of a girl I once loved in vain. Perhaps if I get to know you well enough—who can tell?"

"Not me," she declared. "Let me alone. I'm nervous, and I don't want to spill the soup. The name is Nora Jaret, without an *H*, and the number is Stanhope five, six-six-two-one. The earrings were a present from Sir Laurence Olivier. I was sitting on his knee."

I wrote the number down in my notebook, thanked her, and looked around. Most of the collection of attractive young females were gathered in an alcove between two cupboards, but one was over by a table watching Felix stir something in a bowl. Her profile was fine and her hair was the color of corn silk just before it starts to turn. I crossed to her, and when she turned her head I spoke. "Good evening, Miss—Miss?"

"Annis," she said. "Carol Annis."

I wrote it down, and told her my name. "I am not blunt by nature," I said, "but you're busy, or soon will be, and there isn't time to talk up to it. I was standing watching you and all of a sudden I had an impulse to ask you for your phone number, and

I'm no good at fighting impulses. Now that you're closed up it's even stronger, and I guess we'll have to humor it."

But I may be giving a wrong impression. Actually, I had no special hankering that Tuesday evening for new telephone numbers; I was doing it for Fritz. But that could give a wrong impression too, so I'll have to explain.

One day in February, Lewis Hewitt, the millionaire orchid fancier for whom Nero Wolfe had once handled a tough problem, had told Wolfe that the Ten for Aristology wanted Fritz Brenner to cook their annual dinner, to be given as usual on April 1, Brillat-Savarin's birthday. When Wolfe said he had never heard of the Ten for Aristology, Hewitt explained that it was a group of ten men pursuing the ideal of perfection in food and drink, and he was one of them. Wolfe had swiveled to the dictionary on its stand at a corner of his desk, and after consulting it had declared that "aristology" meant the science of dining, and therefore the Ten were witlings, since dining was not a science but an art. After a long argument Hewitt had admitted he was licked and had agreed that the name should be changed, and Wolfe had given him permission to ask Fritz to cook the dinner.

In fact, Wolfe was pleased, though of course he wouldn't say so. It took a big slice of his income as a private detective to pay Fritz Brenner, chef and housekeeper in the old brownstone on West 35th Street—about the same as the slice that came to me as his assistant detective and man Friday, Saturday, Sunday, Monday, Tuesday, Wednesday, and Thursday—not to mention what it took to supply the kitchen with the raw materials of Fritz's productions. Since I am also the bookkeeper, I can certify that for the year 1957 the kitchen and Fritz cost only slightly less than the plant rooms on the roof bulging with orchids.

So when Hewitt made it clear that the Ten, though they might be dubs at picking names, were true and trustworthy gourmets, that the dinner would be at the home of Benjamin Schriver, the shipping magnate, who wrote a letter to *The Times* every year on September 1 denouncing the use of horseradish on oysters, and that the cook would have a free hand on the menu and the Ten would furnish whatever he desired, Wolfe pushed a button to summon Fritz. There was a little hitch when Fritz refused to commit himself until he had seen the Schriver kitchen, but Hewitt settled that by escorting him out front to his Heron town car and driving him down to Eleventh Street to inspect the kitchen.

That's where I was that Tuesday evening, April 1, collecting phone numbers—in the kitchen of the four-story Schriver house on Eleventh Street west of Fifth Avenue. Wolfe and I had been invited by Schriver, and though Wolfe dislikes eating with strangers and thinks that more than six at table spoils a meal, he knew Fritz's feelings would be hurt if he didn't go; and besides, if he stayed home who would cook his dinner? Even so, he would probably have balked if he had learned of one detail which Fritz and I knew about but had carefully kept from him: that the table was to be served by twelve young women, one for each guest.

When Hewitt had told me that, I had protested that I wouldn't be responsible for Wolfe's conduct when the orgy got under way, that he would certainly stamp out of the house when the girls started to squeal. Good Lord, Hewitt said, nothing like that; that wasn't the idea at all. It was merely that the Ten had gone to ancient Greece not only for their name but also for other precedents. Hebe, the goddess of youth, had been cupbearer to the gods, so it was the custom of the Ten for Aristology to be waited on by maidens in appropriate dress. When I asked where they got the maidens he said through a theatrical agency, and added that at that time of year there were always hundreds of young actresses out of a job glad to grab at a chance to make fifty bucks, with a good meal thrown in, by spending an evening carrying food, one plate at a time. Originally, they had hired experienced waitresses from an agency, but they had tripped on their stolas.

Wolfe and I had arrived at seven on the dot, and after we had met our host and the rest of the Ten, and had sampled oysters and our choice of five white wines, I had made my way to the kitchen to see how Fritz was making out. He was tasting from a pot on the range, with no more sign of fluster than if he had been at home getting dinner for Wolfe and me. Felix and Zoltan, from Ruster-man's, were there to help, so I didn't ask if I was needed.

And there were the Hebes, cupbearers to the gods, twelve of them, in their stolas, deep rich purple, flowing garments to their ankles. Very nice. It gave me an idea. Fritz likes to pretend that he has reason to believe that no damsel is safe within a mile of me, which doesn't make sense since you can't tell much about them a mile off, and I thought it would do him good to see me operate at close quarters. Also, it was a challenge and an interesting sociolog-ical experiment. The first two had been a cinch: one named Fern Faber, so she said, a tall blonde with a wide lazy mouth, and Nora Jaret with the big brown eyes and dimples. Now I was after this Carol Annis with hair like corn silk.

"I have no sense of humor," she said and turned back to watch Felix.

I stuck. "That's a different kind of humor and an impulse like mine isn't funny. It hurts. Maybe I can guess it. Is it Hebe one, oh-oh-oh-oh?"

No reply.

"Apparently not. Plato two, three-four-five-six?"

She said, without turning her head, "It's listed. Gorham eight, three-two-one-seven." Her head jerked to me. "Please?" It jerked back again.

It rather sounded as if she meant please go away, not please ring her as soon as possible, but I wrote it down anyway, for the record, and moved off. The rest of them were still grouped in the alcove, and I crossed over. The deep purple of the stolas was a good contrast for their pretty young faces topped by nine different colors and styles of hairdos. As I came up the chatter stopped and the faces turned to me.

"At ease," I told them. "I have no official standing. I am merely one of the guests, invited because I'm a friend of the cook, and I have a personal problem. I would prefer to discuss it with each of you separately and privately, but since there isn't time for that—"

"I know who you are," one declared. "You're a detective and you work for Nero Wolfe. You're Archie Goodwin."

She was a redhead with milky skin. "I don't deny it," I told her, "but I'm not here professionally. I don't ask if I've met you because if I had I wouldn't have forgot—"

"You haven't met me. I've seen you and I've seen your picture. You like yourself. Don't you?"

"Certainly. I string along with the majority. We'll take a vote. How many of you like yourselves? Raise your hands."

A hand went up with a bare arm shooting out of the purple folds, then two more, then the rest of them, including the red-head.

"Okay," I said, "that's settled. Unanimous. My problem is that I decided to look you over and ask the most absolutely, irresistibly beautiful and fascinating one of the bunch for her phone number, and I'm stalled. You are all it. In beauty and fascination you are all far beyond the wildest dreams of any poet, and I'm not a poet. So obviously I'm in a fix. How can I possibly pick on one of you, any one, when—"

"Nuts." It was the redhead. "Me, of course. Peggy Choate. Argyle two, three-three-four-eight. Don't call before noon."

"That's not fair," a throaty voice objected. It came from one who looked a little too old for Hebe, and just a shade too plump. It went on, "Do I call you Archie?"

"Sure, that's my name."

"All right, Archie, have your eyes examined." She lifted an arm, baring it, to touch the shoulder of one beside her. "We admit we're all beautiful, but we're not in the same class as Helen Iacono. Look at her!"

I was doing so, and I must say that the throaty voice had a point. Helen Iacono, with deep dark eyes, dark velvet skin, and wavy, silky hair darker than either skin or eyes, was unquestionably rare and special. Her lips were parted enough to show the gleam of white teeth, but she wasn't laughing. She wasn't reacting at all, which was remarkable for an actress.

"It may be," I conceded, "that I am so dazzled by the collective radiance that I am blind to the glory of any single star. Perhaps I'm a poet after all, I sound like one. My feeling that I must have the phone numbers of *all* of you is certainly no reflection on Helen Iacono. I admit that that will not completely solve the problem, for tomorrow I must face the question which one to call first. If I feel as I do right now I would have to dial all the numbers simultaneously, and that's impossible. I hope to heaven it doesn't end in a stalemate. What if I can never decide which one to call first? What if it drives me mad? Or what if I gradually sink—"

I turned to see who was tugging at my sleeve. It was Benjamin Schriver, the host, with a grin on his ruddy round face. He said, "I hate to interrupt your speech, but perhaps you can finish it later. We're ready to sit. Will you join us?"

THE DINING ROOM, ON the same floor as the kitchen, three feet or so below street level, would have been too gloomy for my taste if most of the darkwood paneling hadn't been covered with pictures of geese, pheasants, fish, fruit, vegetables, and other assorted edible objects; and also it helped that the tablecloth was white as snow, the wineglasses, seven of them at each place, glistened in the soft light from above, and the polished silver shone. In the center was a low gilt bowl, or maybe gold, two feet long, filled with clusters of Phalaenopsis Aphrodite, donated by Wolfe, cut by him that afternoon from some of his most treasured plants.

As he sat he was scowling at them, but the scowl was not for the orchids; it was for the chair, which, though a little fancy, was perfectly okay for you or me but not for his seventh of a ton. His fundament lapped over at both sides. He erased the scowl when Schriver, at the end of the table, complimented him on the flowers, and Hewitt, across from him, said he had never seen Phalaenopsis better grown, and the others joined in the chorus, all but the aristologist who sat between Wolfe and me. He was a Wall Street character and a well-known theatrical angel named Vincent Pyle, and was living up to his reputation as an original by wearing a dinner jacket, with tie to match, which looked black until you had the light at a certain slant and then you saw that it was green. He eyed the orchids with his head cocked and his mouth puckered, and said, "I don't care for flowers with spots and streaks. They're messy."

I thought, but didn't say, *Okay, drop dead.* If I had known that that was what he was going to do in about three hours I might not even have thought it. He got a rise, not from Wolfe and me, or Schriver or Hewitt, but from three others who thought flowers with spots and streaks were wonderful: Adrian Dart, the actor who had turned down an offer of a million a week, more or less, from Hollywood; Emil Kreis, chairman of the board of Codex Press, book publishers; and Harvey M. Leacraft, corporation lawyer.

Actually, cupbearers was what the Hebes were not. The wines, beginning with the Montrachet with the first course, were poured by Felix; but the girls delivered the food, with different routines for different items. The first course, put on individual plates in the kitchen, with each girl bringing in a plate for her aristologist, was small blinis sprinkled with chopped chives, piled with caviar, and topped with sour cream—the point, as far as Fritz was concerned, being that he had made the blinis, starting on them at eleven that morning, and also the sour cream, starting on that Sunday evening. Fritz's sour cream is very special, but Vincent Pyle had to get in a crack. After he had downed all his blinis he remarked loud enough to carry around the table, "A new idea, putting sand in. Clever. Good for chickens, since they need grit."

The man on my left, Emil Kreis, the publisher, muttered at my ear, "Ignore him. He backed three flops this season."

The girls, who had been coached by Fritz and Felix that afternoon, handled the green turtle soup without a splash. When they had brought in the soup plates Felix brought the bowl, and each girl ladled from it as Felix held it by the plate. I asked Pyle cordially, "Any sand?" but he said no, it was delicious, and cleaned it up.

I was relieved when I saw that the girls wouldn't dish the fish— flounders poached in dry white wine, with a mussel-and-mushroom sauce that was one of Fritz's specialties. Felix did the dishing at a side table, and the girls merely carried. With the first taste of the sauce there were murmurs of appreciation, and Adrian Dart, the actor, across from Wolfe, sang out, "Superb!" They were making various noises of satisfaction, and Leacraft, the lawyer, was asking Wolfe if Fritz would be willing to give him the recipe, when Pyle, on my right, made a face and dropped his fork on his plate with a clatter.

I thought he was putting on an act, and still thought so when his head drooped and I heard him gnash his teeth, but then his shoulders sagged and he clapped a hand to his mouth, and that seemed to be overdoing it. Two or three of them said something, and he pushed his chair back, got to his feet, said, "You must excuse me, I'm sorry," and headed for the door to the hall. Schriver arose and followed him out. The others exchanged words and glances.

Hewitt said, "A damn shame, but I'm going to finish this," and used his fork. Someone asked if Pyle had a bad heart, and someone else said no. They all resumed with the flounder and the conversation, but the spirit wasn't the same.

When, at a signal from Felix, the maidens started removing the plates, Lewis Hewitt got up and left the room, came back in a couple of minutes, sat, and raised his voice. "Vincent is in considerable pain. There is nothing we can do, and Ben wishes us to proceed. He will rejoin us when—when he can."

"What is it?" someone asked.

Hewitt said the doctor didn't know. Zoltan entered bearing an enormous covered platter, and the Hebes gathered at the side table, and Felix lifted the cover and began serving the roast pheasant, which had been larded with strips of pork soaked for twenty hours in Tokay, and then—but no. What's the use? The annual dinner of the Ten for Aristology was a flop. Since for years I have been eating three meals a day cooked by Fritz Brenner I would like to show my appreciation by getting in print some idea of what he can do in the way of victuals, but it won't do here. Sure, the pheasant was good enough for gods if there had been any around, and so was the suckling pig, and the salad, with a dressing which Fritz calls Devil's Rain, and the chestnut croquettes, and the cheese— only the one kind, made in New Jersey by a man named Bill Thompson under Fritz's supervision; and they were all eaten, more or less. But Hewitt left the room three more times and the last time was gone a good ten minutes, and Schriver didn't rejoin the party at all, and while the salad was being served Emil Kreis went out and didn't come back.

When, as coffee and brandy were being poured and cigars and cigarettes passed, Hewitt left his chair for the fifth time, Nero Wolfe got up and followed him out. I lit a cigar just to be doing something, and tried to be sociable by giving an ear to a story Adrian Dart was telling, but by the time I finished my coffee I was getting fidgety. By the glower that had been deepening on Wolfe's face for the past hour I knew he was boiling, and when he's like that, especially away from home, there's no telling about him. He might even have had the idea of aiming the glower at Vincent Pyle for ruining Fritz's meal. So I put what was left of the cigar in a tray, arose, and headed for the door, and was halfway to it when here he came, still glowering.

"Come with me," he snapped, and kept going.

The way to the kitchen from the dining room was through a pantry, twenty feet long, with counters and shelves and cupboards on both sides. Wolfe marched through with me behind. In the kitchen the twelve maidens were scattered around on chairs and stools at tables and counters, eating. A woman was busy at a sink. Zoltan was busy at a refrigerator. Fritz, who was pouring a glass of wine, presumably for himself, turned as Wolfe entered and put the bottle down.

Wolfe went to him, stood, and spoke. "Fritz. I offer my apologies. I permitted Mr. Hewitt to cajole you. I should have known better. I beg your pardon."

Fritz gestured with his free hand, the wineglass steady in the other. "But it is not to pardon, only to regret. The man got sick, that's a pity, only not from my cooking. I assure you."

"You don't need to. Not from your cooking as it left you, but as it reached him. I repeat that I am culpable, but I won't dwell on that now; it can wait. There is an aspect that is exigent." Wolfe turned. "Archie. Are those women all here?"

I had to cover more than half a circle to count them, scattered as they were. "Yes, sir, all present. Twelve."

"Collect them. They can stand"—he pointed to the alcove— "over there. And bring Felix."

It was hard to believe. They were eating; and for him to interrupt a man, or even a woman, at a meal, was unheard of. Not even me. Only in an extreme emergency had he ever asked me to quit food before I was through. Boiling was no name for it. Without even bothering to raise a brow, I turned and called out, "I'm sorry, ladies, but if Mr. Wolfe says it's urgent that settles it. Over there, please? All of you."

Then I went through the pantry corridor, pushed the two-way door, caught Felix's eye, and wiggled a beckoning finger at him, and he came. By the time we got to the kitchen, the girls had left the chairs and stools and were gathering at the alcove, but not with enthusiasm. There were mutterings, and some dirty looks for me as I approached with Felix. Wolfe came with Zoltan and stood, tight-lipped, surveying them.

"I remind you," he said, "that the first course you brought to the table was caviar on blinis topped with sour cream. The portion served to Mr. Vincent Pyle, and eaten by him, contained arsenic. Mr. Pyle is in bed upstairs, attended by three doctors, and will probably die within an hour. I am speaking—"

He stopped to glare at them. They were reacting, or acting, no matter which. There were gasps and exclamations, and one of them clutched her throat, and another, baring her arms, clapped her palms to her ears. When the glare had restored order, Wolfe went on, "You will please keep quiet and listen. I am speaking of conclusions formed by me. My conclusion that Mr. Pyle ate arsenic is based on the symptoms—burning throat, faintness,

intense burning pain in the stomach, dry mouth, cool skin, vomiting. My conclusion that the arsenic was in the first course is
based, first, on the amount of time it takes arsenic to act; second,
on the fact that it is highly unlikely it could have been put in the
soup or the fish; and third, that Mr. Pyle complained of sand in
the cream or caviar. I admit the possibility that one or both of my
conclusions will be proven wrong, but I regard it as remote and I
am acting on them." His head turned. "Fritz. Tell me about the
caviar from the moment it was put on the individual plates. Who
did that?"

I had once told Fritz that I could imagine no circumstances in
which he would look really unhappy, but now I wouldn't have to
try. He was biting his lips, first the lower and then the upper. He
began, "I must assure you—"

"I need no assurance from you, Fritz. Who put it on the plates?"

"Zoltan and I did." He pointed. "At that table."

"And left them there? They were taken from that table by the
women?"

"Yes, sir."

"Each woman took one plate?"

"Yes, sir. I mean, they were told to. I was at the range."

Zoltan spoke up. "I watched them, Mr. Wolfe. They each took
one plate. And believe me, nobody put any arsenic—"

"Please, Zoltan. I add another conclusion: that no one put
arsenic in one of the portions and then left to chance which one of
the guests would get it. Surely the poisoner intended it to reach a
certain one—either Mr. Pyle, or, as an alternative, some other one
and it went to Mr. Pyle by mishap. In any case, it was the portion
Pyle ate that was poisoned, and whether he got it by design or by
mischance is for the moment irrelevant." His eyes were at the girls.
"Which one of you took that plate to Mr. Pyle?"

No reply. No sound, no movement.

Wolfe grunted. "Pfui. If you didn't know his name, you do now.
The man who left during the fish course and who is now dying.
Who served him?"

No reply; and I had to hand it to them that no pair of eyes left
Wolfe to fasten on Peggy Choate, the redhead. Mine did. "What
the heck," I said. "Speak up, Miss Choate."

"I didn't!" she cried.

"That's silly. Of course you did. Twenty people can swear to it. I looked right at you while you were dishing his soup. And when you brought the fish—"

"But I didn't take him that first thing! He already had some!"

Wolfe took over. "Your name is Choate?"

"Yes." Her chin was up. "Peggy Choate."

"You deny that you served the plate of caviar, the first course, to Mr. Pyle?"

"I certainly do."

"But you were supposed to? You were assigned to him?"

"Yes. I took the plate from the table there and went in with it, and started to him, and then I saw that he had some, and I thought I had made a mistake. We hadn't seen the guests. That man"—she pointed to Felix—"had shown us which chair our guest would sit in, and mine was the second from the right on this side as I went in, but that one had already been served, and I thought someone else had made a mistake or I was mixed up. Anyway, I saw that the man next to him, on his right, hadn't been served, and I gave it to him. That was you. I gave it to you."

"Indeed." Wolfe was frowning at her. "Who was assigned to me?"

That wasn't put on. He actually didn't know. He had never looked at her. He had been irritated that females were serving, and besides, he hates to twist his neck. Of course, I could have told him, but Helen Iacono said, "I was."

"Your name, please?"

"Helen Iacono." She had a rich contralto that went fine with the deep dark eyes and dark velvet skin and wavy silk hair.

"Did you bring me the first course?"

"No. When I went in I saw Peggy serving you, and a man on the left next to the end didn't have any, so I gave it to him."

"Do you know his name?"

"I do," Nora Jaret said. "From the card. He was mine." Her big brown eyes were straight at Wolfe. "His name is Kreis. He had his when I got there. I was going to take it back to the kitchen, but then I thought, someone had stage fright but I haven't, and I gave it to the man at the end."

"Which end?"

"The left end. Mr. Schriver. He came and spoke to us this afternoon."

She was corroborated by Carol Annis, the one with hair like corn silk who had no sense of humor. "That's right," she said. "I saw her. I was going to stop her, but she had already put the plate down, so I went around to the other side of the table with it when I saw that Adrian Dart didn't have any. I didn't mind because it was him."

"You were assigned to Mr. Schriver?"

"Yes. I served him the other courses, until he left."

It was turning into a ring-around-a-rosy, but the squat was bound to come. All Wolfe had to do was get to one who couldn't claim a delivery, and that would tag her. I was rather hoping it wouldn't be the next one, for the girl with the throaty voice had been Adrian Dart's, and she had called me Archie and had given Helen Iacono a nice tribute. Would she claim she had served Dart herself?

No. She answered without being asked. "My name is Lucy Morgan," she said, "and I had Adrian Dart, and Carol got to him before I did. There was only one place that didn't have one, on Dart's left, the next but one, and I took it there. I don't know his name."

I supplied it. "Hewitt. Mr. Lewis Hewitt." A better name for it than ring-around-a-rosy would have been passing-the-buck. I looked at Fern Faber, the tall blonde with a wide lazy mouth who had been my first stop on my phone-number tour. "It's your turn, Miss Faber," I told her. "You had Mr. Hewitt. Yes?"

"I sure did." Her voice was pitched so high it threatened to squeak.

"But you didn't take him his caviar?"

"I sure didn't."

"Then who did you take it to?"

"Nobody."

I looked at Wolfe. His eyes were narrowed at her. "What did you do with it, Miss Faber?"

"I didn't do anything with it. There wasn't any."

"Nonsense. There are twelve of you, and there were twelve at the table, and each got a portion. How can you say there wasn't any?"

"Because there wasn't. I was in the john fixing my hair, and when I came back in she was taking the last one from the table, and when I asked where mine was he said he didn't know, and I went to the dining room and they all had some."

"Who was taking the last one from the table?"

She pointed to Lucy Morgan.

"Whom did you ask where yours was?"

She pointed to Zoltan. "Him."

Wolfe turned. "Zoltan?"

"Yes, sir. I mean, yes, sir, she asked where hers was. I had turned away when the last one was taken. I don't mean I know where she had been, just that she asked me that. I asked Fritz if I should go in and see if they were one short and he said no, Felix was there and would see to it."

Wolfe went back to Fern Faber. "Where is that room where you were fixing your hair?"

She pointed toward the pantry. "In there."

"The door's around the corner," Felix said.

"How long were you in there?"

"My God, I don't know, do you think I timed it? When Archie Goodwin was talking to us, and Mr. Schriver came and said they were going to start, I went pretty soon after that."

Wolfe's head jerked to me. "So that's where you were. I might have known there were young women around. Supposing that Miss Faber went to fix her hair shortly after you left—say three minutes—how long was she at it, if the last plate had been taken from the table when she returned to the kitchen?"

I gave it a thought. "Fifteen to twenty minutes."

He growled at her, "What was wrong with your hair?"

"I didn't say anything was wrong with it." She was getting riled. "Look, Mister, do you want all the details?"

"No." Wolfe surveyed them for a moment, not amiably, took in enough air to fill all his middle—say two bushels—let it out again, turned his back on them, saw the glass of wine Fritz had left on a table, went and picked it up, smelled it, and stood to make noises, and, hearing them, he put the glass down and came back.

"You're in a pickle," he said. "So am I. You heard me apologize to Mr. Brenner and avow my responsibility for his undertaking to cook that meal. When, upstairs, I saw that Mr. Pyle would die, and reached the conclusions I told you of, I felt myself under compulsion to expose the culprit. I am committed. When I came down here I thought it would be a simple matter to learn who had served poisoned food to Mr. Pyle, but I was wrong.

"It's obvious now that I have to deal with one who is not only resourceful and ingenious, but also quick-witted and audacious. While I was closing in on her just now, as I thought, inexorably approaching the point where she would either have to contradict one of you or deny that she had served the first course to anyone, she was fleering at me inwardly, and with reason, for her coup had worked. She had slipped through my fingers, and—"

"But she didn't!" It came from one of them whose name I didn't have. "She said she didn't serve anybody!"

Wolfe shook his head. "No. Not Miss Faber. She is the only one who is eliminated. She says she was absent from this room during the entire period when the plates were being taken from the table and she wouldn't dare to say that if she had in fact been here and taken a plate and carried it in to Mr. Pyle. She would certainly have been seen by some of you."

He shook his head again. "Not her. But it could have been any other one of you. You—I speak now to that one, still to be identified—you must have extraordinary faith in your attendant godling, even allowing for your craft. For you took great risks. You took a plate from the table—not the first probably, but one of the first— and on your way to the dining room you put arsenic in the cream. That wasn't difficult; you might even have done it without stopping if you had the arsenic in a paper spill. You could get rid of the spill later, perhaps in the room which Miss Faber calls a john. You took the plate to Mr. Pyle, came back here immediately, got another plate, took it to the dining room, and gave it to one who had not been served. I am not guessing; it had to be like that. It was a remarkably adroit stratagem, but you can't possibly be impregnable."

He turned to Zoltan. "You say you watched as the plates were taken, and each of them took only one. Did one of them come back and take another?"

Zoltan looked fully as unhappy as Fritz. "I'm thinking, Mr. Wolfe. I can try to think, but I'm afraid it won't help. I didn't look at their faces, and they're all dressed alike. I guess I didn't watch very close."

"Fritz?"

"No, sir. I was at the range."

"Then try this, Zoltan. Who were the first ones to take plates— the first three or four?"

Zoltan slowly shook his head. "I'm afraid it's no good, Mr. Wolfe. I could try to think, but I couldn't be sure." He moved his eyes right to left and back again, at the girls. "I tell you, I wasn't looking at their faces." He extended his hands, palms up. "You will consider, Mr. Wolfe, I was not thinking of poison. I was only seeing that the plates were carried properly. Was I thinking which one has got arsenic? No."

"I took the first plate," a girl blurted—another whose name I didn't know. "I took it in and gave it to the man in my chair, the one at the left corner at the other side of the table, and I stayed there. I never left the dining room."

"Your name, please?"

"Marjorie Quinn."

"Thank you. Now, the second plate. Who took it?"

Apparently, nobody. Wolfe gave them ten seconds, his eyes moving to take them all in, his lips tight. "I advise you," he said, "to jog your memories, in case it becomes necessary to establish the order in which you took the plates by dragging it out of you. I hope it won't come to that." His head turned. "Felix, I have neglected you purposely, to give you time to reflect. You were in the dining room. My expectation was that after I had learned who had served the first course to Mr. Pyle you would corroborate it, but now that there is nothing for you to corroborate I must look to you for the fact itself. I must ask you to point her out."

In a way Wolfe was Felix's boss. When Wolfe's oldest and dearest friend, Marko Vukcic, who had owned Rusterman's restaurant, had died, his will had left the restaurant to members of the staff in trust, with Wolfe as the trustee, and Felix was the *maître d'hôtel*. With that job at the best restaurant in New York, naturally Felix was both bland and commanding, but now he was neither. If he felt the way he looked, he was miserable.

"I can't," he said.

"Pfui! You, trained as you are to see everything?"

"That is true, Mr. Wolfe. I knew you would ask me this, but I can't. I can only explain. The young woman who just spoke, Marjorie Quinn, was the first one in with a plate, as she said. She did not say that as she served it one of the blinis slid off onto the table, but it did. As I sprang toward her she was actually about to pick it up with her fingers, and I jerked her away and put it back on the plate with a fork, and I gave her a look. Anyway, I was not myself.

Having women as waiters was bad enough, and not only that, they were without experience. When I recovered command of myself I saw the redheaded one, Choate, standing back of Mr. Pyle, to whom she had been assigned, with a plate in her hand, and I saw that he had already been served. As I moved forward she stepped to the right and served the plate to you. The operation was completely upset, and I was helpless. The dark-skinned one, Iacono, who was assigned to you, served Mr. Kreis, and the—"

"If you please." Wolfe was curt. "I have heard them, and so have you. I have always found you worthy of trust, but it's possible that in your exalted position, *maître d'hôtel* at Rusterman's, you would rather dodge than get involved in a poisoning. Are you dodging, Felix?"

"Good God, Mr. Wolfe, I *am* involved!"

"Very well. I saw that woman spill the blini and start her fingers for it, and I saw you retrieve it. Yes, you're involved, but not as I am." He turned to me. "Archie. You are commonly my first resort, but now you are my last. You sat next to Mr. Pyle. Who put that plate before him?"

Of course I knew that was coming, but I hadn't been beating my brain because there was no use. I said merely but positively, "No." He glared at me and I added, "That's all, just no, but like Felix I can explain. First, I would have had to turn around to see her face, and that's bad table manners. Second, I was watching Felix rescue the blini. Third, there was an argument going on about flowers with spots and streaks, and I was listening to it and so were you. I didn't even see her arm."

Wolfe stood and breathed. He shut his eyes and opened them again, and breathed some more. "Incredible," he muttered. "The wretch had incredible luck."

"I'm going home," Fern Faber said. "I'm tired."

"So am I," another one said, and was moving, but Wolfe's eyes pinned her. "I advise you not to," he said. "It is true that Miss Faber is eliminated as the culprit, and also Miss Quinn, since she was under surveillance by Felix while Mr. Pyle was being served, but I advise even them to stay. When Mr. Pyle dies, the doctors will certainly summon the police, and it would be well for all of you to be here when they arrive. I had hoped to be able to present them with an exposed murderer. Confound it! There is still a chance. Archie, come with me. Fritz, Felix, Zoltan, remain with these women. If one or more of them insist on leaving do not detain them by force, but have the names and the times of departure. If they want to eat, feed them. I'll be—"

"I'm going home," Fern Faber said stubbornly.

"Very well, go. You'll be got out of bed by a policeman before the night's out. I'll be in the dining room, Fritz. Come, Archie."

He went and I followed, along the pantry corridor and through the two-way door. On the way I glanced at my wristwatch: ten past eleven. I rather expected to find the dining room empty, but it wasn't. Eight of them were still there, the only ones missing being Schriver and Hewitt, who were probably upstairs. The air was heavy with cigar smoke. All of them but Adrian Dart were at the table with their chairs pushed back at various angles, with brandy glasses and cigars. Dart was standing with his back to a picture of honkers on the wing, holding forth. As we entered he stopped and heads turned.

Emil Kreis spoke. "Oh, there you are. I was coming to the kitchen but didn't want to butt in. Schriver asked me to apologize to Fritz Brenner. Our custom is to ask the chef to join us with champagne, which is barbarous but gay, but of course in the circumstances . . ." He let it hang, and added, "Shall I explain to him? Or will you?"

"I will." Wolfe went to the end of the table and sat. He had been on his feet for nearly two hours—all very well for his twice-a-day sessions in the plant rooms, but not elsewhere. He looked around. "Mr. Pyle is still alive?"

"We hope so," one said. "We sincerely hope so."

"I ought to be home in bed," another one said. "I have a hard day tomorrow. But it doesn't seem . . ." He took a puff on his cigar.

Emil Kreis reached for the brandy bottle. "There's been no word since I came down." He looked at his wrist. "Nearly an hour ago. I suppose I should go up. It's so damned unpleasant." He poured brandy.

"Terrible," one said. "Absolutely terrible. I understand you were asking which one of the girls brought him the caviar. Kreis says you asked him."

Wolfe nodded. "I also asked Mr. Schriver and Mr. Hewitt. And Mr. Goodwin and Mr. Brenner, and the two men who came to help at my request. And the women themselves. After more than an hour with them I am still at fault. I have discovered the artifice the culprit used, but not her identity."

"Aren't you a bit premature?" Leacraft, the lawyer, asked. "There may be no culprit. An acute and severe gastric disturbance may be caused—"

"Nonsense. I am too provoked for civility, Mr. Leacraft. The symptoms are typical of arsenic, and you heard Mr. Pyle complain of sand, but that's not all. I said I have discovered the artifice. None of them will admit serving him the first course. The one assigned to him found he had already been served and served me instead. There is indeed a culprit. She put arsenic in the cream *en passant*, served it to Mr. Pyle, returned to the kitchen for another portion, and came and served it to someone else. That is established."

"But then," the lawyer objected, "one of them served no one. How could that be?"

"I am not a tyro at inquiry, Mr. Leacraft. I'll ravel it for you later if you want, but now I want to get on. It is no conjecture that poison was given to Mr. Pyle by the woman who brought him the caviar; it is a fact. By a remarkable combination of cunning and luck she has so far eluded identification, and I am appealing to you. All of you. I ask you to close your eyes and recall the scene. We are here at table, discussing the orchids—the spots and streaks. The woman serving that place"—he pointed—"lets a blini slip from the plate and Felix retrieves it. It helps to close your eyes. Just about then a woman enters with a plate, goes to Mr. Pyle, and puts it before him. I appeal to you: which one?"

Emil Kreis shook his head. "I told you upstairs, I don't know. I didn't see her. Or if I did, it didn't register."

Adrian Dart, the actor, stood with his eyes closed, his chin up, and his arms folded, a fine pose for concentration. The others, even Leacraft, had their eyes closed, too, but of course they couldn't hold a candle to Dart. After a long moment the eyes began to open and heads to shake.

"It's gone," Dart said in his rich musical baritone. "I must have seen it, since I sat across from him, but it's gone. Utterly."

"I didn't see it," another said. "I simply didn't see it."

"I have a vague feeling," another said, "but it's too damn vague. No."

They made it unanimous.

Wolfe put his palms on the table. "Then I'm in for it," he said grimly. "I am your guest, gentlemen, and would not be offensive,

but I am to blame that Fritz Brenner was enticed to this deplorable
fiasco. If Mr. Pyle dies, as he surely will—"

The door opened and Benjamin Schriver entered. Then Lewis
Hewitt, and then the familiar burly frame of Sergeant Purley Stebbins of Manhattan Homicide West.

Schriver crossed to the table and spoke. "Vincent is dead. Half
an hour ago. Doctor Jameson called the police. He thinks that it is
practically certain—"

"Hold it," Purley growled at his elbow. "I'll handle it if you don't
mind."

"My God," Adrian Dart groaned, and shuddered magnificently.

That was the last I heard of the affair from an aristologist.

"I DID NOT!" INSPECTOR Cramer roared. "Quit twisting my words
around! I didn't charge you with complicity! I merely said you're
concealing something, and what the hell is that to scrape your
neck? You always do!"

It was a quarter to two Wednesday afternoon. We were in the
office on the first floor of the old brownstone on West 35th
Street—Wolfe in his oversized chair. The daily schedule was
messed beyond repair. When we had finally got home, at five
o'clock in the morning, Wolfe had told Fritz to forget about breakfast until further notice, and had sent me up to the plant rooms to
leave a note for Theodore saying that he would not appear at nine
in the morning and perhaps not at all. It had been not at all. At
half-past eleven he had buzzed on the house phone to tell Fritz to
bring up the breakfast tray with four eggs and ten slices of bacon
instead of two and five, and it was past one o'clock when the
sounds came of his elevator and then his footsteps in the hall,
heading for the office.

If you think a problem child is rough, try handling a problem
elephant. He is plenty knotty even when he is himself, and that day
he was really special. After looking through the mail, glancing at
his desk calendar, and signing three checks I had put on his desk,
he snapped at me, "A fine prospect. Dealing with them singly
would be interminable. Will you have them all here at six o'clock?"

I kept calm. I merely asked, "All of whom?"

"You know quite well. Those women."

I still kept calm. "I should think ten of them would be enough. You said yourself that two of them can be crossed off."

"I need them all. Those two can help establish the order in which the plates were taken."

I held on. I too was short on sleep, shorter even than he, and I didn't feel up to a fracas. "I have a suggestion," I said. "I suggest that you postpone operations until your wires are connected again. Counting up to five hundred might help. You know damn well that all twelve of them will spend the afternoon either at the District Attorney's office or receiving official callers at their homes—probably most of them at the DA's office. And probably they'll spend the evening there too. Do you want some aspirin?"

"I want *them*," he growled.

I could have left him to grope back to normal on his own and gone up to my room for a nap, but after all he pays my salary. So I picked up a sheet of paper I had typed and got up and handed it to him. It read:

	Assigned to	*Served*
Peggy Choate	Pyle	Wolfe
Helen Iacono	Wolfe	Kreis
Nora Jaret	Kreis	Schriver
Carol Annis	Schriver	Dart
Lucy Morgan	Dart	Hewitt
Fern Faber	Hewitt	No one

"Fern Faber's out," I said, "and I realize it doesn't have to be one of those five, even though Lucy Morgan took the last plate. Possibly one or two others took plates after Peggy Choate did, and served the men they were assigned to. But it seems—"

I stopped because he had crumpled it and dropped it in the wastebasket. "I heard them," he growled. "My faculties, including my memory, are not impaired. I am merely ruffled beyond the bounds of tolerance."

For him that was an abject apology, and a sign that he was beginning to regain control. But a few minutes later, when the bell rang, and after a look through the one-way glass panel of the front door I told him it was Cramer, and he said to admit him, and Cramer marched in and planted his fanny on the red leather chair and opened up with an impolite remark about concealing facts connected with a murder, Wolfe had cut loose; and Cramer asked him what the hell was that to scrape his neck, which was a new one to me but sounded somewhat vulgar for an inspector. He had probably picked it up from some hoodlum.

Ruffling Cramer beyond the bounds of tolerance did Wolfe good. He leaned back in his chair. "Everyone conceals something," he said placidly. "Or at least omits something, if only because to include everything is impossible. During those wearisome hours, nearly six of them, I answered all questions, and so did Mr. Goodwin. Indeed, I thought we were helpful. I thought we had cleared away some rubble."

"Yeah." Cramer wasn't grateful. His big pink face was always a little pinker than normal, not with pleasure, when he was tackling Wolfe. "You had witnessed the commission of a murder, and you didn't notify—"

"It wasn't a murder until he died."

"All right, a felony. You not only failed to report it, you—"

"That a felony had been committed was my conclusion. Others present disagreed with me. Only a few minutes before Mr. Stebbins entered the room, Mr. Leacraft, a member of the bar himself an officer of the law, challenged my conclusion."

"You should have reported it. You're a licensed detective. Also you started an investigation, questioning the suspects—"

"Only to test my conclusion. I would have been a ninny to report it before learning—"

"Damn it," Cramer barked, "will you let me finish a sentence? Just one?"

Wolfe's shoulders went up an eighth of an inch and down again. "Certainly, if it has import. I am not baiting you, Mr. Cramer. But I have already replied to these imputations, to you and Mr. Stebbins and an assistant district attorney. I did not wrongly delay reporting a crime, and I did not usurp the function of the police. Very well, finish a sentence."

"You knew Pyle was dying. You said so."

"Also my own conclusion. The doctors were trying to save him."

Cramer took a breath. He looked at me, saw nothing inspiring, and returned to Wolfe. "I'll tell you why I'm here. Those three men—the cook, the man that helped him, and the man in the dining room—Fritz Brenner, Felix Courbet, and Zoltan Mahany, were all supplied by you. All close to you. I want to know about them, or at least two of them. I might as well leave Fritz out of it. In the first place, it's hard to believe that Zoltan doesn't know who took the first two or three plates or whether one of them came back for a second one, and it's also hard to believe that Felix doesn't know who served Pyle."

"It is indeed," Wolfe agreed. "They are highly trained men. But they have been questioned."

"They sure have. It's also hard to believe that Goodwin didn't see who served Pyle. He sees everything."

"Mr. Goodwin is present. Discuss it with him."

"I have. Now, I want to ask your opinion of a theory. I know yours, and I don't reject it, but there are alternatives. First, a fact. In a metal trash container in the kitchen—not a garbage pail—we found a small roll of paper, ordinary white paper that had been rolled into a tube, held with tape, smaller at one end. The laboratory has found particles of arsenic inside. The only two finger-prints on it that are any good are Zoltan's. He says he saw it on the kitchen floor under a table some time after the meal had started, he can't say exactly when, and he picked it up and dropped it in the container, and his prints are on it because he pinched it to see if there was anything in it."

Wolfe nodded. "As I surmised. A paper spill."

"Yeah. I don't say it kills your theory. She could have shaken it into the cream without leaving prints, and she certainly wouldn't have dropped it on the floor if there was any chance it had her prints. But it *has* got Zoltan's. What's wrong with the theory that Zoltan poisoned one of the portions and saw that it was taken by a certain one? I'll answer that myself. There are two things wrong with it. First, Zoltan claims he didn't know which guest any of the girls were assigned to. But Felix knew, and they could have been in collusion. Second, the girls all deny that Zoltan indicated which plate they were to take, but you know how that is. He could have done it without her knowing it. What else is wrong with it?"

"It's not only untenable, it's egregious," Wolfe declared. "Why, in that case, did one of them come back for another plate?"

"She was confused. Nervous. Dumb."

"Bosh. Why doesn't she admit it?"

"Scared."

"I don't believe it. I questioned them before you did." Wolfe waved it away. "Tommyrot, and you know it. My theory is not a theory; it is a reasoned conviction. I hope it is being acted on. I suggested to Mr. Stebbins that he examine their garments to see if some kind of pocket had been made in one of them. She had to have it readily available."

"He did. They all had pockets. The laboratory has found no trace of arsenic." Cramer uncrossed his legs. "But I wanted to ask you about those men. You know them."

"I do, yes. But I do not answer for them. They may have a dozen murders on their souls, but they had nothing to do with the death of Mr. Pyle. If you are following up my theory—my conviction, rather—I suppose you have learned the order in which the women took the plates."

Cramer shook his head. "We have not, and I doubt if we will. All we have is a bunch of contradictions. You had them good and scared before we got to them. We do have the last five, starting with Peggy Choate, who found that Pyle had been served and gave it to you, and then—but you got that yourself."

"No. I got those five, but not that they were the last. There might have been others in between."

"There weren't. It's pretty well settled that these five were the last. After Peggy Choate the last four plates were taken by Helen Iacono, Nora Jaret, Carol Annis, and Lucy Morgan. Then that Fern Faber, who had been in the can, but there was no plate for her. It's the order in which they took them before that, the first seven, that we can't pry out of them—except the first one, that Marjorie Quinn. You couldn't either."

Wolfe turned a palm up. "I was interrupted."

"You were not. You left them there in a huddle, scared stiff, and went to the dining room to start in on the men. Your own private murder investigation, and to hell with the law. I was surprised to see Goodwin here when I rang the bell just now. I supposed you'd have him out running errands like calling at the agency they got the girls from. Or getting a line on Pyle to find a connection between him and one of them. Unless you're no longer interested?"

"I'm interested willy-nilly," Wolfe declared. "As I told the assistant district attorney, it is on my score that a man was poisoned in

food prepared by Fritz Brenner. But I do not send Mr. Goodwin on
fruitless errands. He is one and you have dozens, and if anything is
to be learned at the agency or by inquiry into Mr. Pyle's associa-
tions your army will dig it up. They're already at it, of course, but if
they had started a trail you wouldn't be here. If I send Mr. Goodwin—"

The doorbell rang and I got up and went to the hall. At the rear
the door to the kitchen swung open part way and Fritz poked his
head through, saw me, and withdrew. Turning to the front for a
look through the panel, I saw that I had exaggerated when I told
Wolfe that all twelve of them would be otherwise engaged. At least
one wasn't. There on the stoop was Helen Iacono.

It had sounded to me as if Cramer had about said his say and
would soon be moving along, and if he bumped into Helen
Iacono in the hall she might be too embarrassed to give me her
phone number, if that was what she had come for; so as I opened
the door I pressed a finger to my lips and *sshh*ed at her, and then
crooked the finger to motion her in. Her deep dark eyes looked a
little startled, but she stepped across the sill, and I shut the door,
turned, opened the first door on the left, to the front room,
motioned to her to enter, followed, and closed the door.

"What's the matter?" she whispered.

"Nothing now," I told her. "This is soundproofed. There's a
police inspector in the office with Mr. Wolfe and I thought you
might have had enough of cops for now. But if you want to meet
him—"

"I don't. I want to see Nero Wolfe."

"Okay, I'll tell him as soon as the cop goes. Have a seat. It
shouldn't be long."

There is a connecting door between the front room and the
office, but I went around through the hall, and here came Cramer.
He was marching by without even the courtesy of a grunt, but I
stepped to the front to let him out, and then went to the office and
told Wolfe, "I've got one of them in the front room. Helen Iacono,
the tawny-skinned Hebe who had you but gave her caviar to Kreis.
Shall I keep her while I get the rest of them?"

He made a face. "What does she want?"

"To see you."

He took a breath. "Confound it. Bring her in."

I went and opened the connecting door, told her to come, and escorted her across to the red leather chair. She was more ornamental in it than Cramer, but not nearly as impressive as she had been at first sight. She was puffy around the eyes and her skin had lost some glow. She told Wolfe she hadn't had any sleep. She said she had just left the district attorney's office, and if she went home her mother would be at her again, and her brothers and sister would come home from school and make noise, and anyway she had decided she had to see Wolfe. Her mother was old-fashioned and didn't want her to be an actress. It was beginning to sound as if what she was after was a place to take a nap, but then Wolfe got a word in.

He said dryly, "I didn't suppose, Miss Iacono, you came to consult me about your career."

"Oh, no. I came because you're a detective and you're very clever and I'm afraid. I'm afraid they'll find out something I did, and if they do I won't have any career. My parents won't let me even if I'm still alive. I nearly gave it away already when they were asking me questions. So I decided to tell you about it and then if you'd help me I'll help you. If you promise to keep my secret."

"I can't promise to keep a secret if it is a guilty one—if it is a confession of a crime or knowledge of one."

"It isn't."

"Then you have my promise, and Mr. Goodwin's. We have kept many secrets."

"All right. I stabbed Vincent Pyle with a knife and got blood on me."

I stared. For half a second I thought she meant that he hadn't died of poison at all, that she had sneaked upstairs and stuck a knife in him, which seemed unlikely since the doctors would probably have found the hole.

Apparently, she wasn't going on, and Wolfe spoke. "Ordinarily, Miss Iacono, stabbing a man is considered a crime. When and where did this happen?"

"It wasn't a crime because it was in self-defense." Her rich contralto was as composed as if she had been telling us the multiplication tables. Evidently, she saved the inflections for her career. She was continuing. "It happened in January, about three months ago. Of course, I knew about him—everybody in show business does. I don't know if it's true that he backs shows just so he can get girls, but it might as well be. There's a lot of talk about the girls he gets, but nobody really knows because he was always very careful about it. Some of the girls have talked but he never did. I don't mean just taking them out, I mean the last ditch. We say that on Broadway. You know what I mean?"

"I can surmise."

"Sometimes we say the last stitch, but it means the same thing. Early last winter he began on me. Of course, I knew about his reputation, but he was backing *Jack in the Pulpit* and they were about to start casting, and I didn't know it was going to be a flop, and if a girl expects to have a career she has to be sociable. I went out with him a few times, dinner and dancing and so forth, and then he asked me to his apartment, and I went. He cooked the dinner himself—I said he was very careful. Didn't I?"

"Yes."

"Well, he was. It's a penthouse on Madison Avenue, but no one else was there. I let him kiss me. I figured it like this, an actress gets kissed all the time on the stage and the screen and TV, and what's the difference? I went to his apartment three times and there was no real trouble, but the fourth time—that was in January—he turned into a beast right before my eyes, and I had to do something, and I grabbed a knife from the table and stabbed him with it. I got blood on my dress, and when I got home I tried to get it out but it left a stain. It cost forty-six dollars."

"But Mr. Pyle recovered."

"Oh, yes. I saw him a few times after that, I mean just by accident, but he barely spoke and so did I. I don't think he ever told anyone about it, but what if he did? What if the police find out about it?"

Wolfe grunted. "That would be regrettable, certainly. You would be pestered even more than you were now. But if you have been candid with me you are not in mortal jeopardy. The police are not simpletons. You wouldn't be arrested for murdering Mr. Pyle last night, let alone convicted, merely because you stabbed him in self-defense last January."

"Of course I wouldn't," she agreed. "That's not it. It's my mother and father. They'd find out about it because they would ask them questions, and if I'm going to have a career I would have to leave home and my family, and I don't want to. Don't you see?" She came forward in the chair. "But if they find out right away who did it, who poisoned him, that would end it and I'd be all right. Only I'm afraid they won't find out right away, but I think you could if I help you, and you said last night that you're committed. I can't offer to help the police because they'd wonder why."

"I see." Wolfe's eyes were narrowed at her. "How do you propose to help me?"

"Well, I figure it like this." She was on the edge of the chair. "The way you explained it last night, one of the girls poisoned him. She was one of the first ones to take a plate in, and then she came back and got another one. I don't quite understand why she did that, but you do, so all right. But if she came back for another plate that took a little time, and she must have been one of the last ones, and the police have got it worked out who were the last five. I know that because of the questions they asked this last time. So it was Peggy Choate or Nora Jaret or Carol Annis or Lucy Morgan."

"Or you."

"No, it wasn't me." Just matter-of-fact. "So it was one of them. And she didn't poison him just for nothing, did she? You'd have to have a very good reason to poison a man, I know I would. So all we have to do is find out which one had a good reason, and that's where I can help. I don't know Lucy Morgan, but I know Carol a little, and I know Nora and Peggy even better. And now we're in this together, and I can pretend to them I want to talk about it. I can talk about him because I had to tell the police I went out with him a few times, because I was seen with him and they'd find out, so I thought I'd better tell them. Dozens of girls went out with him, but he was so careful that nobody knows which ones went to the last ditch except the ones that talked. And I can find out which one of those four girls had a reason, and tell you, and that will end it."

I was congratulating myself that I hadn't got her phone number; and if I had got it, I would have crossed it off without a pang. I don't say that a girl must have true nobility of character before I'll buy her a lunch, but you have to draw the line somewhere. Thinking that Wolfe might be disgusted enough to put into words the way I felt, I horned in. "I have a suggestion, Miss Iacono.

You could bring them here, all four of them, and let Mr. Wolfe talk it over with them. As you say, he's very clever."

She looked doubtful. "I don't believe that's a good idea. I think they'd be more apt to say things to me, just one at a time. Don't you think so, Mr. Wolfe?"

"You know them better than I do," he muttered. He was controlling himself.

"And then," she said, "when we find out which one had a reason, and we tell the police, I can say that I saw her going back to the kitchen for another plate. Of course, just where I saw her, where she was and where I was, that will depend on who she is. I saw you, Mr. Wolfe, when I said you could if I helped you, I saw the look on your face. You didn't think a twenty-year-old girl could help, did you?"

He had my sympathy. Of course, what he would have liked to say was that it might well be that a twenty-year-old hellcat could help, but that wouldn't have been tactful.

"I may have been a little skeptical," he conceded. "And it's possible that you're oversimplifying the problem. We have to consider all the factors. Take one: her plan must have been not only premeditated but also thoroughly rigged, since she had the poison ready. So she must have known that Mr. Pyle would be one of the guests. Did she?"

"Oh, yes. We all did. Mr. Buchman at the agency showed us a list of them and told us who they were, only of course he didn't have to tell us who Vincent Pyle was. That was about a month ago, so she had plenty of time to get the poison. Is arsenic very hard to get?"

"Not at all. It is in common use for many purposes. That is, of course, one of the police lines of inquiry, but she knew it would be and she is no bungler. Another point: when Mr. Pyle saw her there, serving food, wouldn't he have been on his guard?"

"But he didn't see her. They didn't see any of us before. She came up behind him and gave him that plate. Of course, he saw her afterward, but he had already eaten it."

Wolfe persisted. "But then? He was in agony, but he was conscious and could speak. Why didn't he denounce her?"

She gestured impatiently. "I guess you're not as clever as you're supposed to be. He didn't know she had done it. When he saw her she was serving another man, and—"

"What other man?"

"How do I know? Only it wasn't you, because I served you. And anyway, maybe he didn't know she wanted to kill him. Of course, she had a good reason, I know that, but maybe he didn't know she felt like that. A man doesn't know how a girl feels—anyhow, some girls. Look at me. He didn't know I would never dream of going to the last ditch. He thought I would give up my honor and my virtue just to get a part in that play he was backing, and anyhow it was a flop." She gestured again. "I thought you wanted to get her. All you do is make objections."

Wolfe rubbed the side of his nose. "I do want to get her, Miss Iacono. I intend to. But like Mr. Pyle, though from a different motive, I am very careful. I can't afford to botch it. I fully appreciate your offer to help. You didn't like Mr. Goodwin's suggestion that you get them here in a body for discussion with me, and you may be right. But I don't like your plan, for you to approach them singly and try to pump them. Our quarry is a malign and crafty harpy, and I will not be a party to your peril. I propose an alternative. Arrange for Mr. Goodwin to see them, together with you. Being a trained investigator, he knows how to beguile, and the peril, if any, will be his. If they are not available at the moment, arrange it for this evening—but not here. Perhaps one of them has a suitable apartment, or if not, a private room at some restaurant would do. At my expense, of course. Will you?"

It was her turn to make objections, and she had several. But when Wolfe met them, and made it plain that he would accept her as a colleague only if she accepted his alternative, she finally gave in. She would phone to let me know how she was making out with the arrangements. From her manner, when she got up to go, you might have thought she had been shopping for some little item, say a handbag, and had graciously deferred to the opinion of the clerk. After I graciously escorted her out and saw her descend the seven steps to the sidewalk, I returned to the office and found Wolfe sitting with his eyes closed and his fists planted on the chair arms.

"Even money," I said.

"On what?" he growled.

"On her against the field. She knows damn well who had a good reason and exactly what it was. It was getting too hot for comfort and she decided that the best way to duck was to wish it on some dear friend."

His eyes opened. "She would, certainly. A woman whose conscience has no sting will stop at nothing. But why come to me? Why
didn't she cook her own stew and serve it to the police?"

"I don't know, but for a guess she was afraid the cops would get
too curious and find out how she had saved her honor and her
virtue and tell her mother and father, and Father would spank her.
Shall I also guess why you proposed your alternative instead of
having her bring them here for you?"

"She wouldn't. She said so."

"Of course she would, if you had insisted. That's your guess.
Mine is that you're not desperate enough yet to take on five
females in a bunch. When you told me to bring the whole dozen
you knew darned well it couldn't be done, not even by me. Okay, I
want instructions."

"Later," he muttered, and closed his eyes.

IT WAS ON THE fourth floor of an old walk-up in the West Nineties
near Amsterdam Avenue. I don't know what it had in the way of a
kitchen or bedroom—or bedrooms—because the only room I saw
was the one we were sitting in. It was medium-sized, and the
couch and chairs and rugs had a homey look, the kind of homey-
ness that furniture gets by being used by a lot of different people
for fifty or sixty years. The chair I was on had a wobbly leg, but
that's no problem if you keep it in mind and make no sudden
shifts. I was more concerned about the spidery little stand at my
elbow on which my glass of milk was perched. I can always drink
milk and had preferred it to Bubble-Pagne, registered trademark,
a dime a bottle, which they were having. It was ten o'clock
Wednesday evening.

The hostesses were the redhead with milky skin, Peggy
Choate, and the one with big brown eyes and dimples, Nora
Jaret, who shared the apartment. Carol Annis, with the fine profile and the corn-silk hair, had been there when Helen Iacono
and I arrived, bringing Lucy Morgan and her throaty voice after
detouring our taxi to pick her up at a street corner. They were a
very attractive collection, though of course not as decorative as
they had been in their ankle-length purple stolas. Girls always

look better in uniforms or costumes. Take nurses or elevator girls or Miss Honeydew at a melon festival.

I was now calling her Helen, not that I felt like it, but in the detective business you have to be sociable, of course preserving your honor and virtue. In the taxi, before picking up Lucy Morgan, she told me she had been thinking it over and she doubted if it would be possible to find out which one of them had a good reason to kill Pyle, or thought she had, because Pyle had been so very careful when he had a girl come to his penthouse. The only way would be to get one of them to open up, and Helen doubted if she could get her to, since she would be practically confessing murder. So the best way would be for Helen and me, after spending an evening with them, to talk it over and decide which one was the most likely, and then she would tell Wolfe she had seen her going back to the kitchen and bringing another plate, and Wolfe would tell the police, and that would do it.

No, I didn't feel like calling her Helen. I would just as soon have been too far away from her to call her at all.

Helen's declared object in arranging the party—declared to them—was to find out from me what Nero Wolfe and the cops had done and were doing, so they would know where they stood. Helen was sure I would loosen up, she had told them, because she had been to see me and found me very nice and sympathetic. So the hostesses were making it sort of festive and intimate by serving Bubble-Pagne, though I preferred milk. I had a suspicion that at least one of them, Lucy Morgan, would have preferred whiskey or gin or rum or vodka, and maybe they all would, but that might have made me suspect that they were not just a bunch of wholesome, hardworking artists.

They didn't look festive. I wouldn't say they were haggard, but much of the bloom was off. And they hadn't bought Helen's plug for me that I was nice and sympathetic. They were absolutely skeptical, sizing me up with sidewise looks, especially Carol Annis, who sat cross-legged on the couch with her head cocked. It was she who asked me, after a few remarks had been made about how awful it had been and still was, how well I knew the chef and the other man in the kitchen. I told her she could forget Fritz. He was completely above suspicion, and anyway he had been at the range while the plates were taken. As for Zoltan, I said that though I had known him a long while we were not intimate, but that was irrelevant because, granting that he had known which guest each girl would serve, if he poisoned one of the portions and saw that a certain girl got it, why did she or some other girl come back for another plate?

"There's no proof that she did," Carol declared. "Nobody saw her."

"Nobody *noticed* her." I wasn't aggressive; I was supposed to be nice and sympathetic. "She wouldn't have been noticed leaving the dining room because the attention of the girls who were in there was on Felix and Marjorie Quinn, who had spilled a blini, and the men wouldn't notice her. The only place she would have been noticed was in the corridor through the pantry, and if she met another girl there she could have stopped and been patting her hair or something. Anyhow, one of you must have gone back for a second plate, because when Fern Faber went for hers there wasn't any."

"Why do you say one of us?" Nora demanded. "If you mean one of us here. There were twelve."

"I do mean one of you here, but I'm not saying it, I'm just quoting the police. They think it was one of you here because you were the last five."

"How do you know what they think?"

"I'm not at liberty to say. But I do."

"I know what I think," Carol asserted. She had uncrossed her legs and slid forward on the couch to get her toes on the floor. "I think it was Zoltan. I read in the *Gazette* that he's a chef at Rusterman's, and Nero Wolfe is the trustee and so he's the boss there, and I think Zoltan hated him for some reason and tried to poison him, but he gave the poisoned plate to the wrong girl. Nero Wolfe sat right next to Pyle."

There was no point in telling her that she was simply ignoring the fact that one of them had gone back for a second helping, so I just said, "Nobody can stop you thinking. But I doubt very much if the police would buy that."

"What would they buy?" Peggy asked.

My personal feelings about Peggy were mixed. For: she had recognized me and named me. Against: she had accused me of liking myself. "Anything that would fit," I told her. "As I said, they think it

was one of you five that went back for more, and therefore they have
to think that one of you gave the poison to Pyle, because what other
possible reason could you have had for serving another portion?
They wouldn't buy anything that didn't fit into that. That's what
rules out everybody else, including Zoltan." I looked at Carol. "I'm
sorry, Miss Annis, but that's how it is."

"They're a bunch of dopes," Lucy Morgan stated. "They get an
idea and then they haven't got room for another one." She was on
the floor with her legs stretched out, her back against the couch. "I
agree with Carol, there's no proof that any of us went back for
another plate. That Zoltan said he didn't see anyone come back.
Didn't he?"

"He did. He still does."

"Then he's a dope, too. And he said no one took two plates.
Didn't he?"

"Right. He still does."

"Then how do they know which one he's wrong about? We were
all nervous, you know that. Maybe one of us took two plates
instead of one, and when she got to the dining room there she was
with an extra, and she got rid of it by giving it to some guest that
didn't have any."

"Then why didn't she say so?" I asked.

"Because she was scared. The way Nero Wolfe came at us was
enough to scare anybody. And now she won't say so because she
has signed a statement and she's even more scared."

I shook my head. "I'm sorry, but if you analyze that you'll see
that it won't do. It's very tricky. You can do it the way I did this
afternoon. Take twenty-four little pieces of paper, on twelve of
them write the names of the guests, and arrange them as they sat
at the table. On the other twelve pieces write the names of the
twelve girls Then try to manipulate the twelve girl pieces so that
one of them either took in two plates at once, and did not give
either of them to Pyle, or went back for a second plate, and did not
give either the first one or the second one to Pyle. It can't be done.
For if either of those things happened there wouldn't have been
one mix-up, there would have been two. Since there was only one
mix-up, Pyle couldn't possibly have been served by a girl who
either brought in two plates at once or went back for a second one.
So the idea that a girl *innocently* brought in two plates is out."

"I don't believe it," Nora said flatly.

"It's not a question of believing." I was still sympathetic. "You might as well say you don't believe two plus two is four. I'll show you. May I have some paper? Any old kind."

She went to a table and brought some, and I took my pen and wrote the twenty-four names, spacing them, and tore the paper into twenty-four pieces. Then I knelt on a rug and arranged the twelve guest pieces in a rectangle as they had sat at table—not that that mattered, since they could have been in a straight line or a circle, but it was plainer that way. The girls gathered around.

"Okay," I said, "show me." I took *Quinn* and put it back of *Leacraft.* "There's no argument about that, Marjorie Quinn brought the first plate and gave it to Leacraft. Remember there was just one mix-up, started by Peggy when she saw Pyle had been served and gave hers to Nero Wolfe. Try having any girl bring in a second plate—or bring in two at once if you still think that might have happened without either serving Pyle or starting a second mix-up."

My memory has had a long stiff training under the strains and pressure Wolfe has put on it, but I wouldn't undertake to report all the combinations they tried, huddled around me on the floor. They stuck to it for half an hour or more. The most persistent was Peggy Choate, the redhead. After the others had given up she stayed with it, frowning and biting her lip, propped first on one hand and then the other. Finally, she said, "Nuts," stretched an arm to make a jumble of all the pieces of paper, guests and girls, got up, and returned to her chair.

"It's just a trick," said Carol Annis, perched on the couch again.

"I still don't believe it," Nora Jaret declared. "I do not believe that one of us deliberately poisoned a man—one of us sitting here." Her big brown eyes were at me. "Good Lord, look at us! Point at her! Point her out! I dare you to!"

That, of course, was what I was there for—not exactly to point her out, but at least to get a hint. I had had a vague idea that one might come from watching them maneuver the pieces of paper, but it hadn't. Nor from anything any of them had said. I had been expecting Helen Iacono to introduce the subject of Vincent Pyle's *modus operandi* with girls, but apparently she had decided it was up to me. She hadn't spoken more than twenty words since we arrived.

"If I could point her out," I said, "I wouldn't be bothering the rest of you. Neither would the cops if *they* could point her out. Sooner or later, of course, they will, but it begins to look as if they'll have to get at it from the other end. Motive. They'll have to find out which one of you had a motive, and they will—sooner or later—and on that maybe I can help. I don't mean help them, I mean help you—not the one who killed him, the rest of you. That thought occurred to me after I learned that Helen Iacono had admitted that she had gone out with Pyle a few times last winter. What if she had said she hadn't? When the police found out she had lied, and they would have, she would have been in for it. It wouldn't have proved she had killed him, but the going would have been mighty rough. I understand that the rest of you have all denied that you ever had anything to do with Pyle. Is that right? Miss Annis?"

"Certainly." Her chin was up. "Of course, I had met him. Everybody in show business has. Once when he came backstage at the Coronet, and once at a party somewhere, and one other time but I don't remember where."

"Miss Morgan?"

She was smiling at me, a crooked smile. "Do you call this helping us?" she demanded.

"It might lead to that after I know how you stand. After all, the cops have your statement."

She shrugged. "I've been around longer than Carol, so I had seen him to speak to more than she had. Once I danced with him at the Flamingo, two years ago. That was the closest I had ever been to him."

"Miss Choate?"

"I never had the honor. I only came to New York last fall. From Montana. He had been pointed out to me from a distance, but he never chased me."

"Miss Jaret?"

"He was Broadway," she said. "I'm TV."

"Don't the twain ever meet?"

"Oh, sure. All the time at Sardi's. That's the only place I ever saw the great Pyle, and I wasn't with him."

"So there you are," I said, "you're all committed. If one of you poisoned him, and though I hate to say it I don't see any way out of that, that one is lying. But if any of the others are lying, if you saw more of him than you admit, you had better get from under quick. If you don't want to tell the cops tell me, tell me now, and I'll pass it on and say I wormed it out of you. Believe me, you'll regret it if you don't."

"Archie Goodwin, a girl's best friend," Lucy said. "My bosom pal."

No one else said anything.

"Actually," I asserted, "I *am* your friend, all of you but one. I have a friendly feeling for all pretty girls, especially those who work, and I admire and respect you for being willing to make an honest fifty bucks by coming there yesterday to carry plates of grub to a bunch of finickers. I *am* your friend, Lucy, if you're not the murderer."

I leaned forward, forgetting the wobbly chair leg, but it didn't object. It was about time to put a crimp in Helen's personal project. "Another thing. It's quite possible that one of you *did* see her returning to the kitchen for another plate, and you haven't said so because you don't want to squeal on her. If so, spill it now. The longer this hangs on, the hotter it will get. When it gets so the pressure is too much for you and you decide you have got to tell it, it will be too late. Tomorrow may be too late. If you go to the cops with it tomorrow they probably won't believe you; they'll figure that you did it yourself and you're trying to squirm out. If you don't want to tell me here and now, in front of her, come with me down to Nero Wolfe's office and we'll talk it over."

They were exchanging glances, and they were not friendly glances. When I had arrived probably not one of them, excluding the murderer, had believed that a poisoner was present, but now they all did, or at least they thought she might be; and when that feeling takes hold it's good-bye to friendliness. It would have been convenient if I could have detected fear in one of the glances, but fear and suspicion and uneasiness are too much alike on faces to tell them apart.

"You *are* a help," Carol Annis said bitterly. "Now you've got us hating each other. Now everybody suspects everybody."

I had quit being nice and sympathetic. "It's about time," I told her. I glanced at my wrist. "It's not midnight yet. If I've made you all realize that this is no Broadway production, or TV either, and the longer the payoff is postponed the tougher it will be for everybody, I *have* helped." I stood up. "Let's go. I don't say Mr. Wolfe can do it by just snapping his fingers, but he might surprise you. He has often surprised me."

"All right," Nora said. She arose. "Come on. This is getting too damn painful. Come on."

I don't pretend that that was what I had been heading for. I admit that I had just been carried along by my tongue. If I arrived with the gang at midnight and Wolfe had gone to bed, he would almost certainly refuse to play. Even if he were still up, he might refuse to work, just to teach me a lesson, since I had not stuck to my instructions. Those thoughts were at me as Peggy Choate bounced up and Carol Annis started to leave the couch.

But they were wasted. That tussle with Wolfe never came off. A door at the end of the room which had been standing ajar suddenly swung open, and there in its frame was a two-legged figure with shoulders almost as broad as the doorway, and I was squinting at Sergeant Purley Stebbins of Manhattan Homicide West. He moved forward, croaking, "I'm surprised at you, Goodwin. These ladies ought to get some sleep."

OF COURSE I WAS a monkey. If it had been Stebbins who had made a monkey of me I suppose I would have leaped for a window and dived through. Hitting the pavement from a fourth-story window should be enough to finish a monkey, and life wouldn't be worth living if I had been bamboozled by Purley Stebbins. But obviously it hadn't been him; it had been Peggy Choate or Nora Jaret, or both; Purley had merely accepted an invitation to come and listen in.

So I kept my face. To say I was jaunty would be stretching it, but I didn't scream or tear my hair. "Greetings," I said heartily. "And welcome. I've been wondering why you didn't join us instead of skulking in there in the dark."

"I'll bet you have." He had come to arm's length and stopped. He turned. "You can relax, ladies." Back to me: "You're under arrest for obstructing justice. Come along."

"In a minute. You've got all night." I moved my head. "Of course, Peggy and Nora knew this hero was in there, but I'd—"

"I said come along!" he barked.

"And I said in a minute, I intend to ask a couple of questions. I wouldn't dream of resisting arrest, but I've got leg cramp from kneeling too long and if you're in a hurry you'll have to carry me." I moved my eyes. "I'd like to know if you all knew. Did you, Miss Iacono?"

"Of course not."

"Miss Morgan?"

"No."

"Miss Annis?"

"No, I didn't, but I think you did." She tossed her head and the corn silk fluttered. "That was contemptible. Saying you wanted to help us, so we would talk, with a policeman listening."

"And then he arrests me?"

"That's just an act."

"I wish it were. Ask your friends Peggy and Nora if I knew—only I suppose you wouldn't believe them. *They* knew, and they didn't tell you. You'd better all think over everything you said. Okay, Sergeant, the leg cramp's gone."

He actually started a hand for my elbow, but I was moving and it wasn't there. I opened the door to the hall. Of course, he had me go first down the three flights; no cop in his senses would descend stairs in front of a dangerous criminal in custody. When we emerged to the sidewalk and he told me to turn left I asked him, "Why not cuffs?"

"Clown if you want to," he croaked.

He flagged a taxi on Amsterdam Avenue, and when we were in and rolling I spoke. "I've been thinking, about laws and liberties and so on. Take false arrest, for instance. And take obstructing justice. If a man is arrested for obstructing justice and it turns out that he didn't obstruct any justice, does that make the arrest false? I wish I knew more about law. I guess I'll have to ask a lawyer. Nathaniel Parker would know."

It was the mention of Parker, the lawyer Wolfe uses when the occasion calls for one, that got him. He had seen Parker in action.

"They heard you," he said, "and I heard you, and I took some notes. You interfered in a homicide investigation. You quoted the police to them. You told them what the police think, and what they're doing and are going to do. You played a game with them with those pieces of paper to show them exactly how it figures. You tried to get them to tell you things instead of telling the police, and you were going to take them to Nero Wolfe so he could pry it out of them. And you haven't even got the excuse that Wolfe is representing a client. He hasn't got a client."

"Wrong. He has."

"Like hell he has. Name her."

"Not her, him. Fritz Brenner. He is seeing red because food cooked by him was poisoned and killed a man. It's convenient to have the client living right in the house. You admit that a licensed detective has a right to investigate on behalf of a client."

"I admit nothing."

"That's sensible," I said approvingly. "You shouldn't. When you're on the stand being sued for false arrest, it would be bad to have it thrown up to you, and it would be two against one because the hackie could testify. Can you hear us, driver?"

"Sure I can hear you," he sang out. "It's very interesting."

"So watch your tongue," I told Purley. "You could get hooked for a year's pay. As for quoting the police, I merely said that they think it was one of those five, and when Cramer told Mr. Wolfe that he didn't say it was confidential. As for telling them what the police think, same comment. As for playing that game with them, why not? As for trying to get them to tell me things, I won't comment on that at all because I don't want to be rude. That must have been a slip of the tongue. If you ask me why I didn't balk there at the apartment and bring up these points then and there, what was the use? You had spoiled the party. They wouldn't have come downtown with me. Also I am saving a buck of Mr. Wolfe's money, since you had arrested me and therefore the taxi fare is on the city of New York. Am I still under arrest?"

"You're damn right you are."

"That may be ill-advised. You heard him, driver."

"Sure I heard him."

"Good. Try to remember it."

We were on Ninth Avenue, stopped at Forty-second Street for a light. When the light changed and we moved, Purley told the hackie to pull over to the curb, and he obeyed. At that time of night there were plenty of gaps. Purley took something from a pocket and showed it to the hackie, and said, "Go get yourself a Coke and come back in ten minutes," and he climbed out and went. Purley turned his head to glare at me.

"I'll pay for the Coke," I offered.

He ignored it. "Lieutenant Rowcliff," he said, "is expecting us at Twentieth Street."

"Fine. Even under arrest, one will get you five that I can make him start stuttering in ten minutes."

"You're not under arrest."

I leaned forward to look at the meter. "Ninety cents. From here on we'll split it."

"Damn it, quit clowning! If you think I'm crawling, you're wrong. I just don't see any percentage in it. If I deliver you in custody I know damn well what you'll do. You'll clam up. We won't get a peep out of you, and in the morning you'll make a phone call and Parker will come. What will that get us?"

I could have said, "A suit for false arrest," but I made it, "Only the pleasure of my company."

There was one point of resemblance between Purley and Carol Annis, just one: no sense of humor. "But," he said, "Lieutenant Rowcliff is expecting you, and you're a material witness in a homicide case, and you were up there working on the suspects."

"You could arrest me as a material witness," I suggested.

He uttered a word that I was glad the hackie wasn't there to hear, and added, "You'd clam up and in the morning you'd be out on bail. I know it's after midnight, but the lieutenant is expecting you."

He's a proud man, Purley is, and I wouldn't go so far as to say that he has nothing to be proud of. He's not a bad cop, as cops go. It was a temptation to keep him dangling for a while, to see how long it would take him to bring himself to the point of coming right out and asking for it, but it was late and I needed some sleep.

"You realize," I said, "that's it's a waste of time and energy. You can tell him everything we said, and if he tried to go into other aspects with me I'll only start making cracks and he'll start stuttering. It's perfectly useless."

"Yeah, I know, but—"

"But the lieutenant expects me."

He nodded. "It was him Nora Jaret told about it, and he sent me. The inspector wasn't around."

"Okay. In the interest of justice, I'll give him an hour. That's understood? Exactly one hour."

"It's not understood with me." He was empathic. "When we get there you're his and he's welcome to you. I don't know if he can stand you for an hour."

AT NOON THE NEXT day, Thursday, Fritz stood at the end of Wolfe's desk, consulting with him on a major point of policy: whether to switch to another source of supply for watercress. The quality had been below par, which for them means perfection, for nearly a week. I was at my desk, yawning. It had been after two o'clock when I got home from my chat with Lieutenant Rowcliff, and with nine hours' sleep in two nights I was way behind.

The hour since Wolfe had come down at eleven o'clock from his morning session with the orchids had been spent, most of it, by me reporting and Wolfe listening. My visit with Rowcliff needed only a couple of sentences, since the only detail of any importance was that it had taken me eight minutes to get him stuttering, but Wolfe wanted my conversation with the girls verbatim, and also my impressions and conclusions. I told him my basic conclusion was that the only way she could be nailed, barring a stroke of luck, would be by a few dozen men sticking to the routine—her getting the poison and her connection with Pyle.

"And," I added, "her connection with Pyle may be hopeless. In fact, it probably is. If it's Helen Iacono, what she told us is no help. If what she told us is true she had no reason to kill him, and if it isn't true how are you going to prove it? If it's one of the others she is certainly no half-wit, and there may be absolutely nothing to link her up. Being very careful with visitors to your penthouse is fine as long as you're alive, but it has its drawbacks if one of them feeds you arsenic. It may save her neck."

He was regarding me without enthusiasm. "You are saying in effect that it must be left to the police. I don't have a few dozen men. I can expose her only by a stroke of luck."

"Right. Or a stroke of genius. That's your department. I make no conclusions about genius."

"Then why the devil were you going to bring them to me at midnight? Don't answer. I know. To badger me."

"No, sir. I told you. I had got nowhere with them. I had got them looking at each other out of the corners of their eyes, but that was all. I kept on talking, and suddenly I heard myself inviting them to come home with me. I was giving them the excuse that I wanted them to discuss it with you, but that may have been just a cover for certain instincts that a man is entitled to. They are very attractive girls—all but one."

"Which one?"

"That's what we're working on."

He probably would have harped on it if Fritz hadn't entered to present the watercress problem. As they wrestled with it, dealing with it from all angles, I swiveled my back to them so I could do my yawning in private. Finally, they got it settled, deciding to give the present source one more week and then switch if the quality didn't improve; and then I heard Fritz say, "There's another matter, sir. Felix phoned me this morning. He and Zoltan would like an appointment with you after lunch, and I would like to be present. They suggested half-past two, if that will suit your convenience."

"What is it?" Wolfe demanded. "Something wrong at the restaurant?"

"No, sir. Concerning the misfortune of Tuesday evening."

"What about it?"

"It would be better for them to tell you. It is their concern."

I swiveled for a view of Fritz's face. Had Felix and Zoltan been holding out on us? Fritz's expression didn't tell me, but it did tell Wolfe something: that it would be unwise for him to insist on knowing the nature of Felix's and Zoltan's concern because Fritz had said all he intended to. There is no one more obliging than Fritz, but also there is no one more immovable when he has taken a stand. So Wolfe merely said that half-past two would be convenient. When Fritz had left I offered to go to the kitchen and see if I could pry it out of him, but Wolfe said no, apparently it wasn't urgent.

As it turned out, it wasn't. Wolfe and I were still in the dining room, with coffee, when the doorbell rang at 2:25 and Fritz answered it, and when we crossed the hall to the office Felix was in the red leather chair, Zoltan was in one of the yellow ones, and Fritz was standing. Fritz had removed his apron and put on a jacket, which was quite proper. People do not attend business conferences in aprons.

When we had exchanged greetings, and Fritz had been told to sit down and had done so, and Wolfe and I had gone to our desks, Felix spoke. "You won't mind, Mr. Wolfe, if I ask a question? Before I say why we requested an appointment?"

Wolfe told him no, go ahead.

"Because," Felix said, "we would like to know this first. We are under the impression that the police are making no progress. They haven't said so, they tell us nothing, but we have the impression. Is it true?"

"It was true at two o'clock this morning, twelve hours ago. They may have learned something by now, but I doubt it."

"Do you think they will soon make progress? That they will soon be successful?"

"I don't know. I can only conjecture. Archie thinks that unless they have a stroke of luck the inquiry will be long and laborious, and even then may fail. I'm inclined to agree with him."

Felix nodded. "That is what we fear—Zoltan and I and others at the restaurant. It is causing a most regrettable atmosphere. A few of our most desirable patrons make jokes, but most of them do not, and some of them do not come. We do not blame them. For the *maître d'hôtel* and one of our chefs to assist at a dinner where a guest is served poison—that is not pleasant. If the—"

"Confound it, Felix! I have avowed my responsibility. I have apologized. Are you here for the gloomy satisfaction of reproaching me?"

"No, sir." He was shocked. "Of course not. We came to say that if the poisoner is not soon discovered, and then the affair will be forgotten, the effect on the restaurant may be serious. And if the police are making no progress that may happen, so we appeal to you. We wish to engage your professional services. We know that with you there would be no question. You would solve it quickly and completely. We know it wouldn't be proper to pay you from restaurant funds, since you are the trustee, so we'll pay you with our own money. There was a meeting of the staff last night, and all will contribute, in a proper ration. We appeal to you."

Zoltan stretched out a hand, arm's length. "We appeal to you," he said.

"Pfui," Wolfe grunted.

He had my sympathy. Not only was their matter-of-fact confidence in his prowess highly flattering, but also their appealing instead of demanding, since he had got them into it, was extremely touching. But a man with a long-standing reputation for being hard and blunt simply can't afford the softer feelings, no matter what the provocation. It called for great self-control.

Felix and Zoltan exchanged looks. "He said 'pfui,' " Zoltan told Felix.

"I heard him," Felix snapped, "I have ears."

Fritz spoke. "I wished to be present," he said, "so I could add my appeal to theirs. I offered to contribute, but they said no."

Wolfe took them in, his eyes going right to left and back again. "This is preposterous," he declared. "I said 'pfui' not in disgust but in astonishment. I am solely to blame for this mess, but you offer to pay me to clean it up. Preposterous! You should know that I have already bestirred myself. Archie?"

"Yes, sir. At least you have bestirred me."

He skipped it. "And," he told them, "your coming is opportune. Before lunch I was sitting here considering the situation, and I concluded that the only way to manage the affair with dispatch is to get the wretch to betray herself; and I conceived a plan. For it I need your cooperation. Yours, Zoltan. Your help is essential. Will you give it? I appeal to you."

Zoltan upturned his palms and raised his shoulders. "But yes! But how?"

"It is complicated. Also it will require great dexterity and aplomb. How are you on the telephone? Some people are not themselves, not entirely at ease, when they are phoning. A few are even discomfited. Are you?"

"No." He reflected. "I don't think so. No."

"If you are it won't work. The plan requires that you telephone five of those women this afternoon. You will first call Miss Iacono, tell her who you are, and ask her to meet you somewhere—in some obscure restaurant. You will say that on Tuesday evening, when you told me that you had not seen one of them return for a second plate, you were upset and flustered by what had happened, and later, when the police questioned you, you were afraid to contradict yourself and tell the truth. But now that the notoriety is harming the restaurant you feel that you may have to reveal the fact that you did see her return for a second plate, but that before—"

"But I didn't!" Zoltan cried. "I told—"

"*Tais-toi!*" Felix snapped at him.

Wolfe resumed. "—but that before you do so you wish to discuss it with her. You will say that one reason you have kept silent is that you have been unable to believe that anyone as attractive and charming as she is could be guilty of such a crime. A parenthesis. I should have said at the beginning that you must not try to parrot my words. I am giving you only the substance; the words must be your own, those you would naturally use. You understand that?"

"Yes, sir." Zoltan's hands were clasped tight.

"So don't try to memorize my words. Your purpose is to get her to agree to meet you. She will of course assume that you intend to blackmail her, but you will not say so. You will try to give her the impression, in everything you say and in your tone of voice, that you will not demand money from her, but expect her favors. In short, that you desire her. I can't tell you how to convey that impression; I must leave that to you. The only requisite is that she must be convinced that if she refuses to meet you, you will go at once to the police and tell them the truth."

"Then you know," Zoltan said. "Then she is guilty."

"Not at all. I haven't the slightest idea who is guilty. When you have finished with her you will phone the other four and repeat the performance—Miss Choate, Miss Annis, Miss—"

"My God, Mr. Wolfe! That's impossible!"

"Not impossible, merely difficult. You alone can do it, for they know your voice. I considered having Archie do it, imitating your voice, but it would be too risky. You said you would help, but there's no use trying it if the bare idea appalls you. Will you undertake it?"

"I don't . . . I would . . ."

"He will," Felix said. "He is like that. He only needs to swallow it. He will do it well. But I must ask, can he be expected to get them all to agree to meet him? The guilty one, yes, but the others?"

"Certainly not. There is much to discuss and arrange. The innocent ones will react variously according to their tempers. One or more of them will probably inform the police, and I must provide for that contingency with Mr. Cramer." To Zoltan: "Since it is possible that one of the innocent ones will agree to meet you, for some unimaginable reason, you will have to give them different hours for the appointments. There are many details to settle, but that is mere routine. The key is you. You must, of course, rehearse, and

into a telephone transmitter. There are several stations on the
house phone. You will go to Archie's room and speak from there.
We will listen at the other stations: Archie in the plant rooms, I in
my room, Fritz in the kitchen, and Felix here. Archie will handle
the other end of the conversation; he is much better qualified than
I to improvise the responses of young women.

"Do you want me to repeat the substance of what you are to say
before rehearsal?"

Zoltan opened his mouth and closed it again.

"Yes," he said.

SERGEANT PURLEY STEBBINS SHIFTED his fanny for the nth time in two
hours. "She's not coming," he muttered. "It's nearly eight o'clock."
His chair was about half big enough for his personal dimensions.

We were squeezed in a corner of the kitchen of John Piotti's
little restaurant on 14th Street between Second and Third
Avenues. On the midget table between us were two notebooks, his
and mine, and a small metal case. Of the three cords extending
from the case, the two in front went to the earphones we had on,
and the one at the back ran down the wall, through the floor,
along the basement ceiling toward the front, back up through the
floor, and on through a tabletop, where it was connected to a
microphone hidden in a bowl of artificial flowers. The installation,
a rush order, had cost Wolfe $191.67. Permission to have it made
had cost him nothing because he had once got John Piotti out of a
difficulty and hadn't soaked him beyond reason.

"We'll have to hang on," I said. "You never can tell with a redhead."

The exposed page of my notebook was blank, but Purley had
written on his. As follows:

Helen Iacono	6:00 P.M.
Peggy Choate	7:30 P.M.
Carol Annis	9:00 P.M.
Lucy Morgan	10:30 P.M.
Nora Jaret	12:00 P.M.

It was in my head. If I had had to write it down I would certainly have made 1:00 "P.M." do, but policemen are trained to do things right.

"Anyhow," Purley said, "we know damn well who it is."

"Don't count your poisoners," I said, "before they're hatched." It was pretty feeble, but I was tired and still short on sleep.

I hoped to heaven he was right, since otherwise the operation was a flop. So far everything had been fine. After half an hour of rehearsing, Zoltan had been wonderful. He had made the five calls from the extension in my room, and when he was through I told him his name should be in lights on a Broadway marquee. The toughest job had been getting Inspector Cramer to agree to Wolfe's terms, but he had no good answer to Wolfe's argument that if he insisted on changing the rules Zoltan wouldn't play. So Purley was in the kitchen with me, Cramer was with Wolfe in the office, prepared to stay for dinner, Zoltan was at the restaurant table with the hidden mike, and two homicide dicks, one male and one female, were at another table twenty feet away. One of the most elaborate charades Nero Wolfe had ever staged.

Purley was right when he said we knew who it was, but I was right too—she hadn't been hatched yet. The reactions to Zoltan's calls had settled it. Helen Iacono had been indignant and after a couple of minutes had hung up on him, and had immediately phoned the district attorney's office. Peggy Choate had let him finish his spiel and then called him a liar, but she had not said definitely that she wouldn't meet him, and the DA or police hadn't heard from her. Carol Annis, after he had spoken his lines, had used only ten words: "Where can I meet you?" and, after he had told her where and when: "All right, I'll be there." Lucy Morgan had coaxed him along, trying to get him to fill it all in on the phone, had finally said she would keep the appointment, and then had rushed downtown and rung our doorbell, told me her tale, demanded that I accompany her to the rendezvous, and insisted on seeing Wolfe. I had to promise to go to get rid of her. Nora Jaret had called him assorted names, from liar on up, or on down, and had told him she had a friend listening in on an extension, which was almost certainly a lie. Neither we nor the law had had a peep from her.

So it was Carol Annis with the corn-silk hair, that was plain enough, but there was no salt on her tail. If she was really smart and really tough she might decide to sit tight and not come, figuring that when they came at her with Zoltan's story she would say he was either mistaken or lying, and we would be up a stump. If she was dumb and only fairly tough she might scram. Of course, they would find her and haul her back, but if she said Zoltan was lying and she had run because she thought she was being framed, again we would be up a stump. But if she was both smart and tough but not quite enough of either, she would turn up at nine o'clock and join Zoltan. From there on it would be up to him, but that had been rehearsed too, and after his performance on the phone, I thought he would deliver.

At half-past eight Purley said, "She's not coming," and removed his earphone.

"I never thought she would," I said. The "she" was of course Peggy Choate, whose hour had been 7:30. "I said you never can tell with a redhead merely to make conversation."

Purley signaled to Piotti, who had been hovering around most of the time, and he brought us a pot of coffee and two fresh cups. The minutes were snails, barely moving. When we had emptied the cups I poured more. At 8:48 Purley put his earphone back on. At 8:56 I asked, "Shall I do a countdown?"

"You'd clown in the hot seat," he muttered, so hoarse that it was barely words. He always gets hoarser as the tension grows; that's the only sign.

It was four minutes past nine when the phone brought me the sound of a chair scraping, then faintly Zoltan's voice saying good evening, and then a female voice, but I couldn't get the words.

"Not loud enough," Purley whispered hoarsely.

"Shut up." I had my pen out. "They're standing up."

There came the sound of chairs scraping, and other little sounds, and then:

Zoltan: Will you have a drink?

Carol: No. I don't want anything.

Zoltan: Won't you eat something?

Carol: I don't feel . . . maybe I will.

Purley and I exchanged glances. That was promising. That sounded as if we might get more than conversation.

Another female voice, belonging to Mrs. Piotti: We have good Osso Buco, madame. Very good. A specialty.

Carol: No, not meat.

Zoltan: A sweet perhaps?

Carol: No.

Zoltan: It is more friendly if we eat. The spaghetti with anchovy sauce is excellent. I had some.

Carol: You had some?

I bit my lip, but he handled it fine.

Zoltan: I've been here half an hour, I wanted so much to see you. I thought I should order something, and I tried that. I might even eat another portion.

Carol: You should know good food. All right.

Mrs. Piotti: Two spaghetti anchovy. Wine? A very good Chianti?

Carol: No. Coffee.

Pause.

Zoltan: You are more lovely without a veil, but the veil is good, too. It makes me want to see behind it. Of course I—

Carol: You have seen behind it, Mr. Mahany.

Zoltan: Ah! You know my name?

Carol: It was in the paper.

Zoltan: I am not sorry that you know it, I want you to know my name, but it will be nicer if you call me Zoltan.

Carol: I might some day. It will depend. I certainly won't call you Zoltan if you go on thinking what you said on the phone. You're mistaken, Mr. Mahany. You didn't see me go back for another plate, because I didn't. I can't believe you would tell a vicious lie about me, so I just think you're mistaken.

Mrs. Piotti, in the kitchen for the spaghetti, came to the corner to stoop and whisper into my free ear, "She's wearing a veil."

Zoltan: I am not mistaken, my dear. That is useless. I know. How could I be mistaken when the first moment I saw you I felt . . . but I will not try to tell you how I felt. If any of the others had come and taken another plate I would have stopped her, but not you. Before you I was dumb. So it is useless.

Needing only one hand for my pen, I used the free one to blow a kiss to Purley.

Carol: I see. So you're sure.

Zoltan: I am, my dear. Very sure.

Carol: But you haven't told the police.

Zoltan: Of course not.

Carol: Have you told Nero Wolfe or Archie Goodwin?

Zoltan: I have told no one. How could I tell anyone? Mr. Wolfe is sure that the one who returned for another plate is the one who killed that man, gave him poison, and Mr. Wolfe is always right. So it is terrible for me. Could I tell anyone that I know you killed a man? You? How could I? That is why I had to see you, to talk with you. If you weren't wearing that veil I could look into your beautiful eyes. I think I know what I would see there. I would see suffering and sorrow. I saw that in your eyes Tuesday evening. I know he made you suffer. I know you wouldn't kill a man unless you had to. That is why—

The voice stopped. That was understandable, since Mrs. Piotti had gone through the door with the spaghetti and coffee and had had time to reach their table. Assorted sounds came as she served them.

Purley muttered, "He's overdoing it," and I muttered back, "No. He's perfect." Mrs. Piotti came over and stood looking down at my notebook. It wasn't until after Mrs. Piotti was back in the kitchen that Carol's voice came.

Carol: That's why I am wearing the veil, Zoltan, because I know it's in my eyes. You're right. I had to. He did make me suffer. He ruined my life.

Zoltan: No, my dear. Your life is not ruined. No! No matter what he did. Was he . . . did he . . .

I was biting my lip again. Why didn't he give them the signal?

The food had been served and presumably they were eating. He had been told that it would be pointless to try to get her to give him any details of her relations with Pyle, since they would almost certainly be lies. Why didn't he give the signal? Her voice was coming:

Carol: He promised to marry me. I'm only twenty-two years old, Zoltan. I didn't think I would ever let a man touch me again, but the way you . . . I don't know. I'm glad you know I killed him because it will be better now, to know that somebody knows. To know that *you* know. Yes, I had to kill him, I *had* to, because if I didn't I would have had to kill myself. Some day I may tell you what a fool I was, how I—Oh!

Zoltan: What? What's the matter?

Carol: My bag. I left it in my car. Out front. And I didn't lock the car. A blue Plymouth hardtop. Would you . . . I'll go . . .

Zoltan: I'll get it.

The sound came of his chair scraping, then faintly his footsteps, and then silence. But the silence was broken in ten seconds, whereas it would have taken him much longer to go for the purse and return. What broke it was a male voice saying, "I'm an officer of the law, Miss Annis" and a noise from Carol. Purley, shedding his earphone, jumped up and went, and I followed, notebook in hand.

It was quite a tableau. The male dick stood with a hand on Carol's shoulder. Carol sat stiff, her chin up, staring straight ahead. The female dick, not much older than Carol, stood facing her from across the table, holding with both hands, at breast level, a plate of spaghetti. She spoke to Purley. "She put something in it and then stuck something in her dress. I saw her in my mirror."

I moved in. After all, I was in charge, under the terms Cramer had agreed to. "Thank you, Miss Annis," I said. "You were a help. On a signal from Zoltan they were going to start a commotion to give him an excuse to leave the table, but you saved them the trouble. I thought you'd like to know. Come on, Zoltan. All over. According to plan."

He had entered and stopped three paces off, a blue handbag under his arm. As he moved toward us, Purley put out a hand. "I'll take that."

CRAMER WAS IN THE red leather chair. Carol Annis was in a yellow one facing Wolfe's desk, with Purley on one side of her and his female colleague on the other. The male colleague had been sent to the laboratory with the plate of spaghetti and a small roll of paper that had been fished from inside Carol's dress. Fritz, Felix, and Zoltan were on the couch near the end of my desk.

"I will not pretend, Miss Annis," Wolfe was saying. "One reason that I persuaded Mr. Cramer to have you brought here first on your way to limbo was that I needed to appease my rancor. You had injured and humiliated not only me, but also one of my most valued friends, Fritz Brenner, and two other men whom I esteem, and I had arranged the situation that gave you your opportunity; and I wished them to witness your own humiliation, contrived by me in my presence."

"That's enough of that," Cramer growled.

Wolfe ignored him. "I admit the puerility of that reason, Miss Annis, but in candor I wanted to acknowledge it. A better reason was that I wished to ask you a few questions. You took such prodigious risks that it is hard to believe in your sanity, and it would give me no satisfaction to work vengeance on a madwoman. What would you have done if Felix's eyes had been on you when you entered with the plate of poison and went to Mr. Pyle? Or if, when you returned to the kitchen for a second plate, Zoltan had challenged you? What would you have done?"

No answer. Apparently, she was holding her gaze straight at Wolfe, but from my angle it was hard to tell because she still had the veil on. Asked by Cramer to remove it, she had refused. When the female dick had extracted the roll of paper from inside Carol's dress she had asked Cramer if she should pull the veil off and Cramer had said no. No rough stuff.

There was no question about Wolfe's gaze at her. He was forward in his chair, his palms flat on his desk. He persisted. "Will you answer me, Miss Annis?"

She wouldn't.

"Are you a lunatic, Miss Annis?"

She wasn't saying.

Wolfe's head jerked to me. "Is she deranged, Archie?"

That was unnecessary. When we're alone I don't particularly mind his insinuations that I presume to be an authority on women, but there was company present. I gave him a look and snapped, "No comment."

He returned to her. "Then that must wait. I leave to the police such matters as your procurement of the poison and your relations with Mr. Pyle, mentioning only that you cannot now deny possession of arsenic, since you used it a second time this evening. It will unquestionably be found in the spaghetti and in the roll of paper you concealed in your dress; and so, manifestly, if you are mad you are also ruthless and malevolent. You may have been intolerably provoked by Mr. Pyle, but not by Zoltan. He presented himself not as a nemesis, but as a bewitched champion. He offered his homage, making no demands, and your counteroffer was death."

"You lie, " Carol said. "And he lied. He was going to lie about me. He didn't see me go back for a second plate, but he was going to say he did. And you lie. He did make demands. He threatened me."

Wolfe's brows went up. "Then you haven't been told?"

"Told what?"

"That you were overheard. That is the other question I had for you. I have no apology for contriving the trap, but you deserve to know you are in its jaws. All that you and Zoltan said was heard by two men at the other end of a wire in another room, and they recorded it—Mr. Stebbins of the police, now at your left, and Mr. Goodwin."

"You lie," she said.

"No, Miss Annis. This isn't the trap; it has already been sprung. You have it, Mr. Stebbins?"

Purley nodded. He hates to answer questions from Wolfe.

"Archie?"

"Yes, sir."

"Did Zoltan threaten her or make demands?"

"No, sir. He followed instructions."

He returned to Carol. "Now you know. I wanted to make sure of that. To finish, since you may have had a just and weighty grievance against Mr. Pyle, I would myself prefer to see you made to account for your attempt to kill Zoltan, but that is not in my discretion. In any case, my rancor is appeased, and I hold—"

"That's enough," Cramer blurted, leaving his chair. "I didn't agree to let you preach at her all night. Bring her along, Sergeant."

As Purley arose a voice came. "May I say something?" It was Fritz. Heads turned as he left the couch and moved, detouring around Zoltan's feet and Purley's bulk to get to Carol, and turning to stand looking down at her.

"On account of what Mr. Wolfe said," he told her. "He said you injured me, and that is true. It is also true that I wanted him to find you. I can't speak for Felix, and you tried to kill Zoltan and I can't speak for him, but I can speak for myself. I forgive you."

"You lie," Carol said.

Cheese Blinis

Blini:
1 cup flour
½ tsp. salt
1 tsp. baking soda
2 Tbsp. sugar
2 eggs at room temperature, beaten until light yellow
⅔ cup milk
⅓ cup water
1 tsp. vanilla

Filling:
1½ cups smooth-curd cottage cheese
¼ cup egg substitute
1 Tbsp. butter, softened
1 Tbsp. vanilla
Butter-flavored Pam
Sour cream to garnish
Confectioner's sugar to garnish
Cinnamon to garnish

MAKE FILLING:
Mix cottage cheese, egg substitute, butter, and vanilla together. Beat until smooth.

MAKE BLINI:
Sift flour, salt, baking powder, and sugar together. Mix eggs, milk, water, and vanilla together in a bowl. Add dry ingredients all at once. Mix just until blended. (Over-beating makes them tough.) Batter will be thin.

SPRAY A SKILLET with Pam. Heat until drops of water dance on the surface. Pour batter onto skillet two tablespoonfuls at a time and spread thinly across the pan by tipping it or by spreading batter quickly about with the back of the spoon. Cook on one side only.

Slide each cake off the grill to a damp tea towel when it is done—
top will no longer be glossy. Cook until batter is gone, respraying
grill with Pam as needed.

ASSEMBLE BLINI:

Place two tablespoons of filling in the center of each pancake.
Fold over sides of cake to make burrito-like shape with filling
inside. Place filled cakes seam-side down on a serving plate. Garnish each cake with a dollop of sour cream, a shake of cinnamon,
and a shake of confectioner's sugar.

Authors' Biographies

Stanley Ellin (1916–1986) stood the mystery genre on its head with his evocatively written crime fiction. His style, as pithy and poignant as any literary writer's; his ideas, the equal of such great idea-men as Roald Dahl and Saki; and his worldview, which was every bit as complex as some of his darker protagonists, all combined to create a paradigm that was a breath of fresh air from the delicate cozies and hard-boiled noir that until then had been staples of the genre. For all this, though, he also had a sense of everyday life and everyday people that few in the genre ever came close to matching. Perhaps this was because, early in his life, he was a steelworker, a dairy farmer, and a teacher. While he is primarily thought of as a short-story writer, he wrote a number of excellent novels, among them *The Eighth Circle* and *Mirror, Mirror on the Wall.*

Joyce Christmas is the creator of two mystery series, one featuring a retired office manager named Betty Trenka, the other centered on an English noblewoman, Lady Margaret Priam, who lives and sleuths in New York City. A former book and magazine editor, she has also written three other novels and several children's plays. Recent novels include *Mood to Murder* and *Dying Well.*

Ruth Rendell's stories of psychological suspense always reveal a new twist in the human psyche that seemed to be just waiting for an author like her to reveal it. The author of more than twenty novels and innumerable short stories, she explores the dark recesses of the mind that make men and women do inexplicable things. Her short fiction has regularly appeared in the year's best anthologies, as well as *The Best British Mysteries of the 20th Century.* Recent novels include *Bloodlines, Keys to the Street, The Reason Why,* and *Road Rage.*

Walter Satterthwaite is adept at all facets of the mystery genre, as his nominations for the Agatha and Shamus Awards indicate. His two series are as different as night and day. In his historical series, Harry Houdini and Sir Arthur Conan Doyle team up to solve a baffling crime in the novel *Escapade,* which won the French Prix du Roman d'Aventures Award. His second series is contemporary, featuring Santa Fe sleuth Joshua Croft and his partner Rota Mondragon. A former encyclopedia salesman, proofreader, bartender, and restaurant manager, Satterthwaite lives in Santa Fe, New Mexico.

M. D. Lake's fiction has appeared in anthologies such as *The Mysterious West* and *Funny Bones.* His most recent novel is *Death Calls the Tune.* A writer with a gift for dialogue and a natural talent for description, here he is at his best in this rather one-sided conversation over a nice cup of tea where several not-so-nice discoveries are made.

Linda Grant is the pseudonym of Linda V. Williams and the author of a detective series featuring private investigator Catherine Saylor and her partner, Jesse. Her short fiction has appeared in *The Mysterious West, The First Lady Murders,* and *Women on the Case.* Twice nominated for the Anthony Award, she lives and works in Berkeley, California. Recent novels include *Vampire Bytes* and *Remind Me Who I Am, Again.*

Bill Pronzini is one of those writers whose long career shows steady and remarkable progress. While he was always an above-average professional, the fourth decade of his career saw him produce novels of true distinction, *Blue Lonesome* and *A Wasteland of Strangers* among them. His "Nameless" novels, popular now for three full decades, are really chapters in the life of a working-class private investigator who lives in the spiritual epicenter of modern-day San Francisco. Students of history as well as crime fiction will be reading his fiction a hundred years from now.

Bill Crider won the Anthony Award for his first novel in the Sheriff Dan Rhodes series. His first novel in the Truman Smith series was nominated for a Shamus Award, and a third series features college English professor Carl Burns. His short stories have appeared in numerous anthologies, including past *Cat Crimes II* and *III*, *Celebrity Vampires*, *Once Upon a Crime*, and *Werewolves*. His recent work includes collaborating on a series of cozy mysteries with television personality Willard Scott. The first novel, *Death under Blue Skies*, was published in 1997, and the second, *Murder in the Mist*, was recently released.

When you write about **Ed Hoch**, the temptation is to dwell on his prolific writing career. Probably the most abundant short-story writer in the history of mystery, with a story in every issue of *Ellery Queen's Mystery Magazine* for more than twenty years, what is often overlooked is the sheer quality of his work. Whether he's working on a locked-room setup featuring his police detective Captain Leopold, or going rustic with one of his more laid-back series characters, or even getting tough (his collection of hard-boiled stories will be published soon), he is always totally in charge of his material. And what wonderful material it is. His stories are classic treatises on the proper execution of the mystery story.

Caroline Benton was born in Somerset, England, in 1947. She now lives in France and is currently working on a full-length mystery. This is the first time her work has been published in book form.

Peter Crowther is the editor or coeditor of nine anthologies and the coauthor (with James Lovegrove) of the novel *Escardy Gap*.

Since the early 1990s, he has sold some seventy short stories and poems to a wide variety of magazines and chapbooks on both sides of the Atlantic. He has also recently added two chapbooks, *Forest Plains* and *Fugue on a G-String*, and a single-author collection, *The Longest Single Note*, to his credits. His review columns and critical essays on the fields of fantasy, horror, and science fiction appear regularly in *Interzone* and *Hellnotes* Internet magazine. He has also served on the board of trustees of the Horror Writer's Association. He lives in Harrogate, England, with his wife and two sons.

Janwillem van de Wetering, born in Rotterdam, the Netherlands, is a former policeman and businessman now living in rural Maine. In 1971, when he was forty-one, he launched his writing career by publishing *The Empty Mirror*, an autobiographical account of his experiences in a Buddhist monastery. Inspired by the mystery fiction of George Simenon, he tapped into his experience in the Amsterdam Special Constabulary, which he joined in lieu of being drafted into the military. He has written more than thirteen novels featuring Adjutant Grijpstra and Sergeant de Gier, as well as nonfiction and children's books.

Barbara Collins's other short fiction can be found in *Marilyn: Shades of Blonde, Till Death Do Us Part,* and *The Year's 25 Finest Crime and Mystery Stories, Third Edition.* Adept at many forms of mystery fiction, she lives in Muscatine, Iowa, with her husband, novelist Max Allan Collins, and their son Nathan.

Nedra Tyre is a prolific contributor to the mystery magazines, especially *Alfred Hitchcock's Mystery Magazine* and *Ellery Queen's Mystery Magazine*. She has also written several mystery novels, notably *Hall of Death* and *Twice So Fair.*

Joyce Carol Oates, a master of psychological fiction in both novel length and short form, is arguably among the top authors in the United States. She examines the usually fragile bonds that hold people together, whether it be by marriage or blood, then introduces the catalyst that more often than not tears that relationship apart, all the while imbuing her characters with a fully realized life of their own that practically makes them walk off the page. Her most recent novel is *My Heart Laid Bare*, and she recently edited the anthology *Telling Stories: An Anthology for Writers*. Her most recent book is *Blonde*, an exploration of the life of Marilyn Monroe.

Gillian Linscott is known for her series of Edwardian novels featuring radical suffragette Nell Bray, which now includes five books. A former Parliamentary reporter for the BBC, she has also written a historical mystery set in Alaska as well as a contemporary mystery series featuring ex-policeman-turned-physical-trainer Birdie Linnett. Her short fiction appears in such anthologies as *Murder, They Wrote* and *Murder Most Medieval*. She lives with her husband, nonfiction author Tony Geraghty, in England.

Barbara D'Amato is an accomplished writer whose short fiction has appeared in *I, P.I.*, *Cat Crimes*, and *Malice Domestic V.* The main protagonists of her short fiction, Chicago police officers Suzanne Figueroa and Norm Bennis, made their first novel-length appearance in *Killer.app*. Her other series features Catherine "Cat" Marsala, an investigative reporter in Chicago. Her mystery tales range from poignant to parsimonious, cozy to chilling, and always leave a reader wanting more.

While **Rex Stout** (1886–1975) will be fondly remembered for his creation of the corpulent detective and gourmet Nero Wolfe, during his writing career of more than forty years he produced mainstream and science fiction novels and also founded his own publishing house, Vanguard Press. After serving as a U.S. Navy yeoman on President Theodore Roosevelt's yacht, he worked as a bookkeeper and hotel manager before turning to writing in 1927. During his lifetime, he was active in many authors' organizations, including the Author's League of America, the Author's Guild, and the Mystery Writers of America.

Copyrights and Permissions

Murder Most

FELINE

Cunning Tales of Cats and Crime

CONTENTS

INTRODUCTION

Oyez! Oyez! Oyez! The court is now in session!

On the surface, one would think that cats and the court system do not have much in common. After all, most people consider the modern legal system to be a slow, massive, unwieldy (possibly even out-of-control) institution where injustices are perpetrated on a daily basis while the rights of the innocents are overlooked. Cats, on the other hand, are living symbols of grace and dignity, quick to deal out their own idea of justice in the form of a claw or bite when necessary, and only occasionally ignoring the rights of their innocent owners.

But upon closer examination, there are several similarities between felines and the American legal system. For example, the justice system (when it works) is reputed to be impartial, and often is, deciding good and evil without regard for race, social status, or gender. Cat owners know that a cat is impartial in many ways, deciding who is worthy of his or her affection also without regard to race, status, or gender, but according to some mysterious private agenda only the cat knows. When the court's attention is brought to bear on a person or event, the scrutiny can be overwhelming, causing many to break down under the all-encompassing eye of the law. The feeling is very much like being stared at by a cat who wants something you have, that inscrutable feline gaze which, if one is not careful, may lead to the confession of all kinds of sins or to the surrender of whatever item that will take those all-knowing eyes off their target. Finally, there has been a recent trend in the judicial system of turning the participants—from the alleged criminals and/or victims to the legal teams on both sides of the case—into celebrities, raising them to an exalted (or sometimes lowering them to a reviled) position in the nation's consciousness. And anybody who has ever owned a cat knows the type of star treatment they expect to receive—and the punishment that may occur if they don't get it.

With these similarities in mind, it seems only natural to combine cats, crime, and the courts and see what the verdict is. The results are the seventeen stories collected here, all of which make jurisprudence more fun than any televised trial could ever be. From a private detective who goes to bat for a cat's inheritance to a feline companion who is a crucial, albeit unknowing, witness in a courtroom unlike any other, cats take the stand in their own defense to catch criminals, provide evidence, and turn the legal system on its collective ear—all in the name of justice.

The jury has returned, the bailiff is calling the court to order, and the judge is entering the courtroom. So sit back on the courtroom bench and get ready to watch law meet paw in these cases of cats and crime.

—The Editors

Murder Most
FELINE

The Witness Cat

Parnell Hall

Steve Winslow was having a bad day. It started off with a witness giving him fits and ended up with his secretary not speaking to him.

Steve was getting nowhere with this witness. The more he cross-examined, the worse it got. Russ Overmeyer sat on the witness stand, smug, self-satisfied, fielding all his questions and turning them back against his client. And this was the key witness. If Steve Winslow couldn't shake Overmeyer's testimony, the defendant was sunk.

Steve Winslow glanced over at the defense table where his client sat. A wizened old man with a stubborn streak and an irascible nature, Clinton Hobbs was glaring at him with cranky eyes. Which was not surprising. Steve Winslow was Mr. Hobbs's court-appointed lawyer, assigned because the defendant was indigent and could not afford to hire an attorney for himself. And Mr. Hobbs could not have been less happy with the choice. With long hair, blue jeans, and corduroy jacket, Steve Winslow looked like a leftover from the sixties. That, coupled with the fact he was much too young to actually be from the sixties, did not exactly inspire Mr. Hobbs with confidence. Steve Winslow was acting as his attorney only because the judge would not allow him to choose another.

Which had to be rather frustrating for someone accused of murder.

Steve Winslow pushed the hair out of his eyes and cocked his head at the witness. "Well, then, Mr. Overmeyer. Getting back to the night in question when you claim you saw my client leaving the bedroom of the decedent—"

The prosecutor, Assistant District Attorney Harvey Beerbaum, was on his feet. "Objection to the word *claim,* Your Honor. The witness isn't claiming anything, he's stating what he saw."

Judge Judith Weston banged the gavel. A tough, no-nonsense jurist, Judge Weston did not take kindly to technical objections. "Overruled," she snapped. "I have confidence the witness can take care of himself. And I would thank you to state your objections at the sidebar, not in front of the jury."

"Yes, Your Honor," A.D.A. Beerbaum said.

"Would the court reporter read back the question?"

"Actually, I believe I was interrupted *before* I asked the question," Steve Winslow said.

"Then ask it now," Judge Weston said irritably.

"Yes, Your Honor." Steve Winslow glanced at the prosecutor. Their eyes met, and Steve smiled. It dawned on A.D.A. Beerbaum that Steve Winslow had deliberately goaded him into annoying the judge.

"Now then, Mr. Overmeyer," Steve Winslow continued. "On the night in question, the night your uncle was killed, the night you claim you saw the defendant coming from his room—just what time did this supposedly happen?"

Russ Overmeyer had a round face, shiny bald head, and twinkling eyes. "It was 9:35."

"Really? How do you fix the time?"

"By television. I was watching a nine o'clock sitcom. It had just ended, and I was on my way to the kitchen to make myself a sandwich."

"Where were you watching television?"

"In my bedroom."

"Were you alone at the time?"

"Yes, I was."

"And where was your bedroom with relation to the decedent's?"

"It's in another wing."

"Another wing?"

"Yes. My uncle's mansion has thirty-four rooms. His bedroom is part of a suite of rooms on the east wing of the second floor. My bedroom is a single room in the west wing. I should explain I do not live in the house.

I have an apartment in Manhattan. When I'm out on Long Island, I often stay over."

"And this was one of those nights?"

"That's right."

"So you were in your bedroom watching television. The show ended, and you went to the kitchen to make a sandwich. And just what happened then?"

"As I say, I saw the defendant, Clinton Hobbs, come out of my uncle's bedroom."

"You're certain it was the defendant you saw?"

"Yes, I am."

"You know him well?"

"Of course. He's been the caretaker for years."

"Do you know him personally? Have you ever spoken to him?"

"I have spoken to him. As to knowing him personally, he's not an easy person to get to know. But I certainly know who he is."

"Did you speak to him on this occasion?"

"No, I did not. And I wouldn't have wanted to."

Steve Winslow frowned. The witness had thrown it out tauntingly, daring him to ask. If he didn't, he'd lose considerable points with the jury. If he did, it would probably be worse.

Steve Winslow took a breath. "Why wouldn't you have wanted to speak to him?"

"Because of his manner. He was irritated, angry, and upset. As if he'd just gone through some emotional trauma."

Steve Winslow didn't object, just nodded thoughtfully. "That's how you would characterize it?"

"That's right."

"You had reason to be concerned?"

"Of course."

"Because you'd seen him coming from your uncle's room?"

"That's right."

"So you rushed to your uncle's room to see what had happened."

"No, I didn't."

"You didn't?"

"No."

"Why not? If you were so concerned, why didn't you check on your uncle?"

"It didn't occur to me."

"It didn't occur to you to check on him?"

"No."

"So you weren't concerned about him, were you?"

"I was concerned. I knew that they'd had a fight. But it never occurred to me that Clinton had killed him."

"You find that hard to believe?"

"Actually, I do. Mr. Hobbs had been the caretaker of my uncle's house for more than twenty years. I knew he was a difficult man with a violent temper. But I did not know he would stoop to murder."

"And you don't know it now, do you?"

Russ Overmeyer smirked. "No, I don't. Because I didn't actually see him do it. I am concluding he did it from the circumstantial evidence. From the fact I saw him leaving the room. From the fact he had a fight with my uncle. From the fact I saw him return the murder weapon to the tool shed."

Steve Winslow raised his finger. "Now, that's the other point I wanted to take up with you. You say you saw the defendant storm out of your uncle's bedroom and down the stairs. And this was while you were on your way to the kitchen to make a sandwich. And Mr. Hobbs was so agitated you decided to follow him instead?"

"I didn't decide to follow him. I just looked out the window to see where he went."

"You looked out the window?"

"Yes, I did."

"And where was the window?"

"Downstairs," Russ Overmeyer said. "If I may say so, this was actually on my way to the kitchen. So, it's not as you say that I decided to follow the defendant. My attention was attracted to him by his agitated manner, so when I followed him downstairs on my way to the kitchen and heard him slam the back door, I did look out the window to see where he went."

"And where was that?"

"He went right to the tool shed behind the house. Where the police found the murder weapon."

"Move to strike," Steve Winslow said.

"Granted," Judge Weston said. "It will go out. Mr. Overmeyer, just testify to what you personally saw."

"That's what I'm doing."

"No, it is not," Judge Weston said. "Unless you were personally present when the police found the murder weapon, don't testify to them finding it. And call me 'Your Honor.'"

"Yes, Your Honor."

"You saw the defendant go into the tool shed," Steve Winslow continued. "Did you see him come out?"

"Yes, I did."

"How soon was that?"

"Right away."

"You mean he just stuck his head in the door?"

"Well, longer than that."

"How much longer?"

"Long enough to have left something there."

Clinton Hobbs's eyes blazed. "That's a lie," he snarled.

Judge Weston banged the gavel. "Silence. Order in the court."

"But he's lying, Your Honor. I never went near that shed."

Judge Weston banged the gavel again. "That will do. Counselor, control your client or I'll have him removed."

Steve Winslow turned to the defendant. "Hang on, Mr. Hobbs," he said. "It's their turn at bat. Don't worry, you'll get your chance." He turned back to the witness. "Now, Mr. Overmeyer, after the defendant left the tool shed, what did he do?"

"He headed in the direction of his cabin."

"His cabin?"

"That's what we call it. It's a little outbuilding near the garage where he lives."

"Mr. Hobbs went back to his cabin?"

"He went in that direction. I didn't watch to see where he went."

"What did you do?"

"I went to the kitchen and made myself a sandwich. Which is what I'd been intending all along."

"Then you weren't concerned about what you'd just seen."

"No, I was not. I knew there'd been an altercation. I didn't know there'd been a murder."

"What changed your mind?"

"On my way upstairs, I noticed my uncle's door was ajar. That was strange. He always kept it closed. I went to the door and stuck my head in. I could see at once something was wrong. The bedclothes were mussed, and my uncle was lying half in and half out of the bed. And his head. It was awful. The blood."

"Yes, you described the scene quite vividly on direct examination. Did you notice anything else at the time?"

"At the time?"

"Yes."

"No, I didn't. All I could see was my uncle."

"And what did you do?"

"Picked up the phone and called the police."

"The phone in the bedroom?"

"Yes."

"It didn't occur to you that you shouldn't touch it?"

"At a time like that? It certainly didn't. I ran to the phone and made the call."

"You were there when the police arrived?"

"Yes, I was."

"You took them to your uncle's room."

"Yes, I did."

"Now, on direct examination you testified that your uncle's jewelry box was open."

"That's right."

"Who noticed that?"

"I beg your pardon?"

"Did the police discover that, or did you point it out to them?"

"I think I may have pointed it out."

"You think?"

"Well, they didn't know what it was. I did. I appreciated the significance of it being opened."

"Which you pointed out to the police?"

"That's right."

"So the police didn't discover the jewelry box until you pointed it out to them."

Overmeyer frowned. "I suppose that's right."

"When did you notice the jewelry box was open?"

"Almost at once."

"Really? Your uncle's lying there dying, and the first thing you see is the jewelry box?"

"Yes, well, after overhearing the conversation."

"Ah, yes, the famous conversation," Steve Winslow said. "Would you tell me again just how you happened to overhear that?"

"It wasn't hard," Overmeyer said. "They were talking very loud."

"Where did this conversation take place?"

"In the study."

"Your uncle's study?"

"That's right."

"Would that be on the ground floor?"

"It would."

"And how did you happen to overhear this conversation? Aside from the fact that it was rather loud."

"I was on my way to the kitchen."

"Again?"

Several of the jurors smiled. Overmeyer was rather pudgy, and the inference was obvious.

Overmeyer looked at Steve Winslow coldly. "This was before the other incident."

"Yes, of course," Steve Winslow said. "At any rate, you overheard the conversation. Now could you tell us again just what was said?"

"Mr. Hobbs was furious. He was shouting at my uncle, calling him names. A thief and a liar."

"And what was that all about?"

"It was over the cufflinks."

"The cufflinks?"

"Yes. As I said before, my grandfather had a pair of diamond-studded cufflinks. Apparently, he promised them to Mr. Hobbs. At least Mr. Hobbs seems to think so."

"He sure did," Hobbs said.

Judge Weston scowled. "Mr. Hobbs, I'm not going to warn you again. The next time you speak out of turn, you will be removed from the courtroom. Proceed, Mr. Winslow."

"Yes, Your Honor," Steve said. "Now, Mr. Overmeyer, you say your grandfather had a pair of diamond-studded cufflinks?"

"Yes. According to Mr. Hobbs, they were promised to him. Be that as it may, they were not mentioned in his will. Instead, everything went to his son. My uncle. The decedent."

"Your father is deceased?"

"Yes, or he would have inherited. He was the older brother."

"Uh-huh. Who inherits under your uncle's will?"

"I have no idea."

"Are you his closest living relative?"

"I am."

"Then can we assume—"

"Objection, Your Honor."

"Sustained," Judge Weston said. "You may not assume, Mr. Winslow. You may question as to fact."

"Yes, Your Honor. Mr. Overmeyer, is it not a fact that in your own mind you consider yourself your uncle's closest living relative and expect to inherit the majority of his estate?"

"Objection, Your Honor. That's not a fact at all. That's sheer speculation."

"Goes to bias, Your Honor."

"Exactly," Judge Weston said. She turned to the jurors. "Ladies and gentlemen of the jury, you are instructed that this question is being asked not to establish a fact but merely to establish the witness' interest in the case which might affect his testimony. You are to consider it only for that purpose. Proceed, Mr. Winslow."

"Thank you, Your Honor. Mr. Overmeyer, do you expect to inherit your uncle's estate?"

"I would think it is likely. Though I am not familiar with the contents of his will."

"Thank you. Now, with regard to your grandfather's will—the one that neglected to mention these diamond-studded cufflinks—you claim that that is what the argument you overheard was about?"

"Yes, it was."

"Specifically, what was said?"

"Mr. Hobbs wanted the cufflinks. He was yelling at my uncle, cursing him. Specifically, he said, 'They're mine'; 'You have no right to keep them'; and 'You'll pay for this.'"

"'You'll pay for this'?"

"That's right."

"You're certain he said, 'You'll pay for this'?"

"Yes, he did."

"Little melodramatic, don't you think?"

"Well, he's your client."

Several of the jurors smiled at this.

"Yes, he is," Steve Winslow said. "But it's your testimony. And your testimony alone. Isn't that right? When you say the defendant told your uncle 'You'll pay for this,' we only have your word for it."

"That's not true. Because I mentioned the conversation to the cook, and she'd heard it too."

"Uh-huh," Steve Winslow said. He put his hand to his head and paused for a moment, as if thinking up the next question. Actually, he was taking a standing nine-count. Someone else had overheard the argument? That was news to him. He needed time to recover.

Steve Winslow glanced around the courtroom. Behind the defense table, just outside the rail, his young secretary, Tracy Garvin, waved her hands to attract his attention.

Steve Winslow said, "One moment, please," walked over to her, and bent down. "What is it?" he whispered.

Tracy Garvin pulled off her large-framed glasses, pushed the blonde hair out of her eyes, and leaned in to whisper back. "I have a woman who wants to see you right away. Says it's urgent."

"Who is it?"

"Her name's Margorie Wilkins. She's a friend of the defendant."

"What does she want?"

"She wouldn't say except it's very important."

"Fine," he said. "At the moment I'll take anything I can get."

Steve Winslow straightened up, turned to the judge. "Your Honor, a matter has arisen which requires my immediate attention. I would ask for an adjournment."

A.D.A. Beerbaum was on his feet. "May I ask if you have completed your cross-examination?"

"No, I have not."

"Then I would object to an adjournment at this time. Let counsel complete his cross-examination."

"I have a matter to attend to first," Steve Winslow said.

Judge Weston frowned. "Sidebar," she snapped.

The judge came down to the side of the bench, where she conferred with the attorneys in low tones.

"Now, what is this all about?"

"I have just been informed that a woman needs to see me right away. She says it's urgent. I don't know the details, but it has something to do with the case, and it is my duty to check it out."

"Oh, for goodness sakes," Beerbaum said.

Judge Weston turned to him. "You have a problem with that?"

"I most certainly do. Don't you see what's happening here? He's losing. The witness has corroborating testimony, he's unhappy to hear it, so he turned around and signaled his secretary, some sort of secret sign or distress call, to which she responded. Then he pretends she's the one who signaled him, goes over, confers with her, and announces he needs an adjournment to talk to a witness. In all probability what he said was,

'I need an adjournment; find anyone I can talk to as a pretext to get one.'"

"Your Honor, in the first place, that's not true. However, I am struck by Mr. Beerbaum's statement that I was surprised to find there was a corroborating witness. I most certainly was. In light of discovery, I hardly expected to find the prosecution had an additional witness."

"Not an additional witness, Your Honor. You will find the cook, Gretchen Rudall, has been on the witness list from day one."

"Yes, with regard to finding the body. I don't recall any reference to her having heard this conversation in her testimony before the grand jury."

"Come, come, Counselor, we don't present everything to the grand jury, just enough to get an indictment."

"That will do," Judge Weston said. "Mr. Winslow, the prosecution contends that you are merely stalling. I would like some assurance that is not true. Who is this woman who needs to see you so urgently?"

"Her name is Margorie Wilkins, Your Honor."

"And where is this Margorie Wilkins?"

"I understand she's right outside."

"Then an adjournment is unnecessary. A short recess should suffice."

Judge Weston returned to the bench and announced that the court would stand in recess for half an hour.

As the jurors filed out and the court officer led the defendant away, Steve Winslow hurried to Tracy Garvin. "This better be good, Tracy. I'm in real trouble here."

"It's not that bad, is it?"

"Yes, it is. Not that there's a witness. That I didn't know it. It's a court-appointed case, and I didn't do my homework. I feel awful. It's like I'm letting my client down because he can't pay."

"How can you say that? You hired Mark Taylor to work on this case out of your own pocket."

"I put up the money. That doesn't mean I don't have to do my job. Where's this woman?"

"Right outside."

"Well, she better have something to help."

Steve Winslow and Tracy Garvin came out the back door of the courtroom. The corridor was mobbed with people. Steve Winslow looked around. "Where is she?"

"I left her sitting on a bench."

"Where?"

"Over there."

Steve Winslow followed Tracy Garvin down the hallway.

Sitting on a bench was an elderly woman in a gingham dress. She wore too much perfume and too much costume jewelry, including several strands of large pearls which were obviously fake. Next to her on the bench was a huge fur coat, also obviously fake, though what actual fur it was attempting to represent Steve couldn't even begin to guess. The woman had a broad face, accentuated by cat's-eye glasses, made of blue plastic with embedded glitter. She wore slightly more eye shadow than a vampire, slightly less lipstick than Bozo the Clown.

Steve Winslow grimaced. *This* was the witness he was pinning his hopes on? He glanced at Tracy Garvin as if asking her to tell him it wasn't so.

But Tracy Garvin turned to the woman and said, "Miss Wilkins, this is Mr. Winslow."

Margorie Wilkins raised her head and batted her eyes. She looked anything but pleased. "Well," she said. "It's about time."

Steve Winslow smiled. "Sorry to keep you waiting, Miss Wilkins, but I was in court."

"So they tell me. You're Mr. Hobbs's lawyer?"

"That's right."

"When is he going to get out of jail?"

"I was hoping you could help me with that."

Her eyes widened in surprise. "Me? What do you mean, me?"

"Well, do you have some information that might help?"

"Information? What sort of information?"

"That would prove he didn't commit the crime."

"Commit the crime? Of course he didn't commit the crime. Mr. Hobbs wouldn't hurt a fly."

"Which is just what I'm attempting to prove, Miss Wilkins. Now, do you think you could help me with that?"

"No, I don't," she said irritably. "And it's the second time you've asked me. That's not my job. That's your job. Now, when are you going to get him out of jail?"

Steve Winslow frowned. "I don't know how long the trial will last."

"Well, will it be this afternoon?"

"I can almost assure you it won't."

Miss Wilkins snorted. "Well, then that's enough for me."

"I beg your pardon?"

"In that case, I wash my hands of the whole affair. I mean, a favor is a favor. But there are limits. I mean, did he think I would keep her forever?"

"I beg your pardon?" Steve Winslow repeated.

"No, sir, she's yours," Margorie Wilkins said.

She reached under the bench and pulled out a large, brown carrying case. It had a handle on the top and air holes in the sides. She lifted it up on the bench, opened the top, and reached in and pulled out the biggest, blackest cat Steve Winslow had ever seen.

"Oh, what a sweetheart!" Tracy Garvin said.

"Isn't she?" Margorie Wilkins said. "This is Molly, Mr. Hobbs's cat. He asked me to look after her when they took him away. Then he didn't come back. Now what do you think of that?"

Steve Winslow didn't know what to think of that. He was gawking at the cat, which was staring at him with large green eyes, as if recognizing him as the new master and challenging his authority. *Oh yeah,* Molly seemed to say. *You just think you're in charge. Well, think again.*

"Miss Wilkins," Steve Winslow said, "I know nothing about cats."

"What's to know? You feed her when she's hungry—Molly makes her wishes known. And you let her run around your apartment. Don't worry, she'll make herself right at home. Here, you want to hold her?"

Steve Winslow blinked. He had never had much luck with cats. He wouldn't want to hold one under normal circumstances, even if he weren't in the middle of a murder trial. But he couldn't be out and out rude to the woman. He found himself lifting his hands to receive Molly.

It didn't happen. Before he could take the cat, Molly bared her teeth, hissed, snaked out an enormous paw, and raked him across the wrist.

Steve Winslow flinched, then gawked at the cat. "Good lord," he said. "That's the biggest paw I've ever seen."

Margorie Wilkins actually smiled. "Yes," she said. "Molly has double paws."

"Double paws?"

"Yes. Some cats are born that way. She has ten toes on her feet. It makes her paws very big."

"And gives her a lot of claws," Steve Winslow observed, examining the scratches on his wrist. "I'm sorry, Miss Wilkins. I'm afraid this cat doesn't like me."

"Oh, she just doesn't know you," Margorie Wilkins said. "You reach for her, she sees it as a threatening gesture. Here now, you sit down on the bench. There, that's right. Sit right down, and I'll put Molly on your lap. Here, Molly, sit on the nice man's lap."

Steve Winslow's whole body tensed as Margorie Wilkins lowered the cat onto him, particularly since Molly didn't lie down but instead stood on his lap with her enormous paws. She swiveled her neck around and looked up at his face. Satisfied, she turned back and began to tread on his lap.

Steve Winslow nearly jumped off the bench, but Margorie Wilkins put her hand on his shoulder.

"It's all right. She likes you, and she's going to lie down."

Sure enough, after tromping on his legs, Molly swiveled around in a one eighty, curled up on his lap, and began to purr.

Margorie Wilkins beamed. "See," she said, "she likes you."

"I'm flattered," Steve Winslow said. "Look here, Miss Wilkins. I'm not prepared to handle a cat."

"Really?" she said. She stroked the cat and patted Winslow on the cheek. "Then you'd better get your client off."

With that, she smiled at him and walked away.

Steve Winslow looked up at Tracy Garvin. "Tracy—"

"Don't look at me," Tracy said. "I don't have room for a cat."

"You think I do?" Steve Winslow ran his hand over his head. "Good lord, what a position to be in. If I can't get my client off, I'm stuck with her."

"Well, here's Mark Taylor," Tracy said. "Maybe he's got something to help."

The private detective approached them hurriedly. "Hi, Steve. Tracy. What you got there?"

"Clinton Hobbs's cat," Steve Winslow said. "If I can't get him off, she's mine."

"Then you better start buying cat food," Mark Taylor said. "'Cause I got nothing good. Everyone I question says the same thing: Clinton Hobbs had it in for the decedent, felt he'd dorked him out of a pair of cufflinks. Hobbs was obsessed with it, talked about it to everyone he'd meet. In short, nothing contradicts Overmeyer's story, and everything supports it." Mark Taylor ran his fingers through his curly, red hair. "Didn't the police find those cufflinks under your client's bed?"

"Under the mattress."

Mark Taylor grimaced, shook his head. "I don't want to tell you your business, Steve, but if I were you, I'd plead him out."

"I can't plead him out, Mark. I'm stuck with the cat."

"What?"

"I'm kidding, of course," Steve Winslow said. "But Clinton Hobbs says he didn't do it, and if he didn't do it, I can't plead him out."

"It's an assigned case, Steve. You're not making a dime."

"That's got nothing to do with it."

"Well, you're payin' me out of your own pocket. I'm billin' you at cost, but still."

"Bill me at your regular rates, Mark. Mr. Hobbs isn't entitled to anything less just because he can't pay. Now, did you get me anything, anything at all I can use?"

The P.I. frowned, shook his head. "No."

"Great," Steve Winslow said. He scratched Molly under her chin. "Looks like I'm stuck with a cat."

When court reconvened, Steve Winslow took a seat next to his client.

"So?" Clinton Hobbs demanded. "Did you get anything?"

"Frankly, nothing that helps."

"Helps?" Clinton Hobbs said. "The witness is lying. What more do you need?"

"It would help to prove it."

"So prove it," Clinton Hobbs said. "The man says I went into the shed and planted the murder weapon. I didn't do it, I didn't go near the shed, the man is lying."

"But you did have the argument?"

"Yes, I had the argument. That afternoon. But I didn't go to his room that night, I didn't go to the shed, and I didn't steal a pair of cufflinks and hide 'em in my bunk. I mean, how stupid do they think I am?"

"And where were you all that time?"

"I told you where. Sitting down by the boat dock cooling off."

"And having a little drink?"

"So I was drinking. So what?"

"Anyone see you there?"

"You think I wouldn't have mentioned that?"

"No, I'm sure you would. As I recall, it was just you and your cat. Is that right?"

"Yeah, that's right. You gonna put my cat on the stand?"

"That's not what I have in mind," Steve Winslow said.

"Yeah, well what do you have in mind? Listening to your cross-examination, I would say not much. I suppose that doesn't matter to you since I'm the one going to jail."

Steve Winslow sighed. Clinton Hobbs was cranky and irascible, just like his cat. They were certainly well suited for each other. It was up to him to keep them together.

Judge Weston called the court to order. "Mr. Overmeyer, I remind you you are still under oath. Mr. Winslow, you may proceed with your cross-examination."

"Thank you, Your Honor." Steve Winslow approached the witness and smiled. "Now, Mr. Overmeyer. When we left off, I believe you had just testified that the cook had also overheard the conversation between your uncle and my client."

"That's right. She did."

"This was the conversation where they argued over the cufflinks?"

"That's right."

"You heard my client threaten your uncle?"

"Yes, I did."

"And as a result of this conversation, you had reason to notice the jewelry box was open when you entered your uncle's room. That's why you pointed it out to the police. Now, were you present when the police subsequently made a search of my client's cabin?"

"Yes, I was."

"Can you tell us what they found?"

A.D.A. Beerbaum was on his feet. "Your Honor, the officers will speak for themselves."

"If he knows, he may tell," Judge Weston ruled. "Provided he was personally present."

"I was," Overmeyer said. "I directed the police to Clinton Hobbs's cabin. I watched them search it. I was there when they found the cufflinks."

"The cufflinks that were missing from your uncle's jewelry box?"

"That's right."

"Is it, Mr. Overmeyer? I ask you, is it possible that you were mistaken in any part of your testimony?"

"No, it is not."

"Your entire testimony is true?"

"Yes, it is."

"If any portion of your testimony is untrue, is it possible your entire testimony is untrue?"

"Objection, Your Honor."

"I'll withdraw it," Steve Winslow said. "Mr. Overmeyer, you have testified that you saw my client, the defendant, enter the tool shed where the murder weapon was found on the night in question."

"That's right."

"Are you aware of the fact he denies going anywhere near that shed?"

"I know that's what he claims."

"How do you account for that?"

"He's lying."

"Because his statement contradicts yours?"

"Because he's testifying to something I know isn't true."

"Well, that would certainly seem to be the case," Steve Winslow said. "He says one thing, you say the other. These things are diametrically opposed, therefore one of you is lying. I put it to you, Mr. Overmeyer, that the one who is lying is you. Is it not a fact that my client never went anywhere near the tool shed? Is it not a fact that you yourself put the murder weapon in the tool shed after you used it to kill your uncle?"

"No, it is not a fact. And I resent the insinuation."

"It's more than an insinuation," Steve Winslow said. "It's a direct accusation. Did you or did you not kill your uncle?"

"Oh, Your Honor," A.D.A. Beerbaum said.

"Goes to bias," Steve Winslow said.

"I'll allow it," Judge Weston said. "But under very narrow grounds."

"Did you kill your uncle?"

"No, I did not."

"Thank you," Steve Winslow said. "Now, Mr. Overmeyer. You say you were present when the police searched the defendant's cabin and found the cufflinks?"

"Yes, I was."

"Did you tell them where to search?"

"No, I just told them where the defendant lived."

"And they proceeded to search his cabin?"

"That's right."

"And you were present during the search?"

"Yes, I was."

"And did you direct the officers to search any portion of the cabin in particular?"

"No, I did not."

"And where were the cufflinks discovered?"

"Under the mattress."

"Under the defendant's mattress?"

"That's right."

"By under the mattress you mean . . . ?"

"Between the mattress and the box spring. The defendant had a small single bed, but it did consist of a mattress and a box spring."

"Was that one of the first places the police searched?"

"Not really. They went through his dresser drawers. His bathroom things. His kitchen alcove."

"And you never directed them to the mattress?"

"No, I did not."

"But you knew the cufflinks were under the mattress, didn't you?"

"No, I didn't."

"Sure you did. You knew they were there because you planted them there after you killed your uncle and placed the murder weapon in the tool shed."

"I did none of those things."

"None of them?"

"That's right."

Steve Winslow frowned. "That's what bothers me, Mr. Overmeyer. See, my feeling is if you did one of them, you did them all."

"Objection, Your Honor."

"Sustained. Mr. Winslow, this is not the time for an argument."

"Yes, Your Honor. Mr. Overmeyer, I cannot prove you killed your uncle, and I cannot prove you placed the murder weapon in the tool shed. But I can prove you planted those cufflinks under my client's mattress. Would it change your story to know I have a witness?"

"Objection, Your Honor."

"Overruled. The witness may answer."

"No, it would not. You can't have a witness because what you say isn't true."

"Is that so, Mr. Overmeyer? Before you answer any more questions, I'm telling you now that I have a witness who saw you on the night in question enter Mr. Hobbs's cabin, lift up his mattress, and place something under it. In light of that, would you like to change your testimony?"

"No, I would not."

"Is that so?" Steve Winslow looked at the judge. "One moment, Your Honor."

He turned and walked back to the defense table. But he walked right on by and went out through the gate.

"Mr. Winslow," Judge Weston said. "Are you leaving the court?"

"No, I'm not, Your Honor," Steve Winslow answered.

He stopped next to Tracy Garvin, who was sitting in the first row. He bent down and unsnapped the top of the cat case.

"Nice kitty," he said. "Now, Molly, it's time for you to be a very nice cat. Easy does it. Come here, sweetie."

Steve Winslow couldn't see the cat, just the green eyes glowing in the dark. They fixed on him. He heard the hiss, saw the paw snake out.

"Not yet, Molly. Not yet. Come on, now. There's a good girl."

Steve Winslow got his hands under the cat, managed to lift her out of the box. Cradling her in his arms, he pushed his way back through the gate.

"Here's the witness," Steve Winslow said. "Molly, Mr. Hobbs's cat. She was in the cabin that night. She saw you come in, she saw you lift the mattress, and she saw you plant the cufflinks. She knows you did it, and she will identify you now. Molly, where's the man you don't like? The man who was in your master's cabin where he shouldn't have been?"

Steve Winslow marched up to the witness stand, holding the cat.

Molly's head swiveled around. Her eyes fastened on the witness. Suddenly she yowled and her huge, double paw reached out and batted the witness across the face.

Overmeyer shrieked and half rose from his chair.

A.D.A Beerbaum lunged to his feet, spouting objections.

Steve Winslow, paying no attention, bore in on Overmeyer. "The cat identifies the witness as the man who was in her master's cabin that night."

"It's a lie," Overmeyer cried. "It means nothing of the sort. It's a trick. The cat wasn't even there."

Steve Winslow turned from the witness stand, a huge smile on his face. "That's right, Mr. Overmeyer. The cat wasn't there. But you were. That's how you know she wasn't. The cat wasn't there when you planted the cufflinks. She's accused you falsely. She may be guilty of perjury." Steve Winslow smiled and chucked Molly under the chin. "Just like you, Mr. Overmeyer. Just like you."

With that, Steve Winslow turned his back on the disconcerted witness, walked to the defense table, handed the cat to his client, and sat down.

Mark Taylor was duly impressed. "I've got to hand it to you, Steve," he said later that afternoon in the lawyer's office after the cranky Mr. Hobbs had departed with his cranky cat. "I mean, getting the charges dismissed. You sure pulled off a miracle this time."

"Well, I had to," Steve Winslow said. "I have a small studio apartment. Where am I going to keep a cat?"

"Don't let him kid you, Mark," Tracy said. "He'd do anything for a client."

"Don't I know it," Mark Taylor said. "But tell me how. I mean, this was brilliant stage managing on your part. You got the cat up there, you got the witness on the stand, and right on cue the cat lashes out and rakes him across the face. I mean, you couldn't have staged it any better."

"I guess not."

"So how did you do it? I mean, if what the witness said was true, if the cat wasn't there that night, why would Molly hate Overmeyer?"

"She's a cranky cat," Steve Winslow said. "She doesn't like anybody very much."

"Yes, but right on cue," Mark Taylor said. "She swiped the guy's face right on cue. When you lifted her out of the box, you had her all calmed down and everything, so how did you get her to do that?"

"Professional secret," Steve Winslow said.

"Don't give me that," Mark Taylor said. "I've seen you do some crazy things in court, but this takes the cake, having a cat accuse a witness. So how did you get her to do it?"

Steve Winslow stole a look at Tracy Garvin and bit his lip. "Ah, gee, Mark . . ."

"Come on. What did you do?"

"Well," Steve Winslow said, "when I held her up to Overmeyer, I had her cradled in my arms. And my right hand was underneath her."

"And?"

Tracy Garvin's eyes widened. "And?"

Steve Winslow exhaled. "I pulled her tail."

Which is why Tracy Garvin wasn't speaking to him.

JUSTICE KNOWS NO PAWS

Jon L. Breen

*T*he judge asked the fourteen citizens seated in the jury box all the expected questions. Did they know the plaintiff, Iris Stapleton Goodhew? (Of course they must have heard of her—she's a celebrity; but it was doubtful they had the pleasure of knowing her personally as I do.) Did they know the defendant, Elmo Gruntz? (Some of the cruder looking male members of the panel might have been acquainted with that low creature and his work, but most of them looked far too civilized.) Did they know the lawyers on either side of the action, the lovely and highly capable Andrea Frost for the plaintiff, the slickly unpleasant Forrest Milhaus for the defendant? Had they or any of their family members ever sued someone or been sued in this overly litigious society? Had they ever worked in the publishing field? Had they ever written anything for publication? Had they ever been party to a plagiarism case? Had they read about the case of Goodhew versus Gruntz in the newspapers? Were there any for whom serving more than a week as a juror would be a hardship?

Then the judge got to the really important question, or at least, judging from the smirk on his face, the one that seemed to give him the most pleasure to ask. "Are any of you allergic to cats?"

That question was indignity number three for me in the sessions leading up to the trial. What, I ask you, could be more prejudicial than to ask the jurors, "Are you allergic to the plaintiff?"

Yes, I realize that, technically, a cat doesn't have status as a plaintiff in a human court. That had been explained to Iris and me at length by our lawyer before we even entered a courtroom. But in-court indignity number one had come a few days earlier when my mere *presence* in the courtroom was questioned by Gruntz and his sleazy lawyer. After a lot of wrangling and some superbly well-reasoned arguments by Andrea, I was allowed to sit in (or sometimes lie or slink in) on the proceedings.

I suppose I must introduce myself, in the unlikely event you don't know me already. I am Whiskers McGuffin. Yes, yes, *the* Whiskers McGuffin. You have undoubtedly seen my name and photograph on numerous dust jackets, even seen and heard me on the TV talk show circuit, as co-author of a very successful series of detective novels with my longtime human companion, Iris Stapleton Goodhew. If you are a true collector, you may also have acquired an autographed copy with my distinctive paw print on the flyleaf. They are called novels, but in truth they are only lightly fictionalized accounts of my real-life exploits as a feline detective. While I, in the tradition established by Ellery Queen, appear in the novels under my own name, Iris adopts an alias as the younger, slimmer, but no more beautiful and charming, Winona Fleming.

The dubious question to the jury also reminded me of indignity number two. Though Iris, via Andrea, successfully insisted that as a full collaborator on the books, I had the right, nay the duty, to be present, there was some talk of requiring me to stay in a cage on or under the counsel table, as if I were some kind of wild animal whose freedom to wander the courtroom would somehow endanger human life or otherwise subvert the cause of justice. No sooner was that battle won than the defendant, Elmo Gruntz, asked for similar rights for his own animal companion, Fang, a huge and fierce German shepherd on whom he said the attack dog Rip in his novels was closely modeled. That led to a long legal confab as well, precipitated by the possibility that Fang really could be a danger to others in the courtroom, though Gruntz claimed he only ripped the flesh of drug lords, child molesters, and other human scum, leaving the pure of heart alone.

What weighed most heavily in the decision that I could attend the trial and Fang could not was the fact that I actually had a collaborative byline on the novels in which I appeared and Fang did not. Either Gruntz was less prone to share credit or, more likely, members of the canine species lack the necessary intelligence for literary achievement. I hope you won't take that as an instance of dog-bashing. Dogs have many fine qualities, and in some respects may even be superior to cats. I don't think a dog could commit premeditated murder, do you? But I'm sure a cat could.

Anyway, back to the courtroom. I'll leap forward, though. A lot of trial action really is boring; in fact, I don't know how people can sit still for it all. At least I could wander around the room and explore without missing anything important. Once the jury had been seated and opening arguments presented, Andrea Frost called to the stand the expert witness who would lay out the basics of our case against Elmo Gruntz. He was the renowned crime fiction critic and historian Merv Glickman, a kind and cheerful man who seemed to know every author, every title, and every continuing character in the history of the form.

I confess I had been dubious about making Merv Glickman our major witness. He is on record as not loving cat mysteries, though he seems reasonably fond of cats, and some of the points he would make in his testimony would not be wholly complimentary to our work. But Andrea assured us that his obvious objectivity could only make our case more persuasive, and Iris seemed to agree.

Andrea spent some twenty minutes establishing Merv's credentials: the publications he'd reviewed for, the books he'd written or edited, the university courses he'd taught, the awards he'd won. Had I been less keyed up, I might have catnapped through much of this. Then Andrea got to the key questions.

"Mr. Glickman, are you familiar with the works of Iris Stapleton Goodhew and Whiskers McGuffin?"

"Yes, I am."

"And are you also familiar with the works of Elmo Gruntz?"

"Yes."

"Did I ask you to make a close study of one novel from each of these, uh, bylines?"

"Yes, you did."

"And what were those two novels?"

"*Cat on a Hatpin Pouffe* by Goodhew and McGuffin, published in 1997 by Conundrum Press, and *Devour* by Elmo Gruntz, published in 1999 by St. Patrick's Press."

"Did you find any points of similarity in the two novels?"

"I found many."

"Could you summarize them for us?"

"Certainly. I'll begin with the more superficial. Each of the books has a title that fits in with a pattern the author has established to create brand recognition. Each of the books has exactly 450 pages and 26 chapters. Of those chapters, in each case half are told from the point of view of an animal character. Every other chapter of *Cat on a Hatpin Pouffe* is narrated by the animal companion of the heroine, free-lance journalist Winona Fleming. That, of course, is Whiskers McGuffin." Merv smiled in my direction, and I meowed in gratitude at his politically correct choice of words.

"Every other chapter of *Devour*," he went on, "is told from the viewpoint of Rip, the dog belonging to unlicensed homeless private eye Abel Durfee." I knew, of course, that the distasteful imputation of animal ownership embodied in this second identification was no accident. Gruntz and his character would naturally think in terms of ownership, master and slave, rather than equality.

"While the chapters about Rip follow his thoughts," Merv went on, "they are not actually written in his voice but from an omniscient narrator. Third dog rather than first dog, you might say.

"Both novels are, of course, whodunits. And in each novel, about twenty of the 450 pages are devoted to advancing the plot."

Andrea raised a disingenuous eyebrow at that. "Twenty pages out of 450? What did the two authors do with the other 430 pages?"

"Well, in the case of *Cat on a Hatpin Pouffe,* there is much attention to descriptions of the scenes, how the various characters are dressed, landscaping, interior decoration, meals, including recipes for selected dishes, things like that. And of course everything must be described twice, once from the viewpoint of a human character and once from the quite different and distinctive, and I might add frequently entertaining, viewpoint of Whiskers McGuffin."

Frequently entertaining? I bristled at the faint praise.

"The approach in *Devour*," Merv went on, "is quite a bit different, with much of the needed page-filling provided by descriptions of physical action: fistfights, car chases, menaces in parking garages, sex, torture, rape—and of course the vengeance finally taken on the baddies by Durfee and Rip is described in loving detail, without a cracking bone or a bleeding wound neglected. Also, Gruntz can go on for pages of monosyllabic, macho posturing dialogue between Durfee and one or more of the villains. Enough speeches of one word to a paragraph and those 450 pages fill up fast."

Forrest Milhaus made some kind of an objection to the slighting tone of Merv's description of Gruntz's repellent novels. Really quite mild, I thought, and he *had* been accepted as an expert witness.

"Please go on, Mr. Glickman," Andrea said, after the judge had, quite appropriately, overruled the objection.

"In both books, there are several chapters made up of the detective summarizing the previous action, all of it well known to the reader, for the benefit of another character. And of course each series has a number of continuing characters who must recur in every book, even if they don't really have anything to do with the story."

"How many continuing characters are there in the series about Winona Fleming and Whiskers McGuffin?"

"May I refer to my notes?"

"Certainly."

Merv drew out a vest-pocket notebook and flipped a few pages. "Seventeen," he replied. "That's not counting Winona and Whiskers."

"That seems like a considerable number."

"They do mount up."

"And how many continuing characters are there in the Abel Durfee and Rip series?"

"Remarkably enough, the same number, seventeen, apart from Durfee and Rip."

"Could you briefly list them for us?"

"From both series, you mean?"

"If you would."

"Well, in the Goodhew/McGuffin series, you have, of course, Winona Fleming's police contact and on-and-off boyfriend Detective Lieutenant Brent Hooper; her upstairs neighbor and best girlfriend Adele Washington; her elderly protective landlord Iggy Lamplighter; veterinarian and on-and-off boyfriend Dr. Curt Hamilton; gossiping hairdresser–cum–cat groomer Sadie McCready; Winona's loving but eccentric parents Hank and Minerva Fleming; her somewhat wild sister Stacy Fleming Tracy; her sister's abusive ex-husband Lester Tracy; her lovable but troubled teenage niece Morning Tracy; her priest brother Father Phil Fleming; her sometime editor and former boyfriend Axel Maxwell; the demented cat psychiatrist Dr. Ephraim Entwhistle; cat food manufacturer Ingo Dominguez and his domestic partner, cat sculptor Fred von Richtofen, who also, by the way, is Brent Hooper's police partner; wealthy and snobbish cat breeder Muffin Esterbrook; and nosy neighborhood druggist Pops Werfel."

"And in the Abel and Rip series?"

"Let's see now. There's Abel's main police contacts, good cop Lieutenant Al Corelli and bad cop Captain Ed McBride; his social worker and sometime girlfriend Estelle Magdalini; his crazy Vietnam-vet sidekick Thorn; local newspaper columnist Manny Graves; good rackets boss Claude Willis; Reggie and Pedro, Claude's two enforcers; bad rackets boss Itchy McAllister; Grog and Amadeus, Itchy's two enforcers; Livia Gravel, local madame and Abel's off-and-on girlfriend; Abel's sociologist brother, Dr. Max Durfee; his naïve and danger-prone niece Megan Durfee; bartender and A.A. advocate Clancy Esposito; lawyer Sholem 'the Shyster' Schuster; alcoholic unlicensed veterinarian Dr. William 'Carver' McTweed; punchdrunk newsy and ex-boxer Bobby 'the Bandaid' Whistler; and—did I miss anybody? No, I think that's seventeen."

"And all seventeen have to appear in each and every book?"

Merv shrugged. "As I say, when there are 450 pages to fill . . ."

"Could you now briefly summarize the plot of *Cat on a Hatpin Pouffe* for us?"

"Yes. Winona and Whiskers are visiting Sadie McCready to get their respective fur done. Sadie says a friend of hers, fleeing an abusive husband, needs a place to stay. Sensitive to the situation because of her sister's experiences, Winona quickly offers her guest room, though Whiskers is dubious. When their boarder is found strangled with a distinctive designer necktie, suspicion falls on the victim's husband, who sells that line of necktie at an exclusive men's shop he owns. But the detective work of the human-feline team eventually pins the crime on the husband's business partner, whose amatory advances had been rejected by the victim. In the last chapter, Whiskers comes to Winona's rescue by upsetting a poisoned cup of tea served her by the murderer."

"Now tell us the plot of *Devour.*"

"Abel Durfee hears from bartender Clancy that a friend fleeing out-of-town loan sharks needs a place to crash. Abel helps the man vanish into the homeless community, though Rip is suspicious. When the fleeing man is found carved to death with a broken Thunderbird bottle, the cops arrest one of Claude Willis's enforcers, who they think was working for the out-of-town loan sharks. Abel finds out the real murderer was the loan shark's apparently legitimate business partner. He had started a child forced-labor and prostitution ring. The victim had found out, and the killer had come after him. In the last chapter, Rip rescues Abel, who is being force-fed cheap vodka preparatory to being sent over the cliff in his car to an explosive death, and pretty much devours the killer."

"Would you say that is the same plot, Mr. Glickman?"

"I'd have to say it's pretty similar."

"I have no further questions. Your witness."

Forrest Milhaus, who had been smirking through much of Merv's testimony, rose to cross-examine. As he approached the witness chair his shoe grazed my fur, and I scurried under the defense table. He apologized, but I was not fooled, nor, I think, were Iris and Andrea. That had been no accident.

"Mr. Glickman, may we look at some of the supposed similarities between my client's work and the plaintiff's?"

"Certainly."

"You referred to a title pattern to establish brand loyalty. I don't see many similarities between Ms. Goodhew's titles and Mr. Gruntz's."

"Their titles aren't similar. It's the use of a title pattern that is similar."

"Perhaps you could explain. What is Ms. Goodhew's title pattern?"

"Punning versions of famous titles or phrases including the word *cat* or a related word. For example, when Winona and Whiskers invaded Steinbeck country, the title was *The Cat and the Cannery*. A novel with a computer industry background was called *Cat and Mouse*. Their Florida novel offered a slight variation, *Kitten on the Keys*. And of course, the book at issue here is *Cat on a Hatpin Pouffe*."

"Do those strike you as good puns, Mr. Glickman?"

"Maybe some of them are rather strained, but that's not the point, is it?"

"The lawyer asks the questions, Mr. Glickman. And what is my client's continuing title pattern?"

"One word titles, as short as possible. The first in the series was *Rip*, named of course for the dog character. The others referred to what Rip and/or Abel Durfee do to the unfortunate villains. *Tear, Shred, Cut, Flay, Slice, Slash, Gouge, Gash,* and of course *Devour.*"

"Not so similar to Ms. Goodhew's titles, are they?"

"Only in that they are title patterns. That wasn't one of my major points."

"No, I suppose not. Shall we move on then? Have you heard of the designations *tough* and *cozy* referring to mystery fiction?"

"Certainly."

"What do they represent?"

"Differing approaches to the crime story, or you might say different schools of mystery writing. I think the terms are self-explanatory."

"Do my client and Ms. Goodhew take the same approach or belong to the same school?"

Merv smiled at that. "Not at all."

"Would Ms. Goodhew be classified as a cozy?"

"Cozy as you can get, yes."

"And would Mr. Gruntz be a tough?"

"None tougher."

"Ms. Goodhew and Mr. Gruntz begin to sound more and more dissimilar."

Andrea was on her feet, and about time. "Objection. Counsel should ask questions, not comment." I had hoped she would call Milhaus on his continuing refusal to include my name as co-author of the books, but I supposed she knew what she was doing.

"Comment withdrawn, your honor." Milhaus picked up from the clerk's table the copies of the two books Andrea had entered into evidence. "Mr. Glickman, I am handing you a copy of *Cat on a Hatpin Pouffe*. I direct your attention to the photograph on the back of the dust jacket."

"Yes, that's a photograph of Ms. Goodhew and of Whiskers." Better of her than me, I always thought, but they don't give me jacket approval.

"What is that object that Ms. Goodhew is holding up to the camera so proudly?"

"That's a Martini."

"Really! It doesn't look like a drink."

"It's an award," Merv explained. "A sculpture of a cat named Martini."

"And what does this award honor?"

"The best cat mystery of the year."

"Why the unusual name?"

"They wanted to call it the Macavity, but that was already taken, so they named it after one of Mr. and Mrs. North's cats."

"And what organization grants this award?"

"The FCC. No, not the one you think. The Feline Crime Consortium. It's an organization of people who write cat mysteries."

"Why did they need such an organization and such an award?"

"Lack of respect accorded cat mysteries. The writers didn't feel that cat mysteries were getting sufficient attention from the other crime fiction awards. They didn't expect much of the Edgar, but the more cozy-oriented fan-voted awards like the Anthony and the Agatha were ignoring them, too. So they formed their own organization and came up with their own award."

"And Ms. Goodhew has won this award?"

"She and Whiskers"—thank you, I meowed—"have won three of them. They have been nominated nearly every year."

"Is it true the same four writers are nominated nearly every year?"

"With minor variations, yes, that's true."

"Now I'd like to hand you this copy of Mr. Gruntz's novel *Devour,* the other work we are considering in this trial. And again I direct your attention to the author photo on the back of the jacket."

"Yes, there's Elmo Gruntz and his dog Fang."

"And what is Mr. Gruntz holding in his hand?"

Merv smirked. "As the caption to the photograph explains, that's called a Baskerville, ostensibly an award for the best dog mystery of the year."

"Why do you say ostensibly, Mr. Glickman?"

"Because it's a gag. There is no such award. Your client made it up and awarded it to himself because he thought it would be a funny joke on the cat ladies."

"Ordinarily, I would object to your apparent ability to read my client's thoughts, Mr. Glickman, but let's say you're correct, that the similarity between the two jacket photographs is intentional and satirical in nature. Would you call that an example of plagiarism?"

"No, of course not. But you'll have noticed that wasn't one of the similarities I pointed out in my direct testimony."

"So noted. Now tell me, Mr. Glickman, to your knowledge is Mr. Elmo Gruntz himself a member of the Feline Cat Consortium?"

"Yes."

"Does he come to their conventions?"

"Never misses one."

"Was there some controversy over his membership?"

"To put it mildly. They didn't want to accept him for membership, thought he only wanted to join to make fun of them, make them uncomfortable. But he was able to point to cat characters in several of his books. According to their own rules, they had to let him in."

"Mr. Glickman, are you aware of the relative commercial success of Ms. Goodhew and Mr. Gruntz?"

"It's about a tossup. Goodhew and Whiskers have probably sold more copies overall, including paperback, but Gruntz makes the hardcover bestseller lists and they don't."

"Would you say that Iris Stapleton Goodhew has many reasons for personal rancor against my client that might explain this incredibly frivolous lawsuit?"

Andrea was on her feet. "Objection, your honor. Argumentative. Prejudicial. Calls for speculation." Why couldn't she have said "incompetent, irrelevant, and immaterial"? I always liked that objection. Anyway, the damage was done.

There's no need to describe the rest of the proceedings in detail. Truthfully, it's too painful. Merv Glickman was undoubtedly the key witness, though both Iris (extremely impressive) and Elmo Gruntz (egregiously offensive) were called as witnesses. I'm not sure whether Elmo Gruntz was technically a plagiarist, but the jury let him off. Andrea explained to us afterwards how very difficult it was to bring a successful plagiarism action without copied passages you could compare side by side with the originals. Gruntz was far too clever to leave tracks of that kind. It bothered me that there was so little I could do to help, apart from providing the occasional encouraging nuzzle to the ankles of those I favored. Murder cases are my métier, not civil trials.

Yes, that was a depressing ending, but we're not quite done yet. As you know if you've ever read one, you never close the book on my stories at the end. You always are treated to a preview of what is to come, an abridged version of the first chapter or two of the next book in the series. Now, I know this isn't a book but a short story, but it's very important you get the teaser anyway. Call it crass commercialism, if you must.

Now, an advance look at the next Winona Fleming/Whiskers McGuffin *mystery,* Curio City Called the Cat, *by Iris Stapleton Goodhew and Whiskers McGuffin, coming to bookstores this spring.*

Chapter One

Fred von Richtofen was in a bad mood. He had been interrupted at a crucial point in the creation of an unusually original and beautiful piece, one that would probably double his price at the gallery he regularly supplied with cat images in clay, bronze, papier-mâché, and other media. But it wasn't the art but the police work that paid his half of the bills, and unless he was prepared to live off Ingo's salary as CEO of the Purrfect Cat Food Company, he had to answer Brent Hooper's call:

"What took you so long?" Brent demanded, as his partner appeared at the front door of the large imposing mansion.

"It's the traffic headed for that damn antique show up the block at the fairgrounds." Fred had been out to his partner for years, but he still affected what he took to be a macho posture. In truth, he'd rather have been at the antique show than here.

As they stood over the body lying at the foot of a tall bookcase, Fred looked at a bloodstained trophy with the figure of a dog lying near a wound in the dead man's head. Shoddy work, his artist's eye told him, but he didn't think Brent would appreciate aesthetic observations at a murder scene.

Brent said, "This is a strange one, Fred."

"Murder, Lieutenant?"

"Has to be. I climbed up the ladder to look at the top of the bookshelf above where the victim is lying. There's a circle of dust where this big dog trophy stood up there. That's a heavy piece, Fred. It couldn't have fallen off by accident, unless there was a 6.0 earthquake this morning we didn't feel or hear about. And I don't think the guy could have brained himself with it, do you?"

"But who could have swung it at him with sufficient force with him just standing there? It must have been pushed off, but how from that height? Who could have got up there to do it without him knowing and being suspicious? And what is the thing anyway? Some kind of award?"

Brent squinted at the part of the lettering that was visible. "I think it says basketball, but we better not move it till the scene-of-crime boys and girls have been here. Wasn't this guy kind of short for a basketball player?"

"Writer, wasn't he? Elmer Fudd, something like that."

Chapter Two
(from the memoirs of Whiskers McGuffin)

The massive antique tent show called Curio City must have covered two acres of the fairgrounds. I like to wander into various nooks and crannies where humans can't go and follow moving things people aren't interested in, so it was to be expected I would get separated from Winona for a while. She was working on a piece about antiques for Axel Maxwell's magazine. As she questioned a man selling art deco lamps, I reestablished contact, rubbing against her ankle and purring. She looked down at me with more love in her eyes than she ever directed toward Brent or Axel or even that Hugh Grant–look-alike vet. I felt relaxed and secure. I knew if she was asked, she'd swear I'd been at her side all morning.

It's in the Bag

Bill Crider

Marilyn Crane had always thought there was something fishy about Roland Bland.

It wasn't just that he was a defense attorney. For one thing, he smelled like fish. Marilyn got the impression that he carried tuna fish sandwiches around in his briefcase, which looked old enough to have been one of Alexander the Great's saddlebags. It was cracking and flaking and coming apart at the seams, and one day when Bland flopped it down on the defense table, a horde of roaches scuttled frantically out of a gaping hole in one corner.

Several people, clearly possessing little fondness for certain creatures of the insect persuasion, had fled screaming in terror and disgust from the Executive Office for Immigration Review, better known as Immigration Court. Bland watched them go and didn't even turn a hair.

"Must have left it in the garage last night," he said, smiling his oily smile as he caressed his ancient briefcase and cooly contemplated the stampeding pests.

Marilyn had stood her ground against the roaches, too, though it hadn't been easy not to run like the others. And she usually held her own against Bland as well, which was why the Ramirez case bothered her so much.

"It's not bad enough that Bland calls me names," Marilyn told her friend Emma, who was also an INS attorney, one evening while they were having a frappuccino at the Starbuck's in the Rice Village. "It's that Judge Whittington seems to bend over backwards to give his clients the benefit of the doubt."

"Bland doesn't call you names," Emma said, seizing, as she always did, on the weakest part of the argument.

"He called me a 'Barbie,'" Marilyn said, looking out at the traffic passing by on University Boulevard through narrowed eyes.

"Not exactly," said Emma, who was short, stout, and had very black hair. *She* looked nothing at all like a Barbie. "What he said was, 'Who's that mean Barbie at the prosecution table?' And he only said it because you beat him pretty badly in your first appearance in court."

Marilyn remembered how nervous she'd been and how good it had felt to win. But she still resented the Barbie bit.

And she resented how easily Bland's latest client, Francisco (Frankie) Ramirez, was getting off.

"You know that Ramirez should have been deported years ago," she told Emma. "I don't know how he's managed to avoid it this long."

Emma knew: "He has a good lawyer."

As much as Marilyn hated to admit it, Emma had a point. Bland was good, all right. But she couldn't let it go.

"I think he has something on Whittington."

"No way. Whittington is as clean as they come."

Emma had a point. Again. Which annoyed Marilyn more than it should have, mainly because Emma was right. Probably Judge Whittington was just inclined to be a little sympathetic to aliens. She didn't hold that against him.

"What about the cat?" she said.

It was known to everyone that Whittington was completely nutty about his cat, whose name was Oliver Wendell Holmes and who slept every day in a towel-lined basket in Whittington's chambers while the judge presided over the court. At the end of the day, Oliver Wendell Holmes would still be asleep in his little basket, at which time Whittington would gently carry him out to his antiquated Volkswagen bus and drive him home.

What happened after that, no one knew—the judge didn't have any friends among the lawyers—but Marilyn assumed that the cat continued to sleep in the basket until the next day, when it would come to court and sleep some more. Cats, in Marilyn's experience, were really, really good at sleeping. They were almost as good at that as they were at ignoring people who called them.

"The cat has nothing to do with anything," Emma said, and Marilyn knew that her friend was right. As usual. But it didn't make her feel any better.

🐈 🐈 🐈

The reason that Marilyn felt a bit of hostility toward both the judge and the attorney was that she truly believed that Francisco (Frankie) Ramirez should never have been allowed to remain in the U.S.

Ramirez had admitted in court that he'd entered the country illegally by stowing away on a boat from his native Colombia and then jumping ship when it came into port. Besides that, he'd gotten married to Maria Calderon, a U.S. citizen, during a long delay in his hearing, a result of his first lawyer abruptly leaving the case. To Marilyn the marriage was a transparent attempt to legitimize his own status, but Frankie didn't see it that way at all.

"Maria and me, we lived together for a long time before that, Your Honor," he said at the hearing. "We truly loved each other. It was like we had a marriage already, you know? A marriage of the heart."

When Marilyn questioned him, he'd been unable to recall the addresses where he and his wife had lived prior to their marriage or even the names of the streets they had supposedly lived on. He couldn't remember what she wore to bed or what her pet name for him was. But he did at least remember that they'd lived for a while with a friend of Maria's named Jorge.

"Jorge Galindo?" Marilyn asked.

"That's him."

"And he was a friend of your wife's?"

"That's right."

"Isn't it true that he was your wife's brother?"

Ramirez looked genuinely surprised. "He was?"

"He was," Marilyn said. "Funny that no one ever mentioned that to you."

Frankie shook his head in astonishment.

"Well, no one ever did," he said, looking guilelessly at Judge Whittington with his big black eyes open wide. "Maybe nobody thought about it."

Marilyn had been sure she had him then, but she had yet another shot to fire.

"Do you and Maria have any children?" she asked.

Frankie's dark eyes grew sad. "No," he said. "We have not been blessed."

"But you *do* have a child, don't you?"

Frankie's eyes narrowed, but he knew enough to be aware that he had to answer the question.

"Yes," he said.

"In fact, you have a son in Colombia, born just a week after your marriage, isn't that right?"

Frankie looked furtive. It was clear that he didn't like the question, but he answered it anyway.

"I guess so."

"But I thought you were living with Maria and that you truly loved her at the time this child was conceived. You and Maria had a marriage of the heart, I believe. Didn't you tell us that?"

Frankie's mouth had an ugly twist now. "I don't know this *conceived*."

The interpreter started to explain, but Frankie waved her off. He wasn't really interested in definitions.

At this point, Roland Bland stood up, smiled greasily, and said, "We'll stipulate that Mr. Ramirez has a child in Colombia and that the child was born during the time he was living with Mrs. Ramirez."

Ramirez nodded as if he'd been coached and went on to say that his wife knew all about the child and had forgiven her husband for his momentary indiscretion, committed while he was visiting his parents in his home country. Mrs. Ramirez, her husband haltingly explained, understood that such things happened. Emotions ran high when a man returned to the country of his birth after a long absence.

Naturally, Mrs. Ramirez had testified to exactly the same thing, although not quite as eloquently, gazing lovingly at her wayward husband all the while, much to Marilyn's disgust.

To Marilyn's even greater chagrin, Judge Whittington was apparently ready to rule that because of his perfectly legitimate marriage to a U.S. citizen, Francisco (Frankie) Ramirez was entitled to remain in the United States. The only thing that stopped him was that they were running out of time for the day, which was a Friday, so the judge continued the hearing until the following Monday.

And that was too bad for Ramirez, because that weekend drug money was found in Ramirez's car.

It began as a routine traffic stop for erratic driving out on Interstate 10, just over the line into Texas from Louisiana, but it became more than routine when the state trooper, John Colby, asked for and was given permission to search Ramirez's car. Colby had become suspicious because of the strong odor of alcohol that emanated from Ramirez, his wife, and the other passenger, a Mr. Gomez. And because of the numerous beer cans that were scattered throughout the vehicle: on the floor, in the seats, and on the package rack over the back seat.

The trooper called for back-up, and when it arrived, the two men searched the car while Gomez and the Ramirezes stood and sweated disconsolately on the shoulder of the road under the blistering Texas sun.

The troopers found a little over six thousand dollars in a paper bag lying on the front floorboard. They also found another bag, this one containing nearly fifty thousand dollars, in the right rear door panel.

Knowing more than a little about the kind of people who carried large sums in small bills and traveled Interstate 10 with depressing regularity, the troopers concluded with little hesitation that Ramirez was a drug trafficker. Besides, as they said in their report, the money smelled so strongly of marijuana that the odor was detectable in the outdoors. They didn't even need a lab analysis.

Ramirez claimed that the money in the front seat was his but that the money in the back belonged to Mr. Gomez. And of course it had nothing to do with drugs. When asked where all that loose cash had come from if not from drug transactions, Ramirez said that he and Gomez had won it playing blackjack at a casino in Louisiana, where they'd gone to celebrate his practically guaranteed new status as a Permanent Legal Resident.

Of course the troopers didn't believe a word of it. They arrested Ramirez for driving under the influence and confiscated the money.

When she heard about the arrest, Marilyn was sure she had Ramirez. If he'd committed a criminal act, like drug trafficking, his staged marriage wouldn't save him. He'd be going home.

Marilyn was already seated at the prosecution's table when Roland Bland came in, the odor of fish wafting along in front of him. Ramirez was beside him as he plopped his practically prehistoric briefcase down on the defense table. No roaches fled its interior, for which Marilyn was grateful.

"Good morning," Bland said, and smiled at Marilyn, revealing tiny white teeth with sharp little canines. He and his client remained standing since the clerk had entered the courtroom.

"All rise," the clerk said, and Marilyn stood up along with the interpreter.

Judge Whittington came in. As usual he cut quite a figure. He was at least six and a half feet tall, and skinnier than Ally McBeal after a week of serious purging. His lank hair hung nearly to his shoulders. It had once been entirely black, but now it was thickly streaked with gray. His cadaverous face was unsmiling, and he carried a little basket in one hand.

Marilyn couldn't see what was in the basket because it was covered with a towel. But she had a sneaking suspicion that she knew exactly what was in there.

"Oliver Wendell Holmes," she said under her breath, meaning, of course, the judge's cat and not the famous jurist for whom the cat had been named.

This time, Marilyn thought, the judge's affection for his cat had led him to go too far. She didn't know whether there was any law against having a cat in the courtroom, but she felt it was far outside the accepted bounds of decorum. She could almost hear the wheels clicking as they turned in Bland's head. If Marilyn won the case, Bland would find a way to have it thrown out because of the stupid cat. She just knew he would.

But was she going to call Judge Whittington's hand? She most certainly was not. Elephants were supposed to have long memories, but they were nothing compared to a judge with a grudge.

So Judge Whittington slipped the basket underneath the bench, and everyone was seated without a word.

There were no spectators today, and all the witnesses were outside the courtroom. Judge Whittington looked around the room, turned on the tape recorder and said, "We're going on the record now."

Immigration court did not use court reporters. All the sessions were taped, and the tapes were transcribed later. When the judge turned on the tape, the hearing had officially begun.

Marilyn felt that she did a pretty good job with the defense witnesses, especially when she caught Ramirez in a contradiction.

"And you say the money in the front seat was yours?" she said.

"No," he said, much to Marilyn's surprise. "The money in the front seat belongs to Mr. Gomez. The money in the back seat is mine."

"I don't believe that's what you told Lieutenant Colby," she said. She looked at her notes. "You said that the money in the front seat was yours."

Ramirez appeared flustered, and he looked toward Bland for help.

"My client is just confused, Your Honor," Bland said smoothly. "You can imagine the fear he must have felt after being stopped on the highway by the minions of the law."

Minions of the law, Marilyn thought. *What a load of crap.*

"Objection, Your Honor," she said. "Mr. Bland is offering testimony for the defendant."

"Sustained," Judge Whittington said, though Marilyn was almost certain he had already taken Bland's words to heart.

"I have no further questions, Your Honor," she said.

Bland tried to repair the damage by getting Ramirez to testify as to how confused and worried he had been when arrested and how confused and worried he was even now, a stranger and afraid in this new country.

Judge Whittington did not look impressed, but Marilyn knew better than to let that get her hopes up. Judge Whittington never looked impressed.

The truth was that Marilyn didn't really care about Ramirez's little slip. What mattered was the police report on the drug money. Unfortunately, according to Judge Whittington when he examined the report, it hadn't been properly signed.

Marilyn asked for a continuance, which was granted. Judge Whittington wanted to hear from the officer. He gave Marilyn a week to set things up.

🦙　　🦙　　🦙

Colby waddled into the courtroom, looking like the antithesis of Judge Whittington. He was as squat, thick, and solid as a chopping block. He was smiling, and he had a crew cut so short that his pink scalp showed through.

After establishing his credentials, Marilyn said, "Lieutenant Colby, have you had much experience with drug dealers?"

"You better believe it," Colby said in a gravelly voice. "I've worked out there on I-10 for eight years, and I've encountered all sorts of drugs and drug dealers. And traffickers."

"When you stopped Mr. Ramirez, did you have reason to think he might be trafficking in drugs?"

"I was suspicious," Colby said. "But I wasn't sure till I found all that money."

"Objection," Bland said. "We know my client got that money at a casino, not in a drug deal."

"There's no proof the money came from a casino," Marilyn said.

"Or that it's drug money," Bland said.

Judge Whittington said, "Overruled."

"Did the money have a smell?" Marilyn asked.

"Absolutely," Colby said. "It smelled like a marijuana field."

Marilyn nodded in satisfaction. "And did you later check to see if Mr. Ramirez had any drug-related arrests?"

She already knew the answer, of course. No lawyer likes to ask a question to which she doesn't already have the response memorized.

"Yes," Colby said, shrugging inside his suit, which fit him like the hide of the Saggy, Baggy Elephant, one of Marilyn's childhood icons. "I found out that he'd been arrested in connection with a bag of marijuana found on a bus he rode to Nashville, Tennessee."

Bland stood up. "Objection. My client was never tied to that."

"Overruled," Whittington said. "You can tell your story, Lieutenant."

"The bag was found in an overhead bin right above Ramirez's seat," Colby said. "Everyone knew he'd put it there."

"What else did you discover about Mr. Ramirez?" Marilyn asked.

Colby looked at Ramirez. "There was a piece of paper in his car. It had a bunch of telephone numbers written on it in pencil, and I ran those through the computer later. There were twenty-six numbers. Seventeen of them were the telephone or pager numbers of known drug dealers."

Marilyn thought Bland would interrupt, but he sat quietly at his table. Biding his time, Marilyn thought. She knew all too well the weaknesses he would pick on.

"Had Mr. Ramirez ever called any of those numbers?"

"Yes," Colby said, "he had."

"And when was that?"

"Well, when we catch a guy that we suspect of dealing, we check him out pretty good. Mr. Ramirez said he'd been at a casino in New Orleans, so we checked out his hotel there. He might have been to a casino, but he also made some phone calls from his hotel room. Three of them were to numbers on that list."

Marilyn could hear Bland stirring behind her, but he didn't rise to object. So she kept going.

"Could you tell us about the three numbers he called from the list?"

"All three were numbers of drug traffickers known to the New Orleans police department."

Marilyn smiled. "I have no further questions, Your Honor."

Bland stood up, rubbed his hands together, humble as Uriah Heep, and said, "Lieutenant Colby, was it ever proven that my client had ever touched that bag of marijuana found on the bus to Nashville?"

"Well, no," Colby said, "but—"

"We don't need any *buts*," Bland said. "Isn't it true that anyone on that bus could have put that marijuana there?"

"Well, yes, but—"

"No *buts*. Anyone could have put the marijuana in the overhead bin. No one saw my client put it there. No one saw him touch it in any way, and his fingerprints were not on the bag. Correct?"

"Yes, but—"

"Now, now, Lieutenant. Remember about those *buts*. Let me ask you another question: has it ever been shown that the writing on that paper you say you found in Mr. Ramirez's car was indeed done by Mr. Ramirez?"

"No," Colby said.

He was no longer smiling. He sat stiffly, twining his fingers together, and Marilyn was pretty sure he would have liked to wring Bland's neck. She understood the feeling.

"So anyone could have written those numbers, right?"

"I guess so, but they were in Mr. Ramirez's car."

"There go those *buts* again. I hope the judge doesn't have to warn you about them. At any rate, I have another question: Can you prove that my client made any of those phone calls you claim were made from his hotel room?"

"It was his room," Colby said.

"True. But could his wife have made the calls? What about the person who cleaned the room? What about Mr. Gomez? Couldn't any of those people have made those calls?"

"Well, sure, possibly, but—"

Bland waggled a finger. "Ah-ah-ah. Remember about the *buts*."

Bland was on a roll, which really irritated Marilyn. She could see her case going down the tubes, and she had a sudden vision of Ramirez happily growing old in the United States, running drugs and sending illegal dollars home to his son in Columbia.

"Your Honor," Bland said, "I don't believe I have to say any more. It's clear to me, as I'm sure it is to you, that my client is entirely innocent of everything he's been accused of."

"Would you like to make your closing argument, then?" Judge Whittington asked.

"Yes," Bland said. "My client, Mr. Ramirez, obtained the money found by the troopers in a legal manner, and the note found in his car could have been written by anyone, just as the phone calls from his room could have been made by any one of several people."

Judge Whittington said, "What about the drunk driving?"

"There's that, true," Bland said, "but who among us hasn't had one too many on occasion? It's a common failing, and certainly not one that should cause anyone to be deported."

"Gambling?" Whittington said.

"Perfectly legal in Louisiana," Bland said. "Why, I myself have been over to one of the casinos for a game of chance. More than once, in fact." He pointed to the two grimy paper bags of money on the evidence table. "My client won that money in a legal game, and it should be restored to him when he walks out of this courtroom and goes back to his wife."

Bland turned and walked back to the defense table. He gestured toward Francisco (Frankie) Ramirez and spun on his heel to face the judge again.

It would have been a wonderfully dramatic gesture had it succeeded, not that it would have impressed Marilyn in the least even if it had. But the important thing was that it didn't succeed. The edge of Bland's hand caught on his briefcase, knocking it from the table to the floor, where it fell open, causing an overpowering odor of decaying tuna to reek out into the courtroom. Even Bland's face turned a little greenish around the eyes and mouth, though Marilyn thought he should have been used to the smell.

Everyone looked at Bland, who reached for the briefcase. Just as he grabbed the raggedy handle, there was a sound from the bench.

"Meowrrr?"

Marilyn turned just in time to see Oliver Wendell Holmes emerge from beneath the bench in all his orangeness. He sniffed the air briefly, then jumped to Colby's shoulder and from there to the evidence table, where he skidded into a bag of money, knocking it off the table and sending crumpled bills flying.

Oliver Wendell Holmes was bothered not at all by the sight of flying money. It is, in fact, doubtful that he even noticed it because he, too, was airborne, gliding downward toward the fetid opening in the briefcase. Before anyone could stop him, he was buried inside it.

The briefcase bumped several inches across the floor, coming to a stop against a leg of the defense table. Nothing could now be seen of the cat except for a long orange tail that whipped from left to right.

Bland looked at the tail as if he might grab it and pull the cat out of the case, but he made no move.

Colby appeared outraged that a cat had used him as a launching pad. It was a good thing, Marilyn thought, that the trooper wasn't carrying his sidearm.

Judge Whittington stood looking down, his slit of a mouth open in what might have been horror or possibly a smile. With the judge, it was hard to tell.

Ramirez sat twitching behind the table as if undecided on whether to make a run for it or just stay where he was.

But Marilyn was looking at the money. There was quite a bit of it, scattered all around the evidence table, the bills lying on the floor in crinkled heaps. There was something about the money, and suddenly Marilyn snapped to what it was. That was when she knew that none of the money would be going to Columbia but that Ramirez would.

"Lieutenant Colby," she said, "is that the money you took from Mr. Ramirez's car?"

Colby turned his eyes to her and said, "Huh?"

Marilyn repeated her question.

"Oh," Colby said, sneaking a glance at the briefcase, from which the tail of Oliver Wendell Holmes still extended. "Yeah. I mean, yes. It is."

Marilyn had been to a casino once or twice herself. She'd won fifty-two dollars playing blackjack, not much, but enough for her to have learned something about casino money.

"Then the money in the bag couldn't have come from a casino, could it," she said.

Bland looked away from the cat. So did the judge. And so did Ramirez.

"Huh?" Colby said.

"That money couldn't have come from a casino," Marilyn repeated. "Look at it. It's old, it's crumpled, it's worn, it's been handled over and over."

"Lots of people handle money in a casino," Bland said, but Marilyn was sure she detected a note of desperation in his voice. After all, he said he'd been to casinos more than once.

"Not money like that," Marilyn said. "They don't give you old money in a casino. It messes up their machines if you use crumpled money. I'll bet you could go to every casino in New Orleans and ask them. They'd tell you that it's new money only, or at least money that's not wrinkled or torn."

Oliver Wendell Holmes's tail had stopped moving. Marilyn thought she heard the sound of purring, but she couldn't be sure. Maybe the cat was asleep. Probably was, she thought.

Judge Whittington finally took his eyes off the briefcase and said, "Is that true, Lieutenant Colby? About the money, I mean?"

Colby sighed as if ashamed of himself. "I don't know why I didn't think of that from the beginning. It's just like she says, Judge. Casinos don't want any old money. It screws everything up. They might take in a few old bills, but they never give any out. That stuff on the floor there? It's drug money, just like I told you."

Judge Whittington nodded slowly. "I do believe you're right," he said.

🐈   🐈   🐈

"So," Emma said, sipping her frappuccino, "there's one less criminally inclined illegal in the country today, thanks to you." She paused. "And a cat named Holmes."

"Oliver Wendell, not Sherlock," Marilyn said, watching the traffic. "I never thought I'd have a cat to thank for beating Roland Bland."

"What was in that briefcase of his, anyway? Tuna fish?"

"Worse," Marilyn said.

"What could be worse?"

"Canned cat food."

"Cat food? Why would anyone carry cat food in a briefcase? I mean, even Bland has to be smarter than that."

"Cats make people do strange things," Marilyn said, thinking of Judge Whittington. No one had said a thing when he'd walked down from the bench, retrieved his cat, and stowed it away in its basket.

"Yeah," Emma said. "But cat food in a briefcase?"

"Bland was feeding a cat at his office," Marilyn said. "He didn't know where it lived or where it came from, but every day it would show up at the door and cry. So he started feeding it. Sometimes, when he was in a hurry, he'd just put the empty can in his briefcase. There wasn't anywhere to throw it, and he didn't want to leave it in his doorway."

"It would have been better for him if he had," Emma said. "But you have to give him credit for being nice to animals. How did he take losing to you again?"

"Pretty well," Marilyn said.

"Did he say anything?"

"Uh-huh."

"Well?"

"He said, 'Only a mean Barbie would send a legally married man back to Columbia.'"

"What about the drug money?" Emma asked.

"He didn't mention that."

"Ramirez will probably be back here within a month, you know."

"Probably," Marilyn said.

"Maybe he'll get caught again."

Marilyn nodded. "I hope so."

"And maybe Bland will defend him. You might enjoy that."

Marilyn smiled. "Especially if I can get some help from Oliver Wendell Holmes."

Animal Sounds

Dulcy Brainard

Both had been married before, and although he was older by thirteen years, her one marriage had lasted longer than his two combined. They had in common a wariness of personal commitment, a preference for intimacy, and the internal unease that results from those conflicting inclinations. They had other things in common too—each was a native New Yorker, each had a career in publishing, and each was passionate about cats: she for, he against.

Bob Neely was a literary agent. He started out in patent law, parlaying an undergraduate degree in engineering and a J.D. from NYU to an invitation from a white-shoe law firm in downtown Manhattan. Soft-spoken and well-mannered, with a slight build, a round face, and a predilection for good grooming, Bob appeared born to the firm's paneled halls. Illness in the associate ranks his third year led him to a spot on the team representing a writer who was suing her publishing house for underpayment of royalties on a trade-paper mystery that had been made into a prime-time mini-series. Bob relished working on that case, so when the firm pointed him back to his patent desk, he declined and lit out on his own as an agent. That decision brought a quick end to his first marriage just as his wife, an investment banker at J.P. Morgan, had promised it would.

Within ten years he developed an expertise as perfectly tailored to the newly meshing media as his Savile Row suits were to his 5' 8" frame. He represented celebrity authors and lesser-known ones, capitalizing on his ability to recognize subjects that were just about to capture popular interest. His agency, which he operated by himself, thrived as the publishing industry wrenched itself into a big business and editors and authors began to move among houses much as rush-hour commuters moved among PATH, LIRR, and subway lines at Penn Station.

Next he married a client, a famous British novelist who was being sued by her previous agent. She and Bob mistook the flash of cameras in her high-profile case (she'd been sleeping with that agent too) for stars in their eyes. Their marriage was effectively over within months.

Laurie Michaels was a bookseller, owner of the Bookshelf, a small, tony store on the upper East Side. Twelve years earlier, she had inherited the shop from the founder, a crusty lesbian named Blackie who had known more about books—popular or esoteric—than any other single individual in the city.

An inch taller than Bob, long-limbed and energetic, Laurie was as full of movement as he was self-contained. She had begun work at the Bookshelf as a freshman at Hunter College. In her senior year, she accepted Blackie's offer of an escalating partnership deal, which didn't provide much more than a living wage but gave Laurie 5 percent of the business at the outset, with an additional 2 percent accruing each successive year. Blackie was a robust, cranky fifty-five at the time, and Laurie's dad, a dentist in Queens, cautioned his daughter against the deal. But Laurie loved books and the business of selling them and had only to agree to five years' employment, after which Blackie would buy back her share if she wanted out. That's less time, she told her father, than it would take to get an MBA at night school.

Three years later, Blackie was dead from heart failure. In her will she gave the store and the four-story building in which it was housed to Laurie, the only person, so read Blackie's lawyer, who had ever made her see value in being straight and having kids.

Bob and Laurie knew each other's names on the Thursday evening in April when they first met. Both were guests at the Edgar Awards Banquet. He sat at a Random House table (the incoming MWA president, a Pantheon author, was a client), and she was with St. Martin's Press. One of the latter's authors had won the Best First Mystery award for a novel set in the Bookshelf's neighborhood and featuring a blind English teacher, his grown daughter, and her very smart Standard Poodle. Laurie, who had hosted the author's first reading and sold hundreds of copies of the book, felt like the book's godmother. She stood with the ecstatic St. Martin's contingent (which had so often been a bridesmaid and rarely the bride), her face aglow, accepting kisses, high-fives, and a series of hugs as the crowd filed out of the hotel ballroom.

Bob stopped to congratulate the winner's editor, Mim Towers, a legendary figure in the genre and an old friend.

"Didn't you promise that you were never, ever going to publish an animal story?" Bob asked.

"I did," said Mim with an unapologetic grin. "But this manuscript came in nearly flawless. Plus, the heroine is an old bitch with curly white hair. How could I resist?"

Introductions were mixed in with congratulations.

"You must know Laurie Michaels of the Bookshelf. She's been a huge part in the book's success."

"Actually no," Bob answered Mim, smiling at Laurie. "I'm delighted to redress the oversight."

Laurie offered her winningest smile as they shook hands and gave in to an urge born of the moment's giddiness.

"Woof," she said brightly. "Woof."

After a moment of startled silence, everyone roared.

"Best line award," said Mim, wiping her eyes.

"Did I ask for that?" Bob asked Laurie as they moved with the group toward the escalators. "Or were you making a statement for canines?"

"Neither," Laurie answered, still trying to squelch a giggle. "Something just came over me."

They met up with Bob's client, the new MWA president, whom Bob introduced as a literary lion.

"Private joke," he said as the man began to demur. They were headed for a party being thrown by the lion's publisher. Laurie surprised herself again by accepting Bob's invitation to join them.

🐱   🐱   🐱

The following Sunday afternoon Bob stopped in at the Bookshelf.

"I thought you'd have a shop dog," he said, nodding at the Abyssinian asleep in the afternoon sun flooding the front window display.

"That's Ffolio," Laurie answered. "There were three cats here when I got the store. Only he's extant. The one near your feet is Clause, in training for succession."

"Booksellers' school for cats?" Bob said, stepping gingerly away from the small Siamese that pressed between his legs and the walnut paneled side of the counter.

Laurie laughed and pushed her hair back from her face. Black and curly, it sparkled in the same sun that shone on the dusty gray-blue cat. Her eyes, the color of Ffolio's fur, shone with a softer gleam. She had enjoyed Bob's company at the Random party more than she'd anticipated. She'd been delighted to see him come in the door.

"I don't like cats much," he said, suddenly needing to get that straight.

"I thought it was animals in general."

"Especially cats. Too secretive. Superior." He shook his head. This woman, this really beautiful, bright woman, could not care in the slightest whether he liked animals or not.

But she did. And she had an idea of what prompted his revelation. Something was starting between them. So unexpected, this excitement. "Supposedly, we don't like in others qualities of our own," she answered.

"Are you suggesting that I'm superior and have things to hide?"

"I don't know if you're superior. And I expect that we all have some secrets."

The bell over the door rang. Laurie spoke with the customer, leaving Bob to look about on his own. He had asked a friend, director of marketing at a small Manhattan publisher, about the Bookshelf at a party the night before. Laurie Michaels had been among the first booksellers to strategically oppose the discounters, the friend had said. She had enlarged the store after taking it over and set up a big space for readings and signings. The Bookshelf was now a must-stop on any author tour, with a decent-sized audience guaranteed. Laurie lived in the top two floors of the building, alone. Her ex-husband, a high-school sweetheart who had been a long-term Ph.D. candidate in economics, had left her for an undergraduate right after the store's renovations.

A wide gallery ran along three sides of the store, accessed via a handsome curved stairway on one side. The floors and furnishings were deep walnut color, the fittings brass, the lighting subtle, abundant, and inviting. Moving backward to better see the mezzanine, Bob stepped on the Siamese. Its cry was sharp and menacing. He leapt away, his heart racing, while the cat fled to the back of the store.

"Sorry," he said to Laurie as she and the customer turned to him with concerned expressions. "I don't think I hurt it."

A pretty, pale young woman came forward with the Siamese in her arms. "Are you all right?" she asked Bob. He told her yes, embarrassed and irritated—he was the stepper, not the steppee. The woman's hair, the same color as the cat's, was absolutely straight and hung to her shoulders in one piece like a curtain.

"How's the injured party?" Bob nodded at the cat and stepped aside as Laurie returned to write up a sale.

"She's fine," answered the young woman, eyeing him through small wire-framed glasses. "Just a little put out."

Laurie handed the customer her package and turned to pat the Siamese.

"Bob Neely, Gina Bellson, my assistant and right hand. Also in line for succession."

They shook hands. "I'm going to show Bob the store and upstairs," Laurie told Gina. "Let's keep the cats down here." As they walked away, Laurie wondered whether he, like her, found the prospect of viewing the rest of the shop less compelling than the prospect of touring her apartment.

🐈 🐈 🐈

That's where they ended up that night; Bob had asked if it was presumptuous to invite her out for dinner that evening. Laurie thought fleetingly of saying she wasn't free. But the chemistry was imperative; she hadn't responded so powerfully to a man for a very long time.

"He's balding, a little bossy, probably too successful for his own good, and he doesn't like cats," she said to her father on the phone a few weeks later.

"Does he have any bad points?" asked the modestly successful former dentist who'd lost most of his hair by the time his only child was in kindergarten.

Laurie laughed. "He's intelligent and funny and he accelerates my heart rate."

Dr. Michaels had retired to Boca Raton as a widower and rarely ate dinner alone. "That's what counts, Princess. The rest you deal with."

Their romance lasted. Laurie and Bob were surprised, but not their friends, who agreed they were a natural pair and wondered why no one had introduced them years ago.

Only two problems marred the relationship. One was the difficulty of getting across town between his apartment on West End Avenue at Eighty-seventh Street and her place at the corner of Sixty-third and Second Avenue. The other was the cats. The obvious solution to the first problem only highlighted the second.

"If you're not really allergic, then you simply adjust," said David Aggrand, Bob's best friend and deputy editor of the *New York Times Book Review.* They sat at the bar in an Italian restaurant on West Twentieth Street, waiting for Laurie and David's wife.

"It's an emotional allergy," Bob answered. "As threatening as anything physiological. They jump on the bed, sleep on the pillows, make mewling noises all night long, dig their claws into my back or my butt, and shed hair everywhere. And the only way she says she'd even consider moving in is if they come with her. I hate the thought."

Finally, however, on Thanksgiving weekend, Laurie did move in, with both cats, whom she transported back and forth to the store with her every morning and night. She wouldn't allow them to stay in the store or her apartment alone. "Gina offered to take them home with her at night, but they belong to me and the store. They're part of my life."

It was an experiment, both agreed. As besotted as Bob remained with Laurie, a state he was beginning to think of as love, he was unable to reconcile himself to the cats. He recognized that part of it was a childish jealousy that they could claim her immediate, undivided attention. The only concession he'd gotten in that regard was that the cats be closed out of the bedroom when they were making love.

The week before Christmas, Laurie moved back to Sixty-third Street. Bob told Dave that the cats were an insurmountable obstacle. "It borders on the tragic. The two of us get along so well, as though we truly were made for each other. I think of her all through the day. Thoughts that warm my heart." He shrugged helplessly at Dave's incredulous look: no one expected such sentiments from buttoned-up Bob Neely.

"If you're not splitting up, where will you sleep together?" asked Dave, an acute reader.

"At her place, with the beasts pacing outside her bedroom door until the deed is done."

"Well, maybe it's not all bad. Couldn't you get used to it? Going out with her, staying over at her place when you can?"

"But I want to marry her, God help me. Not in a package though, dragging along these two creatures like meddling in-laws. I don't know what I'm going to do."

🐾 🐾 🐾

Late in the morning of February 16, Dave got a call from Bob's secretary. Bob was at Mt. Sinai Hospital. He'd fallen at Laurie's apartment and broken his leg. Would Dave please come to the hospital?

"I tripped over the old cat, the fat one," Bob said from the hospital bed. His left leg was wrapped in a massive cast, ankle to hip. His face was mottled with two days' growth of beard, his thin hair was unkempt, and his hospital gown was stained. Dave was astonished at the sight and could only nod for him to continue.

"It was about midnight. I was going home, had a breakfast meeting. I stepped on the cat right below the landing—never saw it—and slid down to the bottom of the stairs. I couldn't get any breath and was sure I'd punctured a rib, didn't even notice my leg. When the EMTs came, Laurie went to look at the cat. They were lifting me on the stretcher when she cries out, 'He's dead. He's dead!' This big bearded guy says, 'No he's not, lady. Just his leg is broke.'

"I didn't see her until late that afternoon, Thursday. She took the cat to the vet, she told me. There weren't any broken bones so she asked for an autopsy, just to satisfy her curiosity. She was going to call me back last night but she never did.

"Then this morning her assistant calls. Turns out the cat was poisoned."

"God! How?"

"Rat poison. Warfarin to be exact, in some salmon. In some salmon that I had brought."

"You brought the cat poisoned salmon?" A smile threatened to crack Dave's rapt expression.

"I brought the cats salmon," Bob said slowly. "I brought Laurie candy. It was Valentine's Day. Hell, I even brought Gina candy. I was asking Laurie to marry me. I did, in fact, and she said yes. That night. We'd been miserable since she moved back and had decided that somehow we could figure out where we'd live, what to do with the cats. There wasn't any rush; I just wanted her to marry me. I gave her a ring too, a ruby for Valentine's Day. Everything was great. But now my fiancée thinks I poisoned her cat, for which she is apparently going to sue me."

"For cat murder?"

"I did *not* intentionally harm the cat. I don't know what she can file for. All I know is I did not poison the cat, even if I might have wanted to, and that its bereaved owner won't return my calls. Apparently she's having the candy tested too."

By that evening word of Bob's accident and Laurie's accusation had polarized their friends. Those backing poor Bob were mainly successful New York City males, the majority divorced, and a lot of up-and-coming young editors. There were also a couple of cat haters, a bookseller (although his retail enterprise was made up of superstores) and everyone they knew who had ever fallen down a flight of stairs. Those taking Laurie's side were predominantly female, pet-fanciers, small business owners, and divorced women.

🐪   🐪   🐪

"Of course I didn't believe it," Laurie said to Mim early Saturday afternoon on Second Avenue. The day was sunny and mild. A strong breeze tossed Laurie's hair, increasing her air of agitation. "I didn't even think of his being involved until the toxicology report."

Mim had called Laurie that morning to ask if they could have lunch. Laurie's extra Saturday sales help was out with the flu, so they'd gotten salad at the Korean grocer down the street to eat at the store.

"But why would he need to get rid of the cat—and only one of them—if you'd already agreed to get married?" Mim asked.

"My father raised that same question. Neither of you has any idea of how much Bob really hated these cats. Gina says that Clause must have been in another part of the store when Bob was feeding the fish to Ffolio."

They walked into the store. Laurie told Gina to call her from the back if she needed help. "Plus," she added as they passed the stairway to the mezzanine, "he may have thought that this was precisely the time to do it, while I was committed and willing."

Mim scooped her lunch out of the clear plastic container onto the plate Laurie handed her. "Tell me what happened, step by step," she said, feeling like a character in a manuscript that she'd surely reject.

"It was Wednesday, Valentine's Day," Laurie said, pulling her chair up to the small oak table tucked in the corner. Scarred and stained, it had belonged to Blackie's Irish grandmother. "He came in just before closing with a sail bag full of packages. It was an awful day, remember? Rained and sleeted all afternoon. 'Great day for surprises,' he said. He pulled out a bottle of wine, gave me a huge pink-satin heart-box from Neuhaus, and handed a smaller box of Godiva to Gina. 'Nor could I forget the four-legged guardians of Manhattan's finest independent bookstore.' He had a quarter-pound of lox from E.A.T. He was super-charged, said the weather outside might be foul but for some reason his heart was as light as a summer morn.

"He must have thought he was keeping our engagement a secret from Gina, but he was so transparent, and of course I'd already told her.

"Anyway, then a man came in wanting all the short-listed fiction titles for National Book Awards. Bob swept the packages off the counter and brought them back here. I helped the customer, and Gina straightened up the children's section. She left right after closing, about 8:15, and Bob opened a bottle of cabernet. We had a drink down here, and he gave me a ring. It was lovely, a ruby with diamonds, the same color as the wine. We thought about canceling our dinner reservations at Felidia's." Laurie smiled dreamily, then frowned and stabbed at her salad. "But I was starving.

"We were back here by 10:30, and then it was after midnight. Next thing I hear is this horrible thumping. I leaped out of bed and found him crumpled up at the bottom of the stairs, making this awful wheezing sound. I called 911 from in here, propped the door open," she gestured behind Mim at the door that led to the small hall and her private stairs, "and turned on the store lights in back and waited with Bob. Then I saw

Ffolio near the top of the stairs. I must have jumped over him getting to Bob. I could tell he was dead just by looking.

"I sat up the rest of the night on the stairs, scared about Bob, who must have tripped over Ffolio, and feeling bereft. Ffolio had been with me through Blackie's dying, my marriage, divorce, every part of my adult life.

"Gina finally came, and we decided I should take Ffolio to the vet. There weren't any broken bones, so the vet said he'd do an autopsy if I wanted. I must have had some hidden suspicions. He called with the report around 8:00. Stomach contents revealed Tender Vittles, chicken and rice, smoked salmon, and Warfarin, a common rat poison."

Laurie grimaced as she twisted a strand of hair around one finger. Mim, so proud of her role in precipitating her friends' romance, was also distressed. She leaned over to stroke the Siamese as it wound around her leg. "Does this one miss the other?"

"I don't think so. Ffolio was pretty solitary, and Clause has always been independent. Gina found her on the street right after the penulti- mate of Blackie's cats died." The cat sprang noiselessly onto the table and let Laurie run a hand down its back.

Mim noticed the small refrigerator under the counter. "Was there any salmon left? Did you get it tested?"

"No, it was gone by the time I thought about that. The cleaning ser- vice came that night and did their periodic clearing out of the fridge. Gina called E.A.T. to ask if anyone had reported getting sick from the salmon, but they hadn't heard anything, or so they said. The candy tested okay."

Mim, who had picked up a thing or two from reading thousands of mystery manuscripts, was pondering motive and opportunity. "What's next?"

"My lawyer will be back from vacation Monday. I'll talk to her, find out what I can charge Bob with, and then get to it. Emotional cruelty, criminal negligence, willful intent to harm. There have to be a lot of angles. Sandra will know."

Mim stood up, lifting her coat from the old-fashioned coat rack. "I stopped in to see Bob before I came this morning. He's in lots of pain, of different kinds, I think, and not much like himself. Looks an unholy mess. He says he'd never have acted so unfeelingly toward you, and even if he had, he would not have been so stupid."

"But, don't you see? It didn't seem stupid to him! He knew what he wanted, and he went after it. You know him. It's why he's so successful, isn't it?" Laurie stood up fast, scraping her chair on the floor.

"But he's not devious."

"Well, he fooled me for quite a while, and I'd gotten to know him pretty well. Don't forget, Mim, he was caught nearly red-handed."

Mim buttoned her old reliable trench coat. "There's so much that's still unclear, Laurie. Don't you think you should get some more information before you take any big steps?"

"Are you suggesting something in particular?" Laurie challenged. She looked electric, her hair standing away from her head, long arms akimbo, one knee sharply bent.

Mim saw Gina watching them from the register and bent down to tie her sensible brown walking shoes. "No. But maybe your cleaning service could add to the store of facts. Or your veterinarian might tell you if the poison was in the salmon for sure. Ffolio might have gotten into something else somehow while you were at dinner."

They walked past the register to the door, which Laurie held open against the wind. "But Clause is okay," she pointed out. "She didn't 'get into anything.' This had to have been deliberate, Mim."

"Oh, I'm not disputing that at all," Mim said, heading down the street and leaving Laurie standing in the doorway, wondering. Exactly as she'd intended.

Never slow on the uptake, Laurie went right upstairs and called Insta-Cleen. It took fifteen minutes to convince Mr. Hameed that she wasn't accusing anyone of stealing food. She just wanted to know what happened to some food that had been in the fridge. He would call her back.

Laurie told Gina that Mim had tried to persuade her that she was overreacting.

"People who don't like cats never really understand," Gina answered quietly, keeping her eyes on the register's computer screen. Her hair was tangled. She's a mess, like Bob, Laurie thought. This business is hitting her hard, too.

Renata and Tony had simply cleaned out the refrigerator as the note had requested, Mr. Hameed's voice reported from her machine after closing. Mrs. Michaels would please call again if she thought of more questions.

Laurie poured herself a glass of wine from the bottle that Bob had brought, reminding herself that she'd safely drunk from it before. She remembered that she had left no note for the cleaners; in fact, it was usually the cleaners who left a note reminding them that they'd be cleaning the refrigerator next time. She thought about her assistant.

Gina had been different from Laurie's other staff from her first day nearly five years ago, taking to the business as naturally as Laurie had. From the beginning the two of them had worked comfortably together, as only women can. They learned to talk through problems before they escalated and, while they didn't often do things together outside of the store, their relationship extended well beyond the workplace. Blackie and Laurie had navigated the shoals of employer/employee relations as friends. She and Gina were furthering the evolution.

Lightly rolling the glass between her hands, Laurie gazed at the moving wine. It dawned on her: Bob's appearance changed that dynamic.

What else don't I know, Laurie repeated Mim's question.

She thought back to the morning after Bob's fall. "Maybe it was something in the salmon," Gina had said.

Then later, after Laurie had come back and said the vet was doing an autopsy, Gina had said she'd seen Bob feeding the fish to Ffolio.

"Hi. It's Sandy. I'm back, got your message. I'm so sorry about Ffolio. How awful of Bob! Are you holding up?" It was twenty years since they were in college, but Sandy's breathless energy hadn't diminished an iota.

"I'm all right. I thought you were coming back tomorrow."

"Got in late last night. Patrick and I had a fight, the weather was horrible, no point in staying. I can't believe it about Bob."

"Well, actually . . ."

"Listen," Sandy barrelled on. "I did some research this afternoon. Looks like you can't file a civil suit in New York for the loss of a pet. Here, this is from a ruling last year: 'It is well established that a pet owner in New York cannot recover damages for emotional distress caused by the negligent destruction of a dog,'" she read in an authoritative voice.

"You can bring a criminal charge here, based on old farming law, but it's only a misdemeanor for the death of an animal from things like overwork, neglect, or torture. Maximum fine of $1,000 and/or a year in prison, if you got the district attorney's office to take the case. I wouldn't bother trying. I'm so sorry. And I'm so angry at Bob. How are you standing it all?"

"I think I was wrong," Laurie answered. "I think it was Gina, not Bob."

"God, that may be worse! You haven't eaten, have you? I'm coming over. We'll go out."

"So why aren't you worried about her putting something in *your* food?" Sandy asked over steamed mussels at a small Italian restaurant on First Avenue.

"Because I think it was an aberration. For years she had reason to think, with my tacit agreement, that her life would go like mine would have if Blackie hadn't died. She and I would work in the store, and one day I'd invite her to be a partner. Then last April Bob entered the picture, shaking up everyone's expectations. Hers too, I bet."

"But she could be seriously crazy."

"If she poisoned Ffolio, it's appalling, I agree. Before I decide anything, though, I want to talk to her."

"Well, I'm staying over tonight. No argument. You may be right, but she could still be nuts and plotting a crime against a higher species."

"I was planning to call you again, too," Bob said. It was 7:30 Sunday morning. He had groped groggily for the phone, but the sound of her hello brought him fully alert. "I've tried to reach you, do you know?"

She told him everything, her anger at him, her regret at blaming him so readily, her suppositions about Gina.

"I'd gotten used to the trajectory of my life, too," she said. "Before you changed its course. That's why I needed to cling more closely to the familiar, like having the cats around all the time. The store, Gina, Ffolio defined me. You said, in effect, that that dictionary was out of date. It's scary. Do you understand?"

"That somebody can knock you completely off course? I think so."

"Well, I suspect it was something like that for Gina. I'm going to call her now, and get her over here before Sandy wakes up, throws papers around, and terrifies her."

Gina arrived at the store twenty minutes later, the bell ringing as she unlocked and opened the door. Her face was blotchy, her hair was matted, her clothes were thrown on. Laurie didn't need to raise the topic.

"Tell me what happened," she said as they sat with coffee at Blackie's table.

"I didn't want him to die, really! Just to get a little sick, so you'd pay more attention. To the store, I thought then, but that doesn't make any sense now." She lifted her head.

"I was petrified when I saw that he had died. I couldn't let you find out it was me. The salmon just popped into my head. I didn't even think about Bob."

"What exactly did you do?"

"I got rat poison from my super, for rats in the basement here, I said. I put just the littlest bit into Ffolio's food that night, while you were in the front with that customer and Bob was in the bathroom. And then I gave him some of the salmon. I thought he'd just get a little sick and that would make things like they were again." She shook her head slowly. "It sounds so dumb. It *was* so dumb."

"What about Clause?"

"I was going to give it to her too, but I just couldn't. She's been here as long as I have.

"That's what's so awful—I know what Ffolio meant to you. I'll do whatever you want. I'll quit, you can fire me. You can sue me. I'll pay whatever you say."

"Then we talked about what's next," Laurie reported that afternoon from the chair next to Bob's bed. He had on ironed pajamas that he'd made Dave bring over. He was clean shaven and as kempt as possible under the circumstances. Laurie held his hand, tracing the lines on his palm with her thumb.

"I told her I understood what she might have been thinking. Even so, the process of rebuilding trust will be really hard. I said I wasn't bringing any charges but showed her the statute that Sandy had brought.

"In effect, she's on probation. We'll see how it goes. If this turns out to be the isolated incident I believe it is, maybe it'll all smooth over. I'd like it to work out with her. In some ways it's kind of interesting to think about not being so wedded to that place."

"Is wedded the problem?" Bob asked. His tone was light, his expression anxious.

Laurie gave him another winning smile. "Not if it's to you. If you'll still have me, I mean. Clearly, Gina hasn't been the only victim of lapsed reason."

Bob turned his hand so that he was holding hers. "I'm going home on Tuesday. I know I'll be a terrible patient, but can I ask you to spend some time on West End? Can you leave Gina in charge to make sick calls?"

"I've made arrangements already. One of the deals is that she's taking Clause home with her at the end of the day. I'm going to be your night nurse, the only animal you'll have to contend with." She drew a finger slowly down his chest, muttering a ridiculous, low growl.

Bob leaned back on the pillow and closed his eyes.

"Meow," he said softly. "Oh, meow."

The End

Special thanks to Stacy Grossman, Esq., of Legal Fiction, Inc., for research.

BLUE EYES

Janet Dawson

"ey, Jeri," Cassie Taylor said with a chuckle. "Have I got a case for you."

I cradled the phone receiver between chin and shoulder as I switched off my computer, glancing at my watch. "I can give you half an hour. Then I've got to take Abigail to the vet."

Cassie's chuckle escalated into outright laughter.

"Why is it so funny that I have to take my cat to the vet?" I asked.

"It's not. Abigail, I mean. It's just that . . ." She stopped talking as she tried to get her laughter under control. "Come on over and I'll explain."

Mystified, I locked the door of J. Howard Investigations, located on the third floor of a building near Oakland's Chinatown. The front suite of offices is occupied by the law firm of Alwin, Taylor and Chao. Cassie's the middle partner. She and I have been friends since we were legal secretaries many years ago. Cassie went to law school, and I went into the private investigating business.

Cassie was in her office, dressed as usual in one of her spiffy lawyer suits. The elegant effect of the classy navy blue wool was spoiled somewhat by the fact that she'd removed her leather pumps and replaced them with a pair of battered running shoes, which were much more suitable for walking several blocks to the Alameda County Courthouse. At the moment, however, she was leaning back in her chair with her running shoes propped up on an open desk drawer, offering a excellent view of her sleek legs.

With Cassie was her partner, Mike Chao. Short and stocky, he wore gray pinstripes, though he'd removed his jacket. The cuffs of his white shirt had been rolled up, and he'd loosened the knot on his red tie. He was sitting in one of the two client chairs in front of Cassie's desk, holding a document in his hands. I sat down in the other client chair. "What's this case that has you in stitches?"

"I'm not in stitches, Cassie is," Mike said, looking glum. "Mainly because it's my problem and not hers. And I can't very well take it to court, because the judge will toss it back in my lap. It's about a cat. And a will."

"Don't tell me some little old lady died and left her estate to her cat Fluffy."

"Sort of," Mike said. "Only the cat's name is Ermengarde."

"Ermengarde! Who names a cat Ermengarde?" I shook my head. "That's cruel and unusual punishment."

"This from a woman who named her cats Abigail and Black Bart," Cassie commented.

"Let me give you some background," Mike said. "My Aunt Mae had a friend named Sylvia Littlejohn. She was only in her early sixties, but she had cancer, and she died about ten days ago. She named Aunt Mae as executor of her will."

"I'm with you so far," I said. "When do we get to Ermengarde?"

Mike ran a hand through his straight black hair. "Mrs. Littlejohn gave Aunt Mae sealed envelopes containing her will and her funeral instructions. And she asked that Aunt Mae look after Ermengarde until the instructions in the will were carried out. So Aunt Mae's had the cat ever since Mrs. Littlejohn went into the hospital for the last time, which was the day before she died. The funeral was last week. Aunt Mae didn't open the envelope containing the will until after the service."

"So the problem is in carrying out the instructions in the will," I guessed.

"Exactly," Mike said. "As soon as Aunt Mae read the will, she called me. For the most part, the document is fairly straightforward. Mrs. Littlejohn wasn't rich, but she was certainly well off. She left a number of substantial bequests to a number of friends as well as several charities."

"I take it one of these large sums was set aside for the care, feeding and upkeep of her cat Ermengarde," I said. Mike nodded.

"It's not worded that way, of course," Cassie chimed in. "The money is left to Mrs. Littlejohn's niece, for the specific purpose of Ermengarde's care, until such time as Ermengarde departs for that great cat tree in the sky."

"So Ermengarde's rich, or rather well off," I said. "Or her caretaker is. Unless the caretaker, or one of the other beneficiaries, decides to eliminate the cat."

Mike waved the document he was holding. "Mrs. Littlejohn anticipated that possibility, and took care of it. She states in her will that if the cat dies of anything other than natural causes, Ermengarde's bequest goes to several charities, not the caretaker or the other beneficiaries."

"And if the cat dies of natural causes?" I asked.

"The caretaker gets what's left," Cassie said.

"Aha." I digested this for a moment. "So what's the problem?"

"The problem's the niece. Or rather, the nieces. There are two of them."

I frowned. "Does the will specify which niece?"

"Nope," Cassie said.

Mike leafed through the pages until he found the offending clause. "It says here that the money is bequeathed to Mrs. Littlejohn's niece, who will have full control of the money as long as it's spent to provide Ermengarde with all the comforts to which she's accustomed."

I reached for the will and read the clause, raising my eyebrows at the number of zeros after that dollar sign. "Wow. That's a lot of cat crunchies. Who the hell drew up this will anyway? A summer law clerk would have known better than to leave a beneficiary unnamed."

"For an attorney to make a mistake like that borders on legal malpractice," Cassie said, with a look that would have withered the yellow chrysanthemums on the credenza behind her desk.

I had to agree. I glanced through the rest of the will. Every other bequest specified a beneficiary by name, whether it was a person or an organization. The clause relating to Ermengarde was the only one that didn't.

It could have been a mistake. It was possible whoever typed the will had left out the name by accident. But if that was the case, the attorney— or Mrs. Littlejohn—should have caught the error when they proofread the will. Unless neither of them had read through the document. I looked at the date the will was signed. Earlier this year, ten months ago.

Somehow I didn't think the omission of the niece's name was a mistake. It smelled deliberate, not accidental.

"Aunt Mae says Mrs. Littlejohn's attorney was named Bruce Cathcart," Mike said. "She found his name and address on some other papers Mrs. Littlejohn left with her. Cathcart's also the one who notarized the will, as you'll see from the last page."

"But you can't find Cathcart," I finished.

"He's done a bunk," Cassie said. "Or so it appears. Which means we can't ask him just what he was thinking when he drafted up this will. If he was thinking at all."

"He's disappeared?" I asked.

"When I went looking for him," Mike said, "I couldn't find him. He rented an office in another law firm, Burke & Hare. When I contacted them, the office manager told me he'd left. And she claimed he didn't leave a forwarding address. But I got the feeling she wasn't telling me everything. All she would say was that he was there two years."

"What about before that?" I asked. "Was Cathcart associated with another firm? Did he have a partner?"

"According to the bar association, he was practicing solo when he rented space from Burke & Hare," Cassie said. "Before that, three years ago, he was with the Bestwick firm over in San Francisco. Nobody there will answer any questions about him. All the human resources manager will do is confirm that he worked there for five years. The bar association doesn't have a current address for him. Nor did they have any record of complaints against him. That doesn't mean there weren't any, of course, just that they didn't get reported to the bar."

"The guy definitely sounds like he's had some problems. If people don't want to talk about him, that could mean they have nothing good to say."

"That's what I thought," Mike said. "He must have had a secretary, though. If you could locate the secretary, maybe that would lead us to Cathcart."

"Worth a try," I said. "That's the first problem. I assume the nieces are the second problem. Only two so far?"

"So far," Mike said. "Aunt Mae organized the funeral according to the instructions Mrs. Littlejohn left, and she notified everyone in Mrs. Littlejohn's address book. She also put a notice in the *Oakland Tribune* and the *San Francisco Chronicle*. Both of the women showed up at the funeral, introduced themselves to Aunt Mae as Mrs. Littlejohn's nieces, and said they'd read the death notice in the *Chronicle*. Aunt Mae had never met either of them before. Neither had anyone else at the funeral. My aunt had heard Mrs. Littlejohn speak of a niece, but she was under the impression that they weren't close, and that the niece lived in another state."

"So you're not even sure the nieces are really nieces," I said. "Let alone the real niece."

"Their names are Cathy Wingate and Mary Hooper." Mike reached for a yellow legal pad on which he'd scribbled some notes. "Aunt Mae's got Mrs. Littlejohn's address book, and she says she didn't see either name there."

"And neither woman is listed as a beneficiary elsewhere in the will," Cassie added.

"Do they know about the will?"

Mike shook his head. "No. I thought it best not to bring up the matter until I was sure which one of them actually is Mrs. Littlejohn's niece. That's where you come in." He tore off a sheet of yellow paper. "Fortunately, Aunt Mae had the presence of mind to get their addresses."

I looked at the sheet. Both of Ermengarde's potential guardians lived in San Francisco. I asked Mike for his aunt's address and phone number, then I glanced at my watch, mindful of Abigail's vet appointment. As I stood up, I folded the paper and tucked it into my purse. "I'm on it. I'll get back to you as soon as I have anything."

"The sooner the better," Mike said. "I can't get this will admitted to probate until this mess is straightened out."

🐪   🐪   🐪

Abigail was not thrilled with the prospect of going to the vet. Neither of my cats are. They have been known to vanish at the rattle of a cat carrier latch. However, Abigail is old and fat, and I'm faster than she is. I scooped her up, ignoring the flailing paws and the outraged meows of protest, and wedged her through the door of the carrier. Then I strapped her into the passenger seat of my Toyota and set off for Dr. Prentice's office, with Abigail muttering imprecations all the way.

Mike didn't know how old Ermengarde was, I thought, as I watched the vet examine Abigail. My own cat was nearing twelve, and I didn't want to think about losing her, but it was hard to know how long a cat would live, even the most pampered feline. Whether Ermengarde lived another year or ten years, she was going to live in style, considering the sum of money Mrs. Littlejohn had left for her care and feeding. And the niece who administered Ermengarde's money would also benefit quite nicely.

My vet conceded that Abigail had slimmed down some since our kitten Black Bart came to live with us. That had upped the cat's exercise level, plus I'd been monitoring her diet. Dr. Prentice administered the required vaccines. That done, I opened the door of the cat carrier and Abigail retreated inside. Coming home from the vet was the only time she ever willingly got into the carrier.

"Do you by any chance have a client named Sylvia Littlejohn?" I asked Dr. Prentice. "With a cat named Ermengarde?"

"Yes, as a matter of fact, I do," the doctor said. "Why do you ask?"

"Mrs. Littlejohn died recently," I said.

"Oh, no," Dr. Prentice said. "I'm sorry to hear that. I hope someone's taking care of Ermengarde. She really loved that cat."

"Yes, the cat's being cared for," I said. "How old is Ermengarde? Is she in good health?"

"I'll have to check my records." Dr. Prentice left the examining room and came back a moment later with a file. "Ermengarde's four. And she's in excellent health. If she doesn't have any major medical problems in the future, she could live another ten to twelve years."

I took my cat home, promising her that if she stayed healthy she wouldn't have to go to the vet again for another year. Then I headed over to an address in the Oakland hills to see Mike's aunt, who was caring for Ermengarde pending resolution of the mystery of her friend's will. I was eager to meet the newly rich cat.

🐈 🐈 🐈

She had blue eyes, slightly crossed. And there was a Siamese somewhere in her gene pool. She was small and elegant, with a luxuriant, long, fluffy coat, mostly white veering into pale champagne and dark brown in places. The dark patches on her dainty pointed face had the look of a harlequin's mask. Her ears and tail were tipped with brown, and so were three of her four paws.

Ermengarde was indeed a gorgeous cat. She gazed at me, unconcerned, with those big blue eyes, rested regally on a dark blue towel on Mae Chao's sofa. I held out my hand and let the cat take a delicate sniff. I knew I'd passed inspection when Ermengarde rubbed her pointy chin against my fingers and allowed me to stroke her silky head.

I saw a white electrical cord running from under the towel to an outlet on the wall. "There's a heating pad under that towel," Mrs. Chao said.

"Sylvia always had heating pads for this cat to sit on. She said cats are like heat-seeking missiles. They always find the warm spot."

I smiled, thinking of Abigail and Black Bart, and how fond they were of my down comforter, especially in winter. I'd have to try the heating pads for them.

I'd seen no other evidence of felines in residence, the sort of evidence I saw at my own house. Mrs. Chao's sofa, dark green with a floral motif of large pink peonies, showed no signs of cat claws shredding through the fabric. The beige carpet didn't have stray bits of cat food and kitty litter, at least none visible. And I didn't see the usual buildup of cat hair anywhere else except the blue towel on which Ermengarde rested. That was covered with long white strands. Either Mae Chao wasn't a cat owner, or she was extraordinarily tidy and had extremely well-behaved cats. If there is such an animal.

"I take it you're not a cat person," I said. Mrs. Chao had made tea, and I sipped at the fragrant jasmine brew.

"Not really," she admitted. "Although I really like Ermengarde. She's such a sweet, good-natured kitty. And very well-mannered. Of course, she's been subdued since she came to live with me. I'm sure she misses Sylvia."

I looked at Ermengarde, wondering what dark secrets of feline misbehavior lurked behind those crossed blue eyes. "Ermengarde's an odd name for a cat."

"Sylvia named her after an old nanny who took care of her when she was child," Mrs. Chao said. "She said Ermengarde—the woman, not the cat—practically raised her and her sister after their mother died. Sylvia was about eight when that happened. Her sister was four or five. Their father was a wealthy businessman here in Oakland, and he traveled a lot. So Sylvia and her sister were frequently left alone, with the original Ermengarde, who was a German refugee. She came over here right before World War II."

"I wonder why the cat reminded her of the woman."

"Oh, she told me." Mrs. Chao reached over and ruffled the cat's fur. "The original Ermengarde had blue eyes that were slightly crossed. When Sylvia saw this little white kitten at the Oakland SPCA four years ago, she immediately thought of Ermengarde. Who has been dead for years, of course."

"What was the sister's name?"

"Oh, dear, let me think." Mrs. Chao reached for the cup of tea she'd set on the lamp table at her end of the sofa. "Lucille, that was it. And I believe her married name was Fanning. From the way Sylvia talked about her, I gathered that the sister was dead. And that they'd been estranged for many years."

That would explain why no one among Mrs. Littlejohn's contemporaries seemed to know that she'd had a niece, until the two women claiming kinship had shown up at the funeral.

I asked if I could look at Sylvia Littlejohn's address book, the one Mrs. Chao had used to notify people of the funeral. It was a worn leather volume that looked as though its owner had used it for many years. I leafed through the pages slowly, looking at the names listed, as well as for scribbles in the margins and bits of paper tucked into the pages. As Mike had said, neither of the purported nieces was listed in the address book.

Which struck me as odd. Presumably Mrs. Littlejohn really did have a niece. Why else would she have designated the niece as the person to look after Ermengarde?

Mrs. Chao interrupted my thoughts with a question of her own. "What happens if they're not really Sylvia's nieces?" She scratched Ermengarde behind the ears, and I heard a contented purr rumbling from the blue-eyed cat.

"I guess we'll have to figure that out when the time comes," I said. "It might be up to the probate judge."

"Well, if nobody else wants her, I'll take care of her," Mae Chao said. "I don't care about the money. But I'm getting to be quite fond of this cat."

The law firm of Burke & Hare, where Bruce Cathcart had rented an office, was located in a suite on an upper floor of a high rise near Lake Merritt. The whole building was lousy with lawyers. I was surprised the management company dealt with anyone who didn't have a *juris doctor.*

The office manager at Burke & Hare wasn't all that thrilled about discussing the missing perpetrator of Mrs. Littlejohn's will, at least not at first. But in my business all it usually takes is a little cajoling. In the end, she and the secretaries in the firm dished the dirt.

They hadn't liked Bruce Cathcart much. He was arrogant, they said, and treated the administrative staff as though they were talking pieces of furniture. The attorneys at Burke & Hare didn't care for him either. In fact, the office manager finally admitted Cathcart had been asked to leave. She wouldn't tell me exactly why, but something in the way she skated around the edge of it indicated that it was about money. Wasn't paying his bills, I guessed.

What about Cathcart's secretary? I asked. Which one? came the reply.

Cathcart had several secretaries. Several left, no doubt because of the way he treated them. Others he hired through staffing agencies, then fired before he was due to pay the agencies for their fee for finding the employee. After pulling that stunt several times, word got out and the staffing agencies refused to work with him anymore. So he'd resorted to ads in the local newspapers to find temps and part-timers, none of whom stayed for very long.

Except the last one. She'd worked with Cathcart for several months. And she'd registered on the view screen at Burke & Hare for reasons other than her job proficiency.

"They were having a thing," the office manager said. "It was more than just a working relationship, if you know what I mean."

"Office romance?" She nodded. "What was her name? And do you remember what she looked like?"

"Kay Loomis. She was . . ." She stopped and thought for a moment. "Late twenties, medium height, dark hair, blue eyes."

I went back to my office and cruised several investigators' databases, looking for information on Bruce Cathcart and Kay Loomis, as well as the purported nieces, Cathy Wingate and Mary Hooper. Cathcart seemed to have vanished completely. A look at his credit report gave ample evidence why. The attorney's finances had gone down the tubes long before he took a powder.

Interestingly enough, Loomis had dropped out of sight about the same time Cathcart had. Maybe they'd run off to a desert island together. I quickly squelched that romantic notion. It was more likely they were in this scam together. I just had to figure out exactly what the scam entailed and how they were pulling it off.

There wasn't much information on either Wingate or Hooper. It looked like they'd both surfaced in San Francisco earlier this year, just before Mrs. Littlejohn had signed that new will Cathcart drew up for her. And not long before the attorney disappeared. Wingate lived in Bernal Heights, Hooper in the Richmond District. When I dug further, I discovered that both women worked as secretaries, temping for one of the staffing agencies that specialized in legal support staff.

I had a late lunch at the nearby deli, then drove across the Bay Bridge to San Francisco. My first stop was in the city's Financial District, which was also lousy with lawyers. The firm of Bestwick, Martin & Smithson, where Cathcart had worked before hanging out his shingle in Oakland, occupied several floors in a highrise on California Street.

I took the elevator to the Bestwick reception area and worked my way through a receptionist and an office manager before I found anyone with an axe to grind. She was an associate in Wills and Trusts. Her opinion of Bruce Cathcart was, in her words, lower than snail snot. But she really couldn't go into detail, not right here in the office. She told me to meet her downstairs in the lobby in fifteen minutes. It was more like twenty. We went outside, then across the street to one of the espresso joints that spring up in this part of town like weeds in a garden.

"The guy's a loser," Beth Fonseca told me, slugging down her cappuccino as though she needed a late afternoon infusion of caffeine. "I'm surprised they didn't fire his ass sooner."

"They fired him? Why?"

"Misconduct, negligence, misappropriation of funds. You name it."

I asked her to name it. She was reluctant at first, but I assured her that we'd never had this conversation. So she gave me a few examples of Cathcart's skullduggery, the kind that could get him disbarred or jailed.

After the attorney went back across California Street, I finished my latte. Time to meet the nieces, I thought, glancing at my watch. It was late enough so that even if they'd worked that day, they should be home.

I retrieved my car and headed west in the thickening rush-hour traffic. Mary Hooper lived near the intersection of Twenty-first Avenue and Lake Street. Finding a parking place anywhere in San Francisco is always a chore, and it took me several passes before I wedged my Toyota into a space between a fire hydrant and someone's driveway. The apartment was on the lower level of a house in the middle of the block, looking as though it had been converted from a garage.

I rang the bell. No answer.

I went back to my car and kept an eye on the place until I saw a gray Ford pull up outside the house. The driver was a man. The woman in the passenger seat leaned over and kissed him, then got out, walking toward the house. I jotted down the plate number as the Ford pulled away. By the time the woman entered the apartment I was out of my car and headed toward the house.

Definitely a converted garage, now a bare-bones studio, I thought, judging from what I could see when Mary Hooper opened the door. Late twenties, medium height, I thought, looking her over. Her dark brown hair fell to her shoulders, and she had blue eyes. Just like Kay Loomis, Cathcart's last secretary. Was that Cathcart in the Ford? I wondered.

I introduced myself, telling Mary Hooper that I worked for the attorney handling her aunt's will. "He's a little concerned about some irregularities," I said. "For instance, you're not named directly as a beneficiary. There's just a reference to a niece."

"I'm surprised she mentioned me in her will at all." She poured herself a glass of orange juice, then held the carton up and asked if I wanted some. I declined. She took a seat on the end of the futon on a frame that served as both bed and sofa, and crossed her legs.

"Mother and Aunt Sylvia weren't close. I don't know why, and now that Mother's dead, I can't ask her," she added regretfully. "When I moved here earlier this year, I decided to make contact. I wish I'd done it sooner. Aunt Sylvia was really a nice lady." She sipped her orange juice. "What's going to happen to her cat? She really doted on that cat. I'd be happy take it."

I looked at her face, trying to detect signs of duplicity. I saw none, only concern for Ermengarde's fate. "The cat's being cared for. How did you know she had a cat?"

"Oh, I was over at Aunt Sylvia's house a couple of times."

"It's interesting," I said, "that you weren't listed in her address book."

"Really? That's odd. Maybe she had my number written down someplace else."

"Maybe. It was lucky that you saw the notice of the funeral in the newspaper."

"Yeah, it was," she said, smiling again. "I would have hated to miss the service."

"And it would have made it more difficult for me to find you," I said, "if you hadn't given your name and address to Mrs. Chao. Then I had to wait until you came home. Were you at work?"

She nodded. "Yeah, it's just a temp job, in a law office. I'm doing that until I find a job I like."

"More job opportunities here than where you lived before?" I asked.

"Definitely more," she agreed. "There weren't as many jobs back home." She took another swallow of juice and smiled at me again.

"Where was that?"

Her smile grew less welcoming. "Detroit. That's where I grew up. Say, what is this, some kind of test?"

It was, but at this point I didn't know whether she'd passed or failed. I'd have to go back and do some more database research to see if her story about living in Detroit was true. And I wanted to put a trace on the license plate of that Ford that had dropped her off.

I took my leave. "You'll let me know about the cat," she said. I assured her I would.

🦙 🦙 🦙

Cathy Wingate's apartment was on Cortland Avenue in Bernal Heights. When she opened her front door, somehow I wasn't surprised to see that she, too, matched the description of Kay Loomis. Late twenties and medium height, again, with blue eyes looking at me from a face fringed with short brunette hair.

I gave her the same spiel I'd given the other niece, and asked if I could come in.

"You mean Sylvia left me something?" she asked, amazed. "I'll be damned. What a sweet old gal." She held the door open wider. Her apartment was also a studio, sparsely furnished and with an air of impermanence. She looked tired, as though she'd had a rough day.

"I'm looking for a job," she volunteered, popping the top on a soda from her refrigerator. She asked if I wanted one, and I shook my head. She sat down on what looked like an old sofabed and kicked off her shoes. "I had two interviews today. I'm bushed. It takes a lot out of you."

I went right to the questions. "What do you do?"

"Legal secretary, legal word processor. Whatever I can get that will pay the rent. At least for now." She sipped her soda. "Both of my interviews today went really went well." She held up her hand, and I saw that her fingers were crossed. "Wish me luck."

"Better job prospects here than in . . ."

"Denver," she said. "I moved here from Denver, not quite a year ago. I don't know about job prospects, but the weather is sure as hell better. So, what did Sylvia leave me? I don't mean to sound greedy or anything, but at this point, an extra fifty bucks would be a godsend."

"We'll get to that. Is your family still in Denver?"

She frowned. "Why all the questions?"

"I'm just curious about why Mrs. Littlejohn would leave you some-thing in her will."

"Well, so am I," she said with a shrug. "I mean, I'm her niece. But it's not like we were close. I never even met her till I came out here. I decided since she was in Oakland, I'd look her up."

"Why weren't you close?"

"She and my mom had a falling out, years ago. Mom didn't like to talk about it. And Mom's dead now, so I can't ask her."

"What about your father?"

"He's dead, too."

"What was his name?"

"George Cooper."

I digested this. Funny how Cooper and Loomis both had double Os. And it was a short walk from Cathy to Kay.

The phone rang. She made no move to answer it, instead letting her answering machine pick up the call. It was a man's voice. He didn't leave his name, just, "Hi, call me when you get in."

"Boyfriend?" I asked. Bruce Cathcart? I wondered, but I didn't say any-thing.

"Just a guy I've been out with a couple of times." Cathy Wingate set her soda on an end table and gave me a hard look. "I get the feeling you don't think I'm Sylvia's niece."

"Just exercising a little caution," I said, leaning back in my chair.

"If it will make you feel any better, I've got some old pictures that belonged to my mother. They show her and Sylvia when they were kids."

"I'd love to see them," I told her.

She got up and moved over to a desk that had been pushed against a wall. She opened a drawer and then walked back toward me, opening the flap on a large accordion folder. She rummaged in one of the pockets and drew out a handful of snapshots. She sifted through the photos in her hand, then held one out to me. "Here. That's Mom on the left and Sylvia on the right."

I glanced at the photo, a faded color snapshot showing two youngsters in frilly dresses who could have been anyone's kids. "Did you know your aunt had a cat?" I asked.

"Oh, my God," she said, concern written on her face. "I forgot about her. Is somebody taking care of her? I should have asked that Mrs. Chao I met at the funeral. Sylvia loved Ermengarde. Did you know she named that cat after her old nanny? I knew why, too, the minute I saw the cat."

"Why is that?"

She handed me another photograph, this one a larger reproduction showing the two little girls standing on either side of a seated woman in a dowdy black dress. Cathy Wingate pointed at the woman's worn round face. "Ermengarde and the cat have the same eyes."

I looked at the photo and smiled. The woman's eyes, like those of her namesake, were blue, slightly crossed.

"But Aunt Mae said she thought Lucille married a guy named Fanning," Mike said. "You're telling me Cathy Wingate's father was George Cooper."

"Lucille's first husband was Tom Fanning. In fact, that's why Sylvia and Lucille had their falling-out. Tom was courting Sylvia, then changed his mind and went after her younger sister. After he was killed in a car accident, Lucille married George and they had one child, Cathy. She was in Sylvia's address book, by the way. As Mary Catherine Cooper, instead of her married name, Wingate. Sylvia never bothered to change the name."

"What happened to Mr. Wingate?" Cassie asked.

"He died of cancer last year, which is one reason Cathy decided to leave Denver for California. At the same time, Sylvia knew she was dying and wanted to make arrangements for Ermengarde. That's when she went to see Cathcart."

I smiled, this time with grim satisfaction. "I traced Cathcart from the plate number of that Ford. He was living in the Sunset District, as John Benson, a deceased client whose social security number he'd appropriated for new identification. Now that both Cathcart and Loomis have been arrested and charged, Kay's singing long and loud. Says it was all Bruce's idea. Turns out Sylvia did specify her niece Mary Catherine Cooper as Ermengarde's caretaker. After she'd signed the will, he substituted the altered page, then set up Kay in the role of the niece, Mary Hooper. What tripped them up was Ermengarde. Cathcart knew what the cat's name was. But he didn't know why Sylvia chose that name."

"So Mike gets the probate judge to sign off on your affidavit," Cassie said, "Cathy Wingate gets designated as Mrs. Littlejohn's one and only niece. And Ermengarde gets a home."

"Well, there's just one problem," Mike said, frowning. "And I don't think Jeri can fix it. Cathy Wingate's allergic to cats."

Cat, the Jury

Catherine Dain

"**I**f there ever was an excuse to get out of jury duty, this is it. Show me the notice again."

"Wait till we get to our table." Michael headed purposefully toward the one vacant table near the small lunch counter and grill.

Two burly, bearded men wearing Harley-Davidson vests above their swim trunks glared as Michael cut them off. He pretended not to notice.

"We shouldn't have come to the beach." Faith stopped, ready to retreat, but the two men moved away without comment.

"Of course we should have come," Michael replied. "Although next time we're going to rent one of those tables with the yellow umbrellas."

"Making reservations for the beach seems un-American. Still . . ." Faith let the sentence trail away. If the bikers had wanted to argue, they would be eating sand with their sandwiches.

The August heat had rendered West Hollywood uninhabitable. When Michael had called that morning asking Faith to cancel whatever appointments she had and join him in a trip to the beach, Faith had confessed that the two clients scheduled for the afternoon had already cancelled. She lived in an older building, with only a window unit to cool her combination office and living room, and one client had explained politely that suffocating heat was not conducive to productive psychotherapy. The other had left a message on her answering machine while she was in the shower.

Michael had read about a European-style area of the Ventura beach where yellow umbrellas had been set up near a small espresso and sandwich bar, allowing spur of the moment beach-going and instant picnics. Ventura sounded like a long drive for nothing to Faith, but since Michael was driving, she agreed to go.

Once they had walked the length of the rickety old Ventura pier and back, stopping to watch the group of fishermen at the end, she was too tired and hungry to walk down the beach to the yellow umbrellas. The lunch counter on the pier was as far as she was willing to move. Besides, the area with yellow umbrellas was packed with escapees from the city. They hadn't thought to make reservations, so they would have had to wait.

The topper was that she was almost cold. Not quite, but almost. The Los Angeles basin was well over a hundred degrees when they left. The Ventura beach wasn't even eighty, and there was a stiff breeze from the ocean. With just a light terry cloth jacket over her bathing suit, Faith wanted shelter. The pier provided it, the beach didn't.

Still, she had to admit that the Ventura beach had its charms, with its clear green water and slightly hazy blue sky. The ocean ended not at the horizon, but in an offshore mist that hid the Channel Islands from view. That was why the breeze was so cool—the marine layer.

Faith set the plate with her grilled veggie burger on the small table next to Michael's teriyaki ahi sandwich. She took a long swallow of her iced tea.

"Elizabeth is a cat," she said. "A cat can't be a juror. How did they get her name?"

"From the voter registration rolls. I bet Bobby that the system was so lax that I could register Elizabeth and no one would check. I was right. And so Elizabeth—my cat—has been summoned to jury duty."

Faith examined the summons. Municipal Court in Van Nuys. She took a bite of her veggie burger and thought about the heat. The pervasive heat, the heat that she had been wandering through malls and going to afternoon movies to get away from. The heat that they had come to the beach to escape. The heat that would be waiting for her when she returned to the city, returned to an apartment with only a fan in the bedroom and a window unit in the combination office/living room.

"I'll go," she said.

"My God! Why?"

"The courthouse will be cooler than my apartment—anything would be—and all my clients are cancelling until the end of the heat wave. I don't blame them, either. I might as well do something useful. They have an on-call system, so I don't have to go every morning. And it's for Municipal Court. That means even if I get a trial, it'll be somebody fighting a traffic violation, or petty theft, or a minor dope bust, something like that. It'll only take a few hours. I'll take a book with me and read in the jury room the rest of the time. Elizabeth will have done her civic duty, and no one will know you diddled with the political system."

"What will you use for identification? I didn't get her a driver's license, and you don't look like a six-year-old blue-point Himalayan anyway."

"The last time I was a juror, no one checked for identification. I showed up with a badge, and they took my word for it. People try to get out. They don't try to get in. If you're worried, ask Bobby to make me a driver's license. He can get something out of his computer that I could flash in a pinch."

"That's breaking the law," Michael pointed out.

Faith rolled her eyes and took another sip of her iced tea.

"I'll only have to lie about my name. The rest of it is close enough. Elizabeth is a television actress—television commercials are the art form of the new generation—and I used to be a television actress. Would you rather explain why Elizabeth can't be a juror?"

"I'll get you something that will pass."

Faith nodded. She picked up her veggie burger and prepared to enjoy the rest of the afternoon.

When the alarm went off on Monday morning, Faith awoke with a jerk that scattered Amy and Mac, her two domestic longhairs, from the bed. It took a few startled, puzzled seconds for her to remember why she had set it the night before.

"Jury duty," she muttered.

Mac stared at her, wild-eyed.

"It's for Elizabeth," she explained. "Michael's cat. A long story."

Amy headed for the kitchen, certain food would be forthcoming soon.

And Faith headed for the shower, not certain that it was going to do much good. The day was going to be another scorcher.

Even getting dressed and made-up required taking breaks in front of the wheezing window unit. She was damp before she left the building. With a book under her arm and a jacket over it, in case the courthouse was actually refrigerated, she dashed for her car, the one place in the world where the temperature was under her control.

Surely jury duty would be better than another day in the heat.

She took Coldwater Canyon over the hill, past Ventura Boulevard and on to Victory Boulevard, where she turned left toward the government complex that included two courthouses, one Municipal, one Superior. Following the directions on Elizabeth's summons, she found the jury parking lot. A young man glanced at the card and waved her through. He had waved at the car before hers, and he waved at the car after hers, too.

The new jurors were all arriving at the same time, causing quite a bottleneck, and the line of cars moving slowly into the structure meant that they would all be late.

Faith parked between the two cars that had been in front of and behind her coming in. She fell into step with the fiftyish man in a work shirt and jeans who emerged from one and the sixtyish woman in a cotton blouse and skirt who emerged from the other, as all three walked briskly across the street and right, toward the building that housed Municipal Court.

There was another bottleneck just inside the door. Everyone had to pass through the metal detector. Nobody set it off, and the guard seemed bored.

The herd moved as one to the jury room. Faith sat and waited for her name—Elizabeth's name, that is—to be called. Whoever had summoned them clearly had done this before and knew they would all be late. The public address system came to life about half an hour after she arrived.

Faith sat and waited through the orientation, first listening to a clerk explain the routine, then watching a videotaped judge explain the system. She sat and waited through a long silence. The room felt uncomfortably like a bus terminal, and she didn't really feel like reading the paperback novel she had brought. But at least it was cool. And not too cold.

Shortly before noon, the speakers came to life again, and an amplified voice called out, "Municipal Court will not be seating a jury today. Superior Court, however, needs jurors. At one-thirty, the following prospective jurors will report for duty at the Superior Court building on the other side of the walkway. If your name is not called, you are dismissed for the day. Walter Ivey, Jane Guerin, Elizabeth Haver . . ."

Faith was picking up her things, getting ready to leave, when she realized unhappily that she was now Elizabeth Haver.

The voice gave directions to the courtroom.

As ordered, Faith reported to the Superior Court building after lunching in the crowded cafeteria. No one wanted to leave the area. It would have meant exposure to the heat.

The man and woman she had met in the parking structure were among the group in the hall waiting for the courtroom door to open.

"Bad luck," the woman said brightly, nodding at Faith. The woman had short white hair and wore heavy bifocals that reflected the light from the windows.

Faith nodded in return. She didn't really want to get caught in small talk. It would mean establishing her identity as Elizabeth Haver, and she wanted to keep the lies to a minimum.

It was almost two o'clock when the bailiff opened the door and motioned them all inside.

More waiting, more listening to instructions.

And it dawned on Faith as the first twelve prospective jurors were questioned that if she were seated, and if she told them her name was Elizabeth Haver, she wouldn't simply be lying. She would be committing perjury—actually breaking the law. She thought about explaining to the bailiff that this was all a mistake, that she had to leave. She thought about suddenly becoming ill.

She imagined the cold eyes of the judge penetrating her heart.

There was no easy out, no way she could tell the truth without making things worse. Perjury it would have to be.

She tried to figure out from the questions what kind of crime the defendant was charged with. It had to be violent, and serious, or the judge wouldn't care so much which of the prospective jurors had recently been victimized.

The defendant was a woman, a grossly obese woman with a spiky halo of flaming red hair. She didn't look particularly violent, although she did look vaguely familiar. Faith had seen her face before. On television. She remembered the protruding blue eyes with the dark shadows beneath.

The voir dire questions that weren't about crime all seemed to do with belief in extrasensory perception. The prosecutor was using his peremptory challenges to get rid of jurors who absolutely believed in psychic phenomena. The defense attorney was using hers to get rid of skeptics.

The judge was excusing people who said they had seen so much media coverage of the case that their minds were made up.

Faith remembered who the woman was: Molly Jupiter, billed as the World's Greatest Psychic. A few months earlier she had been arrested for the murder of Charles Bennis, operator of a psychic hotline that was advertised extensively on late night television. Faith hadn't paid too much attention to the media coverage because too much had been happening in her own life at the time. All she remembered was the fat psychic, who had seemed even fatter on television, refusing to talk.

If Faith wanted to avoid this jury, all she had to do was tell them her mind was closed, one way or the other. Closed on psychic phenomena, certain the woman was a murderess.

Unfortunately, her mind was open on both issues. It was one thing to lie about her name, another to lie about her tolerance and sense of fair play.

At the end of the afternoon, Faith—now Elizabeth Haver—was one of twelve jurors sworn in to decide the case of Molly Jupiter.

Opening arguments were scheduled for ten the following morning.

Faith glumly trudged out of the courtroom. The white-haired woman, also on the jury, caught her at the escalator. "What do you think?" she asked. "By the way, my name is Jane."

"I think we shouldn't discuss it," Faith said. "And my name is— Elizabeth."

"Glad to meet you, Elizabeth. You mentioned when the judge was asking questions that you're an actress. Might I have seen you in anything? You do look familiar." Jane seemed determined to strike up a conversation.

"Uh, no, I don't think so. I've been living on residuals, nothing recent."

Faith was almost glad to hit the heat. Walking from the courthouse to the parking structure left both women short of breath, ending all talk.

They waved goodbye as they reached their cars.

Turning the air conditioner to maximum cool restored Faith's good humor. She considered driving until morning, until it was time to return to court.

She went home because her cats were there. And she needed to confess her crime to Michael.

"Faith, you knew it would be perjury," he said when she called.

"I didn't think. Could I be prosecuted?"

"I don't know. Probably not—or at least not unless you cause a mistrial. Are you sure you want to go ahead?"

"Forward is easier than back."

"And it's for a good cause."

"I know. You read about all these lousy court decisions. Maybe I can do something right."

"Don't flatter yourself. The cause is staying out of the heat, and you know it."

Faith sniffed. "Partly true. Besides, I want to know what happened. This was a case that got some attention. I'll tell you about it just as soon as I can."

"Of course. You don't want to add misconduct to perjury."

"That's enough. I'll call you tomorrow."

🐱   🐱   🐱

The bottleneck at the door to the Superior Court building reached all the way down the stairs. Faith was perspiring heavily by the time the guards passed her through the metal detector. And she was not in a good mood.

"Elizabeth!"

A hand tapped Faith's shoulder. Startled, she turned to see the juror named Jane, smiling at her.

"I was thinking about you last night," the older woman said. "What good experience this will be, if you're ever cast in a crime series."

Faith made a weak attempt to smile back.

"I suspect it isn't the same," she said, moving purposefully toward the escalator.

Jane scurried to catch up. "Well, we'll certainly find out, won't we?"

The crowd had thinned in the hall, but the escalator renewed the now-familiar bottleneck.

Faith realized that she would be doomed to chat with Jane for the duration of the trial. She turned, calling on all her reserves of charm, and found a smile that was almost sincere. "Yes, we surely will," she said.

She smiled through the wait in the hallway, smiled as the bailiff called them in, smiled as Jane kept talking.

Once seated in her spot as Juror Number Four, Faith began to study Molly Jupiter, who was having a whispered conversation with her attorney.

The woman could have gone straight from the courtroom to the Renaissance Fair. She was wearing several layers of dark blue cotton, including a blouse, a long ruffled skirt, and an equally long sleeveless vest. Her pudgy hands were clasped in front of her in a manner that seemed to Faith too relaxed for the circumstances. She searched for signs of tension.

As if sensing Faith's gaze, the woman glanced at her, focused the protruding eyes for a moment, eyes that seemed an even deeper blue this morning, nodded, and returned to her conversation. The attorney, whose beige tailored suit offered a striking contrast to her client's dress, didn't seem to notice the momentary shift in attention.

"All rise," the bailiff called.

The judge, a dark-haired woman with a friendly face, entered and took her place. She greeted the jurors and called for the opening arguments, and the trial was underway.

The prosecutor was a young black man who looked barely out of law school.

"Ladies and gentlemen of the jury," he began, looking each of them in the eyes, one at a time. "The defendant is charged with brutally murdering her former employer, a man who had built her professional career. Because of the nature of the crime, I will have to describe acts and show photographs that will offend some of you. Let me apologize in advance. But there is no other way."

The prosecutor proceeded to tell them how Charles Bennis had advertised in several magazines catering to those with an interest in the occult, looking for someone who could be billed as the World's Greatest Psychic. He auditioned close to a hundred psychics before hiring Molly Jupiter. Bennis set her up as star of her own psychic hotline, complete with infomercials on late night cable. The money poured in. Then Molly Jupiter decided she wanted to be in business for herself. Bennis threatened to sue. He was bludgeoned to death two days later. A piece of skin matching Molly Jupiter's DNA was found under Bennis's fingernails, and the defendant had a scratch on her arm. Plus, she had no alibi for the time of the murder.

"Circumstantial evidence, yes," the prosecutor said. "But circumstantial evidence can be convincing. Think of the light inside your refrigerator. How do you know it goes out when you close the door? Can you see it? No. You know there is a light switch, and you believe that the door hits the light switch when it closes, and the light goes out. Circumstantial evidence. But you have no doubt that the light goes out."

Molly Jupiter sat quietly, looking at her hands, as the prosecutor dramatized the story. Faith wondered again if she was truly that calm, even as the prosecutor had the jury seeing the fat woman as a murderous refrigerator door.

The defense attorney's statement was short.

"Much of what you have heard is true," she said. "One thing is not. Molly Jupiter did not commit the murder. This is a case of mistaken identity. The police arrested the wrong psychic. The real perpetrator was not Molly Jupiter but her cousin, Melinda Parris, who was passed over originally for the title of World's Greatest Psychic, and then passed over a second time when Molly left the hotline. Molly Jupiter was framed. What you will hear is circumstantial evidence. Nothing places Molly Jupiter at the crime because she wasn't there. Someone cut off the victim's light. But it wasn't Molly Jupiter."

The defense attorney looked each of them in the eyes, just as her counterpart had previously.

Reasonable doubt, Faith thought. All she has to do is convince one of us that there is a reasonable doubt. A case of mistaken refrigerator doors.

At the end of the opening statements, the judge ordered a lunch break.

"Do you mind if I join you, Elizabeth?"

"Not at all, Jane." Faith sighed. It was going to be a long trial.

The assistant district attorney took four days to present his case. First he established a motive, calling several witnesses to testify that Molly Jupiter had been struggling to survive when she had answered the ad, that Charles Bennis had saved her from certain bankruptcy, and that there had been loud, ugly arguments when she wanted to leave the hotline and go out on her own. Two psychics who worked the hotline confirmed that threats on both sides escalated when Bennis said he would sue Jupiter for everything she was worth if she started a competing service.

During cross-examination, both psychics admitted that they had trouble imagining Molly Jupiter as a murderess.

Then the assistant district attorney called the coroner to the stand and showed the promised photographs of the bludgeoned body. He was right. They were ugly. Faith was more disturbed by them than she had expected to be.

There was also a photograph of Molly Jupiter's arm, showing what appeared to be a partly healed scratch.

The circumstantial evidence tying Molly Jupiter to the crime scene was mostly built around the DNA. When cross-examined, the DNA expert had to admit that sometimes first cousins were genetically close enough to confuse the issue. No one had checked Melinda Parris's DNA.

There was a lot of hypothesizing about Jupiter going to Bennis's house on the pretext of settling differences, most of which the defense attorney objected to and the jury was told to ignore.

The defense attorney had her turn the following Monday morning.

She called Melinda Parris to the stand.

The cousins certainly looked alike. Melinda Parris was as round as Molly Jupiter, with the same protruding eyes, although she had spiky black hair and dressed in layers of white cotton. Faith wondered about the choice. It made her think of refrigerator doors again.

The testimony was short. Melinda Parris denied committing the murder.

"I had no motive," she insisted. "I was in a position to take over the hotline. In fact, if you check the phone records, you'll see that I was signed on to the computer that evening, taking calls. I have an alibi."

"One of those calls was well over an hour," the defense attorney pointed out. "You could have faked the call to yourself, which would have given you plenty of time to commit the murder."

Melinda Parris rolled her eyes. "But I didn't."

That was the entire defense. Molly Jupiter didn't take the stand.

The closing arguments were much the same as the opening ones.

The judge instructed the jury to decide whether Molly Jupiter was guilty beyond a reasonable doubt.

Faith looked again at Molly Jupiter. The woman responded to Faith's gaze almost as she had at the beginning of the trial. But this time as she met Faith's eyes, she seemed to mouth the word "meow" before she turned away.

🐾   🐾   🐾

"Remarkable," Michael said as he refilled Faith's wine glass. "But you probably imagined it."

They were sitting on Michael's deck. The late afternoon sun was obscured by smog, but the worst of the heat wave had passed.

"Of course. That's what I thought, too. Still, I had a sense of a meeting of the minds. As if she knew what I had done, that I had assumed a cat's identity, and knew at the same time that I wasn't a criminal. I believed that she was a victim of mistaken identity. And I couldn't believe the woman was a murderer."

"Oh, Faith! So you persuaded the others to agree?"

Faith shook her head. "No need. We elected a forewoman— Jane—and she suggested a preliminary vote. Twelve not guilties. We were back with the verdict in under an hour."

Michael pushed the half-empty bottle of chardonnay into the ice bucket with a practiced hand.

"Was that really doing your civic duty?" he asked. "I thought you were supposed to discuss the evidence."

"I suppose we decided that our civic duty didn't include wasting the court's time when our collective mind was made up. Anyway, that wasn't the truly remarkable thing."

Michael waited as Faith took a sip of her wine, drawing out the moment.

"Well?" he prompted.

"The remarkable thing was that as Jane and I rode down the escalator, she told me that Molly Jupiter had looked at her and mouthed 'meow.' And Jane remembered a time that the refrigerator door hadn't shut off the light because of a problem with the switch. It was her parents' refrigerator, a very long time ago, which was why she hadn't remembered sooner. Her mother discovered the cat playing with this little plastic switch that came from the refrigerator door."

"And 'meow' reminded her."

"Yes. And then Walter, who was right behind Jane, said that Molly Jupiter had looked at him and mouthed 'meow' just as he was thinking she was probably guilty. He realized that the scratch on her arm could have been a cat scratch—he said it looked more like a cat scratch than a human scratch."

"I suppose you're going to tell me nine more stories proving each juror was swayed by Molly Jupiter's eyes, and that each one took 'meow' personally."

"No. I was afraid to ask because I couldn't tell mine."

"She may not be the World's Greatest Psychic, but she has to be the World's Greatest Hypnotist."

"Possibly."

"Did it occur to you that the two women were in it together?"

"Of course it did." Faith glared at Michael, then took another sip of wine. "But I wasn't about to make that hypothetical case for the other jurors. It was up to the prosecution to prove guilt beyond a reasonable doubt, and they didn't do it."

"And you were really afraid that someone, somehow, would expose you. You wanted to end the charade, and not guilty was the easiest way to do it."

"I don't know. I rather liked being Elizabeth." Faith looked at the cat, who was curled up on the chaise a few feet away.

"Good. That means you can vote twice in November," Michael said.

Elizabeth opened her eyes, her deep blue, protruding eyes, and met Faith's gaze.

"No. I got away with it once, and I'm not doing it again." Faith shivered as she said the words. "Besides, if the district attorney comes up with new evidence, I may have to confess my misdeed. I get fifteen minutes of fame and the prosecutors get a second shot at conviction. My cat impersonation may turn out to have been a good idea after all."

Elizabeth yawned, nodded in forgiveness, and went back to sleep.

The End

The Memory Pool

Tracy Knight

My grandfather's law office was cavernous and musty-smelling, with formidable cobwebs suspended from the upper corners. He and his two best friends were seated around a card table in the middle of the large waiting room while I huddled on the floor against a wall, my arms and legs as crossed and closed as my attitude.

My grandfather, Farley Bellson, leaned back in his chair and stuck his hands down the front of his pants. Then he said to his Gang of Two, "Gentlemen, it's time for today's memory pool."

As I watched him and his two decrepit cronies nodding emptily to one another as they swallowed the dregs of their after-lunch coffee, my late adolescent body filled again with the harsh restlessness that I had felt often in recent days. It had been only three weeks since I'd arrived in Lamoine—"to show some responsibility, learn to care for someone other than yourself, and help out your family," to quote my mother—but if there was anything to be learned here in the torpid drone of my grandfather's world, it wasn't conspicuous. He didn't seem to have any clients (which didn't surprise me, given his age of eighty-seven and the Alzheimer's), and so we spent four hours a day sitting alone in his office, pretending to be comfortable around each other, staring at a telephone that rang only when it was a wrong number. The highlight of his daily existence was when his two best friends dropped in and ate lunch with him, after which they played their foolish game.

Grandpa cleared his throat as if he were preparing to give a campaign speech and continued, "Let me remind you of the rules of our memory pool, gentlemen."

He turned over the envelope he held and studied his own scrawled handwriting on the back. Obviously he'd completely forgotten what was written there. "We meet once a day, at noon," he read, "and after lunch, we each see a photo that we must remember. The photo is sealed in this envelope and secured in the possession of my recently arrived grandson, uh . . ."

"Ellery," I muttered from my place in the shadows.

"Ellery. The most trustworthy twelve-year-old boy a man could hope to have as a grandson—"

"I'm nineteen," I reminded him for the thirtieth time.

"Of course. Anyway, gentlemen, when we meet the subsequent day, we each must announce what picture we remember being sealed in the envelope. The first person to utter the correct answer is treated to lunch the next day by the other two. Everybody clear on that?"

The other two old men nodded like jostled mannequins.

"Okay, now it's time for today's challenge. Son," he said, turning to me, obviously having forgotten my name again, "please count to three."

Maintaining a dour expression I knew he didn't see, I quickly and flatly said, "One-two-three."

Larry Beckwith nearly screamed, "Sammy Davis Jr.! Right? I saw him on the *Dean Martin Show* last night. Or a few years ago. Sometime." Beckwith was an eighty-year-old bachelor, a retired pastor. He was as round as Curly Howard and even sported a haircut identical to the Stooge's. But Curly, unlike Beckwith, had possessed the sense to shuffle off his mortal coil before his appearance went from amusing to pitiful.

Nodding, Morris Tittweiler, a widower and retired veterinarian who lived two houses down the block from my grandfather's, said, "Sammy Davis. Yes. He's right. I always enjoyed the noises he made."

"They call it singing," I said under my breath. I remembered Morris Tittweiler's name easily because of his initials: M.T. Empty. And he was. Of the three, he was most deeply submerged in Alzheimer's Lake, rarely surfacing for a breath of reality.

Tittweiler proudly wiped a hand across his skeletal, liver-spotted face as if he'd just correctly answered a Final Jeopardy question. Then he suddenly shot straight up in his chair. "One thing, Farley."

"Yes?"

"Why are we doing this? I, uh . . ."

"You forgot," my grandfather said, raising an index finger into the air. "That's the entire point, Morris. Each of us is showing compelling evidence of encroaching senility, Alzheimer's. Having our little memory pool every day permits us to exercise what memory we have and to commiserate with one another during our declining days. Interpersonal food for the soul. Remember?"

"Oh, yeah." A vacant smile. He had no clue.

Grandfather opened the envelope and pulled out a rumpled newspaper photo of Richard Nixon. "Well, your answers were incorrect," he said, "but at least *you* answered. I, on the other hand, had no notion whose picture was in the envelope. It appears the decay of our memories is continuing apace. Hmm. I guess this means I lose. I'll bring lunch for the three of us tomorrow. I must remember to make a note of it." He smiled, but the irony was lost on his two friends.

The office's front door opened, and in strolled the city police chief, Bill Grandling. He wrenched his middle-aged simian face into the semblance of a smile and said, "Good afternoon, gents. How are things going today?" Then he shot me a suspicious glare that only I saw.

"Why, we're fine, Chief," my grandfather said. "Will you join us for coffee? We'll give you the honor of selecting our target picture for tomorrow's memory pool."

Grandling dragged a chair from the perimeter of the waiting room and sat. "You guys are still having your pool every day, huh? Sure, I'd be happy to help out." He began thumbing through a tattered copy of the *National Enquirer* in search of a photo. "By the way, you fellas locking your doors these days?" he asked absently as he continued turning pages.

The three men laughed in unison.

"Of course not, Chief," my grandfather said. "This is Lamoine, remember?"

Chief Grandling said, "Well, you might want to consider it. There's been a bunch of break-ins around the county recently and—this should be of special interest to you, Farley—in three cases people's pet cats have been stolen. I'm starting to wonder whether the thieves are selling them to medical labs or something terrible like that. You'd better be more careful, all of you."

"How horrible," my grandfather said. He gestured in my direction. "Will you go find Lucy for me, uh . . . ?"

"Ellery," I said. I stood up and shambled into my grandfather's private office.

I quickly scanned the pictures that hung on the walls. Seeing my grandparents as a young couple made me vow to myself that I'd never end up like my grandfather, an all-but-retired attorney who had never lived anywhere but this tiny nowhere town. I wouldn't be like him, sitting around waiting to die with nothing useful to contribute or accomplish. My life was going to mean something right up until the very end.

Lucy was asleep on my grandfather's plush desk chair. She was a sleek black cat with small splashes of white: a vest, a band at the tip of her tail, and a lopsided spot on her chin that made her look like she was sneering. I related to that.

I picked up Lucy—who immediately uttered a complaining yowl— and carried her out to my grandfather. When I dropped her in his lap, he smiled.

"I'll have Lucy sing a tune for you gents before you leave." With that declaration, he hugged Lucy close to him, closing his eyes and tipping his head to one side as he carefully listened to her thunderous purrs.

He nodded, then quickly but delicately squeezed her.

She emitted a sound much more articulated than a simple meow: two syllables, something like "Ngeeee-rowwwl!"

All four men laughed uproariously. I remained silent, but confessed to myself that if this were being done in my dorm room with a couple of buddies, it'd be hilarious. Here, with these four, it was just sad. Sad and stupid.

"It's magically harmonic, don't you think?" my grandfather said.

Two squeezes. Sure enough, Lucy released two more garbled verbalizations.

"That last one was a B-flat if I'm not mistaken," my grandfather said with a grin. He petted Lucy gently on her head and kissed her cheek. "What a good girl you are," he whispered. "You can talk and you can sing. What a talented, sweet girl you are."

Maintaining his monkey grin, Chief Grandling stood up, licked the envelope flap and handed the sealed envelope to my grandfather. "Okay, now that you've all seen it, here's your answer for the next memory pool," he said, hitching up his pants for good measure. "You fellas take care of yourselves. And remember what I said about locking your doors."

As soon as the police chief departed, my grandfather turned to me and said, "Keep this safe and secure for us, won't you, son?"

I walked to the table and, as my grandfather handed the envelope to me, I noticed the skin on his hands, how paper-thin and transparent it was. As thin and transparent as his life appeared to my nineteen-year-old all-seeing, all-knowing eyes.

I nodded impatiently. I was already bored to death with this town and the grandfather I'd visited exactly twice before being forced to move here. "I'm going out," I said, folding up the envelope and stuffing it into my back pocket.

I left the office, as I did every day at this time. A daily walk was necessary just to keep a bridle on my sanity. It was still hard to believe that I was being held hostage in Lamoine, a town of three thousand, when only a few months ago I'd been cavorting with my friends at the University of Wisconsin in Madison.

I'm not sure when I crossed the line with my parents. Maybe it was the conviction for Driving While Intoxicated when I was apprehended navigating my VW bug across a frozen pond while wearing no pants; maybe it was the fact that I was on academic probation because I missed half of my classes and slept through the other half, most likely it was the episode in which I and three other neo-hippies held a sit-down strike in the University Union to protest the high price of textbooks, then tied up the campus policeman who had been summoned to remove us.

Regardless, my parents informed me that neither their emotional nor financial support would be forthcoming for the time being. My solitary option was to live with my grandfather for a semester, to tend to him in his failing health and hopefully learn a bit of responsibility in the process. Only then would my return to school be considered.

The whole thing stank.

Trudging around the town square, I did my best to divert my attention from self-pity by examining all the old buildings encircling the square and the towering trees whose autumn leaves were only beginning to turn. I proudly basked in the double-takes of passers-by when my long stringy ponytail or the small tattoo of a dove on my Adam's apple caught their attention.

Within a half-hour, however, I tired of my walk. As I did every day. I returned to my grandfather's office.

"Who's there?" he said, sitting up in his chair and looking me straight in the eyes.

"Ellery."

"Who?"

"Ellery. Your grandson. Your daughter Ann's son."

"Of course," he said, rubbing his eyes. Undoubtedly as soon as I'd left the office they'd all fallen asleep. As they did every day.

Sure enough, Larry Beckwith and Morris Tittweiler were still sitting at the card table, heads bowed backward, mouths open, ragged snores erupting like spews from tiny volcanoes.

But something was wrong. Several chairs in the waiting room had been tipped over.

I quickly walked into my grandfather's private office. Files full of papers were scattered across the floor and all the framed photographs had disappeared from the wall.

Then I realized there was no sign of Lucy.

Returning to the waiting room, I said to my grandfather, "Who's been here?"

"What do you mean?"

"Someone was here. All the pictures in your office are gone. Lucy's gone, too."

"Lucy?" His eyes widened and he barreled into his office as he called his cat's name over and over.

By then, Larry and Morris had been restored to vague sentience, looking befuddled as always.

My grandfather said, "Did you two see anybody come in here? There's been a burglary and, more importantly, a kidnapping. Lucy is gone!"

The two old men exchanged bewildered glances, then shrugged in unison.

Soon, Morris and Larry arose from the card table like frazzled robots and mutely exited the office, leaving my grandfather and me standing there staring at each other.

His eyes were moist, and that got my attention because the rest of him looked so dry and withered. In fact, his eyes reminded me of the beagle I had as a child; it used to look at me with that same pleading expression once in a while.

He stood silently for a few moments, just like that, frozen. Then he furrowed his brow. "Who are you again?"

"Ellery Marshall. Your grandson."

"Hmm. And who am I?"

Sighing, I said, "You're just an old man who's lost his cat."

A single tear dripped down his wrinkled cheek.

"Why isn't he talking?" Police Chief Grandling asked.

We were in my grandfather's living room, steeped in dusk's lengthening shadows. Even though I'd called the police department early in the afternoon, the Chief had only now arrived. For all his talk about area cats being stolen, he apparently didn't consider my call an emergency. And by the time he arrived, my grandfather had fallen into silence.

"He just gets like this," I said. "Usually when it's getting dark. He becomes more confused and, a couple of times, it's like he's forgotten how to talk. Like now."

Chief Grandling patted my grandfather's hand. "It'll be okay, Farley. I'll keep looking for your cat."

My grandfather smiled and nodded, feigning awareness of what was going on.

"And you," the Chief said to me, narrowing his eyes to pinpoints, "you need to be taking better care of your grandpa."

My face instantly swelled with heat. That moment I wanted to empty my gut of the frustration and anger that filled it. Instead, I gritted my teeth and nodded amiably.

I walked him to the front door. Before leaving, Chief Grandling said, "This grandfather of yours has done more for this little town than anyone I know. He donated a big piece of property to the county, and they named the city park after him. He's helped more families than I can imagine who were down on their luck, lost their houses or jobs. And he treats everyone he meets with dignity and respect. He's one in a million and we're lucky he lives here. *You're* lucky he's your granddad. See what you can learn from him."

Even as I was inwardly trembling with rage at the condescending way the police chief treated me, I was equally concerned about my parents' reaction to the news. Finding out that I had allowed my grandfather's pet cat and family pictures to be stolen wouldn't exactly speak to my responsibility and competence as a caregiver.

But I still had the opportunity to show them I could handle myself like a grown man. I could take care of my grandfather. And I could take care of myself.

A half-hour later, my grandfather slowly emerged from his fog of confusion and I persuaded him to take a walk with me.

"It'll be good for you to get some fresh air," I said. "And we can go visit your friends. Maybe they'll remember something now." It was a slim

chance, but worth a try, even though there could be nothing more difficult than solving a mystery when all the witnesses had memories like
weeping colanders.

🐈   🐈   🐈

The streetlights were flickering to life and a cool breeze was blowing.
Several times my grandfather abruptly stopped in his tracks, stood at
attention and inhaled deeply, beaming like a fool, as if the wind itself had
become a sudden joy.

We walked to Larry Beckwith's, about three blocks away. When we
knocked on Beckwith's door, no one answered, even though all the lights
in the house were on.

"Sometimes he doesn't hear so well," my grandfather said. "Let me
take a peek. He won't mind."

We stepped to one side of the house and peered through a curtainless
window.

I could barely contain myself. I wanted to shout with joy, proclaim
my victory.

In the den of his home, Larry Beckwith sat in a recliner. On the coffee table in front of him sat the framed photos of my grandparents,
arranged in a perfect semi-circle. He examined them one by one, all the
time petting Lucy, who sat in his lap.

"There's Lucy!" I said. "And all your pictures! It was him!"

I moved to rap on the window but my grandfather reached up and
caught my arm so quickly it startled me. He pressed a finger to his lips
and nodded.

"We've got to confront him," I whispered.

"Very well," he responded without a hint of enthusiasm.

The front door was unlocked and we walked in. My grandfather told
me to stay put while he went in and talked to Beckwith.

As I waited, I could almost picture my parents congratulating me on
helping my grandfather to so quickly retrieve his lost cat and photos. I'd
be welcomed back at my parents' with open arms and returned to the
U of W before I knew it.

When he emerged from Beckwith's den, he said simply, "Let's go."

"Wait a minute. What about the pictures? What about Lucy?"

My grandfather sighed deeply. "Larry says they're his."

"What do you mean? That's nuts!"

He shrugged.

"I'm calling the police," I said, hoping Beckwith would hear me. "I'm not going to let you just give away your stuff I like this. We're getting it back!"

He put his arm on my shoulder and guided me out of the house.

We were silent most of the way home and, right before we entered my grandfather's house, he said, "Okay, son. If you absolutely insist, we'll do something about this dilemma. I'll make you a deal. Don't call the police. We'll resolve this in another forum."

"What's that?"

"Small claims court."

"Okay . . . but I still think you're being silly for not just walking in there and taking back your stuff. You have a right to it! I don't care if it was your friend who stole everything. It's your property!"

"At my last count, there are twenty-three important things in life," my grandfather said. "This ain't one of them."

🦙   🦙   🦙

Because we were in a county that was virtually crime-free, my grandfather was given a court date only two days after filing his complaint, and yet he still bemoaned the fact that he'd suspended the memory pool until the case was decided.

It must have been the last case of the day, since the judge (who looked even older than my grandfather) struck his gavel at exactly 4:30.

Larry Beckwith was there. Next to him was a cardboard box full of my grandfather's pictures and a carrier that contained the insistently meowing Lucy. Beckwith was leaning back in his chair, asleep.

Twice the judge banged his gavel, possibly in an attempt to wake Beckwith. Beckwith released a louder, wetter snore.

"Farley," the judge said, "I understand that you're saying Larry stole these items from you. Am I right?"

There was no reply. My grandfather stared straight ahead. He had that beagle look in his eyes again. They were moist, frightened, lost.

"Farley?" the judge said. "Are you with us, my friend?"

After several uncomfortable moments inched past, I raised my hand like I was in math class. "Sir . . . Your Honor, may I speak for my grand-father?"

The judge furrowed his brow. "You're who? Farley's grandson?"

"Yes."

"Humph." The judge didn't seem impressed with my appearance. Whether it was the nose ring or the Metallica tee-shirt I couldn't say. "Well, I suppose you can," he barked.

In a consciously polite manner I presented what I knew about the memory pool, and about how Larry plainly had stolen my grandfather's belongings after Chief Grandling had left and the others had gone to sleep.

"Do you know this as a fact? Did you see it happen?" the judge asked.

"Well, no, but—"

"You didn't see evidence of a crime yourself or talk to Mr. Beckwith, right? And, heck, you haven't been here that long. You can't even say for sure that the items belong to Farley. Maybe he was just keeping them for Larry."

"But I—"

Suddenly, out of nowhere, Larry Beckwith yelled, "My cat sings!"

The judge smiled and said, patiently, "We'll get to you soon, Larry." He looked again to me and said, less patiently, "Son, I'm going to need some testimony from your grandfather. I don't see any way around it. You're not a part in this case. You have no standing."

"Okay," I said. Then, thanks to Beckwith's inappropriate comment, a brilliant idea struck me. "Your Honor, my grandfather isn't able to speak right now, but I still think I can get answers from him. Can I do that?"

"What do you need?"

I pointed in Larry Beckwith's general direction. "I need the cat."

Astonishing me, the judge shrugged. "Well, sure, give him the cat, Larry."

Beckwith looked shocked, but he let me open the carrier and remove Lucy, who meowed even louder now, as if I were pulling out her claws one by one.

I laid Lucy in my grandfather's lap and she fell momentarily quiet.

Operating on pure instinct, my grandfather smiled vacantly while he hugged Lucy close to his body.

"What now, son?" the judge asked, coming dangerously close to picking his nose.

"Watch, Your Honor. Grandpa, listen to me. I want you to use Lucy to answer me. Do you understand?"

He looked me in the eyes and I thought I saw one corner of his mouth lift in an effort toward a smile.

"Once means 'yes,' and twice means 'no.' Understand?"

Without missing a beat, my grandfather tipped his head to one side to listen to Lucy's purring, then squeezed her quickly.

"Ngeeee-rowwwl!" Lucy said.

"B-flat!" Larry Beckwith shouted.

The judge banged his gavel. "Order!"

"That's a yes," I said to the judge. "And what's a no?" I asked my grandfather.

"Ngeee-rowwwl. Ngeee-rowwwl," sang Lucy.

"Proceed," said the judge.

Amazing. Here I was, a raging mutant who looked like he'd just stomped away from a fistfight at a grunge concert, and the judge was actually cooperating with me. More than that, he seemed to be enjoying the show.

I was the hip, gifted city kid showing the supposedly wise minds of Lamoine a thing or two about problem solving.

I asked my grandfather a series of questions. When I showed him a photo of himself and my grandmother, he squeezed Lucy once to indicate that it was him in the picture. When I asked him whether he'd had Lucy since she was a kitten, he carefully teased a "yes" out of her.

Then I asked him the central question: "Is it true that Larry Beckwith stole all these items from your office, including your pictures and your cat Lucy?"

With grandfather's help, Lucy emitted a B-flat. I slid my hands into my back pockets, mentally preparing my closing argument.

Then, to my complete surprise, Lucy released another "Ngeee-rowwwl."

"Wait a minute," I said. "You just answered that Larry Beckwith *didn't* steal the items."

A single B-flat.

"What?" My brief legal career was crashing down around me. "Grandfather, listen to me. If these items belong to you, and Larry Beckwith now possesses them, you're saying that you gave them to him."

A lone B-flat.

"That decides it then," the judge said. "They were gifts. Case dismissed!"

He pounded his gavel and left the bench.

I stood there, speechless, gazing at my grandfather, who smiled weakly and winked at me.

Larry Beckwith yelled, "My cat! She sings!"

The bailiff removed Lucy from my grandfather's lap and returned her to the carrier.

Larry carried his bounty out of the courtroom with the help of a couple of observers including Morris Tittweiler, who had wandered in late thinking he was at the coffee shop and ordered toast from the court reporter.

Within minutes, only my grandfather and I remained.

I felt my face flushing as I grabbed him by the wrist and led him out of the courtroom. I didn't know what to say.

We had just stepped out onto the courtyard when he turned to me. "I'm proud of you, son."

"What? You're talking."

He smiled. "Indeed I am."

"But I thought—"

"I had planned to stay mute and let things run their course, but I must admit, your thinking to use Lucy as a means of communication was highly creative. And entertaining, to boot."

"Why did you lie?"

He paused momentarily, then said, "I didn't lie. Even if I had, son, there's lies and then there's lies. Maybe lies that don't hurt anyone and help people realize their dreams, become more of who they are, are something different, better than ordinary lies. Wait until it's dark and I'll show you something. You'll see."

After supper, my grandfather and I walked the three blocks to Larry Beckwith's home. At this point, I admitted to myself that I was truly intrigued for the first time since I'd come to Lamoine.

"Right this way," he said, leading me around to the side of the house. He arrived at the window, peeked inside, then motioned for me to take a look.

Larry Beckwith was sitting in a recliner in his den, just like before. On the coffee table before him sat the family pictures from my grandfather's office. On his lap sat Lucy.

"Isn't it nice?" my grandfather said.

"Nice? You gotta be kidding. He's sitting in there with a roomful of stolen goods. *Your* goods!"

Grandfather shook his head. "No. He's sitting in there with memories of life."

"What do you mean?"

"Larry never married. He spent his life serving the community. With his Alzheimer's getting worse all the time, I think he found himself float-ing away. He needed something to anchor him."

"Anchor him?"

The light from Beckwith's den illuminated my grandfather's face. It looked strong and noble, almost young. "That's right, anchor him. He's sitting in there right now, son, thinking how lucky he is to have shared in a family like those in the pictures, and to have the company of a cat who loves him. He's anchored, at least for now. His life means something. He's not alone."

"What about you?"

He patted me on the shoulder. "I'm not alone either."

"But . . ." I began, but then realized I had nothing further to say.

"I must confess something, Ellery. For weeks I'd been thinking of giv-ing Lucy and the pictures to Larry. I could tell how much he wanted them. Needed them. He needed them more than I did, and even more than Morris. As bad off as Morris is these days, he still remembers his wife and family."

"There wasn't a theft. So everyone was in on this whole charade?"

"Larry wasn't. But, yes, everyone else was. It was something we wanted to do for our friend. Chief Grandling returned to the office after you left for your walk that day. He and Morris and I carried everything out to his car and Grandling took all of it to Larry's house while Morris and I messed the place up. We didn't even have to miss our naps."

"So the police didn't need to be involved? There didn't need to be a court case?"

"True. But it's perfect that everything happened as it did. We all par-took of a brief but memorable adventure and, most important of all, the town got to see what a good grandson I have."

I was still puzzled, trying to sort out everything. "So the point was . . . ?"

Still watching his friend Larry Beckwith with Lucy and his make-believe family, my grandfather said, "There are twenty-three important things in life. That, my son," he said, pointing toward his old friend, "is one of them."

My grandfather and his friends never met for another memory pool.

Two days later, Grandpa suffered a stroke, serious enough that he was hospitalized, then transferred to the nursing home.

The last time he spoke, he spoke to me.

We were in his room late one night, after the squeaks of the passing aides' shoes had become tolerably infrequent. I'd taken to bringing books to read to my grandfather when he didn't feel like talking. That night, I was reading aloud from *Venus on the Half-Shell* when I heard a sudden, sharp intake of breath.

I looked up. He had the beagle look in his eyes. He pulled the covers up to his chin.

"What's wrong?"

"Who are you?" he asked, voice trembling.

"I'm Ellery Marshall. I'm your grandson."

"And . . .who am I?"

"You're my grandpa. You're Farley Bellson."

"Ahh." He went silent for a moment, then asked, "My life. Was it a good one?"

"It was the best," I said. "You were the most accomplished and generous man around, the most amazing attorney in the world, you had the most beautiful wife and children a man could ever dream of, and you touched every person you ever met in a way that made their lives larger. There is no one walking the earth who's better than you, Grandpa."

"That's nice to know," he said, closing his eyes.

During sleep that night he had a massive stroke and, this time, he didn't return.

My parents came for the funeral, helped me pack my belongings, and took me home. I'd be re-enrolled at U of W for the next semester. Simple as that.

One day some three weeks later I found a folded-up envelope in the back pocket of the jeans I hadn't washed for months. It was the envelope from my grandpa's last memory pool.

But instead of a picture inside, there was a note.

"You're a good man," it said in my grandfather's hand. "Please don't forget us." Below the message were four signatures: Grandpa's, Larry Beckwith's, Morris Tittweiler's, and Police Chief Grandling's.

There are twenty-three important things in life, I reminded myself, placing the note in my front pocket and patting it there.

Twenty-two to go.

The Lawlessness West of the Pecos

Jan Grape

The judge was on a rampage again, throwing papers and tearing his hair and yelling. The yelling was the worst part. "Get that goldarn silly cat out of my courtroom." Judge Roy Bean had been known to cuss in two languages for two hours and never repeat himself. In all fairness, however, his Southern breeding kept him from turning the air too blue in the presence of a female.

"Your honor, this courtroom, as you call it, is that cat's home," said Sarah Jane Austin. She tried not to sound defiant but was unable to sound meek either. As the defendant currently before Judge Roy Bean, the man also known as "The Law West of the Pecos," Sarah Jane couldn't help it if Judge Bean had convened court in a barn. It certainly wouldn't be her choice. Of course, being in a court of justice wouldn't be her choice either. She'd much rather be on the stagecoach heading to California. She'd always thought she wanted to be married, but now she had many doubts.

Langtry, Texas, wasn't much of a town, but it was Judge Bean's town, and he ran it to the best of his ability. Well, he ran it with the backing of the Texas Rangers, and if he wanted his court convened in a barn, then who was Sarah Jane to argue. Especially when she was being accused of something she had not done.

Judge Bean's authority had begun with the railroad being built. The savage and barren Texas wilderness covered many square miles, but the populated region on the banks of the Rio Grande some twenty miles from the Pecos River had its beginnings as a construction camp or tent city. The saloons, sporting houses, and gambling halls were full of faro men, poker men, monte men, dice men, wheel men, and card sharks of all ilk, mingling with railroad workers, young Easterners trying to make their stake, runaway farm boys, pickpockets, gamblers, and a few foreigners. The dancehalls also nourished a few women who fought and hustled in the dives. The place was ripe for thievery, robbery, fights, duels, and plain old murder. Trouble swarmed like blue-tail flies buzzing an aggravated cow. The region was often called "Hell on Wheels" by right-thinking folks.

Several citizens of Langtry *were* law-abiding. Ranchers, cattlemen, soldiers, railroad workers, salesmen, and preachers—the general make-up of most small Texas towns, good people who would do anything for you. But the ruffians were the ones who made the loudest noise and caused trouble. They were the ones who gave Judge Bean his opportunity to be "The Law West of the Pecos."

Since the nearest hall of justice was in Fort Stockton, two hundred miles away, the governor sent a troop of Rangers hoping to keep problems to a minimum along the migratory towns until the railroad was completed. Roy Bean, saloon owner and profiteer, the nearest thing to an honest man in those early days, had been appointed a justice of the peace by the commissioner's court on the recommendation of Captain Oglesby and General King.

Judge Bean didn't hear Sarah Jane's remarks regarding the cat, or if he did, he was not about to admit it. All the judge cared about was having this trial over with, sentencing this bar-room floozie so he could finish off the new bottle of fine Kentucky whiskey a lady mule skinner had left for him just this morning.

A lady mule skinner. If that didn't gall your gullet then nothing would, thought Judge Bean. A dadgum female trying to drive a supply wagon out here in the desert, where some of the wildest men who ever rode worked and lived. Woman must be crazy.

Now where did that stupid cat go? Bean drew his revolver and began searching for the cat. "Here, kitty. Here, kitty."

"Judge Bean," Sarah Jane said. "Judge Bean?"

The judge finally looked at Sarah Jane. "What is it, child?" He looked down at the gun in his hand. "Awww. I ain't going shoot the cat, just gonna scare her a little."

He put the gun away, sat back down and focused squinty eyes at Sarah Jane. "Don't you realize you're on trial for horse thievery here? How dare you keep interrupting this court."

Sarah Jane knew she had to pacify the man or there was no telling what he'd do. "I'm terribly sorry Your Honor, sir. But the cat you are looking for, Tinta, lives here in this barn. I wouldn't be surprised to discover she's recently had kittens. She's only upset because she's not used to people being in her barn disturbing her babies."

"*Tinta*? Means 'ink' in Spanish, don't it?" the judge asked, ignoring the rest of the girl's explanation.

"Yes sir. Ink or inky. I named her that for obvious reasons—she's black as midnight."

"Well, she's going to be one dead cat if she doesn't quit squalling."

"Maybe Your Honor can finish this trial up over at the Jersey Lilly, and Tinta can go back to her babies." Sarah Jane patted her blonde hair back into place and smoothed her blue gingham dress. She was eighteen years old and too innocent looking for this dry, dusty country.

"Look, young lady. Mr. Conrad says you stole his horse from this here barn. Your attorney sent word that I needed to ass—er—tain," he stumbled over the long word. "Ascertain that you'd been out here before. Like if you knew your way around and such."

"Well, Judge. You know I've been inside here many times. I've worked in here, cleaning stalls, feeding the animals because I'm engaged to be married to Mr. Conrad."

"Which doesn't prove a single thing in my book," a contralto voice spoke up from the doorway.

Judge Bean looked up and blinked as the bright morning sun suddenly streamed in, nearly blinding him. When he could focus again, he saw a vision of loveliness. She had dark hair and was wearing a high-fashion dress of green brocade and a hat with two white doves on one side. "It can't be. Can it? Miss Langtry? Darling Lily, I knew you'd come one day. . . ."

"Judge Bean, I'm not Lily Langtry. I'm Dallas Armstrong, and I represent Miss Austin. Is her accuser in the courtroom?"

"Miss Armstrong. Ahem, uh . . . I thought you were a drover—a mule skinner. I had no idea you were a lawyer, too." Judge Bean kept looking at her. She looked so much like the picture he had hanging on the wall of the Jersey Lily. His own true love, the British actress, Miss Lily Langtry.

"I am, but I've also read for the law—although I've not taken the bar examination."

Judge Bean banged the gavel. "Court's taking a ten minute recess." He uncorked a bottle of whiskey and poured a hefty slug in his cup. "And what are you doing in Langtry?"

"I'm employed by Mr. Allen Pinkerton."

Roy Bean nearly choked on the bourbon. "The detective agency?"

"Yes. While I was vacationing in San Antonio I heard of Miss Austin's plight. Her mother asked if I'd help." She smiled sweetly at Judge Bean. "And where is her accuser?"

"Mr. Conrad had business elsewhere this morning," said the judge.

"In that case, may we have a few hours? I need to confer with my client and have time to verify her story."

"All right. Court's dismissed until tomorrow morning." The judge banged on the makeshift table and jumped up. He was only too happy to bring matters to a close for the day. He wanted to finish his bottle of whiskey and try to figure out how Miss Lily Langtry had slipped into town disguised as a mule skinner and lawyer. Of course, she is an actress, he thought, as he walked outside, got on his old dun horse, Bayo, and rambled toward town.

Sarah Jane called to the cat, "Tinta. You can come in now. That nasty man has left." The cat jumped into the young woman's arms and began purring. "Thank you, Miss Armstrong." Sarah Jane breathed into the cat's fur. "You and Tinta may have saved my life. If Tinta hadn't upset the judge in the first place, I'm sure he would have found me guilty and hung me right here on the spot."

"Well, he doesn't have the authority to do such a thing. All he can do is arraign you."

"What does 'arraign' mean?"

"It just says you will be bound over for a trial. Most likely one of the Texas Rangers would take you to Del Rio."

Sarah Jane began crying.

"Oh, merciful heavens. Don't do that. There's nothing to cry about. I don't think either the judge or Mr. Conrad thinks you're guilty, so we've just got to prove you're not." Dallas looked at the girl closely. "You're not, are you?"

"Not what?"

"Not guilty."

"Oh gosh. No. Mr. Conrad is only mad because I wouldn't go to the big dance with him over to the King Ranch."

"You mean Mr. Conrad is just a frustrated beau?" The young girl nodded. "Why did you refuse to go to the dance with him?"

"Because he can't dance. Who wants to go to the dance with some old cowboy who can't even dance?"

"Who indeed," said Dallas. It must be the heat down here, she thought. They're all addled by the hot sun. The girl's remarks made no sense at all.

"Come on," Dallas told Sarah Jane. "Let's go to my camp. I need to figure out a plan of action."

"Okay. Can I bring Tinta with me?"

Dallas looked at the black cat snoozing peacefully in the girl's arms. "I thought she had babies to take care of."

The girl laughed. "No. They haven't been born yet, but I was hoping to get Judge Bean's mind off of shooting her." The cat had her own agenda however; she jumped down, scrambled up a pole, and jumped to the floor of the loft.

"Pretty good. You're a quick-witted young lady."

Sarah Jane smiled at the compliment and started to climb into the back of Dallas's wagon, but Dallas told the girl to sit up front with her. "You'll get bounced around too much back there."

"Tell me what you're doing out here in this God-forsaken country. Where do you live, by the way?" Dallas clucked her tongue and the mules started walking slowly in the direction of Langtry.

"I'm boarding at Mrs. Shaw's right now. After Mr. Conrad fired me, I rented a room with her and got a job at the general store. I plan to apply for the schoolteacher's job in the fall."

"What did you do for Mr. Conrad?"

"Kept his books."

"Business or household?"

"Both. Say, did my mother hire you to bring me home?"

"Not exactly." Dallas looked at the girl. "She just wanted me to be sure you were okay. She'd had word you were in trouble out here—all on your own and. . . ."

"Well, you can just stop this wagon and let me out. . . ."

"But that's no solution."

"You let me out right now. Stop."

Dallas stopped the wagon and Sarah Jane jumped down. "I thank you for the few extra hours of freedom. But I'm perfectly capable of taking care of myself, and I don't need help from you or my mother." The girl took off walking.

Dallas followed along for about a mile and kept trying to persuade the girl to get back into the wagon but finally gave up when Langtry appeared in the distance. Dallas turned the mules in the direction of her campsite, but she watched until Sarah Jane had reached the outskirts of town.

Wonder what the full story is there. Why is this pretty girl out here in this wild territory with all these hard-nosed ruffians? Mrs. Austin had not been very forthcoming when she hired Dallas.

"Miss Armstrong?" the slender, pale woman had said. "I've received word my daughter is in serious trouble. She's going to be tried for stealing a horse from her future husband."

Dallas could have corrected Mrs. Austin by saying she was a Mrs. instead of a Miss, but didn't want to explain how she actually was a widow. "Has the man accused her?"

"Not only that—it's possible she could be found guilty."

Mrs. Austin had contacted the Pinkerton agency and had been given Dallas Armstrong's name and informed that Agent Armstrong would call on her in due time. When Dallas received the telegram from the agency, she had gone directly to the Austins' home.

Dallas had made arrangements to leave immediately for Langtry, and Mrs. Austin didn't explain how her daughter had managed to get herself to the area in the first place other than the mention of marriage plans.

"See if you can bring her back," Mrs. Austin had pleaded. "I would like to have her home again. Back among civilized people instead of those barbarians where she is now."

"I'll ask her, but if she's as headstrong as you've said, that will be all I can do. She is a grown woman after all. I won't force her to come back here."

Dallas packed her wagon, hitched her horse Vinegar to the back, and found herself several miles down the trail when the sun had set. Some people actually liked this wilderness, but Dallas didn't think she could ever feel completely comfortable here.

The canyons *were* beautiful, though, she thought, gouged out by the Rio Grande and the Pecos, but the endless miles of nothing gave out such a sense of desolation. That and the constant wind blowing and blowing, sometimes gently but more often shrieking and screaming out of the arroyos and canyons.

The wild animals—coyotes, foxes, bobcats, and mountain lions—didn't bother Dallas too much. They stayed away from people the majority of the time. Even the rattlesnakes and the lizards didn't bother her much. She usually left them alone unless a snake got too close—Dallas was a pretty good shot with her old long-barrel .38 Colt—but the prickly pear cactus and other harmless-looking bushes with hidden spines and thorns drove her crazy. She hated stepping or sitting on something that looked so innocent and getting stuck in unmentionable places.

Dallas had to admit March was a nice time of the year. Spring brought color to the desert: even the prickly pear had wonderful yellow blossoms, and the yucca sent up tall spikes that turned into pillows of white bell-shaped flowers. An occasional scarlet patch of some minor little cactus pincushion showed up on a hillside along with the greenery, softening the landscape somewhat. You did have to keep alert, however, because danger often lurked around the corner of this boulder or that mesquite tree.

Dallas noticed the dust the two horses stirred up long before the riders appeared. She poked her campfire and set the coffee pot back on the flame. Earlier, she had changed into her riding clothes—pants, shirt, and jacket—packing away her dress and fancy hat. She double-checked the Colt before placing it in the holster under her jacket. She finished eating her rabbit stew and was ready for the coffee when the men arrived. She liked the fact they stopped a little distance back and both took off their hats.

"Miz Armstrong," the older man said. "I'm Ira Conrad and this is my son, Lucas. May we join you for coffee?"

"I've only got one extra cup, so if you're packing a cup or can share, you're welcome to what's left in the pot. Have you eaten? It's rabbit stew."

The men dismounted, and both pulled a cup out of their bedrolls. "We have eaten, thank you." Both men were lean and tall. The older man had gray hair and a gray and black moustache.

Dallas poured the coffee and watched as the men settled down. She waited for them to begin.

"Miz Armstrong," said Lucas, the younger man. He was more attractive than his father, with startling blue eyes and light brown hair. "I'm sorry to have troubled you to come all this way. Sarah Jane is a very head-strong young woman, and sometimes she needs a firm hand. When that doesn't work, I have to resort to drastic measures."

"Such as accusing her of stealing a horse?"

"That's about it."

"But that's a bit harsh, and the accusation could get her hung."

"Not in Roy Bean's court. He's only a justice of the peace. He has no authority to hang anyone," said Ira.

"We all know that, but people in San Antonio don't know it," said Dallas. "The word got to Sarah Jane's mother, and naturally she became quite upset to think her daughter was in imminent danger."

"But she never was," said Lucas. "It was only to scare her a little."

"Of course, but you understand Mrs. Austin's perception." Dallas wondered what these two really wanted. Everything they were saying could just as easily have been said tomorrow in town.

"I have instructed Sarah Jane to write a note to her mother explaining how it was all a misunderstanding. I hope you will take that letter back to Mrs. Austin when you leave tomorrow." Lucas held an envelope out to Dallas. "You are leaving tomorrow, I take it?"

Dallas didn't answer, but he obviously took her silence for an affirmative answer.

"I will pay for your time, of course, and also for your expenses in coming all the way out here. It was simply my fault. Since Sarah Jane and I are to be married, I shall have to find other ways to persuade her—to counteract her bullheadedness." Both men stood.

Dallas stood also, took the envelope he handed her, glanced at it, and placed it in her jacket pocket.

"We are looking forward to a wedding in June," said Ira. "Sarah Jane has high hopes that her mother will be able to travel by then." The older man had not said too much, obviously preferring to let his son state his case.

"Mrs. Austin's health seemed poorly, but perhaps she will be better by June," Dallas said.

"We do thank you for the coffee," Ira said. "Shall I give you payment in paper or in gold coins?"

Ah, thought Dallas. Papa is the one controlling the purse strings. "I would not take money from you, Mr. Conrad. Mrs. Austin has already paid my fee, and I shall be happy to take Sarah Jane's letter to her mother for no charge. It's part of the job I was hired for."

"And what exactly were you hired for, Mrs. Armstrong?" asked Lucas as he put his hat back on his head.

"Normally that information is strictly confidential between my client and myself, but since you are part of the family, as it were . . . I was hired to be sure Miss Austin received a fair trial and to escort her back to San Antonio if she wished to go. But she's already made it clear she wants to stay here, so my job is finished."

"And you'll be leaving tomorrow morning?" Ira said, mounting his horse.

"As soon as things are clear with Judge Bean that Miss Armstrong won't be tried for horse thieving." Dallas forced a small smile and wondered why they seemed so anxious that she leave. "You will talk to Judge Bean first thing tomorrow?"

"Yes indeed," said both men in unison. They tipped their hats and rode back towards town.

"What was that all about?" Dallas wondered aloud to Vinegar. He huffed air through his nostrils and shook his head as if he understood. "I never saw two men so antsy about me staying someplace. We might just have to hang around a bit to see why."

The next morning Dallas rode Vinegar into Langtry. When she reached Judge Bean's saloon, she almost fell off her mount as a mountain lion let out an eerie sound. That's when she noticed all the cages in front of the Jersey Lily. Each had an animal in it: a coyote, a fox, a mountain lion, and some type of black cat that must be a panther. She got off Vinegar and tied him to the hitching rail. A large bear chained to a pole came shuffling around the side of the building just as she stepped onto the porch. She let out a soft scream until she realized he couldn't reach her. "He must be tame," she whispered.

A horrid smell reached her nostrils as she neared the door, and she stopped immediately.

Smells like someone died in there, she thought. She stood in the doorway and peered inside, looking down a long hallway, unsure of what she'd find. On her right was a big room, and as her eyes adjusted to the dimness she saw a pool table with a young man laid out on it. "My stars and nightgown," she said. "Somebody did die."

But the young man moved and rolled over, opening one eye as he did so. "And just who are you, pretty darlin'?"

"That there is Miz Armstrong, son." Judge Bean walked out of a room on the left of the hall and out onto the porch. "She's a mule skinner and a lawyer and not someone you want to even think about tangling with."

"I thought from the smell he had died," said Dallas. Then she realized this establishment obviously was also Roy Bean's home. "I am sorry; I don't mean to sound rude."

"No, ma'am, you're quite right. The odor coming from a drunk often smells like death and my Sam usually smells like a cantina this time of day."

Judge Bean's huge stomach poked through his vest, showing his red longjohns. His shirt-tail hung out in back, and his hair and beard looked as if they'd not been cleaned nor combed in days. The man didn't smell like a lilac himself, but Dallas tried not to show her shock. He certainly had not looked so unkempt yesterday. An evening of drinking didn't set well on him.

She asked if the Conrads had spoken to him about dropping the charges against her client.

"Yes. They did. She's free as a bird."

"Judge Bean, you and I both know that young lady didn't steal a horse. What do you think is going on there?"

"Miz Armstrong, I wouldn't dwell on it too much. The Conrads are almost as rich and powerful as the King family. You don't want to cross 'em."

A young boy came running up, interrupting, "Señor Judge, Señor Judge!"

"What is it, Manuel?"

"They found a woman's body out in Meyers Canyon," said the boy.

"Do they know who it is?" the judge and Dallas asked at the same time.

"Somebody said it was that lady that works at the General Store."

Dallas gasped and turned away quickly as she felt nausea rise up.

"Oh migo . . . uh, er . . . uh, my good gosh," stammered the judge. "Let me get the buckboard."

"May I go with you?" Dallas asked. "I must know if it is Sarah Jane."

When they arrived at the canyon, they found that the railroad men had brought up the young woman's body and wrapped her in a saddle blanket. Judge Bean pulled the blanket back and took a quick look. "It's Sarah Jane Austin all right."

"Did anyone see anybody around?" asked Dallas.

The railroad workers shook their heads.

One of the men stepped forward and removed his sombrero. "Nothin', Judge. We were the onliest ones out here this mornin' I think."

The second man spoke up. "I just saw that piece of blue material flappin' in the breeze, and something told me we needed to look closer. I climbed down and could see it was a body."

"So you men got her out?" asked Dallas. "Was she shot?"

"I couldn't see no bullet hole," said the second man. "Back of her head is smashed like a gourd."

"And have either of you men ever seen Miss Austin before?"

The first man spoke up. "I knowed she worked at the general store, but I didn't really know her."

"This here is Ramon Rodriguiz," said Judge Bean. "He's a good man. And over there is his brother-in-law Pedro. Both are hard workers and honest men."

"You 'cusing me?" asked Ramon. "I didn't do nothin'."

"No, no," said Dallas. "I'm just wondering what happened."

"Well, we best get her loaded into the wagon and back into town," said the judge.

In a few minutes the men had Sarah Jane's body loaded into the wagon, and they started their three-mile journey back into Langtry.

Once in town the men took Sarah Jane's body to Mrs. Shaw's house. Normally Judge Bean, also the coroner, checked the bodies at the Jersey Lily and made a ruling or determination of the cause of death. But it wasn't in him to treat Miss Austin's body in that crude manner.

After a thorough examination—which included consulting with Mr. Shaw, who had had some medic training during the Civil War—Judge Bean ruled that Sarah Jane Austin had fallen off the bridge at Meyer's Canyon—suffering a severe head injury, and it was death by accident.

When he told Dallas his ruling, she was furious. "Judge, how can you say her death was an accident?"

"You want me to rule it what it actually is, a suicide? That's too harsh and would be devastating to her poor mother."

"No. She was killed."

"And just what makes you think somebody killed her, murdered her? Do you know anything that could make me change my ruling?"

"No. But I know as sure as I'm standing here that she didn't kill herself, nor did she have an accident. The only thing left is murder."

"And may I deduce you think Lucas Conrad is guilty of something?"

"Look, he accused her of stealing his horse for no more reason, she said, than she refused to go to the dance with him. Doesn't that strike you as pretty dumb? Why did she lie to me? And then the Conrads, both father and son, rode all the way out to my campsite to try to pay me to leave Langtry immediately."

Dallas paced the floor in front of Judge Bean's desk in his office inside the Jersey Lily. "Judge Bean, why did the Conrads want me out of town? I think it was because they didn't want me to be here when Sarah Jane's body was found."

Judge Bean looked thoughtful. "Miz Armstrong, you could very well be right, but there is no proof. Bring me some proof, and I'll make a different ruling."

"You can bet that's exactly what I will do—find you some proof." Dallas turned and practically stomped out of the Judge's saloon.

When she reached her wagon, she remembered the letter Lucas Conrad had given her to take to Mrs. Austin. She got it out and opened and read it without any qualms:

Dear Mother,

> *The court thing was only because of a silly argument between Lucas and myself. He only meant it to make me stop and think how I might be hurting him. I'm sorry you heard about it and got worried. I did not need nor want an attorney, but I'm thankful Mrs. Armstrong is willing to bring this letter to you and tell you herself how happy I am. I am looking forward to my wedding in June, and if you are unable to travel—well then we shall come to San Antonio to be married.*

> *Always,*
> *Your loving daughter, Sarah Jane*

The letter was bland and pointless. It really didn't say much, but reading the letter gave Dallas the idea for a plan of investigation.

Dallas stopped in at Mrs. Shaw's house. "Has anyone notified Sarah Jane's mother?"

"Yes," said Mrs. Shaw. "Judge Bean sent a telegram. He expects to hear something back before long."

"Do you mind if I look in her room? She said she would give me a letter today to take to her mother. If I can find it, I'll see that Mrs. Austin gets it. It might be of some comfort to the poor woman."

"Of course. It's the first door on the left upstairs. Oh my, oh my." Mrs. Shaw wrung her hands and wiped her eyes. "I just can't believe this poor girl is gone."

Dallas entered the room where Sarah Jane had lived. She didn't know what she thought she'd find, but she felt compelled to look at the dead girl's things.

She searched through the tall oak wardrobe and found nothing except the girl's dresses and shoes. A large chest of drawers stood on the other side of the bed next to a wash basin. On top was a Bible and a photograph of a woman and man. The woman was Mrs. Austin, and presumably the man was the girl's father, Mr. Austin.

Dallas pulled open the top drawer and found several letters written to Sarah Jane from her mother, two copies of *Harper's Weekly* magazine, and a small sewing kit holding two needles stuck in a pin cushion and two spools of thread—one black and one white—and a thimble.

A little box was hidden under a pair of kid gloves and a scarf. Dallas opened it and found a ring with an opal stone, several pins, two necklaces, and three hat pins with jeweled topknots. She poked her finger through the jewelry, and just as she was ready to close the lid she spied a tiny key. She picked it up and looked carefully at it. She couldn't be sure, but thought the key might open a small jewelry or music box. Since she found the key in the girl's jewelry box, Dallas reasoned the key might fit a music box. Maybe the girl had hidden a letter or some papers inside that could explain things. Nothing made sense to Dallas, but the girl was dead. That part was real. Maybe it *had* been a tragic accident, but why had the girl been out at Meyer's Canyon anyway? It was a lonely spot, and not a place a young woman would go all by herself, especially in the evening.

Dallas searched the room thoroughly and could find nothing the key might be used for, but she wasn't ready to give up on the matter. She heard masculine voices downstairs and thought one sounded very much like Judge Bean. She slipped the key in her pocket and hurried downstairs.

"Hello, Judge. Do we know yet what to do about poor Sarah Jane's body?"

"Here's the telegram I just received." He handed her the paper.

AM TOO ILL TO TRAVEL STOP CAN MRS. ARMSTRONG HANDLE BURIAL? STOP LUTHERAN CHURCH PLEASE STOP HOPE TO VISIT THERE ONE DAY STOP —MRS. SAM AUSTIN

"Of course I'll take care of things. How sad not to be at your child's funeral," Dallas said. "And sadder still for her to be buried so far away, but I guess it can't be helped."

Mrs. Shaw sniffed in the background. "Did you find a suitable dress for her?"

Dallas nodded, thankful that Mrs. Shaw came up with a likely reason for Dallas to have been upstairs in the girl's room. "She has a lovely dark blue silk that will be perfect."

Judge Bean left after offering to take care of things with the Lutheran preacher. "I'll be back soon as we have a time set."

Dallas started back up the stairs then stopped to ask Mrs. Shaw, "Did Sarah Jane have a wedding dress being made?"

"Yes. Claire Lenander is the town dressmaker. I think Sarah Jane had something being made there. Or she bought a dress in San Antonio and Claire was fitting it. I'm not sure of all the details."

Dallas couldn't imagine that Sarah Jane would leave an important box at the dressmaker's, but maybe she had had no other place to hide something.

After bringing down the burial clothes for the woman, Dallas excused herself and headed to the dressmaker's shop.

Claire Lenander said that, yes, Miss Austin had a dress on order and had planned to have it fitted at her shop when it came in. Claire was also making the going-away dress for the honeymoon trip. But, no, nothing had been left there for safekeeping.

Dallas could only think of the general store where Sarah Jane worked as the last resort. Surely the girl wouldn't leave something important out at the Conrads' ranch. Maybe she only had sentimental things that she didn't need to hide from her future husband.

She wasn't sure how to ask the Conrads about it.

Dallas made a quick trip out to her campsite to get a dress and hat to wear to the funeral, and on the way she remembered when she first saw the girl—out at that barn where Judge Bean was holding his court. Sarah Jane had mentioned something about being out in that barn often, doing chores, and she knew all about the black cat—how the cat was expecting kittens.

Could she have hidden something there? It didn't seem likely as the barn did belong to Lucas Conrad, but Dallas didn't have any other ideas. Could she do any serious looking in that barn without getting caught?

Dallas rode out to the barn and had a cover story ready when she arrived. She decided not to go up to the ranch house but to talk to a ranch hand instead. One cowboy looked to be in charge of the bronco-busting going on in the nearby corral, so she approached him.

"Hi," she said, when he turned to her. "I'm Dallas Armstrong, and I was here the other day for the court hearing? I think I lost my favorite hat pin here. Do you think anyone would mind if I look?"

After the cowboy's initial shock at seeing a woman at the corral, he was quite cooperative. "Mr. Lucas is over at his father's place today. His father is in Galveston awaiting a cattle shipment, but I'm sure Mr. Lucas won't mind. It's okie-doke by me. Can I help you look?"

"Oh goodness, no. I don't want to take you away from your work. I won't be long, I'm sure."

He nodded and turned back to the horse training.

Dallas walked into the barn and looked around. "Where would a good hiding place be?"

"Meooow."

Dallas looked up and saw Tinta standing at the edge of the loft. "Well hello, Missy. Have you had your babies yet?"

Tinta stretched, scampered down the nearest pole and hopped into Dallas's arms. Dallas thought of her own cats who had been expecting throughout the years, especially one years ago who had had kittens on the Fourth of July and spoiled an evening out with her husband-to-be, Hank Armstrong. The night had not been wasted, however, as the two young people fell deeply in love that evening. She decided if Tinta *was* expecting, it was way too early to tell because her tummy seemed completely unchanged.

Tinta kept looking up at the loft, and Dallas wondered, could Sarah Jane have hidden something up there?

You'll never know until you look, she thought, and climbed the ladder to the loft.

Tinta, purring and dancing, led Dallas to a snug little alcove hidden behind several huge bales of alfalfa.

Dallas noticed a nest Tinta obviously had made, but the cat had not pulled out fur to line it yet, so it probably was for sleeping not for birthing. Dallas also spotted a saddle blanket nearby and what looked like an old milking stool, as if someone had made a place to sit and daydream or contemplate her life.

It's Sarah Jane's hideaway, thought Dallas. She began searching further, and back in the corner where the wall and the roof beams came together, Dallas felt the rough edges of something hard. She pulled it out. It was a book. More specifically, it was a diary. And it had a lock.

Dallas took the key she'd found in Sarah Jane's jewelry box from her pocket. The key fit. Dallas opened the diary. It only took a few moments of reading to realize what had gotten Sarah Jane killed. Cattle rustling. The Conrads were stealing cattle from nearby ranches and selling them to Europe for three times the going price. Sarah Jane wrote that Lucas Conrad said he would kill her and her mother if she ever told anyone what she had found out. She knew he would do it, too. She was afraid to tell anyone the truth—even when she went to court.

Dallas heard a slight noise and looked up.

Lucas Conrad was at the ladder, his head and shoulders already above the loft floor.

"Mrs. Armstrong. So you found it?"

Dallas had laid the diary on the old stool before she stood up. "Found what?"

"Sarah Jane's journal."

"So you did have a reason to kill her. You knew Sarah Jane had found out about the cattle rustling?"

"Of course. That's why she broke our engagement and why she threatened to turn me over to the Texas Rangers due here next week."

"So you accused her of stealing a horse in hopes she would be sent to jail over in Fort Stockton. That way she wouldn't be around when the Rangers came. That's when you threatened her too. When it all backfired you had to get rid of her."

"Well, she did know too much, and she claimed to have written everything down in case something happened to her. But I didn't believe her. And I looked everywhere last night for any place she could have hidden her journal."

Lucas Conrad's face turned ugly then, and Dallas felt fear as he pulled a gun and pointed it at her. This man had killed one woman already and wouldn't hesitate to kill again. She glanced to her right and then to her left for a way past him.

"You can't get around me. But even if you do, I'll chase you down."

Lucas laughed and the sound was cold, sending shivers down Dallas's backbone.

Suddenly, a loud "meooow" startled the man.

He turned and looked behind him.

That was all the distraction that Dallas needed. She rushed toward Conrad with both her arms out straight and rigid.

Tinta meowed again, dancing around, and Conrad tried to sidestep her. Dallas's outstretched hands shoved against the man's body.

He tried to keep his balance but couldn't, then staggered and went over the edge of the loft, screaming as he fell and landed with a thud.

Dallas hurried down the ladder and over to Conrad. He was breathing, but he was knocked out cold. She darted outside to her horse and grabbed a lariat from her saddle. Conrad was trussed up like a calf when he woke up, both legs tied to his right arm. His left arm was broken, or it would have been tied up also.

Dallas had worried that the cowhands would come running to Conrad's aid when he woke up and called out, so she had gagged him with his neckerchief. She pushed and pulled until she got him inside a grain storage room. "You can just stay there until I get Judge Bean. Looks like he'll be holding justice court out here once again."

Conrad moaned and tried to talk but the gag did its job. "You better lie still and rest while I go to town for Mr. Shaw. You could have internal injuries."

Conrad groaned again.

She ignored him and closed the door. She climbed back up to the loft to get Sarah Jane's journal and to check on Tinta. The cat was calmly cleaning her face. "You yelled at just the right time, little miss Tinta."

Tinta jumped into Dallas's arms and began purring. "And what's this story about you having babies? Was it just a false alarm? It better be, 'cause I'm taking you back to San Antonio with me."

Tinta put one paw up to the woman's face and purred extra loud.

Catnip

Dick Lochte

1 was sitting in my favorite chair in the den, going over my notes for the Donna Seaton trial—the most important trial of my short, heretofore undistinguished prosecutorial career—when a tall redhead of uncommon beauty walked in wearing a gorilla suit. She was carrying the gorilla head in one furry hand, a wooden box in the other.

"I'm bored, Billy," my wife Jenny said, flopping down on the over-stuffed sofa.

I continued staring at her.

"Oh, this old thing?" She pointed to the gorilla suit as if she'd forgotten she was wearing it. "I found it in the attic. Found this, too." She held up the wooden box. "What the heck is it?"

It was about half the size of a good tool kit, with screen mesh windows on either side and a metal door at one end. "My turtle box," I said. "My grammar school buddies and I used to have turtle races. Line up four or five boxes. We stole the remote clickers from our parents' TVs, and Guy Terriot, this incipient electronic genius who's now working for Bill Gates, rigged the doors so they opened on the click. First turtle to crawl out of the box was the winner."

"Sounds like you boys were pretty starved for entertainment," Jenny said, pulling the metal door open. "Clicker's still inside." She reached in and found it. "These were inside, too." She withdrew a pack of pink envelopes held by a rubber band. "The hottest, wildest mash notes I've ever read, written by somebody. named Tara to somebody named Wild Willy."

"Wild Willy, huh? Can't imagine who that might have been."

"They're addressed to William Quinlan, this house, New Orleans, Louisiana," she said, accusingly. "Wouldn't that be you?"

"My uncle William," I replied, employing the guile that comes naturally to members of the legal profession. "I was named for him. He lived with us for a few years around the time I was at Tulane. Dashing bachelor type. The ladies loved him. Can't imagine how his letters wound up in my turtle box." Not for the first time, I questioned the wisdom of moving back into the family home on Henry Clay Street.

My intention had been to sell the old place, unused since my mother's death two years before, and buy one of those nice, clean, all-amenities-included condos along St. Charles Avenue. But Jenny wouldn't hear of it. "This house is hurricane-sturdy and mortgage-free," she'd argued. "It's completely furnished, Billy. Think of the money we'll save. Remember, I'm not working anymore."

So I agreed. But the ambiance was getting to me—sleeping with Jenny in my parents' big bed, for example. And having her root mercilessly through my past.

"I assume this is a Mardi Gras costume," she said, indicating the ape suit.

"No. The whole family had 'em. Saturday nights we'd put 'em on and dance around the back yard in the moonlight."

"I wish that were true," she said. "We've only been in New Orleans for eight weeks and already I sense you're turning conservative on me."

"Me? Conservative?"

"One of us is still wearing his tie from work."

With a sigh I lowered the lid on my laptop and placed it on the floor where an assortment of manila folders formed a druid's circle around my chair. "Why don't I go slip into my biker leathers? We'll get out the chopper and zoom through the Quarter terrorizing tourists."

"You're kidding, but I'd love to. I'm bored, Billy," she repeated. "I've been a good girl for nearly a year. But that was in L.A., where there were other things to do. Here, I just loll around, reading books on local lore and remembering the excitement of my old life."

I met Jenny at a large cocktail party held at the sprawling estate of the mayor of Los Angeles. I was one of the up-and-coming deputy district attorneys tapped for attendance. Trying to stay out of everyone's way, I walked into our host's study and found the most beautiful woman I'd ever seen perusing his honor's bookshelf.

It was lust at first sight.

Not until Jenny was certain the lust had firmly congealed into a love stronger than civic duty did she confess to me that she'd crashed the party. She'd been looking for the mayor's wall safe when I stumbled into the room. She preferred stealing from politicians, she said, because there was always a little something you could find in their safes that amounted to a "Get Out Of Jail" card.

The discovery that my one true love was a professional thief caused quite a bit of anxiety on my part. I was, after all, an officer of the court. I won't bore you with the arguments that ensued, encompassing such dreary topics as good and evil, crime and punishment, male chauvinism and female rights to an occupation of one's own choosing. Let it suffice to say that, four months after that fateful meeting in the mayor's study, Jenny agreed to hang up her burglar tools, make several handsome anonymous donations to local charities and become my bride. In that order.

When New Orleans District Attorney Timothy Mathern, a friend of my late father, offered me a job in my hometown, I leapt at it. I envisioned it as the ideal way for both of us to start our married life relatively afresh. But the slow pace of the city had only succeeded in giving Jenny more time to recall the joys of burglary.

"Why don't we go somewhere for a drink?" I suggested.

"What about your trial prep?"

"I'd rather spend time with my beautiful ape girl."

She shook her head, red tendrils whipping her face. "No-no-no. I know that look on your face, Billy—that pinched, beetle-browed, squinchy combination of frustration and panic. You're in trouble on this one."

"No trouble. The case just isn't as strong as I'd like."

She moved in front of me and offered me her back. "Unzip me while you fill me in," she said. "I'll give you the felon's perspective."

"How much do you know?" I asked, digging through the fake ape fur for the zipper.

"Well," she said, emerging from the costume in her bra and panties, "I know that it was a gross murder with lots of blood. Ritualistic. The carved-up victim was a not very pleasant old lady named Laura Denecheaux, one of the richest women in New Orleans. Petroleum, I guess. Inherited from her father."

"And grandfather," I amended, admiring her lithe figure as she began folding the ape suit.

"The point is she was loaded, and she had this house tabby that she dearly loved."

"That would be Lulu, an extremely rare black Burmese," I said.

"Rare, huh?" Jenny asked. "How would that translate into U.S. currency?"

"Usually anywhere from several hundred to several thousand dollars. But if you're talking Lulu, about $40 million," I said. "Regardless of whether the jury finds Ms. Denecheaux's ward, Donna Seaton, guilty or innocent, Lulu still inherits the bundle."

"A forty million dollar cat," Jenny said. I wasn't happy with the way her green eyes were glistening.

"You ever engage in dog- or cat-napping when you were working?" I asked.

She sat on my lap and began to remove my tie. "I stuck to strictly inanimate objects," she said. "But a forty million dollar cat . . . Anyway, if the cat is the heir, why did Donna Seaton sic some maniac slasher on Ms. Denecheaux?"

"She'd been set to take over Lulu's legal guardianship in the event of the old lady's death. But, according to the lawyer for the estate, Maurice Fortier, Laura Denecheaux was about to change her will, dumping Seaton in favor of one Louise Hendry, the president of People For Animals."

"Uh-oh," my darling wife said. "People For Animals. Scam alert!"

"I think it's legit," I said. "They've got veterinary clinics in three southern states, offering their services free to those who can't afford them. I know these things because I had a long chat with Ms. Hendry, who seems like a genuinely dedicated woman."

"Don't tell me. In her thirties, blonde, wears glasses she doesn't really need and even with them on manages to curl your toes."

"Absolutely wrong," I said. "She's myopic. Needs the glasses."

"And I bet she's taking care of little Lulu while the nasty trial goes on."

"Well, yes," I said, feeling oddly defensive. "Somebody has to care for the heiress. Lou . . . Ms. Hendry has fixed up a nice room for the cat at her home."

"So," Jenny said, pretending to study my hair and pat down little errant tufts, "why would Donna Seaton want the ordeal of caring for a forty million dollar cat?"

"It's a matter of naked ownership and usufruct rights," I said.

"According to Ms. Denecheaux's will, Lulu has the naked rights, that is, the house, the stocks, the bonds, the various holdings. She owns them, but being a cat, she can't really do anything with them. As guardian, Seaton has the usufruct. Which means she can use and enjoy the forty mil to make life comfortable for herself and the cat. She just can't sell, lease or dispose of it."

"That's okay, but is it worth murder?" Jenny asked, running her fingers through my hair.

"Lulu's nine years old. When she goes to cat heaven, assuming she dies a natural death, Seaton gets both naked ownership and usufruct. The inheritance will be hers, free and clear."

"Why did Ms. Denecheaux want to change her will?"

"The lawyer says she 'overheard' one of Seaton's phone conversations with, in her words, 'an obvious member of the demimonde.'"

"Now you're talking," my wife said, snuggling closer. "They were discussing her gruesome death?"

"Not at all. They were discussing sex. Pretty steamy stuff, according to Ms. D. She was shocked that this woman who'd been under her roof for nearly six years could be so 'brazen.' She told lawyer Fortier she wanted to fire Seaton on the spot but was canny enough to consider the possibility of a wrongful termination suit. She requested that Fortier hire a private investigator to secure proof of Seaton's lack of moral turpitude."

"I love that kind of talk. Moral turpitude," Jenny said, wiggling closer. "Were there pictures, Billy? The kind you guys snigger about down at the D.A.'s?"

"Nothing even vaguely snigger-worthy, I'm sorry to report. The sleuth, a colorful gent named Lou Cronin, who speaks like something that just crawled out of an all-night forties movie festival, took some shots of Seaton in the company of a thug named Joe Gordon."

"Thug?"

"A lower echelon rackets guy. Anyhow, Cronin had shots of Seaton and Joe Gordon necking up a storm."

"Shocking," my wife said, adrip with sarcasm.

"It wasn't exactly the kendo chop Ms. D. had been hoping for, but she believed that because Gordon was a wiseguy, she had reason enough for the dismissal. Lawyer Fortier thinks she must have made the mistake of confronting Seaton, possibly giving her notice, before she had the chance to change the will."

"And Seaton got the wiseguy to carve up the old lady?"

"That's the problem. She and Gordon were seen at a cheesy casino in Bay Saint Louis at approximately the time Laura Denecheaux was meeting her fate. But, only a few days before, Cronin the private eye followed them both to an establishment on Magazine Street named Le Bistro Voudou, where they chatted up the owner, Henri Lebord. Cronin identified Lebord as an associate of thieves—"

"Look who's talking," my wife whispered against my neck.

"—and murderers," I completed my statement, trying to ignore the way my neck was tingling. "Cronin's snitches told him that Lebord has, in the past, acted as buffer for a hit man known as The Reverend. The Rev is a knife artist who really loves his work, as is evidenced by the remains of Ms. Denecheaux."

"The lawyer knew in advance about The Reverend?" she asked, nuzzling my ear.

"Yep. But when he relayed Cronin's information to Ms. Denecheaux, suggesting she might be in danger, she called him a melodramatic idiot."

"Well," Jenny whispered softly into my right ear, "She was concentrating too much on Seaton's hot phone call. She wasn't thinking murder; she was thinking sex."

"I know precisely how that feels," I said, straining every muscle in my body to stand with her still in my arms. Having passed that hurdle, carrying her, staggering, to the big bedroom was a snap.

🐾   🐾   🐾

Eventually, we got back to our discussion of the Seaton trial. We were in the kitchen where I used to eat my Cream of Wheat every morning before biking off to Holy Name of Jesus grammar school. We were sipping hot cocoa, cozily wrapped in thick terry robes from the Ritz in Paris where we honeymooned. (To this day Jenny thinks we stole them, and I would never dream of ruining her fun by admitting I had them added to the bill.) "So what was it that convinced Big Tim to indict Donna Seaton?" she asked, watching her marshmallow melt in the liquid.

"Well, we've got the lawyer's statement about the will. We have Seaton's bank records indicating a withdrawal of thirty thousand dollars three days before the murder. That transaction was in cash, according to the bank manager, and Seaton refuses to explain what she did with the money.

"Then we have Cronin's photos of Seaton and Gordon and Henri

Lebord. Plus, and this is a big plus, the P.I. overheard the lady make the comment to Lebord, 'It has to be done Tuesday night.' That was the night of the murder."

"Any hard evidence?" Jenny asked, zeroing in on the big problem. "The knife the Reverend used? The Reverend's prints in the house? The Reverend himself?"

"Haven't found the weapon. There was a windowpane removed from one of the French doors at the side of the house, which is how the Reverend has been entering his victims' homes. That's how he did it in Metairie last summer and in Baton Rouge a year ago. Both deaths were just as bloody as Laura Denecheaux's. As for locating the guy, the cops are clueless."

"But Big Tim thought you had enough to go to trial." Big Tim being my boss, the District Attorney.

"Big Tim was being pressured by lawyer Fortier, a man of influence in this city."

"Who's defending Seaton?"

"A pit bull named Gene Bethune. He destroyed poor old Lou Cronin on the stand. He translated all his old-fashioned hard-boiled slang for the jury, as if the guy were speaking Hindi. I objected, but Judge Bascombe Seymour, who has more than a touch of sadism in his Southern soul, said he was having trouble understanding the witness, too.

"Then Bethune mumbled a question, and before I could object Cronin asked him to repeat. And Bethune shouted, 'Are you sure you heard Ms. Seaton's comment in that noisy bistro correctly?'"

"Ouch."

"Thanks for your sympathy," I said.

"No weapon," she said. "No killer. But you still have the missing money."

"As Bethune has pointed out to the jury, it's no crime to withdraw money from a bank. Not even in cash. And if his client wanted to, say, make ten or twenty anonymous donations to various church poor boxes throughout the city, it is entirely within her rights to do so."

"This Bethune is an evil man, isn't he?"

"I've put his number on my speed-dial," I told her. "In case one of us should ever need the services of a criminal lawyer."

She sipped her cocoa, licked away a bit of residue with the tip of her pink tongue and said, "What've you dragged out of the boyfriend, Joe Gordon?"

"His name, address, and phone number. He denies any association with this city's criminal element and would have us believe that he's an entrepreneur. He says he and Seaton are engaged and will marry as soon as this annoying little trial is over."

"Unless I've miscounted," Jenny said, "that leaves only restaurateur and hit man agent Lebord. Why's that name sound familiar?"

"Don't know, honey. But he's joined our team. The cops tossed his establishment and found several cases of booze without any kind of tax stamp on them. In return for our forgetting to notify the Alcohol, Tobacco and Firearms folks, Lebord has agreed to tell the jury that Seaton asked him to arrange for an introduction to the Reverend."

"He admits fronting for a hit man?"

"No. He says he told Seaton she'd made a mistake, that he had no connection whatsoever to the Reverend."

"You believe that?" she asked.

"Not for a second. But that's all he'll give us. I'd love to put this Reverend away, but right now I'll settle for him telling the jury that Seaton was shopping for an assassin."

"Her Rambo of a defense lawyer is going to go after Lebord with tooth and fang. How reliable is a guy who peddles illegal booze?"

"He claims he doesn't know how those cases of whisky got in his locker. He thinks they may have been put there by a previous owner."

"Like your uncle Will's love letters," she said.

I sighed.

"He's a liar, Billy," she said. "No telling what he'll say or do on the stand."

"A wild card is my Lebord."

"I'd love to see how you play him," she said. "When are you going to call him?"

"I'm not sure."

"Of course you are, Billy. When?"

"Tomorrow."

"Please, oh please, can I come?"

It was the first time she'd ever asked to watch me prosecute a case. "I'd rather you saw me on a day when I felt more confident. . . ."

But she was there in the packed courtroom the next afternoon when Henri Lebord took the stand. The jury was a pretty cosmopolitan collection of truth-seekers, but I'm not sure they were ready for Lebord. He was an odd duck, five-six or so, with long braided black hair and a face white as whey, made even paler by his preference for black clothing. Black long-sleeved shirt. Black trousers, held together on his wiry frame by a unique snakeskin belt. His sockless feet wore scuffed sandals. A variety of items were pinned to his shirt, including several little cloth bags, a bright yellow feather, and a hank of hair. When we'd met in my office to discuss his testimony I'd suggested he leave the decorations at home before taking the stand. Wasted breath.

He sat bent forward nervously in the witness chair while responding to my introductory questions. Yes, he was Henri Lebord, owner of Le Bistro Voudou on Magazine Street. Yes, he recognized the defendant, Donna Seaton.

"Have you ever spoken with Ms. Seaton?" I asked. I expected his response to be, as it was in my office, "*Oui*. On the night of April 17 of this year, Ms. Seaton entered my *taverne* with a man I know slightly, Joe Gordon, to ask me to arrange a meeting with someone called 'The Reverend.'"

What he said, after a moment's hesitation, was, "*Oui*. On the night of April 17, Ms. Seaton entered my bistro with a man known to me as Joe Gordon. He stopped by to tell me they are engaged to be married."

Feeling my stomach and lower bowels lurch unpleasantly, I said, not too desperately, I hope, "Didn't Ms. Seaton have a particular request?"

"Objection. Leading the witness."

"Let me restate," I said. "Was there any other reason for Ms. Seaton's visit?"

A frown creased Lebord's forehead, fingers fondled the objects pinned to his shirt. "*Non*. Not as I recall. We just discussed their good fortune."

"Do you know the man who calls himself the Reverend?" I asked.

"I know *of* him. I read about him in the *Times-Picayune*. They speak of him on television."

I indulged in a short fantasy of choking Henri until his eyes popped out. "Did you not say to me, in the presence of two New Orleans police officers, that Ms. Seaton told you she wanted to contact the Reverend?"

"If I say anything like that," Henri Lebord said, "it would not be truth. Maybe you misunderstand me, sir." He was not being cute or smart-alecky. He seemed uncomfortable, tense, obviously not enjoying himself. That made two of us.

I turned to Judge Seymour, who was grinning at me. A sadist, like I said. "Your Honor, in light of Mr. Lebord's, ah, confusion over statements he has previously made, I'd like to request a brief recess to gather—"

"Your Honor," the pit bull said, rising from the defense table, "Mr. Quinlan has had more than ample time to prepare his witness and himself for this trial. There are at least another two hours left in the day. I owe it to my client to request that we use them."

"Ah am inclined to side with Mistah Bethune on this point, Mistah Quinlan," Judge Seymour drawled, happy as a clam. "Please carry on."

I saw my beautiful wife leave her chair and move to the bar, shoving a slip of paper at my clerk, Jay Hodel. "That being the case," I said to Judge Seymour, "I'd like to designate Mr. Lebord a hostile witness."

"Soun's lak a fine idea."

"Hostile?" Lebord asked. "I am not hostile."

While the judge explained the term to the creepy nerd, I moved quickly to the prosecution table and glimpsed Jenny's note. *Has he been in Denecheaux's house?* it·said.

Lebord avoided my eyes as I approached.

It was the worst sort of situation for a lawyer. One of the prime rules of the game is that you never ask a question unless you already know the answer. From this point on, I was flying blind, working with a flopped witness who didn't mind lying under oath. A prudent prosecutor would have stepped back and turned Lebord over to his new friend, Bethune. But I wanted to rattle his cage a little first.

"To your knowledge, have you ever told me a falsehood, Mr. Lebord?" I asked.

"I . . . a falsehood . . . ?"

"A lie, then. Yes or no?"

"I, uh . . . *non.* I do not recall doing such a thing."

"And you don't recall saying anything about Ms. Seaton wanting to get in touch with the Reverend?"

"Asked and answered, Your Honor," the pit bull objected.

"Sustained. Gettin' all this, mah deah?" His "deah" was a sixty-year-old court steno.

"Do you sell illegal merchandise in your tavern, Mr. Lebord?" I asked.

"*Non.* Not to my knowledge."

"Didn't the police find cases and cases of untaxed whisky stacked up in your liquor locker?"

"*Oui.*" His fingers were hopping from one little pinned bag to another. Very distracting. "But, sir, I do not know where the bottles come from. I do not put them there."

"You're trying to tell us that behind your back, somebody snuck into your bistro and loaded up your locker with cases of smuggled scotch and bourbon?"

"Your Honor," Gene Bethune squawked. "Mr. Lebord's not on trial here. The legality or illegality of alcohol found on his premises has no bearing on this case."

"Goes to credibility of this witness, Your Honor."

"Ovah-ruled. You may continya, Mistah Quinlan, but don't press yoah luck, son."

"Mr. Lebord," I said, "how close a friend are you to Mr. Gordon?"

Henri frowned. "We talk a few times."

"More of an acquaintance?"

"*Oui.* I guess."

"You ever work with Mr. Gordon?"

"*Non.*"

"For Mr. Gordon?"

"*Non.*"

"So this guy you know slightly made a special trip to come to your place to tell you he was getting married?"

"Asked and answered!" Bethune shouted.

"Okay," I said and was about to let Bethune sing his duet with Henri when I remembered Jenny's note. "Mr. Lebord, did you ever see Ms. Seaton at some location other than your bar?"

"Huh?"

"Have you ever met with her where she lives, at the late Ms. Denecheaux's home?"

"*Non.*"

"Ever been inside the Denecheaux home?"

He hesitated before replying, "*Non.* Why would I?"

I didn't have the foggiest idea, not having had the opportunity to ask my wife about it. Fortunately, lawyers don't have to answer witnesses' questions. Instead, I told Judge Seymour that I was temporarily finished with Mr. Lebord but might have some other questions for him at a later time.

Ms. Seaton's pit bull stood and said, "I have no questions for this witness, Your Honor. Mr. Quinlan's done my job for me."

Judge Seymour dismissed Lebord and called it a day.

Jenny was waiting for me.

"I bet I know who could use an Old Fashioned right about now," she said.

"Were you just guessing or did I miss something?" I asked.

"About the Old Fashioned?"

"No. About Henri Lebord being in the Denecheaux house."

"Drink first. Then a nice filet mignon at Chris' Steak House. But no more talk about the case until we get home tonight. Then I'll tell you what you missed. You're so lucky to have a wife with a devious mind."

❧   ❧   ❧

At nine-thirty, weary and woozy from beef and bourbon, I sat on the too comfortable sofa in the den, watching my devious-minded wife through rapidly lowering lids as she made a selection from the wall-length book-shelf. "Shouldn't've let you talk me into that last shot of whisky after dinner," I said. "You know too much booze puts me to sleep."

"It relaxes you," she said. "And after the day you've had, you need a little relaxation."

"Yes, indeed," I said. "Come on over here."

She remained where she was. "Billy, why do you suppose Lebord did his flip?"

"I imagine Bethune and Company outbid us somehow."

"Exactly," she said. "But if he'd gone along with you, his tavern would stay open, and he'd avoid a lot of trouble. What could Bethune have offered? Money? What's money when you're facing Treasury hounds? They're notoriously bad news."

I liked what she was saying, but I was feeling weary and unloved. "Couldn't we talk about this in bed?"

"You know we don't talk in bed," she said. "Right now I have a point to make."

"You could make it sitting here next to me," I said, patting the cushion.

She remained where she was. "I think Bethune is holding something heavier over Lebord's head than the illegal sale of alcohol."

"I agree one hundred percent. Now come over here."

She approached, but only to hand me a book.

I blinked at it. *New Orleans Voodoo,* by Michel Beauchamps. Then I blinked at her.

"That thing I knew and you didn't," she said. "It's in there."

I flipped through it. "Three hundred and twenty pages," I said.

"That's the nature of books," she said. "Lots of pages. I know. I've got so much time on my hands, I've been reading one of these every day."

"Even if I were sober and not two-thirds asleep, it'd take me hours to leaf through this. Give me a little hint."

"Think Reverend, mister," she said, starting for the door.

"Whoa. Wait. Where're you going?"

"Just to the kitchen for some cocoa."

I stared at the book. *Reverend*. Great. I started flipping the thin pages, blinking at the tiny type. I was having trouble focusing. That one drink too many. I was squinting at the beginning of a chapter on Marie Laveau, the Voodoo Queen, when my eyelids turned out the light and I went to sleep.

🐈   🐈   🐈

What sounded like the cry of a baby woke me at a little after one. I felt vaguely hung-over and sweaty. Mouth full of damp, ill-tasting, moist lint. The book had fallen to the floor.

Yawning, I left it there and dragged myself up to the bedroom.

The bed was pristine. Empty. No wife anywhere.

I retraced my steps to the top of the stairwell and called Jenny's name. No response.

On the main floor, I called her name again.

The door to the downstairs bathroom opened and she emerged, smiling. "Hi, honey," she said. "Feeling refreshed after your cat nap?"

"I heard a baby cry," I said.

"That's so sweet," she said. "You're dreaming about babies. Could be a sign."

"I don't think I was dreaming about babies." But I couldn't remember dreaming about anything. I started for the bathroom. "Aspirin in there?" I asked.

"Kitchen," she said, taking my arm. "Any luck with the Voodoo book?"

"Luck? No. It put me right out. Look, I feel like hell, and in another eight hours I'm going to have to walk back into that courtroom like Samson with a buzz cut at lion-feeding time."

"It was Daniel with the lions," she said. "But you get points for buzz cut."

"If you've got something I can use in court, please let me have it."

She stopped off in the den to get the book. Then she led me to the kitchen where she presented me with a glass of water and two aspirin. I swallowed the pills and asked, "Why are you feeling so chipper?"

"Because I didn't have two Old Fashioneds before dinner, one with dinner, and three straight shots of bourbon after. Anyway, the section you want is the one titled 'Fit for the Morgue.'"

It was the seventh chapter in the book. It told the gruesome story of a follower of the infamous voodoo Dr. John who, at the end of the 1800s, began performing blood rituals on fresh, unclaimed corpses purchased from corrupt morgue attendants. When the venal attendants were booted out and his supply of dead bodies dried up, the witch priest turned to living creatures—women in the main, though not exclusively, for his ceremonies.

The oddest thing about the man was that, in addition to his bloody voodoo sacrifices, he performed more conservative religious services in his own chapel in what would eventually become the uptown area of New Orleans. His name was Reverend Claude Lebord.

"Reverend Lebord," Jenny said when I closed the book. "What do you think?"

"A great-grandfather of our Henri?" I asked.

"If not then at least a role model," she said.

"A little thin," I said.

"Think about it, Billy. Lebord isn't just a front man for a paid killer. He is the killer. And the defense crowd knows it and that's how they got him to join their team."

"I like it," I said. "But it's all mush. Nothing solid. What can I do with it?"

"You're the lawyer."

I mulled it over. It seemed just this side of hopeless.

"When you recall Lebord," Jenny said, "get him going on his name."

I tried to imagine Bethune sitting still for that. "What's in a name?" I asked.

"Have faith," she said. "Recall the maniac to the stand."

"Dr. Boudreaux's up first thing in the morning." Boudreaux was the coroner. "I could probably pull Lebord back in the afternoon. You're convinced he's the Reverend?"

"Does a horsefly eat Spam?" Jenny replied, as if that were an answer.

"Well, we can check his alibis for the nights of the Rev's murders. But the bag of tricks is really empty. No fingerprints worth noting. No witnesses. Just probabilities."

"Some of my best friends have been convicted on circumstantial evidence, Billy."

"Well, I'll do my best," I said. "Speaking of which, shall we go to bed now?"

When the phone woke me at seven the next morning, I was alone. I grabbed the receiver from the nightstand and grumbled, "Yeah?"

"You hear the news?" my boss, Tim Mathern, asked.

"Not really," I said. "What's up?"

I heard him inhale and exhale and knew he was smoking. It probably wasn't his first of the day. "Somebody stole the damned black cat," he said.

"Come again?"

"Lulu, the forty-million dollar feline," Big Tim said. "Somebody broke into Louise Hendry's home in the Garden District last night and made off with the animal. The cops say it probably wasn't the Reverend, mainly because Hendry's still intact. Also, whoever did this was a real pro. Just a scratch or two on the rear door lock. Hendry was asleep in her bedroom right next to the room with the cat. She didn't hear a thing. Didn't know the puss was missing until this morning."

I didn't like any of it. I particularly didn't like the fact that Jenny, who usually slept in until nine or ten, seemed to be missing. "Any idea what time the theft occurred?" I asked.

"Hendry says she went to bed at ten-thirty. Give her another half-hour to nod off, I suppose it could have happened any time after that. They're set up at her place to tape and trace any ransom call. But my guess is the Seaton woman arranged for the catnap just like she arranged for Miss Denecheaux's murder. That the way you see it?"

"Right," I lied.

"This going to impact on the trial, do you think?"

"Hard to tell," I said, sitting on the edge of the bed.

"Well, give 'em hell today, podnah," he said.

"Will do." I was staring at the black, rubber-soled shoes lying on the carpet. Part of what my wife used to call her neo-Ninja nightwork outfit.

"Give Jenny a big, wet kiss for me," Big Jim said before ringing off.

🐾   🐾   🐾

I left home thirty-five minutes later. There'd been no sign of Jenny. No sign either of the cat whose cry I had mistaken for a baby's the night before. But I did find shiny black hairs on the rug in the downstairs bathroom and a toilet paper ring that had been gnawed on.

Edgy, anxious, dehydrated, and despondent, I drove to the Crescent, a tavern not far from the Criminal Courts Building. There, I joined Officer

Ray Ponetta, some twenty pounds past the NOPD guidebook for a man barely six feet, who was at a table eating something brown and messy while sweating through his shiny, lime-colored sports coat. Ray was in charge of the Denecheaux murder investigation.

"Hey," he said, good-naturedly, "how about that cat gettin' snatched, huh?"

I dispensed with the amenities and moved directly into the reason I was there. Lebord had told us he was working the night of the murder. I wanted Ray to check that out and let me know the results before court convened at two that afternoon.

"I'll get right on it," he said. "You hungry, you oughta try some of this gree-ards an' grits."

"I, ah, already ate," I said. "Is that warrant you used for Lebord's bistro still good?" When he nodded, I asked if it included his residence. Again a nod. "Perfect," I said. "I want you to check out both places for every knife with a serrated edge you can find."

"What's this all about, counselah? You p.o.'ed at the man for jackin' you up in court yestaday?"

"Yeah, I am," I said. "But I'm not just doing this for spite."

"You figyah Lebord's the Reverend?"

"Maybe, but let's keep that our secret for a while."

I spent a little over an hour of the morning session taking the coroner, Dr. Boudreaux, through information from his autopsy and various other elements of physical evidence. Then I used up another twenty minutes comparing the fatal cuts on Laura Denecheaux's body with the wounds of other victims presumed to have been dispatched by the Reverend. Dr. Boudreaux, a very serious, slow-talking man, nearly put the jury to sleep. But they perked right up when Judge Seymour, over Bethune's objection, allowed us to flash a few grisly crime scene photos of the victims. The three murders, Dr. Boudreaux concluded, had been performed by the same hand.

Bethune didn't use much of the hour and a half I'd left him before the noon break. "Dr. Boudreaux," he asked, "have you discovered any physical evidence, any blood, incriminating fingerprints, anything at all to suggest that Ms. Seaton had anything whatsoever to do with the murder of Ms. Denecheaux?"

Boudreaux took his time before replying. But it didn't change his answer, which was "No."

I was working on my notes and an oyster po'boy at my desk when Ray Ponetta showed up. "Man, they was knives grammaw at both them places. We picked up twenty-seven. They's another twenny-five or so steak knives at the bistro, but you didn't want them, too?"

"Maybe," I said. "But let's see what the lab can do with the ones you did grab first."

"Man, there wuz all this spooky stuff at his place, too. Dragon's Blood. Goofah Dust. Devil's Shoestrings. Gambla's Luck. Voodoo stuff. Ah doan like to be in the same room with some o' that junk. Lebord is one serious voodoo."

"He around when you were going through his stuff?"

"Naw. The day man let us in the bistro. The buildin' managah opened up the apawtment fo' us. I'm sorry, cap, but I let ya down about Lebord's alibi. I got nuthin' for ya. Couldn't find the night bawtenda and he don't come on 'til fo'. I'm gonna drop by the bistro then, tawk to him an' the regulah boozahs, see what they can remembah."

"Okay. And after you're through, hang a padlock on the place and we'll notify the ATF about the illegal booze."

He chuckled. "Teach the weasel not to renege on a deal."

"How quickly can the lab get us some results on those knives?"

"Usually they're like molasses in wintah," Ray said.

"I'll call over there and see if I can thaw 'em a little," I said. "And thanks for the fast work."

He smiled. "Feels good to run a little. Build up an appetite."

The afternoon session was to begin at two o'clock. My clerk, Jay Hodel, and I arrived a little early, just in time to see my wife on a waiting bench outside the courtroom, sitting thigh to thigh with Henri Lebord. He was chattering away like a Paris magpie.

"Isn't that—" Jay began.

"I'm afraid so," I said.

She spotted us headed their way and moved her head in a quick "no" gesture.

Annoyed and a bit dismayed, I took my confused clerk and led him quickly to the closed courtroom door, which was still locked. We were five minutes too early. I spent the time talking to Jay about nonsense, just to keep both of us from gawking at my wife while she flirted with a man who was probably wondering how she'd look with her throat slit.

The hall was filling up by the time the courtroom door was unlocked. Jay and I were the first in. As we approached the prosecution table, we both noticed the pink envelope at the same time. Jay picked it up. "It's for you," he said, frowning. "But it's old. And it's postmarked eighteen years ago. Damn, this is a weird afternoon."

I snatched it from him. It was one of the envelopes Jenny had found in the attic. But instead of one of Tara O'Neill's damn fine love letters, it now housed a slip of white paper on which my wife had written: *Ask Lebord about Lulu.*

"How'd it get in here?" Jay asked. "The door was locked."

"For every lock there is a key," I said, turning to watch the spectators file into the courtroom. *Ask Lebord* what *about Lulu?* I wondered.

Gene Bethune bounced jauntily to his table, where he stood sneering at me until the jury began to file in. Then he immediately exchanged his sneer for a warm and confident smile and sat down.

Judge Seymour entered, robe aflutter. As the call for order came, I took another glance at the crowd. My reckless wife had found a spot five rows back at the far right of the room. She smiled at me and gave me a wink.

At the sound of my name, I turned to find Judge Seymour looking at me expectantly. I told him that I wanted to recall Mr. Henri Lebord to the stand.

The voodoo had lost some of the sparkle he was showing Jenny out in the hall.

"Mr. Lebord," I said, "Yesterday you mentioned that you'd heard of the homicidal maniac who calls himself the Reverend. Is that correct?"

"Heard of him, *oui*."

"Where do you suppose he got his nickname?"

Lebord shrugged. "I imagine he thinks it makes him soun' *un type cool*. You know, like a cool guy."

I smiled at his rather quaint usage. "So you think he gave himself the name?"

"*Oui*, I suppose."

"You don't think it was something the media came up with?" I said.

"They're the ones who usually invent a name for serial murderers. The Bayou Strangler. The Kissing Killer."

"Maybe they did. I dunno."

"No. You're right," I said. "He gave himself the name. At least, according to a couple of the Reverend's competitors who're now behind bars."

Henri stared at me.

"You think the name's cool, huh, Mr. Lebord?"

"It is . . . different."

"Can you think of some underlying reason why this murderer might have selected that particular nickname?"

"Object, your honor," Bethune complained, "What's the point of all this?"

"Gentlemen, would you both gathah 'round the bench?" the judge requested.

When we'd done so, he said, "Care to explain what you're up to, Mistah Quinlan?"

"Your honor, we've heard from various experts, including our coroner Dr. Boudreaux and Officer Ray Ponetta, that it's relatively certain Laura Denecheaux was murdered by the man known as the Reverend. It's the people's contention that Donna Seaton hired him to commit the murder. What I'm hoping to do here is clarify that connection."

"Mr. Lebord has already stated under oath that he knows nothing about the Reverend," Bethune said.

"Mr. Lebord owns a popular bistro," I said. "I assume that means he hears a lot of things about a lot of people. Perhaps he knows more about the Reverend than he thinks he does. That's all I'm trying to find out."

The judge gave me a mildly skeptical look. "Let me remind you about hearsay evidence, Mr. Quinlan," he said. "Okay, son, I'll give you another few casts of yo' line. Then you're gonna have to find yourself a different pond to fish in."

As I turned back to Lebord, my eyes caught something odd and yet familiar on the floor against the rear wall. Not twenty feet from where I was standing was my old turtle box. And through the screen side I could see there was something inside it. Something moving around. I suddenly realized what Jenny had in mind.

A chill went through me, prompted by the sheer outrageous, *I Love Lucy*–ness of her scheme. Maybe I could avoid it by taking another tack. "Mr. Lebord, I've been wondering about your use of language," I said. "You were born *here*, were you not?"

"Yes."

"Then the accent, the occasional use of French words, are, what . . . affectation?"

"It is the way I speak. *En Français* with friends. In English, when I must."

"Did your parents speak French?"

He nodded. "Parents. Gran'parents. We have been here for genera-tions, but we have always maintained our ties to France."

"Any of your ancestors members of the religious community?"

He smiled and his eyes sparkled, but he remained silent.

"I was thinking of Claude Lebord. Was he your great-grandfather, by any chance?"

A slight nod of the head.

"Could you please answer yes or no?" I asked. "For the stenographer."

"*Oui.* Yes."

"That would be the *Reverend* Claude Lebord?"

"*Oui.*"

"The Reverend Claude Lebord who performed ritual sacrifices involv-ing the bloodletting of his victims?"

"Object, your honor," Bethune wailed. "Mr. Lebord's ancestry is not at issue here."

"Mistah Quinlan," the judge faced me, smiling, "we can all see where you're headed. I'd be happy to let you continya, if you've got something concrete to put into evidence."

Would that I had. "No physical evidence, your honor. Not at this time."

"Well then I guess you been wastin' the aftahnoon so fah, because we're jus' gonna have to strike all those questions about Mistah Lebord's lineage from the record. You finished with this witness?"

"Just one or two questions more, your honor."

"They bettah be more appropriate than the last."

Not in this lifetime, I thought. "Mr. Lebord," I said, "yesterday, you stated you'd never been inside the Denecheaux home. Right?"

"This is true."

"What about Ms. Denecheaux's cat, Lulu? You ever come in contact with the cat?"

"Of course not."

"Somebody stole it this morning," I said. "It wasn't you, was it?"

Bethune objected, of course.

Judge Seymour frowned and shook his head at me. "That washes you up, Mr. Quinlan," he said. "From here on . . ."

His sentence trailed off as his attention drifted to something happening to the left of me.

I followed his line of sight. A few feet in front of my now-open turtle box, a lovely, long, and muscular cat was enjoying her sudden freedom by stretching luxuriously. Lulu's face and body and legs were a satiny black, but her rather large pointed ears were a dark brown. She made a little "brrrrr" sound and moved her small rounded head from side to side, her wide-apart bright golden eyes surveying the courtroom. She was a handsome animal, all right. Not worth forty mil, maybe, but handsome.

It was not until she took a step in our direction, her shiny coat glistening as if it were liquid, that I noticed the effect she was having on Lebord. Maybe it was some voodoo thing—Marie Laveau the voodoo queen assuming feline form. More likely it was simple guilt. In any case, he was petrified, unconsciously drawing back as Lulu approached.

I heard Judge Seymour yelling "Somebody get that damn animal outta mah courtroom."

Lulu moved closer to Lebord. Sniffing him. She lifted her right paw and placed it on his leg.

With a yelp of *"le chat noir,"* he leapt from the witness chair.

"Get the damn cat," the judge was shouting. "Grab him, Quinlan."

I didn't bother to correct him on the sex of the cat. And I certainly didn't grab Lulu. Instead, I turned to the stunned members of the jury and shouted above the increasing din, "Mr. Lebord, are you trying to tell us you've never seen this cat before? That you've never set foot inside the Denecheaux home? That you didn't murder Laura Dene—"

I was interrupted by something very sharp entering my back near the left shoulder. A pain more intense than any I could recall shot down my arm. I staggered, tripped on the stenographer's chair, and fell head first into the court clerk's table.

When I awoke, lying on my stomach in a bouncy ambulance, a paramedic gave me a shot of something. Before it did its job, he told me Lebord had been carrying a long thin knife in an ankle sheath. He drew it to use on the cat, but Lulu had been too swift for him. So he settled for me.

"My wife?" I asked. "Is she . . ." I looked around the vehicle.

The paramedic seemed a nice, empathic guy. "Some ladies would rather not ride with us. I'm sure she'll show up at the hospital."

🐈 🐈 🐈

She was there when I awoke the next day. "How're you feeling?" she asked.

"About like your average knife victim." I was lying on my side in a hospital bed, trapped in some foam rubber device that kept me from rolling back on the wound, which my doctor had said was deep but not devastating.

"I'm sorry it got so crazy," she said. "It seemed like such a good idea at the time. Henri Lebord would say he'd never had contact with Lulu, and then out she'd pop to head straight for him. Maybe hop up on his lap. It's the kind of image a jury would remember. No matter what the judge instructed them, they'd be certain the cat knew him. I just didn't dream that Lebord would freak like that."

"It made for an interesting session."

"But," she said brightly, "now the jury has that image of him stabbing you, which is even more damning."

I nodded.

"The *Picayune* says they found traces of several blood types on the knife. Yours, of course. And Laura Denecheaux's. So we were definitely on the right track."

"I feel a little dizzy," I said. "Think I'll go back to sleep."

"Oh, Billy, according to the morning news, Judge Seymour is calling some sort of hearing about how Lulu got into the courtroom. I imagine you'll be invited."

"All I can do is tell them the truth: that I didn't have anything to do with stealing the cat or putting it in the courtroom. I suppose I could pass a polygraph, if they insist. Though if they ask me about the turtle box. . . ."

"Don't worry about that," she said. "With the bailiff and Lebord wrestling over the knife and those policemen charging into the room and everybody screaming and yelling, I managed to hide the box behind the judge's bench. He'd vamoosed by then. I wanted to be with you in the ambulance, but the box could have been a problem. It's now back in the attic where it belongs."

She is sort of amazing.

"What happened to Lulu?" I asked.

"One of the jurors caught her. The big man with the square head who looks a little like the Frankenstein monster."

"Claude Appleton," I said.

"Whatever. Your girlfriend at People For Animals says she's going to reward him handsomely as soon as they retry and fry Donna Seaton."

"Well, I suppose a new trial was in order anyway."

"I don't feel good about Louise Hendry having the dear cat back in that amazingly unsafe apartment of hers. You know, Billy, I rather liked having Lulu around. And we have our big old house."

I glared at her.

"I didn't mean Lulu," she said. "Any cat. A pound kitty."

"It's not the impossible dream," I said. "Jenny, something's been bothering me, as I lay here in my delirium and pain. I can see how you broke into the courtroom at noon and planted Lulu. And how you used the old remote clicker to set her free. But what made you so sure, out of all the people there, the cat would seek out Lebord?"

"Good Lord, Billy, what in the word did you think I was doing with him on that bench? Flirting? I was slipping catnip into his pants pocket."

"You never cease to amaze me," I said.

"I hope not. Oh, aren't you just too lonely in that nice bed? Wouldn't you like a little company?"

"We're in the Hospital of the Sacred Heart of Jesus, with nuns popping in here with pills and prayers every ten minutes. I've got a serious back wound and a possible concussion and I'm stuck in this rather limited position." I stared at her and could feel my heart start beating faster. "But, yeah, I would like a little company."

She smiled, sat on the side of the bed, then swung aboard, moving close. "You're *my* catnip," she said.

The End

ḋOSKIN'S CAT

Shirley Rousseau Murphy

The Greeley courthouse rose just above the false-fronted store buildings that crowded along three blocks of Main Street. The courtroom was on the second floor of the hundred-year-old granite landmark which housed, as well, all of Farley County's offices. Folks came there to renew drivers' licenses, apply for hunting permits, and settle land disputes. The atmosphere was casual. Men appeared in court wearing bib overalls, coming directly from the fields. On hot summer days, dogs wandered the halls looking for a cool spot in which to nap. The town was small and clannish, everyone knew everyone, and all stores were closed on Sunday, which was rightly reserved for God and a big dinner; everything about the town was old, much of it unchanged since the War Between the States except for its bright new pickups and tractors, and computers in all the stores.

Hidden within the courthouse walls and ceilings was a warren of old, abandoned air ducts and peculiar niches from various remodelling projects over the years. Here generations of mice had proliferated, their colonies becoming so bold and clever that they sprang the janitor's traps and would not touch the little yellow packets of poison bait he distributed. The week before the Bobby Hoskin trial, Judge Blane, sick and tired of mice chewing his desk blotter and his papers, ordered George Figley, who took care of maintenance, to procure some cats from the volunteers at Animal Rescue and set them on the mice. He then forgot about the matter as he prepared for Hoskin's trial. Three cats were duly obtained, good mousers all, and were housed in the courthouse basement and given the run of the building.

Bobby Hoskin had shot his mother and father with a twelve-gauge shotgun and had blown away his two small brothers at the same time. The town of Greeley took swift action. Within an hour of the 911 call, Hoskin was in jail on suspicion. Within seventy-two hours he had been arraigned and charged with murder. Judge Blane didn't consider moving jurisdiction to another town: Hoskin lived in Greeley. Hoskin's family was murdered in Greeley. Hoskin would be tried in Greeley by his peers and neighbors.

When Ada Whitney was selected as a juror, she could hardly wait to convict Bobby. Of course, she didn't divulge this to the defense attorney when he querried prospective jurors. She simply said she was capable of being fair. Though Ada had never served on a jury before, she felt she was very fair.

There was no motel in Greeley, so the jury was to be sequestered two miles from town in the small, simple bedrooms of the Christian Retreat. Ada cancelled her housecleaning jobs for the next three weeks, bought some frozen dinners so her husband Carl wouldn't starve, and packed her suitcase. As jurors were allowed to choose their roommates, Ada and Lithecia Flowers naturally roomed together, they being neighbors and members of the same church.

Ada, sun-browned and sturdy, made the younger woman seem as white and insubstantial as gauze. Poor Lithecia was not a happy juror. She quaked at the prospect of hearing the gory details of the case, but she felt that serving on the jury was her civic duty.

Bobby Hoskin had shot his father in the blue and white family kitchen at eleven-thirty on a Saturday morning as John Hoskin was making a grilled cheese sandwich. After Bobby blew away his father, smattering Nell Hoskin's pretty kitchen with gore and bone, Bobby turned off the stove and went in the living room, where he sat on the couch and waited for his mother and two little brothers to return home from the Piggly Wiggly. James was ten, Billy seven. Bobby, at twenty-seven, was a strapping, handsome lad and a major stud around Greeley. He was quiet and mannerly, though, until he got a few beers in him. The morning he killed his family he had not been drinking.

When Bobby's mother and brothers entered the house just before noon through the front door, loaded down with Piggly Wiggly bags, Bobby rose from the couch. He fired five rounds into them, emptying his shotgun and scattering bits of iceberg lettuce, hot dogs, white bread, paper bags and blood across the living room ceiling and the flowered wallpaper. The new damask couch and matching loveseat that May Hoskin had got on sale at Sears and didn't have to pay for until next summer were not in returnable condition.

With three members of his family dead in the living room and his father's body sprawled bleeding in the kitchen, Bobby stepped outside to his '94 Ford pickup with the killer wheels and roll bar and drove twenty miles north. Parking beside the Worley River, he threw his good shotgun into nine feet of water and watched it sink down through the river silt.

Driving back to town, he made several conspicuous stops at local stores then drove home where he "discovered" the bodies and called 911.

The sheriff, arriving with two backup cars, found Bobby standing by the phone still holding the receiver, weeping and weakly cursing whoever had done this terrible thing. When Bobby saw the sheriff, he looked up at the ceiling and shouted at the Lord to strike down the killers.

Bobby's gun was found three days later when an alert twelve-year-old boy fishing along the river came upon fresh, oversized tire marks, grew suspicious, and called the newspaper—the papers were full of the murder. Jury selection began the day Bobby was indicted.

Ada Whitney was accepted for the jury only after she swore she had not known the Hoskins well, had known them only to speak to, and after reiterating that she was capable of being totally fair. She did not say that she was determined to fry Bobby; she considered that convicting Bobby of first-degree murder was extremely fair. If she could have drawn and quartered him, or pilloried him like in the old days to die of thirst in the summer sun she would happily have done so.

She did tell the judge that after the Hoskins were found dead and Bobby was taken off to jail, their tomcat, with nothing to eat in its deserted home, found its way to her place half a mile up the road, where she'd fed it with her cats for a week then put it in a box and carried it to her friend who ran Greeley Animal Rescue, so they could find it a new home. The judge didn't think her short relationship with Bobby Hoskin's cat would prejudice her judgement.

The cat had in fact been the only one in the Hoskin family to whom Bobby had shown any affection. He ignored his parents and his two little brothers as if they were pieces of furniture. But you'd see Bobby sitting in the front yard on a rusted lawn chair taking a break from working on his truck, and the cat would be winding around his feet or on his lap. Or you'd see it, a huge red-tabby tomcat with big balls and one white foot, sitting on the truck fender as Bobby tinkered under the hood. Ada had heard people say that when Bobby whistled the cat would come running to him just like a dog.

The jury convened on Monday the seventh of June. The jurors had left their suitcases in the sheriff's bus. The day was hot and all twelve jurors were dressed in summer cottons, the women in sleeveless dresses, their fleshy arms still pale from the winter. But Judge Blane kept the air-conditioned courtroom so cold that the women all sent home for sweaters, which were duly deposited in the sheriff's office by their husbands or one of their children. The first night after court, the jurors ate supper together at a long table in Donna's Family Cafe with a sheriff's deputy sitting at each end to guard them and keep them from talking about the case. Later, Ada and Lithecia were getting ready for bed when Lithecia began to cry.

"What's wrong?" Ada said, pulling off her pantyhose.

"It's so terrible. Those poor people, his own parents and those precious little boys. All this talk about blood and the—remains. How can you stand to listen?"

"It's what we're here for, Lithecia. If we don't know the facts, we can't make a judgement."

"Well you read mysteries all the time. You're used to those terrible things. I just feel all shaky inside." And Lithecia wept so hard that Ada wondered if the younger woman would get through the trial without getting physically ill. Then Lithecia began to pray aloud, beseeching God for His guidance. She kept on until Ada had to snap at her to make her go to sleep.

But Lithecia received her sign from God quickly.

Word from God, in fact, reached her the very next morning.

The jury had been sent out of the courtroom while Defense conferred with the judge. The jury room, where they waited, was a twelve-by-twelve cubicle that hadn't seen paint since Sherman burned Atlanta. The windows were so filthy you could hardly see out, and hard wooden chairs surrounded a wooden table around which the seven men of the jury sat smoking. There was one dinky bathroom shared by men and women, with just a thin door separating the toilet from the gathered jurors and no soap in the basin. Ada complained about the soap until the bailiff put in a bar of Ivory. She'd used the facilities, trying not to make a tinkling noise, and had washed her hands and come out, when she glanced up at the air return above the table where the seated men were talking baseball and saw, through the air grate, two eyes looking back at her.

She made out a big red cat with one white paw. That was Bobby Hoskin's cat crouching behind that vent as big as a terrier and glaring twice as bold.

She could see that the vent grid was loose, and after a while the cat, evidently wanting human company, leaped down, banging the grill behind him, and trod smiling across the table. All but two men ignored him. Will Breen from the barber shop scratched the cat under its chin, and the cat waved its tail and purred. Maybe it missed Bobby. She wondered if it was looking for Bobby. She wondered how it had found its way here.

"That'll be one of the cats Millie Sayers brought," Lithecia said. "From Animal Rescue. For the mice, you know. She brought three cats. I saw her in the drugstore before we came on jury duty. The maintenance man takes care of them in the basement."

"Well isn't that the limit. Bobby Hoskin's cat ending up right here in the courthouse where Bobby's being tried."

"That's the Hoskins' cat?"

"Sure is," Ada said. "I'm the one took him to Animal Rescue. Couldn't see him go hungry. Five cats of my own is enough."

That night when they were alone in their room, Lithecia prayed again, and this time she thanked God for giving her a sign.

"What sign?" Ada asked.

"Why the cat, of course. Bobby Hoskin's cat." She turned to look at Ada. "God sent that cat. It's God's sign, sure as you're sitting on that bed. You may have taken the cat to Animal Rescue, Ada. And Millie may have brought it over here. But that's how God works. The cat," Lithecia told her with a level look, "is God's sign. The Lord sent Bobby Hoskin's cat to intercede. Sure as the nose on your face, the Lord wants mercy for Bobby."

Ada looked hard at Lithecia. But she kept her mouth shut. Lithecia seemed near the edge after the second day of gory details and was probably in no state to be reasoned with.

They didn't see the cat again until the fourth day of the trial. Sheriff Larsen was on the stand, testifying that Bobby's fingerprints were on the shotgun his department had pulled from the Worley River, and Bobby's prints were on the shell casings they had found at the scene. Ada thought it amazing that Bobby hadn't picked up the casings. During the sheriff's testimony, the cat entered the courtroom from the back hall. Walked in bold as you please, waving his tail, and padded toward the judge's bench. Laughter rippled through the courtroom.

When Bobby Hoskin, sitting beside his lawyer at a table between the judge's bench and the jury, saw the cat, his face lit up in a huge smile.

This was the first expression of any kind that Ada had seen on Bobby's face. The young man, for four days, had sat as still and expressionless as a stone, staring down at the table as if he heard nothing of the testimony. As if he'd gone into some kind of trance. Lithecia said he was grieving for his murdered family.

But now, seeing the cat, Bobby's entire being seemed to brighten—as if his only friend in all the world had come to comfort him. He looked so much younger suddenly and so open and boyish that Ada felt a pang of pain for him.

Beside her, Lithecia was weeping. Snivelling and blowing her nose. Ada could just hear what she was thinking, that God had given his sign, that God in his wisdom had sent this innocent animal to intercede for Bobby Hoskin. That God had sent Bobby's small, helpless friend to show how gentle Bobby was. To show that he, God, wanted the jurors to be merciful. And Ada realized that Lithecia had begun to make her nervous.

At the judge's amused nod, one of the deputies scooped up the cat and deposited it back in the hall and shut the door. The courtroom quieted. The next witness to take the stand was the checkout girl at Piggly Wiggly who testified that May Hoskin and the two little boys had bought hotdogs that Saturday morning, had paid in cash, and had not seemed disturbed or upset in any way.

That night at supper, which was served family-style with big bowls of vegetables and meat filling the center of the long table, the two deputies, both hearty eaters, sat packing in the groceries and laughing about the cat.

"I wondered," Deputy Harn snickered, "how long it'd be before that tomcat came in the courtroom. That animal's all over the building, bold as the devil. Not about to move if it wants to sit on your desk. Looks you right in the eye, daring you to make it jump down." Harn grinned. "Seen it twice in Judge Blane's chambers. Sitting right there on his papers lashing its tail. Judge seems to get a kick out of it."

Judge Blane was an elk hunter and a skilled fisherman. There was nothing soft about him. If he took a liking to a cat, which was typically a woman's animal, no one could call him a sissy.

"It keeps the mice out of his desk," Deputy Green said, helping himself to mashed potatoes. "I hear the judge talking to it, and the cat just winding around him and purring away." He grinned, his mouth full of potatoes. "That cat's a real piece of work."

Lithecia hung on their words—as if everything about the cat had special meaning. Ada was growing impatient and short-tempered with Lithecia. She wanted to ask the deputies if the cat visited Bobby Hoskin in the holding room where he was confined during court recess, but she didn't want to give Lithecia any more ammunition in the matter.

That night when they were alone, Lithecia went on about God's sign until Ada turned on her.

"God," Ada snapped, "wants Bobby Hoskin to fry. Use your brain, Lithecia. Bobby's fingerprints were on the gun. The way forensics figured out the tire marks in the Hoskin yard, Bobby was there when his mother and brothers got home. He left after they were dead, and came back later to find them and call 911." She was nearly shouting. She glanced at the thin walls and lowered her voice.

"His mother's blood was spattered on his shoes and pants, Lithecia, that the cops found in that Dumpster north of Worley. His mother's blood was flecked on the floor mats of his truck."

Scowling, she held Lithecia's gaze. "If God has his way, Lithecia, Bobby Hoskins will fry like a fly in a bug zapper."

"God *saves* souls," Lithecia snapped. "He doesn't burn them."

It was against the judge's instructions for the jurors to discuss the case between themselves, same as discussing it with anyone else. But Ada's patience was gone. Sure as piglets squeal, Lithecia was building to a vote of not guilty. It would take only one dissenting vote to hang the jury and set Bobby Hoskin free.

Well it was bad enough being shut up in that pokey little jury room thick with cigarette smoke, with her bowels out of order because she wasn't getting any exercise sitting in the jury box all day and then eating huge meals at night. Now, to top it off, she had to listen to Lithecia's crazy theories. When Bobby wept on the stand, mourning his departed family, Lithecia wept. When Bobby gave his emotionless testimony, describing his supposed actions on the fatal day, Lithecia listened wide-eyed, believing every word: that he left the house that morning after his mother had used his truck to run over to the Laundromat because their washer was broken, that she had cut her sandaled foot on those sharp rocks in the Laundromat drive. That after she had gotten home he'd gone to run some errands, had returned home to find his parents and his two little brothers brutally murdered. He told it all with a fake look of pain twisting his face like a painted mask.

Lithecia was so riven with pity for Bobby that she practically wrung her hands. She stared at him with those big, pale eyes until Ada felt her stomach go sour. And when the cat appeared again two days later, strolling directly into the jury box to rub against the jurors' ankles, Lithecia glanced at Ada with a look of pure vindication: This time, God had sent the tomcat intimately among them. God intended his message to rub off and cling to them just like the red-tabby cat fur that clung to Ada's stockinged ankles.

She didn't know how Lithecia could be so foolish. The testimony against Bobby was overwhelming. No other suspect had been implicated. No other scenario seemed possible but that Bobby Hoskin had brutally murdered the four members of his family.

She'd wondered more than once why the defense hadn't gone for temporary insanity. Seemed to her, that was the only way to win this case.

But she had her own theory about that. She thought maybe this court-appointed lawyer found the crime so horrible that he meant only to go through the motions, that he'd be happy to see Bobby Hoskin fry.

The cat did not appear again until the ninth day of the trial as the prosecution cross-examined Bobby for the last time before the jury was sent out. Again the beast entered the courtroom, striding boldly, and again when Bobby saw his cat his blank expression exploded into such wild joy that it wrenched even Ada's heart. Bobby must be terrified for his life; and he had no one, no family now, only this big, scruffy tomcat.

Reaching out over the witness stand, Bobby softly whistled for the cat, as if he expected the big tom to leap into his arms and cuddle against him.

The jurors didn't take their eyes from the small, intimate scene. The gallery sat hushed. Defense council, seeing the courtroom drama shaping in Bobby's favor, remained utterly still.

The district attorney and the assistant D.A. glanced at each other and began to fidget. Ada could see them wondering how many of these jurors would convict a man of blood-cold murder when one of God's helpless creatures loved and trusted him—loved Bobby so much that it had found its way from Bobby's home five miles south of town directly to the courthouse, just to be with him.

If a cat trusted him so completely, how could Bobby Hoskin be capable of this chilling murder?

Bobby whistled again and made a faint clucking noise. The cat, sitting on the carpet before the witness stand, looked up at him for a long time.

Then it turned and leaped onto the judge's bench and sat staring intently into Judge Blane's face. The judge looked back with interest until the cat turned and fixed his gaze on the jury, his eyes blazing into the jurors' eyes.

Lithecia cast a sharp *I-told-you-so* look at Ada. As if to say that God's final word was, at this precise moment, being transmitted for each juror to understand. The pale woman looked so certain that Ada wavered; she wasn't sure what to think.

Had God led her, Ada, to take the cat to Animal Rescue so the beast would end up here at the courthouse? *Had* God meant for the cat to find Bobby and save him? *Could* Bobby Hoskin somehow be innocent? Could his soul not, after all, be filled with cold malice?

Or, she wondered, even if Bobby had done the bloody deed, was he, as Lithecia claimed, not deserving of death? Would the jury, if they convicted him, kill a young man desperately in need of another chance at life?

She kept going back to the coincidence of the cat. If the cat was not a direct messenger, if there was not a divine purpose for his being here, then his timely arrival at the courthouse, and his insistent appearances in the courtroom, added up to a mighty strange set of events.

She had, she decided, been around Lithecia too long. She shook her head, trying to clear it, and glanced at Lithecia again. Lithecia's gleam of righteousness was contagious, Lithecia's arguments were, despite Ada's own good judgement, beginning to make sense.

From the bench, the cat continued to stare deeply into each juror's eyes—until Judge Blane picked him up and dropped him gently to the floor. The judge said not a word. No one rose to remove the cat. The beast sat down at the foot of the judge's bench and began to wash his paws. The judge nodded impatiently to the prosecutor, who proceeded with questioning Bobby Hoskin.

It was after the prosecution presented its closing statement and court recessed for lunch—or dinner, as she and Lithecia and most everyone else called their noon meal—that Ada noticed the change in Lithecia.

The younger woman sat at the lunch table as white and frail looking as ever but now, beneath Lithecia's palor, Ada saw something different.

Lithecia's features had hardened. Were rigid with a taut determination. As if the young woman was preparing to do battle.

But not until after lunch, after the final plea by the defense, during which Bobby's court-appointed lawyer actually wept, did the cat make his move.

Just before the jury was instructed and sent out to decide their verdict, the cat began to pace the courtroom, swaying boldly between the bailiff's box and the jury, between the judge's bench and the tables where sat the prosecution, the defense, and the accused. Circling the courtroom lashing his tail, swaggering with all the importance of a practiced trial lawyer, the cat held the audience captive. He was so full of himself that he seemed to have grown larger and broader, to have grown considerably in stature.

Bobby watched him, his eyes widening.

Lithecia clasped her hands together and directed her look at the ceiling where, presumably, God was looking down.

As the defense wound down its plea, the cat leaped to the rail of the bailiff's box. While the jury was formally instructed and court was adjourned, the cat sat unmoving.

Bobby Hoskin rose to be led back to jail. There was expression in his eyes now. A thin gleam of triumph—overlaying the look of a trapped beast. And suddenly the prisoner, in one violent lunge, had a choke grip on Deputy Green's neck, had jerked the deputy's gun from its holster and cocked and pointed it at Green's throat.

The courtroom was still. At Bobby's nod, the other four deputies stepped back. At his command they laid their guns on the rail of the bailiff's box and retreated to the far wall.

Pressing his hostage ahead of him, Hoskin started for the back door, the four-inch barrel of Green's .38 jammed so hard into Green's throat that the deputy choked for breath.

At the same instant, from the rail, the red tomcat rose and in a flying six-foot leap slammed straight into Bobby's face, clawing so wildly that Bobby dropped the gun screaming, snatching at the cat with both hands.

Jerking the cat free—and ripping his own skin in the process—he heaved the cat above his head and threw it hard at the wall. Bobby's face was a bloody mask of hatred and cold rage.

The cat hit the wall hard and fell. It lay still at the feet of four deputies as they grabbed Bobby.

There wasn't much of a scuffle. They had him on the floor and in cuffs when the cat rose again, shook its head, and began to stalk Bobby Hoskin.

No one moved. The cat swaggered across Bobby's prone, manacled body and dove for Bobby's throat.

A deputy said later that if they'd shot the cat, they would have shot Bobby. And no one, not even the Sheriff's finest, had the nerve, or the heart, to grab that cat and pull him off. Ada didn't see the expressions on the deputies' faces. She couldn't take her eyes from the cat and what he was doing.

The cat finally turned away, his whiskers gory, and stalked out of the courtroom. Three deputies knelt to try to stop the bleeding and save Bobby, and as the amubulance siren screamed down Main Street, Ada looked at Lithecia.

A terrible change had come over the younger woman. Beneath the shock of reality, Lithecia had crumpled; she looked thinner and smaller— as insubstantial and white as if she were indeed made of gauze. All her religious verve seemed to have drained from her. She appeared, now, to be looking only inward.

God had spoken, just as Lithecia predicted. Trouble was, Lithecia got the message wrong.

The End

Missing the Cat

Mat Coward

I've only been up in court once in my life, and that was mainly because of a dog.

For about three months in the summer of 1979 I was going out with a Cuban girl called Jay, which was short for something or other Hispanic which I've now forgotten. She was a student at London University, and the fact that I can remember neither her full name nor what she was studying perhaps suggests that I was not as in love with her as I thought I was. She was amazingly beautiful, though, and sexy, and generally excellent company—that much I do remember.

Her sister was also living in Britain then, and the sister had a boyfriend, Mahmood, who worked as a kitchen hand at a restaurant not far from Leicester Square. Although by the time I met him, he wasn't actually working there anymore because he was on strike.

"Conditions in the catering industry are unbelievable," Jay told me one night in a pub in the Charing Cross Road. "Literally unbelievable! What is London—a great capital city, or a third world sweathole?"

"A bit of both, I suppose," I replied. "That's how it is with capital cities." Not that I was really arguing with her. The catering industry was notorious for long hours, low pay, and an immense shit-eating requirement. The employees were mostly new immigrants, too scared to stand up for their rights.

Mahmood and his pals must've been made of sterner stuff than most of their fellow sufferers, because they joined a union and attempted to open negotiations with management. Management responded in the time-honored fashion of sacking them all and replacing them with a fresh lot of semi-slaves. Two months later, Mahmood and the boys were still holding that picket line, living on strike pay and fresh air and the enriched vitamins that are contained in the substance known to science as Human Dignity.

Quite how I came to be standing alongside them, one warm Friday night in late August, is still a matter of some confusion to me. Certainly I had never stood on a picket line before, nor ever expected to, being myself the sole employee of a dingy, unprofitable second-hand record shop in Kentish Town. Put it down to being in love, I guess.

"Put this round your neck," said Mahmood, plonking a sandwich-board over my shoulders.

"What does it say?" I said, trying to read the placard upside down.

"Same as these," said Mahmood, handing me a sheaf of poorly dupli-cated handbills. "It says 'On strike for the right to join a union. This restaurant staffed by scabs. Please eat elsewhere. Thank you for your kind support.'"

"It says that?" Maybe I needed glasses. All I could see was squiggles and gibberish.

"In every known tourist language," said Mahmood. "German, French, Arabic, Spanish—"

"Not English?"

Mahmood frowned. "If they're English, you can employ the spoken word, no?" He put a hand on my arm. "That is why we are so grateful for your help tonight, Malcolm. Some of the fellows here don't speak English too well, so you will be of great assistance. I can see why Jay is so fond of you: you are a young man of courage and conviction."

Courage? I didn't like the sound of that: *courage*. . . . On the other hand, I was too scared to ask Mahmood what he meant.

After about half an hour, I was feeling a lot calmer. Nothing particularly alarming had happened. Five parties of tourists had been successfully turned away, while one group of Englishmen in suits had slipped past the blockade, despite my most eloquent efforts.

"Look, gents, would it actually kill you to eat somewhere else, huh?"

"Yes," said their spokesman. "It would actually physically kill us." His friends' chins wobbled as they laughed.

"In that case," I said, "could you at least read this before you go in?"

The spokesman glanced at the handbill. Turned it over. Frowned. Turned it over again. "This is crap," he said, sounding quite affronted. "It's total gibberish." He screwed it up and tossed it over his shoulder.

They entered the empty restaurant, to be met by a manager who appeared to be in training for the World Fawning Championships. I heard the words *"all lies, gentlemen, I assure you"* before the door swung shut behind them. The "gentlemen" made the arrogant tactical error of choosing a table right by the window, where they were treated to the sight of me scratching my bottom with unnecessary vigour and thoroughness throughout their first course.

All in all, I felt I was getting the hang of this "Solidarity with the Proletariat" lark. It wasn't skilled work. It didn't require courage. All it required was an ability to do what one was told by beautiful girls from Latin America, which was well within my capabilities. Plus, it provided a rare opportunity to be terribly rude to posh bastards in a good cause.

Yup, I was beginning to enjoy myself. Which was when a guy walked straight up to me out of the blue and gave me a cat. Just like that.

I started to protest, but by the time I got the words out, the silent man had vanished back into the early evening crowd from whence he'd sprung.

Odd, I thought, holding a cat in my arms, where previously there had been only handbills. *Most people just drown 'em in buckets.*

The policeman arrived about thirty seconds later.

🦙   🦙   🦙

Bow Street Magistrates Court, for all its leather and mahogany, its ancient dusty air, and its echoing corridors, was not a grand palace of justice. More like a conveyor-belt system for dealing rapidly with minor offenses.

In answer to the charge of obstruction, I pled not guilty. I'd been taking part in a perfectly legal protest, I insisted, obstructing no one and nothing. I had no idea why I'd been arrested.

Police Constable Arthur Groyne was happy to explain. "The matter of obstruction, sir, arose due to the fact that the accused was accompanied by a large and fearsome dog, the presence of which was a clear deterrent to persons entering the restaurant situated at—"

"I didn't have a dog," I said.

"Mr. Hurst," drawled the chairman of the bench. "Please be quiet. You will have your say in a moment."

"But I didn't have a dog," I said. "I've never had a dog."

"This police officer says you did have a dog, Mr. Hurst. Are you calling him a liar?"

I wasn't falling into that trap. Twenty years ago, you did not accuse cops of lying under oath. "No, sir, but I believe he was mistaken. There was no dog."

"Certainly was a dog," said P.C. Groyne.

The chairman gave me a look that said, *You see? There was a dog, the nice policeman says so.*

"But there was a cat," I blurted, and immediately cursed myself. I hadn't intended to mention the cat—didn't want to complicate matters— but all this nonsense about a dog had disoriented me.

"A cat?" said the chairman, as if the word were unfamiliar to him. PC Groyne, I noted with interest, was blushing behind his beard. The chairman turned his mildly offended gaze upon the officer. "The accused says there was a cat, Constable?"

"It was a dog," said P.C. Groyne. "I have been a police officer for fifteen years, sir. I know the difference between a dog and a cat."

The magistrates conferred for a moment in whispers, and then the chairman spoke. "Can you describe this dog, Constable?"

"Certainly, sir. With pleasure." P.C. Groyne produced his notebook from his tunic pocket. "If I may refer to my contemporaneous notes, sir? The aforementioned dog was a large animal of canine demeanour, black with a white muzzle, four-legged, with a short tail, a dog-like face, and large teeth."

"And fearsome, I believe you said?"

"And fearsome, sir, indeed. A dog of a most fearsome nature."

Having elicited such incontrovertible testimony, the chairman did not bother to hide his sneer as he turned to me. "Doesn't sound much like a cat, does it, Mr. Hurst?"

"Doesn't sound much like the animal in question, sir," I said. "Which, for the record, was small, quite young, predominantly ginger, with a distinctive double kink in its tail."

"For heaven's sake, this is intolerable," the chairman muttered. He conferred once more with his colleagues. "Mr. Hurst. Can you produce this alleged cat?"

"No, sir. The cat ran off at the moment of my arrest."

"Most convenient, Mr. Hurst."

I pointed at the policeman. "OK, then—can *he* produce the dog?"

This brought a smug shake of the head from the chairman. "It is not up to P.C. Groyne to produce or not produce the dog, young man. It is not, after all, his dog. It is your dog."

"But I haven't *got* a—"

"I trust you have a license for this fearsome dog of yours, Mr. Hurst," said the Chairman, clearly enjoying himself now. "Otherwise you may be fined, you know." P.C. Groyne gave an appreciative chuckle.

I sighed and surrendered. I felt angry, frustrated, and even embarrassed, but most of all I felt stupid. Everyone knew that Bow Street magistrates always sided with the police, rarely troubling themselves with such trivia as evidence. I had to be an idiot, wasting my time arguing about cats and dogs with this bunch of asses. It was Saturday, for heaven's sake, and the pubs were open.

"If I admit the charge, sir, can we get this over with?"

I was fined three pounds—roughly the price, back then, of a reasonable weekend's pubbing.

Having handed over my beer money, I went to the Gents, where I found myself standing next to P.C. Groyne. Keeping careful rein on my temper, I asked him: "Just as a matter of interest, Constable, what was all that about?"

He didn't answer until I was washing my hands at the basin (he didn't bother washing his; probably thought it an effeminate affectation). "People like you," he growled, grabbing the lapels of my suit coat in his surprisingly small, pink fists, "are ruining this country. Do you know that? You don't even work at that bloody restaurant; you're just a professional trouble-maker! Well listen, sonny—I won't forget your name."

I won't forget yours either, I thought. But then, to be fair, anyone would have a hard time forgetting a name like Groyne.

🦙   🦙   🦙

Mahmood didn't drink alcohol. Instead, in a dark corner of a crowded pub, he sipped a tiny bottle of alleged orange juice which cost more than my Guinness.

"Yes, Malcolm," he confirmed, "this policeman, Groyne, we know. He does not arrest us so much, but if he sees white people supporting us, this angers him. Yes, he has played this trick before."

"The trick with the cat?"

Mahmood's orange juice paused at chin level. "Cat? You mean dog, yes?"

Don't you start, I thought. "Cat, dog, whatever. You didn't see me being given the animal that evening?"

"I saw nothing, sorry to say. We had a rush of customers at the other entrance. First I have known of it is when P.C. Groyne is arresting you."

"OK, but can you describe the man who usually dumps the cats?" I held up my hands. "Sorry, Mahmood—I meant dogs."

"Ah. The Dog Man. No, I only ever snatch a glimpse. He moves fast, you have seen yourself."

"True enough. But it's definitely not P.C. Groyne?"

"No, no. Him I know, only too well. He's in very thick with the management, as probably you have guessed. But the Dog Man is a similar looking man, I can say. Quite big, made of both fat and muscle together, you know? Mostly bald, though not old. A big face, as if made of dough."

Well, that narrowed it down a bit. To half the adult male population of London.

🐾   🐾   🐾

My brief picketing career was over, perforce. I didn't dare imagine what treats P.C. Groyne might arrange for me if he saw me there again. But that wasn't the end of it for me, because I just couldn't get that cat (the one that wasn't a dog) out of my mind.

I like cats. I like dogs, too; I'm not prejudiced. I suppose it's just that cats remind me of happier days. The first cat I ever knew, a black and white named Tricksy, had been given to my mother as a birthday present when she was seven. Mum was twenty-eight and divorced with two children when Tricksy died on her lap, purring to the end. Imagine that: twenty-one years. And my mother's bereavement was long and deep, let me tell you. This'll sound crazy to anyone who doesn't know cats and cat people, but the truth is I don't think Mum ever fully got over Tricksy's death. It marked a kind of turning point in the life of our family, certainly. A bad turning.

I felt that I ought to make at least a token effort to find out what had happened to the missing cat after it leaped from my arms when I was arrested. I had to fear the worst. There was lots of traffic in the West End of London . . . and, with all those restaurants, lots of rat poison.

Jay agreed, which, I admit, was another factor in maintaining my determination. "This poor cat is as much a victim of the slave bosses and their tame police as are the strikers," she pronounced, in that erotically serious way of hers. "Yes, Malcolm, you must search for the cat who is missing."

"Missing"—not a bad name, I thought, for a nameless cat. Fine. But where to start?

Assuming the overzealous cop and his bulky-but-swift accomplice usually used a dog for their frame-ups (probably as a kind of furry insurance policy against the unlikely presence of passers-by naive enough to offer themselves as witnesses for the defense), then why had they employed a cat on this occasion? Presumably their regular dog was ill or dead or working another gig. So the accomplice had, at the last minute, substituted a cat. A stray, I guessed: easily available and unlikely to hang around long enough to contradict P.C. Groyne's story.

Knowing—or guessing—all this did me no good at all. I had no leads, so to speak, on the Dog Man. Which left just one option: prowling around the back alleys at night after the restaurants had closed, jangling a can opener against a tin of smelly sardines, in the hope, however forlorn, that Missing might still be in the area.

I had to be careful. This was P.C. Groyne's patch, after all, and I soon came to know his routines: which restaurants and bars he liked to pop into for a friendly chat and free refreshments.

On the third night of my vigil, I was loitering in the shadows of a rubbish skip, waiting for Groyne to emerge from a steak house on the edge of Leicester Square. There'd been no sign of Missing: I'd met a couple of hedgehogs, many pigeons, and a fox, but no cats at all. The pointlessness of my quest was becoming more obvious with every minute.

I hated the thought of quitting. I felt a kind of connection to that cat which even now I can't fully explain. (Two strays thrown together by chance in a big city? Nah, too corny. Forget it.)

Groyne eventually left the steak house, burping his appreciation. I shrank further back into the shadows, but the sweat froze under my T-shirt as Groyne seemed to look right at me and then started marching towards my hiding place. My trousers were saved from ruin, though, when Groyne stopped some yards away and spoke some words I didn't catch. From the shelter of another skip there emerged, sheepishly, a man of roughly the same size and shape as the cop.

The Dog Man: it had to be.

"You prat, Vince! What the hell are you doing here?" Groyne gave the Dog Man (Vince, apparently) a clip round the ear, the sort you sometimes see mothers giving to kids they regret owning.

"I'm sorry, Arthur, honest! I was only—"

"Get away home, you moron," Groyne snarled, and this time Vince took a flat-handed slap to the face hard enough to raise a bruise.

P.C. Arthur Groyne strode off in the direction of Trafalgar Square.

"Excuse me mate, I'd like a word."

Vince jumped. He hadn't heard me come up behind him; he hadn't been meant to. But it was obvious he recognized me the instant he saw my face.

"This is all your fault! Arthur won't pay my rent, thanks to you. You and that cat."

"It's the cat I'm interested in," I reassured him. "Not you—just the cat."

Vince wasn't listening. "Clint was poorly that day; he had a chill. I couldn't take him out like that, could I?"

"Clint?"

"Dogs are same as us, yeah? They got a chill, you got to wrap 'em up with a hot water bottle."

Clint. "So you used a cat instead."

"Arthur says I made him a laughing-stock down the nick. I don't think that's fair. It's all your fault. If you hadn't been making trouble for Arthur's friends outside their restaurant, none of this would have happened, and Arthur wouldn't have hit me."

Vince looked to be on the verge of tears. Outwardly, sure, he was off the same shelf as P.C. Groyne. But he lacked the swagger, the confidence.

"Listen, mate, I never meant to get you in trouble with Arthur. He often hit you?"

"Sometimes," the big man sniffed.

"I am sorry, honest." I was, too. Almost. "Thing is, Vince, I just need to find that cat. That's all. If you can remember where you got it from, or what happened to it—"

Vince sprang away from me. "I never touched it! I never hurt it, I swear, I never. I wouldn't!"

And he was off. That Dog Man, he truly could move, for a big guy.

Even if I could've caught him, what was I going to do? Beat the truth out
of him?

It was only on the journey home that a somewhat pertinent question
entered my skull. What had Vince been doing there, that he didn't want
Arthur Groyne to know about? Answer: same as me. He was looking for
Missing.

Which raised several other questions, of course, but I was tired and
fed up, and I tried to put them out of my mind. For the next twenty years,
I tried to put them out of my mind.

Twenty years later, I was still working in the record shop and still living
alone in the small flat over the shop. My life was good enough. Plenty of
friends, a few lovers, no serious illnesses. A warm place to sleep: us strays
don't ask for much more.

Jay and Mahmood and poor, scared Vince remained only as half-
forgotten walk-ons in my mental biopic. But I still worried about Missing,
every now and then. That might sound daft—after all, I'd lived a life full
of loose ends. But most of those ends were ones I'd left dangling deliberately. Missing the Cat was one I'd tried, and failed, to tie up.

Realistically, there was nothing more I could do, following my con-
frontation with Vince. Realistically, with each month, and then each year
that passed, the likelihood that Missing was still alive faded. Street cats
are not noted for spectacular longevity. But still, some lonely nights, into
my mind would drift unbidden a picture of that double-kinked tail.
"Realistically," after all, is just a word frightened humans use to shield
themselves from their own hearts.

I forgot, and didn't forget, and then, about five years ago, I met a
girl called Sammy who worked as a clerk at Bow Street Magistrate's
Court, and I had an idea. Only a small idea, a little token of an idea,
really.

The Metropolitan Police Service had changed some during those
years, and cowboys of the Wild West End like P.C. Groyne were no longer
quite so welcome in its ranks. Plus, Groyne was an unusual name.

"If you ever hear of a man named Groyne being brought before the
courts on any sort of charge," I asked Sammy, when I thought I knew her
well enough, "let me know, would you?"

And she did. She didn't forget, and last month, after all these years, she rang me. *Well,* I thought, *this is nothing to do with a stray cat any. more, but still I'd like to be there. For auld lang syne.*

There had been no press present when I'd had my day in court, but there were one or two journalists at Bow Street that morning. I sat behind them on the public benches and waited for the accused to be led in. When he appeared, I got the shock of my life.

Vincent Groyne, unemployed decorator, pleaded guilty to the manslaughter of his brother, retired police sergeant Arthur Groyne, and was committed for trial at Crown Court. Committal hearings are brief, anti-climactic affairs, but this one did have a small, pathetic moment of excitement at the end, as the prisoner was being taken from the room.

Turning to the Bench, that big, sad man cried out: "Please, who's going to feed my cat?"

"Cat?" I said aloud, though no one heard me above the scraping of chairs and the clasping of briefcases. "Don't you mean dog?"

🐈   🐈   🐈

Two hours later, I arrived at the address given by the accused in court— a small, paint-peeling, semi-detached house in the middle of a long, tedious road in the working-class suburb of Leytonstone.

"Are you a friend of Vincent's?" asked Mrs. O'Donnell, Vince's landlady, as we sat in her clean, under-furnished living room.

"It's some years since I'd seen him," I told her. "I was sorry to hear about what happened."

Mrs. O'Donnell looked away, as if ashamed of what she was about to say, but determined to say it even so. "I'm only surprised it didn't happen long ago. That brother of his treated poor Vincent like a slave. Worse than ever since Arthur retired from the police." The way she said *retired* suggested there might be a story there, but if so, it wasn't the story she was telling today. "Then when Arthur announced he was moving in here with Vincent—he'd been thrown out of his last place for drunkenness, I happen to know that for a fact—well, that was the last straw. There was a fight, and . . . I'm sure Vincent didn't really mean to hurt him. But Arthur said he'd have to get rid of the cat—he'd always hated it."

We sipped our tea in respectful silence for a moment, and then I got to the point. "About the cat—" I began.

"Will you take her in? Oh, bless you! I'll fetch you a box to carry her in. I can't keep the poor thing, you see. She doesn't see eye to eye with my budgie." She leapt to her feet and led me to Vince's room, which was almost empty except for a dirt tray, a feeding bowl, and a bed, upon which snored an ancient, ginger cat. "He had a dog, too, when he first moved in. But that's long gone."

"Does she have a name?" I asked.

Mrs. O'Donnell smiled, sadly. "He just called her Sweetie. She was a stray, you see, originally."

The cat on the bed stretched, and I got my first good look at her. "She had her tail amputated?"

"It had been damaged in a fight, the vet thought. Or by a car, maybe," said Mrs. O'Donnell. "I don't suppose she'll be a burden to you for long. She must be twenty years old if she's a day. You're doing a kind thing, God bless you."

"Not really," I said. "It just so happens I've been thinking lately that my life has a cat-shaped hole in it. Yes, indeed, Mrs. O'Donnell, I've been thinking that for quite a while."

I'd never know for sure, of course—not really. But I didn't care. She was a fine, friendly old cat in need of a home. And for whatever reason, I was in need of her.

As I carried her home on the bus that day, speaking softly to calm her in her box, I said to her, "Well, Sweetie, whoever you are, one thing's for certain. You're not Missing any longer."

PRINTS

Ann Barrett

Gordon McKay cast a sideways glance at his client and sighed. Or rather, yawned then sighed. He'd been up half the night mulling over how to avert what he feared was a foregone but unfair verdict. But there had been no 2 A.M. flash of brilliance.

Besides, court-appointed cases disheartened him. While McKay was the lead proponent of his firm's carrying out its share of community service—his partners had nicknamed him "Good-do Gordon"—the overly complicated lives of his non-paying clients typically gave him insomnia. The more lucrative side of his business seemed a degree insulated from their legal tangles. And Shays, McKay and Crimmons, Attorneys at Law, had a reputation that appealed to the blessedly endowed. Money cushioned. Money also afforded McKay enough emotional distance to view his endeavors as a game. A game he mostly won.

But this case, *this* case. . . . Light from a low winter sun streamed through the courtroom windows, making the sweat on his client's forehead shine. Joe Richards was a tall man, thirtyish, with abundant dark hair and a muscular build. Handsome but hapless, thought McKay, reflecting that Richards's goods looks were unfortunately unaccompanied by mental prowess. McKay had had to explain every legal detail at least three times, with a confused stare Richards's typical response.

And worse, handsome was a sinker this time—in a murder rap. An obviously premeditated murder rap, to boot. Richards's girlfriend had been found stabbed. Several witnesses were slated to testify about conflict in the relationship—make that cat fights, rather, from what McKay knew. And Richards had been off camping by himself in the White Mountains the weekend she was killed. No alibi. And no hope.

But still, McKay believed him. He'd seen plenty of lying and evasion before, and this was different. Richards seemed bewildered at his predicament and, more importantly, genuinely unmoored by the loss of his girlfriend. He'd even depleted McKay's supply of Kleenex.

McKay had gone through the tissues, too, but from allergies rather than tears. The back of Richards's only sport coat carried a dusting of white fur that McKay knew, from the tickle in his nose, had originated from some cat. He was beginning to sniffle now. Should have suggested Richards have it cleaned, he thought, reaching for his handkerchief.

McKay was stifling a sneeze as the prosecution began questioning their first witness, the police detective. Peter Shribman peered from the stand through rimless glasses that magnified his brown eyes. The compactly built man sat, hands folded in his lap, with a stillness that seemed at odds with the violent details of his testimony.

"Mr. Shribman," asked Alfred Gomes, the district attorney, "on September second of last year, did you have occasion to investigate apartment #352 at 48 Rock Street in Lowell, which had been occupied by Miss Anita J. Olney?"

"I did."

"And what did you find there?"

"A murder victim, identified as Anita Olney."

Gomes paused to allow the words to acquire weight, then looked toward the jury. McKay had always thought that Gomes, who was a frequent courtroom rival, had been cursed with a vaguely rat-like countenance. Gomes's small but protruding black eyes, set above a long nose and unfortunate chin, rarely blinked as they fixed upon a witness. His handlebar mustache didn't help matters either. While it was a judgment that McKay expected to pay for with a few additional moments in purgatory, he suspected that Gomes thought even worse of him. McKay had prevailed in all but a few of their encounters, and Gomes's pique had turned personal. He now generally refused to negotiate settlements with McKay and forced most of their cases to trial. Not that there had been any wiggle room in this one, anyway. It was either acquittal or murder one. And McKay was afraid that this was the case that might even Gomes's score.

Gomes turned back to the witness. "Please describe for the jury the scene as you came upon it in Miss Olney's apartment."

"Well," Shribman began, "the victim was lying facedown on the kitchen floor. She had sustained multiple stab wounds, primarily in her back and neck. She had been dead approximately twenty-four hours. There was blood surrounding the body—on the floor and on one of the walls. Some blood had also been tracked into the living room by an animal, apparently the victim's cat. Two kitchen chairs were overturned, and objects knocked off the counters."

"Your Honor, the prosecution submits to the jury photographs of the crime scene."

"Any objection, Mr. McKay?" asked the Honorable Gareth Simmons, glancing over half-glasses poised at the end of his nose.

McKay shook his head no and the projector whirred on, lighting a yellowed, slightly torn screen. The first slides were as Shribman had described. What had been Anita Olney lay crumpled. Masses of blond hair streamed away from the slight figure, contrasting vividly with blood pooled on the floor. McKay noticed two men on the jury averting their eyes. Another juror, an elderly woman, covered her open mouth with her hand. McKay thought fleetingly of his own daughter and suppressed a shudder.

The last slide displayed a baseball cap. A smear of dried blood stained the top of the blue hat and half-obscured the letters "G. E. I." emblazoned on the front. McKay stared at the screen for a long time. Something was off about that hat.

Gomes cleared his throat. "Mr. Shribman, where was Mr. Richards employed?"

"At Grady Enterprises, Incorporated. As a mechanic."

"Did you determine that the hat belonged to Mr. Richards?"

"His prints were all over the visor."

"And you found it next to the body?"

"Yes. It—"

"Tell us about the locks in the apartment," Gomes cut in.

"The door was set to automatically lock. The windows were also locked and unbroken."

"No sign of forced entry?"

"No."

"Mr. Shribman, in your opinion, how could the perpetrator have gained access to Miss Olney's apartment?"

"Well, he would've had to have had a key. Or been let in."

"He would have had to have had a key, or been let in," repeated Gomes with gravity. "Thank you, Mr. Shribman. Your witness, Counselor."

McKay unfolded his rangy frame from his chair. His legs were stiff as he approached the stand. I'm feeling this case in my bones, he thought, as he ran a hand through his graying hair.

"Mr. Shribman, did you test the blood found in Miss Olney's apartment?"

"Yes. Everything originated from the victim."

"And where were those samples taken from?"

"From the floor next to the body, and also from splatters on the wall."

"Nowhere else?"

Shribman looked at him blankly. "That's where the blood was—the floor and the walls."

"But you said that there were also animal prints."

"Oh. Yes, well—"

"And you didn't test those prints?"

Shribman shrugged. "They were tracks from the body."

"So you didn't test *all* the blood stains, did you?"

The detective squirmed slightly. "No."

"And you said these tracks were in the living room. Did they extend all the way to the body?"

Color drained from Shribman's face. He held McKay's eyes. "Oddly, no."

"Yes—very odd, isn't it, Mr. Shribman? Odd unless the blood in those prints came from someone else, correct?"

"Objection. This is ridiculous, Your Honor!" Gomes cut in.

"Overruled, Counselor. The witness will answer the question." Judge Simmons absently touched a crystal statue of a curled and sleeping cat, which he always placed on his bench. Attorneys had long debated the significance of this cat after hours, and it had prompted an enterprising few to send the judge Christmas cards graced with pictures of cats or kittens. The statue had evolved into something of a courtroom talisman: Supposedly, its placement on the left side of the bench favored the prosecution; a right side orientation meant sympathy for the defense. McKay noted that the statue's current position was dead center in front of Simmons.

Shribman regained some composure. "I can't see how that's possible."

"But it *is* possible, is it not?"

"Yes. But unlikely."

"Now, sir, tell us about that baseball hat. Where did you find it?"

"About four feet from the body."

"Did you find it right side up?"

Shribman's eyebrows rose. "Yes, I did."

McKay rubbed his chin. "If a hat just accidentally fell off someone—say if it were knocked off, or if the person bent over—how would that hat most likely land?"

"I suppose upside down. But that depends—"

"And how would you characterize the bloodstain on the hat?" McKay interrupted.

"The top of the cap was stained."

"In what manner?"

"A solid stain. It was a smear."

"Now, if a garment worn by a killer during a knifing were blood-stained, what form would that stain usually take?"

Shribman paused, then pushed his bangs back with the palm of his hand. "Probably a splatter."

"And where would the splatter be?"

There was another moment of silence. "In the front."

"Now again, Mr. Shribman, how would you characterize the blood-stain on Mr. Richards's Grady Enterprises cap?"

"A solid smear on top of the cap." Shribman's voice was quiet but clear.

"A solid *smear* on *top* of the cap," McKay repeated. "And the cap right-side up, too. Mr. Shribman, that hat looked placed to you, didn't it?"

Shribman was silent.

"Mr. Shribman?"

"Yes."

Gordon McKay's eyes were briefly lit from within. "Thank you, Mr. Shribman."

🐜 🐜 🐜

As he returned to his chair, McKay reflected that Anita Olney had been near the age of his own daughter, Clarissa, whom he had met for break-fast that morning. The pictures had gotten to him because Clary had hair like that. In the restaurant he had admired his daughter's long golden curls when she turned around to signal their waiter. She had her mother's hair. And her mother's eyes, smile, and laugh, he thought wistfully—at least the way he remembered them. They'd lost her so long ago.

But Clarissa, a lawyer like her father, was alive and spirited and most likely arguing a case that very moment. She was engaged to a man McKay thought highly of, and he knew they both looked forward to children. McKay vicariously savored their anticipation of the future. What, he wondered, would Anita Olney's future have been?

Gomes called his next witness. Cameron Elliot Westfield, a tall, slim man wearing a charcoal Hart, Shafter and Marks suit, strode purposefully to the stand. Reflections of the brass ceiling lights glinted off Westfield's shoes.

"Mr. Westfield, would you tell us how you knew Anita Olney?"

Westfield cleared his throat. "I am president of the Lowell Bank and Trust. Miss Olney had been my secretary for approximately six months."

"And did you ever observe Miss Olney's interaction with the defendant?"

"Yes. Mr. Richards occasionally visited her at our office."

"And how would you characterize those interactions?"

"Hmmm. . . ." Westfield straightened his yellow silk tie. "I'm afraid she was always slightly fearful of him. She often looked worried. Eventually I asked if anything was troubling her."

"And what did she tell you?" Gomes paced in front of the witness stand, hands balled in his pockets, his nose elevated as if sniffing the air.

"She confided in me, but only slightly. She said that things weren't going well at home—er, with Mr. Richards. But she didn't elaborate. I assumed that it was a garden-variety relational problem. That is, until she came to work with a black eye—"

"Objection, Your Honor! Conjecture!" McKay half-rose from his seat.

"Overruled, Mr. McKay," replied Simmons. "We need to follow this. Continue please, Mr. Westfield." Simmons unconsciously fingered the crystal cat and moved it a few centimeters to the left.

Westfield shrugged his shoulders. "Well, she didn't want to talk about it. She seemed embarrassed—understandably, I guess. She said something about falling down the stairs." He stopped to smooth his close-cropped graying hair. "I took her explanation at face value until I actually saw the fellow in action—screaming obscenities at her right in our office."

"I never!" The shout came like a shot.

McKay put a hand on Richards's shoulder. "Mr. Richards . . ."

"But he's lying!"

Simmons gaveled the rumbling crowd into silence. "Once more and you're in contempt!" he snapped. "Go on, Counselor."

Gomes cleared his throat. "Mr. Westfield, did you discern the reason for the altercation that you witnessed between Miss Olney and Mr. Richards?"

"As I said, I walked in in the middle of it. But I gathered that it involved jealousy. I distinctly remember that he called her a 'slut.'"

Gordon McKay imagined one hundred pairs of eyes burning the back of Richards's head, boring into what was prejudged to be his black, evil soul. He studied the frowns on the faces of the jury—mostly middle-aged or elderly women, with a smattering of well-scrubbed young men who looked to him like recent graduates of a seminary. One woman was clutching the varnished rail of the jury box, shaking her head.

"Your witness, Counselor," said Gomes. His mustache twitched above a slight smile.

McKay leaned back in his chair and folded his hands behind his head. He took a long breath before speaking.

"Mr. Westfield," he began, "you never saw Mr. Richards lay a hand on Anita Olney, did you?" He noticed that the man took a long time to meet his eyes.

"Well, we were in a bank—in an office environment."

"You never saw him hit her."

The witness coughed. "I saw the aftereffects. Other employees at the bank did, too."

"But you just said she never directly told you that she was struck by Mr. Richards."

"She was embarrassed about it."

McKay rose and moved toward the stand. "But it's true that she never specifically said Mr. Richards hit her?"

Westfield turned and spoke directly to the jury. "She was afraid of him. I saw her bruises. I heard him scream at her."

"Answer the question, sir."

Westfield shifted in his seat. "I wouldn't have expected her to. Battered women . . ."

"Yes or no, sir."

He paused for several seconds, considering.

"No."

"Thank you," McKay replied, adding "sir" as he turned toward his chair.

Clary had remarked that morning, as they sipped coffee, "People are rarely what they first appear to be. Many of my clients, many of the people I see in court, have 'fronts'—or projections. The truth, if you ever find it, is buried in layers. A trial's a little like peeling an onion." She paused to bite into a muffin, then giggled. "And sometimes it makes you cry."

McKay had laughed, then rejoined, "And it smells stronger the more you unpeel!"

McKay reflected that this one was beginning to stink.

🐈 🐈 🐈

The next witness, Ellen Doyle, had been Anita Olney's neighbor. She was a plump woman who wore a too spring-like flowered dress that billowed above too-high pink sandals. She sashayed rather than walked. Ellen gave Gomes a bright smile that faded quickly. She just remembered she's in a courtroom and not a garden party, McKay thought.

"Miss Doyle," Gomes began, "how long had you and Miss Olney been neighbors?"

"Oh, neighbors two years. Friends almost as long. The way I met her was, when our building lost its power one winter and I had *fifteen* pounds of steak—that's prime rib, not chuck, mind you—in my freezer for a party, and I was just beside myself. Well, Anita had a balcony, so—"

"Did Miss Olney confide in you?" Gomes cut in.

"Oh definitely! Poor girl had no family left. And that's another story—you just wouldn't believe how her Mom suffered with her cancer. Just about took over her uterus and—"

Gomes raised his palm in front of the witness. "Miss Doyle. Miss Doyle, please!" Ellen stopped and stared blankly at him.

"Were you observant of the relationship between Miss Olney and Mr. Richards?"

"I should think so! I had dinner with them at least a couple times a month. Anita and I both loved to cook, see, and we'd taken this Chinese cooking class—" McKay could see that Gomes was trying to keep from rolling his eyes.

"And how would you characterize their relationship?"

Ellen sighed. A little longer than necessary, thought McKay.

"Well . . . definitely rocky, I'd say. Anita was frequently upset. She'd come over to my place after they'd had a spat."

Gomes's eyes glistened. "They argued frequently?"

Ellen for the first time looked hesitant. "Yes."

"About what?"

"Of course I don't know the *whole* story. But Joe seemed jealous a lot. And I know they had a lot of conflict about her new job."

"Why? It was an excellent position. Executive secretary to a bank president was a significant step up for her. Would you say," Gomes asked as he smoothed down the lapel of his suit, "that Mr. Richards felt somehow threatened, or undermined, by her advancement?"

McKay sprang to his feet. "Objection, Your Honor!"

"Sustained. A bit more slack, Counselor."

Gomes took a step back, folded his arms, and smiled. "Yes, Your Honor." He turned back to Ellen. "Miss Doyle, were you aware of specific issues involving Miss Olney's position that resulted in conflict between her and Mr. Richards?"

Ellen shrugged her plump shoulders. "Well, maybe the hours."

"Mr. Richards objected to her not being available?"

"That, and I gathered Joe didn't go for Anita's boss—and him so good to her! Anita got a pay raise after only three months. And Mr. Westfield's so nice. Took such an interest in her career! You know, he'd give her rides home, too, so she wouldn't have to deal with the bus—and he'd even drop by to pick up work so she wouldn't have to carry in so much in the morning." McKay suddenly stared hard at Ellen. His scalp tingled. "I always told Anita she was lucky to work for someone who cared. I could tell you stories about some of the bosses *I* had. There was this one—"

"Thank you very much, Miss Doyle. Your witness, Counselor."

McKay's chair scraped against the wood floor as he backed away from his table. He paused in front of Ellen Doyle for several seconds, during which he noticed the ticking of the clock over Judge Simmons's head. He crossed his arms before speaking.

"Miss Doyle, why would you suppose Joe Richards objected to Mr. Westfield?"

Ellen shrugged. "I just can't imagine. He was so wonderful to Anita."

"And in your opinion, Miss Olney appreciated Mr. Westfield as a boss?"

"Oh yes! It was always 'Cameron this' and 'Cameron that.'"

"They had a close working relationship?"

"Anita would've *slaved* for Mr. Westfield."

"And exactly how often did you see Mr. Westfield at Anita Olney's apartment?"

"Objection—"

"Your Honor," McKay cut Gomes off, "I'm pursuing an avenue of questioning that the prosecution itself introduced."

"I really don't see the relevance, Counselor. Sustained," Simmons said gruffly.

McKay sighed. "Miss Doyle," he began, "I understand that you were the one to alert the police after Miss Olney was murdered. Tell us how you came to determine that there had been an attack."

Ellen looked suddenly solemn. "Well, the cat, actually. I found Casper wandering around the hall, meowing pitifully—and Anita never let him out of the apartment. I thought he'd just been shut out, so I knocked but got no answer—which was odd for a Sunday morning. Anita liked to sleep in and then cook a good breakfast. Often, I'd join her."

"What did you do?"

"I took Casper into my place and gave him some food. The poor kitty's still with me. Then, all day, I knocked to see if Anita'd come home. Toward night, I got a funny feeling that something was wrong. Anita had left a key with me the last time she went away on vacation—with Joe," Ellen sniffed and wiped at a tear underneath her eye, "so I could go over and feed Casper for her. She said to keep it for the next time—or in case she locked herself out or somthing."

McKay crossed his arms and looked down at the floor before continuing. "Miss Doyle, did you hear anything, see anything, *notice* anything strange the weekend that Miss Olney was murdered?"

Ellen held his eyes for a long moment. "Let me think. . . ."

"Did you see anyone go into or come out of her apartment that weekend?"

"Only Mr. Westfield."

Murmuring filled the courtroom. McKay whirled around to glance at Westfield, whose face was white, then turned back to the stand.

"Mr. Westfield was in Anita Olney's apartment the night she was murdered?"

"I ran into him Saturday evening, leaving with a sheaf of papers. He told me Anita'd been typing an important document at home. . . . Oh!" Ellen's hand flew to her mouth.

McKay turned to the bench. "Your Honor," he began in a resonant voice, "I move for a suspension of this trial pending an investigation of an additional suspect who has just been determined to have been at the scene of the crime, Mr. Cameron Westfield."

"This is an outrage!" Westfield shouted.

"Order! Order!" It took five strikes of Simmons's gavel to silence the crowd. "Bailiff, remove the jury! Gentlemen, in my chambers immediately!"

McKay and Gomes followed Simmons's billowing robes through the courtroom doors and down the hall. The judge swept into his chambers and abruptly turned to them, arms akimbo. He fixed Gomes with a wide-eyed glare.

"Counselor, I expect this to be the last half-baked case I see in my courtroom! You have more work to do."

🦙   🦙   🦙

McKay parked across the street from Joe Richards's building and picked his way around mud-streaked snow banks to reach the front steps. The day was nasty. Wind-driven sleet seemed to aim for the half inch of exposed neck between his hat and scarf. He stepped through the door quickly, then tried to ignore the urine stench permeating the foyer.

He was tired. The call from the D.A.'s office had awakened him from a sound sleep that morning. He'd groggily punched at his alarm clock, mistakenly believing that it was the source of the offending ring, then wrestled with his sheets as he hurried out of bed. He had just entered the living room as the message was ending, and he caught the words ". . . results implicate a third, unknown party." There had been no going back to sleep.

McKay searched through the names printed on bits of masking tape stuck next to the line of doorbells and pushed the one marked "Richards." The inner door buzzed immediately. He climbed one flight of steps and found Richards waiting outside his apartment, holding a fluffy, loudly purring white cat.

"Hello, Joe. New roommate?" McKay immediately felt an itch gathering in his nose.

"Hey, Gordon. Meet Casper. He was Anita's, remember?" Joe rubbed the top of Casper's head. "Damn cat always followed me around when I visited and glued himself to my lap. Figured the furball would be company."

"I thought he was with Ellen."

"Yeah, well. I guess Ellen had to let him go. She's allergic. In fact, I found him outside her place, stuck in a tree—he started meowing when he saw me. Come on in and sit down."

The only furniture in Richards's living room was a sofa, television, and small dinette set. But the room was clean and neatly picked up, except for a dish of cat food that trailed several Friskies nuggets. McKay peeled his coat off and sank onto the couch. "So, you've seen Ellen?"

Richards smiled and colored slightly. He put the cat down and sat. "She keeps calling me. Telling me how sorry she is about Anita and about all the shit I've been through. Things like that. And, she started bringing dinner over. And—well . . . in fact, she's coming by this afternoon."

"Joe, I came by to tell you that Westfield was let go. The DNA results didn't match. Those paw prints were human blood that wasn't Anita's or yours, or Westfield's either. So the case is still open."

"God, I hope they find that bastard. You know, I suspected all along that Anita and 'Mr. Pinstripe' were carrying on, but—"

"They were. He admitted it."

Richards's jaw tightened. "Yeah. Well."

"And, while we can't prove it, I suspect that he may have found her— I mean after she was killed—when he came by that day. Found her and didn't say anything. He's married. He's prominent. He's not supposed to have a key to his secretary's apartment."

"And Anita wasn't worth going to the police for," Richards muttered bitterly.

"Worse than that, I think. Joe," McKay leaned forward and clasped his hands, "was your G.E.I. hat in Anita's apartment before the murder?"

"She had one. I'd given her one a while back."

McKay nodded slowly. "Westfield might have also tampered with the crime scene. He may have been worried that someone knew about his relationship with Anita, so he placed that hat."

"Asshole!" Richards stood up. "Why can't you do something about that?"

McKay sighed. "Because we can't prove anything, Joe. We don't know. I'm just trying to piece things together in my own mind." They looked at each other for a long minute.

The doorbell startled both of them. "Ellen," Joe said and got up to buzz her in. He opened the apartment door.

She arrived a few seconds later, flinging her arms around Joe's neck as she walked into the apartment. Joe briefly patted her back then released himself.

"Ellen, Mr. McKay's here."

Ellen looked around, startled. It took a second for her to compose her face into a tentative smile. "Why hello, Mr. McKay." She walked over to shake his hand. "How nice to see you."

"You too, Ellen. Actually, I was on my way out."

"Why don't you have dinner with us?" Richards asked. "We have plenty of the spaghetti sauce that Ellen made. Please stay."

Ellen noticeably blanched, then smiled weakly. "Yes, Mr. McKay. Joe appreciates what you did so much." She slid out of her coat and handed it to Richards, then reached up to remove her hat. The left cuff of her dress sleeve was unbuttoned and the fabric fell away from her wrist.

"Oh, thank you, but I—" McKay stopped when he noticed the four parallel scratches running the length of her forearm. "Well sure. I'd like that. Thanks."

She quickly buttoned her sleeve. "Joe, do you have any wine? I could really use a—"

Ellen was interrupted by a low, unearthly growl from the floor. Casper stood facing her with his back arched and fur on end. The cat hissed, baring his teeth. Ellen took a step back.

"Casper! Be nice!" Joe scooped the cat into his arms. "I don't know what gets into him when Ellen's around. He's so friendly with everyone else."

Ellen's hand shook as she smoothed her hair. She gave a brittle laugh. "I guess I'm just not a cat person. So tell me, Mr. McKay, is the case sewn up yet?"

McKay rubbed his chin. "Well no, Ellen, it's not. But I don't think it will be long now. Not long at all. . . ."

MR. BIGGLES FOR THE DEFENSE

Matthew J. Costello

The phone intercom produced a soft tone that made Ernest K. Thorp stop doodling on his Palm Pilot 5 with its expanded memory and never-used 33.6 kps modem.

"Yes, Connie?"

Connie was actually Conseula Romero, wife to Antony, spelled thusly, with a giant emphasis on the 'An'. Whenever Consuela—Connie—referred to her husband by name, her jaw opened wide as if she were about to engulf a hoagie with the works.

Or something.

And old An-tony Romero made periodic visits to the office, to scarf up his wife's check or just lurk in the outer office for a few minutes, marking his territory. He was big, solid, a Latino tank of a man; one would not want to get old Antony mad by hitting on his pretty, petite wife.

Besides, she was a good secretary and budding paralegal. His other paralegal, Molly, was—Ernest imagined—president of the local Harley and Jack Daniel's shooters club. But she, too, was more than competent.

Competence was good. Made the wheels of enterprise roll. Kept the bucks flowing into Ernest's small but growing practice in criminal law.

"Mister Thorp, I have the County Jail on the line."

Except, despite her competency, Connie pronounced it "Meeester Thorp." Someday, when Antony wasn't around, he'd have to suggest to her to get some elocution or diction lessons. Lose the accent. Play a little Pygmalion with the bright-eyed lady from the Dominican Republic.

"Thanks, Connie. I'll pick up."

Ernest knew the man on the other end of the phone. When he had been with the prosecutor's office, he had had lots of dealings with James Tidyman, County Jail Supervisor. It paid to be nice to old Jimbo since he could make life a piece of cake—or hell—for any of Earnest's clients.

And the current request on the table was . . . definitely one for the books.

"James, thanks for getting back to me."

James grumbled something in reply, something that sounded like, "Sew rye, Urn."

As in, "It's all right, Ern."

"So have you run our request through the powers that be?"

While Jimbo processed the question, Ernest brought up the handy-dandy calendar on his Pilot. Tomorrow afternoon was clear, had been wiped clean in anticipation of getting the green light for his little court-approved experiment on behalf of his client.

"Well—" Ernest heard the word *whale*—"there's one little problem. The D.A.'s office doesn't rightly mind you taking Mrs. Jerryman out of the jail—as long as you have two of my deputies with you."

Why, thought Ernest? Did they imagine that petite Mrs. Jerryman would make a getaway and head south? Pick up a dinghy to Castro's Cuba and ask for political asylum? *I murdered my husband with his claw hammer. Can I stay here please?*

"So, what's the problem, Jimmy? We'll bring the deputies along."

Jimmy grunted. Not exactly a grunt, but some sort of primal sound that represented a *problem.*

"Well you see, Ernie . . ." Another *whale* sighting. "We have this *problem.* Gotta take the two deputies. And that's time away from jail, maybe, Ern, even overtime, plus the bookkeeping. What I'm trying to say here—"

What he's trying to say, Ernest knew, was . . . where's the beef? Or at least the grease to make this little road-show work. Money makes the world go around, and nowhere more so than in the court system of this great country of ours.

"Oh, is that all? Don't you worry about that, Jimmy." As in, take the damn gun from my head, the cash is coming. "I'm sure Mrs. Jerryman can cover the expense of the deputies and, of course, your own personal over-time dealing with bookkeeping."

A bit of hesitation on the other end of the line. Ernest guessed that Jimbo was wondering if he should nail down that figure right now. But Jimmy must have thought the better of it.

"Alrighty then, Ern. We're all set." The "we" of the "we're" was a pig-calling sound. Ernest could picture the man's mouth widening to a big satisfied grin. "You can come by this afternoon and take her to her house. Just one question, Ernie, about your little plan."

Ernest wanted the call ended. He needed to call the judge's office to get a court observer to meet them at the jail.

"What's that, James?"

"Well . . ."

There she blows.

"I was wonderin' . . . will you pick it up, or should I send one of my deputies?"

Ernest was half listening, scrolling through his phone numbers until he reached the one for Judge Pillbord's office.

"Pick up?"

"Yes, the cat, the kittie? Want us to get it?"

Ernest laughed. The cat. The creature at the center of this whole lit-tle road trip.

"No, James. Don't worry. I'll take care of that."

Yes, Ernest would pick up Mr. Biggles from the kennel on the way to the jail. After all, Mr. Biggles was about to be the defense's star witness!

Ernest waited on the street by the side exit to the County Jail. The sun was blistering, and he wondered if he should have waited in the car. But he had a whole entourage with him: the two officers of the jail and the court reporter. It was a regular little circus train heading to the house where William Jerryman was murdered with a claw hammer by—it would seem—his petite wife.

It fell to Ernest Thorp to disprove that claim.

The side door of the jail opened. Mrs. Linda Jerryman walked out, blinking in the sun. She wore a green county-issue jumpsuit that did lit-tle to hide the fact that, though she was small, she was more than an attractive package. Obviously the sixty-two-year-old Mr. Jerryman must have thought so, bringing her back from a business trip to Las Vegas, already married.

Linda Jerryman came up to Ernest and grabbed his hand.

"Ernie, did you get him?"

Ernest nodded. "He's in my car, Mrs. Jerryman, meowing like crazy."

Linda Jerryman ran to the car and opened the back door. Ernest could only see the small tufts of orange sticking out, but Linda draped herself over the carrier.

"Mr. Biggles, mommy's missed you soooo much!"

In response, Mr. Biggles produced a long, soulful meow. The meaning, Ernest imagined, was probably less "glad to see you, too" than "get me the hell out of here."

Linda turned back to Ernest. "Can I take him out?"

Ernest shook his head.

"No. Not till we get to the house. Then you can"—he looked at her two guards and the court observer—"show us everything you told me about."

Now Linda stood up, all business. She sniffed as if the reunion had overcome her just a tad. "Right. Well, you'll see. You'll all see. Mr. Biggles will show you. Then," she said with a big smile, as big as the yawning emptiness of the Great Plains states where cornfields stretch from Omaha to Mars, "everything will be fine."

Right, Ernest thought. *Maybe.* Though not too fine for Mr. Jerryman, who was already six feet under with a nasty hole in his forehead. Fine was a word Mr. Jerryman had left behind forever.

"We better get going," one of the guards said. This test wasn't supposed to take too much time.

Ernest nodded. Mr. Biggles was in the car, and now they were ready to see how cute little Linda's defense all boiled down to one mangy, orange cat.

🐾 🐾 🐾

As they pulled up to the house, Ernest glanced over at the two guards to catch their reaction to the size of the mansion. He could see from the expressions on their faces that they suddenly had a deeper understanding of who it was Mrs. Jerryman was accused of killing.

The victim, her hubby, had major bucks.

The house resembled a giant cruise ship, a mammoth boat of a mansion that only went up two stories but occupied an entire block, shrouded by tall palm trees dotted with tropical pines. It was all but invisible from the street, but once through the electronic gates, everyone in the car was treated to an unobstructed view of one mighty big house. In fact, the only place Ernest could compare it to, at least in the environs of Miami, was the castle occupied by Al Pacino in *Scarface*.

Come to think of it, he ended up getting whacked too.

Anyone who came to kill Mr. Jerryman would have to get past the electronic gate, then past the house's own security system, then—God!—somehow find the billionaire in this expansive warren of rooms.

Didn't seem worth the effort.

Especially since, in this case, the murderer didn't steal anything.

All of which made it doubly, even trebly, worse for Mrs. Jerryman's case.

Only one person stood to gain from Mr. Jerryman's sudden and violent demise—pert Linda Jerryman.

"Whoa—"

That was the reaction of one of the beefy guards to the house.

Linda made a derisive noise in response that sounded like the last belch of air escaping from a popped balloon, as in—"*You* try to keep it clean!" But Ernest was more than sure Linda Jerryman never had to deal with the day-to-day running of this stucco Tara.

They pulled up to the front. The shiny ribbon proclaiming a "Police Scene" rustled in front of the giant double-door entryway.

On cue, Mr. Biggles spoke up. Another long, low disgruntled meow filled the car.

"Oooh, Mr. Biggles," Linda purred. Then she turned to Ernest. "See, he knows." Then, nodding to the guards and then Ralph, the court-appointed observer, she said again, "See, he knows." And one more time for good measure, lest anyone missed the point. "He *remembers*."

The car stopped. The guards got out first and stood by the door while Linda got out, holding the cat carrier. Ralph was sitting beside Ernest in the front. He slid out and, Ernest noticed, began his official observing. A sworn court officer, his testimony about what happened during the next few minutes would be vital to the case.

Linda Jerryman turned to the entourage.

"I don't know if I can stand it."

Ernest nodded. Linda was undoubtedly talking about being overwhelmed by her memory of discovering hubby with the claw hammer buried in his forehead.

"It's okay," Ernest said. "We'll be out here." Then, in case she needed some honest encouragement, "You have to. For your case."

Was there ever any real doubt that she'd do it?

Do monkeys fly?

She took a deep breath. Everyone watched the intake of breath and its results with barely guarded appreciation.

"Okay," she said. "I'll go in now." She looked down at the cat. "Are you ready, Mr. B? Such a good kitty."

The words seemed almost to be a cue. But then how many times has this woman walked into a crime scene?

She walked to the giant double doors, entered the monster house, and shut the door behind her, while the guards, Ralph, and Ernest waited outside under the hot mid-summer Miami sun.

The ride back was quiet. Ralph took notes on a large yellow pad documenting what had just transpired inside the house.

Mr. Biggles, about to be returned to the pound, was also subdued, though based on what they had just witnessed, Mr. Biggles wouldn't be doing much more time in the feline slammer. Nor would his owner be incarcerated much longer.

Hard to believe, thought Ernest, *I may actually win this case.*

He looked over at Ralph, writing furiously on his fourth page of legal-sized yellow lined paper. Ralph was the court's eyes and ears on what happened. Then the jurors would decide.

He looked back at Linda, sandwiched between the two guards.

She smiled at him.

And, thought Ernest, *if I get Mrs. Jerryman off there will be no question that I'll get paid. None at all.*

He smiled back.

Not that he was such a great lawyer. But that was one hell of a cat. As the court was about to learn.

The downtown courthouse was stifling hot despite being sealed and air-conditioned. Perhaps so many bodies were overwhelming the cooling system. The tabloid "media"—if you could call those parasites by that name—were all over this story, grabbing pictures of Linda. The Internet had pictures of the murdered Jerryman only hours after the crime, though no one knows how the official photos got released. The pictures were extraordinarily grisly, but the murder mavens on the Web gobbled them up.

The Internet is so *educational!*

The courthouse was packed, obviously fueled by the day's testimony. Ernest looked around at the noisy crowd and thought, *they'll get their money's worth today. That's for sure.*

Ernest's assisting lawyer, a sleepy-eyed woman who knew criminal law like most people know their social security number, was ready to deal with all of the prosecution's expected objections.

The prosecution had the report from Ralph. They knew what was ahead. They didn't look happy.

Finally, the bailiff entered and asked the noisy assemblage to stand for Judge Pillbord. The judge, an unattractive woman with dark hair, bore a surprising resemblance to Judge Judy. So far during the trial she had kept a tight rein on what could have been a runaway freight train.

After everyone sat down, Judge Pillbord looked at Ernest, then at the prosecution team, and then she signaled that she'd like to talk quietly to both sides.

Ernest hurried up.

"Look, I don't want this turning into a circus today," she said, snorting a slight lateral S. Ernest nodded. "We're going to deal with this . . . evidence . . . the same way we've dealt with everything else about this trial."

She looked at the lead prosecutor to make sure he understood exactly what she was saying.

The prosecutor nodded. "Your Honor, I'd like to reserve a challenge to—"

Judge Pillbord held up a hand. "Your time to challenge has passed. You agreed to this test, you have the—" she waved some typed pages in the air "—documentation. It's up to the jury now, and what they make of it."

"But—"

"Let's get going!" Pillbord barked, her sloppy S's kicking up spittle as she sent the opposing lawyers back to their desks.

Well, that was good, Ernest thought. *The state will have to sit there and take it.*

"Counselor?"

Ernest sprung to his feet. "The defense calls Ralph Guttentag."

The audience spun around to watch the short, squat man make his way down the aisle to the witness seat. After being sworn in, Ralph sat back, smiled at the judge and looked right at Ernest.

"Mr. Guttentag, would you please tell us in what capacity you serve this court."

Ralph cleared his throat. "Yes. I am a court-appointed, legally bonded impartial observer."

Another smile.

"Yes, and in that capacity you do what?"

"Oh, I observe or note things for the court, provide depositions—"

"And in general, act as the court's eyes and ears?"

"Exactly."

"Objection." The lead prosecutor was starting his attempt to stem the tide of the upcoming testimony.

Pillbord looked right at him. "Your honor, Mr. Guttentag's testimony is still subject to interpretation. He can't suggest that his observations represent fact."

"Overruled," Pillbord said.

So much for that objection, and probably any more to come. Ernest smiled at the prosecutor. *Suck it in,* he thought, *because you're going down.*

"Now, Mr. Guttentag, would you please tell us what you saw on the thirteenth of this month, just yesterday."

"Yes, it's in my report, but I will tell you." Ralph started in by describing the trip to the Jerryman house, with the cat in tow.

"If it please Your Honor, the defense would like to produce the just-mentioned cat, Mr. Biggles, as defense exhibit A."

The prosecutor jumped up again but was again waved away by the judge, who gave the order for Mr. Biggles to be brought in and placed on an evidence table. In moments, the cat carrier, with Biggles's yellow fur sticking out of the holes, was part of the show in the courtroom.

"It was this cat that went with you, isn't that right, Mr. Guttentag?"

Guttentag leaned forward as if trying to see more of the cat in the carrier.

"I assume so." He smiled. "I mean, if that's Mr. Biggles."

In response to its name the cat meowed, and the courtroom burst out in laughter. It *was* funny, but Ernest had to keep a firm hold on the proceedings, otherwise the absurdity of it all would get in the way of the defense.

"Now, if you'd tell us what you saw yesterday?"

A deep breath. "Well, Mrs. Jerryman entered the establishment with Mr. Biggles while we waited outside."

"We?"

"Yourself, Mr. Thorp, me, and the two guards."

"And can you tell us why we waited?"

"Yes, I can," Ralph said. "The point was to demonstrate what would happen when an intruder entered the house."

"An intruder?"

"Yes, someone who didn't belong there."

"I see. Go on please."

"Well, we waited—I don't know—about five minutes, and then we walked up to the front door."

"With you in the lead?"

"Yes."

"And could you tell us what happened then?"

"Sure. I entered the house."

"Using a key?"

"Yes."

"So you didn't make any big noise, nothing alarming or disruptive?"

"Oh no, we entered very quietly."

"And then?"

"Well, I knew Mrs. Jerryman had gone to her room just as she had the night of the unfortunate encounter—"

"Objection, Your Honor, to the witness' terminology. It's not an 'unfortunate encounter,' it's a murder. Cold blooded. Bloody, a—"

"Sustained." The judge turned to Ralph. "The witness will be directed to call the 'encounter' a murder."

Ralph nodded. "Y-yes, Your Honor."

Ernest looked at the beleaguered prosecutor and rolled his eyes. Is that the best he could do—hairsplitting over terminology?

"Mr. Guttentag, would you please continue?"

"Yes. We entered, me in the lead."

"And you didn't see anyone?"

"Didn't see anyone . . . except for the cat, Mr. Biggles."

Ernest walked over to the cat carrier. "Your Honor, may I?"

Pillbord nodded. Ernest opened the carrier and pulled out the fluffy orange cat.

"You saw *this* cat?" Ernest gave the cat a little scratch under its chin. The cat arched up, obviously starved for affection after his time in the pen.

"And tell us what happened then."

"Mr. Biggles was there, at the foot of the stairs, and as soon as we entered, he started hissing, howling . . . it was weird. Like he was some kind of alarm cat."

"Obj—"

"Overruled. Continue, Counselor."

I'm on a roll, Ernest thought. *Everyone wants to hear what old Mr. Biggles did.*

"Continue, Mr. Guttentag."

"Yes. Mr. Biggles hissed and growled, and then he hacked up this giant, reddish hairball."

"Really?"

"Yes, and in a flash, after more hissing, another."

The courtroom grew quiet.

"Two hairballs? Right there?"

"Yes . . . and then one final one, all in a row. It was some kind of reaction to strangers, I guess."

"Objection, Your Honor, Mr. Guttentag is simply interpreting what could have been—"

The judge hesitated. Sustain it, and she'd have to tell the jurors to ignore what had been said. Overrule it, and then Ernest could deliver the *coup de grâce.* Courtesy of Mr. Biggles.

"Overruled. The witness is simply providing what he saw to be happening at the time. Mr. Thorp, continue."

Swish! He shoots and scores. Ernest looked back at Mrs. Jerryman, who looked pleased, mighty pleased. In fact, from the twinkle in her eyes, *way* more than pleased.

"Thank you, Mr. Guttentag. You may step down."

Ralph left, hairball testimony delivered, while Ernest turned to the judge.

"Your Honor, I would like to re-admit to evidence the crime scene photograph, enlarged, as defense exhibit B." Ernest went to the side of his desk and produced a poster-sized enlargement of the crime scene.

It was a cropped close-up, showing a portion of Mr. Jerryman's head, which looked like a disfigured moon of Jupiter with an erupting volcano gushing red lava.

The vision of the head was horrible, so enlarged as to be unreal but revolting nonetheless. But the little circles behind the head were what Ernest wanted everyone to see—the three clumps that, as could be confirmed in the official detective's report, were three reddish hairballs in a line.

Mr. Biggles had this odd response to strangers. Soon as they came in the house, he'd hack up fur . . . right in a line.

He did it the other day, and he did it the night Mr. Jerryman was killed. And he left the evidence right there, at the foot of the stairs for everyone to see. Some stranger killed Mr. Jerryman.

And as they say: case closed.

A week layer, Ernest was once again back at the Jerryman mansion, this time sitting cozily on a couch with the widowed mistress of this lavish domain—and all the money attached to it.

She handed Ernest an envelope.

"Thank you," she said, pressing the envelope of cash into Earnest's hand. She smiled, and the room felt a bit on the warm side.

Mr. Biggles meowed, a jealous lover, and wandered in. He hopped up beside Ernest and gave him a steely-eyed stare.

"Hope he doesn't—" Ernest laughed and made a gagging gesture.

Mrs. Jerryman didn't laugh. "Don't worry, he wouldn't. Not without my permission." She hesitated. "After all, you're not a stranger, and I don't want you to be."

The temperature climbed another few degrees.

Mr. Biggles growled again. Mrs. Jerryman made a cooing noise.

"Ohh, Mr. Biggles, you're upsetting Ernest." Then she made a little whistling noise, and Mr. Biggles literally leaped off the couch and jumped onto an empty chair like magic.

Ernest laughed. "Some trick."

"Oh, Mr. Biggles knows lots of tricks!" She made another whistle, and this time Mr. Biggles threw himself into the air and turned 360 degrees around.

Ernest gasped. "That's amazing. You should do a show."

Mrs. Jerryman's smile broadened. "Oh, but we did do one."

Ernest nodded. And he had a funny feeling, like when you've eaten something that you know won't agree with you. But the trouble was still mere moments ahead.

"A show?"

"Yes. In Vegas. 'Mr. Biggles and Linda.' We did the lounges. That's, where I met my—" she took a deep cleansing breath "—husband."

"A show." Now Ernest took a breath. "What kind of show?"

"Mr. Biggles did tricks. Lots of tricks."

"Lots?"

"Yes. There wasn't anything I couldn't teach him, isn't that right, Mr. B?" On cue, the cat spun around in the air again.

"Could teach him anything, could you?"

Mrs. Jerryman smiled broadly. "Anything."

Ernest looked over at Mr. Biggles. He was tempted to ask the question about what exactly were the limits of Mr. Biggles's performing talents.

But the trial was over.

The verdict was in.

Besides, maybe Mr. Biggles could learn to stop growling at him.

After all, he can learn to do anything!

Family Ties

Richard Chizmar and Barry Hoffman

1

A couple years ago, my momma told me about the one and only time she saw her daddy cry. It was a very long time ago at his youngest brother's funeral. Uncle Bobby was her favorite uncle in the whole world, Momma said, and he'd got himself killed at the factory. Momma told me it broke her heart to see her daddy that way. Felt like something inside of her was dying, like her heart was just ripping apart.

That's how I felt when they brought Jason into the courtroom.

Like something inside of me was dying.

He seemed so small. So scared. His arms looked so skinny in the handcuffs. And he wouldn't look at me.

He hadn't been the same big brother for a long time now, that's for sure, but the old Jason still lived inside my head. The way he used to wink at me and laugh when he was up to no good or fooling around teasing Momma. The way he used to take charge of a bad situation out on the street and turn it around. Or the way he could look at you with those big brown eyes of his and make you believe you could do almost anything, even fly if you wanted to. I was his Little One, and he was my big brother. Always so strong and sure of himself.

Now, sitting up there on the witness stand, as the lawyers and the judge asked him questions, he mostly just stared at the floor in front of him. Nodded his head every now and then. And when he did look up, it was like staring at a stranger. Like someone you passed on the street corner and never thought twice about.

A tear rolled down my cheek, and before I could wipe it away with my shirt sleeve, Momma did it herself with a balled-up Kleenex. "You okay, honey?" she whispered.

I nodded and tried to smile.

Momma knew I wasn't okay. She'd been through this before—a couple of times with one of her nephews—but this was my first time inside a courtroom. It sure looked different than on television. Everything was so big and the ceilings were so high and the furniture didn't look all shiny and pretty. And there weren't a lot of fancy-dressed people running around yelling and screaming like on television either. Just me and Momma and Jason, the judge, and a bunch of fat lawyers and policemen. And some lady with curly red hair who was typing everything that was being said.

It was cold too. Real cold. Didn't they have heat in a place like this?

I hugged myself and shivered. It all made me feel so small. Like a little girl. Much younger than fourteen years old. It all made me want my big brother even more.

"I'll always be there to watch your back, Little One," he used to tell me. "Try not to worry so much. I'll take good care of you."

And he had. Up until six or seven months ago. Until everything changed. . . .

2

Jason had been more than just a big brother to me. He'd been my father, protector, teacher, playmate, my best friend in the whole world. He and Momma were everything to me. Our daddy had taken off soon after I was born. Left one morning for work and never came back, Momma told me. Rumor was he moved down to Baltimore with some other woman. Jason was three at the time. I saw a picture of my daddy once. It was old and wrinkled and faded, but he didn't look a thing like Jason or me. Just some stranger is all.

From the time he was old enough, Jason took care of me. Took good care of me, too. Making sure I was dressed for school on time and had some breakfast. Making sure I did my homework before watching television. Teaching me to read better than anyone in my class and how to write cursive. How to wash my clothes and help keep the apartment clean. Always checking on me after school and making sure I wasn't smoking cigarettes or hanging around with what he called "the bad kids."

Momma did the best she could with both us kids. And her best was pretty darn good. We started out in the projects. Rats, roaches, brown water, and a whole lot worse. But Momma worked two jobs all day long and took in some baby-sitting whenever she had a couple of free hours. When I was six, we moved three blocks north to a two-bedroom apartment. It was still pretty cold in the winter—heck, I've never lived anywhere where the heat works the way it's supposed to—but we had hot food on the table and store-bought clothes on our backs. No more food stamps or charity for us. Momma was a proud woman, and she taught us kids to be the same way. Most nights, she'd come home from her first job, shower, grab a bite to eat or squeeze in a nap, and then she was gone to the bus stop and her night job. Seven days a week it was like that. Sometimes we teased her and called her the Phantom.

"It won't always be like this, kids," she'd promise us. "It'll keep getting better and better. Just you wait and see."

And we believed her, too.

In the meantime, it was up to us to take care of ourselves. But it wasn't all work either. We had fun together. Lots of it. We'd play board games when it was raining outside and watch movies on television. Jason even pretended to like to watch cartoons with me. Sometimes we'd play Stratego or Monopoly or cards at the kitchen table and bake chocolate-chip cookies or cupcakes. I can still see Jason now, walking over to check on the cookies and me pretending to sneak a peek at his game pieces. He'd give me one of those I-know-exactly-what-you're-doing looks and wink at me. He never once yelled or got mad because he knew I wasn't really cheating; just teasing him and trying to get a rise outta him.

The summer I turned ten years old, Jason taught me how to play basketball. How to dribble and pass the ball. How to shoot and play good defense. He was a great teacher; he was real patient and hardly ever got mad, even when I didn't listen to him. And he was tough with me, too. Didn't treat me like a sissy or anything. Later, when I started playing rec ball at the YMCA on Saturday mornings, he came to every game and sat in the stands with his friends from school. I could tell he was proud of me.

And, of course, it was Jason who brought Simon home three days before my twelfth birthday.

Simon was a skinny little runt of a gray kitten. The first time I laid eyes on him he looked more like a baby beaver than a cat. Jason had found him inside a Dumpster behind the Laundromat meowing away in a rainstorm. Said he was afraid the poor thing might've drowned if he hadn't come along. Figured the kitty could keep me company when he was at basketball practice after school or working down at the video store. That evening, we went down to Fisher's Pet Store, and he bought me a collar, a food and water dish, some cat food, and a place for Simon to use the bathroom. He gave me a big hug out on the sidewalk in front of Fisher's and wished me an early Happy Birthday. That's how I like to remember my big brother.

A few months later, when I started whining that Simon liked Jason more than me, he really surprised me and brought home another kitty. A girl this time. He named her Samantha—after the mom on *Bewitched*—and we made a return trip to Fisher's Pet Store. Simon and Samantha took to each other like brother and sister, and Samantha grew to be as fond of me as Simon was of Jason. Some nights she would sit on my lap for hours and watch television, and she slept at the foot of my bed every night, curled inside the covers.

It was around that time that Momma got her promotion at the store, and she was finally able to quit her night job. Good thing too, because before long she was busy at the store every night until eight or nine o'clock. She usually came home about an hour before my bedtime. *But just wait and see, kids,* she told us a few weeks into her new schedule. *It'll be worth it. It comes with a good pay increase and a lot of responsibility.* My God, we were so proud of her. I remember we celebrated with dinner at Pizza Hut and a movie afterwards. Jason gave a toast at the restaurant, and Momma started crying and laughing at the same time, and then I did, too. Jason said we were both crazy ladies and acted all embarrassed.

So things were good for all of us—no, they were great—for about a year after that. We both kept on missing Momma, but Jason and I understood why she had to be gone so much. And we still had each other. It was probably the happiest time of my life.

Then, just like that, things started to change.

Jason started to change.

It was little things at first. I noticed he didn't smile as often as he used to. He wasn't as funny as he once was—not as many wisecracks or practical jokes or silly faces. He didn't spend as much time hanging around with me either—watching television, playing games, or playing with

Simon and Samantha. Some days after practice he went right to his bed-room and stayed there until dinnertime. Some mornings I had to wake him up for school, when it had usually been the other way around.

And then it got worse. He went from being a little moody to down-right grumpy. Some days he was mean to me; other days he just ignored me. I couldn't believe it. I hadn't done anything at all to make him act this way. Some nights we'd sit at the kitchen table eating dinner and not say a word to each other. It was like living with a different person.

I talked to Momma about it, and she told me it was probably just "girl trouble." That's exactly what she called it—*girl trouble*. Promised me that she would talk to him. Said all teenagers went through it, and you just watch and see, he'll be back to his old self before we know it.

But she was wrong. It kept getting worse.

Soon I started noticing other things. Jason didn't shower as often as before. Sometimes I could smell the sweat and the stink on him all the way across the room. And his clothes were always wrinkled and dirty. For someone like Jason, this was a big deal. In the old days, he used to be such a sharp dresser, so handsome and cool; all my girlfriends used to say so.

And then there was school. Once basketball season was over, he started missing classes. Some of my friends would tell me they saw him leaving school early, or once in a while, he would tell me he was sick and for me to leave without him in the morning. He would promise that he was coming in late, and then he'd never show up at all.

I tried to tell Momma what was going on, but she was real busy at work, and Jason always had an answer for her anyway. He was good like that; he always had it covered.

One of the worst things of all was how Jason started treating Simon and Samantha. First he just ignored them. He didn't feed them anymore or clean their litter boxes when it was his turn. He didn't play with them. He pretty much just pretended they didn't exist. That was bad enough, but then he got mean. He started pushing them away when they slinked over to him for attention. He tried to kick them when they got in his way. That kind of thing. I couldn't believe he could do those things, but he was like that pretty much every day.

Then, one day, I found out his secret. His dirty little secret.

I came home early from practice one Saturday afternoon and walked in on him in the bathroom by accident. The door wasn't locked, and I didn't even know anyone was home. Jason was bent over the sink, smok-ing a little glass pipe. His face was all red and sweaty and his eyes were wild and glassy. I knew what he was doing right away—smoking crack cocaine. I ran into the kitchen crying, and he followed me, the pipe still in his hand. I was hysterical, screaming and crying. Jason sat me down at the table and calmed me down, but first I made him put the pipe away; I couldn't even stand to look at it. We talked for almost two hours that night, and this is what he promised me:

He said it was only a phase he was going through. Kind of an experiment. Everyone was doing it at school, and he wanted to try it. But he knew it was stupid, and he'd already decided that it wasn't for him. Today was only the third or fourth time he'd tried it, he swore to me. So, no problem, he would stop. He didn't like the cocaine, and he certainly didn't need it. He would stop. It was as simple as that.

I wasn't sure if I should believe him or not, but he was so convincing. So much like the old Jason. God, it felt so good to see and hear him like that and to be able to talk to him again. He wasn't at all like the stranger I'd grown to know.

So by my bedtime that night, Jason agreed not to take drugs ever again. And I agreed not to tell Momma anything and to trust him. We were sister and brother again, and we watched television—Simon and Samantha on our laps—until Momma came home from work. I thought things were going to be better from that night on. This time it was my turn to be wrong.

Things were better for about a week.

But then came the next couple of months—Jason losing so much weight and quitting his summer-league basketball team; Momma complaining that money was missing from her purse and a necklace was gone from her top dresser drawer; Jason quitting his job at the video store. . . .

Call me stupid but I never thought it was the drugs. People got hooked on dope all the time—especially in my neighborhood—but not my brother. He was too smart for that, for goodness sake. I just thought Jason had changed. That happens lots of times, you know. Plenty of my friends were close to their sisters or brothers when they were younger and then as soon as they reached a certain age, they drifted apart. I just thought that's what was happening with Jason and me.

It all came to a head a few days after Jason's seventeenth birthday. I came home from school and found him sprawled on the kitchen floor. His face was a bloody, swollen mess, and his arm was bleeding. The kitchen table was overturned, and a chair was broken. Samantha was going crazy in the corner behind the trash can, meowing and whimpering louder than I had ever heard her.

Jason refused to go to the hospital, so I wet a washcloth and started cleaning his face. I kept asking him over and over again what had happened but all he would say was: "I'm sorry. I'm sorry. I'm so sorry. . . . "

I was just finishing with his arm when suddenly a sick feeling came over me and I asked him: "Where's Simon?"

He shook his head and started crying.

I felt the panic in my stomach. "Jason, what happened to Simon?"

"I'm sorry. . . ."

Louder this time. "Jason, where's Simon?"

And that's when he broke down and told me everything: about the drugs and the money he owed. About how they warned him this would happen. How they were waiting for him inside the apartment . . . and finally, about what they'd done to poor Simon, as his final warning to come up with the money or else.

My hands were shaking. I couldn't believe this was happening. Happening to us. Inside our own apartment. I picked up Samantha and walked into the living room. Sat on the sofa and cried for a long, long time. Poor Simon. God, I was going to miss him.

Before Momma came home, we cleaned up the mess and made up another story. I never asked exactly what happened to Simon; I was afraid to.

And, of course, Jason promised to stop again. He owed the men two hundred dollars. I loaned him all the money I had—just over forty—and he swore he would make good on his debt and never do drugs again. He swore he would borrow the money from his friends and get his job back at the video store and repay me. He promised me and I believed him. He was my best friend in the whole world.

Two weeks later, money wasn't a problem any more. But he wasn't working at the video store. Instead, he came home one evening, and I noticed the changes right away: a fancy gold watch on his right wrist, a thick bracelet on his left. A beeper clipped to his belt. A new jacket and boots. And a swagger to his walk that hadn't been there before. He walked up to me, pulled a wad of bills from his front pants pocket, and peeled off two twenty dollar bills and handed them to me. Walked into his bedroom without saying a word and closed the door.

I knew the truth then. He was never going to stop. Never. He was dealing now. Out on the street to pay off his habit. Using was bad enough, but dealing. . . .

For the next few days, I tried to think of how to tell Momma without breaking her heart. She was working so hard and was so proud of us, I couldn't bear the thought of telling her, of disappointing her. But she had to know.

That weekend, Jason brought home another cat for me. He had a gold-studded collar and a fancy gold tag that read *SIMON 2*. I kept the cat but threw away the collar and tag. I named him Jordan, and by Monday he and Samantha were old friends.

Jason had no problem flaunting his newfound wealth in front of me, but Momma was another story. If he knew she was going to be home, there was no jewelry, no flashy new clothes or pager on his belt. To Momma, he was still the old Jason, a little more distant maybe, a little more grown-up, but still her baby boy. He still came home every night, but he'd started sneaking out after Momma fell asleep.

One night, when I knew he was gone, I heard a story on the news about a drive-by shooting over on Madison, two blocks north from where we live. The man on the news said it was drug-related and three young men were killed. I cried myself to sleep that night with worry, and when I saw Jason the next morning in the parking lot in front of our apartment building, getting out of the passenger side of a shiny new Jeep Cherokee, I was relieved and furious at the same time.

I ran up to him and hugged him as the truck drove away.

"Oh my God, Jason," I cried. "I thought you were one of those men on the television, the ones that got killed—"

"Hey, hey, Little One. It's okay," he said, wrapping his arms around me. "It's okay. I ain't never gonna be the one, so you just stop your worrying."

I looked at him, at his glazed eyes, his crooked smile. He was high as a kite.

I hugged him as tight as I could, and he hugged me back. I kissed him on the cheek and said, "I love you, big brother," and I walked to school.

A couple days later, on a Sunday afternoon, it finally happened. Three policemen knocked on our door. They had their hands on their guns and a search warrant. There had been a middle-of-the-night robbery at Hardesty's Pharmacy, where Momma worked, and evidence at the scene pointed to Jason: a spare key, which was evidently used for entry, was found there, and the serial number was registered to Momma. And a wallet with Jason's identification was also found on the floor.

Although it was almost noon, Jason was still asleep when Momma let the officers into his bedroom. He was in handcuffs before he was fully awake. The policemen discovered five stolen watches and several baggies of cocaine underneath the mattress of his bed.

Jason never said a word when the officers walked him out of the apartment. Not to Momma, not to me, and not to the policemen.

3

Even Jason's voice sounded strange to me. The courtroom was so big and empty that it echoed off the walls. Or maybe it was the microphone, but he sounded like an old man, not my seventeen-year-old brother.

I listened to him talk:

"I didn't steal no watches."

"I wasn't in no fool store."

"No, sir, I don't know where they came from."

"No, Your Honor, I don't take drugs. Never have, never will."

I could tell he was trying to sound strong and smooth and in control—like the old Jason—but his voice reminded me of that afternoon when I found him beat-up and laying on the kitchen floor. Right before he'd started to cry and tell me how sorry he was.

I reached over and took Momma's hand. I gave it a little squeeze, and she did the same.

Twenty minutes later, with Jason sitting next to his lawyer, the judge pronounced Jason guilty and shook his head sadly as he handed down his sentence. "You leave me with no choice, young man. The evidence was found at the crime scene. You were caught with stolen property and crack cocaine in your bedroom. Yet you refuse to take any responsibility for the crime. I've taken into account the fact that you are a first-time offender, but . . ."

And then the judge sentenced Jason to a juvenile bootcamp upstate until his twenty-first birthday.

I heard Momma start to cry. I squeezed her hand again. I knew how hard this was for her.

"Removing you from this environment may be the best thing for you," the judge continued, and for the first time Jason met his eyes. "It's still not too late to turn your life around. There are people in this courtroom," he said, pointing to Momma and me, "who are counting on you. You've let them down. And now you have three and a half years to straighten yourself out and become the man you think you are."

And just like that, the judge banged his gavel and walked out of the room.

Suddenly the room was full of conversation and activity. The sound of shoes on the hardwood floor. Lawyers chattering away and shuffling papers. Briefcases being closed. Police officers huddled together talking. In a matter of minutes, Jason was headed for a side door, on his way out of the courtroom. He looked over his shoulder at us. There were tears on his face.

Momma stood on her tip-toes and waved and cried, "I love you, baby! I love you!"

And then he was gone.

We hugged right there in the courtroom. We hugged tight and for a long time, searching for hope in each other's arms. And then we headed home on the subway.

Three and a half years wasn't forever. And then we would be a family again. In the meantime, it was just Momma and me, and Samantha and Jordan. Just the four of us, waiting for Jason to come home again. Waiting for things to be the way they used to be.

All the way home, I thought about Jason. I thought about only the good times. Back when we were kids, playing those silly games and watching television for hours. Running around the apartment chasing Simon and Samantha. I thought about that smile of his and how he used to wink at me. How much he used to love me and Momma.

And I knew I had done the right thing. Stealing Momma's key from her purse and sneaking into the store that night. Taking those watches and hiding them under Jason's mattress. Leaving his wallet behind.

That night I fell asleep on the sofa with my head in Momma's lap, and I dreamed about my big brother coming home again.

For the Benefit of Bootsy

A John Francis Cuddy Short Story

Jeremiah Healy

"Let me get this straight," I said to the man sitting in the client chair on the other side of my desk. "You're being sued by a . . . cat?"

Oscar Mudge squirmed a bit, the reverse stenciling of "JOHN FRANCIS CUDDY, CONFIDENTIAL INVESTIGATIONS" on my office door arching over his head. "No, Mr. Cuddy. I've been served with process by Dana Jeffers, who is in charge of a trust for the benefit of . . . Bootsy."

"Which you told me is a cat, though."

Mudge squirmed a little more, now seriously stressing the old chair, since he went about two-fifty on maybe five-eight of height. Well past forty, Mudge wore a gray tweed suit that looked a good ten years out of style, even with my limited appreciation of fashion trends. His tie was regimental, the black, straight hair parted slightly to the right of center, which I'd bet would parallel the man's politics as well. Boston's weather can be raw in November, and Mudge kept leather driving gloves on his hands.

He said, "Perhaps I should explain a little further."

I leaned back in my swivel chair. "Perhaps you should."

Mudge squared himself, and wood squeaked against torqued screws and glue. "For years I represented Felix Felber. Does the name ring any bells?"

"Textile magnate. Got out of the mills before they went south, then moved to Brookline and began doling out his money to various charities." I tried for more, but all that came back was, "And he died recently, from a fall, right?"

Mudge pursed his lips. "Quite good, Mr. Cuddy. Felix passed from us a week ago, but he allegedly executed a codicil to his will a week before that. A codicil drawn up by the Jeffers woman."

Allegedly stuck in my ear. "So Ms. Jeffers is a lawyer?"

"Yes, though rather a young one. And the amendment she drew provides that the bulk of Felix's estate goes to one legatee."

Uh-oh. "Not . . . Bootsy?"

The current expression on Mudge's lips would curdle the cat's cream. "Absurd, isn't it?"

"And you think that therefore Mr. Felber might not actually have . . ."

"It would have been so out of character for him, it's beyond absurd."

I stared at Mudge for a moment. "I think you need a lawyer."

His eyes closed and opened once. "Mr. Cuddy, I *am* a lawyer."

"Oh."

"One who is being sued for alleged malfeasance in the prior management of Felix's investments."

"You were his investment advisor?"

"Investment *manager,* actually. I had handled things for him ever since he had suffered a partial stroke three years ago."

"What about the attorney who did the original will?"

"I handled that as well."

"But Mr. Felber didn't ask you to do the amendment."

"No. In fact, in his last weeks, he never even mentioned the possibility to me."

"Why do you suppose that was?"

"Because," said Mudge portentously, "I don't believe the codicil's valid."

"Now it sounds like you need a handwriting expert."

"No. No, it's Felix's signature, all right." Mudge wrung his gloved hands, the leather making almost as much noise as my poor chair. "I've seen it affixed to hundreds of documents. To be sure, though, I did run the codicil by an expert against the possibility of tracing, and so forth. The signature is definitely the handwriting—even the pressure of pen—that Felix would have applied since the stroke."

"And so your theory is . . . ?"

"Felix couldn't have known what he was signing."

"And you want me to substantiate that this codicil therefore is fraud-ulent?"

"Yes. Two individuals allegedly witnessed the execution, Jeffers her-self and the man who kept the grounds."

"Meaning the gardener?"

"Yes."

I reached for a pen of my own. "And his name?"

"Warren. Suh-*dell* Warren."

"Spelling?"

"S-e-d-e-l-l. One of their made-up names."

"Their?"

"Warren is a black, Mr. Cuddy. As is Dana Jeffers."

I put down my pen. "And because they're both of the same race, you automatically think they're in cahoots somehow?"

Mudge made the chair creak more than just squeak this time. "That, and the fact that Ms. Jeffers's mother, Lorraine, was Felix's housekeeper and cook."

"Lorraine Jeffers worked in the house, too, but didn't witness the signing of the codicil?"

"I imagine *law*-yer Jeffers didn't think *ma*-ma Jeffers would be suit-able for that task."

I was about to ask Mudge to take his business elsewhere when he said, "You see, Mr. Cuddy, Bootsy the feline—legatee to an estate of nearly seven million dollars—belongs to Jeffers Senior."

"Oh."

A smug smile. "So, you appreciate my predicament. I feel responsi-ble as Felix's long-term steward and confidante to prevent this prepos-terous fraud from being carried off, yet now that Jeffers Junior has sued me—*me*—for malfeasance, I must defend myself in the public's eye and in court against . . . against . . ."

"A cat."

Even the smug smile disappeared. "If you'll promise to stop repeat-ing that," said Oscar Mudge, "I'll increase your daily rate by 10 percent."

I knocked on the door to an office in one of the older buildings fronting Massachusetts Avenue near Beacon. The painting on the exterior needed a major overhaul, and neither the lobby nor the elevator had impressed, either. But when a female voice on the other side of the fourth-floor door told me to enter, I saw an interior painted a bright and pleasing yellow, with hanging spider plants and a vase of tulips centered on the desk. The only woman in sight was African-American, late twenties, with corn-rowed hair bunched behind her head with a scrunchy. The hair band picked up one of the minor colors in her print dress and matched the polish on her nails.

She smiled, one gold incisor among the otherwise gleaming white teeth. "Can I help you?"

"Dana Jeffers?"

"Yes?"

"My name's John Cuddy." I opened my identification holder so she could read the laminated copy of my license. "I'm here about the estate of Felix Felber."

Jeffers took her time reading, the greeting smile fading. Then she looked up. "Maybe you should have a seat."

Her client chairs were more modern than mine, with chrome struts supporting caned seats and backs. I took the one to her right as she sat down in a padded judge's chair.

Jeffers said, "You're working for Oscar Mudge, I imagine."

"That's right."

"And what did he tell you?"

"Client confidence, counselor."

"Let me guess, then." Jeffers smiled again, but more like a predator sensing prey. "I'm aiding and abetting my greedy mother, who somehow snowed the late Mr. Felber into moving his millions."

"Are you?"

A blink. "Am I what?"

"Aiding and abet—"

"Mr. Cuddy," said Jeffers, coming forward in her chair and planting her elbows on the desk as though she wanted to arm wrestle. "Oscar Mudge thought he ran that poor old man's life. And I guess in a lot of ways—on account of the stroke—somebody had to. But Felix's *quality* of life jumped off the scale thanks to my mother's cat. Apparently, when he was a young boy, he loved Felix the Cat cartoons because 'Felix' was his name, too. And, as an old man, he just took a shine to Bootsy, and Bootsy to him. I visited Mama often enough in that house, I should know."

"And on one of those visits, you witnessed Mr. Felber signing the codicil you drafted."

"Sedell Warren and me, both."

"And Mr. Felber knew what you'd put in front of him?"

Jeffers stiffened. "I had him read it out loud, then explain it in his own words. He even talked about the cartoon stuff. Then Felix signed, without any coercion and in his own house."

"Does your mother still live there?"

Jeffers seemed a little thrown by the change of pace, the braided hair shimmering behind her like a beaded curtain. "Until Mr. Mudge tries to kick her out. But he won't, because somebody's got to keep everything looking nice for the Realtor to sell it."

I processed that. "My client is still the executor of the estate?"

"Of course he is. I do mostly criminal stuff, including that DNA case you might have read about last week?"

The *Boston Herald* had done a piece on a defendant getting off because his lawyer—apparently Jeffers—had matched some hair found at the scene of a murder to a suspect the police had overlooked. "But you felt competent enough to do the codicil?"

"Simple paragraph incorporating a simple trust. In one sentence, Felix left most of his estate to Bootsy. The proceeds of the house'll still go to Mr. Mudge's charities."

"*His* charities?"

"He didn't tell you?" A triumphant smirk. "Well, then, let me. Mr. Mudge is the 'investment manager' for every one of the charities named in the will. Which is fine with me."

"I thought you were suing my client for malfeasance in handling Mr. Felber's money."

"Look, Mr. Cuddy," Jeffers angled back in her chair, "the original will was done before Felix suffered his stroke. If he wanted to leave Mudge in charge of the charity things, that's fine with me. I just need an accounting for the trust of what's supposed to be in the estate, and Mudge won't give it to me. What else could I do but sue him?"

"How much did your mother receive under the original will?"

"Felix had provided for Mama to the tune of two hundred and fifty thousand dollars."

Pretty nice melody. "So you're saying she wouldn't need the other seven million?"

"I'm the trustee for Bootsy, not my mother."

"And who inherits when the cat dies?"

Another predator smile, the gold tooth glinting. "Maybe you should ask whoever's trying to kill it."

"What?"

"Same night that Mr. Felber took his header down the stairs, some-body nearly clawed Bootsy to death."

"Clawed?"

Dana Jeffers extended the three middle fingers of her right hand, curving them so that the polished nails seemed to be talons. "With one of those three-tined things, like you use in the garden?"

Brookline is a lovely town that borders Boston on the west. Though it's been civilized since the seventeenth century, some of the settlers must have thought they'd reached the Rockies, because I've never seen any other relatively flat topography sporting so many switch-back roads.

The Felber place occupied a cul-de-sac at the end of one of the switchbacks, with probably a commanding view of the city from its third-story windows. There were white pillars, red bricks, and cement cornices over every window, to the point that you might have mistaken it for an Ivy League dormitory.

I left my old Prelude in the circular drive and pulled a fob on the massive, paneled front door. The woman who answered a minute later was black and stolid. She wore a polka-dot blouse, denim skirt, and run-ning shoes with white socks. Her hair was buzzed short, hoop earrings dangling from each lobe.

And she didn't look happy to see me.

"Mrs. Jeffers?"

"My daughter told me you'd be coming around."

"Did she tell you why?"

A scowl the older Jeffers might have learned from Oscar Mudge. "Said you thought we was stealing from Felix."

"That might be what my client thinks, but I'm trying to keep an open mind."

The scowl stood down a notch. "Suppose you'll be wanting to see things for yourself."

"That would help."

"Well," said Jeffers with a huff, "come on then."

I followed her through a high-ceilinged foyer that ended at two internal arches flanking a staircase to the second floor.

"These the stairs?"

"Where Felix fell down?"

"Yes."

"Uh-unh. The cellar ones."

"Cellar?"

"For his wines and such." Another huff. "I'll show you."

When we reached the kitchen, a cat was curled up on the sill of a small bay window, taking in the weak November sunlight. His head perked up, maybe at my unfamiliar step. He was all black, except for a white nose and four white paws and the three nasty scabs that ran longitudinally along his back where the fur had been shaved down to his skin.

I said, "Bootsy."

The cat rose to its feet and hissed at me.

Jeffers crossed the room to her pet. "Ain't nothing wrong with your instincts, Boots."

"I don't want to upset him any more, but I would like to get a look at his wounds."

She picked the cat up tenderly, then brought him over toward me, Bootsy growling all the way. "He don't like for you to touch him," she said.

I didn't, but Bootsy snaked a front paw at me anyway.

"You should teach him not to lead with his right," I said.

"Don't matter much. He don't have but two claws on his whole body."

"Two?"

"I got him as a stray. The people at the animal-shelter place didn't know how he got like that, except maybe somebody abused him. But he set you up with that little powder-puff right, then he cut you to the bone with the claws on his left."

I advanced my hand, Bootsy giving me the one-two and nearly grazing me with his dangerous paw, those remaining claws separated by a missing member. "You keep him indoors, then?"

"Try to. Once in a while, though, he escape, don't you, Boots?" The cat stopped growling at me and looked up at Jeffers. "Yes, that time the other cat got you, and you wouldn't come out even for food?"

I saw a door off the stove area. "That lead to the cellar?"

"Uh-huh." Jeffers put Bootsy back on the sill. "You can open it, you want."

The knob was old glass, and the steps below looked even older. Some were swayed in the middle, others listed a bit to port or starboard. No railing on either side.

I said, "Seems like it would have been kind of tricky for Mr. Felber to negotiate these."

A grunted laugh behind me. "Felix, he growed up in this house. Took those stairs two at a time till his stroke, when he got kind of frail and tentative." I went down tentatively myself. Ten degrees cooler, but what you really noticed was a stain on the cement floor at the bottom.

"That's poor Felix's head blood, where he landed. I tried to wash it out, but once blood comes, it want to stay, make you remember whose it was."

"What time did Mr. Felber fall?"

"Round ten at night, best as I can figure."

I moved toward the wine bottles stacked in columns of diamond-shaped boxes standing a foot from the cellar walls. "You didn't find him right away?"

"Not till the next day. Sedell and me went to the movies, and when we got back around ten-thirty, we was real quiet so's not to wake Felix. But come morning, I went to bring him breakfast, and his bed was empty."

Nice collection of wines, mostly reds and many of those Californian, with a sheet of stainless steel over the floor beneath them and some wooden blocks that matched the boxes to keep the lowest wines above any minor basement flooding. "Did it look like Mr. Felber had been sleeping in his bed?"

"That's what I mean about when he must've fell. Felix, he went upstairs to sleep every night at ten sharp to get his eight hours in. And I know he didn't fall after we got home, or one of us would've heard."

"Where were you and Mr. Warren?"

No hesitation before a firm, "I was in my room, and Sedell was in his."

"Were you present when Mr. Felber signed the codicil to his will?"

Jeffers hesitated a moment this time, then said, "I was there, alright, in the den. But Dana didn't want me signing, too. Just her and Sedell done it so everything be all legal."

I was about to ask for confirmation on Felix Felber reading and explaining the codicil aloud when I heard a rattling noise to my left. Turning, I was blinded by a blazing light that might have come from heaven itself.

"Sedell," said Lorraine Jeffers above me, "You close those doors before you let every bit of heat out of this house."

🐈 🐈 🐈

"I'm kind of dirty for sitting in the parlor."

Pointing to the left, I said, "That bench over there would be fine."

Sedell Warren led me toward a stone bench in the middle of a proud garden humbled by November's frosts. Reaching the bench, I saw a fat cherub carved in the middle of the top, seeming about to spit from its puffed cheeks.

"Puffed" didn't apply to Warren, though. Maybe six feet tall, he was so wiry that every bone his work clothes didn't hide seemed covered merely by skin and not by flesh as well. Pushing the bill of a stained John Deere ballcap off his forehead, Warren eyed me warily from sunken sockets. I said, "You know why I'm here?"

He nodded. "Lorraine's girl called her. I don't know one thing about what happened to Mr. Felber."

Both the Jeffers women had called him "Felix."

I said, "Actually, I'm more interested in what happened to Bootsy."

Warren frowned. "The kitty-cat?"

"Why would somebody attack him?"

A cracked and leathery hand rubbed a stubbly chin. "I know that's what Lorraine thinks, but could be he just run under one of my tools."

"You don't keep them hanging up?"

"I do, but Bootsy, he kind of a devil."

"How do you mean?"

Warren gestured with both hands. "He all the time getting into things, and whopping at them with his little feet, even though he don't have but the two claws left." Warren finished in a flourish of fists, like a boxer windmilling the speed bag. With authority.

I said, "You ever in the ring?"

A sheepish smile. "Some, back when I was a boy. Fight game ruint a lot of my friends. I got lucky, though. All's it did was knock some sense into me. I learned about flowers and plants." Warren sighed. "Mr. Felber, he just loved this garden to pieces."

"Back to Bootsy," I said, "you think he pulled one of your tools down on top of himself?"

"That's what I told Lorraine." Another sheepish smile. "Her and me, we been keeping company, if you get my drift?"

"That's what she told me, too."

"All right, then. When Lorraine and me come back from the picture show that night, I thought I heard something in my shed."

"Your shed?"

Warren waved his hand over beyond a clump of trees. "For Mr. Felber's garden. Well, I don't like for nobody to be messing around there, so I walked over before I went to bed. And one of my tools was off the hook."

"Off the . . . ?"

"Off the hook I hang it from. Was my 'claw-fork,' I call it. On the floor, and with blood dripping from the pointy parts. Must've been Lorraine's kitty-cat, whopping away with his paws till that claw-fork fell down and scratch him."

I thought about the wounds I'd seen on Bootsy's back. "Kind of deep and even scratches."

Sedell Warren gave me a wise smile this time. "Us peoples ain't ever gonna know all the things God's creatures can do."

I asked Warren if he'd walk me to the shed. Its door swung inward, so Bootsy could have pushed his way through. And the "claw-fork"—maybe twelve inches long including its wooden handle—was hanging low enough that the cat could have knocked it off. But the tool was also too low to build much momentum falling toward Bootsy, and I had trouble seeing how the wounded cat could have exited the shed without somebody holding the door.

Back in my office, I sat behind the desk and stared out my window at the Massachusetts statehouse across Boston Common. Most of the trees had dropped their leaves, and except for the capitol's gold dome, the scene looked as bleak as the Felber case felt.

Which is when it struck me that I thought of it as the "Felber" case instead of the "Mudge" case.

Opening a drawer, I pulled out some three-by-five notecards and started writing down the impressions I'd acquired. Oscar Mudge appearing so indignant in coming to see me; Dana Jeffers, the criminal specialist, seeming stubborn in her law office about the codicil and trust she'd drawn for Felber; Lorraine Jeffers projecting discomfort in speaking with me but defiance in defending her cat; Sedell Warren opining that Bootsy might have hurt himself on a gardening tool.

And then I tried to write down everything I'd learned about the late Felix Felber. His reliance on Mudge for investment management; his interest in the garden Warren maintained; his frailty from the stroke; his partiality to the housekeeper's cat.

Finally, I listed everything I'd learned about Bootsy himself, which made me think of a question I hadn't asked.

Picking up the phone, I dialed the Felber house. When Lorraine Jeffers answered, I said, "This is John Cuddy again."

"What you want now?"

"When I was over there today, you told me that Bootsy had once been in a fight with another cat?"

A pause before, "That's right."

"And you also said something like 'He didn't come out for days.'"

"Boots be licking his wounds, account of that other—"

"Mrs. Jeffers?"

Another pause. "Yeah?"

"Where was Bootsy hiding?"

"What in the world?"

Oscar Mudge stared at the two of us as I closed his office door behind Dana Jeffers. He struggled to rise from the other side of a large, mahogany desk, but I don't think his effort grew out of courtesy for us as visitors.

I said, "I think you ought to sit down, Mr. Mudge."

"How dare—"

"Maybe lie down," said Jeffers as she took a red-leather, brass-tacked armchair herself, the corn-rowed pony-tail flogging the back of it.

I settled on her seat's mate as my "client" plopped back into his, Mudge's left hand reaching for the telephone. "I'm calling the police."

I gave him my most ingratiating grin. "I have the direct number for the Homicide Unit, you want to save everybody some time."

Mudge froze with the receiver halfway to his face. "The Homicide . . . ?"

Jeffers nodded. "Or you can talk to us."

The phone was still hovering when I said, "We've figured it out, Mr. Mudge."

Very deliberately, he put the receiver back in its cradle, then folded his left hand over his right and across the broad stomach. "Cuddy, you're supposed to be representing *my* interests."

"As I recall, you asked me to find out if Felix Felber knew that he was signing a significant amendment to his will. He did, but then, you were already aware of that."

"I was?"

Jeffers said, "Felix told you."

Mudge looked at her. "What a preposterous—"

"He told you," I broke in, "and you immediately went to 'visit' him."

"Only you stopped by Sedell Warren's shed first," said Jeffers.

I nodded. "To pick up a little 'friendly persuasion,' in the form of a claw-fork."

Mudge's cheeks burned. "This is ridicu—"

"Problem was," I added, "for all his frailty, Mr. Felber wasn't about to die without a fight. Or at least without running.

"Toward the cellar," said Jeffers. "Where he figured you wouldn't dare try to follow him, what with those bad stairs and your . . . body type."

"I want you to leave now. In fact, I *order* both of—"

"Except that you got to him at the door from the kitchen, and gave him a shove, so you didn't need to use the garden tool after all."

"At least," Jeffers interjected, "not on Felix."

Mudge began to seethe. "Now look here, you little—"

I said, "But you hadn't counted on the cat."

He turned to me. "What?"

"Bootsy. He'd taken a real liking to Mr. Felber, and when you chased after the old guy with that claw-fork, the cat pitched in to help him. And Bootsy got you with his two remaining claws."

"Nonsense."

I said, "When you came to see me, you were still wearing driving gloves. I chalked it up to the weather at the time, but I notice you're not wearing them now."

Mudge seemed to steel himself so his eyes wouldn't wander downward. "What I wear, and where I—"

Dana Jeffers said, "We also found your blood."

He turned to her, baffled. "My . . . ?"

"Blood." She waved her hand, the gold tooth peeking out from between her lips. "Just a little, of course, but it was right where my mother told Mr. Cuddy it would be."

"You're both . . . insane."

I said, "Bootsy has a favorite hiding place after battle, Mr. Mudge. Under one of the wine racks in Mr. Felber's basement. On top of a stainless steel sheet beneath it."

Jeffers's turn to nod. "We found a paw print of your blood from where Bootsy scratched you. That stainless steel and cool temperature preserved enough of it for the DNA analysis."

Mudge's voice quavered as he repeated, "DNA?"

"Yes," I said. "They can do wonders now, Counselor. And it'll take just a tape measure to show the scratches on your right hand are exactly the same distance apart as Bootsy's own rather distinctive claw pattern."

Mudge's face fell, and he actually raised his right hand to his eyes, seeming to study the back of it.

Jeffers lowered her voice an octave. "You found out about the codicil, and you couldn't risk an independent investigation into your handling of Mr. Felber's money."

"No," said Mudge, still studying his hand. "No, I couldn't."

I spoke quietly now. "I've checked the records on your 'charities' filed at the state offices. You control all of them."

"And steal from each of them," said Jeffers.

"Felix . . ." Mudge cleared his throat, starting again. "Felix had always trusted me, and it was only just a little . . . dipping at the beginning, just enough to carry me through a lean month here and there. But the lean months started mounting up, so I couldn't get even with the board. And then came the stupid codicil Felix felt he **had** to let me know about. Which would have . . . which did provoke. . . ."

". . . you to kill him," I said. "And to hire me to try and bluff Ms. Jeffers off."

"I didn't know what else to do! Until Felix's house sold and I could get at the proceeds, I barely had enough money to pay for a private investigator, much less the retainer any substantial law firm would require to litigate the malfeasance case. And another killing would have looked so . . . strange."

"Even the cat's?"

"I meant that stupid creature no harm! He was the one who attacked **me,** and I simply lashed out with the claw-fork."

"In self-defense," I said.

"Yes."

Dana Jeffers smiled grimly. "Jury's gonna love that."

"You don't understand." Oscar Mudge looked from her to me before trying to take in both of us at once. "If it weren't for that accursed feline, I'd have been set for the rest of my days."

I said, "And thanks to that 'accursed feline,' you still will be."

Dana Jeffers stood. "At least, that's how my clients doing life look at it."

The End

In the Lowlands

Gary A. Braunbeck

Do you know how a hobo feels?
Life is a series of dirty deals
Except for a kind word, a cup of coffee
And the song of the wheels . . .

—*Anonymous message scrawled on boxcar wall, Kansas City, 1934*

There's an old superstition among hoboes—especially those whose camps are made near the switch yards—that a 'Bo's death is mourned by the whistles of two passing trains; the sounds meet overhead in the night and, though each might be a bit mournful when heard by itself, they combine to create a pleasant song of welcome for the 'Bo's soul as he takes himself that last, great freight to Heaven.

When you hear that sound, you're supposed to remove your hat (if you wear one), close your eyes, and wish that fellow's soul good travel to the Pearly Gates, then say a little prayer that the body he left behind finds its way to the Lowlands—that is, that some good soul will see fit to give it a proper burial and not just leave it where the fellow shuffled off the ole mortal coil.

A second blast of the dual train whistles serves as a message to let you know that his soul found its way home and his remains have been properly sent to the Lowlands. That's about the best a 'Bo can hope for when he leaves this world.

Fry Pan Jack told me about that legend right before the TB finally overpowered his body and he passed on, leaving his cat, Billy, in my care. I heard the trains cry for him that night. And I put his remains in the Lowlands myself, reading a passage from Jack's Bible after I finished tamping down the soil.

Now I've got to stand trial for my life before a jury of my peers.

All of this in the same week.

It happened like this:

It was as good a jungle as a 'Bo could hope for in that spring of 1933: On the sunny side of the hills, within walking distance of a fairly clean creek, and not too far from a couple of switchyards and coal bunkers; a thick patch of trees offered shelter from the chilly night winds, and the town dump was within spitting distance and ready for scavenging. Add to that the friendly atmosphere that greeted a fellow upon his arrival— sometimes just getting past the railroad bulls was cause for major celebration on the parts of all residents—and, well, you'd be crazy to think you could do better.

Billy and I had decked a rattler—that is to say, rode spread-eagle atop a passenger train—for about the last half-hour before we jumped. (I did the actual jumping; Billy just sort of curled himself up into a ball inside my pack and hung on for dear life.) My landing was nothing to write home about—in fact, I thought I might've twisted my ankle (not the case, I'm pleased to tell you)—but luckily we were far enough away from any yards or stations that I didn't have to worry about any bulls seeing me.

Not that I've got anything against railroad police, understand. Most of them are fairly good sorts, but there's always a couple wherever you go who make sport of cracking open a 'Bo's skull. Seems those types can't tell the difference between a bum and a hobo—and believe you me, there's a difference. As Jack used to say: "Bums loaf and sit; tramps loaf and walk; but a 'Bo moves and works and he's clean."

Even on the road there's a hierarchy—and I learned myself that word from a dictionary Jack gave to me. "Nothin'll catch folks off-guard quicker than a 'Bo with a good vocabulary, son; shows 'em you got brains, and folks're more likely to give a decent meal to a man with some brains who's willing to work than a moron."

Add to that formula a hungry pet—like a cute cat—and you're hardly ever turned away.

I suppose that's one of the reasons Billy and me found ourselves so welcome at this particular jungle that evening.

There were a couple of fellows standing watch over a pot of Mulligan stew in the center of the camp; they were the first to spot me. They'd been talking up 'til then, but once they got sight of me their conversing stopped and they just stared at me.

One by one, the other men in the camp took notice of their silence and had to have themselves a look at what was going on.

Every man there was staring at me as I walked toward the fire and the pot.

"Evenin'," I said, tipping my hat.

"Where you coming from, stranger?" asked one of the Mulligan Stew Boys.

"Michigan way. Found a couple days' work helping to unload coal at the River Rouge auto plant."

"Was they still needin' workers when you left?"

"That they were."

He considered this for a moment.

I knew what was going through their minds: *Is he on the level or is he a damned yegg?*

A *yegg* was any one of a number of disreputable fellows who posed as a 'Bo but didn't want to be bothered with actually *earning* his keep, and so made his way by robbing an honest traveling laborer. A yegg wouldn't think twice about beating up or even killing a 'Bo for whatever the man had on him.

I set down my pack and untied it—not enough that Billy could stick his head out and attract even more attention—but enough so that I could reach inside and remove a potato and an onion, which I offered to the Mulligan Brothers. They were more than happy to take it.

You never, ever walk into a 'Bo camp and not offer something to go with the evening's meal if you can help it. That's part of the code. Not that they'd let you go hungry—if there's a meal being cooked up in a camp, then that meal is for everyone there and anyone who might happen by. Just because there's a code, that in no way means that fellow 'Bos would let a man starve.

The camp warmed up to me fairly quickly after that, and when I later pulled out some recent newspapers and detective magazines that I'd managed to pick up along the way, well, you'd have thought I was one of the Permanents there. The three things you can have in your pack that will

always make you welcome in any camp are coffee (or tobacco), food, and
something for the fellows to read. Life on the road is lonely—that's a
given—but it can also be boring as hell, and a recent newspaper or a story
magazine can offer a man something to occupy his mind with besides the
worry of where his next job and meal might be coming from.

It was only when we were sitting down to dinner that Billy woke up
and started raising a ruckus inside my pack. I reached in and pulled him
out, and from the way the rest of the camp reacted, you'd have thought
I'd produced a wad of greenbacks.

"Well, damn my eyes," said the bigger of the two Mulligan Brothers—
who went by the name of Cracker-Barrel Pete (you never use your real
name in a camp and never ask a man for his)—"Why didn't you tell us
you had yourself a little fur-ball with you?"

"He was sleeping when I got here, and he doesn't take kindly to being
woke up from his beauty rest." The fellows laughed at this.

"You know, don't you," said Pete, "that there's a couple restaurants in
town that'd be happy to give a day-old fish to a cat like your, uh—he got
a name, your cat?"

"Billy."

Pete nodded. "Yessir. Never fails to amaze me, human nature, that is:
Folks who wouldn't give you a slice of moldy bread would hand over
something small and fresh for a hungry cat."

I knew that to be true enough. Many was the time when Jack and I
almost met with the business end of a proprietor's shotgun until they
caught sight of Billy; then we almost always left with a tin of sardines or
tuna. A can of tuna, mixed with some crushed cracker, sometimes lasted
the three of us a couple of days.

Pete's words did not go unheard by the others.

"Say," he said, leaning over and refilling my coffee tin, "think you and
Billy there might be up for a little excursion in the morning? Might find
yourself a decent day's work, plus old Billy there might snag us some special goodies for tomorrow's dinner."

"Don't see why not," I said, letting Billy get comfortable in my lap. I
picked a small square of potato from my stew and fed it to him. Billy liked
potatoes—onions, too, which often made his breath a holy terror. "Folks
seem to take a quick shine to him."

"Then it's settled," Pete said just loud enough that the others would
know I was more than willing to do my share. "First thing tomorrow,
we'll go into town with Billy and hit the bakery there, see if we can't

get ourselves some day-old bread or pastries—he like pastries, does he?"

"Billy's a pastry fool."

Pete laughed. "Ain't that something? A cat that likes pastry!"

We all had ourselves a good laugh then at Billy's expense, but he didn't seem to mind; an animal of sweeter nature you'd be hard-pressed to find.

I couldn't help noticing, though, that the other Mulligan Brother—a thin reed of a fellow calling himself Icehouse Willie—wasn't laughing like the rest of us; oh, sure, he was chuckling away so's to fit in, but I caught something in his eyes as he looked at Billy that didn't sit right with me.

Maybe I'm just tired, I thought, and would not allow myself to think unkindly of anyone in the camp that night.

I read a few news articles to some of the men who couldn't read themselves, then we passed another hour or so passing around one of the detective magazines, taking turns reading serial chapters (and a juicy one this yarn was, too!), then, long about ten, with the stars above us in abundance, we found our spots for the night and got as comfortable as the ground would allow.

Just before I dozed off, with Billy's terrible breath on my cheek on account he'd decided to sleep on my arm, I heard a train whistle in the distance, echoing low and lonely, and I closed my eyes, wishing Jack a good night, as well.

As if to echo my sentiments in his own unique way, Billy sneezed in my ear, yawned, then dug in his claws and conked out.

Long about three in the morning (I checked the position of the stars, something Jack had taught me to do, in order to guess about the time) I woke up and pulled Billy off my arm, sitting him down next to me. He gave a grumpy, sleepy-faced look—*You'd better have a damned good reason for this*—then sat back on his hind legs and stared.

"Shh," I whispered so as not to awaken anyone nearby. "Just . . . just stay right there."

I reached into the bottom of my pack (which I'd been using as my pillow) and pulled out a small piece of smoked salmon wrapped in tinfoil—a little treat I'd bought for Billy with some of my Michigan wages at a Japanese place in Cedar Hill, Ohio, the day before. I would've offered it to put in with the stew, but Billy had been a little out of sorts lately—Jack having only left us a week ago—and I figured the fellow would enjoy a little late-night treat.

That's when I heard the cry.

It wasn't so much a scream—it had been strangled in the throat before it could get to that point—but there was enough panic and underlying misery in the sound to let me know that whoever had made it was either being killed or in the middle of a right terrible dream.

I took a quick look round the camp and saw Pete a few yards away with the other Mulligan Brother, Icehouse Willie, the one who'd been looking at me and Billy so strangely. Pete had Willie's head pressed against his chest and was covering Willie's mouth with one of his hands. Willie was crying fiercely, deep, body-wracking sobs, his eyes closed tight, his face getting redder and redder, and as I gently put Billy down and started over to see if there was anything I could do to help, I saw that Pete was rocking his buddy back and forth like he would a baby and all the time whispering, "It's okay, Willie, there you go, there you go, no fires, okay? It's a nice, cool night, and you're out here in the open with me and you're okay, shhh, there you go, it's okay. . . ."

It took a few more minutes of this before the other man finally fell back to sleep.

I hoped for his sake that it was a peaceful slumber.

Another quick look-round showed me that the man's cries had awakened a few of the residents, but they acted as if they were used to it and simply rolled over and went back to sleep.

Pete came over to me, shaking his head. "Sorry about that. Guess we should've told you about Willie."

He gestured toward the far end of the camp and we set off walking. When we were almost to the edge of the camp he stopped for a moment, a sad look crossing briefly over his face. "I don't mean to sound cold-hearted, but Willie, he's . . . he's not quite right in the head, understand? Lost his wife, Carol, and his little girl, Sandy, to a boxcar fire about a year ago when they were riding to Chicago. I was riding that same train, only I was in a different car. Terrible thing. He tried to get to them, but they were in a hay car on account the train was hauling a lot of cattle, and the flames . . . well, you get the idea."

"Yeah . . ." I whispered.

"Sometimes he talks about 'em like they're still alive." He reached up and squeezed the bridge of his nose. "Damnedest thing, though. The folks who were ridin' in that car . . . well, shit, you just *know* better than to light any kind of match in a hay car. I mean, light's a bad idea in the first place on account it can tip off the bulls, but in a *hay car!*" He shook his head. "We had just pulled out from a stopover when the fire broke out, understand? And most of the people in that car had been asleep. Willie and his family, they were sitting way in the back of the car so's they'd face everyone."

"Best way to protect a family, under the circumstances."

"That may well be, but I heard later from a couple of the folks who got out that a bull set that fire—just came running up alongside and tossed in a match. Someone hadn't closed the door all the way." He shrugged. "It happens. Them cars, they can get damned stuffy." He looked back to where Willie was sleeping quietly, then looked at me and lowered his voice. "Just between you and me, though, I always thought Willie must've gotten a look at the bull who done it, and maybe part of what makes him . . . not quite right anymore is that there just ain't enough room in him for both his grief and his wanting to get revenge on the sumbitch what set that fire."

By now we'd started walking back into camp. I looked at Pete and grinned. "It's really decent of you . . . I mean, taking him on like you have."

Pete grinned back. "That obvious, is it?" A shrug. "What the hell else was a God-fearing man supposed to do? Couldn't very well leave him to his own devices, not in the shape he's in. Yeggs'd make a meal of him and not even leave bones for the dogs. And lately—hell, ever since we came to this camp three, four weeks ago—he's been gettin' a lot worse. Not just the dreams, those're bad as ever, but he's . . . he's acting less and less . . . uh . . . ."

". . . rational?"

"Yeah, that's the word. He's been actin' less rational when he's awake. Scares me, y'know? Man's been a good traveling companion, and I think of him as a friend, but if he gets to the point where I can't handle him no more. . . ." He let the words and thought trail off. He knew I didn't need to hear him complete that sentence.

"How'd he come to be called 'Icehouse' Willie?"

Pete told me, and his answer damn near broke my heart.

I stopped by my sleeping spot where Billy was still sitting impatiently, waiting for his late-night treat.

"Cute little bugger, ain't he?" said Pete.

"Not so loud. He's full enough of himself as it is."

Pete smiled, reached down, and petted Billy's head, then gave me a tip of his hat and went back to his spot beside Icehouse Willie.

I laid back down and got as comfortable as I could, then peeled away the foil wrapping Billy's treat and placed the chunk of salmon in front of him. "There you go, pal, enjoy yourself."

Billy sniffed at it, decided it was to his liking (why he always made a show of deciding whether he wanted to eat something I could never figure out), then dug in, savoring every bite.

I had to admit it looked sort of tasty and made my mouth water slightly—and it wasn't as if I'd never shared Billy's meals before—but I figured he deserved this special treat all to himself.

I stroked the fur on top of his head. "You're a good traveling companion, Billy."

He sniffed once in mid-chew as if to say, *Yeah, yeah, yeah, I'm a prince and so're you, now can I please get back to the business at hand?*

I laughed under my breath, then rolled over and fell back asleep.

The last thing I remember thinking was how I hoped that Willie could sleep the rest of the night without hearing the cries of his wife and daughter.

Damnedest thing, really, the trouble that little secret snack of Billy's caused later.

🐈 🐈 🐈

Jack was an old-timer on the road (he admitted to being "in spitting distance of seventy, but I ain't gonna tell you in what direction"), and many was the night he'd regale me with tales of his adventures on the road before I hooked up with him.

One of his favorite memories was of a house in Portage, Wisconsin, he'd spent time at a few years back.

"The mother there, her husband had died a year or so before, and what with a family to care for, she had to find a way to make herself a respectable living. She took in washing, cooked meals for others, and baked up something like forty or fifty pies a day for a little restaurant called the Pig-n-Whistle. All that pie-cooking, it took a powerful lot of stove wood.

"Now, her children couldn't keep up—poor woman had to have at least five long rows of stacked wood that needed to be split—so she was more than happy to offer a 'Bo a job splitting the logs. You could earn yourself a fine, fine meal splitting wood for her. The jungle we lived in was just a few hundred yards from her back yard, on the other side of the rail yard in a grove of trees by Mud Lake. 'Bos tended to hang around that jungle for a good long while, not just because of the work and meals this lady'd provide us with, but because if it was your birthday and her kids got wind of it, she'd bake up a little cake and send it over, and her kids . . . well, they always managed to come up with some sort of present for you, a magazine or book or old toy. Yessir, it was a good place. Many's the night, after the wood had been split and the pies baked and the evening meal served, she'd invite any 'Bo who wanted to come over and sit on her porch and listen to the radio. She always served something to drink on those nights. I remember her lemonade best, on summer evenings with the radio playing and the train whistles calling in the distance.

"Yessir, that's my idea of Heaven. In fact, that's where I first found old Billy here. He was one of a litter of kittens that someone tossed in the river one night, all tied up in a bag. If me and this other fellah—can't recall his name now—but if we hadn't been where we was and seen this happen, all them kittens would've drowned. Terrible thing, the way people treat their pets."

"What about the way they treat each other?"

He looked at me and shook his head, grinning. "You expect too much of others, son. Take my advice: If you expect no kindness, then you won't be disappointed when none is given; but, Lord, are you all the more grateful for it when it is!"

I was awakened from my pleasant dream of Jack and the Pie Lady when someone slammed a steel-toed boot into my hip. I came awake with a shout, grabbing my pack and spinning around on the ground, ready to swing at whoever'd done that to me, when I found myself staring up at one of the most unpleasant-looking bulls I'd ever seen. He stood there, big as life and three times as ugly, holding his club in his hands and looking all-too-ready to open up my skull.

And if he wasn't up to messing up his uniform with my brains, one look at the younger fellow with him told me *he* was ready.

A little too ready, from the glint in his eyes.

The big bull stared down at me. "Understand you came in here around six, six-thirty last night, that right?"

"Yessir," I said, looking around for Pete and the others. They were gathered together near the cooking area, trying not to be too obvious about looking at me.

I looked around quickly myself, wondering where Billy had wandered off to.

"Look, officer," I said, "I don't want any trouble. If you'd be so good as to tell me what this is all about—"

He snapped the business end of his club forward and thrust it into my chest. I took this as a request to shut up and listen.

"There's been rumors about a yegg moving through these parts," the bull said to me. "Don't get me wrong, boy: I got nothing against the likes of 'Bos, but last night—early this morning, actually, around four-thirty, five—someone from this camp broke into a couple of stores and stole themselves a bunch of food, liquor, and a little bit of money."

He squatted down to get his face close to mine, still keeping the club in my chest. "Reason I know they were from this camp is because it wasn't enough for them to be happy with the stores. No, they had to go and break into some folks' *homes*." He made a quick sideways gesture with his head. "Pete over there told me you're the only new fellah what's come around here lately. Sorry to say, but that makes you—"

"—your best suspect, yessir."

He studied me for a moment. "The only reason I don't have the sheriff out here with me is because, one, I didn't think you'd be stupid enough to come back here and, two, I think it would sit better with the folks who were robbed if I could go back and tell them that the 'Bos took care of the problem in their own manner . . . if you read my meaning."

And I did, all too clearly.

You live in a camp, you don't rob from another hobo. You live in a camp, thievery of any kind was to be avoided outside the camp as well—or at least kept to a minimum: a pie lifted from its cooling spot in an open bakery window every now and then, some vegetables hurriedly snatched from a garden, or an old shirt clipped from an outside line, that was acceptable if the circumstances warranted thieving, but if it could be avoided, you did so. Townspeople were your only source of jobs and handouts, and you did not—repeat, *did not*—do anything to anger them. One dirty yegg could muck it up for everyone in the camp, and a good camp near a good town—especially one where the bulls didn't run you off on a regular basis, as this one seemed to be—well, that was to be respected in the same way people respect the church they go into every Sunday.

The bull looked at his partner and said, "Watch him while I search his pack, Carl."

Carl's idea of watching me was planting one of his feet right into my chest and pressing down. Hard.

"*Carl,*" said the other bull. "What'd I tell you about that?"

"Bastard broke into *my house,* McGregor."

"I know that your place was one that he hit, but until we find something of yours or one of the other folks'—" He stopped, then looked down as he pulled a half-empty bottle of whiskey from my pack. He followed that with some bread, cheese, and a couple emptied cans of salmon.

None of which had been in my pack the night before.

"Looks like we got our man, Carl." Then McGregor pulled out an envelope with some writing on it. He read it, looked at me, then his partner, and handed the envelope to Carl.

"What's this?" asked his partner.

"You tell me. It's got your name on it."

Carl glared at me—now I was sure there was a craziness barely hiding behind his eyes—and snatched the envelope from McGregor, tore it open, and removed the letter inside.

He tried to control it, that I could see, but whatever was written on that page rattled him something fierce.

"Well?" said McGregor.

"Huh? Oh—it's, uh . . . it's just a letter I got from, uh . . . my grand-dad." He folded the paper up in a hurry and stuffed it into his pocket. "You piece of—" he said to me, pulling back his foot to kick me.

"Carl!" snapped McGregor. "This ain't that Illinois rat-trap you moved here from. We don't strike a man without bein' provoked."

"I can't help it! It's bad enough to break into a man's house and steal his food and whiskey, but what the hell kind of yegg steals a man's personal *mail?*"

"The kind we just caught."

McGregor stood up and gestured that I should do the same. As soon as I was on my feet Carl spun me around slapped handcuffs on me—none too gently, I might add—then marched me into the center of the camp and sat me down on an old tree stump.

"One way or another," Carl snarled in my ear just low enough so only I could hear him. "One way or another you're going to the Lowlands."

My mouth went dry. The violence in his voice was like nothing I'd ever heard before, and there was no doubt in my mind that Carl wanted to kill me with his own bare hands . . . and whatever was in that letter was the reason.

"Okay, fellahs," said McGregor loudly enough to get the camp's attention. "My shift ends at five. I got three other guys from the yard who're willing to sit on the jury. I'll stand in as bailiff. You got until then to pick out the other nine jurors."

Pete stepped up and said, "You be the one who calls Judge Carson?"

"I'll take care of it—and I'll make damned sure the people in town know that you fellahs are gonna take care of this problem. I'll offer apologies, if it's all the same."

Pete nodded. "And if it's all the same to you, McGregor, I'll be defending our friend here."

"Ain't no friend of mine." He turned to me real quick and said, "Nothing personal. If you're innocent, I'll apologize to you. Until then, you're as good as a crook in my eyes." He grabbed up a small coil of rope someone had scavenged from the dump and ordered a couple of men nearby to tie my legs and ankles to the stump.

"Be seeing y'all this evening," he said, tapping the end of his club against the brim of his hat.

Carl walked by me real slow.

Real slow.

Not blinking.

One way or another . . .

Everyone in camp watched the two bulls make their way over the hill and back toward the rail yard. Then Pete put a hand on my shoulder and said, "You know what the penalty is for that kind of thieving, don't you?"

I nodded my head.

If found guilty, they were bound by the code to either kill me or exile me.

You exile a 'Bo by marking his face; that way, he'll not find himself welcomed in any camp he comes across thereafter.

I have seen such marked men in my travels. Burned faces, faces missing an eye, an ear, a nose . . . a simple scar would be treasured as a symbol of mercy. But mercy was something you rarely found under these circumstances. Not only was a marked 'Bo not welcomed in a camp, damn few people will give him work or a handout.

Death or marked exile; wasn't much of a choice, when you got right down to it.

The rules of the road can be brutal when a bad element threatens to ruin it for the innocent.

I looked up at Pete. "You seen Billy?"

"No, I ain't. And that's how come McGregor went right for you."

"Beg pardon?"

"Whoever broke into them places had a cat with him. A couple of witnesses saw it. Guess the guy stole a fish or two from one of the markets to feed it."

"Oh, brother. . . . There were a couple of empty cans of salmon in my pack."

"Not yours, I take it?"

"No."

"Now let me ask you something."

"Anything."

"Am I the only one who's noticed that Willie is conspicuously absent this morning?"

I looked at his face and knew there was no need for me to answer.

🐈 🐈 🐈

The trial got under way a little after four P.M.

It didn't help my chances much that Eastbound Earl, the prosecutor, dumped the contents of my pack onto the ground to reveal the evidence that McGregor and Carl had found there.

It also didn't help much that Billy finally put in an appearance a few minutes before the trial started, his breath stinking of fish. He bounded right up to me and jumped into my lap, rubbing himself against my coat.

"I have to say in all fairness," whispered Pete, "that this does not bode well for your, uh . . . your—"

"Acquittal?"

"I was going to say something a little more colorful—mentioning a particular point on your anatomy—but 'acquittal' will do. Look, we both know full well that Willie's the one who snatched Billy up and took him into town when he did all that stealing. I *told* you he ain't been actin' like himself since we got here. Probably figured things would go just like they have up to this point. Hell, wouldn't surprise me one bit if he actually made an effort to be seen."

"He knew that any witness would remember the cat more than his face?"

Pete nodded. "If there was even enough light for them to see his face."

"Yeah," I whispered.

"Don't get me wrong. He's the one who did this, but the rules don't allow for his, uh, condition to be taken into account. Thief's a thief, and that's all there is to it."

We both searched the crowd of faces until we found Willie, standing way in the back of the spectators and looking for all the world like a man who was walking in his sleep.

"We'll hear the defense's arguments now," said Judge Carson, a hard-looking older gentleman whose voice sounded like he gargled with moonshine three times a day. Pete told me that Carson had ridden the rails once himself and had been treated well by the hoboes he encountered and so always oversaw these trials. "He's as fair as you're going to find."

"*Pete,*" said McGregor, our bailiff.

Carl stood off to the side, trying to look like he didn't want to slit my throat.

"If it please the court," said Pete, standing just a bit taller than usual, "I would like to call Mr. Icehouse Willie to the stand."

There was a murmur among the spectators, and when Willie didn't come forward right away, McGregor, our inspiring bailiff, said, "All right, Willie, let's . . ."

And that's when Pete pulled me to my feet and led me up to the witness chair.

McGregor stopped and stared but said nothing.

He knew damned well—as did every other resident of the camp—that I was not Willie, but no one said a thing.

"What the hell're you doing?" I whispered.

"You remember our talk last night?"

"Yeah . . . ?"

"Just try and follow my lead. And remember that Willie stammers."

I glanced in Willie's direction; he gave me a nervous, almost apologetic look as Pete started in on his questioning.

"Okay, Willie, why don't you tell us why you—"

"Thief!" someone shouted.

The camp crowd reacted with appropriate shock.

Judge Carson banged his gavel, calling for order.

"Would you please tell us," said Pete, "why it is you're called 'Icehouse' Willie?"

I was never much for play-acting, but I gave it my best try; can't rightly say why, but I trusted Pete. "Ah, hell, Pete . . . what's that got to do with—?"

"Answer the question, please," said Judge Carson.

"Pete here, he g-gave me that name."

Judge Carson stared at me, then at Pete. "I'm gonna assume here that this has some kind of bearing on the case?"

"It does, Yeronner; it might not seem, ah . . . uh . . ."

"Evident," I whispered from the side of my mouth.

"Evident right away," said Pete, "but it will come to bear on things."

Carson sighed and nodded his head. "Just don't go off on any tangents, understand? My daughter's bringing my new granddaughter over for supper tonight, and I'll be damned if I'm gonna miss seeing them."

"Understood, Yeronner." Pete turned his attention back to me, but not before making a quick gesture with his head and eyes that told me I should look over at Carl.

I did so, and saw a 'Bo offering the bull a bottle of beer. Carl accepted—not gratefully, big surprise—and had a little trouble getting the top off. While he struggled with the bottle opener, the 'Bo who'd given him the beer brushed back behind him—

—and slipped something from his pocket.

I looked at Pete to let him know I'd seen it. I'd told him about the letter earlier that day. Evidently he'd taken it upon himself to obtain the thing without Carl's cooperation, Carl being so warm-hearted toward hoboes as he was. It probably would have seemed like taking advantage of the man's good nature to ask him for it.

I went on, remembering as best I could what Pete had told me of Willie's story last night. ". . . and after the fire, the bulls put all the bodies in this here icehouse near the yard. I . . . I, uh . . . I w-w-went in there to find my Carol and Sandy, and after I f-found 'em I wanted to sit with 'em awhile, y'know? Sandy, she don't like to be left alone when she's sleeping, and Carol, sh-she'd give me h-h-holy h-hell if I went off while they was resting." I made up this last part, which might have been stupid, but by this time I found I was enjoying playing this part—so much so that I felt a tear slip down my cheek. It wasn't hard to muster tears at the thought of how terrible Carol's and Sandy's last moments had been. Then I simply sat there, staring at the ground and shaking.

"Go on," said Pete, softly.

"Then you come in there after a bit and made me leave before I f-froze to death." Then I remembered something Pete had told me Willie once said: "Sometimes I wish I had. Least then we'd all still be together."

Judge Carson slammed his gavel against the wood tabletop that served as his bench. Someone had scavenged the table from the dump earlier; it smelled of old and rancid food and decay and probably accounted for the pained expression the Judge's face had been sporting since things got under way.

"All right, Pete, that's enough," said the Judge. "Whether or not this has any bearing on your case, I don't care. It's damned depressing, and I, for one, will not sit here and be made to listen to a man relive something as terrible as losing his family."

"May I ask one more question, Yeronner?"

"Best make it a good one."

I saw Pete glance over in Carl's direction; that glance was not lost on McGregor, who, for the rest of the proceeding, kept looking from Carl to Pete to me to Willie, then back again.

"Willie, did you see the man who set that fire in your boxcar that night?"

Carl froze, blanching.

I shot a quick glance in Willie's direction; he looked straight at me with one of the most lonely, scared, and pained expressions I've ever seen deform a man's face, then gave a short, sharp nod of his head.

"I'm a bit deef these days," snapped Judge Carson. "You're gonna have to actually *say* something."

"Oh, yeah," I said. "I saw him real good."

Carl looked about ready to dump in his shorts.

I had just a moment before I figured out what was in that letter and who had written it.

What I didn't understand was the why of the rest of it.

"*O-kay,*" said Judge Carson, slamming his gavel once again, "that is more than sufficient for my tastes. We are here to try this man," he snapped a liver-spotted hand in my direction, "for thievery and breaking and entering. I must be gettin' soft in the head, lettin' you pull a stunt like this."

"But, Yeronner—"

"But *nothin'*, Pete." He looked directly at me. "Are you guilty of the crimes of which you're being accused?"

"N-nosir."

Carson smiled. "All-righty, then." He glared at Pete. "Now, we have heard the prosecution's arguments and seen their evidence, I have the statements of the townsfolk whose businesses and residences were broken into, so now it's your turn. That's how this works, Pete, it's called a *trial*. They go, then you go, I listen to all pertinent statements. Dull, I know, but I *like* dull. So . . . do you have any witnesses to call who might actually have something to say about the case that I'm supposed to be hearing, or should we just go right to the closing statements?"

Pete looked at me, then Carl, then Willie.

"One moment, please, Yeronner," Pete said.

"What the . . . ?" I whispered to him when he came over to me.

"You a gambling man?"

"I don't—"

"Shh, hang on."

The 'Bo who'd picked Carl's pocket came up to Pete and handed him the letter. Pete made a fairly big show of accepting the letter, opening it, reading it, then considering what he'd just read.

"Yeronner," he said, "I have no other witnesses to call, but I would ask a favor of the court."

"Oh, *hoo-ray*," muttered Carson. "What is it?"

"A twenty-four hour recess."

Carson mumbled curses under his breath, then said, "If I ask you why, is the answer going to upset me?"

"Probably."

"I should've retired last year like Mildred wanted." A sigh, then: "All right, why do you want a recess?"

"Some new evidence has just come to light which might prove my client's innocence."

Carson was silent for several moments, then said: "You're kidding."

"Afraid not, Yeronner."

"The man was discovered with several of the stolen items on his person. Not only that, but several of the stolen items were either fresh or canned fish—and *don't* think I didn't get a whiff of his cat's breath earlier. Between its breath and the smell on its fur, it could knock a buzzard off a shit-wagon."

"It looks bad, I know."

"This is such a help," I said under my breath.

"We're talking not only about the thieving here, Yeronner, but a man's life, as well. I'm willing to personally vouch for my client. Twenty-four hours."

Carson looked at his pocket watch. "No, but I'll give you some time. It's just right now six. Even though it's gonna have Mildred spittin' nails at me, we will reconvene at this same spot at nine A.M. tomorrow morning. Is that sufficient time for you to gather and examine your new evidence?"

Pete's smile was almost evil. "That'll be more than enough time, Yeronner."

I looked back to where Carl had been standing.

He was long gone.

One way or another . . .

And Pete, with more than a little help from Willie, had just turned me into bait.

"Nine A.M.," repeated Carson. "But after that, new evidence or no, some sort of action has to be taken, understand? If someone isn't punished, the town's gonna want me to have McGregor and his friends bust up this camp and send all of you on your way. I'd hate to see that happen. I know a lot of you fellahs—if not by name, then by sight—and find you a decent sort for the most part.

"Until nine A.M., then," he cracked his gavel against the table top, "this court stands in recess."

Pete looked at me and winked.

"*Please* tell me you know what you're doing."

"I sure hope so."

I looked down at Billy, whose expression seemed to say, *Me? I wanted to keep going, but you just had to stop and make some new friends, didn't you? If Jack was here, he'd hit you on the head so hard you'd have to unzip your pants to blow your nose.*

"Next time, I'll listen," I whispered to him.

Then Billy yawned. Easy to do when there's no chance your body'll be in the Lowlands come this time tomorrow.

It was close to midnight, and I was freezing.

Billy lay curled up in my lap, fast asleep.

I had been moved outside the camp, to a special "holding area" that McGregor and one of the jury bulls had set up according to Judge Carson's instructions before all the law boys had left for the night.

I was still in handcuffs, though my legs had been untied so I could at least stand from time to time and stretch. McGregor and the jury bull had taken a group of 'Bos down to the dump and hauled back a couple of discarded railroad ties which they proceeded to set upright into a portion of soggy ground. The mud pulled the ties down about two feet before the things hit solid rock and stayed in place. Then one of the cuffs was opened and my arms were stretched behind my back and cuffed again behind the two ties, both of which extended a good three feet above my head. I didn't have a lot of room for moving, but at least it wasn't so tight that I couldn't relax my shoulders a little.

But only a very little.

Pete and Willie had made themselves pretty scarce after I was secured, and for the better part of the last four hours it'd just been me and Billy, sitting in the cold night air with little more than cricket-song and starlight for company.

Trees still surrounded me, in places pretty thick.

A man could hide himself pretty well in those trees.

I had a feeling I knew what was going to happen, and why it was that no one in the camp—McGregor included—had spoken up to say that I wasn't Icehouse Willie.

It was all a crapshoot, and while I don't discourage a fellow from taking himself a big leap of faith every once in a while, it feels a bit different when a possible snake eyes will come attached to a real snake of sorts, one filled with venom and ready to end your life in a heartbeat.

I looked down at Billy's sleeping form and jostled him with my legs.

Nothing.

I tried once more.

Billy made a little mewling sound in the back of his throat, dug his back claws in just a little bit deeper, but still didn't wake up.

"Wish to hell I could sleep like you," I said to him. "You have any idea how that used to burn Jack up when you was on the road together? He used to say that you could probably sleep through a train wreck that was caused by an earthquake that took out an iron bridge." Then I laughed. "There were times he wondered whether or not you were deaf."

"What happened to your stammer, Willie?"

I snapped my head up just in time for my eyes to meet the business end of a .38.

"You should've known better than to try and catch a free ride on any line I worked for, Willie," said Carl, looking crazier than even before. He gave me the once-over, then stepped back and gestured with his gun for me to stand up. "I don't like the idea of killing a man who's not on his feet, even though you goddamn tramps barely qualify as men, you ask me."

I thought that last remark should be left unanswered, so I shimmied myself up into a standing position, much to Billy's chagrin; he finally let go of my leg and dropped onto the ground, stretching, yawning, and hissing.

"Cute cat," said Carl.

"I get a lot of compliments on him, thank you."

Carl stepped forward again and pressed the barrel of the gun to the middle of my forehead. I was amazed that I didn't wet myself, I was so scared.

"Tell me one thing," he said.

"Anything to keep the conversation goin' as long as possible."

A smile slithered across his face like a worm. "Good that you can crack wise right now. Be a good idea if you kept a pleasant thought in your head."

In the distance I heard the whistle of a train.

Far off, from the opposite direction, it was answered—though not yet joined—by the cry of another train.

"How'd you see me, Willie? I mean, I was pretty fast on my feet and that door wasn't opened all that far. I just ran up and tossed in the lit book of matches. How'd you get a look at me?"

"I d-don't quite r-r-remember." The stammer this time wasn't play-acting on my part; I was scared right down to the ground.

Carl considered this for a moment, then shrugged, pulling back the hammer. "So I didn't get everyone in the boxcar. I guess I can live with that."

Billy had by now wandered over down by Carl's legs and was rubbing himself up against the bull's steel-toed boots.

Carl kicked out a bit, but that didn't deter Billy; once he decides he's going to rub up against you, you just resign yourself to it and that's all she wrote.

"Dammit to hell!" Carl snapped, looking down and giving Billy a more insistent kick—

—and that's when the gun slipped away from my forehead, a little off to the side—

—and that's when I heard a voice yell, "Duck!" from somewhere in the nearby trees—

—and then there was a blast from somewhere that sparked right above my head and sent Carl to the ground cussing and flailing and blew away a good foot of railroad tie above—

—and before I knew what was happening, I felt someone toying with the handcuffs.

"Don't make a sound," said Pete, who was in front of me.

"Who's messing with the cuffs—?"

"Willie," Pete replied. "Did I forget to mention that he used to be a locksmith?"

I twisted my neck so as to look beside me. "That true?"

"B-bad locks in t-t-town," said Willie, working the cuffs open with some sort of pin. "Bad and ch-ch-cheap, easy to break in, easy, easy, easy."

The cuffs came off, and I took my pack when Pete offered it.

Carl still lay on the ground a few feet away, cradling his right hand against his chest. There wasn't any blood, but his hand looked to have been burned pretty good. The cylinder of his .38 gleamed in the moonlight pooling near my feet. I looked around and saw the rest of his gun a few feet beyond that.

McGregor came walking up to Carl, holding a mean-looking pump-action shotgun in front of him.

"Helluva shot, ain't he?" said Pete.

"A true marksman," I replied, shaking so much I thought I was going to drop.

Trailing behind McGregor—and looking for all the world like the most cantankerous so-and-so you'd ever want to meet—was Judge Carson. Two sheriff's deputies flanked him.

I looked at Pete. *"And . . . ?"*

"Okay, okay, sorry. Look, me and Willie, we been keeping close to Carl ever since Chicago. We figured it was only a matter of time before he wound up transferred to some little 'burg like this and we'd have time to . . . well, see if we couldn't do something about what he done. The trick was being able to stay in one place long enough to get the trust of the camp."

As he spoke, I noticed the other residents of the jungle, awakened by the gunfire and yelling, shuffling toward us from down below.

"They had a helluva time convincing me," said McGregor over his shoulder. "I know Pete and Willie here fairly well, and I knew when Pete pulled a stunt like he did earlier today—you know, calling you up to testify like you were Willie—I figured something pretty serious must be going on."

I nodded. "That's why you didn't say anything?"

"That's why no one who knows the two of them didn't say anything. 'Course, that letter of Willie's that Carl had on him was a pretty convincing piece of evidence. That, and what he just now tried to do to you."

Carl was still, evidently fascinated by the barrel of McGregor's pump-gun.

"I'm real sorry that we did this to you," said Pete, putting a hand on my shoulder. "But we had to distract ole Carl's attention there in order to have time to convince McGregor and the Judge that Carl here's the fellah that set that fire in Chicago."

"Twelve people died in that fire," said Judge Carson. "Be they hoboes or not, it was murder. Some parts of this country still look poorly upon that."

"Judge," I said, nodding my head.

"That was quite a performance you gave this afternoon," he said. "Mildred's going get herself quite a laugh out of it when I tell her."

"How was dinner?" I asked.

Carson shuddered. "Oh, it was great, seein' my daughter and grand-daughter, but my wife still can't make a decent gravy." He put a hand to his belly. "I was already up when McGregor came by with Pete and Willie. I figured even if this turned out to be a bust, I'd at least be out in the open when that gravy made me start sounding my horn, if you get my meaning."

The judge and McGregor, along with the two deputies, hauled Carl to his feet and cuffed him with the same cuffs he'd used on me. I'd be lying if I said I didn't get a certain amount of enjoyment out of seeing that.

I looked at Icehouse Willie. "Why'd you have to take Billy?"

"Sandy likes cats, that she d-d-does. Likes 'em a lot. Was always asking me for one. Her mother, though—" he whistled quick and low "—can't stand the things. M-m-make her sneeze something terrible."

He was crying as he told me this.

"No one's g-g-gonna burn today, nosir, not while I'm around, nosir. No one's gonna burn. The Lowlands aren't g-g-gonna take anybody today, nosir."

Pete slapped my back. "C'mon, we got to get the hell out of here."

I heard the cry of the approaching train whistles.

"Where's Billy?"

Willie opened his coat. "S-snug as a bug."

Billy was nestled comfortably in one of Willie's massive inside pockets.

Judge Carson looked at us, then toward the train whistle. "You know, this here's gonna draw a lot of attention from folks for a while. Me and McGregor and the deputies, we all heard Carl's confession. The rest'll be fairly easy." He came up to Willie. "Justice will now be served, Willie. Your Carol and Sandy, they can rest easy now. So can you."

And with that, they hauled Carl away.

I turned and looked at the rest of the camp. They had stopped several yards away and were now making their way back to their beds, cricket-song and starlight accompanying them.

Life on the road is hard, but sometimes you make new and good friends.

"You in the market for a couple of extra traveling companions?" Pete asked.

"The more the merrier," I said as the four of us took off up the hill and over the rise toward the tracks.

We decked the rattler just outside the switch yard, disembarking a few hours later just a few miles from the Canadian border. From there we caught a lumber car.

We've been a team ever since.

Some nights Willie wakes up from his bad dreams about his wife and daughter. That's when Billy helps the most, soothing his night terrors while I tell him all about Heaven, as Jack saw it. Then we smile at each other, finding peace in the thought of Jack and Sandy and Carol all sitting on that back porch under a summer night sky and sipping lemonade while the radio plays on. A good end to a good day's labors.

And no train whistles mourning.

The Lowlands can't touch us here.

—end—

Author Biographies

Parnell Hall is the author of the Puzzle Lady crossword puzzle mysteries, the Stanley Hastings private eye novels, and the Steve Winslow courtroom dramas. His books have been nominated for the Edgar and Shamus awards. A former private detective, Hall is also a part-time actor, and he has appeared in summer stock, regional theater, and interactive dinner theater events, as well as motion pictures. He lives in New York City.

Dulcy Brainard is the Editor for the Lifestyles and Mystery sections of *Publisher's Weekly*, the leading trade magazine of the publishing world. She lives in New York.

Janet Dawson is the author of a mystery series featuring Oakland, California, private Investigator Jeri Howard. Her first book, *Kindred Crimes,* won the St. Martin's Press/Private Eye Writers of America contest for best first private eye novel and also garnered nominations for the Shamus, Macavity, and Anthony Awards. Other Jeri Howard cases include *Till the Old Men Die, Don't Turn Your Back on the Ocean, Where the Bodies Are Buried,* and *A Killing at the Track.*

Catherine Dain is the creator of the Freddie O'Neal series, including the novels *Lay It On the Line* and *Lament for a Dead Cowboy,* both nominated for the Shamus Award. After receiving her graduate degree in theater arts from the University of Southern California, she worked as a television newscaster before turning to mystery writing. She has also edited non-fiction books on leadership and global business for the university's Business Education and Research Center. She lives in Ventura, California.

Tracy Knight is a psychologist who uses elements of his work to write stories with keen insight into the human mind. Other fiction of his appears in *Cat Crimes Goes on Vacation, The UFO Files, Werewolves,* and *Murder Most Delicious.* He lives in Macomb, Illinois.

Jan Grape is a co-editor of *Deadly Women: The Female Mystery Writer.* She also has short stories in anthologies ranging from *Deadly Allies I & II, Lethal Ladies I & II, Feline & Famous,* to the recently released *Vengeance Is Hers.* Her non-fiction articles appear in *The Mystery Writers Sourcebook, The Fine Art of Murder,* and *How to Write a Private Eye Novel.* A regular columnist for *Mystery Scene* magazine, she also writes for the British publication *A Shot in the Dark.* She edits the Private Eye Writers of America newsletter and is the vice-president of that organization. Along with her husband, she owns the Mysteries & More bookstore in Austin, Texas.

Dick Lochte is the creator of Leo Bloodworth and Serendipity Dalhquist, who have appeared in several novels, including *Sleeping Dog* and *Laughing Dog.* He is also the creator of Terry Manion, a New Orleans–based private eye. He has been a promotional copywriter for *Playboy* magazine, a film critic for the *Los Angeles Free Press,* and a book columnist for the *Los Angeles Times.* Recently he teamed up with former L.A. prosecutor Christopher Darden to co-author a new mystery series beginning with the novel *The Trials of Nikki Hill.* He lives in Southern California.

Shirley Rousseau Murphy is the author of seven feline mystery novels, *Cat on the Edge, Cat Under Fire, Cat Raise the Dead, Cat in the Dark, Cat to the Dogs, Cat Spitting Mad,* and *Cat Laughing Last.* She lives in Carmel, California.

Mat Coward is a British writer of crime, science fiction, horror, children's, and humorous fiction whose stories have been broadcast on BBC Radio and published in numerous anthologies, magazines, and e-zines in the United Kingdom, United States, and Europe. According to Ian Rankin, "Mat Coward's stories resemble distilled novels." His first non-distilled novel, a whodunit called *Up and Down,* was published in the United States in 2000. Short stories have recently appeared in *Ellery Queen's Mystery Magazine, The World's Finest Crime and Mystery Stories, Felonious Felines,* and *Murder Through the Ages.*

Ann Barrett primarily writes non-fiction, food-related technical articles, but has also won second place in a contest sponsored by the National Academy of Poets and had her work published in an anthology of the contest winners entitled *A Delicate Balance.* In addition, she has received honorable mention in a contest sponsored by the Writer's Journal. She lives with her family and two cats in Needham, Massachusettes.

Matthew J. Costello is the author of more than sixteen novels and numerous non-fiction works, including collaborations with F. Paul Wilson and Craig Shaw Gardner and film novelizations. His articles have appeared in publications ranging from The *Los Angeles Times* to *Sports Illustrated.* He scripted *The 7th Guest,* the best-selling CD-ROM interactive drama, and its sequel, *The 11th Hour.*

Richard T. Chizmar is primarily known for his work in the horror field, most notably as the editor of the World Fantasy Award–winning magazine *Cemetery Dance,* a showcase of dark fantasy and horror fiction. The best of the magazine's run was recently collected in *The Best of Cemetery Dance.* His short fiction, which has appeared in *White House Horrors* and *Cat Crimes at the Holidays,* is both poignant and disturbing. The best of his short stories was collected in the anthology *Midnight Promises* in 1997.

Barry Hoffman's short fiction has appeared in *Return to the Twilight Zone, Werewolves,* and *A Horror Story a Day: 365 Scary Stories.* He lives in Springfield, Pennsylvania.

Jeremiah Healy, a graduate of Rutgers College and Harvard Law School, was a professor at the New England School of Law for eighteen years. He is the creator of John Francis Cuddy, a Boston-based private investigator who has appeared in more than a dozen novels. He was president of the Private Eye Writers of America for two years and is currently the president of the International Association of Crime Writers. A lecturer on mystery writing, he has attended mystery conferences in New York, London, Spain, and Austria.

Gary A. Braunbeck is the acclaimed author of the collection *Things Left Behind* (CD Publications), released last year to unanimously excellent reviews and nominated for both the Bram Stoker Award and the International Horror Guild Award for Best Collection. He has written in the fields of horror, science fiction, mystery, suspense, fantasy, and western fiction, with over 120 published works to his credit. His work has most recently appeared in *Alien Abductions, The Best of Cemetery Dance, The Year's Best Fantasy and Horror,* and *Dark Whispers.* He is co-author (along with Steve Perry) of *Time Was: Isaac Asimov's I-Bots,* a science fiction adventure novel praised for its depth of characterization. His fiction, to quote *Publisher's Weekly,* "stirs the mind as it chills the marrow."

Copyrights